THE MEASURE OF A MAN

MARA O'REILLY

All rights reserved.

The characters and events portrayed in this book are fictitious. Any similarity to real persons, living or dead, is coincidental and not intended by the author.
Commentary regarding the 22nd century is fictitious and speculative. No time travel, tarot card readings, psychic abilities, or prophetic dreams were used.

No part of this book may be reproduced, or stored in a retrieval system, or transmitted in any form or by any means, electronic, mechanical, photocopying, recording, or otherwise, or used for the advancement of AI without express written permission of the publisher.

No part of this novel was created using Artificial Intelligence.
Any errors, typos, or formatting issues are absolutely due to Human Failure.
Please feel free to contact the author for corrections: mara-oreilly.com
Mara.oreilly.author@gmail.com

ISBN-13: 979-8371800459

Printed in the United States of America

For Clan O'Reilly

CONTENTS

PART ONE 1

ONE – THE SANCTITY OF LIFE 5
    The Sanctity of Life Oath 5
    Meeting the Chief 7
    Assessing the Disposal Site and Victims 12
    Burials of the Dead 14
    K9 Cadaver Dogs 15
    Lodgings 17
    Something Unsettled 18

TWO - THE MORGUE AND VICTIMS 19
    Introduction to Officer Stanton 19
    Security and Protocol 21
    Entering the Morgue 24
    Reviewing Victims with the Medical Examiner 26
    Meeting Officer Stanton 32
    Report on Four Victims 34

THREE – SPD MORGUE AND VA 37
    RS—Postmortem Follow-up 37
    AR—Postmortem Follow-Up 39
    The Investigation Team 41
    Meeting the Victim Advocate 43

FOUR – CR —1— INITIATING INVESTIGATION 47
    Preparing to Visit the Randall Farm 47
    Meeting Caroline Randall 48
    Meeting Micah Davidson 55
    Initial Background Check of WA 59
    Arrest Report: AR Farm 60
    Securing Caroline Randall's Missing Person Report 63

    CR's Missing Person SPD Interview 64

FIVE – KU —1— INITIATING INVESTIGATION 67

    Opening the Investigation 67

    Interviews: Parents and Children 70

    Lucya's Missing Person Interview 71

    Oscar's Missing Person Response 72

    After Katarina's Disappearance 73

    Before and After the Great Reformation 74

SIX – KU —2— DEATH NOTIFICATION 77

    Death Notification—I: Meeting Oscar 77

    Death Notification II: Meeting Lucya 83

    Death Notification III: Providing Answers 87

    Death Notification IV: Interview 89

    Moving Forward 92

PART TWO 95

SEVEN - DK AND FN'S —1— 99

    Introduction to Daegan Kyl 99

    Two Foreign Nationals Identified 101

    Establishing Links to Two Foreign Nationals 103

    DK—Initial Background Check 104

EIGHT – RS —1— DEATH NOTIFICATION 105

    Understanding Rebecca 105

    Death Notification 107

    The Father of the Unborn 109

NINE - DK AND FN's —2— 111

    Cameras 111

    DK—Moving Men & Maids 114

    DK—Establishing Links to K&H Textiles 116

    DK—Establishing Links to Victims 118

TEN – INVESTIGATION —2— 119

  Ruling Out Caroline Randall's Involvement 119

  Interview: Rebecca's Roommate 121

  Update and Report on Missing Persons Cases 123

ELEVEN – MP —1— INITIATING INVESTIGATION 125

  The Abduction of Mariam 125

  After Her Missing Person Report 128

  The Eternal Optimism of Mankind 131

  In Her Final Moments 133

  The Watchers On The Wall Speech: The Ripple Effect 136

PART THREE 139

TWELVE – RS —2— 143

  Lost Treasure 143

  Rape or Relationship 145

THIRTEEN – MP —2— 147

  MP—21st Century Crimes Against Women 147

  Despite Every Effort, It Wasn't Enough 150

FOURTEEN - RS —3— 153

  Stanton—Proof of Rape Surveillance 153

  Confirmation From the Medical Examiner 157

  Establishing Links Between Mariam and Rebecca 158

FIFTEEN – MP — DEATH NOTIFICATION 159

  Preparing for Notification 159

  Examining Her Life 162

  The Final Moments Before the World Changed 166

  Death Notification 168

SIXTEEN – KU —3— 171

  The Details of Katarina's Forensic Report 171

  The Watchers On The Wall Speech: A Proclamation To The World 173

SEVENTEEN – RS —4— 177

  Finding Rebecca's Sex Offender 177

    Scope of Campus Security Investigation 178

    The Ripple Effect of Rebecca's Death 179

PART FOUR 183

EIGHTEEN – EVAN HARRISON 187

    Interview: Evan Harrison 187

    All That Evan Harrison Knew 191

    An Introduction to The Angels of Mercy 193

    Initial Search Results—WA and RS After Rape 195

    Willow Amos and the Winter Season Hospice Care Facility 196

NINETEEN – STANTON AND ARRESTS 197

    Stanton Update: Two Foreign Nationals 197

    Progression toward Arrest Warrants 198

    Identification of LeRoy Jones 199

    Meeting with the Chief 200

    Stanton Update: Stalking 202

    Plan for Arrests 203

    Arrests and Search Warrants 204

TWENTY – JARRETT AND KENNEDY 205

    The Stadium 205

    Jarrett and Kennedy at the Stadium 206

    Interview: Kennedy 208

    Interview: Jarrett 212

    Thoughts on Detective Jarrett 218

TWENTY-ONE - DAEGAN KYL — ARRESTED 219

    Meeting Daegan Kyl 219

    Search Warrant: Moving Men and Maids 220

    Establishing Links Between Daegan Kyl and Willow Amos 221

    Establishing Communication: Daegan Kyl 222

    Interview I: Arlan 224

    Interview II: Rebecca 228

Interview III: Cut from the Same Cloth 235

TWENTY-TWO – WILLOW AMOS —ARRESTED 243

Meeting Willow Amos 243

Establishing Communication: Willow Amos 244

Irreconcilable Differences 249

TWENTY-THREE – AOM — ARRESTED 253

Rounding Up the Angels 253

Ideology 255

PART FIVE 257

TWENTY-FOUR - TWO ICE AGENTS 261

Governor Interference 261

Two ICE Agents Arrive 266

The Chief and the Two ICE Agents 270

Government Accountability for Katarina 274

Planning the Next Move 276

TWENTY-FIVE – DK — HOLDING CELL 281

Holding Cell 281

DK and WA Preparing to Meet 285

DK and WA Meeting 288

DK—Military Report 291

DK—Interview IV: LeRoy Jones 292

No Known Motive 297

TWENTY-SIX – FINDING ANSWERS 301

Results of Search Warrant: Willow Amos 301

Results of Search Warrant: LeRoy Jones 302

Arrest of the Doctor 303

Something Missing with The Angels of Mercy 304

DK—Final Interviews: Choices 306

Daegan Kyl, Soldier 308

TWENTY-SEVEN – THE RIDE SOUTH 315

    The Trinity Triangle 315
    Riding Down to the Factory 320
    The Line Between Good and Evil 321
    The Benefits of a Team 324
    Thoughts on Grace 326
    The I-5 Corridor 329
TWENTY-EIGHT – AOM — AFTER ARREST.............................**333**
    An Angel of Mercy Confesses 333
    The Watchers On The Wall Speech: Civil War 335
PART SIX **339**
TWENTY-NINE – THE FACTORY **343**
    The Factory Parking Lot 343
    Touring the Factory 344
    The Third Floor 348
    Meeting the Governor 349
THIRTY – AFTER THE FACTORY **365**
    Grace's Office 365
    Leveling the Playing Field 371
    Protecting the Team 372
    After Urgent Care 375
THIRTY-ONE – END OF DAY **377**
    A Lesser Man 377
    Release from Custody 381
    Back at the Barracks 385
    Sleep 387
THIRTY-TWO – WAKING AFTER THE FACTORY **389**
    Waking After the Factory Visit 389
    Thoughts on the Governor 392
THIRTY-THREE – IN THE BASEMENT **397**
    A Conversation at the Factory: 1300 397

The Basement	405
Upon Finding Katarina	415
After Losing Katarina	421
THIRTY-FOUR – EMERGING FROM THE DARKNESS	**425**
The Walk Back Outside	425
Final Conversation at the Factory	430
PART SEVEN	**435**
THIRTY-FIVE – KU — 4	**439**
The Bearer of Bad News	439
How We Had Failed Katarina and Her Family	442
THIRTY-SIX – WA — CONFESSION	**445**
Getting Willow to Talk	445
Interview I: Regarding Arlan Randall	448
Interview II: Regarding Rebecca Summers	454
Interview III: 2nd Interview Regarding Rebecca Summers	457
Statement I: Regarding The Angels of Mercy	463
Interview IV: Regarding LeRoy Jones	466
THIRTY-SEVEN – WA — STATEMENT	**469**
Compromise and Results	469
Statement II: Regarding The Night in Question	470
Statement III: Regarding Relationship to DK	473
Statement IV: Regarding DK & AOM	474
Statement V: Regarding DK & LJ	475
Statement VI: Regarding DK, RS, MP	476
Interview VII: Regarding RFID-Chip Removal	478
PART EIGHT	**481**
THIRTY-EIGHT – CR —2— DEATH NOTIFICATION	**485**
Arlan—Why He Left	485
Confirmation of Nefarious Misdeeds	487
Upon Learning of Her Husband's Death	488

    Death Notification 490
THIRTY-NINE - CONVICTIONS 493
    Life Evaluations: LJ, Rebecca, and Mariam 493
    Convictions 495
FORTY – CASE CLOSURE 497
    Final Case Summary 497
    Thoughts on Mariam and Rebecca 500
    Thoughts on Katarina 502
    The Weight of it All... 504
FORTY-ONE - SENTENCING 507
    Final Stages... 507
    AOM—Window of Time 509
    The Execution of LeRoy Jones.. 511
    The Execution of The Angels of Mercy 512
    The Watchers On The Wall Speech: Crossroads 513
PART NINE 517
FORTY-TWO – PLAN FOR DEPORTATION 521
    Plan for Deportation 521
    Thoughts on Willow Amos 524
    Alaska, Utopia Realized 529
    Three Drop-Zones 534
    Preparing Daegan Kyl for Alaska 538
    The Transport Station Plan 541
    Awaiting Deportation Dates... 545
FORTY-THREE – EXILE 547
    Marking the Date 547
    Standard Policy Measures for Exile Drop-Off's......................... 548
    WA-SET: The Washington State Exile Transport Station 550
FORTY-FOUR - DEPORTATION 551
    Transportation Hub Deportation: Phase I 551

- Transportation Hub Deportation: Phase II 556
- 268th DOY, 1700 Hours: Return from Patos Island 562
- 268th DOY, 1800 Hours: Waiting 563
- 268th DOY, 1900 Hours: The Chief's Daughters 567
- 268th DOY, 1900 Hours: The Man in The Mirror 570

FORTY-FIVE - TIMESTAMP 1-8 .... **575**
- Timestamp: 1 575
- Timestamp: 2 580
- Timestamp: 3 581
- Timestamp: 4 583
- Timestamp: 5 587
- Timestamp: 6 591
- Timestamp: 7 594
- Timestamp: 8 595

FORTY-SIX - TIMESTAMP 9-15 .... **599**
- Timestamp: 9 599
- Timestamp: 10 600
- Timestamp: 11 603
- Timestamp: 12 608
- Timestamp: 13 610
- Timestamp: 14 612
- Timestamp: 15 615

PART TEN **619**

FORTY-SEVEN – AFTER A CASE IS CLOSED **623**
- Traveling by Train 623
- The Call from the Chief 627
- The Designated Location 628
- Assessment, Planning, Departure 632

FORTY-EIGHT – COLLATERAL DAMAGE **637**
- A Fragile Edge 637

Before I Go ~ A Testament of Love	639
A Love Story for the Ages	643
All the Reasons I Could Not Stay	645
FORTY-NINE - TO LOVE SOMEBODY	**651**
To Love Somebody	651
The Want of Her ~ Submission	659
A Love Divine	663
Surrender	665
FIFTY – WINTER WINDS	**669**
Winter Winds	669
A Graceless Exit	671
FIFTY-ONE – BROKEN CROWN	**677**
Broken Crown	677
All That Remained	679
The Measure of a Man Worthy	682
MILITARY OATH OF ENLISTMENT	**695**
LAW ENFORCEMENT CODE OF ETHICS	**697**
THE AMERICAN'S CREED	**699**
The Watchman On The Wall	701

*"And in Thy book they were all written,
the days that were ordained for me."*

Psalm 139:16

PART ONE

For thus has the Lord said to me:
"Go, set a watchman,
Let him declare what he sees."

Isaiah 21: 6

For we are God's masterpiece.
He has created us anew in Christ Jesus,
so we can do the good things he planned for us long ago.

Ephesians 2:10

ONE – THE SANCTITY OF LIFE

The Sanctity of Life Oath

"Blessed are *the peacemakers, For they shall be called sons of God."*
Matthew 5:9

I regarded working within Law Enforcement as a Calling, not merely a profession. This was a common sentiment. My professional duties may have seemed mundane and grim to some. I conducted Investigations for the Deceased Victims of Violence, and for many, working under such circumstances was impossible to consider.

My job was the gateway between the Living and the Dead, and I was one of the gatekeepers. Our purpose as Investigators was to secure Justice for the Victim. We investigated Crime Scenes and the Disposal Sites of Victims. Along with this, we gathered and documented evidence, and conducted research through comprehensive fact-finding, forensic analysis, and personal interviews. Our purpose was to secure incontrovertible evidence so no Guilty Offender ever went free, and no miscarriages of Justice ever occurred.

We were Peacekeepers—defenders of Law and Order. But we were also Guardians of our Fellow Man, appointed to investigate the Cause of Death of each Victim. Through our efforts, we gave a voice to the voiceless, and our work created a lasting legacy of each individual in their Final Moments. We produced public records of every life lost through the Unnatural Act of Violence. We catalogued the Stolen Lives of our Fellow Citizen and their Loss to our collective society.

The sacrifices never mattered. The time served, the lost associations with friends and family, the secrecy and discretion our cases required—none of those specifics mattered to us while we served. We understood that for the duration of time we were under contract they expected us to prioritize Investigations.

My time in service was voluntary, and I could opt out at any point. There was never a moral or ethical obligation for staying and signing on tour after tour. I was free to check out anytime, and would receive commendation for having worked within the field for as long as I already had.

An entire career spent traveling the nation as an Investigator was a substantial contribution to public service. It meant a career without stability and routine; it made marriage extremely difficult for both partners, and active parenting almost impossible. For both spouses and children, it was an entirely unreasonable professional commitment. It was one of the primary reasons they made the job mirror military enlistments, and our travel duties resemble deployments. Signing contracts for yearly commitments allowed for the best of the best to serve their nation in reasonable timeframes, take time off as needed, and forgo reenlistment when the time came for Investigators to move on.

It would otherwise be too difficult; it meant countless missed holidays and important events along with usually over 300 days a year spent on assignments throughout the US. There were no other professions within Law Enforcement or the Military that required as much travel without making relocation an option for family members. Most did not manage over a decade before transitioning back to being a Detective for their local PD or transferring into another government job with local ties and fewer demands. Staying in the fight meant plenty of sacrifices, but it all came down to why men such as myself were doing it to begin with, and why it was all worthwhile.

Like many other Investigators, I believed in what I was doing and believed it was an important Calling. It was a profession that I had spent many years working toward, and it was a meaningful part of the man that I had become over the last two decades of my life. Deep in my heart, I knew that what I was doing was for a purpose. It was who I was, and it was who I was meant to be.

This work was exactly what I believed God wanted me to be doing. I was sharing the truth, that each Victim's life mattered, that each story had a right to be told, and that every Human Life—every American Citizen—had a Divine Right to live within our borders without fear of Premature Death caused by the Violent Actions of Others. I was here for a reason, and that reason, shared with so many other Investigators and members of Law Enforcement within America, was to Protect and Defend the Sanctity of Human Life.

Meeting the Chief

After taking my motorcycle from Olympia, I made my way through the Seattle Police Department in search of the Police Chief. Seattle hadn't had a highly publicized or noteworthy Homicide case in several decades, and many people credited the strength of their Police Department—and Chief—for those numbers. Although I hadn't ever worked a case for him—or even worked one in Seattle before—the Chief had requested me by name. There were a few hundred Law Enforcement Investigators around the country, but I was one of only four that were permanently stationed in my home state of Washington.

Although as an Investigator I was used to working throughout the nation, the bulk of my work was usually done at the request of smaller Police or Sheriff's departments. Because of the rarity of Violent Crimes in their area, they were not as well-versed in the procedures and intricacies related to comprehensive investigations like many of the more urban areas. The SPD, however, was one of the largest Police Departments in America, and as such, they had internal departments for both Homicide and Missing Persons. By electing to secure an Investigator rather than using his own Detectives, I could surmise that the case was significant enough he wanted to ensure it was handled independently.

Even though we were Investigators, we were still Emergency Response Personnel; most Requests for Service were made by random selection and based on our availability. If we agreed to accept the assignment, we sent a notification to the department that had issued the request, allowing them to get things ready for our arrival. It was customary to head out the same day as requested, and usually the sooner the better. For many cases, they needed assistance processing Crime Scenes, so there was a sense of urgency for Investigators to get there as quickly as possible. Our acceptance also included a commitment to remain until we completed the case.

I had just returned to my home station in Olympia after having finalized my last case in New York, so it was a simple drive on my bike, and I had made it within a few hours of notification. I wasn't sure of the details of the case yet, but after having been home for a week, I was ready to get started again. I checked in with the secretary outside of the Chief's office and had barely made my way to the seating area before one of the local Officers—a man that was far too young to be the Chief but was likely his Assistant—opened the door from the inside and waved me in. As I entered the room, I raised the visor shielding my face. With my eyes visible, the Chief and I could engage in eye contact freely.

Chief Monty, standing behind an oversized desk on the far wall, was a tall, broad-shouldered man, and it did not appear that the years of working in an elevated position of authority rather than out in the field had affected his desire to maintain a fit appearance. If I were a betting man, I would have put my money on him being capable of holding his own against any of the younger men in his ranks without question. Even though he was allocated a higher body fat percentage because of his age, this man was clearly not one to bend the rules or allow himself a standard deemed unacceptable for his men. This was not an unusual precedent from my experience. Because of my work and the travel involved, I'd met with many Senior Officers all over the US and they were seldom unfit, no matter their age. Leadership, after all, was about setting the bar and upholding agency standards; it wasn't about getting free passes because of rank and title.

All that being noted as I entered the room and stood across from him, I sincerely hoped that he was a man I could follow and get the working conditions I would need in order to be successful with the task at hand. We were only as good as our own contribution, and any myriad of environmental factors could prove detrimental to our success.

The door shut behind me as his Assistant left, and he motioned for me to sit down. I estimated his age to be approximately sixty to sixty-five, based on the telltale signs of his weathered face and the smattering of silver in his otherwise dark hair. Given the overall condition of his body, it seemed highly likely that he would be among the millions that celebrated their Centurion birthdays with a well-deserved vacation on some sunny beach down the road.

"It's nice to meet you, Officer. I've heard good things about you. I've read your file and know you worked on a few of the national multiple Homicides we've had. You did the Bronx case?"

It wasn't really a question; he knew I had. I nodded anyhow.

"From what I've read, the Bronx case was one of our most gruesome. You helped catch one of the worst Serial Killers in the last hundred years with that one. Eight Victims, was it?"

"Yes, Sir. Though they're still recovering Human Remains."

The Chief nodded.

"But they were all his."

"Sir?"

"His Victims. I meant; they were all confirmed to be his Victims. He had a specific type, correct?"

"Oh. Yes, Sir. They were all women in their early twenties, Asian. They presented a small target with minimal resistance. He kept them around for sex until he grew bored with them, and then he would...trade them in. They're still doing aerial scouting and K9 Cadaver patrols on the property that he had up in the mountains, but it will be slow-moving due to the terrain and elevation."

"But you've got it all wrapped up on your end?" he queried.

"Yes, Sir. We were able to secure the Death Penalty at the end of May. They executed him within thirty days, as per policy. The appeals were all denied. He was convicted on eight separate Victims; if they find more, it will only be for the sake of the Bereaved at this point."

"Good. Good. Ok, then. Well, let me get this case brought up."

He tinkered with his remote control that programmed his wall screens for a moment. I could have offered some help, but it wasn't my style to be too imposing or to encroach on leadership. If it were, I'd have just told him to use voice commands; instead, I patiently waited and wondered why his Assistant hadn't bothered to help him keep up with the ever-changing programming within the agency, or at least have the files prepared and set-up before he left the room. It seemed the sort of preemptive work that most good Assistants would do if they were working in the support capacity; most teams were like marriages after enough time. Maybe his Assistant was new—or maybe the Chief was just bull-headed.

He finally got it to activate, and I was immediately staring at a wall showcasing a small handful of images of people. They were all the Missing Persons cases for the Pacific Northwest. Among them, there were all races, both men and women, as well as a few children. I saw no consistent patterning, although it seemed like a high number of active Missing Persons to be open all at once, even for such an expansive geographical region.

"A couple of our guys have found a gravesite down by the waterfront in the industrial district. We've recovered four sets of Human Remains. Four separate graves—each at least six feet deep, hand-dug; no machinery. I'm not sure if any of them were from our list of active Missing Persons cases, but all of Washington State's resources are at your disposal. The satellite and dogs are going over the property now to ensure we don't find any additional graves, but it will be the biggest Disposal Site found in the last fifty years for Seattle either way. My guys have said they were all in various states of Decomposition. You'll have to talk to the ME about all of that.

"Basically, our Front-Line guys responded to a distress signal from a minor child's RFID-Chip. The Chip had been flagged as a Missing Person; it belonged to a little girl, so they had responded immediately to the site. But when they arrived, they couldn't find the location of the Chip, so they called in a K9 unit. It immediately triggered the dogs. They found her location right away; she was buried at the edge of a field. My guys thought that was the end of it, but the dogs had apparently sniffed out three additional graves right next to her. We've had the Crime Scene Units out there all night."

"Why was the girl's Chip activated upon her Death if they had already tagged her as Missing? Why didn't it activate upon her Disappearance?" I asked.

"Those are great questions, and I look forward to reading your report to find out what you learn. The ME can tell you more once he has their Remains. But at least we know the other three were much older Victims and there was only one minor out of the group."

"How long since they discovered the site?" I asked. It would matter because whoever was putting Victims there was bound to show up at some point, though the frequency would depend on the time that had been taken between placing each Victim—something that would be determined by the Medical Examiner upon his work with their Remains and based on their state of Decomposition.

"Last night; just after midnight. So far, we have monitored the road from about halfway in case someone shows up. It will be too late if they make it that far. There's a factory out that way—not visible from the Disposal Site. I sent a couple of Blues over there to check it out; they said it appeared deserted. It seems unlikely that there would be any justifiable reason that anyone should show up unless it was because of the gravesite itself. It's in a remote area."

I nodded. "I'll get out there right away. We should evacuate the area as quickly as we can. Did you call in a team for the morgue to help process the Victims faster?"

Chief Monty stood up and began walking around his desk toward me. I stood as well and followed him to the door. He assured me the team was in place and he'd secured the best available. Motioning to his Assistant through the front window of his office, he opened the door and gave him orders to escort me to where my Authorization credentials were being processed. He also instructed him to make sure I had a vehicle assigned for my use. The eager young Assistant nodded his head and patiently waited for us to wrap up our meeting.

I told him I'd touch base periodically just to keep him apprised. One of the unique qualities regarding my profession was the distinction between my relationship and obligations with the Police Departments I worked with. While his job enabled him to maintain an authoritative position of leadership over the men in the trenches—sometimes many thousands of men depending on the region—Investigators were more comparable to Independent Contractors. We were not subordinate to men such as the Chief, even when they called us in for a job. In almost every case, Investigators held higher credentials, especially regarding education and training.

Our education was comprehensive besides our Law Enforcement training, and as such, we were often among the most highly educated Citizens in our country. It was customary to report our findings to the Chiefs we assisted. I had long since learned that it was far easier to garner any resources I may need if I demonstrated sufficient humility and regard for their position. After all, they were just as concerned about the outcome as I was; we were all on the same team.

The Chief made the obligatory comments about how good it was to have met me and informed me he had procured some additional resources for my use, including some office space within the SPD. He then remarked that since I didn't work with my own team, he had also assigned a Research and Investigation Specialist and a Victim Advocate, both of whom he said he had also hand-selected. He assured me that he believed them to be the best in their field within the SPD and knew I would find them indispensable. I'd never worked with a Chief that was so directly involved with choosing his own staff regarding external investigations, and I wondered if it was an indicator of his desire to do his best by the Victims recently located, or a precursor to a domineering Type-A personality that would soon prove to be a nuisance.

Shaking his hand, I thanked him for his time and consideration and made my way out of his office where his Assistant had been waiting for me, lowering my visor over my eyes once again. From there, his Assistant took me to the Human Resources department where I secured my authorization to work within the Greater Seattle Area through the SPD, updated my electronic credentials and clearance, and then made my way to my assigned vehicle. My lodgings and vehicle had both been secured by the acceptance of the work assignment. I had a small dwelling unit waiting for me at the SPD Barracks when I was ready.

I left my motorcycle in the parking garage of the SPD for the time being so I could head out to the Disposal Site, transferred my two duffel bags of extra clothing and uniforms into the backseat of the SPD Cruiser, and programmed in the coordinates. It appeared to be about fifteen minutes south of the Headquarters back down the I-5 corridor and toward the direction I had just traveled from. I set the Cruiser on autopilot and reviewed the files the Chief had given me as I traveled.

Since they had already been working for several hours, I knew they would have accomplished a great deal of progress. But a Disposal Site consisting of four separate graves and four Victims would require a substantial amount of work, time, and resources to process, so there was a strong likelihood that I would arrive in time to find each of the Victims themselves still on site. At the very least, it would give me an opportunity to review the scene in person rather than through photographs and video alone, so I was grateful that the Chief had taken the initiative from such an early point in the investigation and invited me in from the start.

In too many cases, they only called in Investigators at a point of desperation once the locals realized they were out of their depth and the odds grew against their success. It was refreshing to see how proactive this Police Chief was, and as I made my way toward the Disposal Site, I believed we would work well together for these reasons.

Assessing the Disposal Site and Victims

    I stood on the edge of the field where four Victims had been Disposed of. Their Physical Remains were covered by thick, black, protective layers and rested on stretchers, neatly lined up at the edge of the darkened holes from which they had each been extracted. A solitary Officer stood guard near them, posed as a sentry while two Crime Scene Investigators finished their assessments and notes before all of them traveled together to transport the Physical Remains to the morgue. The entire field was quiet despite there being over two dozen Officers working the land, taking photographs, recording videos, and doing various forensic work.

    Nothing was disturbed beyond what was necessary, and the entire field was treated with reverence by all who worked the area. This was not out of respect for the value of the property itself or because the SPD workers were trying to be courteous for the property owners; when a site was discovered, none of those subjects were even a consideration for the Crime Scene Investigators, nor should they have been. The land would repair itself and leave no memory of Human traffic soon enough.

    The Crime Scene Investigators were dedicated to their duties and maintained a universal Respect for the Dead. Such reverence was important just as surely as it would have been had there been caskets, a funeral procession, or any other memorial type of event from the 21st century being carried out. Although the processing practices had changed over the last century, it had been much more in relation to the cultural and psychological perception of how we cared for our Deceased than anything else. Whoever had buried these Innocent Citizens here may have been doing something that had once been common practice, but it was an antiquated act now—aside from obviously being Criminal. It was not only potentially the Disposal Site of four Homicides, it was an unconscionable means of discarding Human Remains, leaving them to rot in the ground.

    I stared out at the team of SPD Officers, watching them work, and as always, the deference they paid to the site humbled me. They worked efficiently, methodically, and in silence. Each worker carried out their duties without hesitation, impeccable in their organization and attention to detail. There could be no question as to their devotion to their work. The terrain was rugged, covered in high, untamed grass, and the smell of Death lingered heavily in the air. Some wore masks, but many chose not to. It was often remarked that only by smelling the Decomposition could one genuinely appreciate just how fragile each Human Life was and understand that our essence had very little to do with our external packaging.

    They explored each gravesite with meticulous care and dedicated craftsmanship that only true artisans could comprehend. It was obviously a well-made team, each with their own skill set and personal qualifiers that made them desirable assets to one of the most prestigious Police Departments in America.

The LEOs who were in charge of processing Crime Scenes were undoubtedly no different from any of those who were working on the Front-Line, within the Missing Persons Division, or as Homicide Detectives. They were all exceptional, and vital to the intricate tapestry of experience and expertise within their chosen areas of Law Enforcement. As with all their Brothers and Sisters in Blue, they were committed to their jobs and to the deliverance of Justice. Working with the Deceased Human Remains of their Fellow Countrymen on a full-time basis, they responded to all manner of Death, including Bloody, Violent, horrific Homicides, and had seen the very worst of Humanity. They were a testament to the quality and character of those who wore the uniform and badge.

It was highly probable that none of them had ever worked a Crime Scene with this many sets of Human Remains all at one time. In all truth, most had probably never even seen four Deceased Victims in a single setting, except in old video footage from the 21st century. The fact that they were all in various states of Decomposition, of varying ages, and that each had presumably been the Victim of a Violent Crime and Murder was even more staggering.

It was also something that would require every Officer to remember the Oath they had taken; it was an Oath to Protect the Sanctity of Human Life, and that meant discretion. This went beyond the standard confidentiality agreements that Peacekeepers were required to honor; it was a matter of personal integrity and respect for both their profession and for the Citizens they served.

In this modern age, this was the stuff of horror stories; but these were the True Crime events that no one would dream of telling, nor expect to hear about. It was unimaginable that anyone would attempt to capitalize off tragedies such as this for any reason, least of all for a headline, a True Crime novel, or just a back-alley profit for a scoop given to a news agency or tabloid. Exploiting Innocent Victims in their most vulnerable and tragic of circumstances, all for selfish gain, was a low-character action, and they held members of Law Enforcement to a higher standard.

Burials of the Dead

There had not been Burials of the Dead within America in almost a century. The Disposal Site had been so quiet it had reminded me of the photographs and video footage I had seen of cemeteries from the 21st century. Our Ancestors had regarded them with at least some measure of respect and public reverence. Few of them were on consecrated ground, however, and this had opened the doorway for discussions regarding the need for more appropriate solutions for the Deceased.

Traditional burials were expensive, time-consuming, and required valuable real estate in order to house our Deceased. By the mid-21st century, as the Violent Crime rates sky-rocketed and Victims of Homicide were scattered from coast to coast, overwhelmed morgues and funeral homes had needed to find better, and quicker, alternatives to burying Human Remains.

One new process involved using the cremated ashes of Loved Ones, and through a delicate process, turned the ash into gemstones and rocks. These Memorial Stones were widely accepted as a cost-effective and sentimental keepsake. Whatever had finally tipped the scales, by the time of the Great Reformation—long before I was born—things had already changed from the old to the new, and Burials of the Dead had ceased to be common practice.

The choice to bury four persons within unmarked graves in these modern times only seemed to prove that foul play must have been afoot. I wondered about the type of person who would go to such lengths to conceal Human Remains, engaging in a Criminal Act regardless of the Cause of Death for each of the Victims.

Our nation had paid its dues in blood many times over already. We had barely recovered from the darkest chapters in our entire sordid collective history; the 21st century had been responsible for incalculable Crimes Against Humanity. We could not afford to travel down such an ugly and bitter road again, and we never would. Americans would never allow such a blatant disregard for the Sanctity of Human Life to become commonplace as they had during the early decades of the 21st century.

Although their burial plots had been the traditional depth in accordance with historic instruction and known examples, there was something both disturbing and ominous about the deep, black holes from which we had freed our Victims.

The morgue would send over a notification as soon as they were ready for me, as would the head of the Crime Scene Unit currently working around me. I knew they'd be at this task long into the night and probably tomorrow as well. They would pore over this terrain with every available piece of technology, forensic equipment, satellite, and surveillance imagery at their disposal, dividing it into grids and documenting everything from start to finish.

K9 Cadaver Dogs

Although I didn't see them around the field, I knew that there would also be Human Remains Detection Officers and their Canine (K9) partners on site soon. The HRDOs were Law Enforcement Officers that were professionally trained to become dog handlers with the specific intent of working alongside K9s. The carefully selected dogs were also given extensive, rigorous training by professional dog handlers before being partnered with their Human companions.

Once paired with one another, the two Peacekeepers would develop a long-term partnership which often spanned many years and the duration of the K9s Law Enforcement career. This professional relationship and commitment to working together crossed over into their off-duty lives because it was customary for the Officers to take care of their K9 partners full-time.

In the past, there had been many important jobs and responsibilities that Human Beings, particularly Westerners, had explored the idea of working with animals to accomplish. After all the work that Westerners had done over the years in relation to exploratory research and zoology, there were many working animals that carried out tasks that were rich in functionality, purpose, and special importance to the Humans they assisted.

As they had been with many other tasks and professions, dogs had been found to be the ideal animal to carry out duties that were beyond Human ability within certain aspects of Law Enforcement. As a result, there were dogs trained to perform a variety of tasks for the communities they served. There were K9 units that addressed the detection of drugs as well as bomb-making materials. They were most commonly used on the Front-Line, working on securing Criminals and apprehending fleeing Suspects by tackling and corralling them until their Human partners could arrive and secure them. But perhaps their most important Calling was in Emergency Rescue, where they detected both Living Humans as well as Human Remains. Although it was not very respectful, the dogs were given the colloquial name of 'K9 Cadaver Dogs'. They had been a part of US Law Enforcement since the 1970s.

The dogs that were selected to become K9s were predominantly German Shepherds because of their natural aptitude for the work. Their keen sense of smell, high intelligence, and ability to be trained with intricate specificity had made them an invaluable asset to Law Enforcement. German Shepherds did not have an exclusive contract, however; other breeds were used for various purposes as well. Although there were breed characteristics that inevitably made certain dogs either better or less ideal for Police work, what mattered most was their training, heart, desire to work, and willingness to do their jobs with the same dedication and spirit that their fellow Human Officers did.

No matter what their breed or specialty, K9s had been a welcome addition to many government agencies for over one-hundred-fifty years now, and there was no indication that they would be less necessary in the future. Even though we had many tasks and duties that could be done by robotics or other technology, and there would then be no threat to the loss of either Human or K9 life, the tasks performed by K9 units were still arguably only able to be done by them. Their usefulness was not just a matter of tradition or sentimentality; they possessed that inherent connection to their assignments in a manner not unlike their Human partners, and that was something that no amount of artificial intelligence could quantify.

K9s took to their duties with serious purpose and determination, especially the ones that were trained to detect both Living Citizens in Emergency Rescue operations, as well as Deceased Human Remains. Whether it was because they truly were 'Man's best friend' or simply because they were intelligent enough to understand the importance and urgency of their work, K9s had both the instinct and a deeply personal desire to help Humans—even strangers—when called upon.

It was powerful to watch, and when compared to all the automated and impersonal technological advancements at our disposal, it was easy to see the differences. K9s rendered aid with such priceless selflessness and bravery that there could be no question as to their value to the Law Enforcement community and the American People. It was immediately evident to all who watched them work that they carried their actions out with the internal fortitude and genuine desire to help that no technology could ever hope to replicate, and only another living creature could provide.

They would be extremely important for this investigation during these early stages, and I knew they would be hard at work covering the vast expanse of the barren field to be thorough. The satellite imagery would be helpful in some regards and might help find more Human Remains if there were any left to find; but when it came down to it, K9 Cadaver Dogs were always going to be able to do the job twice as quickly and for a fraction of the cost. As grim as it was, a well-trained animal was more effective than the most advanced detection equipment available to us. All the cameras in the sky couldn't compare to a dog's nose on the ground.

Lodgings

I touched base with the Lead Officer of the Crime Scene Investigation Team, shook his hand, and prepared to head back to my lodgings. They had assigned me a small apartment in government barracks, standard fare for all outside Investigators. Without having been there before, I knew I could expect a plain, furnished, one-bedroom unit with a stocked refrigerator and access to other basic amenities, including a pool, gym, and twenty-four-hour cafeteria with room service. It would become my new home for the duration of my stay in Seattle.

I expected the summons from the morgue would be forthcoming in the early hours, since I knew they would begin their work just as soon as they received the Victims into their care.

Knowing the Disposal Site was in well-qualified hands, I made my way to my lodgings. I was eager to hear what the Medical Examiner would have to say.

Something Unsettled

I had been thinking about the case all night and it just wasn't settling well with me. I'd never encountered a case where there were that many variations within the Victims' descriptions. Finding a gravesite was peculiar enough, but from an investigatory perspective, to have found one within twenty-four hours of a Victim being buried seemed very fortuitous.

I realized it was because the young Victim's RFID-Chip had been activated, but even that was odd because her Chip was the only one that had been activated prior to her burial. What had been most interesting to me, however, wasn't only that her Chip had been activated, it was that it had been silent for so long before.

It just didn't add up.

It was concerning, regardless of whether there was one Murderer or multiple. Either way, it was possible that more Homicides might have been committed already. If that ended up being the case, then it was likely that there would be more Victims.

Nothing was known for certain at this point. I would have to meet with the Medical Examiner and receive the reports on each of the Victims before I could even say conclusively what the findings were for Cause of Death. At this point, I couldn't even ascertain that they had been the Victims of Homicide—only that they had all somehow ended up buried in a field together and someone had obviously put them there.

Once I had met with the ME and gained the full outline of each individual Cause of Death, I would at least know if we were looking at one or multiple Suspects. For now, the only thing I knew for sure was that three of my Victims were adults, two women and one male, and the fourth Victim was a young girl.

My first night in Seattle left me feeling unsettled, and sleep was slow to come.

TWO - THE MORGUE AND VICTIMS

Introduction to Officer Stanton

When I awoke in the morning of my first day, I found a notification from the Research and Investigation Specialist awaiting me with a timestamp of 0500, showing he was an early riser. The notification was simple, an introduction stating that he had received his credentials yesterday through the SPD for his new assignment and he would report in today. He stated he would arrive at the office at 0800—a self-appointed time that seemed reasonable enough, although he could have waited until 0900 as it was a standard start time for most government departments. I appreciated his dedication.

According to his email, he was a Research and Investigation Specialist IV, which was the highest rank for that work title. Like many other government jobs, it meant that he had to hold at least a certain number of years within each level before he would be eligible for promotion. By his having reached the glass ceiling within his field, it meant he had to have at least ten years of work experience within his department along with being a fully qualified Law Enforcement Officer. Based on those two facts, without actually seeing his credentials, I could surmise that he must be at least around thirty-five years of age and have a minimum of fifteen years of work history within Law Enforcement.

His name was Officer Stanton—Alexander Stanton, though he signed his note as Alex, and I knew it was highly unlikely I would ever reach a point where I was familiar with him enough to call him by his Christian name. It wasn't my style to be so presumptuous or to create such familiarity before we knew one another well. His professional title, however, had been well-earned. It had always seemed disrespectful not to acknowledge the hard work that went into gaining rank and title and instead use more casual terms.

Officers such as Stanton were invaluable assets for doing the legwork in cases such as this. When so much of my job involved investigating locations and interviewing people, having a well-trained and highly qualified Officer working on my team was worth its weight in gold. I knew I could count on the best coming out of the Seattle Police Department and was grateful that the Chief had assigned someone to my team with Officer Stanton's skill set.

He had attached a link to his Badge ID, which contained an outline of his credentials and qualifications, similar to a resume. It was entirely unnecessary since he had no obligation to provide it to me and I wouldn't have asked, especially since he had been appointed to my team by the SPD Chief. I found it rather amusing in a way. It was either exceptionally earnest or it reflected his efficiency and attention to detail, his being compelled to ensure me he was a suitable and worthy Assistant for the case. It would have been unusual for us to spend much physical time together since I was mostly out in the field and he was working within the realm of technology, but I imagined we would get along well enough.

I readied myself for the day and sent Officer Stanton a quick reply, thanking him for the introduction and ensuring I had the means of contacting him directly before I returned to the HQ where we would eventually meet. After outlining my plans for the morning—to first head over to the Greater Seattle Area Morgue and meet with the Medical Examiner before going over to HQ—I let him know we were also expecting someone from the Victim Advocacy Agency to arrive at our designated office space to set up post. I wasn't sure if he was aware of who she was, but it wouldn't hurt to let him know we had someone else joining our team.

After I sent his message out, I ate the meal I had programmed to have sent up from the cafeteria, and then sent out my coordinates to my bike. I had left it sitting in the SPD garage yesterday when I arrived. Now that I was all checked into the barracks, I could program the autopilot for self-delivery to the garage below. I knew I wouldn't have time to ride it again for a while, but it didn't hurt to have it at the barracks rather than kept at Headquarters.

Once I had sent out the signal and tagged the garage with my badge ID as a notification so the gates would admit my bike upon its arrival, I headed over to the morgue in the SPD Cruiser.

Security and Protocol

The Harborview Center for After-Life Care was a state-of-the-art building built entirely underground in the government district of Seattle. It was one of the largest sub-structures in the Greater Seattle Area and had served as the first architectural prototype after the Great Reformation. No expense was spared, and the square footage was remarkably vast considering its underground location.

The first underground level was the parking lot. It was designed specifically with privacy and respect in mind. Along with the functionality of Law Enforcement being provided with the security and discretion they often required, occasionally a government official or politician would make a pilgrimage down just to get a tour of the process.

After the Great Reformation, many aspects of care for the Deceased changed. The 21st century practice of having family members 'identify the body' of their Deceased Loved One was no longer permitted. Viewing the body caused considerable distress for the family members, and so they had sought other alternatives for verification of Human Remains. The technology to confirm identity through DNA had existed as far back as the mid-1980s, and fingerprinting for over two-hundred years already. They established both forensic tests as the new policy, and from that point forward, we spared family members the gruesome, cruel, barbaric practice of seeing the Deceased body of their Loved One.

As with every other aspect of the Criminal Justice system, the indifference and callous nature of After-Life Care was not only over-hauled in both the legal and physical sense, it was given a social and cultural transformation as well. The time had passed when the Decedents were nothing more than corpses lining the basement walls of overwhelmed hospitals with indifferent staff and inadequate funding issues. One could not examine the Value of Human Life without considering how we, as a society, addressed the bodies of our Loved Ones once they had Passed from this world.

The Morgue was a Level 3 zone, which meant that anyone working within its building had high enough clearance that their identities were secured. It ensured that everyone working or visiting the building had access to criminal investigations in some aspect or another. Access meant they were involved in Law Enforcement, Emergency Response, or the Criminal Justice system in a professional capacity. Qualifying for clearance enabled unveiled, unrestricted communication and connections within the designated areas. When engaging in conversation and establishing valuable working relationships over the years, having that intimacy, even in a professional setting, mattered. It helped to develop trust beyond simply knowing that everyone was working on the same side.

The zoning gave me clearance to remove my visor, which I appreciated but knew I wouldn't take advantage of. Even though I was an Investigator, I was still responsible for wearing a uniform that was only vaguely different from any other member of Law Enforcement in America. Our uniforms were unique regarding color, style, badges, and various other means of establishing our role and rank, but overall, when one observed us, there was not supposed to be any question as to who we were or what our role was. As Peacekeepers, we were Law Enforcement Officers first and foremost; whether we were Investigators, Front-Line Officers, or Forensics, made little difference to the public. They just wanted to know we were there and easily identifiable.

As such, my uniform had the same security standards as all others, and very little to distinguish it from those worn by the SPD. I had a light Kev-Tek helmet for my outerwear with the front composing of the see-through visor much like any other helmet might have but with additional security features. Underneath, I had a balaclava that had a detachable visor secured to it that only cleared my eyes. They required both the visor and helmet whenever we were out in the general population.

The balaclava I wore underneath my helmet consisted of a fabric hoodie that covered my head, fanning out over my shoulders beneath my uniform and protecting my neck. I could raise both the helmet visor as well as the balaclava visor so people could see my face from the top of my eyebrows to the middle of my nose, although it was not recommended or advised to do so as it left me extremely vulnerable. It was designed to prevent anyone from seeing my eyes, facial skin tone, or other personal features directly. There were a variety of tools contained within it, including a voice recognition and distortion program. I could also lighten and darken the tint of the visor while still keeping it lowered and secured, which was the preferred method of interaction with the public. Ultimately, the Kev-Tek material prevented mortal injury, shielding my bare skin from knife wounds such as slashings or stabbings.

Our equipment required our personal biometrics in order to activate and function properly, but when speaking to the Citizenry, all Peacekeepers were required to use the same generic voice programming to help conceal our identities and protect us from potential doxing.

The Medical Examiner had no obligation to allow anyone into his workspace and let them see him without his own visor in place, nor did he have to permit me to go without mine. Protocol dictated that although we both had the right to either remain protected or to lower our guard, it was entirely up to each individual regarding how comfortable we were with the decision. It could not be overstated enough that we were both at much greater risk if we could identify other team members out in public, and it had been that way for well over the last century.

It would be unheard of for us to conduct our duties entirely exposed to the public, especially out on the streets. There had been too many tragic Deaths over the years because of the lack of security measures for them to not be used at this point. After thousands of cases of LEOs and other government agents being subjected to doxing, stalking, Homicides, and even the Raping and Murdering of family members, the People and their government finally demanded action to protect the identities of all those who were willing to work within Law Enforcement. The sharp decline in Peacekeepers during the 21st century illustrated just how dangerous the profession had become.

It had taken years of Violence against government workers, especially LEOs, ICE, and Border Agents before the tech industry took ownership for their intentional inaction regarding their failure to implement protective measures to prevent doxing and to conceal personal information responsibly. After decades of repeated hacking and the distribution of personal information of government employees, which was ultimately used for nefarious purposes, security for Law Enforcement Officers had been reduced to rubble by the mid-21st century.

What was indisputable was that the benefits of concealed identities outweighed any inconvenience or burden the multi-layered uniform and head gear created. The uniforms and concealed identities unquestionably increased the survival rates for all LEOs on a national scale. No Peacekeeper would ever sacrifice their right to anonymity and the security it provided whilst on the job just for the opportunity to avoid wearing their external helmet, nor would they face potential Death just so they could avoid the discomfort of their heavy uniform. The policies were in place for a reason, and they had saved countless lives over the decades as a result. It was worth the discomfort, and seldom did one ever hear a complaint. Even still, it was always a much-appreciated reprieve whenever we could remove our head gear, and I was always among those who were grateful to have a break.

For these reasons, it made working within the field of Criminal Justice both easier and more restrained. We were forced to be cautious, forced to question our relationships and privacy within our own workplace, and mostly, forced to keep our professional lives discreet in public. Most families concealed having a Peacekeeper in their family, instead opting to list their profession as some vague field or industry. This was done for the protection of all, even decades after public perception against Law Enforcement had shifted into more positive and favorable views once again.

Choosing to maintain my anonymity even whilst around others who worked within the field of Criminal Justice wasn't just for my protection; it was meant to help keep everyone safe. I was inclined to be cautious; history had proven that no one was ever as secure or protected as they believed.

Entering the Morgue

I scanned my card and retina at the entry, and then made my way down the hall to the morgue. It was likely that the Medical Examiner would have called in additional help; the level of detail necessary to devote to each examination would be far too great for only one ME to conduct all four examinations properly himself.

There were Detectives and Medical Examiners that went years between cases if they lived in small towns. For many, it was a rare occurrence whenever they encountered Deceased Victims of Homicide or even Suicide. Aside from the infrequent discovery of multiple Homicides due to the work of a Serial Killer, very few Investigators had encountered four sets of Human Remains from a singular Crime Scene or Disposal Site in the same month. It did still happen, however, in the rare event of a national tragedy, natural disaster, or Terrorist Attack.

Any Medical Examiner would understand just how important his contribution would be in relation to the work of the Investigator. I sincerely hoped that the team appointed to do these examinations would be at the top of their game.

I pushed into the double doors and was gladdened by what I saw. There were at least a half-dozen top-level Medical Examiners plus another half-dozen lower-level Assistants.

It was heartening to see that either the SPD Chief or the Lead ME had taken great pains to ensure that the Victims were going to be given excellent care. When it became time to speak to the Families, I would be able to tell them unequivocally that they had given their Loved Ones the best services possible.

The Lead ME caught my eye and signaled for me to approach. He appeared to be working with another ME on the child. There were two additional Assistant ME's (AME's) standing nearby, both observing the examination as their gear provided additional records of the event.

They recorded all examinations in triple form: audio, video, and an internal hand-scribed copy for the records, which were then downloaded and stored at their main department headquarters. Quality assurance was always a top priority with Postmortem Medical Examinations; Loved Ones needed answers, and the Criminal Justice system heavily relied upon the forensic evidence they gathered.

As an Investigator, I had always appreciated the thoroughness of the ME's office. No matter their location, Medical Examiners were more consistent with their professionalism than most factory line work. They were a vital part of the investigative and legal process; one had to respect the work they did. It was important to recognize just how valuable their role was in the Criminal Justice process.

Luckily for us, the Great Reformation helped to give credit where it was due at long last. For all the many hours and classes we took for our education in this field, it never ceased to amaze most of us just how little regard the ME's office and practitioners used to be given. How else, though, could one comprehend the sheer medical complexity of the Violence against the Human Body that then resulted in a person's

Death? The fragility of Human Life was easily snuffed out—but without Medical Examiners telling the Victim's story for them posthumously, how could we possibly hope to understand the most intimate of causation and the ensuing events that led to their demise?

Indeed, as we all knew, there were millions of Deaths that were vindicated solely through the procedural work of the ME. When addressing the concept of the true 'unsung heroes,' the Criminal Justice system would not be very successful without those committed to providing exceptional work through Postmortem Examinations. There were many jobs within the Criminal Justice and healthcare system that were not well known or often acknowledged for their commitment to helping our nation and Citizenry, but without a doubt, I held the work of Medical Examiners at the top.

I shook the Lead ME's hand; he introduced himself as ME-177. Even with our privacy less guarded within the building, personal names were still strictly in violation of protocol. He told me to call him Lee. There was about a one in a million chance that was actually his name, but I introduced myself and told him to call me Ivan. I always went by Ivan.

Our circles were small enough that it was likely we had heard of one another even if we hadn't yet met. Just because we didn't have our true names on record didn't mean our integrity, work ethic, or reputations weren't well-known or well-established. There were probably only a few thousand ME's in the entire country, and fewer who were dedicated to cases specializing in Violent Crimes. As soon as he said his name, I realized I was speaking with an important man; he had been an advocate for change within his department, and his work was incredibly significant within the Criminal Justice field.

ME-177, AKA Lee, was the ME that had transformed Medical Examinations during the Final Wave of the Great Reformation. He had first gained recognition after publishing an article related to the importance of inventorying hair, fiber, and DNA samples found on every Deceased Citizen that crossed the paths of any Medical Examiner in the country. He cited it was imperative for the good of the nation that we gave every single Deceased Citizen the Dignity and Respect of having their Physical Bodies processed and catalogued with meticulous precision regardless of the simplicity of the case or Cause of Death.

Lee, the Medical Examiner now standing directly in front of me, was a brilliant man with a tremendous amount of love for his Fellow Countrymen. I was honored to work with him. It also confirmed my previous thoughts about the SPD Chief; he was dedicated to discovering the truth about what had happened to our Victims.

Reviewing Victims with the Medical Examiner

I followed the Medical Examiner over to the first table. The room was standard for this industry; cement floors with drains, stainless steel everywhere, and brick walls with a white ceiling to contrast all the metal. There were doors in various places leading to unknown areas of their domain, and classical music played softly from the speakers built into the walls. It was not a very welcoming environment, but then, it would not be a simple task to make it so. The lack of windows was common to most government buildings, whether above or below ground, but when sharing an enclosed space with a myriad of people in outfits similar to Hazmat suits, four Deceased Citizens, and a variety of overpowering, and oftentimes unpleasant, odors, it created an oddly claustrophobic effect.

"Sir," I stated.

"I remember your work, Ivan, from the Railway case. Nicely done. I'm glad to see they brought out one of their best for this. It's going to get complicated." His eye contact was strong, and his voice was deep and craggy.

"Thank you, Sir. How are things?" I asked. It had been less than twenty-four hours since the Remains had been discovered.

Lee motioned for his AME to back up a bit and give us a little room. The AME moved over to a wall and began setting up documents along the brick so we could look after the initial physical exam. I followed Lee's lead, and for the first time, took a moment just to look at the Lifeless form on the table below me. In just that split second, everything emotional within myself seemed to disengage naturally, and I could feel the veil of professionalism wash over me like a layer of Kevlar.

It was the little girl, approximately five or six years of age. Her skin was pale, almost translucent. She had a privacy sheet over her hipline and across her little chest area, even though she was clearly too young to be developed. It was simply a small measure of modesty and respect. Her eyes were closed, and her ears were pierced. Her blonde, curly hair was dirty and matted. She seemed small in frame, even for her age.

"Well, from a preliminary standpoint, this one appears to be the last Victim out of the four. Her Time of Death is less than forty-eight hours. We'll narrow that down to a more precise time in our Final Report. They are currently working on confirming her identity and cross-checking with Missing Persons. We believe her age to be six. She's lost her two maxillary incisors—her two front teeth.

"We've done preliminary examinations for DNA under fingernails and swabbed her mouth. We're waiting for the Omniscan report to upload, but we know she's been penetrated vaginally, anally, and orally. I believe her Cause of Death will be Tension Pneumothorax from a collapsed lung. She had significant bruising, and it appears she was severely dehydrated and malnourished. The last few weeks before her Death had not been pleasant. We won't be able to compare her weight until we've gathered more information from her medical records, but she appears to be under-sized for her age besides the obvious malnourishment she'd been experiencing. We'll know more once we get her records squared."

The Omniscan was similar to an MRI machine but capable of doing much more intricate, detailed scans, both internally and externally. It was an integral part of medical exams, both for the living and the dead. Through its advanced technology, it was capable of reconstructing Human Remains and isolating damage to the body—intentionally inflicted or not—even after they had been ravaged by time, the elements, and natural decomposition. It was an indispensable tool for all Postmortem Examinations. Unlike the human eye, the technology was error-free, documenting every abnormality within the materials examined, providing exact measurements of all wounds sustained from the epidermis to the bone.

Her frail body was covered in dark bruises, all various shades, indicating they had occurred at different times.

The faint blonde hairs on her legs were highlighted by the artificial light in the room, and for some reason, the only thing I could imagine was her running around barefoot in the yard on a nice summer day like today. That's what she should have been doing, and yet here we were.

As I listened, my eyes kept zeroing in on her tiny feet. Her toes had once been painted with fingernail polish; what remained was old, faded, and chipping. Her small feet were bare and dirty. There were no cuts or scrapes, but they seemed to have a bit of hardening along the bottom, as if she had been barefoot for a while and her little feet had toughened up to accommodate the lack of shoes. Even so, they appeared small and fragile. And as I listened to the older man speak of the Brutal Assault that had obviously been committed against her on more than one occasion, all I could think about was the mother out there missing her; the same one that had probably held this little girl in her lap and had painted each of those tiny little toenails bubblegum pink, never imagining such horrors would ever befall their family.

While we stood there going over her emaciated body in more detail, one of the AME's came over with his electronic file pad. He had confirmed the match between her DNA and the RFID-Chip information that had initially begun this entire process and helped us find her. Her name was Katarina Urakov, and she was six years old. Confirmation of her identity was the first step toward initiating our investigation; given how many Jane Doe's had been found over the generations, it was always a relief to have the identities of Victims confirmed through DNA. It was a solid starting point.

Moving on, I followed the Medical Examiner as he led me past several tables and into his office. Inviting me to sit down, he shut the door and then took his seat behind his neatly organized desk.

"You're welcome to view the remaining three Victims if you'd like, but their state of decomposition would probably not make it worth your time. They were all buried within a very brief window after their deaths, but the three adults were placed there at least twenty to thirty days before the little girl, and their bodies have undergone significant changes despite the burials."

I shook my head; seeing their bodies in a state of decomposition would not necessarily add anything to my investigation. I would be able to garner all of the information I needed from the reports that the Medical Examiner and his team would provide.

The ME settled back in his chair, pulling out an electronic file pad, and brought up something on his screen.

"They identified the second adult female Victim as Mariam Pembrook, age thirty-four. So far, we're listing her Cause of Death as Strangulation. You might not be familiar with it if you've been out of Washington State recently, but her case has been in the news regularly over the last few weeks."

I shook my head no and waited for him to continue.

"Well, she disappeared from a shopping center a while back. It was a clear case of Abduction. They had some CCTV footage to confirm it, but I don't think it helped much to identify her Attacker. But from it, LEOs knew she was Abducted. They had a lot of coverage and local response, but it didn't lead to anything."

Using his E-File, he brought up several images on the media wall of the outline of a female body. It had been marked in a multitude of places to indicate various injuries Mariam's body had sustained. There were 3D graphics that rotated in a full 360 degrees on the screen, allowing for a full analysis of her Remains without seeing them in person.

Her Abduction meant that her case would be classified as an ARM Attack—an Abduction-Rape-Murder. The ME began outlining all that her body had endured and damage that had been documented. There were some broken fingernails they were swabbing for DNA, blood and semen in the vaginal area, and several bite marks, all of which would require further testing and documentation.

As I reviewed the images of her body with the Medical Examiner, there was no question that the man that had Assaulted her had been exceptionally Brutal, as her body was covered in scratches and scrapes from rough terrain, bite marks, and bruising all around her torso and face. Her wrists and neck were covered in bruises as well. The bruising along her neck confirmed that she had been strangled, and although severe, paled in comparison to the four sizable gouges in her chest area where an obviously oversized, serrated knife had been used on her. Further evidence of the knife was visible with a smattering of defensive wounds along her hands and arms as she had fought against her Assailant.

I imagined she had been beneath him, judging by the patterns of the cuts along her hands and forearms. She had not just been Abducted and Raped; the animal that had done this to her had been excessively angry, Violent, and intentionally Sadistic. This level of animus usually indicated it was a personal relationship with significant hatred to cause this much rage to be directed at a person, and I made a mental note to discuss it with Officer Stanton when we had time.

We spoke of Mariam Pembrook at great length, and I listened closely as the ME outlined noteworthy details pertaining to her injured body. It might not all be relevant at this point in my investigation, but by the time we captured the animal that had done this, and it went to trial, every single scratch and scrape that Mariam had been subjected to would be on display.

When he had finished presenting his findings for Mariam, he moved on to our only male Victim, Arlan Randall, from Carnation, Washington. The ME said he was waiting on a toxicology report, but that his Remains had been the most deteriorated. This indicated that out of the four Victims, he had been the first to die, and had been buried the longest. Although the burial of his Remains had drastically slowed the decomposition process comparative to what would have been done had he been left to the elements above ground, there was still a significant degree of deterioration. For this reason, the ME did not have much prepared for his report yet, and was waiting on more comprehensive work.

The ME closed Arlan's file down into a corner, and then brought up the one for the final female Victim. Her basic information had been entered into the Postmortem Examination report visible on the wall. She had been a woman in her mid-twenties and identified as Rebecca Summers. She was a petite female, approximately 5'2', weight listed as one-hundred-twenty; another example of the type of female that was most often subjected to ARM Attacks.

The Medical Examiner shuffled through files on his electronic pad, eventually closing out Arlan Randall's report entirely and then focusing on the one for Rebecca Summers. It was eerily quiet, with only the faint ticking of the clock breaking the silence.

It was strange to hear, an analog clock in a digital world. My guess was that the architect selected it intentionally as some type of retro-throwback to a bygone era; it certainly seemed as though every morgue in America existed within another dimension where time had no meaning. No matter where I went, every morgue was always the same, and always had been. The clock was fitting; it was on a permanent loop of twenty-four-hour cycles in a place where time no longer had any functionality. Only the Living had need of time; for the inhabitants of this facility, every passing second was another step away from all that each of its guests had once held dear.

Lee's voice broke the air, bringing my wandering mind back into focus. The deep baritone filled the room with warmth despite the cold temperatures and bleak surroundings.

"Ah, all right. Here we have Rebecca Summers, age confirmed to be twenty-three. She Committed Suicide after an Abortion. It was a relatively professional one from what I could discern, but it was still an Abortion. My guess was within a week or so of her Suicide. She probably just couldn't cope."

He shook his head.

"A damn shame, too. She might have pulled through this. Clearly, she just couldn't live with it."

"So, what was the Cause of Death?"

"A couple of things show it was Suicide; officially it was an Overdose by prescription pills. But she had other indications of Attempted Suicide. Look at her arm here. She must have tried it before."

I looked at the image of a long cut running up her left arm.

"And she meant business, given the length of the laceration. But she didn't go deep enough; she probably panicked and stopped the bleeding herself, or she just didn't want to have another go at it when she realized it wouldn't work. Either way, she never finished. But the cut was done recently. So, I'm thinking she probably tried to do it after she found out she was Pregnant; the data verified she was still in her first trimester when she had the Abortion."

"And the second thing?" I asked.

"She took a bunch of different pills. My guess is that they came from the Abortionist; she hadn't been prescribed anything for years through her Primary Care according to her medical records. She had a combination of codeine-based pain relievers and anti-depressants."

Suicide.

What a waste. Suicides were always difficult for me to understand, and this one was no different.

Although the ME had undoubtedly used the chemical component commonly used in recent decades that all but halted the degradation of Human Remains when used in combination with the extremely low temperatures within the morgue, if left unattended, eventually time would decimate all that this woman once was. This was not the case in store for her, luckily. They would halt her Decomposition only as long as necessary for all Postmortem Examinations to be completed. She would then join the millions that had gone before her, and they would convert her Physical Remains into one of a multitude of hard gems for safekeeping.

It was not permanent physical preservation, but it was an eternal one; a reminder of all that she once was—the only one of her kind. I thought of her mother and father and the heartbreak they would surely one day soon know.

It was a beautiful thing to me, the memorialization of our frail Human Bodies through gemstones. There could be no better tribute for our weak, Physical Beings than to be transformed and gloriously preserved into beautiful stones; weathered, tested, and able to shine for eternity.

I prayed that this poor young girl was finally at peace, and secretly regretted that I would soon deliver more heartbreak to her parents than they were already experiencing. Would that I could, I would share this moment with every Suicidal person so they could see a glimpse into their future beforehand; no earthly woe was worth the depth of Suffering their Passing left on those who Mourned them.

Her Pregnancy was an interesting development, and it brought forth a new line of questions. It had been too early for her body to have undergone any type of noticeable physical change. I wondered how she had looked in the mirror and reconciled with herself that Abortion and Suicide had been the only solution.

"One more thing—" I began. "Did you do a check for any STD's or any type of recent infections?"

Lee nodded his head to show he understood where I was going.

"We did, but the results haven't cleared yet. I'll have my AME send over the results when they arrive. Is your Assistant cleared for all case details?"

I nodded my head and thanked him again. We both stood, taking the time to shake hands as our meeting ended. He would send over his reports to Stanton once he was done.

The Medical Examiner walked with me to the door. He patted me on the shoulder as we parted and mentioned that he was still working on a few other bits and pieces he would pass along soon.

I considered what I could now confirm with absolute certainty, even if I still lacked physical evidence. My youngest and oldest female Victims, Katarina and Mariam, were both Abducted and Sexually Assaulted. They had both been Savagely Violated, forced to endure severe Emotional, Physical, and Sexual Trauma, and then discarded when their Abductors were done using them.

It was horrific to see, even in this preliminary capacity. I knew that the reports and exams would expound upon their Assaults in much greater depth when they were concluded, but for now, I knew enough to know that both of them had Suffered unimaginably during their Final Hours.

I left the Morgue with dozens of notes and images filling my head. I certainly had more questions than answers at this point. But as I headed to my temporary office within the SPD, I had to wonder just how dark this road I was traveling down was going to turn. There was much to be done before I would have any answers.

Meeting Officer Stanton

After I went to the morgue, I returned to the SPD Headquarters. The workspace they had provided us with was on the same floor as the Chief's office; it included a centralized conference room and was generous in size considering we were only a team of three. It was there that I found the Research Specialist sitting and waiting for me, quietly working on a laptop.

I approached the room, knocking on the door politely before entering, and waited for his response before I proceeded.

My balaclava and visor were still on, though I raised it once he acknowledged me.

I crossed the room as he rose from his seat, a younger man in his mid-thirties with light brown hair and clear blue eyes. He was about 5'9", and while not a man with a large frame, it was obvious he spent a fair amount of time in the gym developing his natural build to its best. His handshake was firm, and his smile was genuine.

"Ivan," I said.

"Stanton—Alex," he said, eagerly.

"It's so good to meet you. I always told the Chief if they ever called you in on a case I would appreciate being allowed on. I've been reading about your cases since I was a cadet," he shared.

I smiled; his compliment was flattering but his personality was so engaging it was difficult not to like him immediately.

"Well, thank you. Not the best of circumstances, but I'm glad to be here. I've never done a case in Seattle, which seems crazy considering Washington has always been my home station," I responded.

He nodded, indicating he was familiar with enough of my cases to know this already, and then waved toward the empty chairs around the table, inviting me to sit. I pulled the chair out next to his and motioned for him to sit back down with me.

"Thank you for sending out that note already; I appreciated it," I told him.

He smiled again, "Sure thing. If it's a system that works for you, I usually send out anything new I learn as it develops."

I nodded, knowing that the immediacy of the information-sharing was usually far more beneficial than inconvenient. Many times, people didn't appreciate being so tightly connected to their electronics, but in the middle of an active investigation, it was important to know that my lead researcher was on point.

We spent some time chatting, changing topics between previous cases I'd worked on and what we were potentially looking at in terms of the case looming before us. Before I realized it, an hour had passed. My stomach rumbled, reminding me it was time to find something to eat. Officer Stanton and I both rose, shook hands once again, and agreed we would touch base as needed. I let him know I was planning on meeting the Victim Advocate the next afternoon. Following suit, Stanton packed up his laptop and followed me out of the conference room.

As I made my way back to the garage, I found myself grateful for the Chief's intervention regarding the team he appointed. If the Victim Advocate was anywhere near as affable and obliging, I felt confident I would be working with a few of the best professionals available to me.

Report on Four Victims

My newly assigned Research and Investigation Specialist had received the notification from the Medical Examiner's office regarding the confirmed identification of the Victims. He then put together a briefing to let me know the preliminaries that he had discovered about each of them. There wasn't much information available, which seemed strange once I learned that each of them had already been reported to the Seattle Police Department as Missing Persons. Officer Stanton's note mentioned that he had expected to find four individual case files with extensive notes and leads outlined within but had been unable to locate anything substantive.

Even though each of the Victims had been reported as a Missing Person over the course of the last four months, the extent of their 'investigations' had only gone so far as the initial reports filed by the Front-Line Responding Officers, who had then turned their reports in to the Missing Persons Division. None of the cases had gone anywhere after that; the only one that appeared to have made any type of progress had been Katarina Urakov's. Her case was the only one that had been assigned to two Missing Persons Detectives. No one from the Missing Persons Division had put in a formal request to have an outside Investigator conduct an independent investigation.

It seemed improbable that the Seattle Police Department could have four open Missing Persons cases that were all somehow 'overlooked', especially since one was a little girl. If the department was overwhelmed with cases, it was all the more reason why they should have called in outside Investigators to assist, and yet they hadn't. Even if it was just accredited to the local SPD Missing Persons Division choosing to keep it in-house and only assign it to their own Detectives, it hadn't been done. Officer Stanton had noted in his briefing that he couldn't think of a single reason to explain or justify why none of the cases were assigned to anyone, nor could he imagine why it appeared none of them were actively being investigated.

The youngest Victim, Katarina Urakov, was five when she had been reported Missing in March and had turned six during her absence. She had been the most recently Killed but had also been the first one to Disappear. This meant that she had been kept Alive somewhere for over three months before her Death and had most likely been Sexually Assaulted countless times at the hands of her Abductor during those months.

Her parents were Oscar and Lucia Urakov, both living, and residents of the Greater Seattle Area. Katarina had Disappeared outside their Roman Catholic church. There had never been enough evidence to create a single Suspect. Her case was still listed as Active, and there were still two Detectives assigned to it. But until now, there had been no sightings or new clues generated. Although her case was still open, it was clearly stagnant and had been lying dormant until now. Had her Remains not been found, I had little doubt that it would have continued to be unsolved.

The second Victim to have been reported Missing was Arlan Randall. What little we knew from his file indicated that he had been Missing roughly the same amount of time as little Katarina, but unlike her, he had died almost immediately after his

Disappearance. While the Medical Examiner still hadn't confirmed the exact date of his demise, the advanced state of deterioration indicated he had been furthest along in the Decomposition cycle. His Remains had shown no signs of physical violence.

Arlan had been a strange Victim in contrast to the other three females. He had been reported Missing by his wife, Caroline. The circumstances of his Disappearance had not added up. He had suddenly 'Disappeared' from a large farm that not only had more than a dozen farm workers on the property at the time, but also his wife. The man was supposedly immobile and wheelchair-bound while suffering from terminal cancer. And yet, despite all this, he had mysteriously Vanished. I wasn't personally familiar with the case beyond what I had learned from the report.

The third Victim, Rebecca Summers, had been reported Missing by her roommate. We had very little to go on. Her case file was almost an afterthought; it was as if someone had taken the initial notification listing her as a Missing Person and then set the newly created file in a drawer somewhere, forgetting about it entirely.

The fourth Victim was Mariam Pembrook. A wife, mother, and local teacher, she had Gone Missing one afternoon recently from a shopping center parking lot. Chronologically, she had been the third reported as Missing, after Katarina Urakov and then Arlan Randall.

The photograph included in her file by Officer Stanton had shown a plump woman with shoulder-length strawberry-blonde hair and a gracious smile. She had been reported Missing by her husband.

She had been very well known within her circle, and the entire community had rallied behind her Disappearance with search parties. They had scoured miles of city blocks surrounding the site of her Abduction. Although they had surveillance footage of the parking lot she was taken from, there had never been a positive ID of the man that had approached her from behind, struck her, and then shoved her into her backseat before driving her car away. The car had been found a week later, but despite continued efforts in both locations to search for her, Mariam had simply Vanished.

Because there had been surveillance footage and they had proven that she had been Abducted, there had been a state-wide warning implemented by Law Enforcement, along with a BOLO alert for the Abductor. The video footage had been almost useless because of the graininess of the recording. It had been taken from CCTV cameras, but the distance had drastically diminished the quality. It had been vital, though, because it had confirmed that she had, indeed, been the Victim of an Abduction. Despite the publicity and attention, she had not been located. I wasn't sure if they had halted searches yet.

I wondered if the man in the surveillance video was the one responsible for causing each of my four Victims to end up buried in an isolated field, and if he was responsible for what had happened to the little girl as well.

There were no noticeable similarities between the four Victims; they were all in different age groups, had different physical appearances, and didn't seem to have anything obvious in common. But somehow, these four Victims had shared something significant enough that they had all eventually ended up buried side by side in a desolate man-made graveyard.

Meanwhile, I knew that Officer Stanton had plans to get started with some additional research he had outlined on his end, and we would touch base again tomorrow.

I was also planning to meet the new Victim Advocate from the Victim Advocacy Agency that the SPD Chief had assigned to our case tomorrow afternoon. After we had a bit more information gathered, we would begin with the Notifications for the families, and meet with them to get some of our own interviews established. Essentially, we were starting from scratch, since there was so little information to go on. Given the complexity of the case and the Victims involved, this was probably for the best anyhow; we wouldn't have anything presented to us that might be misleading or take us down the wrong path based on notes made by other Investigators in the files before they became ours.

THREE — SPD MORGUE AND VA

RS—Postmortem Follow-up

As I began the drive over to the SPD Headquarters, I thought more about what I knew of Rebecca and her situation thus far.

There had to be more to it than just an Unwanted Pregnancy and a Suicide. There were enough resources out there regarding Unwanted Pregnancy that it seemed unreconcilable that a young woman such as herself would go for an Abortion rather than utilizing any of the other known methods available to address it, and that was ignoring the reality that she could have used a variety of contraceptives in the first place to prevent the Unwanted Pregnancy from even occurring.

Based on this alone, I knew there was more to this young woman's choice to go down this dark path. I had a whole different avenue to investigate. If the ME's report stated that Rebecca had not been using any type of contraception, it could be another indication that she had not been sexually active but had, instead, been Raped. Unless I could confirm she had been involved in a sexual relationship with a man through my investigation, I could not entirely remove the possibility of Rape until I had found the father of her child.

I was eager to see the results of the STD panel because I suspected Rape was the answer. Statistically, there was a high probability that her Rapist would have been infected with some type of STD. If that were the case, even if the girl could have borne the weight of getting Pregnant because of Sexual Assault, what she could clearly not have learned to live with was some manner of sexually transmitted disease that she had been stricken with because of her Rape. It was a possibility; I had seen Suicides by women before for precisely that same reason.

Both Abortion and Suicide were Crimes Against Humanity; there would have been tragic consequences not only for her, but for her entire family. They would have been heart-broken, but they would have also been disallowed to collect on any of the Victim Compensation and After-Life Care funding that they would have otherwise been entitled to. There was also a rather unspoken but quiet connection to shame for many people to have their family lineage connected to such Criminal Offenses. For many people, it was easier to be related to a thief than it was to know that someone in their own family had Taken another Human Life—even if it was their own.

There was nothing to indicate that Rebecca would have felt compelled to avoid Suicide purely to secure the financial compensation paid out through the State following her untimely Death, but it was a well-documented preventative measure that many

Suicidal Citizens had acknowledged had led to their seeking psychological and medical help for their problems rather than following through with their decision to End their own Life. It wasn't a fool-proof measure, and there were still Suicides every year in America. But for many, the decision to hurt their families through their Deaths and then to leave them to struggle financially, as well as bearing the societal burden of their Suicide, was just too costly a price for them to force their Loved Ones to bear.

A Crime Against Humanity is a Crime Against Ourselves.

It was a familiar phrase that they had taught us since our infancy, meant to instill a firm connection between the Sanctity of Human Life and the value we placed on our own life as well as that of our Fellow Man. Aside from that, anyone with a basic grasp of our population numbers understood why every life mattered and could not be so casually thrown away.

There was one last point, although it went without saying. Even if this young woman had chosen to have an Abortion and chosen to End her own Life, she had still somehow managed to bury herself in an unmarked grave along with three of her Fellow Countrymen.

Someone out there had the answers we were looking for.

Someone had impregnated this young woman, taken her to get an illegal Abortion at an undisclosed location, and paid for it to be done. Someone—with medical training—had conducted the Abortion. Someone had driven her home afterward. And eventually, someone had either caused her Death or found her Deceased Remains and then made the conscious decision to bury her in that field.

None of these Victims had buried themselves, regardless of the circumstances that had led them to the edge of those graves.

AR—Postmortem Follow-Up

The ME had assessed that Arlan was terminal and nearing the End of his Life. However, after reviewing his toxicology report, he was listing his Death as an Overdose of Opioids. Whatever my investigation would prove, as far as the ME was concerned, the man had either taken, or been given, a high dosage of morphine. It wasn't up to him to question the motive behind it; he could only base his determination on the information he had to work with, and that meant Arlan's body.

At first glance, seeing an elderly person with a terminal illness die of an Overdose seemed like Suicide or possibly even an Assisted-Suicide. It was highly probable he had Overdosed on his own pain medication, which could have been self-administered.

Even though both forms of Suicide were illegal and socially condemned within American culture, they did still occur occasionally. Having a body being ravaged by such a horrific disease like cancer would be a reason worthy of Ending one's own Life to many people. Debilitating and terminal illnesses had been listed as the number one cause of Suicides and Assisted-Suicides in past years, and many regarded Suicide as a solution to a problem for which there could only be one ending. Given his immobility, Assisted-Suicide was a plausible possibility.

I needed to know more about the surviving members of his family. The important part here was that whatever the motivation was for his Death, it clearly would not be financial since neither Missing Persons nor Suicides could receive Restitution and Compensation per the Victim Compensation Fund. The law was very clear, and Suicide, especially Assisted-Suicides since they required pre-meditation and a secondary person, were automatic disqualifiers.

If Arlan's Death was intentional, the overall goal was unlikely to have been for financial gain. The law required Missing Persons to be Missing for a minimum of five years if their death was presumed, but there were no Human Remains. This meant no physical sightings or financial activity after an investigation. We always investigated Missing Persons upon notification, without delay, and without skepticism. Law Enforcement was free to investigate without time-restricted policies that crippled response times such as those in the 21st century.

The investigatory delays had a high cost to Human Life. For Missing Persons, every single moment and scrap of information was vital. Time mattered. Given the statistics for Abduction, especially for the Kidnapping and Sexual Predation of children, time was a vital factor in reaching positive results. The rate of Death for Missing Children was astronomical. The longer they were unaccounted for, the higher the probability of their ending up Murdered. Statistically, if a child reported Missing was not found within the first forty-eight hours, they were most likely already Dead. When searching for Missing Persons, especially children, every second counted. We treated our elderly population just as we did Missing Children—many were suffering from chronic health conditions, Alzheimer's, and Dementia, and time was of the essence when locating them.

Removing profit as the motivator, it left only Suicide or Assisted-Suicide. The man had cancer. He was terminal. He was likely in severely debilitating pain every day. By the Medical Examiner's own admission, Arlan's body had been plagued with substantial damage internally that was widespread and would have only continued to increase in severity. Cancer was a terrible, painful way to die, and it had long since been the bane of our mortal existence. Millions of American Citizens had lost their lives to the disease. Judging by Arlan's medical status, he had either been untreatable and incurable, or he had finally just accepted his fate and surrendered to it once it metastasized.

Even though Suicide was illegal, those who were committed to Ending their own Lives often found a way. Euthanasia was far less common. And despite there still being a high enough Suicide rate within the US to require a database to track them, the numbers were only in the dozens, not the hundreds of thousands like they were during the latter-21st century. It was rumored that there was a small movement of support for Suicide and Euthanasia, but most Americans regarded both as not only morally wrong, but criminal. Even if there were a select demographic of Citizens who supported ones 'Right to Choose' Suicide or Euthanasia, most people found the cost for such types of Death to be too high to risk it.

Euthanasia would result in a Murder Conviction for anyone found Guilty of rendering assistance to an American Citizen intending to End their own Life. It was one thing to believe that Suicide should be allowed to be fulfilled as a choice as an American Citizen and legalized; the argument could be made for that and had been in the past. True freedom meant the personal autonomy to do as one wanted with one's own person. But Euthanasia, whether Physician-Assisted or by one's family or someone else, was openly classified as Premeditated Murder. Most people would cease to be helpful once they faced the risk of the Death Penalty themselves, and anyone found Guilty of Murder in the First Degree would ultimately be put to Death.

The truth behind Arlan's Death would be revealed all in due course as my investigation developed more answers than questions. Whether or not Arlan delivered the final dosage of morphine to his system and Took his own Life was only part of the question; I needed to know who helped bury his Remains and why.

Did this man choose to End his own Life, or did someone make that decision for him? Who had transported his body to his grave, who dug the hole they buried him in, and who filled the dirt over his body? Was this proof that it was Murder, or could it be evidence that this man had recruited additional help so he could take part in an Assisted-Suicide? Perhaps one of the most obvious questions was whether Arlan had the mobility and dexterity to Take his own Life. He was already wheelchair-bound, but I didn't have any evidence to support either way whether he could deliver the last shot of morphine that had claimed his Final Breath.

Whoever had buried these bodies had not intended for them to ever be discovered. Although it may only be a technicality, we needed to determine if this was Suicide, Assisted-Suicide, or Homicide.

The Investigation Team

In bygone eras there used to be two Detectives usually paired up within most Police Departments, and they spent the bulk of their time doing tedious, slow-moving legwork that progressed at a snail's pace because of the physical work required. But even this would have been preferable to the work product that was able to be accomplished in the early decades of the 21st century as cities defunded entire police departments and Peacekeepers fled the profession in mass exodus.

For decades before the Great Reformation, low numbers within Law Enforcement had affected the manner in which all police work had been conducted, and the lack of trained Detectives had impeded investigations from coast to coast.

Fortunately, by the mid-21st century, the nation began to shift once again, and Law Enforcement numbers slowly began to repair themselves as new policies were enacted. This enabled the previously practiced methods of protocol to be reassessed and improved upon. Progression with technology had a marked influence on how new policies were implemented.

One of these critical changes was regarding Investigations. Rather than having two designated Detectives working cases, Investigations were conducted with small teams of qualified specialists. One lead Investigator was appointed to each case. In addition, he was accompanied by a Research and Investigation Specialist and a Victim Advocate. These teams were federal, allowing for national travel.

Technological advancements had made having tech-savvy researchers a requirement. Having highly qualified Research and Investigation Specialists for all the background legwork became a vital component for all Investigations, and as our society continued to develop in this field, it was well beyond the training and skill of most Investigators, including myself. The work contributed by Research and Investigation Specialists was vital to every successful investigation, and it was not uncommon for the information secured by them to break cases and lead to convictions.

Likewise, the talents and skills that Victim Advocacy Agents brought to the table were also well beyond my general comfort zone. Their job duties were as much of a necessity as either the Investigators or the Research Specialists. The education level was often much lower, but it still required them to have a background in psychology, and they often specialized in counseling services, such as Grief or family therapy. Their primary duties were to assist Investigators and often worked in the field alongside them. They worked with Victims of Violent Crimes and their Families by providing them with a myriad of services throughout the investigations. They provided a substantial support system that had never been provided on the government level prior to the Great Reformation, despite there always having been an obvious need for such an agency.

Their workers, known as Victim Advocacy Agents (VAs or VAAs), were, in most cases, college-educated professionals. But there were also many with lesser credentials, having fast-tracked their usual four-year programs in Social Services or Psychology into a condensed two-year degree. The shorter program resulted in an Assistant Victim Agent (AVA) title and was an extremely specialized degree. Both types of education and training consisted of various courses regarding Body Language, coping strategies, and emotional de-escalation because of trauma and stress. They were always present when Investigators delivered Death Notifications to the Bereaved, and while their work did not focus on crime-solving or the intricacies of the investigations themselves, they were vital for the social and human interactions that were an integral part of every case.

The level of education the VAs held determined whether they could handle cases entirely independently or required supervision. For Investigators, their services were still valuable in any capacity and always welcomed. But for a case of this magnitude, I appreciated that the Chief assigned one of the more advanced professionals so I could hand over more of the workload, which would not have been allowed with the less-credentialed AVAs. The Seattle VAA had an excellent reputation on the national level, and it was mostly because of the quality of Advocates they employed.

Given the serious nature of this case, and the fact that the SPD Chief had personally 'hand-selected' the two that were going to be working with me, I sincerely hoped that they would prove worth their weight rather than having been granted the positions through favoritism or nepotism, both of which were entirely possible even if highly improbable. Our roles were implicitly different and necessary to one another as part of a thorough, well-rounded team. The strength of our investigation depended on the strength of our individual skills, just as surely as it did on our teamwork and communication.

Meeting the Victim Advocate

Promptly at 1600, a woman knocked on the doorframe and smiled through the open doorway. She was exactly as countless other VAs were across the nation: female, neatly dressed, serene smile, outgoing personality, and deep, expressive eyes. This one was younger than most, and probably within five years of my age range; I imagined she was fast-tracked because of her qualifications, education, and work conduct. The Calling was deceptive; it differed greatly from almost any other profession within Law Enforcement or Criminal Justice. It was also one of the youngest agencies within the government, although it had been operational since the late 21st century.

Motioning her inside, we greeted each other warmly and exchanged the usual pleasantries. She was familiar with my work, she stated. Very pleased with the assignment. Certain that we would be an excellent team, and of course, always open to any suggestions or helpful critiques, as I was the Lead.

Introductions within any Law Enforcement agency were always similar; our first impressions were at least based on work performance and reputation rather than appearances since our uniforms required the full external helmet even within our own office space. It set us apart, kept us protected, and yet created an unmistakable disadvantage to anyone meeting us who lacked the same safety measures to protect their identities, such as this woman.

The banality of first introductions, especially among colleagues, was always a tedious endeavor no matter how it was conducted, and I seldom enjoyed them. I'd never been good with small talk, with trying to maintain superficial conversation, or pretending to care when I seldom did. Would that I could, I'd have well-established, long-standing relationships with everyone I ever knew. It was always better to know others well; it ensured you could know what to expect, and provided a certain sense of both comfort and convenience when working together. There was nothing worse than tiptoeing around new relationships, afraid to ask too much or offend the other when there was work to be done. Given my choice, I'd rather have all my companions be as well-worn and familiar as an old family pet or a good pair of slippers; reliable, predictable, comfortably molded to your own personality, and loyal to you above all others. There was something to be said for the relationships that endured the test of time. Unfortunately, because of the travel my career involved, this was seldom achieved with new colleagues.

Nonetheless, I smiled graciously, shook her warm hand, and invited her to sit down across from me. She noted that they gave us Hive Nine. This made it easier; we both had an office, with a shared community space between, and then there were additional empty offices behind. Even with Officer Stanton, we had plenty of room.

As with most government buildings, they had designed the SPD Headquarters based on the traditional Hive architectural style; it allowed simplified building, smaller group placement for specifically inter-connected agencies and groups of workers, and kept a detailed organizational application that even the most OCD personnel could appreciate. Additionally, it allowed for extra layers of protection against terrorist attacks or cases of mass shootings, as it not only drastically reduced the number of occupants allowed in any given area, each hive could also be securely locked both internally and externally if necessary. In many cases, it prevented entry by those who would Inflict Harm. In others, it prevented them from exiting until the appropriate authorities could capture them.

This was also carried over to all national public schools and various other organizations, including prisons. Hive building construction had been so standardized that most probably imagined there was some type of legislation, or maybe a contractor discount for using it. There wasn't, of course; but once it became clearly optimal in design and functionality, it became standardized. In our particular case, however, it was a surplus of space, as I had no interest in bringing in any more team members beyond the three of us.

The woman had red hair and a splattering of freckles across her face; by all accounts, she was very attractive. It was an unmistakable face and was the perfect example to explain why Law Enforcement and anyone working within Criminal Justice was required to wear visors while on duty. The facial recognition program made it too easy to track one's movements. Her face was not one that would easily be forgotten. Given most inter-mixing between nationalities over the last two centuries, it was a rare thing to find—a natural redhead with pale skin and freckles. The green eyes put her in about the rarest of 1%.

She introduced herself as Grace O'Connor, although protocol typically meant she was only obligated to share her Badge ID, which was legible from the lapel of her uniform. It was fairly standard from the VAs, however, to personalize their relationships more so than most of the other departments and employees. Perhaps it was simply another credit to their gender, but most within my field of work appreciated their compassionate and sensitive nature. It was always welcome to witness their desire to establish and build upon their professional relationships with as much Humanity as reasonably allowed. Men still dominated most of the Criminal Justice field, but we would all be living in a drought of formality and fortresses of solitude if we didn't have the Victim Advocates there to remind us that our Souls must be nurtured and replenished as well.

Of all the agencies and transformations that had arrived because of our Great Reformation, the VAA became the most important link between the government being paid to represent the People and the very People who had lived for so many decades feeling as though they were not being heard, let alone understood or respected. And it was because of employees such as this woman.

We exchanged a few moments of casual conversation—without ever getting too personal, of course. We were functionally ghosts; we were government employees working within the Criminal Justice system in a society that wanted to ensure they protected us from all that would choose to Harm us. This included each other and prevented any threat to our personal information should we ever find ourselves in a difficult predicament, with nefarious circumstances working against us.

She had been provided with a copy of the initial case specifics and was prepped for our first visit. We discussed our options and decided that the first course of action would be to speak with the widow of Arlan Randall. However, we would not be delivering a Notification of his Death yet. The idea was simply to establish communication and interview her on our own. This would help us develop a solid background of each of our Victims, the patterns of their day-to-day activities, and the events leading up to their Disappearances.

Officer Stanton, meanwhile, could begin his own research. As I had expected, she agreed we should reach out to the parents of the little girl only after spending some time reviewing the case and possibly re-interviewing witnesses. Her case was one of the more sadistic and heartbreaking, but it was important that we let her parents know her Remains had been found. It had been a lengthy period of time for Katarina to have been Missing, and her parents had already endured enough. It was time to meet with them and put their daughter to rest. They had been waiting for an exceedingly long time to find out any type of news regarding what had happened to their little girl, and while I did not want to have to deliver a Notification of Death, it was part of my duties. I did not want to make them spend any more time than necessary submerged in the blackness of fear and uncertainty.

It was time for them to hear from us, even if it was only to confirm that which they likely already knew in their hearts. As my new colleague pointed out, sometimes simply gaining Closure was better than spending another year, month, week, day, or even an hour in the dark not knowing. There was something to be said for simply knowing that a Loved One had been found and was no longer Suffering—or so they trained us to believe.

The news completely devastated some people; it removed all doubt, and thus all hope. Nonetheless, I knew we must inform them of that which we knew at this point. And for now, that was enough. Their poor, dear little girl, after having been reported Missing just over three months ago, had been found Deceased. Perhaps the most unsettling part of this was that she had only recently Died. I had no intention of sharing this with her parents at this point—or possibly ever. For now, it was enough to know that she had been found and was officially confirmed Deceased.

We made plans to meet in the morning so we could begin our first day together. It was important that we meet with the families together initially, especially if I were going to be delivering news of their Deaths. She was of the highest credentials available within her field, which would be extremely helpful throughout our investigation because of the level of responsibility she could maintain. I was grateful after having met with her that the Chief had provided me with a highly qualified and professional colleague to work with.

FOUR – CR —1— INITIATING INVESTIGATION

Preparing to Visit the Randall Farm

Grace O'Connor would work in the capacity of a Case Manager because of the number of Victims we would address within our investigation.

In most investigations, the Victim Advocacy Agency had routine practices established which outlined the chain of command and other protocols related to standard investigative procedures. It was customary for the VAA to send the caseworker that was assigned to the Bereaved rather than their Case Manager. Grace O'Connor would be the person who came along with me and became the 'introduction' into the VAA for the Bereaved. She would conduct an initial interview with the wife of Arlan Randall, and then with the rest of the Bereaved for the remaining Victims.

After our first meeting and her initial assessments, she would then assign another Victim Advocate to work directly with each of the families, and they would report back to her. If, in the course of their work with the families, they discovered anything related to our investigation, they would report to Grace O'Connor directly and she would report it to me. Both of our agencies would conduct our own field reports and documentation of all Victims, and anything related to the investigation. Both Grace O'Connor and Officer Stanton were in positions of oversight within their divisions.

After I had reviewed the case file for the Randall's, it surprised me to discover that no one had appointed a Victim Advocate Agent to Caroline Randall. Not doing this was a serious breach of protocol, and when I had asked Grace O'Connor about it, even though she was a person of some supervisory standing, she hadn't understood what had happened either. This should have been resolved as soon as they had filed the Missing Persons case for Arlan in the immediate aftermath of his Disappearance.

It was becoming clear that there was a breakdown of communication between the Missing Persons Division and the Victim Advocacy Agency, and it was negatively affecting the Bereaved. Grace O'Connor had reassured me she had already launched an internal investigation to determine what had gone wrong and why her agency had not appointed anyone to represent the Randall's. Additionally, Officer Stanton was doing some elementary research to see if anything seemed out of sorts within the Missing Persons Division of the SPD. For all the time that had passed since these Disappearances had occurred, the lack of progress within each case was appalling. It was difficult not to question if that was not intentional rather than accidental.

Meeting Caroline Randall

After meeting Grace O'Connor at 1100, we drove to the Randall residence. The town of Carnation, Washington, was approximately an hour outside of the Greater Seattle Area.

I'd never been this far north before and was surprised to see just how lush the landscape was. The Randall residence was situated on a private farm outside of city limits. Carnation had roughly five-thousand residents; the contrast in population such a brief drive from the Greater Seattle Area was impressive. Carnation hadn't had a Homicide on record in over fifty years; they hadn't even had a Rape in almost the same time. There were many local dairy and chicken farms in the area. It was an agricultural zoned community, and because of its more rural location, had been untainted by the hard years before the Great Reformation. It still held that wonderfully nostalgic sense of Americana that was often on display outside of the more fast-paced cities.

Arlan was survived by his wife, Caroline, and the four adult children they shared. According to the information provided by Officer Stanton, all of their children were still in the state but had moved further into the more urban areas surrounding the City of Seattle. They were college-educated, gainfully employed, and married with children of their own. No one in the family had any type of criminal history or known societal problems, such as drug-abuse.

I did not notify her ahead of time that we would be visiting. The best way to read a person was to interview them without giving them time to prepare or rehearse. I had no reason to suspect at this point that Arlan's wife or children had anything to do with his Death or the resulting Disposal of his body, but I still wanted to have the element of surprise.

We had used the autopilot to get us to the Randall farm and made good time, discussing various points of the Postmortem Examination along the way. Once the GPS informed us we were nearing the property, I put away my notes and took in my surroundings. The homestead was down a long, fenced driveway, and I noted fields on either side with both horses and cows. The land was fertile and green, so it was apparently good for grazing. It was a remarkable contrast to the concrete jungle we had just left. The entire I-5 corridor from Portland, Oregon through Vancouver B.C. was well-established; the eastern sides of the two states remained far more rural compared to the massive populations of their neighbors along the corridor.

Up ahead, a traditional two-story home with white trim stood next to a large metal shop. About a quarter of a mile off to the right, I could see the outline of another enormous structure—an oversized barn. Beyond that, a row of stables for the plethora of horses and cows grazing in the fields.

I saw several vehicles near the large shop, but none were directly in front of the home in the designated parking area. I slowed down a bit as I neared the homestead but didn't catch sight of a single person. In the distance, I could hear a dog barking.

After we parked, Grace O'Connor gathered her things and stepped out of our vehicle. I walked around to her side of our cruiser, watching as she straightened her skirt and jacket top and then assured herself that her badge was clearly on display over her left lapel area near her collar. The deeply layered curve pattern of her jacket as it ran from the left collar to her right waistline was flattering to her figure considering it was a uniform, but for some illogical female reason, she kept fussing over her appearance as we walked toward the front steps of the large veranda. I placed a customary hand on the small of her back as I followed her up the stairs, noting that her skirt made it a slow climb. The feminine uniforms for the VAA had always reminded me of the 1960s with their cut jackets and pencil skirts that fell below the knee, and I had always liked them. But watching Grace O'Connor struggle as she tried to navigate the stairs made me grateful for my loose-fitting, low-maintenance Kev-Tek uniform.

I guessed she had chosen the skirt because it was a first meeting; I knew that they also had a uniform much like those worn in Law Enforcement for the daily grind, reserving the more feminine, formal version for important meetings and Court appearances. I imagined like most men, I would always choose comfort over fashion, and there was little question that I was far more comfortable than the woman currently fidgeting next to me. How she kept adjusting her slim skirt made me lose all hope that we would stop for a bite to eat on our way back to the office.

Almost absent-mindedly, I raised the visor on my external helmet so my eyes were visible. Then, with my foot propping the screen door open, I scanned my ID against the Entry Bell, and felt the vibration which alerted those inside. If their system was a standard Entry ID Notification System, when a visitor arrived and scanned their Chip, the system would send notification to the resident. They were also equipped with an Emergency Response button that could notify local First Responders of household emergencies. It was likely that Arlan's wife, Caroline, had used this system to contact local Law Enforcement on the day she came home and realized her husband was Missing.

There was a bit of shuffling and movement, and then the click of the locks on the front door. A woman that I knew to be Arlan's wife answered. The lines on her face were deep, but they looked well-earned, and told of years of laughter and smiling. And although there was enough grey to reveal her years, the fading blonde was another reminder of the youthful woman she once was. She opened the door wide, extended her hand, and greeted us warmly.

I introduced myself and Grace O'Connor, and took the opportunity created by the two women immediately engaging in pleasantries to look around the place as I followed them into the formal living room. We believed her to be living alone, but as with everything, caution was paramount at all times.

The formal living room was brightly painted, and the curtains were pulled back, showcasing a view of the stables far in the distance. Since it was June, the room felt happy and full of light; it even smelled like wildflowers and fresh linen created by the gentle breeze coming in through the open windows and filtering through the freshly laundered curtains. It was deceptive, though; anyone that had ever lived in the Greater Seattle Area knew the region was inundated with grey skies and damp weather. I imagined this old farmhouse would become drafty and cold once winter set in. Still, I had to commend this woman for trying to create such a lovely atmosphere; both her views, and the hominess she provided, were refreshing.

Caroline Randall made a wide sweep of her arm as an invitation to select a seat. She took the chair at the end of the overstuffed couch on one side of a large area rug centered in the middle of the room. She asked us politely if we would like something to eat or drink after our long drive. Her thoughtful offer was well-received by Grace O'Connor, and the two of them went off to make some iced tea. They headed for the kitchen before I had even considered objecting or trying to find a discreet way to caution Grace O'Connor to remain vigilant, so I just kept an ear out for them and used the time to look around the room.

I could see the little red button on my visor flashing as it showed that it was recording. My recorder was automatically activated as soon as I had driven onto the property, as per protocol. It activated on both my person and the vehicle. Along with the audio and video recorders, it also monitored my vitals. If anything triggered my heart rate, or if it suddenly jumped or drastically lowered, the closest Police Department was notified. If it stopped, First Responders and back-up were issued. An automated distress call helped to secure immediate medical help for all First Responders and was vital for when Law Enforcement Officers were out doing patrols or investigations on their own. There had been far too many cases where LEOs had been injured or otherwise debilitated and unable to call for back-up on their own. They would lose their lives or face other types of medical crisis that could have resulted in a different outcome if only they had been able to contact Dispatch and summon additional help.

It was peculiar to imagine a time when Law Enforcement wasn't held in high regard, but it was even more concerning knowing that our Ancestors had been out there doing our jobs prior to the Great Reformation with none of the standard issue advancements we now had as a matter of course. They had paved the way for us with both technology and security.

Far greater men than I had done this job, and they had done it routinely, never knowing what was out there just beyond their line of sight. There had been many Detectives Murdered in cold blood simply for doing the very thing we were engaged in, meeting with witnesses and trying to talk to local Citizens about potential Crimes. Anyone wearing the uniform was at risk, even today. But nothing compared to how things used to be. It was humbling, and I never forgot it. One mishap, one time letting my guard down in the wrong place, and it could all be over.

The two women returned, and having spent the last five minutes working together in the Randall kitchen, were now on the best of terms. It was that flair for interpersonal relationship development that had made the Victim Advocacy Agency such an important addition to the federal government.

As they settled in with a tray of iced tea and an assortment of cookies and pastries, I re-established my focus and felt a twinge of sorrow as I realized that this woman sitting before me was as yet unaware that her beloved husband was not merely Missing, but had actually been located and formally labeled 'Deceased.'

Caroline Randall—Caroline, as she had insisted—didn't seem nervous or rushed; she only seemed busy, like I was preventing her from doing a day's work that would still need to be done once I left. I assured her I wouldn't keep her long and informed her she was being recorded via videotape.

Continuing, I stated I was an Investigator that was newly assigned to her husband's Disappearance and that Grace O'Connor was here with me from the Victim Advocacy Agency to help her in any way she could. I told her I had some questions for her, but mostly I wanted to hear from her about the day of Arlan's Disappearance and anything else she might have to say, and then Grace O'Connor could go over everything with her about her agency before we finished up.

Caroline nodded her head and then seemed to let her thoughts and emotions pour out. It appeared she had been holding a lot in since her husband had Vanished, and both Grace O'Connor and I apologized because they had not assigned her a Victim Advocate to help her with the ongoing investigation as she should have been. We explained the process and protocol, outlining the order of events that should have taken place, and told her that both of our agencies were working on finding out the answers regarding why she and her family hadn't been assigned anyone from the VAA prior to this.

It should have been done at the same time the First Responders had submitted their report of Arlan as a Missing Person; the Missing Persons Division should have opened their investigation into his Disappearance and contacted the VAA immediately so they could provide services to Mrs. Randall and any of the children who requested them. A large part of what the VAA did was provide counseling services for the friends and family of Missing Persons and the Bereaved—those Left Behind who had lost a Loved One through Violence. Their duties also included providing medical or financial help as the Bereaved attempted to process the situation. Despite the resources available for this, they had provided none to the Randall family.

These services were often the only lifeline the friends and family of Missing Persons had for their cases, and they were a vital component of helping them through the entire experience. I understood that sometimes 'mistakes' occurred; we were all Human, and there were many steps required for even the slightest task. But if mistakes must occur, this was not the department that they should happen in.

"All I can really remember was that he was so awfully sick that last few months. Cancer had torn up his insides. The treatments had stopped working, and he was nearing the end. He was in constant pain. He could barely move."

Caroline motioned toward the back of the house.

"We'd moved his hospital bed to the spare room in the back. It's on the bottom floor and it has an attached bath. Our kids were here as much as they could be, and we had our farm manager here, too, but he's always been more of an adopted son than anything. And then we had Hospice Care as well. I didn't want them here, but Arlan didn't want me to do all the work myself, and we still had all the farm and business work that needed to be done regularly. So, I let them come, and I let them stay. God, as my witness, I wish I had never let that man sweet talk me into it, but he always managed to."

"Did you ever have any kind of feelings or intuition regarding any of the workers?"

She seemed genuinely surprised by my question. We usually just stuck to the facts, but here I was asking if her instincts had indicated anything. It was a little unorthodox, and I noticed that Grace O'Connor had shifted her attention away from Caroline Randall and directed her eyes toward me for a moment. Unorthodox, perhaps, but it had always been my contention that Loved Ones observed more than they realized, and their opinions were worth paying attention to.

She shook her head no, but then she hesitated.

"I've already told them all I knew about the Hospice workers. I didn't trust them then, and I still think they had something to do with how Arlan disappeared. He wasn't capable of leaving on his own. I know that woman had something to do with it—but what can I do about it if no one else believes me? I told them she was responsible. They haven't even told me if she was ever charged with anything or given me any updates."

I wasn't sure exactly whom she was referring to, but when I probed deeper, she just shook her head, telling me that all of that should be in the report already, and she couldn't remember any of their Badge ID's.

"Every day, when I spent time with him, I watched him fade away a little more, bit by bit. The pain was excruciating. It was difficult to watch. Have you ever watched someone you love fade away into a shell of their former self?" It was a rhetorical question; she didn't really expect an answer as she continued.

"He was my husband, and I was watching him die. Part of me wanted to keep him, and I couldn't imagine having to let him go. But most of me, especially toward the end, just wanted it done because it was tearing him apart. His stomach cancer spread all over. And the worse it got, the worse the pain got. And the more pain he was in, the more we were all just praying for it to be over sooner rather than later."

She paused, and her eyes welled up with tears. Grace O'Connor leaned toward her slightly and placed her hand over Caroline's as the two rested in her lap. She had been fidgeting with her wedding band as she drifted backward in time, recalling her husband as his health faded. Grace O'Connor's warm touch had given her the physical contact and reassurances she had needed, and upon their hands touching, the old woman seemed to calm herself and stopped spinning her ring. It was only a slight motion, but it was one of those examples of how precious compassion and human contact was, and made me grateful that she had joined me for the interview.

"My kids were watching their daddy die a horrible death. I know you didn't know him, but he was a good man. He didn't deserve to suffer like that. He knew how bad it was; he knew he was dying. He went from being strong and healthy to so weak he couldn't even walk anymore. He was 6'3" and had spent almost twenty-five years in the military. He was a Marine, and you know that's in their blood—it's part of their identity 'til the day they die. So here he was, my proud Marine, and he was just fading away, and he knew it.

"He went from two-sixty-five down to a hundred-fifty in less than a year from all the drugs, chemo, and pain. That disease tore through him worse than any of his doctors had ever seen. And all the while, my husband, my strong, good husband, watched his whole sense of self just fade away. We all watched it happen; everyone that loved him. We watched the greatest man we ever knew try to fight against a disease that didn't care one bit about who he was or what he could do. And eventually, he just stopped being himself. He surrendered. One day, you could just see it; he had lost the battle. The cancer had won, and there was nothing we could do. I watched him change on the inside, just like he had on the outside. He finally seemed to just give up."

She sat quietly for a second, staring out the window as tears fell down her cheeks. Somewhere in the distance, we could hear a clock ticking, and further away, the sounds of horses neighing.

"That was when I knew we had lost him; when I saw it change in his eyes. He knew he couldn't fight it anymore. He understood it was only a matter of time. And I don't know if he would have pulled out of it or not; he disappeared right after that. But I'd like to believe that he was still in the game. I'd like to believe that he went down fighting."

She looked directly into my eyes.

"I saw him give up. The man that I knew better than any other person on this earth wasn't a quitter. He was a fighter. The man I knew—my husband, the father of my children and the Love of My Life—the man that I spent forty years of my life with, he wouldn't have just given up. He wouldn't have left us. He wouldn't have left me. Because I know my husband, and I know he was a warrior in his heart. And if it meant that he had to spend his last breath fighting just for the chance that he could come home to us, I believe he would have done that. There's no way he would have killed himself. There's no way that man would have ever given up on this family or himself."

Her eyes were pleading.

"Find out what happened to him. We've been grieving for him for a long time—far longer than people realize—we've been saying goodbye ever since we got the news that he was going to die. We've been letting go inch by inch, and every time he lost another part of who he was, we grieved for him some more. And we kept right on praying and hoping even when it seemed hopeless."

She continued looking at me and speaking with firm conviction.

"And if someone hurt him, we need that person to be brought to Justice. I know he must be Dead by now, but he should have died here, with me. Even if—" her voice broke, but she continued. "Even if my husband actually left here so he could go kill himself, I want to know."

Grace O'Connor had moved from the seat next to me on the couch and had gone to sit next to Mrs. Randall by perching on the edge of her chair, rubbing her back as

Caroline Randall held her hand. I felt terrible for opening these wounds again, but I also knew I needed to be here to get to the truth. The woman was clearly devastated, and I had put a major damper on her otherwise peaceful day.

I took Caroline Randall's other hand into my two gloved hands, and simply held it for a moment, granting her strength. I knew a bit more than she did; it was true. But whether he requested help in his Final Hours or Days or not, he had still Died of an Overdose and there was no way to prove that it had been self-administered. Perhaps the only thing that really needed to be taken into consideration at this point in time was that whether it was Homicide or Suicide, he had not removed himself from the Randall property, and he had not buried himself out there in that field. Whatever had happened to him, it hadn't happened to him solely by his own hand.

Knowing that Grace O'Connor still had to go over some of the basic pieces of information about her agency and the resources she had available for her, I asked Mrs. Randall if she minded if I left the two ladies on their own and explored the farm a bit. Caroline was in excellent hands, and I was confident that Grace O'Connor was in no mortal danger. The two women shooed me away, assuring me they would be fine and would come find me when they were done.

I left the two women to their talk and walked around the property, careful to stick within a quick sprint back to the farmhouse in case I heard any signs of distress from Grace O'Connor. It was a beautiful day and growing hotter by the minute. I let my thoughts drift to the wife of a brave former Marine, and I realized yet again why all of this mattered so deeply. We weren't just solving cases to gain relevant facts; we were creating Closure for families and bringing them Peace. We were helping them gain the truth, and sometimes, protecting them from it when it was just too gruesome or painful. Our duties and responsibility lay not only with the Deceased but also with the families that were Left Behind. Their stories mattered. Their lives had mattered. We as Human Beings had to help those incapable of helping themselves—because each of us, both individually as well as collectively, were all intrinsically linked to one another—and each of us deserved to know such peace.

Before long, I was met by the two women at the SPD Cruiser. I watched as Grace O'Connor gave Caroline Randall a warm hug as they parted, and then I shook her hand while she put her other hand on my arm. Her kind-heartedness was contagious, and I was sorrowed by what I already knew about her husband.

I thanked her for her hospitality and told her we would be in touch. She seemed like a wonderful woman, and it was a tough situation. But we had a lot of work to do before I could return and tell her about her husband, so I put it out of my mind and set our navigation system to the SPD offices as we departed. No matter what had actually happened to Arlan or who was responsible, we would learn the full story before breaking this woman's heart with unfounded half-truths. Arlan's legacy deserved that, and having met Caroline Randall, I was certain more than ever that I wanted to ensure we fully understood everything for the sake of the entire family that had been Left Behind.

Meeting Micah Davidson

As my colleague and I reached the end of the driveway of the Randall residence, we saw a ranch vehicle bearing the Randall Homestead mark. A man was leaning against the driver's side door holding a clipboard. I slowed the SPD Cruiser and parked.

"What are you doing?" Grace O'Connor asked.

"Just hang tight a sec. I'm going to speak with this guy."

She had been looking at her notes and only just then looked back to see the farm worker behind us.

"I'll just be a second. I don't think this will take long. Activate Armor."

I wasn't used to traveling with a partner in any sense of the word. But since she was a VA, there wasn't any need for her to step out with me and see why this guy had been waiting for us.

Immediately, I felt the slightly pressurized additional weight of my uniform and helmet visor engage as I exited the squad car, and I heard the slight whoosh as the car simultaneously entered lockdown mode after I vacated the vehicle. As with all of my equipment and firearms, my physical presence, including my DNA, fingerprints, and optical identification, must be secured before they would activate. Grace O'Connor was safer sitting inside the armored SPD cruiser than she would have been sitting inside a bank vault; a bank vault could be breached simply through force alone, whereas my vehicle could only be entered by verifying my unique biometrics.

I approached the man casually, stopping a few feet away. His clipboard was a rectangle piece of smooth wood with a bracket at the top designed to hold paper products, just like the ones from a century ago. It wasn't odd for small businesses to track records on paper; they were tangible products, less likely to undergo a malfunction or hack, and wouldn't result in a permanent record since it wasn't connected to technology.

"Is there something I can help you with?" I asked.

The deep creases along his forehead were causing little droplets of sweat to pool underneath the brim of his hat.

My visor transmitted a blip identifying the holstered firearm attached to his belt as a common brand with a mid-capacity magazine, which he had loaded to its maximum. The sensors in my visor coordinated with his firearm and ran an instantaneous security check, confirming the firearm was legally purchased and registered by the man standing in front of me. Federal Open Carry laws made firearms commonplace. It was a standard joke that Americans were seen with firearms riding on their hips more often than babies, and in some places, that was probably true.

"My name is Micah Davidson. I've been working for the Randall's for almost twenty years." His voice was low, slow, and southern.

Behind my screen, my system had run his background and confirmed his identity. He was from Georgia, had been in the State of Washington for almost twenty-five years, and had gone to school for Business Management and served in the military for more than a decade.

"I have an office and do the surveillance monitoring for the farm."

He nodded his head in the general direction of the barn.

"I don't know if you were told this, but I was the first to respond after I heard Mrs. Randall screaming. My office is in the big red barn that's closest to the house, and I live on the property, too."

He adjusted himself against his truck, used his right hand to remove his hat, wiped his brow with his arm, and then set the hat back in place.

"Mrs. Randall called me right after she put the call in to the SPD. I could barely understand her over the speaker, she was so upset. I could hear her screaming at the Hospice worker to tell her where he was. I dropped everything and went straight to the house. I could hear her yelling at her through the windows as I ran up the porch. But when I got inside, I don't know, man. It just wasn't right. Mrs. Randall was clearly upset. They were in the back room. It was strange. Nothing about it added up to me. The Hospice worker was just sitting on the bed, not saying a word."

He paused, and I could see he was deep in his mind's eye, recalling the events again. His mouth was taut.

"I didn't know the Hospice lady well, but I'd seen her around. She wasn't that old; twenty-five or so. It seemed like a strange choice of a job for a younger gal. Anyhow, so when I went into the room, she was just sitting there on the edge of the bed while Mrs. Randall screamed at her. She wasn't defending herself; she wasn't apologizing, she wasn't trying to blame someone else—she wasn't doing anything. She just sat there."

"And what did the SPD say about that? Did you say any of this to the SPD later on after they arrived?"

"Yeah, see—that was the thing. I only had a second to take it all in—because as soon as I got into the room it turned crazy. Mrs. Randall was standing there screaming and crying, begging her to tell her where he was. Then I heard the sirens in the background, so I knew the SPD was almost there. And then that gal *smiled*. And as soon as soon as Mrs. Randall saw her smile, she just lunged at her. It was all instant—it all happened in a flash—as fast as I could process what was happening."

"So, then what happened?" I asked.

"I knew that Mrs. Randall was fixin' to wipe that smug look off her face. I don't know what it was about her, but as soon as I saw her smile like that, I just knew she had caused it, whatever had happened to Arlan. And I knew that Mrs. Randall saw it too—that was why she lunged at her."

He made eye contact with me and held my gaze.

"Honestly, man, I almost wish I hadn't stopped her. I shoulda let her do it. At least then we would have felt like she at least got some answers and some justice."

I nodded my head, trying to at least show that I understood where he was coming from, and that I, too, was less than impressed with their results.

"Anyhow, so I immediately reached for her. By the time I got to them, Mrs. Randall had the lady by the hair, and she had another hand grabbing her uniform. She was hysterical."

"So, then what?" I asked.

"So that was pretty much it. SPD arrived, and I pulled Mrs. Randall off the lady. I just kinda put my arms around her middle, pulled her arms back, and then carried her into the other room."

"And then what? SPD just came in and did their assessment? They just interviewed each of you and then left? That was it? They didn't even check your surveillance footage, is that right?"

"Exactly. Yeah, that's what was strange. They interviewed us and took the lady with them. That was it. She never spoke to us as she was being taken through the house and put in one of their cars."

"Anyhow," he continued, "They hauled her away, spent about ten minutes looking around, and then left. I went back and reviewed all the security footage and found some video of a white van showing up around an hour before everything hit the fan. It didn't have any markings, but it looked like one of the Hospice vans."

"So, you think the white van came there on purpose to remove him? But the surveillance doesn't show it?"

It made sense, of course. And although it caused more unanswered questions, it managed to fill in some gaps.

"Yep. No doubt. You'll see. No one even got out of the front of the van. They backed up alongside the house, so you couldn't see much. They must have gone out of the backside of the van and then used the back door. Yeah, I think they took him."

"Do you suspect anything with any of the family? Perhaps one of the kids, or even Mrs. Randall being involved?"

"Absolutely not. I've known all their kids their entire lives; they've all become great adults, and they love their dad. They were a close family; they still are. The missus loved Arlan. Anyone could see that. Heck, we all did. He was a great man. It was tough to see him get so bad."

He wrote out his name and contact information on a piece of paper and then handed it to me with a thumb drive. The paper also had his surveillance monitoring access information and the passcode so I could gain entry. It enabled me to watch the live stream of the property. It wouldn't do me much good, but I knew that Officer Stanton might make some use out of it. At any rate, I was grateful for Micah Davidson's help.

The sun was beating down on us, and I was grateful for my temperature-regulated uniform.

I shook his hand again, thanked him, and told him I was going to get it resolved. It would have been against protocol to let him know we'd already found Arlan's body before the immediate family, but it also wasn't something I was prepared to give up yet. It may become necessary for me to share the information with him at some point, but for now, I didn't want anyone to know that their bodies had already been discovered. This was one of the first leads I'd received in my investigation regarding Arlan's case, and because it had not been included in the initial report, it was entirely unadulterated. I needed to keep things discreet until I had more to go on.

I recalled that Mrs. Randall had stated that her farm manager was 'more like a son' to them than an employee. I didn't have any doubts that the man standing in front of me genuinely cared about the Randall's and only wanted to help. He didn't want to see them hurt, and he hadn't wanted to put any unnecessary strain on 'the missus' with something he couldn't easily verify as significant.

Returning, I remembered I had left my colleague sitting in a locked, armored vehicle with the armor activated. I shook my head at my folly and opened the door.

Lifting my visor so I could see her eye to eye, she looked up from her work.

"Well? What did he say?" she asked.

I climbed back into my seat and looked at the center console screen. The auto sensors had detected there was a living creature within the vehicle and had turned on the ventilation system to increase airflow and regulate the air conditioning to a cool sixty-eight degrees. I could see by the console monitor it was also tracking her vitals. The system would immediately employ Emergency Response services if vital signs dropped below the safety zones, and the GPS system allowed for accurate locations. I believed there was also an automatic Emergency Response sent out if more than four hours lapsed as well, although there was no threat of the system itself failing within that time frame.

The same heat sensor technology that was within our infrared home security units was used in every vehicle and was supplied its energy from a separate solar panel source derived from the paint used on the vehicles. This allowed the ventilation, air conditioning, vitals monitoring system, GPS, and internal call system to operate even if there was damage to the engine components, the vehicles were out of their fuel source, or there were electrical issues preventing the vehicles from starting or functioning. The solar paint receptors made it virtually impossible to ever entirely deplete its power or ability to function, but if it occurred, there was a forty-eight-hour supply stored in the most basic models, while some could last as long as seven days. The result was as predicted; not a single death due to hot vehicles in almost eighty years.

Given that I had completely forgotten I had a passenger for the last half hour on a ninety-degree day, I was once again reminded that while clipboards might be a subtle way to rebel against our advancing society, there were still some undeniably positive attributes about it as well. I set the SPD Cruiser on autopilot, and as we made our way back to Seattle, I told Grace O'Connor all about my visit with Micah Davidson.

Initial Background Check of WA

After Grace O'Connor and I left the Randall Farm, I asked her to send Officer Stanton a message. I wanted him to check on the information we had learned after our visit and see what he could come up with regarding the Hospice Care workers or the company both Caroline Randall and Micah Davidson had each mentioned. I had her ask him to look through all the information we had regarding Arlan's Missing Persons case again and make any note of the Hospice workers by name or routine visits. If it was a professional company, they should have logs outlining their visits to the farm or work with Arlan before his Disappearance.

I also wanted him to check and see if the Hospice Care facility had records indicating they had reached out to the Randall's at any point afterward, or if their communication had simply ended after Arlan's Disappearance. It seemed peculiar that they would be involved in one of their patients' cases, and yet not even manage to conduct an inquiry into the strange circumstances that occurred with one of their employees present. Then again, if no one from the SPD had even contacted them or done any type of review of their facility or employees, that, too, would seem odd.

Still, the Hospice Care facility should have at least followed through with the Randall's to determine if services would be ongoing or not, but according to Caroline Randall, she had heard nothing since the day of Arlan's Disappearance. This wasn't just moderately strange to her, it seemed sketchy to both Grace O'Connor and me, as well. If it did not involve the company beyond having employed the worker that had been Arrested at one point, why did they drop off the earth once they knew Arlan Randall had Disappeared?

Less than an hour after we had reached out to Stanton as we made our way back to the SPD Headquarters, he sent us what little information he had gathered. He had learned that the company was the Winter Season Hospice Care facility.

He stated that he would have to access the facility's records to learn all the employees previously assigned to Arlan's case, but he could confirm that the one who had been working there on the day of Arlan's Disappearance was a woman by the name of Willow Amos. As Micah Davidson had shared, the woman had been on-site during the time in question directly preceding Arlan's Disappearance. She had been removed from the property by the First Responders who had answered the call made by Caroline Randall.

Before we had reached the freeway exit to get back to the SPD HQ, Officer Stanton had secured her current address and let us know he was working on a more comprehensive report. We would have more to go on soon enough.

Arrest Report: AR Farm

Once we got back to the office, we met with Officer Stanton in our conference room. He'd obtained copies of the initial Arrest Record for Willow Amos after the Disappearance of Arlan.

After reviewing it, I was left with even more questions than I already had regarding both Willow Amos and the method in which the SPD conducted their investigatory work. I couldn't help but question if the investigations were intentionally being done poorly.

For now, the best I could hope for was to gather everything we could, override anything that had been done prior to our involvement, and start fresh, carefully selecting the pieces and clues that we determined to be useful for our investigation ourselves.

The SPD LEOs that had responded to the call made by Caroline Randall had detained Willow Amos. She had refused to answer questions at the time, and had chosen instead to sit silently while they investigated the home and surrounding yard area. The physical investigation had been almost unnecessary because Arlan's complete immobility would have made a solo departure impossible, but they had followed protocol and completed the search anyhow.

Her refusal to account for her whereabouts or acknowledge that she had witnessed the Disappearance of Arlan was concerning. She had been the only other person present. Given the peculiarity of the situation because of his immobility and his sudden inability to be accounted for, even the SPD Officers had considered there to be sufficient cause to believe that Willow Amos had somehow been responsible for whatever had occurred. They had determined that she had either helped facilitate his Disappearance, or she had somehow Harmed or Killed him and then found a way to Dispose of his Body or remove him before anyone returned. It was a desperate effort to explain the inexplicable, and because the two Responding Officers couldn't, they had just Arrested her. At the very least, they had wanted to ensure that Willow Amos was removed from the location under their watchful eye so they could avoid any further escalation of events between the two women. Given how emotional Caroline Randall had apparently been in the aftermath of her husband's bizarre Disappearance, it was probably a wise decision.

The circumstances immediately following the Disappearance of Arlan had been so strange that it would have been difficult for any Responding Officer to sort it out in the time frame they had invested upon their arrival. They had interviewed everyone present, addressed the immediate concerns of the Citizen that had called in the distress call, Caroline Randall, and then they had done a cursory review of the immediate area. Based on what little information and evidence they could have gathered given those facts, and since they hadn't known about the white van when they investigated, they had still decided to Arrest Willow Amos and remove her from the property. It seemed they had concluded that she could not have been ignorant of the situation because of her proximity to Arlan at the time of his mysterious Disappearance.

The information provided within the report was almost inconsequential given that the Randall Farm could have been a Crime Scene, but it was all we had to go on. The two Responding Officers hadn't asked Caroline Randall a lot of questions and Willow Amos had provided no answers. Caroline Randall's heightened emotions, compounded exponentially by the fragility of Arlan himself, had increased the urgency of the reactions conducted by the two Responding Officers. Their solution had been to put a few facts down on paper—enough to pass it off as an interview, anyway—Arrest the only apparent Suspect, and then leave as quickly as possible.

The details outlined that Caroline Randall's distress call had been made approximately half an hour after she had last seen him, and she had left him in the well-qualified hands of the Hospice Care Provider, Willow Amos. Caroline Randall had included that Willow Amos had been a regular part-time employee of the Hospice Care facility they had been assigned, had a set schedule with regular hours, and was known to most of the employees on the farm. The report hadn't contained enough information about the behavior of Willow Amos or how calm her demeanor had been, which seemed odd to me considering she had been quiet and stiff in her countenance from the time the Officers had arrived on site and begun recording her.

It seemed, just as a basic observation, that if a person was Innocent of something and was being Falsely Accused of a Crime, that they would be at least a bit indignant or put forth some sort of effort to defend themselves against their Accuser. Even the Guilty would have done this. It seemed even more bizarre, given that Willow Amos was supposed to be a concerned healthcare worker.

Willow Amos had been working with Arlan for quite some time; she knew him personally. She had worked with him directly for several weeks. One would imagine that if someone that was familiar suddenly 'Vanished' that they would express some concern over the situation. Even if I learned nothing else from any of the video captured, just seeing the manner in which Willow Amos had behaved in those moments would have been sufficient to draw both my suspicion and my wrath. Caroline Randall had been beside herself during that time and Willow Amos had only aggravated it and played on her fears. Her behavior had been shockingly cold, and whether or not it was intentional, it had been cruel.

They had taken her to the SPD Headquarters and questioned her. An attorney had been authorized for her during the interview, and they had appointed a secondary attorney to oversee the Victim and his family. Throughout this interrogation, however, she had remained tight-lipped and had volunteered nothing.

The report stated that she had been interrogated and released that same day; they had not even held her overnight. I watched the video made available through the Holding Cell and was not surprised they released her; she had secured an attorney as soon as they allowed her to make a phone call. It was not a state-appointed attorney; it was a private one, and she had known his contact information by heart. This might not have seemed like an unusual detail, but to anyone that paused for a moment to think it through, it was. Her background check revealed that she was a college student that worked approximately ten hours a week at the counseling center on the Greater Seattle Area University campus, and she worked another twenty hours a week at the Hospice Care facility as a Home-Care Provider, which was essentially the lowest-paid rung of the medical field professional ladder.

And yet despite this, she not only had a private attorney, she had one that received her call immediately, arrived at the SPD headquarters within the hour, and either prevented the SPD from filing charges against her, or compelled them to drop them and void the records. No one in her position had that type of clout with a private attorney unless they either had a family with the right sort of connections or they were involved in something unscrupulous.

Given that she had memorized the number and had been patched through immediately—not to mention the attorney's swift arrival by her side—I was inclined to believe that the woman was directly linked to something greater than the SPD LEOs had suspected at the time of her Arrest. Someone was footing the bill for a private attorney; we had missed something.

It was time to dig deeper into her finances and background rather than make assumptions about her financial status; just because she was a student didn't mean she was necessarily in a lower-income bracket. Most who were of modest means did not have their own attorney on retainer. We could conclude two possibilities; she either had someone backing her or she had additional sources of income that we weren't aware of at this point. Either way, further investigation was necessary.

I needed to know who she had called. I had many more questions regarding Willow Amos, and I was left with concerns regarding the SPD's handling of Arlan's case as well. For now, I would ask Officer Stanton to continue digging while we worked toward reaching out to her again. A second interview might yield decidedly different results.

Securing Caroline Randall's Missing Person Report

Stanton located the original SPD LEO Incident Response Report after Arlan's Disappearance. The two Officers that had responded had each submitted their mandatory paperwork, and the Officer that had conducted the initial interview with Caroline Randall that fateful day had also submitted a written summary.

He had made a note on the report when he transferred it over to me, advising me it was the bare-bones minimum, including minimum effort. After reviewing it, it was easy to see that Officer Stanton had not been overselling the paperwork; it was so basic it could have passed for a telegram. I wasn't sure if it was intentional or not, but there seemed to be a recurring theme of indifference regarding how Arlan's case had been handled.

There had been one bonus that had been included in the latest information that Officer Stanton had provided to me, and that was a copy of the video footage that had been recorded during the Incident Response. However, Officer Stanton's note stated that the second LEOs recording had only consisted of his patrolling the grounds; he hadn't engaged with anyone, and his surveillance of the area had recorded nothing worth taking the time to view. He reaffirmed that the Satellite footage supported his story, and that the Satellite imagery had not picked up on anything during their time at the farm.

I trusted his judgment and was grateful for the reprieve. Watching the surveillance footage could be mentally exhausting work. It was almost as tedious as the laborious 'stakeouts' that had been done in the past by many Law Enforcement, trapped in enclosed spaces for days, weeks, and even months at a time while using primitive surveillance devices hoping to capture criminal activity and confessions. Such tasks were both tiresome and mind-numbing; it was fortunate that technology had helped ease much of it along the way, sparing us all the miserable, taxing experience that often yielded little reward for the investment of time and resources.

Stanton had advised that I set aside some time to review the video footage from the other Officer, however, stating that the interview with Caroline Randall was worth taking the time to watch. I made a note to do as he suggested and then forwarded the video to Grace O'Connor as well. Given her background in psychology, and since she worked directly with the Victims and their Bereaved far more intimately than I did, I wanted her to be as familiar with the Citizens represented in our case as I was. Now that she had met Caroline Randall herself, I imagined she would have some insight into how she might have seemed different during each encounter.

I checked my timestamp, said goodnight, and decided to grab something to eat once I got home. I could watch the video before turning in for the night.

CR's Missing Person SPD Interview

    The video from the second Responding Officer proved to be extremely insightful regarding Caroline Randall as it captured her directly in the hours following her husband's abrupt Disappearance. She had provided a very straightforward accounting of the events as they had occurred, and she had disclosed a fair amount of information regarding the general functionality of the farm, business practices, and the Randall's personal lives as a family.
    Caroline Randall, having taken over many of the responsibilities on the farm that her husband had previously done prior to his illness, was always coming and going around the property. She often crossed paths with the Hospice workers throughout the day during their shifts, as Mrs. Randall had the flexibility to travel throughout the property and often checked in with her husband at random times. Arlan's mind was still 'sharp as a tack', and Caroline consulted with him about the daily operations around the farm. She had stated in her report that even though he had lost his mobility, battled chronic pain, and was often tired, he always expressed an interest in the farm and welcomed any of the visitors or farm staff that dropped in.
    She also stated that Micah Davidson, their long-time manager, had spent the majority of his evenings with Arlan once his illness had taken a more serious hold on his health. Along with providing his boss with daily updates and anecdotes of the farm he loved and was likely missing despite being nearby, Micah Davidson had been sharing his evening meals with the Randall's. Mrs. Randall had stated that Micah joining them for dinner was routine, and lifted Arlan's spirits because it reminded him of the early years of the farm when Micah had just taken the position.
    In the beginning, she said, before the growth of their small farm business had required them to hire more employees, Micah had become like one of their own. Unlike the Randall's own children, however, Arlan and Micah had always shared a love of the land. Their children had grown up and eventually ventured further into the Greater Seattle Area and then established their own careers entirely separate from their family farm. Caroline had mentioned that Micah Davidson had always been a part of their family, celebrating holidays with them, building their business with Arlan, and had always gotten along well with their own sons and daughters.
    I could see the much older Arlan passing along his expertise to the younger man, see them planning how to develop the land and increase their profits over the years and transform what was once a small family farm into a very profitable family business. I could also see Micah Davidson sitting alongside the rest of the family and sharing meals; he would have been around when the kids were young and throughout their entire childhoods, educational years, and even attended their graduations. He would have been a staple in their lives just as much as any aunt or uncle, being around them every day just as their own parents were.
    I then thought about Caroline herself; a lovely woman that had given her heart to a man, bore his children, stood by him as he worked the land in a profession that had

almost entirely died out because of the big corporations, and grown old with him. I envisioned them sitting together on their porch swing on a summer evening, the small-framed woman resting comfortably against her oversized husband, secure, content, and protected. It was a tragedy that in his Final Days and weeks they had been separated; Caroline had wanted to be there until his Final Breath. It was an image that filled me with deep sorrow. He had been given many years of good health and had lived a rich and productive life. But Death was almost always a tragedy, especially when one had so much to offer the world. There were many people that had relied on him, that loved him and needed him. He was a vital piece of the tapestry of his farm, and there were certainly reminders of him everywhere.

Caroline's report had made it clear that both she and Arlan had relied heavily on Micah Davidson and had trusted him implicitly. She had emphatically denied the slightest possibility that Micah Davidson could have been responsible for Arlan's Disappearance or taken part in organizing it. Likewise, she had responded to the SPD's questions with a ferocious defense for her own children and their love for their father when the LEO had softly questioned if there was any possibility of impropriety from any of their own.

Anyone watching the video could readily see that she was a woman in complete distress. She was heartbroken, fear-stricken, panicked, and afraid to face the reality that she may never see her beloved husband alive again. Her voice held the unmistakable quiver of one on the verge of tears, and its heightened pitch told me everything I needed to know about how close to hysteria she had been. She was doing her best to maintain composure and address the LEOs questions respectfully and as thoroughly as possible. Nonetheless, there was an air of urgency to her responses, as if she knew that time was already working against them.

The one thing that should have been clear to both SPD Officers by the end of their interview was that Caroline Randall had been very open and direct regarding where her suspicions were aimed, and she made no pretext about pointing her finger directly at Willow Amos. Not only had she informed them she had not been permitted to select the Hospice employees sent to care for her husband herself, but she had never warmed to any of the 'hired staff' that had been sent over from the Winter Season Hospice Care facility.

Out of all the variables and potential red flags, the Hospice workers had been the only variation and change that had occurred within the Randall's environment in the last year. Caroline Randall had provided the SPD Officers with everything they needed to pursue an investigation, and yet despite having gone so far as to Arrest Willow Amos directly following the report of Arlan's Disappearance, it had gone nowhere. The two Responding Officers had somehow found enough cause to Arrest the Hospice worker, remove her from the homestead, drive her all the way to the SPD Headquarters, and detain her for questioning, and yet they had then simply turned her loose and essentially tossed the entire case. It made little sense, and I was glad that Officer Stanton had forwarded the video interview to me rather than just the summary report.

After I viewed it, I felt even more disheartened over how this case was developing. Caroline Randall was a woman that had built her life around her husband and children; the Disappearance of her husband had deeply affected her from the very first moment she sensed something was amiss. It was difficult to watch her as she realized what was happening and struggled to understand that something tragic was unfolding.

In those moments, even as I watched it through a video that had occurred months earlier, I felt a mixture of emotions that reminded me just how important this case was to resolve. It was almost voyeuristic to watch, and I felt both saddened and strangely guilty for viewing the footage now that I had met the woman in person. She was now presented in front of me through two different recordings, surrounded by a screen full of techno-jargon that was recording everything the human eye could not possibly hope to catch. Her eye movements, her body posturing, the elevation in her body temperature, even the increased inflections of her words as she spoke were all being documented. All of it was entirely unbeknownst to her, and all with the soulless, mechanical intent of tracking everything as the starting point of a potential Crime Scene Investigation.

It was a deeply personal moment in this woman's life; an unforgettable event that had probably seemed to drag on for an eternity to her as she desperately struggled to cope with the situation being presented and its implications. There was no doubt in my mind that this event had left an indelible impression upon her Soul; there was no need for another Human Being to bear witness to such a raw moment of tragic, emotional vulnerability, let alone store it for all time and eternity. I was left in quiet reflection as I thought about Arlan's wife and all that she had endured. Grief was such a profoundly personal experience I felt an almost primitive desire to protect this woman from any further pain, and yet I knew it was only a short time before I robbed her of the marginal stability she had found since her husband's Disappearance.

The next time this woman experienced this level of Grief it would be because of my own words, and I could not prevent it from occurring; the news of her husband's Death was going to be heartbreaking for her.

FIVE – KU —1— INITIATING INVESTIGATION

Opening the Investigation

With the assistance of Officer Stanton and Grace O'Connor, we reviewed all the information provided within the files related to the Disappearance of Katarina. We now had the benefit of knowing that she had, indeed, been Abducted from the parking lot of the church they had reported her Missing from. In the immediate aftermath of her Disappearance, neither her parents nor the Responding SPD Officers had been afforded that same luxury.

The file was as comprehensive as it could be, considering it had been an open, ongoing investigation in which there had been little to go on from the onset. The facts were extremely basic, easily verified, and provided next to nothing to move forward with. They knew that Katarina and her mother had arrived at the church together, that there had been other children around the playground and parking lot area who had observed them, and that there were no other reported adults in the vicinity—especially on church grounds. They could verify that the little girl had been wearing a pink sweater, riding a pink bike, and some had noted that she had also worn a pinkish-purple bike helmet. Beyond that, they had determined that Katarina's mother, Lucya, had left her daughter at the bottom of the steps along with multiple other girls who had been sitting in the same area. Katarina had been standing either next to, or over, her bike—she had been stationary, not riding it—when her mother had entered the building.

Lucya Urakov had been the last known adult to see Katarina before she Disappeared.

When she had returned to the parking lot after approximately ten minutes, the same young girls had been sitting there and had not stirred. The only thing that had changed during that time, from Lucya's perspective, was that both her daughter and her bike had been Missing, and they had both Vanished Without A Trace.

As time had progressed, the Detectives had done a fair amount of work. They had conducted extensive interviews with every potential witness, verified statements, and followed any leads that crossed their path.

Finding the Physical Remains of Katarina had immediately elevated us to a higher vantage point than the two Missing Persons Detectives that had been assigned to her case over three months ago.

They had not brought me on until after the Physical Remains of Katarina had been located, but that was a long way from a little girl being reported as 'Missing' with no one having come forward with any type of leads. Despite the time span being greater than three full months having passed, and despite what appeared to be a pair of efficient local Detectives working on her case, there had been little information gathered.

Everything had been working against them, and while we had the distinct advantage of being able to conduct our investigations with better advancements in technology, forensics, and investigative research than we had ever before known in the history of our nation, ultimately everything still depended on being able to build cases on a solid foundation, and the Disappearance of Katarina had anything but.

Most Missing Persons cases had at least something of substance with which to go on, and at least had some leads, a helpful background, witnesses, potential motives, or enemies. There were concerned Loved Ones who were volunteering their time and knowledge about the Missing Person, offering their own ideas and theories, and usually working diligently both with Law Enforcement and on their own to help the case. They spent their time, resources, and funding to canvas neighborhoods, put up reward money, and follow leads. For generations, Americans had gone above and beyond to do everything in their power as friends and family members of Missing Persons—as well as Victims of other Violent Crimes such as Rape and Murder—to help bring Closure and Justice to those who had been affected by the horrors brought about by their Fellow Man.

It was frequently said that while Law Enforcement did their best, and undoubtedly had better equipment and tools at their disposal, Investigators and Detectives were still not 'family', and therefore incapable of pushing themselves as hard as Loved Ones did to secure resolution. It wasn't that they were indifferent or that they didn't have a genuine care for the fate of their Missing Loved One. It was only that they were unlikely to be as invested in the outcome. What was a mere job for them was the world to others

Besides that, when Detectives were handed a dozen or more cases because of understaffing, it only reaffirmed that Loved Ones needed to offer as much of their own skill, time, and resources possible so they could contribute to the groundwork for their case. It might not have been the same for other types of cases, when friends and family were deemed to be more 'underfoot', but in the event of a Disappearance or known Abduction, time was of the essence, especially with children. Of all the times when a bridge between Law Enforcement, members of their community, and the Loved Ones of a Victim was necessary, it was in the immediate aftermath of a Citizen having been reported as Missing.

But after three full months, statistics had proven that their investigation would have transitioned from a search to a wishful prayer that they could find her Physical

Remains, and then be able to gather forensics from that. Even so, I was not unimpressed with the level of work that the two SPD Missing Persons Detectives had applied toward the search, and one, in particular, had kept extensive journal entries into both his actions and his thoughts regarding leads and information he had gained.

He had tried, which was at least something. Statistically, we had all known the odds were stacked against our being able to find her, and they had waned more and more with each passing day. But Katarina had been different from the beginning. They hadn't even been able to confirm she had been Abducted rather than simply wandered off and gotten lost.

This was not the case, of course, and despite records showing that they had made considerable efforts to scour the entire neighborhood, they had not come up with anything substantial within the first twenty-four hours. This time frame was critical regarding finding Missing Children because statistics had demonstrated shockingly painful realities regarding the reduced odds for survival the more time progressed. More than seventy-four percent of the children that had Gone Missing were Murdered within the first three hours directly following their Abduction.

The SPD Missing Persons Detective that had been assigned to the case had made a note stating that there had been no cameras in the area between the Urakov home and the church, so there had been no surveillance footage.

The SPD Detective had done some legwork regarding canvassing the area and interviewing all the locals. Eventually, he had found a home with a security camera that had captured Katarina and her mother walking to the church. The surveillance wasn't very clear, and as it was from an inexpensive, low-quality unit, the recording was grainy, low-resolution, and had some flickering. But it was the last known footage of Katarina Urakov.

If nothing else, the video footage verified that the child had not met with an Accidental Death or Died at the hands of her mother in their home or while under her care. There had been times where parents had attempted to create Missing Persons cases to conceal truths which might otherwise have implicated them in some form of Wrongful Death. The security system was terrible, to be sure. But it was more than adequate to verify the mother's accounting of events, clear her own name, and at least help establish, and confirm, a potential Point of Abduction.

Interviews: Parents and Children

I proceeded with the investigative end of Katarina's Disappearance by re-doing all the interviews that the previous two Detectives had conducted, choosing to leave no stone unturned and to start fresh with my own eyes. I drove to the church, walked the property and block, and even retraced the pathway taken by Lucya and Katarina on their last day together. I wanted to get a feel for what I could expect, and given the complexity and solemnity of the situation, I wanted to be certain I knew as much as I could before delivering the Notification of Death to little Katarina's parents.

The records provided by the previous Detectives were well-done and detailed. Stanton and I spent some time contacting each of the parents and establishing communication, and for two days I worked solely throughout the church community, re-interviewing families one at a time, speaking with clergy, parents, children, and the women in Lucya Urakov's sewing circle. I found my own notes lining up exactly with all those already on record, with almost no variance—even in the children's testimonies. Katarina had simply Vanished.

All the children that had been outside when Katarina had Disappeared had been interviewed by well-qualified professionals who could extract relevant information from young children while being equally careful not to plant anything or pose leading questions. Despite this focused effort to be thorough as they tried to gather evidence and potential witnesses, none of the children observed anything out of the ordinary. The children had ranged in age; the oldest on site had been fourteen years of age, while the youngest had been a set of three-year-old twins in the care of several older siblings.

It was a casual situation among the members of their congregation, and most parents allowed their children to play in the parking lot unsupervised.

As concerned as some parents were upon hearing of the mystery surrounding Katarina, there were still those who remained skeptical. When asked, many of the adults had seemed rather unperturbed by the practice, even as one little girl had remained Missing. Some of them had simply declared that it was how things had always been done; there had never been a sufficient cause for concern before, and although the circumstances of the Disappearance of Katarina were tragic and mysterious, they simply lacked evidence to confirm she had, indeed, been Abducted.

None of them had ever considered that there could be any risk involved in regard to leaving children unattended in the parking lot—either by other church members or by Stranger Abduction. They were all a part of a community; they were around one another's children routinely, and while they may not have ensured they were watching them, they would never have allowed one to be hurt or approached by a random stranger without intervening.

Everything indicated that it had been a Crime of Opportunity, and as such, there was very little that either Lucya or Katarina could have done to alter that inevitable outcome.

Lucya's Missing Person Interview

    Oscar Urakov had arrived at the church within a half an hour of the SPD Officers. Because Lucya had still been giving her interview and volunteering as much information as she could provide, we were able to witness Oscar's arrival. She had contacted him immediately after she had exited the church and failed to locate her daughter. She had stated that she had called her name out a few times, and, while awaiting her response, had remained at the top of the stairs for several moments, scanning the parking lot for her daughter's pink bike. The church steps had provided her with a critical vantage point because of its elevation, but with three dozen children running around, she had been unable to locate Katarina. She had descended the steps and walked through the parking lot, frantically searching the faces of the children for her daughter. By the time she had used her mobile phone to call her husband, she was already in full panic.

    This served us well as it showed just how powerfully the two had reacted to the situation; they were both highly emotional and beside themselves. Lucya Urakov had immediately apologized to her husband upon his arrival; an indicator of how much guilt over her daughter's Disappearance she had been consumed by.

    She had retraced her steps for the interview, showing the Responding Officers exactly what she had done between the time of her arrival and the time she returned to the parking lot and couldn't find Katarina. Nothing had seemed out of sorts, but she had been extremely distressed, and with each passing moment, became more frightened and panic-stricken.

    During Lucya Urakov's interview, she had emphasized that her young daughter had known the boundaries in which she had granted her permission to roam. She had told her she only wanted her to ride her bike in the area located right outside of the church itself, and to avoid going over into the outer areas of the parking lot. She mentioned she had advised her to avoid the furthest reaches of the black asphalt, citing that there was a road with traffic at the end of it and she had been concerned about her inability to stop easily enough since she was new to riding. The distraught mother was terrified that she had gone so far she had become disoriented and unable to find her way back to the church.

    She had expressed having no misgivings or feelings of potential danger at the prospect of allowing her daughter to ride her new bicycle in front of the church, as she had seen many other children do so in the past.

    My interviews with various church staff and officials confirmed that there had been several classes taking place during this time period, and the church had been overflowing with both adults as well as youth and children. The window for the Abduction of Katarina Urakov had been brief, and seemingly improbable.

    Unfortunately for the Urakov's, a few minutes had been all the time necessary to carry out a horrific series of events which would lead to devastating consequences for all involved.

Oscar's Missing Person Response

Lucya had conveyed her thoughts and fears to her husband upon his arrival. He had asked the two Responding Officers if he could leave rather than stay. As soon as they had granted their consent, he had turned to Lucya Urakov as if to ask her if he could leave her side—if she could forgive him for his desire to flee right then instead of staying and comforting her. She had hugged him fiercely, crying and begging him to go find their little girl, and to not stop driving until he had located her. He had wiped her tears from her anguished face with the wide palms of his hands, pressed her head against his own as he whispered reassurances to her, and then kissed her on the forehead before disappearing from the view of the SPD Officer's camera.

It was unknown just how long he had looked for her that night. But no one was likely to endure such an experience without it exacting its price; I had witnessed many parents—mothers especially—wither away into nothing in the weeks and months following the Loss of a Child through either Abduction or Murder.

Fathers, from my perspective, had often been much more pragmatic at such times; men of action who could not sit idly by and wait for 'the authorities' to do what was necessary. They needed to be involved directly—they needed to see that steps were being taken, that everything that could be done was being done, and that no stone was ever left unturned. Evil men created the problems that Good men spent their entire lives both cleaning up and paying for, and it had always been that way.

I wondered how long that night Oscar had stayed out searching for his daughter, driving around the neighborhood surrounding the church, walking the city blocks, and canvassing every alleyway, parking lot, and dark corner in which he might find her. I wondered how many times he had gone out patrolling the streets looking for her after that, how many evening meals and workdays he had missed, how many sleepless nights, and how many miles he had logged while trying to find even the slightest of leads. Men, by nature, were problem-solvers and fixers, protectors, and providers. They would sooner die than let something happen to one of their children or their Loved Ones.

Since the dawn of time, the world had known the haunted footsteps of the worried father as he searched the streets of his community after his child's whereabouts had become unknown. I wondered how many fathers throughout the history of our nation had also suffered similar situations, canvassed the land, and felt the panicked escalation of fear overtake them as they realized the worst.

It was difficult to imagine anything more tormenting than to watch a father desperately search for his Missing little girl. Every fiber of his Being would reject the sound of silence after he called out to her and heard nothing in return. A father's love would compel him to search endlessly and defy every boundary forced upon him until his body collapsed from exhaustion. It seemed to me that children of such men would have known this; they would have known that their fathers would never give up on them. I wondered how many nights Katarina had cried herself to sleep, calling out for her papa.

After Katarina's Disappearance

The Abduction of Katarina had caused significant turmoil for the small neighborhood in which she and her parents had lived. There had not been an Abduction on record for the Greater Seattle Area of a young female child in over a decade, and Katarina had been taken in broad daylight while outside of her own church in a residential neighborhood. There had been no sightings of her since her Disappearance, and no other children had been reported Missing after her.

It wasn't just an anomaly that a young girl would Vanish from a residential neighborhood; cases involving Missing Children were so rare that the entire state had been placed on high alert. All throughout the Greater Seattle Area, parents had been guarding their sons and daughters with a newfound ferocity. It was highly probable that it had felt more than a little alien to the parents.

A child had been Missing from the Greater Seattle Area that had not been located after more than three agonizingly long months despite all the technological advancements available. They could not find her despite the mandatory RFID-Chipping of every minor Citizen under the age of twenty. The RFID-Chipping, of course, was intended to help parents and Law Enforcement locate their children should any of them need to be tracked in an emergency, and yet it had not worked within the one child that had Gone Missing that needed to be found.

After Katarina's Abduction, parents realized that not only were their children not nearly as safe as they had believed them to be, but that their only method of being able to save their child after a Disappearance might not actually work as expected. Parents were now faced with uncertainties and risks that they had never before known. After decades of almost non-existent Violent Crime, most people were unfamiliar with topics and information related to Child Endangerment. They lacked basic knowledge about Child Safety, including common practices and methods that had been previously used to reduce risks. They were unfamiliar with Law Enforcement procedures and investigative practices for Child Abduction cases.

For the first time in many of their lives, parents had been tasked with educating themselves about the methodology and dangers related to Abduction. It became necessary to teach their young children about topics related to child abductions, including potential risks, hidden dangers, sketchy characters lurking about, and what they should do to handle such events.

The Disappearance of one young girl had changed the perception of Child Safety for countless families in the Greater Seattle Area, and for many parents of young children, it served as a cautionary tale.

Before and After the Great Reformation

Perhaps one of the most heart-breaking aspects of the Disappearance of Katarina was that it had occurred while she had presumably been on the property of her place of worship; a church that she had belonged to her entire life and had undoubtedly considered a sacred place. It was a location that most likely could instill a sense of peace for all who visited, including the children.

She should have felt safe anywhere in her nation, but it was deeply troubling that her life was in imminent danger while only feet away from her mother.

She had been doing something that had been a favorite American pastime for children for hundreds of years all throughout the nation. Whatever had happened—however she had been Taken—she had probably never seen it coming, and at the age of five, she could never have imagined the horrors they would have subjected her to. The children of the 22nd century had not grown up in the same troublesome times as before. They had never been warned or taught to fear monsters because there had been none to fear. The American People had worked extremely hard for many, many decades to ensure this was the reality for our children and future generations.

Even in the 21st century—likely the worst period in our collective history in which our children had routinely Gone Missing—the Abduction and Murder of Children was a relatively small category of Violence. Child Abductions which resulted in Sexual Assault and then Murder had only been less than half of a percentage of all the Homicides on any given year, and as such, had never been an excessively pronounced category.

Of course, these statistics had increased over time as the nation became more engulfed in turmoil during the mid-21st century, but then the number of cases had dropped almost to the point of obsolescence after the Sentence Reform Act. It had been yet another example of how 'Random' Acts of Violence had been decimated once we removed the population of Habitual Offenders from society.

It didn't take a statistician to recognize the merit of having such men removed from the streets of our nation. Harsh sentencing would spare countless Innocent Lives. When more than half of the Violent Crimes Against Children were committed by men with Prior Convictions, it was foolish to presume that they would be 'rehabilitated' if released back onto our streets. The lax policies of the 21st century which allowed for the release of those convicted of Crimes Against Children essentially handed them license to seek new Victims to target. The Sentence Reform Act had ensured that none of them were ever granted the opportunity to commit new Crimes again.

Had such men with Prior Convictions for Violent Crimes Against Children been removed permanently upon their Convictions, more than half of the children Abducted and Murdered every year would have been Alive and free from any Harm or Threat of Harm. That was an irrefutable statistical fact. It was a disgusting example of how our ineffective Criminal Justice system had paralyzed our Citizenry, failed to protect children from entirely preventable and avoidable tragedy, and Stolen the Lives of hundreds of thousands of our Children.

Was not one child's Death too many if someone whom everyone knew to be a high-risk threat did it? If the statistics and facts had already revealed solid truths regarding the likelihood of Re-Offending and Escalation in the depravity and Violence of their Crimes, was there any justification for providing them with another opportunity?

We had safely protected the sons and daughters of America for the first time in history. Likewise, as they had in the years immediately following the onset of the Great Reformation, all public schools had implemented Self-Defense courses, and with every new school year, more advanced courses were both available and required.

Teaching our sons and daughters how to defend and protect themselves had been a proven deterrent for many negative situations. When it became common practice for every child over the age of eight to train in some form of Self-Defense, hand-to-hand combat, MMA, or martial arts, with their training and skill levels increasing each year, it served them well in many regards. Bullying and harassment decreased. Statistics proved drastic reductions in Date Rape, Campus Rape, and Sexual Harassment. Random Stranger Abductions and ARM Attacks had decreased to almost non-existent numbers within a generation.

It was a devastating thought to realize that our world would miss out on all that Katarina was—all that she could have become—because of the abhorrent actions of another. I found it heartbreaking to recognize that a little girl of such a tender age was lost to us forever. Her story was now frozen until the end of time; it immortalized her as a beautiful little girl, left to remain a perfect child, leaving her mark on her parents, our nation, and our Citizenry.

It was, as The Watchers On The Wall had called it, the *Undoing of a Ripple*. Katarina had been a young girl who normally would have—and should have—lived for around a century, and during that time she would have affected many lives. She would have fallen in love, married, had children, gained an education and career, and contributed to our society in countless ways. She may have become one of our greatest national treasures. She might have possessed a talent for art, or math, or wordplay that surpassed us all and would have benefited our entire world.

Whether she could change our world on a grand scale, or if she would have just spent her life as most of us did, only touching and leaving a small Ripple for an intimate collection of Loved Ones, her Death had ended all of it prematurely. Her parents would never have her back again; she would never help take care of them in their old age as she had been taken care of during her brief lifetime. Her story was Undone; the Ripple cut short.

Even in a nation that had done everything possible to ensure that the tragic horrors of the past were corrected through the most comprehensive, intolerant, and unforgiving Criminal Justice system in the history of our nation, there were still Evil men out there that were able to get away with Evil things.

Our nation had done an excellent job ensuring that those who were Convicted for a first-time regarding Crimes Against Humanity and Crimes Against Children were never given an opportunity to be Convicted a second time. We had done everything within our power to obliterate the propensity for Violence by eradicating any Violent Offenders before they became *Repeat* Offenders. The Sentence Reform Act ensured this. Tough sentencing laws, meticulous mental health evaluations, and the permanent Exile or Death of any Convicted Pedophile or Sexual Offender from our nation had all but guaranteed this.

I knew that the case of Katarina was a one in a million Crime—even less than that; it was an almost infinitesimal percentage since the Great Reformation had occurred and the Sentence Reform Act had been put into effect. I knew that most states went years between similar cases, and that there had been states that hadn't had a single Child Abduction resulting in Sexual Assault and Murder by a Stranger in more years than I had been Alive. I knew that our Criminal Justice system worked.

I knew it had not only drastically decreased the number of Victims created, but that we had effectively eradicated all Serial Sexual Deviants with a predilection for Children and purged our nation of our worst Offenders. They eradicated all those who were incapable of being rehabilitated, either through the Death Penalty or Exile, and overall, the vast majority of our children were safe within our nation.

But none of that mattered to Katarina, and none of it would make one ounce of difference to Oscar and Lucya Urakov.

SIX – KU —2— DEATH NOTIFICATION

Death Notification—I: Meeting Oscar

We approached the house slowly and parked across the street. It was a pleasant house on a pleasant street in a pleasant neighborhood. There were flowers growing along the walkway that someone had planted with care. The home was tidy.

It was 1730 on a workday. I had waited an appropriate time for the Victim's father to arrive home from his small storefront where he operated a neighborhood butcher shop. Officer Stanton had reported that the store hours stated he closed shop at 1700 every day except Sunday.

Stanton had stated that the butcher's wife, Lucya, did not work outside of the home and didn't have any professional work history—at least, according to the IRS and going back as far as her US Citizenship background showed. Her social media was virtually non-existent, but posts and online activities showed she belonged to a neighborhood meal program for international cooking lessons and various church activities. Their neighborhood was ethnically diverse and had a high Russian population.

Neither were educated beyond high school. Their immigration records stated Oscar had proposed to his wife in Russia and they were married in a local family church. Her social media reflected this with a series of photos depicting the happy couple posing outside of a Roman Catholic cathedral, smiling, surrounded by family and friends. She appeared to be a woman in her mid-to-late twenties, very slender, with big blue eyes and blonde hair; her skin was so pale it was almost chalky. Her husband, Oscar, had been a short, stocky man in his mid-thirties, broad-shouldered, thick-waisted, and dark-complected, especially compared to his ghostly wife. One picture showed him lifting her up as grooms often did, his stubby, sausage fingers gripping her from underneath, and carrying her off while winking at the camera. They both seemed light-hearted, good-natured, and in love.

Katarina was their only child.

The math showed that at least a decade of marriage had passed before Katarina's birth, and given how fragile both mother and daughter seemed to be, I wondered if poor health had played a role. If the delicate fragility of Lucya Urakov had determined the size of their family, it was only going to be all the more devastating when I broke the news of Katarina's Death to them. It was never a simple job, but I could imagine that for women of a certain age, or women with such difficulties, losing one's only child would be even more difficult to bear. Before we arrived, I had shared these sentiments with my new colleague, Grace O'Connor, just as a manner of courtesy; my observations were merely speculative, but it was always best to be cognizant of the sensitive nature of our work.

Further readings from their Immigration files spoke of strong ties to extended family located both in America and Russia, and each had stated that they could trace their family lineage back several hundred years. They had been in America for almost sixteen years, having arrived the same year they married, and had presumably chosen Seattle because Oscar had relatives that had immigrated to the area many years before. Since then, another half-dozen members of their families from both sides had also immigrated over the years, all of them living and working within the same local community, sometimes immigrating with their own spouses and children. The extended family of Oscar and Lucya Urakov consisted of some fifty locals nearby. Hopefully, this would translate into a strong support system in place once we had met with them and delivered our news. Soon enough, an entire family would be Grieving.

I knocked on the door and heard a man's voice mumble something in Russian. A higher-pitched female voice responded. Within a moment, the front door opened, and I found myself looking downward at the concrete, wide frame of the man whom I recognized to be Oscar Urakov.

As soon as the man saw me, I could tell that he understood. His face fell with a shadowed sorrow, and his eyes dropped to the floor. He shook his head briefly, and with one hand wiping a rogue tear away from his eye, he opened the door wide without a word. With a low, sweeping wave of his arm, he motioned for us to enter his home and have a seat. I stepped aside for Grace O'Connor to enter ahead of me, and she passed through the door without ceremony. We then stood in the entryway, watching as Oscar closed the door softly. It seemed to require all his strength.

Entering the living room, I was immediately struck by how homey it was, filled with warm colors, heavy wooden furniture, and vibrantly patterned rugs covering the hardwood floors.

I noticed Oscar was only wearing his socks, and a row of neatly organized shoes—including several which could have only belonged to a very little girl—lined a carpeted area next to a seating bench. The sight of such small shoes was a sharp reminder once again, and my mind briefly flashed back to the tiny feet with pink nail polish on her toes.

I pushed the thought from my head, regrouped, and concentrated on following Grace O'Connor as Oscar Urakov motioned for us to sit next to one another on an overstuffed sofa lined with plaid pillows. We complied, and Grace O'Connor took the further seat off to my right, and closest to the wall. Oscar took a seat in a high-backed leather chair angled toward us.

From my vantage point, I could see the picturesque window on the opposite wall as it looked out over the front yard.

I released the lens on my external helmet and raised the balaclava visor so he could see my eyes clearly with no barriers separating us. This was protocol for such meetings; the eye contact mattered. Compassion mattered. Their being able to see my earnest desire to help their Loved One, a Victim of Murder, mattered.

I introduced Grace O'Connor by name, rank, and profession as a Case Manager from the VAA, and then myself as the newly appointed Investigator to their case.

He asked quietly if our visit meant we had located his daughter, and I nodded my head gently. His eyes searched mine for a reason to hold on to hope. Finding none, he shook his head with the slow acceptance of a man who had known what he expected to hear, but never wanted to. He inhaled sharply; a man struggling for strength.

He clenched his fists slowly, his jaw tightening, and then took a deep breath as he closed his eyes. He turned his face toward the ceiling and paused for a moment in his silence so he could compose himself.

I wondered if he had been asking God for the strength he would need to go into the other room and retrieve his wife for us, or if he might have been asking for strength to tell her himself. Perhaps he had been asking for guidance, for a moment of Divine Acceptance, for God's Will to be Done even if it meant this, the Death of his only Daughter.

I sat there until he was ready, willing to stay here, follow him, speak in more depth of what we knew—whatever he needed from us at any pace he wished to proceed. But it appeared all he needed from me was the unspoken confirmation of that which he already seemed to at least suspect must have been an inevitability. He then leaned over, and with two firm pats on my shoulder, motioned toward the kitchen and said that he would return shortly.

I knew what these moments were like, having shared in them more times than anyone should in a single lifetime. We were there at his leisure; they were our only priority for the moment, and such moments could seldom be rushed. He knew his wife far better than we did; he knew what to expect. But experience had taught me that most mothers processed this moment with greater difficulty.

As a general rule, it was often better to have them receive the news during a Notification with someone from the VAA right there beside them. Many times, when the spouse or other Loved One was trying to break it to them gently, they either lost their nerve or their will, and then it became an even more difficult process of confusion and distress. They trained us to be certain to clarify matters, to emphasize that their Loved One was Deceased, ensuring that we used the words—Dead, Death, Physical Remains. They were bitter words, impersonal, cold, abrupt. But it was necessary—they needed to know under no uncertain terms that 'Gone' meant 'Gone'—not Missing, not Disappeared, not 'Unable to be Located', but Dead. Deceased. Never Coming Back.

It seemed like the intentional infliction of unnecessary pain, but the words needed to be said; they had to hear them. For many, it was the first step toward Grieving. It was a long enough journey on its own without being able to hide behind Denial because some tender-hearted Law Enforcement Officer or Victim Advocate couldn't be forthcoming, or their compassion impeded protocol. It was protocol for a reason. Long before the Victim Advocacy Agency had been created, Peacekeepers had been delivering Death Notifications, and it had never been easy for any of them, regardless of training. There was never a good way to destroy someone's world.

After Oscar Urakov left us to our own devices, I took some time and looked around the room. I noted that Grace O'Connor was quietly taking everything in, hands folded on her lap, her legs neatly crossed at the ankle. Instead of leaning back into the comfortable, well-padded couch, she sat perched on the edge, artfully angling herself so she was positioned in such a manner that she could address both myself and Oscar Urakov—a Body Language strategy to show a welcoming countenance, inviting and unguarded.

Along with this, she took the time to examine the home just as I did; there was no need for small talk or superficial conversation, and it would have been out of place if there had been. I appreciated professionalism such as that; it was a subtlety that exceeded training and spoke more of her level of respect for the Grieving parents, reverence for the Human Life we were there to address, and the gravity of the situation we were presenting to complete strangers. Such things could not be taught—compassion, tact, discretion, patience, and especially a healthy reverence and regard for the task at hand. It was the most difficult part of my job. But it took willingness to venture into those difficult emotions in order to work through such experiences, and there were few who could do it well. Even being able to exist within the moment, read the situation, and appreciate it for what it was could be challenging for most. There was a very subtle, even delicate, art to being the Deliverer of such a Notification; it required more than just a basic understanding about what our visit meant to the two Citizens in the other room. There needed to be a certain level of personal depth, compassion, and emotional intelligence for the sake of the recipients, and I was glad to see that the woman sitting beside me was seemingly in alignment with how I felt about it.

The house was warm and inviting, but I was never comfortable in such situations, and I knew my Body Language always reflected it. It was another reason why having the Victim Advocates working alongside the Detectives and Investigators was so important; they bridged that gap between the formality of my work and the strangers we were interacting with. Most of us were men, and along with being analytical by nature, delivering the Notifications for Death with sufficient sensitivity and an appropriate investment of time was seldom our strength.

The home was just as tidy on the inside as the outside. There were photographs on the walls. Real, old-fashioned paper photographs, not digital screens; it made for an extremely homey feeling, and once again reaffirmed that this home was well-loved by its owners. Non-digital photographs were extremely rare to see, and it was almost peculiar how antiquated they presented because of their obscurity. They were nothing less than a foolish investment, given their archaic preservation methods, but still very sentimental.

Above the fireplace, a framed photograph of the family stared back at all visitors fortunate enough to be welcomed into their lovely home. There stood Oscar, in a handsome red vest, alongside his petite wife Lucya. Positioned directly before the two of them, each with a hand on one of her shoulders, was their only daughter Katarina. She stared back at me with blonde curls and a red bow in her hair. Her eyes were wide and blue, and a deep dimple graced her left cheek. Her front teeth were both featured in the photograph. The Christmas tree in the background showed this must have been last Christmas; approximately six or seven months prior. Her last Christmas.

I heard Oscar in the other room, talking softly to a woman. Her heightened emotional inflections told me he was already breaking the news to her and telling her to prepare for Final Confirmation from me. I had the technology at my fingertips to zero-in on external conversations and listen via audio, or I could use my visor and have the words placed on the screen. It was often used to transcribe other languages, as well as to ensure that communication was above board when ground troops interacted with regular civilians.

There was no need for any of this now, though. The overall tone was exactly what one should expect; an inconsolable wife trying to deal with the worst news of her life as a Mother. There was nothing translation would offer me other than the deep Sorrow of knowing that neither I, nor her husband, could ever find adequate words to help her during these moments. Listening would only be intrusive. There was nothing more to be done other than simply pause for a moment and give her time.

Of all the Human Suffering imaginable, nothing compared to that of the wailing made by a Mother upon learning of the Death of her Child. Such pain reached into the very coding of our Humanity and was the most direct and immediate Divine Connection between the Human Soul and God. It was, I believed, devoid of label because there were no earthly words capable of describing the incomprehensible depth of Suffering such Loss created. Around the world, the results were the same; it was the descent into a bottomless pit of Sorrow and Grief which no parent could ever entirely climb out of. It placed on display the most profoundly simple testament of Unconditional Love possible through its host's eternal mourning.

A more awesome, Divine example of the depth of our capacity to love one another could never be witnessed. Only God, and God alone, could heal the wound caused by such a Loss, but I was uncertain that it *should* heal. For as long as there was such evidence able to be observed, it stood as testimony for the world to see, illustrating just how beautiful Mankind truly was, despite all evidence to the contrary. Our Grief was a tribute both to our Loved One and our Heavenly Father; it was proof that we were supposed to be here, and when one of us was ripped away from this world through Unnatural Causes, especially outside of the natural order of things, it left a chasm of Empty Space which would remain vacant and unalterable for the rest of time.

I looked over at my companion, saw the pained expression on her face, and wondered if she herself was a mother or had perhaps suffered a similar Loss. Compassion was easy to find in this line of work, but for many, having a tender heart was also a disadvantage. It was difficult to maintain a respectable distance from one's work when it involved such dark subjects. To maintain our perspective, many put up brave fronts, distanced themselves entirely with distractions, and built walls to better protect themselves from forging a direct connection to all those whom they were being paid to assist. Sometimes, though, the walls could not be kept in place, and they crashed down as compassion gave way to empathy and shared experiences.

I wondered, seeing the tears well in her eyes now, if Grace O'Connor had felt the hand of God upon her in such a manner, and with every fiber of my Being I sincerely hoped not. I could not imagine doing this line of work—cases such as this—if one had known such Grief firsthand. Empathy might produce a level of authenticity to one's professionalism the likes of which could seldom be compared, but no one should ever Suffer the Loss of a Child. I prayed for her sake that she was merely one of those exceptional Human Beings so intimately capable of experiencing the emotions of another that she could not help but be drawn into the Tragedy unfolding in front of us, which surely was enough to evoke such Sorrow.

I tried to redirect Grace O'Connor's attention. Motioning to the far wall, I gave a nod to note the objects hanging from it. Oscar's wife, Lucya, worked not just with hand-sewing but with other aspects of needlework, it seemed. It was an old tradition that was long since forgotten by most because of technological advances. But it was one of the Arts that many immigrants and even a small demographic of our own Americans—usually our seniors and Centurions—held on to. They taught classes for such things at most universities, although it was usually an elective provided to Art majors and historians. I recalled reading an article about how they were trying to rejuvenate interest in such Lost Arts. They asserted that such skills were part of our Humanity, and should not be forgotten, comparing them to the Lost Languages of many Native American Tribes and other ancient civilizations of the past.

I watched as Grace O'Connor shifted her focus on the wall art, blinking back her watered eyes, and then spending her time looking around the room and trying to take stock of all the hand-crafted projects. It proved an effective distraction.

Out of the corner of my eye, I noticed another knitted item; a sweater in pale pink, neatly hanging from the coat rack. It was almost the size of doll clothing; no bigger than that of a toddler's winter coat. *She had been such a frail girl to begin with…*There had been little chance for any child, but especially not for her after that long of a period of malnourishment.

This home had once been an idyllic fairy tale for them, cozy, warm, safe. Now, it was nothing more than a museum, reminders everywhere of a little girl who had once filled these rooms with noise and laughter. She had just *Vanished*; her toys, dolls, stuffed animals, and books were all still sitting here, waiting for her to return and resume their use. It was as if their daughter had simply gone to the store with Oscar; everything was exactly as it must have been on the day she left.

Katarina had Disappeared, and Time had ceased to exist.

Death Notification II: Meeting Lucya

I looked in the direction that I had observed Oscar make his way toward, assuming it was likely the kitchen as it was nearing the evening meal hour. The woman's cries had subsided after a few moments, and I could see Oscar shuffling toward us at long last. I hadn't minded the wait; it gave me an opportunity to assess my surroundings, to get a feel for who Oscar and Lucya Urakov were as people, and it had even given me a glimpse into the sort of girl their sweet daughter Katarina had been.

We had not been granted the best manner of introduction, she and I, so it warmed my heart to spend a moment in her world—the world that she had been raised, the two people whom she had been born out of, and in the home that she had once called her own. She had been loved. They had doted on her, treasured her, and taken care of her. Her presence was everywhere—possibly too much of her for the long-term, but for now, in this interim period without Closure, very little clues to go on, and no way to expect what may come, it was only natural, I thought, for parents to leave their child's belongings exactly as they lay.

Even though I didn't have children myself, several of my brothers already did, and I knew from visiting that they were very much like little rabbits, always leaving their droppings underfoot. If memory served, one of my brothers had said that his girls were the cleaner and quieter of the two, but then he had followed that up with 'the most terrifying', so I wasn't certain if being tidy was necessarily enough to count them as the better of the sexes.

It seemed, though, after looking around the Urakov living room, that Katarina had enjoyed dollies and princesses and other things commonly beloved by all little girls. Her parents had a lovely little table and chair set up over in the corner for her coloring books and artwork. She had drawn a picture of a pink bike with pink and purple tassels hanging from the handlebars, which someone had taped up to the wall near her desk. There were a handful of colorful crayons strewn about the table, and although the floor appeared to have been swept recently, there were three crayons resting on the floor beneath her chair.

Such things, while sentimental, were troublesome to me, and I gently nudged the woman at my side with my knee so she would follow my gaze and note them. We did not need to speak, and for that, I was grateful. The time for talking would come later.

My eyes came to rest on a long black mark that I had first noticed when we had entered the room; it was right in the middle of the floor in the hallway area between the living room and the dining room on the opposite side. It had been oddly out of place in a home that was otherwise very tidy, and I wondered what could have made such a pattern.

Several moments later, Oscar entered the room from the dining area across the hall, and I observed that he made a conscious effort not to step on the black mark running along the floor. His eyes were bloodshot and Grief-stricken.

Lucya Urakov followed, but unlike the woman that I had seen smiling back from wedding photos and the Christmas portrait overhead, the woman that now stood before us was gaunt, emaciated, with a countenance that told of unspeakable Sorrow. She had swollen, puffy eyes from crying only moments before, but it was the large swells of darkness underneath that were immediately concerning to me, as they indicated too many sleepless, stress-filled nights. I felt Grace O'Connor's body tense next to mine upon seeing Lucya Urakov and knew that my concerns were well-grounded.

This woman was in a dangerous state of mind; the months of silence had taken their toll. Confirmation of Death had provided no relief, however. This woman had been Suffering for months already; she had slowly been torturing herself to death.

Her eyes had been a vibrant blue in her photographs and as seen in the large photograph hanging over the mantle nearby. I had looked into them and been reminded of a trip I had taken once; the opportunity to travel into outer space and look down upon our planet. Her eyes had reminded me of Earth; a brightness and familiarity that had seemed immediately welcoming to each of us.

But those eyes were now dull and lifeless. They only changed expression as they welled up with water and overflowed from time to time. Eye contact was painful; enjoyment, spark, happiness—all were out of reach now. She was self-contained, guilt-ridden, trapped in a psychological hell of her own making, separated by a wall so high that not even her husband could enter anymore.

She followed her husband with docile compliance, allowing him to lead her by the hand just as he would a child. She had glanced at us, briefly, when she had rounded the corner at the edge of the room, and then I had observed how she had consciously, carefully, stepped around the black marking on the floor just as her husband had. But then she had looked down toward the floor once more, shoulders sagging, tiny little feet slowly moving toward us only because her husband kept directing her. Her entrance told me two things; she was still in there, somewhere, and I needed to inspect whatever that marking was on the floor, because it had been significant enough to reach her even though she was clearly far away otherwise.

Oscar approached us, his eyebrows furrowed together; he was a man's man, a man of few words who by nature seemed to want to enjoy life. He was out of his element with this situation, a blue-collar man working with a limited toolbox when his wife needed far more than what he could give.

What had happened to the Victim Advocate that should have been assigned to the Urakov family? They had left this woman to drown in her own Grief and fear. Her husband worked all day, leaving his profoundly depressed wife on her own. She had been sitting in this house for over three months—a house where her daughter had once played, shared her days, and filled her hours with joy, but was now overwhelmed by silence.

Our arrival would not help matters. After months of quiet contemplation and fear, the facts were being placed in front of her. Several months ago, she had been instantly struck with her daughter's absence, a complete mystery and lack of Closure, a husband who must continue to work to put bread on the table, and enough guilt and self-recrimination to make most people turn to a bottle or a gun. Now, all that remained was heartache and pain.

I watched as her large blue eyes—the same big blue eyes featured on her lovely little daughter—looked furtively into my face before darting over to Grace O'Connor briefly and then looking downward again. Her head hung low, her eyes downcast as they overflowed with bursts of hot tears, falling like bombs dropping from the sky onto the hardwood floor below. She could barely process what was happening. She was little more than a deer caught in headlights, ready to bolt, terrified of the situation at hand, heart almost visibly palpitating as she fiercely clutched the only protection she felt she had—Oscar.

Both Grace O'Connor and I had risen to greet them as they entered the room and then made their way toward the seating area. I stood quietly and extended my hand toward Lucya, moderately surprised when she released her hold on Oscar long enough to place her frail, trembling hand into my own briefly. She was little more than the size of a child, and her hand had been so delicately carved and cold it had reminded me of a marble statue.

She then allowed herself to be greeted by Grace O'Connor, who, having forged her own course of action, had immediately moved past me, and drawn Lucya into a warm and nurturing hug. It was all that Oscar could bear to see as he heard his wife let out another sob from the depths of her Soul. He hung his head, allowing himself a moment to feel the pain he knew would be present henceforth.

Their tragedy, although shared between them and no doubt of equal measure, was not something they could spare one another from, nor could they share in it entirely. Each would suffer independently—both for their own sorrows as well as that which they knew their spouse was also suffering—and neither would be able to shield the other.

The two women stood there for a moment, Grace O'Connor holding on to her new ward like any mother would have, smoothing the poor woman's hair down as she ran her hand along the back of her neck, whispering into her ear things of which we were not meant to hear. Oscar's face, though strained, was filled with relief; his love for his wife was immeasurable, clearly, but the stress of the last three months had taken its toll. He needed rest, especially emotionally. Their home, like their Grief, had become a prison. Time had stood frozen; this moment had been desperately needed.

Oscar and I sat down, followed by the two women. Grace O'Connor took my place, making herself accessible to Lucya and still holding her hand as they sat in their respective corners of the couch and loveseat. Grace O'Connor had been a Godsend; of this, I was certain.

Even Oscar could sense a change within his wife; a newfound strength to continue, to tell her story, to reach out one last time even if only to ensure that someone would remain steadfast on the case and still try to discover what had happened to her little girl. There was only the slightest breath of life still within her, but by finding refuge in a stranger, in feeling the compassion and heartfelt sympathy conveyed by Grace O'Connor, she had found her will to continue.

I didn't know what she had whispered to her during those moments, and I didn't know by what power of persuasion she had empowered Lucya Urakov to seize control of her Vulnerability and Heartache, but somehow, she had done exactly that, and the ember that had been slowly dying within Lucya had gained strength and momentum once more.

Death Notification III: Providing Answers

Once I was certain that Lucya and Oscar were both in a state of mind that they could process more information, I went through my formal statement using the protocols established on a national level for all Law Enforcement. I recited the passage we were all required to share regarding the Constitutional protections outlining our Right to Life, and then explained that their daughter, Katarina, a minor child and a Citizen of These United States, had been discovered on this date in June in The Year of Our Lord, having been found Deceased in a manner which met the specifications as a Crime Against Humanity and the Violence Against Children Act.

I made the standard formal Declaration of Identity and Intent, pledged to each of them I would do my Due Diligence as an Officer of the Law and their Fellow Countryman to complete a professional and thorough investigation to the best of my ability, and that I would not waiver in my Oath as a Peacekeeper to bring Closure and Justice to this case for their daughter, Katarina, and to them, the Bereaved.

When I concluded my personal Oath, I introduced Grace O'Connor once more, provided a statement granting her Independent Access and Rights within my Investigation, and informed each of the Urakov's that they had the right to withdraw their involvement with either of us at any point, to cease all communication, to employ an Attorney or have one present during our communications, or to route my communication through a 3rd party. I concluded by stating that although the Crimes had been Committed Against their Loved One, because the Crimes were Against a Child, they did not have the authority to halt my Investigation, dictate the terms and conditions, or evict any Assigned or Appointed Investigators or Staff from the case. I concluded my formal recitation by making the proclamation that as a Federal Investigator and a Peacekeeper that I was beyond reproach, accountable to no state or local government, and worked independently to ensure each case was legitimate and immune from hostile acts. I informed them that I had my own team, and the other two Detectives would no longer be working on the case.

Once the formalities were out of the way, I went over as much about the case as I could and included any relevant information that had been learned and verified from the two previous Detectives who had initiated the investigation.

And then finally, after all that, I delivered the Notification of which I had arrived to deliver. In accordance with policy, I did not mention any specifics of her Death. I would not burden the family with the Violent details that would surely haunt their minds and hearts as they visualized them. It was bad enough they would know she had been Intentionally Harmed; there was nothing to be gained by planting seeds of just how Violent or Painful her Death was.

After sharing only the barest minimum of details with them, I explained it had been a Crime Against Humanity, and that the SPD was investigating it. I took my role in relaying information seriously. I left enough scars on the minds and hearts of Innocent People without adding to it needlessly with images of their Loved One's being

Intentionally Hurt. Those were images one could not easily forget, and all too often became permanently associated with the life story of their Loved One. It was important to me, as it should be to everyone that worked within these fields, that the precious memories of their Loved Ones remain pure and based on the lives that they had lived; not on the last few moments, hours, or days of their lives, and above all else, not on the Pain they may have Suffered or Endured at the hands of some Unknown Assailant or Predator.

I shared as much information as I could, offering them reassurances that I was on task while Grace O'Connor reviewed all her information with them, and then I asked for Oscar and Lucya to recount everything they could from the initial Abduction of their daughter, little Katarina. The records I had were already over three months old. We were entering this investigation with fresh eyes, and I wanted to hear from every source myself.

Listening to Oscar speak quietly, Lucya would nod her head in agreement as he offered relevant details that pertained to her case. He shared her daily habits, her travel itinerary between school, home, and sometimes the place where Lucya picked up odd hours doing sewing projects for a local business. Katarina was seldom on her own; even when she was at the sewing business, she was there with her mother.

We comforted the two of them as they absorbed the news that we had found the Physical Remains of their only daughter, allowing ample time for them to process the information and come to terms with it; no small feat given their absolute love for their only child.

Death Notification IV: Interview

My cameras recorded the interview. I asked a few more pointed questions about it, all with monotone professionalism, hopefully conveying a standard line of questioning. I did not want them to feel as though it could be someone within their church, but there were indications that whoever had buried her had done so in a more personal manner than with the other three Victims. This could indicate that she had been known to her Assailant.

The three adult Victims had all been wrapped in outer lining, which was currently being analyzed through the SPD Forensics Department. Young Katarina, however, had not been wrapped in anything; she had been Buried with only a thin layer of clothing that had covered her body. Along with this variation, they had carefully placed her within the Grave with her delicate little arms crossed over, as if in prayer.

She had been cared for.

She had been treated with tenderness.

It seemed contradictory—such Evil in contrast to such gentleness upon her Final Breath. Whoever had taken the time to place her into that grave had done so with care, with compassion, and intended to allow her to Lie in Peace. Whether motivated by guilt, shame, or perhaps even some misguided, broken, warped version of 'love', the person who had Buried her had done so with something akin to actual reverence, and for that reason, I could not rule out anyone at her church.

Likewise, I could not presume that the person was directly linked to the Urakov's lives, or that they were known to them. It could have been an entirely random Abduction that was only based on chance and opportunity. That was what remained to be seen.

"We have been members here since the beginning. Since we arrived, we go to this church. My uncle and his family all go to this church. Our first home, our apartment, was near this church. So, then we buy our house. It is near our church, and near my work. This way I can walk, and we need only one car."

Oscar was very direct; his conversation was brusque, but he spoke with a masculine authority many Russian men were known for. His tone was decisive, abrupt, and his sentences were nondescript because of his language barrier and his Grief. Getting told of his daughter's confirmed Death while also being introduced to the new Investigator and Victim Advocate and then asked to review everything from the beginning was a lot to process. He deserved credit for being able to articulate himself as well as he was, given the circumstances.

"Sir, do you recall any negative interactions with anyone at church? Has there ever been anyone that made your family experience any discomfort? Did Katarina ever express to you that someone at church or elsewhere made her feel uncomfortable, or like they were too familiar with her?" I asked him.

I looked searchingly at both of their faces, leaving it open to each of them to contemplate, but also trying to be respectful toward Lucya, who was obviously bearing the worst of the trauma.

I knew she had been the one who had been watching little Katarina at the time of her Abduction. She had been the one that had determined Katarina could remain outside of the church whilst she went inside.

It was then that I realized what the black mark was on the floor, what the pattern was—it was tire tread.

A black mark left on an otherwise spotless floor.

A reminder of their daughter in motion, much like the crayons that had fallen to the floor beneath her desk.

Contemplating my question, Oscar shook his head and ran his hands through his hair. It was probably a subject each parent had weighed and considered countless times over the months, internally questioning everyone they knew with endless suspicion.

I spent a bit more time going over the basic details once again, double-checking my notes against the original interviewer's notes when Katarina had Disappeared.

Lucya quietly stated that many children were left outside to play while their parents were inside, that they did so with such regularity that the church had eventually placed playground equipment near the front, and that no one had ever experienced anything negative in all their years of having been members there. She said that children played out there even now, despite everything.

She was heartbroken, Guilt-ridden, and Grief-stricken. Her voice broke as she told me, but she wanted me to understand—she had not thought what she was doing was anything she should not have done; all the parents did it. I tried my best to reassure her she had done nothing wrong and that she must not blame herself.

When I believed I had asked everything and gained all that I could for the time being, I offered my credentials to their visitor log system at the door so they could contact me directly should they need me for anything, and then Grace O'Connor followed suit.

I shook Oscar's hand warmly, then Lucya's, holding her hand in both of my own. Today was going to be the first day of the rest of her life without her daughter; the first day knowing for certain that her young daughter had not Disappeared, but that she had been Abducted, and that not only had she Gone Missing, but that she had been Murdered, and she would never return to them.

It was one thing to know that 'something had happened' and yet not have any answers; there could remain some semblance of Hope in that. But now they knew; now she knew, whether right or wrong, intentional or not, what had transpired on that fateful day had resulted in the most devastating of consequences with permanent, unavoidable results. Their daughter's Death was now confirmed, and nothing would ever change that.

After having spent several hours in their company, I knew I was leaving them with a quiet home and many unresolved issues. They would have more questions over time, and many more terrible feelings to contend with as the investigation progressed.

We had just delivered the first of four Notifications of Death for each of our Victims.

As the door gently closed behind us and we took our leave, Lucya Urakov could be heard crying out; an aching, primal sob from deep within filling the air.

Followed by this, Oscar's heart-wrenching lament— *"Katarina, oh, my Katarina!"*

Moving Forward

    We as a nation had never invested much time into examining the long-term consequences of Violent Crime and those who were Left Behind after someone Went Missing. There had been many areas of Human Suffering that the government had overlooked and ignored throughout the 21st century in the years before the Great Reformation, and those who were Mourning the absence of a Missing Child had never garnered much attention.

    But those who worked within specific professions, especially that of psychotherapy and Grief counseling, knew all too well how powerfully guilt and blame affected parents who felt responsible for their Missing children.

    After meeting with Lucya Urakov, I realized she had felt great responsibility for her daughter's Disappearance despite there being no validity to her self-imposed admonition. Lucya Urakov was not a woman that seemed willing to accept forgiveness from either her husband or herself, such was the power of loud, negative reinforcement, and such was the extent of her Suffering and Grief.

    Historical recordings of cases had illustrated well over a century of such parental disquiet; they were often inclined to self-blame, and possessed an inability to forgive themselves for having 'allowed' the Disappearance of their child to have occurred, even when by all rights nothing could have been done differently or changed the outcome. They were known to 'replay' the event repeatedly, haunted by their memories, their actions, their lack of awareness of the impending danger, and their inability to prevent it from occurring. It left many in a vicious cycle of self-torment and contempt; their negative reactions became stuck on a loop much like a broken vinyl record that could never escape the damaged grooves, leaving it to replay the same notes over and over again.

    However, there was not anything that Lucya Urakov could have done differently which would have prevented the Abduction of Katarina from occurring on that fateful day. She had done nothing uniquely different or worse than any of the parents that had allowed their own children to play outside of the church.

    Whether Katarina had been specifically targeted because of who she was, her age, or how she looked, was probably never going to be known. Her Abduction could have been extremely focused, well-planned, and impeccably timed, or it could have been nothing more than random, unfortunate luck of the draw entirely due to chance and circumstance. Just as there were often lingering questions by countless others who were Left Behind to Grieve after the Abduction of their Loved One, the Urakov's might spend the rest of their lives searching for answers which were never forthcoming. Sadly, there may always be unanswered questions and unexplored, unprovable theories, all of which would remain speculative and interwoven with sorrow and remorse.

    Katarina may have been Abducted as a matter of opportunity; it was not so very different from how most women were Abducted—they were simply in the wrong place at the wrong time and noticed by the wrong person. Aside from all that, even if

Katarina had been spared, nothing would have changed the fact that there had been a Predator out there waiting; if it hadn't been her, it was highly probable that it still would have been someone else's child at some point.

The tragic reality was that the Abduction of Katarina, like so many others before, may not have been preventable in any capacity.

There was still much to be discovered about who was responsible for her Abduction and Death. We had the 'Disposal Site', and it would undoubtedly yield a plethora of clues. And though it was often bleak to consider, there was a wealth of information about her case to be found through her Physical Remains. We had more to go on than three months of investigation by two Detectives solely because of those two key components, and that was nothing to scoff at.

Grace O'Connor and I had both felt a compulsion to share with Lucya Urakov how random such events could be. We wanted her to understand that she could not shoulder a sense of blame that was not, by all rights, hers alone to bear. In almost sixty percent of the cases of Child Abduction, the children that were selected were entirely random, and the Abductions occurred because they were Victims of Opportunity.

We had made a tremendous leap in her investigation by the discovery of her Remains. It might not have seemed like much, given it was the worst possible ending to a case, but now we had a fair chance of solving it and getting Justice for their entire family. Now, at least, we knew she had been Taken, and we knew they had intentionally done it for nefarious purposes. It meant that there was still a bad guy out there—that he had Disposed of his Victim through Concealment of her Remains, something that was done by men who Committed Crimes Against Children in more than half of all the cases so they could reduce their risk of getting caught.

We now knew the place where she had been Taken from, which meant that statistically we had a defined geographic perimeter in which to search for our Predator, since most of the time children were Abducted within only a mile or two of where the Child Abductor lived, worked, or had cause to visit. There was a good chance that her Killer lived nearby, or at the very least worked nearby or had social reasons to be right around the neighborhood. And because the Urakov's home was also within a close distance of the site in which she had been Abducted, it drastically narrowed down the search perimeters. We had been extremely fortunate despite the hardship of knowing that her Disappearance had now become a Homicide Investigation.

It was a heartbreaking situation for the parents of Katarina, but it was not without hope. By being able to investigate this with far more information available to us, we could now formulate legitimate theories and establish some geographic, technological, and forensic outlines.

Her Abduction could have just been an unfortunate, random event that had claimed an Innocent young girl when a moment of opportunity presented itself. Sadly, had it not been Katarina, it would undoubtedly have been someone else's child. Even more horrific and eye-opening, we still had no way of knowing for certain that there had not been others before or after her, either.

Moving forward, it was important to bear in mind that while we still had many unanswered questions, we were not entirely without direction and potential. As with all investigations, there was much to be done, and it often required a great deal of time. But we were on the right track, and I was determined to find those responsible for destroying the loving home the Urakov's had once known.

PART TWO

But the very hairs of your head are all numbered.
Do not fear; you are of more value than many sparrows.

Matthew 10:30-31

SEVEN - DK AND FN'S —1—

Introduction to Daegan Kyl

 Officer Stanton had been working on the Transportation Department network and reviewing their surveillance cameras.
 The I-5 freeway system running north and south along Washington State had cameras that monitored traffic. Issues such as congestion, gridlock, and accidents made it necessary to track most roads in real time, and Washington had been using cameras on their roadways for over one-hundred-fifty years already.
 The freeway surveillance was only helpful if it captured the access points to the property, however, and it didn't. The property had two points of access: a northern and southern entrance, both dirt roads connected to a paved road that led to a state highway before connecting to the 1-5 freeway. The nearest freeway entrance and Transportation Department camera was over four miles away from the northern entrance of the property. Because the state-operated surveillance equipment available proved ineffective, it had required Stanton to explore other avenues.
 By accessing the surveillance systems of private homes along the paved road, he found home security camera footage that captured one lone truck leaving the dirt road that ran alongside the neighbor's property. It was a box truck, approximately fourteen feet long.
 There was a full view available that identified the make and model of the vehicle. Since it was dark, there was no way to identify the driver, and according to Stanton's report, no efforts to adjust the footage yielded worthwhile results.
 Stanton said he was working on securing all other surveillance of the vehicle that he could track over the last few months and would keep me apprised if he discovered any other vehicles or activity in relation to the property. It seemed extremely fortunate that we had found any sort of lead given the isolation of the area, so I was cautiously optimistic about his ability to discover anything else. In the meantime, he had provided additional details about the truck, and prefaced his information by saying he was now working on learning more about the owner of the vehicle.
 When he traced the license plate, it came back registered to a local moving company in the Greater Seattle Area. After searching cameras throughout Seattle, Stanton secured footage of the truck as it was being driven. There was a clear image of

the driver, and Stanton could verify that the man driving was the owner of the company.

Being able to confirm that he not only owned it but was actively responsible for its use was important. It proved he had a personal connection to the vehicle. He couldn't state that the truck had been stolen, that others used it, or even simply deny that he ever drove it.

There weren't any photos linking the man directly to the footage related to the roads near the gravesite property, but there was still a connection established.

His name was Daegan Kyl.

Two Foreign Nationals Identified

The gravesite property was owned by a textile company called K&H Textiles and had two men listed as CEOs. The two men were identified as Khalam Athil Harb and Fatik Mahjub Ghazwan, respectively.

Records showed Khalam Harb was the first of the two to fly into the US and secure his official One-Year Work Visa. Then, within six months of Khalam Harb entering the US, Fatik Mahjub Ghazwan had cleared customs and applied for the same US Work Visa with a one-year stay approved.

The information about the factory and the owners was current and indisputable. But after reading Stanton's notes on the matter, I fully understood why he had stated that he was going to continue digging into the background of the factory and the two men listed as its owners. The information made little sense, and it wasn't for lack of facts or verification.

According to Stanton, the textile factory the two men were supposedly working for had not been operational for almost twelve years. That meant twelve long years since there had been employees, a business tax paid, or a product produced. Twelve years of non-existent production and yet these men had lived in the US on Work Visas for almost thirteen years under the pretext of running the company in question.

If the textile company didn't have a factory that was operational anymore, the two men should not have remained within US borders. Yet they were legally in America, had submitted to all the background checks, and had been cleared to live within our nation.

Legally, once their business dealings ended or their company closed, the two men should have left These United States. At the very least, US agents ought to have verified their ongoing business dealings with their yearly Work Visa renewals. Yet somehow, their Work Visas continued to be renewed with no vetting done.

It was highly suspect that such an oversight had occurred, given that the two men hailed from a region that the US had regarded with contention and distrust. Never in my lifetime had These United States, or any other country in the West, sustained an open-door policy with any nation that allowed Political Islam to be practiced or incorporated into their system of government. To my knowledge, every Foreign National that lived in the US had to have a valid reason for being here; their Work Visas and Visitation Visas were carefully examined and validated. We did not permit routine tourism from any Islamic nation, nor were Americans—or any Westerners to my knowledge—allowed to travel to any Islamic nations.

The borders had been closed to the Middle East for over a century now because of Violence and Terrorism. We didn't even allow Islamic nations to have embassies or consulates within the US anymore. Once Islam had been reclassified as a political ideology, every single mosque had been destroyed within the US and throughout the West, turning the buildings to rubble entirely before being cleared away for new construction.

It was not until recently—within the last fifteen years—that our nation's leaders had even attempted to open some sort of communication and begin allowing professional Work Visas.

Knowing this, and recognizing that this situation was extremely problematic, I could anticipate certain possibilities. If I were to encounter any sort of backlash through their Arrest—or even simply through attempting to obtain Warrants for their Arrests—I would know there was some sort of politics at play.

I cautioned myself against this type of thinking. This contradicted the very fiber of the nation that I had always known, believed in, and defended. Sometimes it was better to search for the simplest answer rather than look for conspiracies. It was better to believe the two men were still in the US because of an error rather than the intentional actions or oversight by government agents.

As a Citizen, and a member of Law Enforcement, I was extremely reluctant to assume the worst of my fellow government employees without first allowing them the benefit of the doubt. We would need to proceed cautiously with this case, however, and it was becoming even more clear that discretion was paramount.

Establishing Links to Two Foreign Nationals

Stanton was actively searching for the location of the two Foreign Nationals. It was too early to bring them in for questioning or for Arrest, but we needed to know where they were. The two men had no other known address, which indicated that they were likely living on the property in some capacity or another. The Chief had mentioned that he had sent a few LEOs over to the factory when the gravesite was discovered, but they had reported back that the factory was vacant. Stanton had also concluded it must have been empty because the factory itself had been closed. But it was still possible the men were living on-site, especially since we could not find any other addresses for them.

If they were living in the factory, we should be able to at least confirm there was some type of traffic flow. Because the two men were Foreign Nationals, they would not have qualified to drive or operate our transportation, so that meant they were presumably either getting rides with people they knew, driving illegally, or walking. Given the isolation of the factory location, it was unlikely that they were traveling on foot, so Officer Stanton was securing data from the local public transportation and various ride-for-hire services.

We had found no legitimate surveillance footage of the two men, not on social media or through local public CCTV. Officer Stanton was trying to work with surveillance of the surrounding roads around their property, and we had petitioned the Chief to set up our own surveillance near the two known roads that could access the area.

Officer Stanton would conduct extensive searches for each of the men, Daegan Kyl as well as the two Foreign Nationals, and gather as much personal information as possible. Every inch of their lives, habits, finances, and social media networking would be scrutinized. He would then monitor each of them until we had the information and evidence necessary to either exonerate or prove their guilt.

Officer Stanton had already reviewed all connections with the Roman Orthodox Church employees and volunteers with each of the databases for Convicted Offenders.

He had also checked to see if any past employees of K&H Textiles were members of the congregation, including the two Foreign Nationals and Daegan Kyl.

So far, we had not established any useful connections.

DK—Initial Background Check

Officer Stanton had sent over a hard copy of Daegan Kyl's background information—it was light so far, but that was to be expected. He assured me he was waiting on records from other sources, including those from his time in service.

He had joined the Armed Forces straight out of high school after signing up for an Early Enlistment. His birthday had been at 1520 on 14 June, the 165th day of the year, and as soon as he was legally able, he was Active Duty. He had barely graduated only the week before, and the dates were close enough it made me question if Daegan Kyl would have skipped his graduation entirely if the two dates had been reversed. The day after his Enlistment went into effect, he left his childhood home in South Dakota, said goodbye to both of his parents, and reported to Basic Training at Fort Benning, Georgia.

As an adult, the man had only ever had one legitimate full-time employer, and that was Uncle Sam. Beyond that, he had worked as an Independent Construction Contractor after he got out, apparently tapping into skills he had learned from his father growing up. His father had been the owner of a construction company in South Dakota, and according to the tax information that Officer Stanton had acquired, Daegan Kyl had worked part-time year-round for his father's construction company from the summer of his fourteenth year, starting the very next day after legally becoming old enough to have a part-time job in the US.

After spending a decade as an Army Ranger, for unknown reasons, Daegan Kyl left the military, and got out with an Honorable Discharge. There was always a high possibility that his records wouldn't be forthcoming at all, or they would be so heavily redacted I wouldn't get much use out of them, so I was left to assume he had performed well based on his discharge status and the mere fact that he had qualified to become a Ranger to begin with. Even without his record, it told me a significant amount about who he was—or at least who he used to be twelve years earlier.

Upon leaving the military, he remained in Washington State, although he moved to the Greater Seattle Area from the military base near Olympia. It was then that he became a licensed Independent Contractor and started working solitary construction jobs on his own. He had done this sporadically throughout the year of his separation from the Army. According to Stanton, after a year working as a contractor, Daegan Kyl registered as the sole CEO of his moving company.

Stanton was still securing his taxes.

EIGHT – RS —1— DEATH NOTIFICATION

Understanding Rebecca

Technology had advanced enough over the last century that Rebecca Summers had more options than had ever before been available for those facing Unwanted Pregnancies. That was what was so difficult to understand; Rebecca Summers could have transferred her embryo—she didn't have to get an Abortion. There was no reason for her, or any woman, to choose an Unsafe and Illegal Abortion rather than simply electing to have an Embryonic-Transference.

Had she sought counsel, they would have informed her of all available options beyond Abortion. None of them would have cost her anything financially, none of them would have resulted in her Pregnancy status being revealed to the public or to her Loved Ones, and none of them would have resulted in an illegal Abortion that, if discovered, would have resulted in the Death Penalty for herself. She could have chosen any of the nationally sanctioned approved methods of Pregnancy alternatives. There had been options. It made little sense for her to endure such an emotional burden unnecessarily.

Given that there were long-term birth control options available that could be 100% effective for ten-year increments and entirely free to any Citizen, male or female, it was unnecessary that anyone should find themselves in this situation in this day and age.

Who was the father, where was he, did he know she was Pregnant and had he known she was not on any form of contraception? Why had he not been on a contraceptive? The technology, the means, and the access were universal, and he bore equal responsibility.

Why would a young woman with so many viable alternatives choose to Commit the worst Act of her entire life—an Act that her Suicide obviously showed she was not capable of causing without her Soul being tortured—just to end a Pregnancy that she could have ended through other means? Why terminate the Pregnancy instead of re-appropriating the embryo?

As I prepared to meet with her parents, fully knowing that they were at first going to be filled with hope as I arrived, daring for a moment to believe that their daughter had been located and was Safe and Sound, I desperately wished I had some better answers to give them. I even considered interviewing them first and then returning another day to tell them, but it would have been a cruel and unnecessary prolonging of the inevitable. No, I was better off just tackling it head-on, and doing my best to make sure that I had the Victim Advocacy Agent alongside me to help them through it.

What was quite possibly the worst risk and consequence of parenting was going to happen to yet another set of parents. My visit with the Urakov's was still very fresh in my mind, but here I was delivering another Death Notification. Tonight, I was going to shatter two Lives by telling them that their daughter's body had been found, and I still did not know what had happened to her or why.

Death Notification

We arrived at the home of Rebecca's parents. Her father was a local family medicine doctor and her mother worked fervently in several prominent charities. Rebecca was their only child.

She was an unlikely person to have faced adversities which would have led to Suicide.

Officer Stanton, after reviewing her social media, had determined that she had been raised in a religious family that was known for having traditional values. By all appearances, she came from a stable home, had not suffered any serious circumstantial or environmental traumas, and did not have any known physical or psychological issues that might have led to her decision to End her own Life.

Her parents were engaged in her life and she theirs. They knew their daughter well; probably at least as well as any set of parents could know a daughter who was a legal adult living on her own.

Her mother stated that although she had insisted on moving out and getting her own place that she still checked in regularly with each of them, that they spoke and texted almost daily, and that Rebecca was still very connected to her childhood home, even going to church with her parents when she could.

They were not aware of any history of her ever struggling with depression, anxiety, or anything else that would have placed her on the downward spiral toward this outcome. I could see their minds trying to process both the confirmation of her Death and the news that she had Committed Suicide. They were struggling to understand how she could have gotten to that point without them sensing anything was amiss. Her father mentioned that she'd had no issues with school, with boys, or with drugs or alcohol. He said that she had always been an 'overachiever' who worked hard for everything and that she had been devoted to her art. Rebecca was a full-time student at the Greater Seattle Area University and lived a simple life.

There was nothing—absolutely nothing—in either of their faces that gave away the appearance that either of them understood what could have prompted her to Take her own Life; they were dumbstruck, completely bewildered, and in shock.

Grace O'Connor spent some time going over the materials about the resources that would be available for them, including Grief counseling, support groups, and the standard appointment of a Victim Advocacy Agent. She explained she would periodically check in on their case through their assigned caseworker and that she would come along with me as we carried out our investigation.

I closed out our brief meeting by expressing my condolences.

Her mother's head hung low, but she seemed to keep her emotions well under control despite the harrowing news. Her father gripped her tightly while staring at me with a shattered, dazed expression; he seemed to be struggling more than his wife.

It was news that no parent ever wanted to receive, and it didn't matter how the news was delivered, how old they were, or how they had Died. When it came to the

Death of a child, every parent was reminded of the baby they had carried in their womb and had walked to sleep as they fussed. Every thought was a memory of the life they had shared together—the first time their baby had rolled over, taken a step, said a word, began school or went to their first dance. Every Lost Child was a unique set of memories and experiences, and no matter what their age at the time of their Death, if it was before their own parents, it was always too soon.

The Father of the Unborn

One of the first actions necessary was to find the father of the Unborn Child that Rebecca had Aborted. Her parents had stated that they did not believe she had been dating anyone, but there was still her roommate to speak with, and she might shed some light on the situation.

The father of the Unborn Victim would not be held criminally liable for the Abortion provided he had not consented, encouraged her, or supplied her with the referral or funding. If he was oblivious to the Pregnancy, he was hardly culpable for the decision she had made. However, if she had informed him she was Pregnant, and he had been involved in her actions, he could face Murder charges just as she would have.

As much as our anti-Abortion laws and Equal Rights laws had developed over time to grant protection to both parents, most times it still left the father at a disadvantage. If Rebecca had not informed him of her Pregnancy, he would not have been able to establish any Rights for himself or his offspring. No matter how much he would have been willing to take the child from her, enact a Surrogacy Replacement Plan through Court Order, and accept sole responsibility for his child, if she had committed this Abortion without his knowledge, she had removed his Right to be involved.

I tried to remember the exact year that the Unborn Protection Act had been established, but I couldn't. It was long before my birth, of course, and for someone like Rebecca, the current legislation was all she would have ever known. It was after the first Embryo-Transfer Procedures began being offered for Pregnant women and they established that pregnancies could be successfully removed as a viable option rather than Abortion. Once the medical science nullified the argument that a Pregnancy must be terminated if the mother was 'unwilling' to carry the baby or raise the baby as her own, the 'Right to get an Abortion' became a moot position to hold. The act of Embryonic-Transference was safe, legal, private, and free to any woman that found herself with an unwanted Pregnancy.

Given that this was an option available in any medical clinic or hospital, was a walk-in procedure, and did not even require a 3rd party Surrogate to be established before the procedure could be done, it seemed reckless and dangerous to do anything other than surrender the Unborn. Even if women were steadfast in declaring that they did not know who the biological male parent was, the procedure could still be done.

They could provide the Unborn with a Surrogate Artificial Womb to grow in, and eventually, the DNA testing would provide medical staff with the information they needed in order to have authorities contact the biological father to discuss options with him.

If neither 'parent' was interested in the Unborn, the child would mature in an Embryonic Incubator or Surrogate Artificial Womb until such a time that a Loving Family could be secured for Adoption. Given that there were so many parents in the nation that were dedicated to this alternative, this was never a hardship.

It did not require very many cases to be established in various states before it went to the Supreme Court and it was determined that the biological fathers had the Right to be given the Opportunity to Provide Life and Equal Parental Rights as the mother, nullifying the prior established doctrine that because the Unborn was grown inside of a woman's body that she alone carried the Right to Choose what she did with the Unborn Child.

It was a tremendous advancement for the Equal Rights For Men campaign, as well as for the Right to Life campaign, both of which had been fighting pro-Abortionists for many generations.

Perhaps more importantly than establishing the Equal Parental Rights Act was that it also defined the Unborn Right To Life Act, finalizing once and for all that the Right To Exist began at Conception, and all Human Life was worth defending.

Whoever the father of her Unborn ended up being, his only defense would be that he was unaware of her decision, and not directly involved in her Abortion or Suicide.

NINE - DK AND FN's —2—

Cameras

As many CCTV cameras as there were in the Greater Seattle Area, they were never a point of focus in residential neighborhoods. There were, however, CCTV cameras overseeing all places of worship. The buildings were not monitored anymore, though. It hadn't been necessary for at least fifty years from what I could recall. There had been a time when many religious locations had been subjected to vandalism, shootings, and even arson. During the years leading up to the Last Stand, both Christian, as well as Jewish places of worship, experienced frequent attacks; so much so that most places began having their own armed security staff and employing live security monitoring. It was also not uncommon for such places of worship to keep metal detectors at the doors, as well as vet their prospective congregation members. In a time when both public schools, as well as churches, were at their peak risk for mass shootings and Domestic Terrorism, taking a proactive, aggressive stand for effective security was imperative.

The Roman Catholic church that Katarina and her family had attended was not one that had been under a live CCTV video surveillance feed, however. Because it had been more than sixty years since the last attack against a church on US soil, many churches had dismantled their security monitoring systems. In most cases, Citizens were able to see that when there were no Criminals, Domestic Terrorists, and people with anti-American values living among them, the Random Acts of Violence and Crime were all but obsolete.

Almost every city with a population greater than fifty thousand was under a twenty-four-hour live-feed CCTV monitoring system, all of which was implemented in the years leading up to the Great Reformation in an effort to combat Crime and Violence. This would have been helpful in solving many cases, including the cases involving my four Victims, had it not been for several key points.

The first was that although the systems had been operational and had been monitored with live-feed and fully staffed personnel at one point, the Crime Rates had been so insignificant in the decades following the Great Reformation that continuous live-feed monitoring had been unnecessary. Although monitoring cities had been left in the hands of state Governors, the national Crime Rates had resulted in most states finding no legitimate cause for continuing the programs. Most leadership had opted to hold a vote on the subject and had allowed the People to decide. To my knowledge, the only places that still had a 24/7 live feed for their cities were NYC and Los Angeles, both of which still had the highest demographics for Crime and Violence. Most of the nation had completely dismantled their programs, although many took the middle-ground approach and still maintained surveillance recordings without the live monitoring, choosing to respect individual privacy by minimizing surveillance.

The Greater Seattle Area had been one of the cities that still recorded but had not kept up on the latest advancements in technology.

The land the gravesite was located on had been zoned as Industrial. This area had also been removed from the designated locations still being surveilled. The downtown areas, the shopping centers, all locations of public use and community events, and all educational buildings were monitored. Additionally, business districts and places zoned for commercial use were still heavily surveilled, but this was more in alignment of property and financial protection, since they were frequently subjected to vandalism, anti-capitalism looting attacks, and Crimes for financial gain. Private businesses were much more inclined to pay for their own surveillance rather than use the state-funded options, but even then, nothing was operational in the Industrial zone where the gravesite had been made. Those responsible for these Abductions, as well as for the usage of the gravesite property, knew where surveillance equipment and satellite monitoring were being done, and managed to avoid those areas carefully.

With each of the Victims there had been a blind spot; a black hole in which their Abduction or absence had been able to occur without any type of technological or satellite surveillance being able to access the locations they had disappeared from. Arlan had been taken from his home, and while parts of his property had been both under surveillance on-site and able to be viewed through satellite imagery after-the-fact, there hadn't been a direct connection linking him to the van that had been on the CCTV cameras. Try as he might, Officer Stanton had not been able to follow the mysterious white van to its destination or confirm Arlan had been inside of it. Upon leaving the Randall farm, it had traveled to another location that was also beyond the watchful scope of both monitoring systems available.

Of all the Victims, Rebecca was the only one that was never classified as an Abduction because there had been no evidence to support it, and although she had been originally reported as a Missing Person by her roommate, technically we could not verify that she had 'Disappeared' because of someone else's doing. She had Gone Missing, and she had been a Missing Person at the time when her case was initially reported. But at some point, she may have willfully followed a course of events that had put her into the crosshairs of someone that helped her End her own Life and then conceal her Physical Remains.

Despite all this, even she was unable to be entirely tracked due to the limitations of technology and how it was implemented. Somehow, despite all the surveillance cameras, satellite imagery, and the traffic cameras made available through the Transportation Department that were located throughout the Greater Seattle Area, even Rebecca had managed to leave her home or the university campus, drive herself to a designated location, and completely evade all possible cameras able to be used by Law Enforcement.

It was frustrating, and unlike most Crimes in our time, technology was not working *for* us, but rather *against* us. I was left to conclude that either they had someone that worked within the CCTV system or had in the past, or they just somehow managed to avoid such visual connections through pure luck. With four random strangers involved, a potential host of bad actors committing and facilitating the most heinous of Crimes, and a system so organized that four Human Beings had been able to be buried within the city limits of an urban metropolis with more than a million residents, it was impossible to consider it all luck. Something, or someone, was assisting these people so they could have their footprints erased from our detection.

DK—Moving Men & Maids

Daegan Kyl was not a man that was hiding in the shadows. Officer Stanton was still working on a complete background check. For now, the report showed that Daegan Kyl was the sole owner of a business that was not only well known but was an immensely financially successful enterprise.

'Moving Men & Maids' was a dual moving truck and cleaning business. They did commercial and residential services and employed both movers and house cleaners. The third component, although probably not their primary source of revenue, were the storage facilities that were attached to all their storefronts. I didn't know how many there were, but I knew it was at least state-wide and there were many dozens, if not hundreds, of locations throughout the cities and towns.

Their vehicles, both moving trucks and their line of smaller trucks and vans that were used for their cleaning services, were seen everywhere. The company was probably the largest moving truck business in the Greater Seattle Area; it was large enough to have the brand recognition that everyone knew immediately, and it was probably the first one anyone thought of in that industry. Officer Stanton was doing a comprehensive background check for his business-related expenses, licensing, and insurance.

From the preliminary report, Daegan Kyl had over a thousand full-time employees on the books working out of the main office located within a few miles of the SPD Headquarters, and although it appeared the man was involved in the business at least on some level since he was driving one of their trucks around, the report stated he had a full-time CEO listed as the primary Point of Contact.

The moving and cleaning business did one-time moves that could also clean both the new homes as well as the old after vacated. They utilized automated robot machinery that could lift and carry heavy objects, and were often hired for home remodels, renovations, and a myriad of commercial jobs.

The cleaning side of the business had contracts with major commercial businesses and property management companies that did comprehensive cleaning jobs between renters. They were listed as primary cleaners for vacation home rentals, commercial real estate companies trying to sell homes and businesses, and perhaps most interestingly, they had a division that provided professional cleaning services for Crime Scenes.

According to the report, the commercial side of his company had put him on the 'Top 100 Local Businesses' for the last ten years in a row. He had built a small empire.

It also meant that he was running in the big leagues and would have established contacts with many of the most important, wealthiest, famous, and political people in our state. If a man were to engage in a criminal enterprise that was moonlighting as a Clean-Up and Disposal business for people that wanted to conceal evidence and bury bodies, Daegan Kyl had created the perfect means to do this.

It could mean absolutely nothing, but it could mean everything. There was nothing to show that just because his business was now linked to the property directly, and had associations with Crime Scene investigations, that the man was a Serial Killer. We still had a long way to go.

DK—Establishing Links to K&H Textiles

Reviewing the moving, cleaning and storage businesses had resulted in nothing substantial, but the private background check on Daegan Kyl had struck pay-dirt after Stanton had invested more time. The information discovered had been significant even though Kyl had not been able to be connected to our Victims. Stanton, having done a cursory history of employment through his tax records, had secured one very distant tax statement belonging to Mr. Kyl. According to his taxes, after he had transitioned from his military service, he had only worked a few random jobs over the months before he was eventually hired by a company called K&H Textiles, Inc.—the same company owned by the two Foreign Nationals, with their sole location being the factory.

Judging by the income he declared on his taxes that first year as he transitioned out of the military, it did not seem that he had made a very profitable living. He had not worked consistently, and it didn't seem as if he had been too concerned about it. Maybe it had something to do with whatever led to his decision to end his military career, or perhaps he was just taking some downtime after a decade of action, deployments, and combat zones.

The paychecks from K&H Textiles were inconsistent and of varying amounts. There was no traceable evidence regarding the kind of work that had been done. However, he had not done these jobs for long because only a mere six months later he had transitioned once more, securing his business license and insurance, and then opening his moving company. Within a year, he had twenty full-time workers, and by the fifth year, he had over a thousand employees and a CEO to run things. According to his financials, he had only kept building empires since then, and now his net worth was greater than a significant percentage of the nation.

I found it interesting that he had a personality that had both adapted well to the demands and rigors of being a Soldier but then he could also think and work like an entrepreneur, which generally required a strong, independent personality, sharp intellect, and self-motivation.

What was important, however, was that Daegan Kyl's work history offered evidence that it was highly probable that he had known each of the two Foreign Nationals directly through his employment with K&H Textiles twelve years prior.

We had confirmed, at the very least, that Daegan Kyl was unquestionably connected to the factory, and therefore was the most likely to have been driving the truck seen exiting the property. Regardless of the lack of surveillance footage that could verify it conclusively, the connection was still there. No matter how it was presented or how improbable it seemed, he was somehow involved in the burials found on the factory land. He was an inexplicable Primary Suspect, and yet, for now, he was all we had for certain.

Try as I might, I could not shake the unsettling feeling that there had been insidious, Evil things done on American soil that We the People were oblivious to, even now, after all that we had learned over the decades.

It was a strange thing, to not feel secure in one's own home. It made every ounce of my protective nature and training switch over instantly into high alert status. It was the feeling of distrust and unrest that no American Citizen should feel about anyone or anything else within their country, especially now, so many years after the Last Stand and the Great Reformation—and yet I could not shake the sense of foreboding that I now held deep within.

DK—Establishing Links to Victims

Officer Stanton had also searched to see if Daegan Kyl had any existing relationships with any of the four Victims. His report summarized that he had obtained a list of known contacts and associates, but that he had no known family in the region.

To date, Stanton had secured no connections between Daegan Kyl and any of the Victims or even the Victims' extended families or professional lives. There was no explanation to account for how the man could have been involved. None of the Victims had ever used the professional services owned by Daegan Kyl, and after having accessed his financial statements, nothing supported that he had ever crossed paths with any of the Victims. He found no links between any employment, educational, or professional services that any of their families might have owned or been employed by. There were no social associations either, given that he was among the wealthiest and most elite Citizenry within the Greater Seattle Area.

In the end, Stanton had come up with nothing linking him to the gravesite or the Victims.

His position within the business industry had made him a well-known face and name in certain circles, but he was not linked to anyone other than through social events, including women. He was single, never married, didn't have any children, was an only child, and his parents were both Deceased. Daegan Kyl was not deeply involved with anyone locally and seemed to live a quiet, uneventful life overall; had it not been for Stanton being able to verify his parents and do a full investigation into his youth, he might have seemed almost a ghost.

However, because the man was both the face of a business enterprise as well as an individual with a private life and history, the search perimeters for Stanton were expanded two-fold. The note attached to Stanton's latest message stated he was working on several other angles, and he would send updates as the information became available. He would continue combing through every available piece of information that could be pored over and analyzed until we knew Daegan Kyl better than he knew himself—and like most government agencies, we would do it all without the subject ever even knowing we had looked.

TEN — INVESTIGATION —2—

Ruling Out Caroline Randall's Involvement

Officer Stanton was able to garner a great deal of information through the technology at his disposal. It was one of the greatest advantages of living in a nation that had always taken pride in advancement and innovation.

Although Caroline Randall was not a Suspect in any sense of the word, it was important that we eliminated her from any suspicion of wrongdoing so we could clear the path toward the most obvious culprits. We had established that there was something amiss in both the Hospice Care Providers as well as within the Winter Season Hospice Care facility itself. Stanton was currently working on discovering more information about the facility.

I also still had some questions about how the Randall case had been handled. There were still a lot of things that were unanswered, but now that we were beginning to get deeper into our investigation, it appeared there were questionable elements regarding how the SPD had handled Arlan's Missing Persons case so far.

For the time being, Stanton was doing a cursory check between Willow Amos and Caroline Randall to remove any doubts as to whether or not the two women were linked. I understood his intentions and would have recommended it had I felt it necessary. They trained us as Investigators to never make assumptions about anyone's guilt or innocence, and to never presume that anyone was automatically exempt from scrutiny just because they were—by all appearances—considered to be secondary Victims or among the Bereavement party.

It would have been very easy to assume Caroline Randall was just a victim of circumstance, but until we could remove her entirely as a Suspect, we needed to proceed with the assumption that she could have been involved in her own husband's Disappearance. I was grateful that Officer Stanton could perform every aspect of his job independently without asking me for permission to proceed; he had been very proactive. I also appreciated how efficiently he provided me with each of his new discoveries and results.

Stanton would tap into CCTV cameras available throughout the campus and Greater Seattle Area. Thousands of cameras would be accessed, and the entire last years' worth of footage would be crossmatched with facial recognition to establish a connection between Caroline Randall and Willow Amos if there was one. If the two of them were ever in the same location at the same time—whether because they both paid for an item at a coffee shop on the same date or because a camera had captured them sitting together—the program would identify them.

It wasn't a guarantee of Caroline Randall's Innocence or that she was entirely uninvolved, but it would certainly prove the likeliness of her Innocence well beyond what any Law Enforcement or even herself would have been able to manage through an alibi on her own.

Likewise, it would also incriminate her or anyone else affiliated with Willow Amos, and by the time Officer Stanton was done with his work, we would have a clear outline of exactly who Willow Amos was, as well as everyone she was involved with.

Interview: Rebecca's Roommate

Rebecca's roommate had little to say that proved fruitful beyond providing us with a more definitive timeline of her last known sighting. Although she had considered them decent friends, having been roommates while at college for several years already, they did not seem to share a very close or personal relationship. According to her roommate, Rebecca was quiet and shy. She did not have any guests over, and there had never been a boyfriend or any type of romantic or sexual relationship to her knowledge.

According to her, Rebecca spent most of her time painting, reading, and doing an assortment of crafts around the apartment. Her roommate, Havel, stated that they would go see a movie every few weeks, but beyond that, they socialized little. Because Havel was working on an advanced degree, she did not spend as much time at the apartment as she had the first few years as an undergraduate. Along with this, she was specializing in a technical field and her program required a great deal of lab time. Continuing to stay in the same apartment and with the same roommate for three years was more a matter of convenience for Havel than because of a connection or friendship with Rebecca.

She stated that because of Rebecca's introverted nature that led to her spending most of her time at their apartment, she could rely on Rebecca to take care of her two cats, and emphasized that she was always a wonderful, caring, considerate roommate. She stated Rebecca spent most of her time upstairs in her own space. The apartment was a converted building and had one bedroom on the main floor and a loft upstairs. She said that because Rebecca painted, she had moved into the place because it had the loft. She then found a roommate to help split the costs. Havel was upset by her Disappearance, but she clearly didn't know her well enough to understand the circumstances of her absence or Death.

Grace O'Connor asked most of the questions. Her attention to detail, ability to pick up on clues surrounding eye contact, subtle body movements, and microaggressions were all proving to be remarkably useful. My uniform recorded everything, including noticeable Body Language actions. It could also detect the sound and inflection of voices, noting variations in pitch and tone, which was a helpful lie detection tool. But there was something to be said for having a partner that was observant and able to communicate directly with me in the moments immediately following such an interview, if only to explore my thoughts better.

We discussed how her roommate seemed more preoccupied with how she was supposed to address her financial needs—now a problem because of Rebecca's Disappearance. Financial setbacks were a common difficulty after an unexpected Death. It was one of the issues addressed by the Victim Advocacy Agency.

Unexpected Deaths left people in compromised situations all the time. Given that Rebecca and her roommate were both college students, even if they were working on advanced degrees, they were still living on a fairly meager income. It would be expected that they were living together to help each other offset financial burdens. If one should Disappear suddenly, it was likely the other would face almost immediate financial difficulties. Even the basics, such as rent and various other household expenses, would become catastrophic problems if funding that was once relied upon was to Vanish suddenly. It was understandable that Havel would have concerns regarding the precarious nature of her situation. She was also living in the dwelling which listed Rebecca as the primary tenant.

It was an unfortunate reality that was yet another byproduct of Death, no matter what the circumstances. As time had progressed beyond the Great Reformation, this was a discussion that had become significant. Death was a disruptive force as it was, but people seldom discussed the financial impact it caused, especially when the fallout occurred directly on the heels of the Violent Death of a Loved One.

With all the countless ways the government helped indigent 'Alleged' Criminals, it was easy to see why the financial and emotional crisis directly following the unexpected Death of a Loved One should also be provided assistance—especially when the Cause of Death was often because of Violence. For these reasons alone, the Victim Compensation Fund was a vital component of every Homicide and Missing Persons case and was yet another reason the services of the Victim Advocacy Agency were so important.

Update and Report on Missing Persons Cases

I received another update from Officer Stanton late in the evening. I had returned to the barracks, showered, eaten the dinner I'd had sent up from the cafeteria, and was about to get some sleep when the report arrived.

Officer Stanton had set about on a mission to retrace all the various reports, the First Responders that had done the initial reports, and dig up whatever he could about the Missing Persons Division just in case something turned up. I knew that a full investigation of the Missing Persons Division would require a great deal more access and time than we had in order to be investigated thoroughly, but with Officer Stanton setting the search perimeters, I had felt confident that he would be able to at least catch some broad leads or indications of impropriety.

Our instincts had not been wrong.

The report was not long; in fact, it was a brief message.

The report showed that someone within the Missing Persons Division was intentionally book-marking select cases and placing them into a type of 'inactive' or 'limbo' status. This was only possible through manual directives, and only those with some authority within their division could do so.

Not one of the cases had been handed over to outside Investigators; they had all been put into a grey zone within a filing system that no one would even notice unless intentionally searching for them. Someone had wanted these cases to disappear.

All such cases required authorization to move into this region, and this made it almost like taking candy from a baby for Officer Stanton to discover that one badge had been behind each of the cases being reclassified. The badge in question belonged to Badge number MP-6404, one Detective 'Jarrett'.

Officer Stanton had run a report on Detective Jarrett once he'd identified him as the sole relation between all the cases within the SPD database. The problem with a background check, of course, was that we had such extremely high privacy guards around our identities as members of Law Enforcement that it was almost impossible to breach another Officer's personnel file beyond their basic badge number.

We as Officers were not entitled to have any more personal information regarding our Fellow Officers than anyone else. We could all find ourselves in positions of duress or threat which could then lead to compromising our Fellow Citizens. Even though any such dangers had subsided long ago, the lessons from the past still resonated loudly due to the high number of casualties that had been systematically targeted before the Last Stand.

Information was power, and most would rather be kept in the dark than carry the weight and pressure related to knowing they had knowledge about their Fellow Peacekeepers that could prove dangerous. Too much personal information was not worth being tortured by Evil people intent on doing Harm.

We would need to inform the Chief about his Missing Persons Detective so he could initiate his own internal investigation from his end. It was beyond the scope of my investigation only in the context that I couldn't authorize any of the background searches which would be necessary; whether or not this man had been using his position within the Missing Persons Division to delete records and conceal evidence was a professional misconduct issue. The information he had been deleting, however, was in my domain since it had all been part of my investigation.

    I needed to get deeper access to this Missing Persons Detective, and the only way I could get that level of clearance regarding one of our own was to petition the Chief. It was time to test the loyalties of the man and find out if he was legitimately unaware of these pockets of subterfuge within his own dominion, or if he had willfully chosen to overlook these discrepancies. I was willing to give him the benefit of the doubt, of course. But what I was beginning to realize was that nothing was as good as it seemed on the surface here in the glittering Emerald city.

ELEVEN – MP —1— INITIATING INVESTIGATION

The Abduction of Mariam

Officer Stanton had secured all the notes, reports, statements, interviews, and relevant information related to Mariam's case immediately upon learning her name as one of our Victims.

Her Abduction had been the most recently reported, but according to the Medical Examiner's report, she had been Murdered within a very brief window of time after her Abduction. It was sad to imagine, but as with most known Abductions and Kidnappings throughout our collective history as a nation, it was a familiar story. It was a tragic reality in such cases; most did not result in successful outcomes.

She had been a beloved member of society, and we knew from all accounts that her Abduction was still a current discussion and kept at the forefront of both local and national news stories. Out of each of our Victims, Mariam's Abduction was not only the most Aggressively Violent at the site of the Attack, it was also the most publicized and widely questioned. Even though most Missing Persons cases were a point of public conversation, some cases were more broadly discussed and debated, having captured the attention and concern of the American People.

The surveillance video of Mariam's Abduction had been widely circulated throughout the Greater Seattle Area and the rest of the nation. For many Citizens, officials used it as a reminder that it was important to remain vigilant even when one believed they were in a safe location. It provided reminders to always pay attention when entering and exiting vehicles, to keep hands free of objects and possessions, and to always have keys, fobs, and Access Cards ready to grant immediate access to vehicles and other points of entry.

Unfortunately for Mariam, she had failed on each of these counts, undoubtedly contributing to the ease in which she had been Targeted, Assaulted, and then Abducted. She had been carrying two bags of groceries, her keys were in her purse, her vehicle was locked, and she had left her vehicle on the outskirts of the parking lot away from the main doors and the bulk of foot traffic. While she was not to be held at fault for any of the events which occurred, each of those factors had most likely contributed to her having been selected by her Assailant; she had unwittingly created the perfect storm.

By sheer luck, the prehistoric surveillance system had proven invaluable as the camera became witness to her Abduction, recording each movement as her Assailant came into view of the camera lens from the northern edge of the parking lot. No one had noticed when the man had descended upon her, moving in a direct line, his purpose steady and focused. The parking lot was not a large space. They seldom were if they had been built within the last half-century. And yet no one had noticed the lone woman, her arms full, trying to shift her groceries around as she fumbled to see where her keys were located. No one noticed a man walk up behind her and then strike her along the back of her head. Although he used his fist and only hit her once, his powerful blow was enough to blindside her, causing her to fall instantaneously as her groceries scattered all around.

    The man had taken the light-colored handbag laying on the ground near her outstretched arm as she lay sprawled out alongside the family transport. He then began looking through it, hurriedly searching for the same keys she had been rummaging around for, only stopping to take a quick look in every direction to ensure he was still undetected. After a few seconds of remaining empty-handed, he paused for a moment, and his head could then be seen moving slowly from one area to another as he began looking around at the ground. He was presumably searching for her keys, and as he had not located them inside of her handbag, must have believed the keys had fallen.

    This was confirmed when he finally noticed where the keys had been; she had managed to grab hold of them just at the moment she had been struck and had been lying on the ground with them still clutched in her hand. The man grabbed the keys unceremoniously, took another panicked look around the parking lot to ensure he was still unnoticed, and then unlocked the doors before lifting her into the backseat. He had even taken the time to pick up her groceries, which he then tossed into the backseat beside her—presumably to prevent alerting anyone that something was amiss. It was, sadly, all that had been required for her Abductor to have gained the upper hand in the situation, allowing him to escape unobserved entirely.

    It had been that easy; not one person had noticed it happen, despite there having been a large handful of Citizens situated all around her vehicle within several hundred feet. Had her vehicle been positioned even just slightly differently, it would have exposed the spaces between the vehicles rather than conceal them from observers.

    It had been an indiscreet Assault made in broad daylight whilst surrounded by dozens of residents from her own neighborhood, and yet somehow it had gone completely overlooked by everyone. Unlike the case of Katarina, who had 'Vanished Without A Trace', leaving no witnesses, surveillance footage, sightings of strange vehicles or strangers, or even anything deemed 'suspicious activity', Mariam had been Abducted, and its proof was beyond question. The Detectives that had been assigned to her case knew that they were looking for one man, a man sighted at a specific time, on a specific day, and at a specific location. Compared to the Disappearance of Katarina, there was a bountiful amount of evidence which had been available from the very onset of the case.

    There were still plenty of questions, and given the time that had passed without the Detectives having discovered the identity of the Assailant or having found Mariam, they still could not determine enough about the case to crack it in time—before her Death.

From their notes, the Detectives had determined that it was likely a stranger and that her Abduction had been based solely on opportunity. After reviewing the outline summarizing the daily life of Mariam and her family, I was inclined to agree.

The manner in which she had been approached—in such a public setting—and then struck from behind were both very aggressive, irrational decisions that illustrated low-impulse control. That she was approached while in the middle of an expansive parking lot, during daylight hours, and while surrounded by dozens of people was further evidence supporting that her Abductor had seized a moment without weighing his actions rationally. His actions were extremely high risk.

There were many other locations in Mariam's daily life and routines that would have allowed for her Abduction from different places which would not have been caught on surveillance, and yet she had been taken from a very public space at a busy time of the day.

None of this bode well for the women of the Greater Seattle Area. A man willing to take extreme risks, disregard CCTV cameras, attack women in broad daylight, and choose Murder to conceal Rape was a dangerous person to be unaccounted for. We needed to find this man before he attacked again.

After Her Missing Person Report

It was not until many hours later that Mariam's husband had called Emergency Services to report her as a potential Missing Person, citing that it was unusual for her not to update him if her plans changed. The last time he had spoken to her was as she had been shopping. She had called him to ask for his meal preferences regarding an upcoming family event they were intending to host. He had told the Emergency Responders—and then later the Missing Persons Detectives—that she had mentioned she still had more shopping to do, and for that reason, he had expressed no concern about her not returning home until over two hours had passed and she still hadn't arrived. According to his statement, he then attempted to contact her via text, waited ten minutes, and then attempted to call. It was only then, he said when it went directly to voicemail, that he became concerned and called Emergency Services.

The first report stated that between the time of his initial Emergency call and the time when the First Responders arrived, he had called his brother, Mark Pembrook, and asked him to contact one of his brothers-in-law as well. Once the two men were aware of the situation, they had begun calling the rest of their extended family hoping to track her down. The report stated that Mariam's husband, Matthew Pembrook, was one of four children. All lived locally, as did his parents. Records showed he had first contacted his oldest brother, Mark Pembrook, who had also submitted a statement outlining the protocol and list of names he had contacted in the hour after they made the initial report.

The first call that Mark Pembrook had made on behalf of Matthew Pembrook was to Tyler Waylon, a local dentist in the area married to Mariam's oldest sister, Sarah. Tyler Waylon had then contacted each of his own brothers-in-law—the three men who were married to Mariam's sisters. His report showed that he first made calls to each of the men, notified his office staff to cancel the last appointments on his calendar for the afternoon, and left his dental office for home. He stated his wife was a homemaker, and their four children were already home from school when he arrived. His statement said that he had pulled his wife aside, given her an update, and then the whole family had gone over to the Pembrook's home. In his closing lines, he clarified that they had made it to the Pembrook's approximately one hour after receiving the phone call, and by the time they had arrived, the rest of the extended family on his wife's side had already convened on the home, as well as the First Responders.

When asked why he had been the first brother-in-law to be notified but the last to arrive, he had responded that he had needed to close his office, drive home, address the issue with his emotional wife, and then help her pack up four children all under the age of ten. They thoroughly vetted him in the days that followed and cleared him of all potential involvement. All family members were vetted carefully during the first week of her having Gone Missing. This included the extended families of each of the men who were married to Mariam's sisters. In total, more than one hundred Citizens were carefully scrutinized, and everyone had welcomed the background checks to be done without any reservation. These same people, as the days passed, were at the forefront of the search for Mariam. By the end of the first week, it was evident that Mariam had lived her life among friends and family who had loved her dearly.

Besides this, Mariam was active in a local church, volunteered time in a community child development center for children with learning disabilities, was employed as a grade school level educator, and worked as an adjunct professor at the Greater Seattle Area University. They canvassed every point of contact she had as a matter of routine within her daily life, assessed for security surveillance, and conducted interviews with every staff member and colleague she had come into contact with in the weeks leading up to her Abduction.

I finished reading the report, and then watched the body-camera interview conducted by the SPD First Responder. Mariam's husband presented as a visibly shaken man who seemed on the verge of breaking down. He stated he had expected her phone to have simply run out of power. However, by the third hour, since he had last heard from her, and with no explanation why she wasn't responding and hadn't returned home, he had contacted Emergency Services. He finished his comment by wiping his eyes with his arm as one of his brothers-in-law grabbed his shoulder for support. He said that he didn't care how paranoid he had seemed, he just knew something was wrong when she failed to respond, stating it was entirely out of character for her to ignore him.

The interview was conducted in the first hour after they had reported her as Missing. The cameras were clear enough to see a large group of family all arriving in the background as he went through the questions. I examined each frame carefully, studying the faces of the people as they arrived. Everyone seemed distressed, and all had looked upon Matthew Pembrook with sympathy and sorrow. It did not seem, at least on the surface, that anyone in their families thought the worst of Matthew even during those early hours before the details of her Abduction were known. Although it was highly probable for the spouse to be directly involved in such cases, there seemed no evidence to support that Matthew was anything other than a concerned husband and father.

Less than four hours after Mariam's husband had last heard from her as she shopped, the SPD Missing Persons Division had secured the grainy surveillance footage that covered the grocery store parking lot and verify that she had been Assaulted and Abducted. The response time had been exceptionally brief compared to many Abductions.

The SPD had put out BOLO alerts for her vehicle and had ensured that they placed her picture and the video in every available location throughout the state. Friends and family, joined by thousands of local Citizens throughout the Greater Seattle

Area, had scoured the city streets and surrounding suburbs, while drones searched vehicles and license plates from above. CCTV throughout the region monitored the roads and freeways, documenting every passing vehicle through cameras at stoplights, intersections, overpasses, and on/off-ramps. Despite a minimal amount of time having passed, and an entire state having been placed on high alert, Mariam, her vehicle, and her Abductor had simply Disappeared. The events surrounding her Disappearance had been terrifying for the community, and especially for her friends and family.

Despite all of this, however, her family had entered this unexpected development with an intestinal strength and fortitude that never failed to elicit powerful emotions from deep within as I reviewed such cases. They had never given up hope in her return or faltered in their continued public calls for attention for the Missing Persons cases in the area. Not just for Mariam's own status, but for all the current, active cases.

They were still trying to find Mariam. It spoke volumes about her character, her devotion to her community, and the devotion of the community to her. Everyone held tight to the belief that there was still hope in her safe return, despite the time that had passed and the unfortunate negative impact of inevitability it represented. Their love for her had held them together in those initial hours and days, and it held them together still.

Her Loved Ones had rallied behind the case; they had come together despite the tragedy and had done everything within their power to bring awareness to her Abduction. They had built an army of Citizens who had searched mile after mile of land, used every resource they could, and worked as a cohesive team to do everything within their power to bring her home. Even though the results were quite tragic, even in its worst moments, there was still evidence of Hope and Love to be found.

The Eternal Optimism of Mankind

Time and again, tragedy transformed into something positive. The response to Mariam's Abduction had been no different from any other case I had ever worked on in this regard; the local Citizens had come together, as they were so often prone to do, when facing a crisis that hit close to home.

As Was Done To One Was Done To All.

The Abduction of Mariam had illustrated the worst of Humanity, while the response to her Abduction had exemplified its best.

We were Believers when it came down to it. We were optimistic, full of hope, and more willing to place our faith in God and Divine Prayer than we were to surrender to the bleakness of the situation, the odds of probability, or the cold realities of statistics.

Something drove us to believe in the possibility of a positive outcome. It was in our nature to hold firm to the hope, no matter how slight the chance, that Good may still Prevail over Evil.

It served as a powerful reminder that even as we found ourselves in our darkest hour, we were surrounded by others who were willing to share in our moment of fear and help us. Such events, as tragic as they were, illustrated the Eternal Spirit and Oneness of Humanity, demonstrating that we all desired to help one another, whether called upon or not. Our willingness to stand together, to search together, to lean on one another no matter what the odds—that was what had been on display in the hours and days following the Abduction of Mariam.

It was easy to focus on the negative, to become overly jaded and bitter because of the incessant flow of ugliness my line of work always exposed. But I also recognized that there was love, even amid the turmoil. People would unite, vigils would be held, search parties organized, and a legacy would be borne from each Tragic Death—often resulting in substantial changes that made remarkable differences, even affecting the very laws governing our society. And always, no matter how lost, fragile, or broken the Victim might have been, there were people Left Behind to Grieve for them, to mark their Passage with Sorrow and Tears, and to fight for Justice on their behalf.

The Tragedies of Unnecessary Death—especially the most Violent—were the darkest parts of what we Humans could do to one another. One Evil monster could destroy a singular life and create a never-ending Ripple Effect of Tragedy and Heartache that could last for generations and span thousands of miles. But likewise, those who were Lost to such circumstances were rarely forgotten; their Deaths were a Tribute, a reminder for each of us so we would never lose sight of just how precious each and every day was supposed to be.

Mariam had been Beloved. Her Legacy would live on—through her husband, her children, her extended family, her professional contributions, and her volunteer work.

Like too many others before her, she had been Wrongfully Stolen in such a manner that the world would never fully come to terms with it. There would always be an Empty Space where she should have been.

But her Goodness had been bountiful—as was testament by the rallying war cry on display in the hours and days after her Abduction.

Would that we all could leave behind such a Legacy of our time having been spent so well.

In Her Final Moments

In her Final Moments, as she had lain gasping for air, her body bloodied, bruised, and violated, she surrendered to the trauma that had been Inflicted.

After enduring such horrors—after having fought so hard, so bravely, and having endured so much—her body had finally been forced to let go, succumbing to the fourth and final wound from the blade as she lost her battle for life.

From the instant of her Abduction until her Final Breath, she would have been trying desperately to make sense of what was happening to her. She would have been struggling to understand *why* it was happening, what she had done, and how she could have possibly deserved such horrors. She would have struggled to understand who the man was that had targeted her, and what she had done to provoke him.

And then, as it was all unfolding, as she was struggling against him, struggling to defend and protect herself from his fists, she would have simply been fighting for her life—fighting to maintain consciousness, fighting to remember details about his appearance, to take stock of her surroundings—all because she would have believed and prayed for herself to be free and safe once again, and intent on delivering Justice to her Assailant.

She would have endured as much as she could, blow after blow, wound after wound, all delivered within seconds of one another, as both Victim and Assailant existed solely in the moment, locked in a primal battle as old as time. Mariam, a wife, and mother, the woman that had been voted Best Teacher multiple times throughout her career, would have given it everything she had as she fought for her Right to Exist. A woman with no known enemies, no prior military or combat experience, the one that had been described by her Fellow Educators as 'an inspiration', would have found herself pitted against a man that outweighed her by at least seventy pounds, had endless genetic and physical advantages over her, and was out for blood. She would have done exactly what she did—the same thing that millions of other women had done over the centuries—and fought for her life with every fiber of her Being, knowing that there would be no second chances.

The loving wife and mother, prone to enjoying her sweets much more than exercise, having lived a relatively routine and sedentary lifestyle, would have done exactly as she had, and done her best in every capacity—with every muscle straining, every instinct on high alert, and every resource she could muster as she fought to Survive. The woman who had never raised her voice, nor her hand, in anger or with intent to Inflict Harm—emotional or otherwise—had continued to do everything within her unskilled, untrained, ineffective wheelhouse. She had never Surrendered; she had never Quit.

She would have continued to resist even after her Assailant presented the knife. And at that moment, she would have known an entirely new level of fear. It would have been then that she would have known just how much was truly at stake. She would have gained an immediate understanding that she was in danger of losing more than she ever could have imagined until that point.

Her strength, her bravery, her faith—she may have been driven to fight for her life from the depths of her Soul. She may have reasoned with herself that she could endure anything—Abduction, the Violation of her Body, even the Beating—just so long as she could live. She may well have attempted to negotiate; to bargain with God, pleading with Him to just let her *Survive*, knowing that she could endure and even forgive, just so long as she was left with her life and able to return home to her family, that they would not have to live the rest of their lives without her.

She would have begged God to not let this be how her story would end; for her husband to have to Grieve for her, to become a widower at such a young age. She would have pleaded for mercy, praying that her mother and father never discovered what horrors had befallen their young daughter. She would have known the impact her Death would cause. She knew she was Beloved and would have been missed dearly.

Mariam would have reached a pivotal moment and she would have accepted any terms—just so long as it left her with the only thing that mattered—*her ability to go back home to her family*. She would have surrendered everything so she could retain that which she knew could not be replaced. She would have known that her Death would have been the one thing that would have not only ended her own existence, but would have left a devastating hole in the lives of everyone she loved—and she probably would have done anything just to spare each of them such pain.

What little hope she might have had would have dissipated with the presence of the blade; it would have been enough to make her blood run cold as her mind attempted to grasp the full weight and gravity of everything that was unfolding before her. Until that moment, she might have felt survival was possible. But somewhere, between fighting back, seeing the blade, or feeling it as it penetrated her flesh for the first time, she would have processed the most shocking and terrifying realization of all—that she might not survive; that she really was living the Final Moments of her life.

What she must have felt during her ordeal; what terror she must have endured, helplessly lying below her Assailant, exhausted, overpowered, knowing that the end was near.

The fear. The sorrow.

She would have lain there, still struggling to Survive, fully conscious as the rage-filled man pinning her down drove his weapon into her soft, defenseless body. Her Final Moments were spent trying desperately to stop his blows; her hands and arms had been riddled with defensive wounds bearing this truth. Her Final Hours on this earth had been filled with unimaginable turmoil and psychological terror.

There was a monster out there that had Stolen something from this world that he had no right to take, and there would be a day of reckoning for it.

His actions against her directly violated her personal Rights as a Human Being and as an American Citizen. It was a blatant Violation of her Right to Exist and the Sanctity of Human Life.

Nothing would absolve this Predator from the weight of his Crimes Against Humanity, nor prevent him from receiving the Sentence and Punishment he was so deserving of.

The animal that had Inflicted such egregious Acts of Violence against her was unworthy of being allowed to live after she was not.

I would find him. It was only a matter of time.

The Watchers On The Wall Speech: The Ripple Effect

Fellow Americans,

The Sanctity of Human Life is being disregarded by those who would rather see Dead Americans than a harsh Criminal Justice system or an end to the social agendas that promote selective Murder, including Abortion, Suicide, and Euthanasia.

It is time for Americans to determine whether or not they believe the Sanctity of Human Life is worth preserving, and if Human Life has Meaning and Purpose.

A Life cut short is a Life left unfulfilled.

This creates a Ripple Effect of Undone Actions and Unintended Consequences, none of which can be foreseen.

If one can accept that each Life has Meaning and Value, then one can surely accept that each life must have its own unique path. Each path then leads to a Purpose. That Purpose will envelop many things and touch many lives along the way. Who are we to know the full extent of our Divine Purpose for our time here on earth? We cannot, nor are we intended to.

When a life is cut short through an Act of Violence, it is an Abomination against Nature, against Mankind, and against God Himself. To deny a person their God-given Right to Exist on this planet and within our great nation is a Crime Against Humanity.

An Unjust Death creates a Ripple Effect in the Story of Life. One Soul lost before its natural time creates many changes, intended or not, that cannot ever be recovered from. Their Right to Exist has been extinguished ahead of schedule; they have been denied their natural Right to thrive, to grow, and to blossom.

They have been denied their Right to Procreation; to bear children, grandchildren, great-grandchildren, and die of natural causes at a ripe old age. Whereas they should be able to live to see the twilight of their years and be gently swept away once their Physical Bodies have reached their maximum capabilities, they have lost that opportunity because someone selfishly Stole those years from them.

An Unjustified Murder, the Taking of one's Life before one's lifespan reaches its natural conclusion, is an affront to Mankind. It creates Unnecessary Victims, and it reduces the quality of Humanity that we can be. It has Unintended Negative Consequences upon society and all parties involved, and the Murderer becomes a burden for the rest of the country to contend with.

The Ripple Effect of their Death leaves an Empty Space where the Victim once stood; they are replaced by Grief and Suffering, and a Purpose that will forever remain Unfulfilled. Life is Sacred and must be Protected at all costs.

The Taking of Human Life must not go Unpunished. No one that has Committed Murder once should ever have the opportunity to potentially Take another Life. It is our assertion that any person Convicted of having Taken the Life of Another Human

Being forfeits their own Right to Live, grow, and thrive within Civilized society. Death is the only suitable consequence, and Capital Punishment the only viable solution. They must be stricken from this earth, eradicated from Existence, and their Bodies destroyed as they once destroyed one of their Fellow Citizen's opportunity to Exist. Nothing short of this will deliver true Justice.

By extension, all those who have been found Guilty of Committing other Acts of Violence against their Fellow Man which were still done with the Intentional Infliction of Harm—including all manner of Sexual Deviancy, Rape, Molestation, Abduction, Kidnapping, and Assault—shall be Exiled, just as Corrupt Souls have been Banished since Biblical times. They will never be allowed to return to Civilized society, and never have another opportunity to Cause Harm to another of our precious sons or daughters.

We must restore balance.

The removal of a Lesser Being hardly replaces the loss of those who were Wrongfully Stolen, but it is the only guaranteed insurance the Lesser Being will never Harm Another again.

The Death of an Innocent Victim is permanent, and unalterable. So, too, should the punishment be for this action.

No person shall ever be exempt from the consequences of Crimes Against Humanity.

We have a vision for the future of America, and we pray it is shared by each of you. We envision a future where our sons and daughters are spared from a life where they must live in fear of Random Acts of Violence. In this New Era, we will finally be able to live in peace together as one nation. A nation of law-abiding, civilized Citizens, small government, and an unprecedented Criminal Justice system in which Violent Predators and habitual Offenders with proven Violent Histories are eradicated. We envision a nation where every Life is Valued, every Future is Secured, and every Citizen can create a long-lasting Ripple of Prosperity and Meaning.

My Fellow Americans, we beseech you, if you share our desire to build a better world for our children, vote for the Sentence Reform Act. Show the Bereaved who have Lost a Loved One because of Senseless Acts of Violence that you have heard their cries for Justice, and you are committed to change. Your vote is an affirmation to your family, to your community, and to your Fellow Man that you believe in the Sanctity of Human Life. Most importantly, it is a pledge to God Almighty to do everything within your power to Protect and Defend the Sanctity of the Divine Life that He has bequeathed to each of us.

The Sentence Reform Act is the first, and most important, step toward creating the long-term transformation of America that has been needed for many, many years. It is time for all Americans to stand together against the Evil that walks among us without fear of consequence or retribution. For the sake of every Victim created by Violence, and for the Love of all who are Bereaved, please vote for the Sentence Reform Act.

We alone can create a safe and prosperous future for the children of our nation. Enough of our Fellow Citizens have Suffered. For the sake of our children and the Ripple Effect our decisions today will create, please vote to save our nation, and protect the lives and futures of every Innocent Citizen.

The Watchers On The Wall
On this date, the 1st day of the New Year,
In the Year of our Lord, 2045

PART THREE

Before I formed you in the womb
I knew you,
before you were born
I set you apart.

Jeremiah 1:5

TWELVE – RS —2—

Lost Treasure

Rebecca was a Lost Treasure.

Granted, she was young. But there was no denying her talent.

In the early years of the Last Stand, before the Great Reformation, one of the political platforms set forth by The Watchers On The Wall pertained to the social cost paid by the world entire with each life that was Wrongfully Stolen through Violence.

Each Human Being was valuable in their own right, and certainly to their Loved Ones, but there were those who were born with exceptional gifts. These gifts were special qualities of intrinsic skills and talents that only they could create and provide. Such people had a clear and distinct Purpose for their Lives, a Calling.

The Watchers On The Wall referred to these special gifts as 'The Treasure within the Human Soul.' They believed their purpose in life was to create and share their talents, enriching the world through their contributions as a result. These artists, painters, sculptors, musicians, and singers were known as Artistic World Treasures; they created beauty for our world that no one else could produce.

The brilliant artists from the past, men such as Van Gogh and Michelangelo, would forever be immortalized within the collective history of Mankind and known because of the beauty they created. They were Treasures on Earth—evidence of all that was Good, and Pure, and Beautiful. They were the defining example of what we were capable of becoming and producing when we fulfilled our Callings and lived up to our Potential.

But not all artists gained such fame and recognition during their lifetime, and for some, it was because their lives were tragically cut short by Acts of Violence. To extinguish the light from someone that had unmistakable raw talent and the inherent desire to create beauty for the world to partake in was beyond reprehensible, and the loss was great.

The Watchers On The Wall had spoken out against the many Acts of Violence that resulted in such loss of life, including through Suicide. They had fought against the merciless and unfair taking of Human Life for reasons that were simply never going to be balanced enough to justify it.

They believed that the death of an artist signified the abrupt end to all they could have created. Years of potential creativity and beauty were wiped out, leaving a vacant hole where their future artistic achievements should have been. Just as their death left a Ripple Effect and an Empty Space where they were missing, all future art they could have created would remain unfulfilled and undone. All art created by them ended at the Final Moment of their Death as they drew their Final Breath. The loss of such potential was incalculable.

One didn't have to appreciate the Arts or have an artistic proclivity in order to understand the multi-faceted reasons their Deaths should matter. It mattered because they may have been Killed before they truly mastered their craft, and thus their most recent work before their Death was only a glimpse of what they could have become had they just been given a chance.

The Watchers On The Wall wanted the world to recognize the loss of such people and used them as examples to illustrate how every individual life mattered. Their fight was for the Sanctity of Human Life and the Sanctity of Human Potential.

Their endeavors were not in vain. During the Great Reformation, as our nation began to rebuild, our leaders created The Lost Treasures Clause. To be recognized as a Lost Treasure was a great honor for a person, even as an award that was only given posthumously. It meant that the world could have, and should have, had the opportunity to discover the Deceased Victim's talent.

With the national recognition as a Lost Treasure, a database was created. It was a national archive created to capture and document the valuable, irreplaceable collective works of every Murder Victim. Their artistic legacy could be recognized, cataloged, archived, and displayed. Everyone could then appreciate all that they had done, and all that they might have become.

It was an opportunity for the families and Bereaved to secure the memory of their Loved One. It gave them great comfort and peace knowing that their Loved One would be remembered long after their own Deaths, and future generations could always discover them on their own. This was what mattered.

When it was all said and done, Rebecca Summers had qualified for this title. Her legacy would be cemented along with countless other creators who had left this world through unnatural causes. Suicide or Murder, Rebecca was a Lost Treasure, and it was important that she be granted that honor. Nothing new would ever be drawn or painted by her hands, and all that she could have accomplished over her lifetime would forever remain undone. Just as her death now meant there would always be an Empty Space where she should have been, the walls of our museums would never carry one of her paintings. To be classified as a Lost Treasure was a tragedy, but through it, at least the world would be able to know who Rebecca Summers had once been. Hopefully, her premature death would help another artist find his or her reason to live and inspire them to keep creating. Sadly, aside from being remembered by her friends and family, it would be all that remained of the girl.

Rape or Relationship

After meeting with both Rebecca's parents and her roommate, we could verify that Rebecca had not been romantically involved with anyone. Her parents believed her to be a 'good girl' who was 'saving herself for marriage', and to their knowledge, she had never had a serious boyfriend or love interest. Her roommate reaffirmed this, stating that she was a quiet, studious girl who only loved her art and didn't even go out on dates.

Given that no one was aware of any potential lovers, we were left to consider that her Pregnancy had been the result of an unwanted sexual advance by a man, possibly a situation where things escalated beyond her control, but a greater possibility that her Pregnancy was a byproduct of Rape. Because her roommate insisted that she never went to parties, social functions through the college, or out on dates, it seemed much more plausible that she had been Raped.

We were still waiting for the results of the STD panel from the Medical Examiner's office, but we knew that if anything came back positive that the odds of it being Rape went up exponentially given the statistics.

We were retracing the last few months of her life to the best of our ability, adding up the unique elements that made her who she was. For now, we knew she was traumatized and had been looking for a way out. It didn't explain how she ended up in that field, but unless someone forced those pills down her throat and then buried her, it still left us to go forward with the notion of Suicide after Abortion. If the STD panel came back as positive—especially if we could secure proof of Rape, it would present sufficient motive.

It was entirely possible that there was a man out there somewhere who impregnated her, forced the Abortion, and then cleaned up his mess by feeding her pills and then Disposing of her Body. It was possible—but it didn't explain how or why the other sets of Human Remains were lying alongside her in that field.

Sadly, it seemed most plausible that her Death had been solely by her own hand, and for reasons that only she may ever conclusively know.

THIRTEEN — MP —2—

MP—21st Century Crimes Against Women

Women used to Disappear all the time.

For Mariam to have been blatantly Abducted from a public grocery store parking lot was a modern-day anomaly, but there had been a time when it had been commonplace.

Its rarity now did not make it any less tragic.

There had been a time when America had borne witness to the most staggering number of Missing Persons imaginable; an unfathomable volume of cases that were seldom resolved with successful or positive outcomes. During the early 21st century, there were almost a million Citizens per year that were reported Missing. As the years passed, when Crime and Violence were at their worst in the decades before the Last Stand and the Great Reformation, there were more than a million and a half cases reported every year. Of those, hundreds of thousands were never resolved; they were cases that were never closed out—Citizens had simply Disappeared and were never heard from again.

Our daughters were dying.

Every day, in every major city and small town in America, our daughters were being butchered.

Americans were growing weary of burying their Innocent sons and daughters through the Senseless, Brutal actions of Criminals that simply did not care about the Value of Human Life. As the 21st century continued to decline, Americans knew that mere thoughts and prayers were not enough.

For generations, the roadways, city streets, and back alleys of our country had been strewn with the Deceased Remains of discarded women, who, having been subjected to the Barbaric Savagery of uncivilized men fulfilling their base desires, were used, abused, and then left for Dead. Worldwide, men had always demonstrated that women were little more than useful orifices for their pleasure, creating an unparalleled legacy of female Victims; a trail of Battered, Exploited, Damaged, and Scarred women and girls from every race, religion, and socio-economic station within society.

Despite global campaigns advocating Human Rights for all, despite advancements in civilization allowing for worldwide education and the spread of knowledge, and despite the never-ending work of good Human Beings in their efforts to curtail such Violence, the world had always been riddled with men who destroyed Human Life without a second thought. Men without fear of consequence had continued to dominate the globe throughout the 21st century, and Crimes Against Women remained at the forefront of the epidemic of Violence that pervaded every nation on earth. Historically, even in the most advanced nations, there remained those who, for a myriad of cultural, religious, and psychological reasons, believed that women were little more than disposable second-class Citizens.

It was a tragic reality that her Remains had now been found and Mariam had officially joined the ranks among the millions of women worldwide who had become Victims to the male counterpart of their species.

Every time a woman or girl Disappeared and was then found to have been the Victim of an ARM Attack, it was a shocking realization that there were men living among the rest of society within America that were not only capable of Inflicting Violence, but that they held zero regard for either the Rule of Law or the Sanctity of Human Life. Somehow this was even more abhorrent and shocking when it was done in cases of pure opportunity, and the Victims were strangers, selected randomly by their Assailants.

When this occurred, it left the American People with one simple truth that could not be denied or excused—a simple truth that was profoundly honest enough to leave no question as to the weight of where the responsibility for correcting this problem actually rested. Knowing that there were men out there who were Committing Acts of Pure Evil against the women in America was one thing; knowing that the government and the Criminal Justice system failed to do anything effectively enough to put an end to the Evil men that were living freely among them was another.

The American government failed to prevent the Loss of our most Innocent and Vulnerable. It was something that rested on the minds and conscience of every Citizen; the blame for apathetic indifference was something that fell squarely on the shoulders of every American who claimed to be a Good Human Being. All Americans had a responsibility to rise against such Barbaric Savages, and until that point, the women of our nation would continue to be targeted. Men such as I would never be free of our professional responsibilities to hunt for Evil Predators, and sadly, women such as Mariam, and even little Katarina, would never be Safe.

When we learned as children about the history of our nation, it was to the early and mid-21st century that we were taught our most valuable lessons. Had our government not failed We The People so obscenely, and had our Criminal Justice system not been so incomprehensibly ineffective, the Citizens of our nation might never have had the courage to rise up collectively together to take their Last Stand. But between the predators and career criminals on the streets, and the severe shortages of Law Enforcement, there was very little that could be done in the name of self-protection except to demand change. The combination of Evil men living without fear of consequence, and the lack of Good Men capable of protecting everyday Citizens, could have been the end of our nation as we knew it.

Instead, history taught us that when We The People rose collectively, we were able to put an end to the Crime and Violence. We knew that it was only because of a rogue band of Citizens called The Watchers On The Wall that we had been able to salvage our nation and change the trajectory of our collective future. As with any group attempting to stand up against tyranny, they were branded as Anti-Americans, Anti-Government, and Domestic Terrorists. But it was only because of their actions that we had managed to survive, and overcome, the tyrannical government that had ignored our most vulnerable Citizens for far, far too long.

Through these lessons, we learned the importance of patriotism and solidarity. Studying our history, including the American Revolution, and then our Last Stand and Great Reformation, we were given the most priceless knowledge possible: We The People were the very fabric of our country, and only by our own effort and standards could we be judged. If we were willing to allow Crime and Violence to become the status quo, and if we were willing to allow a corrupt, toxic government to control and dominate us while also destroying our freedom and eradicating our rights, then we had only ourselves to blame.

There was a time when the lives of Human Beings had been without value in our nation. But through the Last Stand and Great Reformation, we transformed this travesty. The death of every woman and girl through an Act of Violence in these modern times served as a reminder of what our Citizens used to tolerate, and we would do well to remember that it would not take much apathy to find ourselves heading down that dark road once again.

Despite Every Effort, It Wasn't Enough

The last one hundred years had been productive regarding many things, but one of the most important progressions had been the implementation of the Victim Advocacy Agency and their tireless work to ensure that no Victim was ever left without a voice and equal representation under a Court of Law.

The Right To Self-Protection Act had guaranteed that no Citizen would ever face criminal charges for any Act of Violence committed against a Violent Aggressor if done in defense of Self or Others, and it, too, had helped reduce the number of Attacks against the Innocent.

But as with many other laws, it still fell short of efficacy on all counts; there were still far too many cases of Violence against Innocent Citizens who were physically inferior and incapable of ensuring their own protection against those who sought to Harm them.

Perhaps the greatest security measure implemented to minimize the risks for Innocent Citizens came through the development of the Sentence Reform Act. It had proven to be the absolute most effective system of governance ever created within These United States for the purpose of saving Innocent Lives.

After the Sentence Reform Act, the revolving door of failed 'transformative justice' and 'reintegration' policies was closed for good. There were no more loopholes or controversial policies designed to serve the interests of Violent Predators or Career Criminals. Nothing provided that opportunity; not hung juries, not mistrials, not early releases, not 'time served'.

Those that had chosen to take a Human Life through an Intentional Act of Violence were never given another opportunity because they never gave their Victims one.

That was Justice.

Whether people would have understood it in the 21st century or not, whether they would have marched against it and spent their time defending the 'Human Rights' of Violent Offenders—it was all irrelevant.

Harsh, permanent sentencing provided two things: It gave a voice to the Victims, and it ensured that there would be no new ones.

Ever.

The Great Reformation had drastically and irrevocably culled almost all Violent Crimes, and the laws had become a reflection of the Will of the People. Such Violence was rare; the nation was fully aware of the Value and Sanctity of Human Life. The strictness of the Criminal Justice system ensured that the casualty rates would be almost non-existent.

But when such cases did occur, convictions were quickly and efficiently done. There were no long, drawn-out trials or years spent on Death Row. The Justice system was effective, thorough, and beyond reproach. It was exactly as it should be and served both as a deterrent and a reminder of what would be exacted by all those who refused to follow the Laws of the Land and respect their Fellow Man.

It had taken decades of Violence and Crime, the internal destruction of our nation and Citizenry, and a final, epic Last Stand by the American People who had stood firm and resolute, demanding drastic change, before we improved our nation and reduced our Violent Crime Rates. But we had done it. Above all else, we had reclaimed both the Rule of Law as well as the sanity and integrity of the nation.

Despite all of this, we still could not eliminate the Violence being directed against women entirely—especially through Abduction, Rape, and Murder.

We had come so far, and yet there were still those among us who were clearly just *incapable* of living decent lives, following our laws, and coexisting in peace. It served as a rough reminder that no matter how extreme the measures, no matter how severe the consequences, no matter what the criminals stood to lose, for those that were Intent on Causing Harm to Others, there simply would be no deterrent. This reality alone should have been enough to understand that there were those among us who were never going to assimilate, never going to live non-violent lives, and could never be controlled, reasoned with, or threatened. Sometimes, a bad seed was just a bad seed, and the only alternative was to discard the rotten fruit before it destroyed everything surrounding it.

FOURTEEN - RS —3—

Stanton—Proof of Rape Surveillance

Stanton had found the evidence that we needed to fill in some of the gaps regarding Rebecca's mysterious Pregnancy and Abortion. After accessing the security cameras on the GSAU campus, he began scouring the footage looking for traces of Rebecca. He had a window of time given the number of weeks that she was possibly Pregnant, so he was able to narrow it down to the last few months.

It didn't take him long to notice an anomaly as he reviewed their security system; there was a date missing from the records. When he sent me the message letting me know, I asked him if he could figure out what had happened to it, how it could be 'missing' without direct Human intervention, and could he do anything to retrieve it. He told me then—more than a week ago now—that he was working on it.

I was sitting at the conference room table going over Rebecca's school records when he finally came bounding in, almost triumphant.

"I've got it. I've got the missing security footage—and you were right—someone tried really hard to make it disappear," he said.

I was surprised—I had written it off as a lost cause. It seldom took Stanton more than a few hours to retrieve information.

He went over to the computer system on the side of the room and brought up the wall monitor, starting what appeared to be GSAU security footage by the numbers and information listed at the bottom of the screen.

He took the wireless keyboard and then sat down at the table alongside me, fast-forwarding through the footage.

"Now watch," he said, his eyes fixed on the screen.

He lowered a dozen of the small squares of video footage—all various locations around the campus—and then brought a final one into full screen.

Within a moment, we could see Rebecca walking along the pathway from the direction of the parking lot toward the buildings. Her arms were full, and she wore a backpack.

I counted five large pieces of canvas between both hands, three of approximately 4x3 and then two more slightly smaller frames as well. She was also carrying a hand-held purse in her right hand.

She was so overwhelmed with items it would have been impossible for her to ward off any potential Attackers. Every self-defense instructor she would have taken mandatory classes from during her years of public education would have advised against what she was doing.

After a few moments of watching her walk, rearranging several times because the paintings were cumbersome and probably heavy, she finally reached the first building. The sidewalk parted, leaving her with the choice of going left or right. If she went right, she would have gone in between the buildings, encountered other students, and been much more visible. Instead, she went left, walking on the outskirts of the building—clearly the most isolated building on the southern side of the campus.

I watched as she walked, a feeling of dread welling up inside of me as I anticipated what was about to happen. A few distracted choices that day had led to what I could now see was going to be a Crime of Opportunity for some degenerate waiting to prey on an unsuspecting young woman.

"Here it comes," Stanton said, his tone low.

As pleased as he may have been about his accomplishment in retrieving the footage, he was now exercising quiet respect for the moment, something I appreciated as much as I did his warning. I could have guessed what and how it would play out—the skulking scumbag lurking behind a tree, some bushes, or the edge of the building, leaping out and grabbing her, and before she knew what was happening, he would have had his way with her. I had studied thousands of similar cases.

I wished more women grasped how opportunistic they made themselves to the Predators out there by failing to remain vigilant and prepared as they were all trained. So many of them took our low Crime Rates and peaceful nation for granted anymore, never believing it could happen to them.

And then it began to unfold, exactly as I had anticipated—a man emerged from the bushes off to her left and crept up behind her, sucker-punching her in the side of the head and sending her reeling toward the bushes. Her arms released everything she was holding as she fell to the ground, dizzy and disoriented.

I saw her hand go up to the side of her face as she tried to figure out what had struck her, and at that moment you could almost see as she looked up at the sky that she thought it had been a tree limb falling. But that moment was short-lived as the man looked around furtively to make sure he hadn't been seen by anyone, and then grabbed her by her long hair and began dragging her into the overgrown shrubbery.

As soon as she felt his hands on her hair and the pressure from him pulling her, she began to fight back. But her small frame was no match for his, and as she tried to free her hair from his hands, we watched as her body was dragged along, her feet desperately trying to attach themselves to anything—dirt, rocks, branches—to help her anchor herself down and prevent his efforts.

Nothing worked, however, and less than a minute after first being struck, she had vanished off the screen and into the brush.

A few seconds later, we watched as the man returned to the sidewalk and began throwing all of her artwork and then her purse out of view, presumably over the same wall of brush where he had taken her.

We could only assume he had struck her and knocked her unconscious in order to have left her there without restraint.

The room was eerily silent as the footage continued to play, but nothing was visible on the screen. I knew we were both imagining what was happening to her during those moments, but neither of us attempted to fast-forward. Instead, we waited, taking special heed of the passage of time. We would need to know such details for the man's trial anyhow.

Finally, Stanton broke the silence and said, "You know that moment when he looked around to see if anyone had noticed him? That's where we're going to get him. I've already got the facial recognition program going. We'll get him."

I nodded. I thought it had seemed like an opportune moment, but it wasn't my field, so I wasn't sure.

"And if he doesn't already have a record?"

"Then I'll keep looking through other databases. No one can stay off-grid entirely anymore. If this guy has so much as a library card, I'll find him," he responded.

I nodded again, still watching the screen.

I felt incredibly sad, sitting there, knowing how the story had ended now that I knew how it had begun.

Finally—after far too long—there was movement.

We watched as Rebecca emerged from the side of the screen. She was completely disoriented and drifting along. One of her shoes was missing. Her hair and clothing were disheveled, covered in leaves and debris, and her stockings were torn in several places.

We watched as she turned around in a full circle, moving so slowly I wondered if she had a concussion. She was looking for her artwork—maybe her shoe.

Disappearing again, she re-emerged a few moments later with her artwork and purse. She still didn't have her other shoe on—a little black flat without a heel or any type of strapping to hold it in place, just a little slip-on sandal.

Taking one last look around, she apparently surrendered to its loss and left without it. We watched her as she continued walking along the same path slowly, still disoriented, and now limping. Her shoulders sagged. She walked with a heavy step on the right and favored the foot without her sandal—indicating that her ankle might have been injured as well.

A moment later, she stopped once again and turned around, looking at the bushes once more. Her face was bloodied and bruised; her right eye was almost swollen shut entirely, her cheekbone and mouth both swollen and bleeding from open cuts. The man hadn't just Raped her; he had punched her directly in the face a multitude of times, possibly to render her unconscious, but likely just because he enjoyed it—and those were just the marks we could see on the screen.

And then she turned, continuing down the pathway once again.

She disappeared from sight, and then Stanton transferred screens to show her carry on slowly down the sidewalk until she reached one of the larger buildings in the center of the campus. She didn't encounter another student or staff member on the path, making that long, lonely walk all by herself.

"What's that building?" I asked, watching as she finally disappeared inside.

"That's a campus administration building. It has campus security, the nurse's office, and the counseling center," he told me.

"That's where I got the footage from. Someone in there didn't want this to be found. They intentionally deleted it—the whole day—which I believe was the only way they could get rid of it. It had to be done through the campus security department, so that's where you need to look. I'm not sure if she went to campus security once she was there, but it might be worth checking with the nurse's station and the counseling center as well."

"How long was she in there?" I asked.

"It's only about a half an hour—I'm going to fast-forward through it if that's all good," he stated.

I nodded, wondering what she had done inside.

He checked his timestamp, slowing down to the time he had marked, and set it to play once again.

Soon enough, Rebecca emerged with a security guard—a young man playing campus cop but seemed to be only twenty-three or -four, probably a student there as well.

"Let's find out who he is," I said, leaning forward in my chair.

"Already did—Evan Harrison. He's a student in the nursing program and a part-time security guard. He walks her straight through the middle of the campus and back to her car. That's it—she never went back to the site of the Rape, the security guard never went there, and there was never a statement issued by the school alerting students to a potential threat on campus. The guy just walked her off campus and then returns to the office—I can't be sure who tried to scrub the system, but we know that at least this guy knew what happened that day."

"And destroyed the evidence," I said.

"But now we have proof of both the Rape and the cover-up," he responded.

I felt my jaw tighten as I thought of it.

"Good work. I mean that; great work," I told him.

"Let me know when you find out who this guy is," I said, referring to the Rapist with a nod of my head toward the screen. "And I think it's time we look into the campus some more. Let's find out who's working inside that building. And let's bring Evan Harrison in for questioning."

Confirmation From the Medical Examiner

Stanton forwarded a notification from the Medical Examiner. Among other details, including the specifics of the toxicology report regarding the medications found within Rebecca's system at the time of her Death, it included the results of her STD panel. He confirmed that she had tested positive for one of the few remaining incurable sexually transmitted diseases that were still prevalent in America. Along with the results, he included some information regarding how the symptoms might have appeared in the hours or days following her Rape, leaving her no doubt as to what was happening to her body.

Stanton confirmed through his investigation into Rebecca's personal computer that she had recently researched symptoms for a variety of transmittable STDs. From this, we could presume she knew what was happening, and although we had found no medical records showing she ever went to an Emergency Room or sought medical help through a gynecologist or her registered family practitioner, we were left to conclude she was fully aware of her diagnosis. All that was left to theorize was that it played into her behavior during her Final Days and Moments alive, and likely affected her decision to End her own Life.

Establishing Links Between Mariam and Rebecca

According to the grocery store that had recorded it, the grocery chain had placed the same security system around the parking lots of each of their stores in the decade before the Last Stand, and had continued to update them with the latest advancements in surveillance technology all the way through the Great Reformation. They had done this as a precaution against Violent Crimes, thefts, assaults, and even the carjackings that had been commonplace during those years when Violence was so widespread that even grocery shopping had become dangerous.

The man responsible for Mariam's Abduction, according to the surveillance footage obtained, had been taller than Mariam by well over a foot in height. Officer Stanton had done his best to review the grainy footage that had been preserved by the security system at the grocery store, but it had been determined to be 'as good as it was going to get' by the SPD technicians that had originally acquired it in the days following her Abduction.

Whoever had done this had been far more aggressive and Violent toward Mariam than a Random Sexual Assault would seemingly merit.

Officer Stanton had established the connection between the Victims and their contacts, employment, education, and daily lives. Mariam was not only a graduate of the same university that Rebecca attended, but she had also just completed a term where she had worked as an adjunct professor. She had been on the campus only a few days before her Abduction. The original First Responders hadn't notated it during their Responding Call investigation because she had walked to the campus rather than driven there, and it wasn't displayed on her GPS.

As a former student of GSAU, Mariam had attended the university roughly a decade before Rebecca had begun her education there. Additionally, when the SPD Officers had conducted their interviews, the administrator that was the spokesman for the school had told them that as a professor, Mariam had worked solely online, and her coursework had seldom required any physical visits to the campus.

At the time of her Disappearance, there had been no connection between her and Rebecca; they were complete strangers other than both accessing the same university. They might have had their education in common, but there had been nothing else to tie them together. The university was the only link between two very different women.

We hadn't 'proven' they were both Victims of the same Assailant; we could presume, since they were both buried alongside one another, but that wasn't the same as finding conclusive proof. If this was the case, then our first clue regarding the man behind the Rape of Rebecca should also be the same man who Abducted Mariam from the grocery store parking lot and then Murdered her. There were many steps to take before we could safely secure this conclusion, but if it *was* the same man, then the escalation between what had happened to Rebecca and then Mariam was not only extremely quick, it was cause for concern since he was still currently unaccounted for and freely roaming our city streets.

FIFTEEN – MP – DEATH NOTIFICATION

Preparing for Notification

Tomorrow afternoon we would deliver the Notification of Death to the family of Mariam Pembrook, and I was hoping to do it in an entirely unconventional way. I thought it would be important for Mariam's parents, the Collins, to be present, as well as any other family members deemed significant by the Pembrook men. I had contacted the same brother of Mariam's husband that he had reached out to during the moments directly after placing the call to Emergency Services, a man by the name of Mark Pembrook. He was not directly related to Mariam's biological family, but he had been the first point of contact selected by Matthew Pembrook when he had first reported her as possibly Missing. It seemed clear that he trusted his brother and had a close relationship with him.

He was going to need that support again soon.

I also wanted Mark Pembrook to reach out to Tyler Waylon. He was married to Mariam's older sister; he had been a part of the Collins family the longest, having married their oldest daughter when they were only twenty-one. He had been part of their lives for over twenty-five years already and had been there as each of the younger sisters had eventually found their prospective mates and gotten married.

Tyler Waylon, alongside Mark Pembrook, were the ones who had coordinated all the searches and campaigning that had been done in the weeks following Mariam's Abduction. According to Officer Stanton, the two men had also employed the services of both a private investigator and a group of private contractors who worked criminal cases. It was unclear if anyone in the family was aware that he and Mark Pembrook had solicited these private agencies to facilitate their own investigations, and even more unfortunate that between the two—and along with the SPD's Missing Persons Division—no one had found her until the gravesite had been discovered. It had not been for lack of effort.

I needed the two of them to coordinate once again so I could meet with the entire family. It was unorthodox, but this family reacted as a unit, and each of them was going to be necessary to keep one another afloat in the upcoming weeks and months. I had discussed the best way for us to deliver our notification of Mariam's Death with Grace O'Connor, and she had been the first to recommend that we give them the opportunity to unify for the news so they could all have access to what little information we had to share. She also suggested it was a good opportunity for us to explore any new leads or ideas they might have, so we could use the time most effectively.

Mark Pembrook worked as an investment banker in a building only a few blocks away from the SPD Headquarters. I had waited for him to finish his workday and had met him near his vehicle. He hadn't been surprised to see me, but I think he was grateful that I had contacted him during his work hours and avoided his home. It had been intentional; I hadn't wanted to alarm his wife or children. I would have done the same thing if I had reached out to Tyler Waylon directly. But I hoped that by going through Matthew Pembrook's side of the family that Mark Pembrook would prove once again to be a level-headed organizer, since this was going to be difficult for everyone in Mariam's immediate family.

It was not the standard procedure for Notification, but I wanted to speak with someone who would be capable of determining the best course of action for the situation. After I had met with him directly, I was certain that I had made the right call in asking for his help. He knew everyone much better than I did and knew the emotional state of the family. I had to trust that if this was the man that Matthew Pembrook had turned to as soon as a crisis was looming, that it was because he viewed him to be a source of strength and guidance. He was going to need those foundations to be firmly in place soon, both as he received the news of his wife's Death and in the transitional period afterward. It was precisely because I had witnessed how close the family was through the video footage, along with their proactive response after Mariam's Abduction, that I wanted to handle breaking the news with special care.

"My recommendation would be to let me reach out to the husbands before we meet as a family. I can talk to all my brothers-in-law, and then they can be prepared to deal with Mariam's sisters after they hear the news from you."

As I had expected, he intended to contact Tyler Waylon first so the two of them could call the Heads of Household and prepare them.

He continued, "All of them have been struggling to come to terms with the situation. The uncertainty is weighing heavily on each of them, but I think everyone is reaching a point where no one is willing to state the obvious. They're all terrified to acknowledge what is likely the outcome."

He raised an eyebrow. "My wife won't even remain in the same room if I bring it up. She begged me not to say anything to anyone else in the family about my concerns. She says it will destroy their hope, and that's all anyone has anymore. Everyone's just holding on by sheer denial."

He sighed. "It's time for the truth. They have to be told so they can finally come to terms with it; they're falling apart even with their silence and denial."

His voice cracked when he tried to express how difficult the last few weeks had been for everyone, but that Matt and the kids were barely coping.

"All the sisters have been stepping in to help with the kids. Her parents are having a hard time, especially her mother."

I realized then just how difficult of a position I had placed him in by asking him to step into the role I had. Nevertheless, I believed it was the right thing to do, and he agreed.

"I don't think any of the men will enjoy keeping the news from their spouses. But if the choice is to tell their wives directly, or have the news come from the Investigator, they would probably prefer not to be the ones delivering it."

He looked at me, mouth grimaced. "It's not going to be easy no matter how it's done. This news is going to crush the family."

"But you agree with this approach? To involve the whole family at the same time? One of the advantages to this will be that no one else will have to provide Notifications to the rest of the family." I replied.

"Oh, yeah, no doubt about it. Let's just get it done."

I shook his hand and agreed to meet him at the home of Matthew and Mariam tomorrow evening at 1730. He assured me he would have all the sisters, husbands, and parents there, however he could manage it.

I offered my sympathies for his Loss, and watched as he choked back his tears.

He held his hand up and shook his head in acknowledgment.

I knew his Grief was most likely because he understood the full weight of the Pain his younger brother was going through. Someone whom he loved dearly was Suffering through a tragedy that he could neither prevent nor control the outcome of.

To compound this, he was now privy to information that only confirmed that which they had been most afraid of learning; that his brother's wife had been Murdered and was never coming back to them.

I understood how heavy this burden was; it was difficult to watch the ones you love experience Pain, and Grief was one of the most personal forms of Suffering possible.

This man's sister-in-law was Dead. His brother, by his own admission, was already barely holding himself together, and he knew it was only going to get worse. He seemed very aware of just how taxing these upcoming days and weeks were going to be for their entire family. Being unable to prevent their inevitable pain weighed on him..

I found myself very moved by it.

All who knew her had loved Mariam, as testament by the depth of their Grief.

I was going to have Grace O'Connor with me tomorrow, and I knew she had already secured the best resources and other Victim Advocates to step in after we had gone.

Nothing was going to be the same for any of them again.

Examining Her Life

After I waylaid Mariam's brother-in-law, Mark Pembrook, outside of his office, I returned to the barracks. It had been a long enough day, and tomorrow was going to be challenging.

I sent a message out to Grace O'Connor letting her know I had made arrangements for us to meet with Mariam's family at 1730. She confirmed the time and sent assurances she had the appropriate resources ready to go and would see me in the morning.

I was tired; it had been a long week already, and I knew tomorrow was going to bring a lot of stress. I wasn't bothered by Death, really. I understood it to be a necessary conclusion to Life. But I had done more than my share of bringing the news of the Passing of a Loved One to strangers, and it was always traumatic.

I wasn't responsible just for informing people that their Loved Ones had Died; I broke their hearts, destroyed their hopes, shattered their faith, and then replaced it with incomprehensible Grief and a broken record of Violent imagery that could never be unseen once it was planted within one's mind.

I was the gatekeeper between the reality that once existed and the new one that no one ever wanted to accept, and no matter how much I desperately wanted to shield people from the horrors on the other side, I knew I was responsible for ensuring that they crossed over.

My only goal, when it was all said and done, was that I wanted to also bring with me some sense of Closure; I wanted to deliver the promise of Justice so that they might be left with some semblance of hope for better days down the road. I knew they were far away in the distance; I knew I couldn't guarantee them or even make promises. But if I could just deliver Justice—ensure that whatever had happened to their Loved One would never happen to anyone else ever again, it would be something, at least. If they could have confirmation that we had removed the source of Evil from the streets, that we had eradicated the plague that had poisoned our nation and caused such irrevocable damage to our Citizens—at least I could know it had not all been destroyed.

Tomorrow I was going to have to go through all of it again—and this time...This time it was really weighing on me.

She had been such a beautiful part of her community. She had done so much good for the people around her. The depth of their love for her only compounded the lack of fairness in her Death.

I set aside my negative thoughts, ordered some food to be delivered from the cafeteria's night menu, and grabbed a bottle of dark ale from the refrigerator.

The food service said it would be approximately thirty minutes, so I took a hot shower before it arrived and then settled down with my beer and meal.

As a matter of tradition, I tried to invest a bit of time into learning who each of my Victims were during their lives before my first encounter with their families, especially before I delivered their Notification of Death after a prolonged Disappearance.

I posted the electronic photographs I had of Mariam onto the media wall and then used my hand sensor to look through them. On another section of the wall, I began scanning through all her social media that I could find. There wasn't much, especially compared to most. But she had a plethora of crafts saved through various sites, including homemade paper crafts and even some small little animal shapes that were made of yarn and different fabrics.

She was a mother.

She was so much more than 'just' a mother, of course, but it only took a moment to realize that she had loved that part of her life very much.

And now there were four children who would never have another new memory of her, and all the paper dolls, hand-sewn clothes, and new toys that would ever come from her had already been given and shared with them. For her children, everything had already happened that ever could. There would never be new experiences, new toys, new things to laugh about, new hugs and kisses, or bedtime stories. Everything she had done for them had ended. All their routines, their daily interactions, and their family outings were over; there would never be more. For all of them, 'family time' would hold a whole new meaning, and her absence would always be felt. They would feel incomplete because something was missing. *She* was missing, and nothing would ever replace the Empty Space she Left Behind. Her children would spend the rest of their lives without her, and their own children would never know the grandmother they should have.

She was a mother, and she was now gone.

She was a wife; the woman that her husband had once met eyes with and felt a connection. She had been the recipient of someone's affection; there had been a love story just for her where she had been the leading lady and had found her match. He had made her laugh, made her heart race, and probably even made her cry a time or two. But she had loved him, and he had loved her. They had been in love, and they had built a life together.

And from that union, they had shared four children. She had probably been very excited when she had discovered she was Pregnant for the first time. I wondered if she had been gleefully secretive about it, waiting for the perfect moment to tell her husband that they were expecting their first child, or if she had just sprung it on him as soon as she next saw him, unable to keep her excitement contained.

I looked through photos of her with her family, her wedding day with her husband and all her sisters and their husbands. An entire wedding party composed of family members, all in matching outfits and evenly paired up along each respective side as they posed for the cameras. The blushing bride, the handsome husband. The look on his face as she walked toward him down the aisle. Two sets of parents beaming at the photographer, an audience full of friends and family. They were in love, and they had wanted to share it with everyone that mattered to them.

And then, a mere fourteen months later, their first-born son. And then a daughter, and another daughter, and then a final little brother to even out the group. A family of six, with three on each side. Their family photos told the tale of happy times, family vacations, and a family home that had been stable and loving.

The two families had been close; everyone, including all their siblings, had lived within a five-mile radius of one another. Their children had all gone to school with one another; cousins from both the mother's and the father's siblings all sharing the same memories of schools, teachers, bus rides, field trips, and graduations.

They had been a happy family before this.

She had been a wonderful mother, a devoted wife, a loving daughter and sister, and a good educator.

She had worked hard, gone to school, gotten married, started a career, raised a family, and paid her taxes.

She had done everything she was supposed to do and had done everything right.

Things like this weren't supposed to happen to people like her.

They weren't supposed to happen to anyone, but certainly not to low-risk, good Human Beings that never did anything to hurt anyone, that never broke any laws, or did anything else to incur bad karma. And yet here we were, a woman who should be here was Dead and yet another Evil, Violent Predator had claimed another Victim.

This was the greatest nation on earth, and we still couldn't figure out how to keep our Citizens Safe against those who lived outside of the Rule of Law and without conscience.

No society could dare call itself 'civilized' if it subjected its Citizens to Random Violence. No government could dare consider itself 'effective leadership' if those whom they have sworn to represent, Protect, and Defend were suffering or incapable of self-defense against the Evil among them.

There was no excuse for this. Not now, not ever.

This woman had deserved better.

The family of Mariam was remarkable. I considered how her Loved Ones had responded to the news of her Abduction. There had been such valiant displays of strength, optimism, and a dedication to push on, never surrendering to their despair even when the passage of time had diminished her odds of Survival. They had all worked with such dedication toward their efforts to shed exposure to the case and *bring her home;* a traditional phrase used for those who were Missing.

I rubbed my eyes, shut off the screen and lamp, and made my way toward the bedroom.

I could see images of Mariam flash through my head, smiling, dancing at her wedding, reading to the children in her class, holding her first baby in a hospital bed, and in a family photograph with her parents, her sisters, their husbands, and all of their children—everyone smiling, happy, safe. Just living their lives.

I pulled off my t-shirt, leaving only my pajama bottoms, and climbed into bed. I shut off the lamp, welcoming the darkness that would bring sleep.

But I wasn't alone. Try as I might, I could not stop my mind from wandering back to the morgue, the first and only place I had ever shared physical space with her. I continued to see Mariam even as I desperately tried to block out the images of her lying on that metal table. I could imagine her—cold, lifeless, her eyes bulging with that all too familiar look of Terror on her face. I could see her neck, bruised purple, and her entire body covered in dark bruising from his fists. I recalled the self-defense cuts on her hands and arms, and the deep, wide, gaping gashes along her chest where she had been repeatedly stabbed.

Sleep was slow to come.

The Final Moments Before the World Changed

At this moment, it was still unknown to the Loved Ones of Mariam that her Physical Remains had been found.

Soon enough, we would make our way to the home she had shared with her husband and four children, and we would break the news to them she had not only been located but that she was Deceased. From there, it would only get worse as I explained the true nature of how her life had been Stolen from her.

I knew, as I always did, that we would convey news they would never be prepared for or want to hear. It was a certainty that I observed many times throughout my career, and it happened in much the same fashion every time. I would share with them the Death Notification, explain to them the information that I was comfortable divulging during my ongoing investigation, and then watch them as their entire countenance would freeze momentarily as they tried to process everything. It was clear, mostly, by expression or Body Language, that as they worked through everything, they were gaining a new awareness of the world that they had never understood or known firsthand. It was at that moment of awakening where they realized that everything—all that they had previously known and thought to be true—the entire reality of their Existence, would forever be changed.

Their world had already taken an enormous hit from the instant they knew Mariam was Missing. Rebecca's parents had been notified by her roommate and would have felt that same moment of shock and fear wash over them. So, too, had Caroline Randall as she had returned from her work on the farm when she entered the house and saw Arlan had Gone Missing, and exactly as Lucya Urakov must have felt when she departed from the church and scanned the parking lot in the hopes of seeing little Katarina out there riding around on her bike as she should have been.

It was a moment of sheer, abject terror.

But until I arrived at the home of the Pembrook's, there was still one minor difference. It wasn't much, but it still existed. In much the same way as the other parents and Loved Ones must have felt, there was a pivotal moment that changed everything. Once there was conclusive evidence to grant Closure to the story, it was the Death of any remaining Hope.

From that moment forward, as soon as I opened my mouth and uttered those words, the truth would shift and change the facts of the case. I was not merely delivering a Notification of Death; I was the eradicator of all things Good, Innocent, and Pure.

I hated to watch their worlds implode.

It was a blessing, I believed, that they had been granted that final moment in time when they were all able to come together as a community to find Mariam rather than discovering her straightaway.

If they had been privy to the knowledge that the Death of Mariam had been carried out exactly as so many hundreds upon hundreds of thousands before her, resulting in her Death almost immediately following her Abduction—and directly proceeding the Rape and complete Violation of her Body—it would have destroyed their hope and faith in a time when they needed it more than ever.

Had they known what was proven to be true and consistent with the statistics—that even as they all rallied and searched, prayed and held vigils, made signs and search parties—that poor, sweet, beloved Mariam had already been Savagely Raped, Beaten, and Murdered, it would have only broken their hearts all the sooner.

Death Notification

The time had finally arrived to deliver the Notification of Death to Mariam's family. Once again, I was grateful for Grace O'Connor sitting alongside me.

It was difficult for me to spend too much time with the Grieving families after I had informed them of their Loved One's Passing. It wasn't because I lacked sympathy or compassion. I was mindful of their Grief, and I understood its significance.

But I didn't want to be the person helping them through it. It was a lifelong process, with many waves.

People like Grace O'Connor were much more qualified to handle the emotional journey commonly experienced as people traveled through the Grief process. Victim Advocates were there because they had the experience and knowledge that was usually unknown to the Loved Ones regarding how to navigate the stages of Grief without being consumed by it.

Their constant attention, check-ins, monitoring, and intercession between resources and those in need of them made them an integral and instrumental component toward the healthy processing and recovery of our Citizenry. They were imperative for the mental health of our nation.

Their role was decidedly different than mine, and as a Calling, it required an entirely different set of qualifications, personality traits, and skills than what I offered.

I was a Sheepdog. I was trained to Protect. I was a man of action.

The best way that I could show someone that I cared about their Loss was to avenge their Suffering. I was here to offer a temporary support, and to let them know I was going to take care of their Loved One. My purpose was to let them see I was cognizant of who she was, that she was loved, and that her life had meaning. They needed to see that I was sincere in my desire to find the person or persons responsible for doing Harm to the Loved One they were now Grieving for, and that I understood the reasons they Mourned.

When they looked into my eyes, they needed to know that I saw that the person I was trying to seek Justice for wasn't just facts in a case, or a number on a list. They wanted confirmation that I understood that she may have been just another Citizen to our nation and part of my assigned job duties, but to them, she was a Mother, a Wife, a Sister, and a Daughter.

What they really wanted, of course, was for her to be safely home with them and for none of this to have happened.

They trusted me to do this for them. I was the only resource they had to carry out that which they could not. They did not possess the tools, the manpower, the skill set, or the technology to investigate the Murder of their Loved One.

Nothing would ever bring their Loved One back. I couldn't undo the damage that had already been done. But as I sat there speaking with them, explaining to them what I knew and was going to do, I wanted them to know that I was in this fight with them, and I would not let them down.

Along the path, they would be introduced to many new people who would be there to help them through this process. They would meet with Grief Counselors, Financial Compensation Advisors, and have an appointed Victim Advocate Agent that would work directly with them to help them through their time of need. They would have Grace O'Connor overseeing their recovery and providing them with any additional help they may need as they came to terms with their Loss. Their emotional needs regarding Grieving, depression, and acceptance of their Loved One's Death would be addressed entirely.

They would have significant anger, and feelings that they may not be entirely comfortable expressing. They would find themselves immersed in resentment and helpless frustration that might overflow into bursts of rage. There would be a desire for revenge, to exact Justice in the physical sense—an eye for an eye. They would want the Killer to Suffer, and to be killed in the slowest, most Violently Savage way possible—and it still would not be enough.

But their own anger wouldn't matter—they would never get the type of Biblical eye-for-an-eye Justice that they wanted. As strict as our society had become—as intolerant of Acts of Violence as we had become because of the Sentence Reform Act and the Great Reformation, they wouldn't get any of that. They would be helpless, and that would make them feel extremely vulnerable, ineffective, and out of control. As much as they might want to fulfill the desires in their heart to exact revenge, they would not be able to.

They needed me to be the channel for their anger, hate, bitterness, and feelings of revenge. And I was happy to provide it. I was happy to be that person for them. I understood what they needed, and needed me to be, and I welcomed it. I embraced it. I could do that for them; I could be *that* person.

And when it was all over, when the person or persons responsible had been found, Charged, Convicted, and Sentenced, my work would be done, and I would move on. It would bring them a nominal sense of Closure. The road ahead for them would still hold many dark days, moments of silence, and a lifetime of family events with an Empty Space at their table.

I observed the tears falling down her mother's cheeks, the way her father clutched his wife's hands with his own, willing himself to stay strong enough for both of them. But the pain in his eyes was undeniable, and as strong of a man as he had believed himself to be, I knew there was nothing that could have prepared him for the bolt of pain that was ripping through his Soul at this moment. The only thing I could do was to meet his gaze, to show him I felt his grief, and to help him understand I would not quit until I had done all that I could to help them.

I saw Mariam's sisters try to console each other, standing behind their mother, each Suffering on their own, but Suffering more knowing how others were also being hurt. I watched as their husbands tried to grapple with the magnitude of what was happening, processing the monumental pain that was flooding the room with tangible shock, disbelief, and a hurt so deep it drew the air from their lungs. It was a pain that they could not stop their wives and in-laws from having to experience, and the helplessness was unbearable for them.

But it was to Mariam's husband that my eyes finally rested, and through him I understood yet again why all of this was so wrong. He was a broken man.

There was a psychologist named Paul Eckman during the 1970s who determined that there were distinct emotions that were universal—a shared series of facial expressions that were identifiable around the globe and shared by the whole of Humanity regardless of culture. But there are some emotions, some expressions, and some Body Language that most people rarely encounter.

Among those are the signs of a man that has completely surrendered, accepting defeat. It was a look that may pass in a moment, or it could be found after years of self-destructive behavior. Sometimes, though, it was a look that followed the news of the Death of a Loved One, and I had seen it before. It was the look of a broken spirit; the absolute last straw that had connected his will to carry on to the last piece of Humanity he had been holding on to. And when it was present, it was worse than Grief. It was worse than anger. It was beyond that scope of rage that bordered on vigilantism and causing Violence in the name of vengeance.

There was nothing more sorrowful than to see that another person had lost their own Will to Live because life had finally dealt a blow that was simply too much to endure. It was a place of darkness that few could ever climb out of, and it was a journey into the unknown that few would ever find the depths of. And Mariam's husband was there.

I could not do my work any better or faster with the weight of his emotional and psychological turmoil pressing down on me, and yet it felt as though I were battling time. Justice, in my mind, was the only thing that could at least make this man realize that this period of horrific, traumatic Grief would someday pass. He couldn't see it now. All he could see was how devastating this was to his world, to his family, and to his children; he couldn't see beyond how he felt in this exact moment.

I couldn't help this man reconcile the reality of his situation or process his pain. Those were the duties of the Victim Advocates and the Grief Counselors. All he could do was try to carry on, if not for himself, then for the love he held for his Deceased wife and the Mother of his children, children who were also going to be hurting and would need him now more than ever.

Looking around the room, I knew that no matter what I said, it would never be enough. But they needed to see me there. I needed to be there with them so they knew I understood Mariam was someone worth fighting for.

SIXTEEN – KU —3—

The Details of Katarina's Forensic Report

The details of what they had done to little Katarina had been sickening to read in the forensic report, and the meticulous work by the Medical Examiner for her Postmortem Examination had all but taken my breath away as I pored through his pages detailing every injury her poor little body had sustained over the months. As with many who have been Abused, her fragile frame told an unspoken story that would not have been able to be concealed through X-rays and a thorough Physical Examination by an astute doctor.

The report verified two separate semen deposits. Although this was horrific, it was also extremely beneficial to our investigation. Every Foreign National was required to submit a DNA sample for the national database in order to secure entry into our nation. This was a long-established law that had been implemented many decades ago precisely for this reason. It gave us the confirmation of identities that we needed and proved that the two Foreign Nationals connected to the textile factory were the Suspects responsible for the Sexual Assault against our young Victim. We would use this to build our case against them regarding her Abduction, Captivity, and Death. We would be able to use the forensic report to obtain Search Warrants for the entire property and factory as well as put out Arrest Warrants for the two men.

Additionally, while it complicated the role that Daegan Kyl had in things, it did remove him from any liability regarding the Sexual Assault of little Katarina. We could still pursue liability for Death and illegal burial, and even possibly link him to her Captivity, but our case was decidedly thinner without his direct connection to the Sexual Assaults we knew to have been committed against her.

She had not been provided with any type of medical care for her injuries after her Abduction that we knew of, and while we could not conclusively say that little Katarina had been Intentionally Hurt by them beyond their Violent Mistreatment and the Callous Disregard for her Safety which was an obvious byproduct of their Sexual Abuse, she had sustained significant trauma to her small frame. The longer she had remained in their prison, the more her body had deteriorated, showing the signs of malnourishment through her teeth, her frail bones, and even through her thin hair. On top of all of that, each of those signs would have been more than apparent to anyone that had taken the time to pay attention to her.

This only seemed to confirm that which was already known—or could have been easily surmised—and it was enough to leave even the most emotionally hardened among us with a lump in our throat and an unquenchable rage at the thought of those responsible. The gradual deterioration of her physical condition revealed that the men responsible for her Abduction had never intended for her to be allowed to Survive, and they had watched her as she faded away and lost her strength, health, and hope from the beginning, for she had begun her slow march toward Death the very first day they had Taken her.

The Abduction and Captivity of Katarina had been the direct causation for the decline in her health; there were no other factors that could have led to her deterioration beyond the environmental ones caused by her Abductor. It was strikingly clear that her Abductor had ignored all signs and evidence of it even as her condition worsened. Worse than that, the men that had used this little girl sexually had continued to use and abuse her despite her Suffering. Throughout those agonizingly long months of Captivity, her painful cries and begging for relief had clearly fallen on deaf ears.

These men had Stolen so much more from her than just her Sexual Innocence; they had Stolen her trust in Humanity, her trust in adults, and possibly her faith. All that she had once known and held dear had been taken away from her, as she undoubtedly struggled to understand why no one was coming to save her and why her parents had never found her. These men had destroyed everything that was Innocent about a young girl's very life, and decimated all hope, magic, and beauty she might have once thought to be found within our world before she finally succumbed to her Death.

All I could see in my mind's eye were her tiny little toes with their pink nail polish and the way her light blonde hair had curled around her angelic face. She was just a little girl, and we had not saved her. *None of us had saved her.* No one had kept her safe—in one of the greatest nations in the world, during one of the safest times in the history of our country, and we still could not keep her safe from the monsters that had come into our nation and preyed upon the most Vulnerable among us. We had failed this little girl, and we had failed her family.

The Watchers On The Wall Speech: A Proclamation To The World

Fellow Americans,

What is worth holding on to when you have lost everything? What is there left to give when everything you have once held dear has been stripped away from you in some tremendous sweep of adversity? How does one find the strength to continue the battle when there is nothing worth fighting for?

As much as it Grieves us that this is the truth of our tenuous situation, it is the current state of the nation in which we Americans are now forced to Live and attempt to Survive. We are surrounded by tragedy, and from that tragedy there will be no reprieve until We The People force it to end. Too many of us have known what it means to Lose a Loved One through Violence, and far too many of us have been forced to endure the debilitating, crippling consequences of such Violent Tragedies within our nation.

The Blood of the Innocent has spilled from coast to coast, from city to city, and from border to border. We have been forced to sacrifice the Lives of our Loved Ones on the altar of permissive Criminal Justice laws, ineffective 'rehabilitation' efforts by a government which allows Known Predators to walk among us, and open borders that have flooded our nation with those who would do more Harm than Good. The Cost for these policies has been paid for with the blood of our Beloved Friends and Family, and that price has been paid immeasurably.

To Lose our Loved Ones through Violence is an incomprehensible Injustice from which we may never recover. It is the Senseless Tragedy and inherently Unjust Act of Evil that can never be justified or excused.

The Death of a Loved One through an Act of Violence causes us to lose parts of ourselves. Our perception of the world changes. Our blind, simple Faith in Humanity is Lost. The naive belief that God will protect us from the most horrific of tragedies is shockingly ripped away from us. We find ourselves being tested by our Heavenly Father in ways in which we never believed we were capable of Surviving, let alone Enduring and Overcoming.

Some tragedies will claim not only the Life Wrongfully Stolen, but the Will to Live from those who could not recover from their Grief and Loss. That is the Ripple Effect of another's actions, the True Cost of Violence. When a Predator Claims a Life, they are not just Robbing the Victim of their ability and Divine Right to Live out the rest of their God-given days as they were entitled to, they are causing a Ripple Effect which will send shock waves throughout everyone's Lives that knew the Victim and Loved them.

But there is one fact that is inescapable, and we are left with the bitter truth of it always:

We must spend the rest of our days upon this earth without the person that we have Loved and Treasured.

Those who have endured such tragedies are Survivors. They are the Bereaved who have been Left Behind, and they must learn to adapt and overcome the circumstances that have forever changed their own Lives as well as all those who were also impacted.

Our 'leaders' have told us that we should have a reasonable expectation that our Loved Ones might end up Losing their Lives through the Violent Actions of Others, and we must accept this as a matter of Random Chance—as part of Living within highly populated areas. They have told us that we should expect it because it is part of Humanity and Life within a 'Civilized society'.

We believe that many of us Americans and Westerners have already proven this to be a contrived fallacy used to excuse the Violence being perpetrated against us.

Those among us that are *law-abiding, Good Human Beings* have already proven that we are more than capable of Living peacefully together without Causing Harm to ourselves or others. We have demonstrated through our Self-Control and Civility that we do *not* have to accept their falsehoods regarding the Inevitability of Violence, their assertion that we must continue to Live within a society that is at the mercy of those who would Commit such Acts of Violence, and the misguided belief that we are somehow helpless to prevent it from being as such.

It is time for every Western Nation to ask some particularly important questions.

Why should we have to come to terms with the Violence being forced upon us? *Why* should we have to learn to make sense of it, to learn to accept that Violence is a 'normal' part of living within a society? *Why* should we as a Civilized society be expected to co-exist with those who would not only Harm us, but also coexist with those who would tell us that we must allow it to occur?

There is no need or excuse for Violent Death; to normalize it and expect the Loved Ones of a Victim of a Senseless Act of Violence to try and simply 'accept' it is an illogical and unfair expectation.

They *should not have to* be able to come to terms with it.

My Fellow Americans, we implore you to pray earnestly about the state of our nation and the tragedies that you have watched your Fellow Citizens contend with. Ask yourself if it is due to the lack of accountability of your government leaders.

Ask yourself if there is adequate action being taken by your government to Protect the Innocent from being Victimized by the Violent Predators that walk among us, or if our failed government leaders are the reason why they have been unleashed among us without any regard for our Safety.

For the sake of Humanity, and for all those who have been Lost under such Violent conditions, I implore you to take action now.

The time has come for all Americans to Rise Collectively Together and put an end to the Butchery that has occurred on American soil unchecked and unchallenged.

We The People must take a stand and make the declaration that we will no longer submit to the Violence being forced upon us, and we have no obligation to allow it.

We hold the power, My Fellow Americans.

Let us never forget this, and let no American Suffer again. Neither the Victim, nor those Left Behind, should ever be created on American soil. Remember who we are, and do not ever forget the power that we collectively hold. By every Citizens' pledge, American Lives will never be subject to Inhumane Cruelty and Devastation again.

American Lives will Bleed No More.

The Watchers On The Wall
On this date, the one-hundred sixty-eighth day,
In the Year of our Lord, 2045

SEVENTEEN – RS —4—

Finding Rebecca's Sex Offender

Stanton went through the database for known Sex Offenders in the SPD area. It was entirely possible that he could use the facial recognition program to identify the Suspect through the campus surveillance footage. Given the likelihood that it was the same Suspect we were looking for in Mariam's Abduction, if we could identify him through the campus cameras, it was going to help connect the two cases. Stanton was currently working to crossmatch the two Suspects captured in each camera. It wouldn't be conclusive, but it could measure height, approximate weight, and a general shape and similarities in movement that could help build a criminal case.

It wasn't a long list. Very few were eligible for reintegration back into society, and the strict requirements made it extremely difficult for most to comply. Exile was far more common, followed with the Death Penalty for those who had caused Physical Harm to an Innocent.

The database did not hold any Violent Sex Offenders, nor did it hold any Pedophiles.

Neither were eligible for reintegration programs following Conviction, and neither would have been capable of Committing an Act of Rape after Sentencing anyhow. There was no recovery from the castration process that was a mandatory part of the Sentencing for such Predators. Removing the desire was one part, removing the ability was essential. The secondary part of their Sentencing always resulted in either Exile or Death.

It was small comfort for the Bereaved who lost a Loved One due to the Violence caused by such Predators, but at least they could take comfort in knowing they would never re-offend.

The price for taking a Life was Life.

Scope of Campus Security Investigation

They had granted officer Stanton full access to the university security system and had been working on compiling all the known data that featured either Rebecca or Mariam. His first order of business had been to take the surveillance footage of the man that had dragged Rebecca into the bushes and work it through the facial recognition program. This process could take anywhere from a few minutes to a few hours or days, depending on how familiar the person was with it.

Once he had gained a positive ID of the Rapist and compiled all the additional footage or information linked to him, he would forward that information to me as well as to the SPD S.W.A.T. so they could go pick him up. It wouldn't take long for the Arrest Warrants and Search Warrants for his home to be processed, and as soon as it was ready, S.W.A.T. would get the man cleared from the streets and placed behind bars until his trial. The facial recognition program had a twenty-four-point recognition grid before it declared a confirmed match, so it was all but taken as gospel when it provided a hit.

Getting confirmation would validate everything required for the Warrants, and the video would provide the evidence necessary for keeping the man incarcerated pending trial. Keeping such Predators off the street was a vital component to protecting the Sanctity of Human Life. The evidence that had already been gathered from the security cameras alone would be enough to secure his Conviction, but that was only the beginning of how the SPD Medical Examiner, along with our forensic and technology experts, would work to ensure that his Conviction was ironclad.

Along with securing the identity of Rebecca's Rapist, Officer Stanton would also continue going through the university cameras to catalog all known surveillance of the two women spanning as far back as he could. Just as a precaution, he would work through the data and see if there were any noticeable stalkers or random men following either of them. If he found anything, it would be added to the case to be used during the trial.

Soon enough, we would know who the man was, and have him behind bars. He didn't know it, but his days of freedom as an American Citizen were soon to be over, and his life forfeit. No man, having Committed such Violence against one of his Fellow Citizens, would have the pleasure of being Sentenced to Exile. Whoever this man was today would no longer matter by the time his trial was over. It wouldn't matter what he had done in his life, what he had accomplished, or how successful his life had been. The true measure of this man had been revealed by the decisions he had made on that fateful day when he chose to Violate the Human Rights of his Fellow Citizen.

Within thirty days of his Conviction, they would sentence this man to Death.

The Ripple Effect of Rebecca's Death

There would be dissenting opinions regarding the choices Rebecca made, but it was not up to me to take sides or lay blame. As compassionate and forgiving as a good deal of people might want the answers to be, the Rule of Law was not meant to be processed through emotions; it applied even-handed, fact-based judgment for all.

Rebecca had faced issues I could never imagine having to experience, nor endure, the consequences of. She was not responsible for having caused any of the events that set her on a downward spiral toward self-destruction. Nothing in her behavior, her actions, or her lifestyle choices had created any type of chain reaction that would have been the catalyst for what had been done to her. Like millions of other Rape Victims, she had been Assaulted as a matter of convenience and ease by an Unknown Assailant in an Attack that she could not have ever expected nor prevented.

All that she was supposed to have become, all that she could have become, would never be known to us in this Lifetime. She would permanently remain exactly as she was, impressed within everyone's memories as a daughter, friend, student, and artist, but never as a girlfriend, fiancé, wife, expectant mother, mother, or grandmother.

There would always be missing sections in her story because it would forever remain unknown and untold. Her parents would never watch their daughter graduate from college, hang her first painting in an art gallery, or meet the love of her life. They would never experience that overwhelming love for their daughter as they grant their blessing to the young man asking for their permission to marry her.

All that Rebecca would have become was forever lost and would never be realized. Her girlfriends would never become her bridesmaids, and she would never be theirs. She would never experience the love of her life as he takes a knee and extends his heart and hand to invite her to share their future together as one. It meant that she would never plan a wedding, run away together on a honeymoon to a private oasis where nothing, and no one, existed beyond herself and her lover—at least for a few brief days or weeks before reality beckoned them back home once again to begin their new life together as husband and wife.

Her parents would never have what was Stolen from them replaced; they, too, were being robbed of their own experiences and treasured memories. Her mother would never help her pick out a wedding dress, help her find her precious traditional items of something borrowed and something blue. They would never share the joy of celebrating the marriage of their daughter and help them welcome a new son into their family. Her father would never walk his daughter down the aisle, or dance with her after he bravely gave her away to a man that he had entrusted with her heart and her physical, emotional, and spiritual well-being. Losing Rebecca meant that instead of being able to let go of his daughter by placing her heart and future into the care of her husband, her father had to bury her instead. It was an obscene abomination of realities that should never have become any parents' nightmare.

It meant that her parents would never see their daughter carrying her first baby, hold her hand as she was in labor, or welcome their first grandchild into the world. The Death of their only daughter meant they would never know how it felt to be grandparents, that they would never know what it felt like to have their daughter's children climb onto their laps for hugs, stories, naps, or comfort. And when they were both old, when their best years were behind them, the Death of their daughter would become even more pronounced. Their home would be filled with silence instead of the laughter and warmth of their daughter and her family, and as their final years were upon them, eventually one would pass from this world and leave the sole remaining Summers' family member here to linger and Grieve entirely alone, trapped only with their memories and sorrows.

It meant that every holiday would have an empty place at the table, every celebration would have an Empty Space where only a memory, a photograph, and an emptiness would remain for the rest of their lives, no matter how long those lives might be. Rebecca was not simply Gone from this world; she was Missing from it. She was a Human Being that was *supposed to be here*, but because poor government inaction and outright Evil existed on the very soil upon which our nation stands was never eradicated as it should have been, one random chance encounter not only changed the life and destiny of this young woman, it permanently affected and altered the lives of everyone that knew and loved her, causing a Ripple Effect of Pain, Loss, Grief, and Emptiness that will never know full restitution or heal properly.

The Death of this young woman did not simply mean that a 'Senseless Tragedy occurred', that Human Beings must accept that horrific events happened within even the most 'Civilized' of societies, or that we must contend with all that is beyond our control and understanding. This was not something that *any* Civilized society should ever have to contend with. In fact, we could challenge that by its very occurrence it was nothing short of confirmation that our society was not *'Civilized'* at all.

The American People had absolutely no obligation to respect or tolerate a system of government that failed to place its own Citizens and their Safety above everything else.

The Citizens of These United States were protected by God-given Rights that were more powerful than any man-made laws.

There was no acceptable form of power, control, or demands issued by a faction of their Countrymen that could supersede the unalienable Right to Life, Liberty, and the Pursuit of Happiness of the American People, and force them to acquiesce and bend to the will of others.

It was an erroneous interpretation of the Constitution to imply or insist otherwise. This had been best observed by the actions of the Activist Judges during the 21st century who had single-handedly transformed the face of Criminal Justice by inserting their own Humanitarian agendas into rulings—causing extensive damage as a result.

The Rights and the Protections afforded to the American People was beyond reproach or interpretation; there was no negotiation to be had.

Nothing would ever be enough to compensate for the devastating Loss of Rebecca—not to the world, and most definitely not to her parents. Some wounds would never fully heal, and the Ripple Effect was magnified all the more because of it.

PART FOUR

For you created my inmost being;
you knit me together in my mother's womb.

Psalm 139:13

EIGHTEEN – EVAN HARRISON

Interview: Evan Harrison

After we watched the surveillance footage of the campus, we knew we had enough to bring Evan Harrison in for questioning. We needed to find out why the campus security guard had walked Rebecca back to her vehicle rather than call the Police. He had obviously witnessed the state of distress that Rebecca had been in when she entered the building, and yet he had elected to dismiss the severity of the situation—or worse, had intentionally ignored it.

Additionally, we knew that someone had deleted the surveillance footage from the security cameras for that day; it stood to reason that it was Evan Harrison since he had been working and was the only logical choice for covering up the evidence. But we still needed to know for certain that he did it, aside from understanding why he would do such a thing.

We went through the process to get his Arrest Warrant and I remained on standby while the SPD brought him in.

It wasn't customary for a Research and Investigation Assistant to sit in with interrogations, but because part of what we suspected Evan Harrison to have done involved the surveillance system, I wanted Officer Stanton to be there. It couldn't hurt to ensure that someone tech-savvy was present and could handle that line of questioning.

A few hours later, we were notified that Evan Harrison was waiting for us in one of the Interview Rooms, and we headed down.

Stanton stayed on my heels, waiting for my lead as we entered the room. We both sat down along the opposite side of Evan Harrison, opting to face him directly. It also allowed us to watch his expression from the clearest vantage point possible, the preferred method for all interviews.

"We've brought you in regarding the Rape of a student on your campus," I began without ceremony.

The man sitting across from us immediately tensed and leaned forward. They did not handcuff him; a courtesy given his position as a security guard, but mostly done intending to relax him.

"I don't know what you're talking about," he declared.

"Her name was Rebecca Summers, if that helps," I responded dryly. "A dark-haired young woman. Perhaps you remember walking her back to her vehicle after she was Assaulted?"

I stared at him, challenging him to look away from my gaze.

He did—in mere seconds, balking at the direct confrontation and slumping his shoulders.

"All I did was walk her out to her car so she got there safely. I did nothing wrong," he offered.

"Wrong again; if you knew what had happened to her and you refused to report it to local Law Enforcement, take her to the hospital, or even take her to the school nurse or counseling office, I'd say you did something very, very wrong."

"I *did* take her to the student counseling office. What are you talking about?" he blurted out angrily.

I felt Officer Stanton look toward me subtly. We had no way of knowing exactly what had happened once they went inside; the building wasn't equipped with cameras. Our line of sight had ended at the front door of the administration building; once she had entered it, we were in the dark until she left again in the company of the security guard sitting across from us.

"If that's the case, what was so difficult to understand—between yourself and the student counseling office—that a young woman that had just been Raped should have been treated by the closest hospital and medical staff? That she ought to have been placed into the care of the SPD at the very least?" I responded sharply.

"I dunno, man, I was just doin' my job. She came into the security office, started crying, and I couldn't make sense of what she was saying, so I just asked her if she wanted to go to the counseling office. She shook her head yes, so I walked her down there. That's it; she went into a room with a student counselor for a while and then later after they came out the student counselor asked me to walk her to her car. So, I did—and that was it. I don't think they even saw a nurse, and I didn't notice any come into the office. But I did nothing wrong, man, I'm tellin' you. They never asked me to take her anywhere else except back to her car."

He was so certain it absolved him from any responsibility. I might have believed him, so adamant was his declaration, had he not been the only one capable of deleting the security footage for the day.

"Who was the student counselor? Do you know her name?" I asked.

"I don't know; some chick," he told me.

"Would you like to think about your answer? Just in case you're uncertain it's the right one?" I asked him patiently.

He sighed, setting both of his arms up on the table. He leaned forward so his hands rested on his forehead, and then began running his hands through his hair.

"I don't understand why I'm even here—all I did was what I was told to do."

"Why did you choose to listen to the student counselor and walk the girl out to her vehicle rather than do what they trained you to do and call the proper authorities?" I asked.

"Because a student counselor told me to!" he growled, frustrated.

"But you don't answer to the counseling office, do you? You're a security guard, aren't you? She wasn't your boss. You *have* a boss—and a manual that outlines what you're supposed to do in the event of a Rape on campus, do you not?"

"I only did what she told me to," he repeated.

"Does that include deleting the security footage?" I asked.

He froze.

"I only did what I was told to do," he said once again, more slowly.

"So, you take orders from a student counselor," I said flatly. "Would you like to tell us her name? The student counselor—the one that somehow persuaded you to drop your security protocols and responsibilities and then disregard the extreme emotional duress of the young woman that had just been Raped? Maybe you would like to reconsider—since you were just following orders and all."

My tone was disparaging, I knew, but he didn't get to sit on the sidelines as if his role wasn't equally culpable. Regardless of whether or not he was instructed by another person, he himself had a professional responsibility to do what was right—aside from a basic Humanitarian obligation. His lack of care, compassion, and effort to do what he was legally expected and required to do was shameful.

"And then I can go home?" he asked. He was completely clueless as to the severity of the predicament he was in.

"And then you can avoid taking the blame for the entire situation that led to a young woman's Disappearance and Death," I retorted.

He shook his head, shoulders slumping.

"Her name was Willow Amos," he stated blandly.

"So why were you following her orders?"

"Because I always do," he responded.

"Now why would a nice guy like yourself, a security guard, and an Honor Roll student, follow the directives of a student counselor?"

He stared hard at me, angry and hostile. He only wanted a way out.

"Did she tell you to delete the surveillance footage?" I asked.

He nodded.

"And you did this once you had returned to your office after walking Rebecca Summers to her vehicle?"

He nodded once again.

"Because Willow Amos told you to."

Sighing deeply, he nodded a third time.

"Did she ever explain to you why she wanted the footage deleted? Did you watch it?" I asked.

"I'm curious," I continued. "If you watched the surveillance footage, you would have seen the girl being Attacked and dragged into the bushes. You must have been able to discern what had happened. Did you see the man on the camera? Did you recognize him?"

He shook his head 'no' and folded his arms across his chest, leaning back further into his chair. It was a familiar look; the look of being beaten and knowing it.

"No, I'm telling you, I only did what I was told to do. I don't know who the guy was, and I had nothing to do with what happened to that girl."

"So, you just blindly followed the orders of a woman who worked in another department for no specific reason," I chastised him.

He sighed.

"Look, man. Willow Amos came with me when I reviewed the security footage. She was there the first time I saw it. After she watched it, she told me to delete all of it, so I did. That's it; that's all I know about it and that's all I did."

"And it didn't seem strange to you she wanted to conceal the evidence which revealed that a Sexual Assault had occurred?"

He looked at me guiltily, shrugging his shoulders.

"Well, I thought I had my reasons," he said. "I thought I had reason to trust her."

"Saying that like you have your doubts is probably the smartest thing you've said since you got here." I told him. "If you want to stay on that track, I recommend you tell me everything you know about Willow Amos and why, exactly, you were so willing to do her bidding. You never know, it might just save someone's life."

I paused, looking him squarely in the eye.

"Who knows? It may even be your own."

All That Evan Harrison Knew

The more I spoke with Evan Harrison, the more information I learned about Willow Amos. Evan Harrison wasn't nearly as tough as one might have imagined given his employment as a Security Guard, but then, he wasn't nearly as ethical as one would have expected, either. Ultimately, when confronted with the fear of severe consequences for his own future, he realized that communication and cooperation were the two best options. He needed to distance himself from Willow Amos.

He cracked like a porcelain doll once he knew he was looking at Exile, and he had no intention of going down alone. Pleading and begging to be overlooked, he declared he was 'just a foot soldier' and that he had done nothing wrong beyond walking Rebecca to her vehicle rather than taking her to the Police Department or hospital. He was perfectly happy to throw Willow Amos under the bus and blame her for all the decisions—including instructing him to delete the surveillance footage from the campus security cameras.

Throughout it all, he never questioned why the Rape of Rebecca needed to be concealed.

Evan Harrison provided confirmation of the resurgence of an underground group known as The Angels of Mercy. The Angels of Mercy had at one point been a serious problem for national Law Enforcement, including the FBI and Homeland Security. To my knowledge, however, there hadn't been a fully functional group active within These United States within my lifetime. There had been occasional Chapters strewn throughout the states over the decades, but they hadn't been a source of serious power since the times of the Last Stand.

Their overall purpose had been to create Chaos and to prevent the changes which had emerged from the days of The Watchers On The Wall, namely the passing of the Sentence Reform Act and other laws that created a decided shift in our culture and Criminal Justice system. To know that there was a modern group with active members who were also taking direct action to commit counter-culture deeds was no small lead.

It was more than worth its weight in gold; it was the confession we had been waiting a long time for. Through him, we learned some very relevant details about this underground movement, and gained at least some understanding of just how problematic and widespread the group was. Most importantly, we learned that its leader was Willow Amos. In all my years working cases, I'd only read about such groups existing. There had been many underground organizations during the years of the Last Stand and the early years of the Great Reformation, some more prone to Violence and Acts of Domestic Terrorism than others, but all driven by a contempt for Law and Order and an intent to disrupt society.

It seemed, after listening to Evan Harrison describe all that he knew about the group, that they were well-funded, organized, and dedicated to their agenda. Willow Amos was the only leader Evan Harrison was aware of, but that wasn't to say she was the only leader out there. According to Harrison, even though he had not ventured beyond his local group meetings, they had given him the impression that there were groups all over the Pacific Northwest, and additional groups were emerging all the time.

When I questioned why he was so quick to jump into such behaviors when he knew them to be outside of the law, he had merely stared straight into my eyes and said, "Outside of the law doesn't necessarily mean doing what is ethically or morally incorrect."

I asked him to elaborate, but he refused to speak any further, and instead asked for representation.

Our interview over, I had to be satisfied with all that he had been willing to divulge, and despite what he may or may not have believed, Evan Harrison had shared a significant amount of new information with me. Thanks to him, I now knew that not only was there some type of anarchist group working within the constructs of the university, but that Willow Amos was deeply involved. It was a solid place for us to look for the identities of these mysterious Angels of Mercy.

What Evan Harrison had done was shameful and disgusting, and above all, weak. But he was a man trying to save himself, and his devotion to Willow Amos—as well as this underground movement he was associated with—wasn't nearly as dear to his heart as his own future was, and for that, I was grateful.

An Introduction to The Angels of Mercy

It was because of the Violence created by The Angels of Mercy organization that they were classified as Domestic Terrorists during the mid-21st century. They were responsible for a plethora of Attacks against Law Enforcement as our nation transformed, but this wasn't always the case. They had originally started out as an underground movement dedicated to ensuring that the Right To Die was accessible regardless of changing laws.

When the Sentence Reform Act was on the ballot and extreme changes regarding the social climate and Criminal Justice system seemed more probable than ever before, the group which became known as The Angels of Mercy had taken root. It began as nothing more than a collective group of individuals all sharing the same mindset: the Right To Die was an individual choice and no government entity or law could deny or criminalize 'free will'. This, of course, was largely directed toward Abortion and Euthanasia, but as the times progressed, Suicide became an additional 'right' that was openly advocated for. Suicides had been increasing not only because of negative mental health reasons such as Depression, Loneliness, and PTSD, but also as the means to thwart the 'global over-population crisis' that was heavily promoted during the 21st century. The result of this ideological group being formed was an organization that became well-funded, popular, and although supposedly an 'underground movement', it was a group that would later openly boast of its famous members, celebrities, and even political supporters.

It wasn't until the passing of the Sentence Reform Act, the Right To Self-Protection Act, and the Equal Parental Rights Act, that The Angels of Mercy truly began escalation on a national scale. What had once been a movement designed to Assist and Enable Individuals so they could have access to Life-Ending drugs, Abortions, and Suicide eventually became one of the most violent Domestic Terrorist Organizations in the 21st century. The more restrictive the laws became, the more The Angels of Mercy openly rioted, burned, and bombed cities throughout the nation. During the height of their movement, they had destroyed hundreds of federal and state buildings in their effort to dismantle government power.

The Angels of Mercy took their name from the earliest references to its usage—people who believed they were helping their fellow man end their suffering by helping them die.

There had been documented criminal cases of Angels of Mercy around the world since the early nineteenth century, some of which were the most prolific Serial Killers known to Law Enforcement. Because the motivation behind such killings was so varied, it was also a demographic that encompassed a uniquely diverse collection of individuals. Adding further to the eclectic nature of those responsible was the wide array of Vulnerable Victims they targeted, as well as the manner in which they chose to help people End their Lives.

Many Angels of Mercy were drawn to the healthcare profession, where they could then access an almost unlimited selection pool of Victims to choose from. An industry which encountered Death routinely was less likely to notice a slight increase in their numbers, especially when the methods employed to carry out the Murders were usually minor enough to escape immediate attention.

It had been difficult for hospitals and other healthcare facilities to detect that they were employing an individual or group of individuals who were Taking Lives.

What was dangerous about them was their disturbing ideological justification for Committing Murder. They were genuinely of the mindset that they were Ending Human Life for justifiable reasons—that they were providing Relief for their Victims—Ending their Pain and Suffering.

Knowing that they were back—that they were being promoted on a college campus as a newly-formed group which was supposedly adhering to the original ideological values—was disconcerting at the very least. It had taken tremendous displays of government force to eradicate the group before, and had resulted in thousands of members being Exiled and Sentenced to Death before it was all said and done.

Knowing such a group was active on US soil once again was incredibly unsettling, no matter how seemingly small they currently were. Furthermore, it was evidence that times were, indeed, changing once again.

Initial Search Results—WA and RS After Rape

Stanton sent over a note regarding Rebecca from his cursory search. He was still gathering information, and I knew it would trickle in as he compiled his data. The information he sent was comprehensive, and I knew he verified everything for accuracy before forwarding it. Just as surely as a lack of information and clues could stifle an investigation, so, too, could misinformation. I was grateful to see that Stanton always listed his citations for verification; he was a man who appreciated the details just as I did.

He was looking for connections between the Victims and Willow Amos. We knew she was working in the counseling center at the same university where Mariam had taught, and Rebecca had attended. We knew she had direct contact with Rebecca through the counseling services on campus following her Rape. We also knew that she was working for the Hospice facility that had taken care of Arlan. This connected her—at least geographically and circumstantially—to three of our four Victims. Stanton was busy trying to trace all of Rebecca's actions following her Attack and find any further communication or interactions between Willow Amos and Rebecca. So far, he had found none.

For now, what I had to go on was that Willow Amos provided counseling to Rebecca Summers after she was Raped. Her direct involvement with this event would have influenced Rebecca's decision to go to the hospital and get the Rape Kit done. This would have included testing for Pregnancy, STDs, and DNA of the Assailant. How Rebecca had proceeded with the situation would have been influenced by information that Willow Amos would have provided.

Willow Amos herself would have been responsible for making sure that Rebecca Summers had followed through with her hospital visit, and yet the school records showed Rebecca had only visited once and had never returned. There were no records of Willow Amos ever attempting to contact Rebecca at any later date, which was surely against protocol for the school counseling services as well.

The question remained, however, for why a group that seemed to mirror the political ideologies of the 21st century regarding self-termination would conceal the Abductions, Rapes, and Murders of multiple Victims. It was contrary to their 'values' and made no sense for purpose or intent.

Aside from all that, there was still no explanation for how little Katarina fit in.

Willow Amos and the Winter Season Hospice Care Facility

The background search had done more than just link Willow Amos to the three separate Victims; it had given us a broad overview of who she was. Perhaps what had been the most interesting aspect of her life was that between the Hospice Care facility and the university, she had created a world that easily allowed her to find new recruits for her underground movement of anarchists. Stanton's investigative work revealed just how dedicated her efforts at recruitment had been.

There were currently fifteen other employees of the Hospice Care facility that were also students in the same healthcare program as Willow Amos. She had been affiliated with the Greater Seattle Area University for the last five years, during which there had been almost thirty students from the same nursing program that had also worked at least part-time for the Winter Season Hospice Care facility. It was possible it was nothing more than a coincidence, but that was what our investigation would either prove or disprove as time went on.

Because Willow Amos was linked to so many students that were also employed with the Hospice Care facility, it widened the entire search perimeter to include the employment and data records of the Winter Season company. Officer Stanton would scrutinize the ownership, business headquarters, history of the company, stocks, and any public news stories.

Every single student linked to the Hospice Care facility would have their entire identity completely dissected. If any of these students were found to be connected to transportation or driving, owned a white van, were hired as drivers, or were assigned in any manner to work with Arlan, Stanton would uncover it.

I didn't have to wait around for the system to do its research. Once Officer Stanton had the information programmed in, the machine set to work on its own, sending out any updates or variables that might need to be addressed before it issued its final report. Officer Stanton had been meticulous about getting me the results of every report and new pieces of information the instant they fell into his hands, and I knew he would work on this with the same urgency a case such as this commanded. We needed answers; we needed to know more about who this woman was. She was deeply connected to several very serious Crimes—Crimes Against Humanity—and there were Victims out there who had lost their entire futures. There were Loved Ones who needed to have answers—the truth—and to be told what had happened.

Soon enough, I would receive more feedback, including the identities of every employee linked between the university, Willow Amos, and the Winter Season Hospice Care facility. Then Officer Stanton would begin the second phase of his research, which was to do an extensive background check of each Suspect identified. With each name confirmed, he would begin searching every known database at our disposal, using all CCTV systems, and known information since the time of Arlan's Disappearance.

NINETEEN – STANTON AND ARRESTS

Stanton Update: Two Foreign Nationals

Stanton had been spending his time doing various research efforts trying to garner any intelligence related to the two Foreign Nationals. All we had to go on was the information made available through the US Immigrations and Customs database; it was old and offered extraordinarily little verification. The only information we knew for certain was through the factory, and gaining access to it was contingent upon securing Warrants first.

As much as Stanton had applied the tools at his disposal, he could not verify any known connections between any of the Victims and the two Foreign Nationals. There was virtually no tangible evidence that they were even in the country or that they ever were. Stanton couldn't link them to any databases, banks, or utilities. They had no credit cards or anything else that created either a cyber or paper trail.

Despite every effort to verify they were not only involved with either Daegan Kyl or the gravesite, but culpable, it had been impossible to link them directly to anything or anyone. The two men were little more than a pair of names and basic descriptions. We had nothing to go on beyond the photos on their Visas and the original documentation that they had used to enter our nation more than a decade earlier.

Since then, although we knew them to be associated with the textile corporation and the factory, we had no conclusive evidence to support that they were still there or even in the country. We needed access to the factory and the rest of the land surrounding it. We needed to go through the building inch by inch and verify that it was abandoned.

As unlikely as it was that they were still there, we needed to see if the factory itself yielded any clues that might help us locate the two men or provide us with evidence which could link them to our Victims. For now, the only proof we had that the two men had been in the US recently was the physical evidence left after the Assault of Katarina Urakov. We knew they existed; it was imperative that we locate them and take them into custody. God only knew if there were other Victims out there or if any new ones were being created.

Progression toward Arrest Warrants

We were making progress within the investigation and working toward Arrest Warrants. After meeting with Evan Harrison and gaining first-hand confirmation of the existence of an underground anarchist movement, it provided the evidence necessary to at least bring in all the employees of the Winter Season Hospice Care facility who were also students at GSAU. I felt confident that once we brought them in for questioning that at least some of them would talk once they realized they were all likely to be charged and found equally culpable for any crimes committed by any of the members.

Evan Harrison's statement, combined with the video surveillance footage of the white van on the property at the time of Arlan Randall's Disappearance, gave suitable cause to detain everyone potentially linked to The Angels of Mercy through their employment at the Winter Season Hospice Care facility.

Evan Harrison had implicated Willow Amos by declaring her a leader of The Angels of Mercy, and by stating that he both received and carried out orders given by her. I now had enough of a confession from Evan Harrison's statements to Arrest him for Obstruction of a Criminal Investigation, Tampering with Evidence, and Intent to Conceal a Crime, as well as linking him to all the same gang-related charges that would be attached to the rest of The Angels of Mercy.

Unless I could find definitive proof of their involvement with the Disappearance and Death of Arlan Randall or any of the other Victims found in that field, the most I believed I could secure would be Exile. Only by directly connecting specific members to the Victims themselves could I hope for stronger charges and the Death Penalty. Still, as it stood, I already felt confident there would be enough to at least reach the Sentencing of Exile. No gangs or person connected to Domestic Terrorism, let alone those responsible for committing Crimes Against Humanity, would ever be allowed to remain in These United States after Conviction. Some things were beyond Reform.

Identification of LeRoy Jones

Officer Stanton finally had the facial recognition results for the man responsible for the Rape of Rebecca Summers. His name was LeRoy Jones, and though he had a history of issues, he had nothing on his record that would have resulted in Reform, Exile, or the Death Penalty.

He had skated under the radar of local Police for years, though, and had a history riddled with questionable actions and an overall lack of accountability. His history was troublesome enough that someone should have detected the personality, anger, and risks contained within; there were obvious red flags.

Immediately upon receiving his name, I applied for an Arrest Warrant. It was approved quickly, and I forwarded the information to the SPD S.W.A.T. Division to bring him in. There was no reason to wait; it was far better to have him removed from the streets as quickly as possible.

Meeting with the Chief

I elected to meet with the Chief and provide him with all the information I had gained so far relating to Daegan Kyl and the two Foreign Nationals. I did this purely because of the political implications posed by their non-Citizenship status. Professionally and legally, I had no obligation to clear anything through any Police Chief or County Sheriff, but in the interest of preserving a good working relationship, I wanted to include him beforehand. I did not want him blind-sided by any fallout the case might receive; I thought it better to confer with him before taking any direct action. Depending on how severe the pushback—if there would be any at all—the weight of it would not only land on my shoulders but also his, as he was the one who called me in.

Sitting at his desk, I watched as he closed out my report and the attachments containing the evidence gathered so far.

"This will not go over well, that's for sure," he began.

I shook my head.

"But you still haven't located either of them?" he asked, referring to the two Foreign Nationals.

"No, I'm ready to put out the Arrest Warrant for Kyl, but so far Stanton has found no trace of the other two men."

"So you're wanting to search the entire property now, including the factory itself."

I nodded.

"Well, that's logical. It is their only listed address on record. Unless you had any other leads?" he queried.

"No, Sir. That's it. Everything comes back to the factory. Now that we have conclusive evidence linking the two men to the Sexual Assault of Katarina Urakov, my next step would naturally be to search everything and issue Arrest Warrants."

"But you know what this could lead to..." he trailed off.

The Chief leaned back into his chair and rubbed the bridge of his nose, closing his eyes and sighing heavily.

"All right, well, if you want my honest opinion, I think you were right to tread with caution and allow me some input. And as much as I hate to do anything to impede your investigation, if you sincerely want my advice, then I recommend we put a hold on everything related to the two Foreign Nationals and run this up the chain of command and see where it goes."

He looked at me.

"I know it's not what you want to hear, but it's what I would do. If any of this got out before we have them securely in custody, God only knows what could happen. This wasn't just any crime; it was a sadistic, obscene, Violent Crime Against a Child. Everyone in our nation would be out for blood."

I agreed.

With that, I left it in the care of the Chief to do with as he saw fit. I wanted to do this as much by the book as possible, but I also didn't want my investigation waylaid by 3rd party characters who ultimately had their own agendas and political interests at heart. I saw the merit of trying to ensure there was no backlash if I were to make the erroneous miscalculation and proceed with Arrests—which was always a matter of public record. I saw and appreciated the Chief's decision to be cautious.

But this was no ordinary case, and these were no ordinary Suspects. We as a society had long since determined that those who crossed our borders and invaded our lands intending to do Harm were not to be provided with any of the Constitutional Rights afforded to our Fellow Countrymen. Above all else, Justice, along with resounding accountability, must be carried out. For this to happen, I needed them Captured, alive and unaccosted, so that I could get their full confessions on record.

Stanton Update: Stalking

After Stanton accessed the GSAU security surveillance, he was able to invest more time into retracing the exact footsteps of both Rebecca and Mariam. The facial recognition software was ideal for such legwork, as it allowed Stanton to go through hundreds of hours of security footage without physically needing to do it on his own. Because of this technological advantage, he accumulated a surprising number of hits for each of our Victims and LeRoy Jones.

It did not take Stanton long to see a pattern of stalking emerge. LeRoy Jones, it seemed, had been watching both Rebecca and Mariam for several weeks prior to his Assaults against them. The compilation of data left extraordinarily little defense for LeRoy Jones to deny his involvement as premeditated Attacks.

By comparing the videos of LeRoy Jones on the campus surveillance and the grocery store security cameras, it also created a 99% probability match based on movement, height, and form. The grocery store footage would never provide conclusive proof of his identity regarding Mariam's Abduction, but combined with the footage gained by the GSAU campus surveillance, it was sufficient evidence to verify that both women had been subjected to Assaults by the same man.

The accumulated data did not provide us with a motive, nor did it explain to us how or why he had selected them. The two women had little in common physically, and Stanton found no connection between the two. LeRoy Jones had never taken a class at the university, nor had he ever registered to attend. Unless LeRoy Jones confessed and provided us with his reasons, we would likely never understand how he came to choose his targets.

Stanton was sure of one thing, however, after having reviewed the surveillance footage. The school kept all security footage for one year, and Stanton reviewed every moment. His conclusion was that LeRoy Jones, although having been sighted on campus randomly over the months with no known reason for it, had stalked no other women during that time. No other patterns emerged, no other Victims were reported, and there were no other Rapes documented on record either through campus security or the nurse's office. This was not to say that prior to Rebecca and Mariam that no other women had been Victimized by LeRoy Jones, merely that there was no evidence to support that any others had been identified on the GSAU campus.

The one last observation noted by Stanton seemed insignificant on its own, but combined with what else we knew, it likely wasn't a coincidence. LeRoy Jones did not seem to wander the campus randomly until he began following first Rebecca and then Mariam. Prior to that, he only visited one location: the building where Willow Amos worked.

Plan for Arrests

At long last, the time had come to proceed with Detainments and Arrests. I felt confident we had established enough connections to at least bring some Suspects in for questioning. The first task was to take the steps necessary to do this with no one getting tipped off or having time to either flee or work out alibis or cover-stories for either themselves or their cohorts.

Daegan Kyl was at the top of my list, along with Willow Amos and LeRoy Jones. As we were still trying to track down any sign of the two Foreign Nationals, my hands were tied until I figured out my next move. For the time being, what was within my control were the three known subjects I could confirm were involved with either the gravesite or our Victims.

It was a solid starting point and marked a decided shift between the research and investigation phase and the point where I could begin extracting information through interviews. It was one of the parts I most enjoyed, as it allowed me to engage directly with the Suspects and put my more analytical perceptions to use. One could learn a lot just through observation, conversation, and reading Body Language.

I relied on Stanton for providing ample clues and the unquestionable evidence necessary to secure Convictions. But it was through Human interaction that motives were often revealed and confirmed, and knowing the reasons 'why' Suspects committed the Crimes they did was not only vital to me, it was the answer most often sought by the Loved Ones of the Victims. Whenever possible, I wanted to be able to share those answers.

Arrests and Search Warrants

We secured Arrest Warrants for Daegan Kyl, Willow Amos, and LeRoy Jones. I wanted them to be carried out simultaneously to eliminate any chance of warning one another. Once that was underway, we would proceed with Phase Two, issuing Search Warrants.

Three different teams would carry the Search Warrants out, put together by the Chief and composed of SPD Peacekeepers. It should minimize risks with the Arrest Warrants being carried out first, and I specified that no Search Warrants were to be conducted until we had each of our Suspects safely in custody. This alone would reduce any Harm to any of the Peacekeepers.

The Search Warrants were similar for each of our Suspects. They allowed us to search virtually every aspect of their lives with unlimited access. For Daegan Kyl, this included all known properties, including his moving company and all trucks and vehicles on-site and registered to the corporation. It also included a penthouse located only a few blocks from the SPD Headquarters in downtown Seattle, and a larger estate located across the waters on Lake Washington.

For LeRoy Jones, our Search Warrant would be much easier to conduct as he didn't own any property, assets, or a vehicle. He only had one place to search. It was a small dwelling unit, a studio comprised of one room.

For Willow Amos, we would search her dwelling unit and vehicle. She rented a small home near the university; it was a bungalow with an attached garage, no basement or attic. We would also go through the GSAU's counseling office and the security department for good measure. We would have access to all of Willow Amos's school and professional records available through the GSAU. And finally, we would access the Winter Season Hospice Care facility.

In addition, we would secure and comb through each of their electronics and any other electronic systems they used with meticulous detail and precision. By the end, with virtually unlimited access and resources at our disposal, we would know our Suspects better than they even knew themselves, and know all the dirty little secrets their past lovers only dreamed of learning. Our Constitution afforded them limited protections, but even following the letter of the law still provided the US government almost unfathomable reach the likes of which our Founding Fathers could never have anticipated or imagined.

TWENTY – JARRETT AND KENNEDY

The Stadium

Officer Stanton sent me a message letting me know where I could find the two SPD Detectives that had initially investigated Katarina. It was serendipitous that they were doing their annual Physical Fitness Assessments over at the sports arena complex where all the professional sporting events were held. Sports complexes such as the one in Seattle were almost always selected for the training, recruitment, and routine fitness testing locations because of the security systems set in place. They were the most secure above-ground facilities for Citizens available in the West.

Being able to locate and confine the two SPD Detectives within the stadium was only something that could ever work to my advantage.

Because their training also involved monitoring their heart rates and sleeping patterns, the three-day training periods allowed for plenty of time for observation by both their Superiors and the medical and fitness staff employed to oversee their performances and evaluate them. What it provided me with, however, was an opportunity to approach them with no warning. They couldn't feign being too busy, previous engagements, or any type of physical injury or distress to extract themselves from meeting with me. Knowing that they could not leave the premises during their training period was only going to make it easier to get them cornered and compliant.

Detective Jarrett's name was attached to the files within the Missing Persons database that were all problematic. His partner, Detective Kennedy, had signed none. The evidence seemed to point to Detective Jarrett acting on his own, but I couldn't verify this for certain without interviewing them or extracting a confession. I had no evidence to clear Detective Kennedy at this point.

I imagined it would be more difficult for them to lie directly to an Investigator, and their paranoia and fear of being caught would affect their calm exterior. Even being questioned about their cases might lead to one of them cracking under the pressure and fear of having been found out. I was going to invite them to come to the Department and make formal statements, and then see which one balked, delayed, or came up with excuses. Body Language and eye contact would go a long way toward seeing which of the two was more culpable.

Jarrett and Kennedy at the Stadium

The men doing their Physical Fitness testing were working hard to do their best, and for most it was obvious they took their health and well-being seriously. They knew the repercussions of being out of shape and unable to sprint while out on the Front-Line. It wasn't difficult to understand that their overall health and fitness equaled strength and power whilst out on the streets, and when any random encounter could result in Physical Violence, Attack, or Ambush, it was imperative that they have the wherewithal to fend off any would-be Assailants. As had always been observed in the past, the men and women working at the SPD were no different from any of the other Police Departments around the US; they knew what was on the line and took their own standards seriously, always striving for the best.

Of course, it was easier for some and harder for others.

I asked one of the group leaders to point out Detective Jarrett and his partner, Detective Kennedy. Jarrett struggled against the cross-fit course from start to finish, although he performed better with the encouragement of his companion—a man who seemed used to carrying his less agile partner as a matter of routine. In all fairness, Detective Jarrett seemed to try, but his physical disadvantages made even the most basic of tasks more work. His height deficit made it harder to reach, his extra weight further hindered him, and somewhere in there, one had to account for the mere possibility that he simply wasn't cut out for physical dominance. Despite all this, the man trudged on, sweating profusely, and tiring more so than his competitors.

After the final Peacekeepers made it through the finish line and their times were marked, one of the group leaders blew his whistle and signaled for a break. I watched as Detective Jarrett bent over, clutched his knees, and remained still for several moments, trying to catch his breath. Sweat drenched his shirt and his bald head glistened in the sunlight.

I spoke with the group leader, asking him to send the two men my way. Nodding his head, he motioned for the man standing alongside him to go collect the two Detectives. The man complied, sprinting out to where they stood, and ushered them back toward us.

As they approached, I watched how Kennedy seemed to support his colleague, patting him on the back, even slowing his own strides to match Jarrett's diminutive steps. I wondered if he had considered the repercussions from having a partner that he needed to carry—if he knew how his own life might be placed into further Danger because of his partner's lack of investment into his own physical health and fitness. Simply being on the shorter side or more prone to being overweight was no reason for any Peacekeeper to subscribe to the notion that he had a free pass for mediocrity.

The two men approached their team leader, then glanced over at me after being told why they had been summoned. Confusion flashed across Kennedy's face; Jarrett didn't seem surprised.

Kennedy reacted first, reaching out to shake my hand and introduce himself. Jarrett followed suit, handing over his squishy little hand as the air filled with ripe body-odor.

"I was called in to investigate a case that overlaps into one of the cases you have been working on. You have a Missing Persons case—a little girl. Katarina Urakov."

Kennedy was immediately obliging. "Absolutely. Tough case. How can we help?"

"I'm reviewing all of your paperwork and findings right now, and was hoping I could meet with both of you to get further insight," I responded.

Jarrett remained silent. Heat flooded his red face. Given how pungent the air was, it was impossible to determine if it was because of the subject matter, or because another wave of heat had surged through his over-worked body. Instinct told me he knew exactly what was going on, but he was being quiet, allowing his partner to carry the conversation for them both.

"Yeah, that would be great. I think we did some steady groundwork initially, but the case has turned completely cold. I'm glad to see you were called in. I'd be happy to meet with you."

I thanked Kennedy for the offer, told him we would be in touch with them regarding their files, and if it wasn't too much of an imposition, I would need them both to come down to the Interview Rooms so I could get their statements on record. It was a subtle request—it wasn't hinged on anything directly threatening, and for a man with nothing to hide, it should have been received as standard protocol. I was, after all, an Investigator simply stepping in and taking over one of the local cases. Accessing all records and files, even interviewing previous Detectives, was not uncommon.

But for the Officer with something to hide, it was likely a terrifying prospect. Given the easy-going smile and dedicated demeanor of Detective Kennedy and then comparing it to Detective Jarrett's tergiversating, it seemed obvious which one knew something more than they were choosing to disclose.

I would have him in a room on his own soon enough—and he wouldn't have his partner to hide behind then.

I shook their hands again, accepted Kennedy's offer to be interviewed in the morning, and then told Jarrett I would expect him to find time no later than the end of the week—giving him a full three days to stew in his own juices and figure out what he was going to say. Given the discrepancies in his records and all that Officer Stanton had uncovered already, I couldn't wait for our meeting.

Interview: Kennedy

Detective Kennedy arrived promptly in the morning at 0900, as he had volunteered to do. In his hands was a paper copy of his files regarding Katarina and a thumb drive. He shook my hand as we met in the hallway, handed me his work product, and led the way into the Interview Room with a smile on his face. He was a seemingly nice, straight-forward character who didn't seem capable of behaving with malice or deception. His blonde hair was cut short, his blue eyes were crisp and clear, and the dimples in his cheeks gave him a boy-next-door look.

Motioning for him to take a seat on the opposite side of the table, I watched as he pulled his chair out and then casually sat down, legs open and hands clasped in his lap. I sat down after him, told him that his statement would be recorded, and asked him if he had questions.

"No, Sir. They reviewed the process with us at the Academy," he responded, comfortably.

"Please state your name and badge number for the record," I began.

"Detective Quin Kennedy, Badge number MP-7311," he replied.

"And how long have you been with the SPD?"

"Since exiting the Academy, ten years."

"And your age?"

"Thirty-six."

"How long have you been with your current partner, Detective Jarrett?"

"Since my seventh year—so three years now."

"How many partners did you have prior to that?"

"Just one—but he was much older; they said he was close to retirement. He died of a heart attack, so they put me with Jarrett."

"Have you ever had any issues with any of the work you've conducted with Detective Jarrett?" I asked.

A sudden realization of what was happening passed across Kennedy's face as he considered for the first time that I wasn't there to investigate the case alone, but also to question him about his partner. It was a time for reflection for some, a crisis of conscience for others, and an opportunity to purge pent-up frustrations for a few; all I needed to know was just how tight Kennedy was with his partner and if he was prepared to cover for him.

He cleared his throat and sat up tall in his chair.

"Sir, if I may ask, is this about the case at hand or my partner?"

He was a straight shooter. It didn't signify loyalty, but Honor at the very least.

"Both, if that's all right. There have been a significant number of discrepancies in his work product, and I'm finding it difficult to reconcile that it's all accidental," I said.

I lost nothing by being honest, but if this man had the integrity that I thought he did, I could gain substantial insight into who Jarrett was. Jarrett had plenty to fear from a partner who conducted his work with more care for his Values and Honor than his loyalty to his partner.

He cleared his throat once again.

"With all due respect, Sir, I'm more than a little uncomfortable with this, but I'm happy to discuss the case in any capacity, and however that overlaps with what you're looking for regarding Detective Jarrett, I'm happy to help. Isn't this more of a matter for Internal Investigations, though?" he asked, concerned.

I wasn't over-reaching; in fact, if I could determine that his actions were linked to my case, I had every right to push for prosecution without handing it over to anyone.

"I appreciate your help, and I'm fully aware that it places you in a precarious situation. I'm not trying to impose on your professional relationship. I think you'll find as we go along that my concerns are all related to the case of one Missing little girl, and it overlaps with everything you've already done. I'm not specifically out to target your partner; I just need some clarification of his role in the reporting process," I explained to him, careful to use a neutral tone—and hopefully setting him at ease once again. There wasn't any point in mentioning that if I gathered the information I needed, I would be Arresting his partner before he would ever need to face him again.

He nodded his head, consenting for me to proceed.

From there, I asked him a myriad of questions about the initial investigative process that he and Jarrett took, going over each of their notes, the steps of their interviews with the church members and staff, and finally, how they had conducted their physical geographic search of the area. I asked him about Oscar and Lucya Urakov, his take on their marriage and parenting, and then finally what he thought had happened to Katarina.

All of it was done with the intent to make him more comfortable before I began asking him deeper questions about how they processed their cases—the part where he would either incriminate or exonerate both himself and his partner. Someone was responsible for shuffling and concealing cases, names of Victims, and openly deleting information from the database. I was inclined to believe it was exactly as it presented to Officer Stanton through his research, and it would all lead to Detective Jarrett. There was enough data collected already to prove it was only done through his Badge number. It was sufficient evidence for his Arrest and likely a Conviction. But it would not hurt to prove that the man sitting across from me was absolved from responsibility, nor would it hurt to gain more evidence. I imagined, as a Peacekeeper, that he would rather his name be entirely free from any hint of impropriety rather than have the stain of a tainted reputation following his entire career.

Detective Kennedy told me he thought the little girl had been picked up by a vehicle without detection, and they probably took her bike with them. He said he believed it was likely she had been Sexually Assaulted and then dumped somewhere the same day—probably far enough beyond the range of investigation that she had remained unfound. He said he thought it was tragic but preventable, had Katarina's mother only taken her inside the church rather than entrusting her care to other children.

I agreed, knowing that we were both likely to be considered cold-hearted simply for daring to say it. Statistically, though, most children went Missing because the opportunity for Abduction presented itself—and the more opportunity, the more possibility. Heartless or not, it rang true.

Wrapping things up, I asked him a series of questions about how the two of them filed their paperwork, who kept track of their technical data and case files, and if anyone else had access to their reports or records. He responded exactly as I had expected, telling me that Jarrett had always taken the lead on it, and as it was not an area that he enjoyed doing, he was happy to have a partner pick up his end of things. Kennedy, it seemed, was the more physical of the two and always did the more labor-intensive work, such as when they scoured the area and Kennedy was the one scaling down embankments and walking along the roadways. After several years of partnership, the two men had worked out their strengths and weaknesses and learned how to maximize them so they could be the most effective team—just as they had been trained to do.

The problem, of course, was that Detective Jarrett was corrupt, and had been doing exceptionally unethical things unbeknownst to his partner.

I thanked Kennedy for his help and shut down all the recording equipment. Standing, we shook hands, and then I walked with him to the door.

"I appreciate all your help. I'll be speaking with Jarrett before too long. I have everything I need for the case—and it was good work initially, just so you know. I wasn't called in because of shoddy work product—you covered a lot of ground and everything you did checked out during my own investigation. They called me in because they found her—Katarina—and it was almost exactly as you described, unfortunately."

His face registered surprise—it hadn't occurred to him I could have been called in after they had discovered her Remains; he had assumed I was taking over his Missing Persons case after it had grown cold over the months.

"That's too bad," he said. "I bet it devastated her parents when they heard the news. They really loved that little girl—that much was obvious."

I nodded.

"I had originally tried to keep an open mind and not rule them out as Suspects right away as we were trained to do—despite how they presented even—but after a while, it was pretty obvious that her parents were completely torn up about it, Lucya especially."

I agreed with him and patted him on the back as we parted ways.

"Thank you for your time, once again, Detective. And thank you for your hard work on the case. You really did a tremendous amount of work and laid the groundwork for me better than I could have hoped for. Have you ever thought about advancing to Investigator?" I asked.

He smiled.

"I did, a while ago. Signed up for school and everything. But then I got married, had a baby, and now the wife is Pregnant again. She'd never let me do the travel required. So, I think this is where I'll stay," he stated. It was an honest answer—and a familiar one.

He extended his hand again, and I shook it.

"It was great to meet you, Sir. Please let me know if there's anything else I can do, or if you need anything. I'm happy to help."

I smiled at him warmly, hoping that my raised visor allowed my eyes to reveal my congeniality toward him, and told him to take care of himself.

As far as I could determine, Kennedy was completely in the dark regarding what was happening in the files and knew nothing of how Jarrett was operating behind closed doors.

It was time to bring Jarrett in, and I felt comfortable we would skip the pleasantries.

Interview: Jarrett

I approached the Interview Room holding Detective Jarrett. He had waited until the afternoon of the third day, electing to push his interview as far off as I had permitted, and only confirming my worst suspicions of his intentional misconduct. He had delayed the inevitable, but at least he had still chosen to show up instead of attempting to reschedule, or worse, try to make a break for it and go off-grid. For the time being, he was still a member of Law Enforcement, even if meeting with him now was under entirely different circumstances than our first encounter at the stadium. The first time we had met had been a courtesy—a request to meet based on a few suspicions of misconduct, a sinking feeling that things hadn't been adding up, and some questionable paperwork in a pattern that suggested that either he or his partner might have been doing something unscrupulous.

Now, however, I knew he was complicit in altering the evidence in his case work just as surely as I had verified that his partner, Kennedy, had been unaware of how things had been. Before, I wasn't sure of the balance within their relationship or how close they were. I didn't know if Jarrett could control his partner or manipulate him, if Kennedy had intentionally been looking the other way, or if he had been working in collusion with him. But my interview with Kennedy had given me a fair assessment of his character, as well as the type of Detective he seemed to be. There was nothing in his demeanor, Body Language, or voice that had indicated his answers had been falsified or were intended to be misleading.

This time, I had the testimony of his partner, Kennedy, verifying that he had not signed off on a single case, and that he had not been present when any of the records had been altered. Having his sworn testimony provided confirmation that Detective Jarrett was responsible for the discrepancies. By disclosing that Detective Jarrett was the only person who submitted their paperwork, Kennedy had inadvertently absolved himself from liability while also substantiating what Stanton had uncovered. It wasn't as solid as a confession directly from Detective Jarrett, and it didn't explain any of the reasons behind his actions, but it was a promising start.

When I entered the room, I did not waste any time with formalities, and I didn't bother to extend my hand. Any respect or patience I previously held was lost at this point; I had seen his culpability well enough that I knew this man was not someone that should be one of my colleagues. No colleague of mine that was a legitimate member of Law Enforcement would have ever done what he had. Whatever had caused this man to travel this path, he had willingly forfeited the right to be classified or respected as an Officer in my book, and by the time my investigation was complete, this man would no longer have the privilege of wearing—or hiding behind—his badge.

I spent several moments sharing the information we had learned regarding how he buried cases within the Missing Persons Division so they appeared inactive.

Knowing that he was caught, he did not attempt to deny it.

He volunteered that there had been occasions where he provided assistance to people who wanted specific cases to fall off the radar or disappear. He was 'compensated' for his work. He had several connections he worked with, but as they approached him, he denied knowing who paid him specifically. There weren't a lot of cases involved, and he never knew who would reach out to him, or when it would happen. He thought he just had a reputation known for helping people out, provided he was well-compensated. He never tried to discover who the people were who hired him.

"You're going to have to make a choice, Detective. Do you want to continue to protect the people who once provided you with a paycheck, or do you want to take a stand for once and try to do the right thing? Because I can assure you, there won't be any further opportunities coming from me."

He sighed heavily, and his shoulders visibly sunk.

"I'm a dead man either way. You don't even know what you're walking into, and you think you can offer me anything that's going to sweeten the pot? You don't even know who you're messing with, and you think I should be afraid of Big Brother?"

"I won't be able to offer any defense without your help, and if you refuse to provide me with anything of substance, there won't be any defense worth declaring. As for those on the outside, I can't protect you from them either if you refuse to talk. But I can assure you of this; if you cannot provide information regarding the people that you're working for and tell me what exactly they've been paying you for, there will be no mercy given. You'll be charged with the Death Penalty regardless of your own culpability. Does this seem reasonable, knowing that you will die to protect those that committed Murder? Have they compensated you enough to justify carrying their Violence and Murders to your grave?"

He stared off into the wall, resigned. I watched him as he weighed out his options; a weak man who had sacrificed his values and his Oath to Protect the Sanctity of Human Life for his own selfish gain and greed.

"You just don't know. You have no idea what you're getting into. This is bigger than just you and me. And they don't care about someone like me. They aren't scared of someone like you, either."

Whoever 'they' were, he regarded them as more powerful than his own government. There could not possibly be that many people in the Greater Seattle Area that had that degree of power or influence.

"And what do you suppose would occur if I were to release you today?" I asked.

"I would be dead before you even finished the paperwork. Come on, you can't really be this stupid."

Detective Jarrett seemed convinced that his life was forfeit either way, but for some reason, he believed he was in more danger at the hands of his employers. It was odd—but only in the context of modern times. If I were to place his behavior and words in relation to another time in history, it seemed much more probable. But post-21st century? After the Great Reformation? He was speaking as though there were diabolical characters out there capable of controlling aspects of Law Enforcement, and that was simply absurd.

There was virtually zero probability of such a level of criminality existing anywhere within These United States. There was no chance of men having the degree of power and influence that he believed they did. It was unfathomable. Even if the local SPD had somehow failed to document men capable of running some sort of criminal enterprise, federal agencies would never have overlooked such activity, nor would they have allowed it to escalate.

"Look, I can only tell you what I know. Sometimes people would contact me. They would already know there was a case filed. They would just ask that the person and their case 'disappear'. So that's what I did. I had a few different people who would ask me to make cases disappear regularly. It wasn't my business to ask them why or how. All I did was shift some files around."

"So, who are they, these mystery men? What can you possibly gain by protecting them now?" I asked. "Explain it to me. You say I don't get it, well, tell me. Help me understand why you would do work like this, especially if you're afraid of them."

Detective Jarrett leaned back in his chair with his arms folded. After a moment of contemplation, he suddenly threw up his hands as if to say, "Why not?"

"I only know there's more than one man at the top. I never met any of them. Two men approached me, offered a lot of cash to look the other way. A while later they came back and offered me more cash if I gave them a few leads every now and again—whenever a MP crossed my desk that fit certain criteria or matched a name, they said they wanted to 'get lost in the shuffle'. Who knows how many work for them because these men—these men are ghosts. You'll never find them. You'll never meet them. You'll never arrest them or even see them. But they already know who you are; I guarantee it. These men are not to be messed around with. They will not have their playthings disturbed. You think that if you catch me, it's going to end. It won't. I'm *nothing* to these people; a mere spoke in the wheel. These men have more power than any that you have encountered, and you're messing around in their playpen now."

Playthings. Playpen.

What was he insinuating? Pedophilia? A pedophilia ring?

There was no database filled with 'Missing Children'. They just didn't 'Disappear' anymore. Statistically, there had never been a safer time for the children of our nation.

Then again, I also knew that this man, Detective Jarrett, had been downgrading Missing Persons Reports, concealing data and crimes, and deleting surveillance footage. Basing our information regarding Missing Persons statistics on the SPD database was no longer an option, because we had no idea how corrupt it had become at the hands of Detective Jarrett. Aside from that, I already knew that the Greater Seattle Area had a higher Missing Persons average than any other major city of its size—something was happening here. Was it possible that there were even more cases out there—cases that had been entirely concealed rather than documented? Was it possible that there had been other Missing Children that had never been investigated because Detective Jarrett had buried their files?

"So, who are they? Why have I disturbed their playpen? Are you talking about the graveyard? Are you calling the Deceased Remains—those Innocent Victims—their playthings?" I asked.

Detective Jarrett looked at me. "You already have them. They own the land. They own a lot of land around here; they have a lot of land everywhere. Why do you think they don't want any of the cases investigated?"

He was talking about the property that they had discovered the gravesites. "But I checked; the land is owned by a defunct corporation. They own the land, but the business went belly-up. The factory shut down, and it's been vacant for years."

"Exactly. But why didn't they ever sell it? Why didn't anyone ever build on it? Come on, buddy. Prime real estate in the Emerald city, and no one ever tried to build on it?"

"So, you've been working for the owners of the property? For how long? And how did you get involved?" I asked. I was skeptical; none of this made any sense, and he was rambling like a man that was about to lose his entire livelihood and life and wanted to make it into something bigger to justify it.

"You don't even know what you're getting into. These guys are going to eat you alive. I'm a dead man, anyway. But you? You're a dead man, too."

Detective Jarrett was scowling at me, and I could feel my impatience rising. The two of us were not mixing well.

"You have no idea what white meat goes for on the black market, do you? Especially *fresh* white meat." He laughed derisively. "I'll be replaced before my body even hits the ground, and they won't even miss a beat. There's a whole other world out there that you don't even know about. As much as our government knows, they can't even see what's right under their noses. All that spying on the American People, and they can't even see that there's a whole separate system at work here."

A wave of contempt washed over me—an internal battle raging between my personal feelings and the professionalism I knew was required. I decided to adjust my approach, to take a deep breath, to keep a level head and play nice in the sandbox. This man wasn't a run-of-the-mill Criminal, after all; he was a member of Law Enforcement until proven Guilty in a Court of Law. I knew what the evidence proved he was complicit in doing, but he didn't know that I had enough to provide a strong Conviction already. It could work in my favor, playing on our shared employment status as if I backed him as another Brother in Blue. And I would have—had he not sold out his Fellow Law Enforcement Officers, our entire profession, and the Sanctity of Life Oaths we had all sworn to uphold, not to mention the very Citizens he was sworn to protect. As it stood, the only goal I had was to see him lose his badge and access to any more potential Victims. But until then, I would moderate my temper and my tone.

"You know how this goes. I can only help you and protect you if I know what's going on. Tell me who they are. Tell me why you're afraid."

Detective Jarrett laughed and sneered at me, boldly staring me down and shaking his head.

"They're already watching you. There's no way you're going to catch them. They're probably long gone already. You're chasing after ghosts, I'm tellin' ya. These men have way more power and money than anything we've seen."

He shook his head and scowled again. "There wasn't enough money for any of this. Whatever I thought I was getting, it wasn't enough. I did nothing that deserved to land here, knowing what it would cost me out there. I never signed up for any of this."

He was defeated. He knew his life was over. Whatever had motivated him to venture off the path of the straight and narrow was now irrelevant, because his course was set, and everything he once knew was about to be removed from him. At the very least, he would face Exile, and would be doomed to spend the rest of his days living in an isolated location filled with all the other social miscreants and aberrations that had been Convicted of Crimes and considered beyond rehabilitation.

Exile was no light Sentence or weight to bear, either. Most would prefer Death than face the Great Unknown. If it were found that he had involved anyone from his family or personal life, or that they knew what he had been doing, they, too, would face Exile alongside him. I hoped for his sake that he had involved no one else.

I sighed heavily, and shifted my body into a more relaxed position, leaning back and crossing my outstretched legs.

"I'll be honest. Your case is sealed, and even if what you're telling me is interesting, it's not enough to even remotely sway the Judges to grant you any leniency. They'll want more. If you want me to help you, you're going to have to give me a lot more information. Are there any other cases or men like yourself out there? How are they picking their targets?"

I leaned toward him.

"If you want me to believe that you never intended to get in this deep, and if you expect anyone to buy that you're not personally responsible for causing Harm to any of the Victims I've been charged with defending, then you're going to have to convince me of both your Innocence and your willingness to help me get the Justice these Victims deserve. You and I both know what you've been helping these mystery people do, and no one is going to blink when it comes time to issuing your Death Warrant."

The more information I could get from him, the more I had to go with as Officer Stanton and I utilized our resources to advance our investigation. It was concerning to me that so much of this had been going on within the Greater Seattle Area outside of the watchful eye of the SPD, as were several other elements regarding how the SPD had conducted their investigations in the past. The combination of Evil happening beyond our knowledge, as well as poorly conducted Law Enforcement work and investigations was a dangerous mix, and it would only result in more Innocent Victims being Harmed and Murdered.

Detective Jarrett gave a slight nod of consent. I knew that he would give me the information I asked for from that moment on, and in exchange, he was counting on me to advocate on his behalf to secure Exile Status for his Sentence rather than Death. It wasn't much of a compromise, but it was a concession that I was prepared to make for his cooperation.

He understood the rules, and he understood the position he was in. He had to choose a side, and when you were down on your luck, sometimes it was better to choose the enemy you knew. For whatever reason, he believed he stood a better chance cooperating with me and taking his chances for Exile rather than going down without a fight. It was a sign that despite his poor choices, he still retained something akin to humanity.

If he wanted to choose to fight for an Exile Sentence, and if he was willing to work with me in order to secure it, I had no problem agreeing to those terms. It was something within my power to recommend and potentially help facilitate, and I was comfortable with this. This man was going to lose a lot before this investigation was complete anyhow. Exile would not result in a free pass; he had effectively destroyed his own life either way.

Thoughts on Detective Jarrett

I felt the disgust rise from deep within as my thoughts turned to the interview with Detective Jarrett. Nothing bothered me more than when Peacekeepers failed to uphold the hefty weight of the ideals of Law Enforcement. They were not just held to average standards; they were a cut above—the best of our society, Set Apart and held to a standard beyond reproach. Every time one of my Brothers failed to measure up, it reflected negatively upon our entire profession.

Detective Jarrett was the worst sort of villain. Sadistic desires did not motivate him. He wasn't driven by revenge, passion, or any sort of deviant sexual or cruel behavior. What made him so offensively reprehensible was that he did it for no other reason than money.

How did one betray one's own Fellow Countrymen? What was the price for turning a blind eye, and enabling Evil people to commit the gravest acts of Depravity? Greed was a shockingly empty reason for how one Human Being could know about the Suffering of Another, especially an Innocent Victim, and not only pretend not to see anything amiss, but actually help facilitate it.

If a person was going to slide among the lowest filth known to Man, to consort with the putrid bile, diseased, and rotting intestinal Human Waste that encompassed all those that would choose to cause the Pain and Horrific Suffering of their Innocent Fellow Citizens, one would think there would be a good reason. Especially if there was Violence Against Children being done—then one would expect it to be because of some sort of depraved psychological issue, malformed understanding of Human relationships because of severe childhood trauma, or perhaps some profoundly rare element of sociopathic Evil festering deep within. But this man allowed Harm to come to Innocent People and Children for no other reason than financial profit.

What could explain the severe degradation of Humanity that could cause such abject moral bankruptcy? How could one account for such cold acceptance of Violence?

But what remained the most incomprehensible element of all was that he was a member of Law Enforcement, and as much as it gladdened me to know he would never have another opportunity to cause Harm to our unsuspecting Citizenry, I knew it could never eradicate the damage he had already done. This man had taken an Oath to Protect and Defend the Citizens of These United States, and he had turned around and sold them out for the weakest of reasons—money.

His actions weren't just reprehensible because of what he had become as a Human Being; he had crossed a line regarding his profession that would only result in the most severe of consequences. No matter how extreme his Sentence was, however, his actions would leave a stain on our entire profession, and regardless of whether the Citizens of our nation knew or not, it would be a stain that would never fade. Detective Jarrett had now joined the ranks of a marginal, yet incalculable percentage of Law Enforcement who had desecrated the very badge and public they had sworn to Protect and Defend, and nothing could ever make amends for that.

TWENTY-ONE - DAEGAN KYL — ARRESTED

Meeting Daegan Kyl

The man stood calmly in the Interview Room, looking around casually as if he were waiting to place an order at his favorite coffee shop. He seemed completely unfazed by the handcuffs that secured his arms in front of him, and even more unperturbed that his tuxedo was exceedingly out of place.

He had been picked up outside of some type of social function, sharply dressed in a sleek black and white tuxedo. His cuffs were silver and boasted a custom-made 'DK'. His watch was obviously expensive, but not too ostentatious, and his shoes held just the right amount of shine.

It was his face that held the most mystery, though, with piercing brown eyes, heavy eyebrows with a distinctive arch, and a dark beard concealing his lower face. His hair was long enough to be pulled back into a ponytail, also brown, and seemed to have some curl to it. He wasn't exactly clean-cut, but he was unquestionably a well-groomed, confident man.

Standing 6'4" and weighing two-hundred and forty pounds, he was a massive, oversized presence in the room, filling out his tuxedo perfectly. He was broad-shouldered, fit, and somehow rugged despite his finery.

I don't know what I had been expecting from a man that had been Arrested for being linked to four Deceased sets of Human Remains and was a potential Serial Killer, but the man standing in front of me was not it.

Looking straight into the double-sided glass on the wall opposite, I found him staring directly into my eyes, and even as I knew he couldn't see me, I still found it disconcerting.

Watching him, he slowly smiled, fearless and arrogant.

Whoever Daegan Kyl was, he was neither surprised, nor afraid, to be here.

I found it off-putting, and mildly irritating.

"Give him a room. Take away his pretty clothes and give him a jumper. Let's let him sleep on it, mull things over, and I'll talk to him in the morning."

It was time to see what Daegan Kyl was made of.

Search Warrant: Moving Men and Maids

We secured Search Warrants for the Moving Men and Maids property and business, and with a team of sixty of SPD's finest, we scoured the building and business, searching for anything that might connect Daegan Kyl to the property or the Victims. Knowing what was at stake, we brought in the K9 Cadaver dogs once again, hoping to rely on their heightened senses to get the results we needed to find.

Despite hours of work, including searches through every moving truck on the property, we found nothing. None of the trucks tested positive for Human Remains either through our technology or with the aid of the K9s. The trucks were clean—as should be expected for a moving business. Human Remains often left trace evidence that even deep, professional cleaning would have likely missed at least once or twice. Nothing materialized, however, even though we carefully searched both the front seating areas and the large box ends of every truck on site.

Strong chemicals and bleach were present in every vehicle—standard cleaning supplies for many businesses, unfortunately—and nothing we could ever prove was purchased or used for nefarious purposes.

After searching through the inventory, eventually Stanton and I found the exact truck that had been captured on video exiting the property. We took a team of K9s and their handlers, several key forensic Officers, and did a comprehensive check. Because the trucks were fairly basic, there seemed little need to impound it for the task at hand; it had one long bench seat, an automatic transmission, standard features, a few floor mats, and a large box end measuring fourteen feet with a ramp. It was as generic as every other truck on the site, and after spending several hours going over it from top to bottom, inside and out, the truck was determined to be just as meticulous as every other truck on the lot.

There were also two-hundred storage units on site—all of which would have required individual Search Warrants to be served to the renters before entering—so we were effectively cut at the knees. We had viewed the rental history and determined which units were being rented and were therefore off-limits. Our Search Warrant allowed us to view and enter only the empty units. Most were active rentals, however, and of the half dozen that were empty, they all came back clean.

We had hit a dead end—there were no Human Remains detected anywhere.

There wasn't much left to go on. We couldn't prove that Daegan Kyl was the only person who used the truck in question. We had no proof he had been the one on the property—other than knowing he had been connected to the property more than a decade earlier.

The Moving Men and Maids lead was a total bust.

Establishing Links Between Daegan Kyl and Willow Amos

Although I believed him to be the person responsible for burying the Victims, I still wasn't sure Daegan Kyl had played a role in any of their Deaths. To date, we hadn't been able to link him directly to any of the Victims in any manner.

However, after the failed search of the Moving Men and Maids corporation and Daegan Kyl's personal properties, Stanton had done more digging. He had considered that Willow Amos might have been in contact with Daegan Kyl, although the two did not have any known connections.

His searches proved fruitful when he was able to establish that the two were in semi-regular communication. Phone records showed regular communication at least on a monthly basis. More importantly, there were GPS records that showed Willow Amos on the Moving Maids property occasionally, and Daegan Kyl was confirmed to have visited the GSAU campus several times. His visits to the campus were too far back for any type of facial recognition to be used through security footage, but the GPS tracker was able to verify that the parking lot used by Daegan Kyl was the one adjacent to the Administration Building that housed the counseling center where Willow Amos worked.

In addition, he was able to verify that both Daegan Kyl's phone and vehicle were documented as having occasionally visited the dwelling unit rented by Willow Amos. In return, her phone and vehicle were also documented as having spent time at the personal residences of Daegan Kyl, with far greater frequency.

We knew they were connected on a personal level, as nothing indicated they knew one another through professional ties. But Stanton had been unable to discover any familial or legal link to bind them. The case against Daegan Kyl was growing stronger, though, with every connection we could establish. Although separated by degrees, we could now verify that Willow Amos was a link between Arlan Randall and Daegan Kyl, however tenuous. We could also confirm Daegan Kyl was connected to the same university frequented by Rebecca Summers, Mariam Pembrook, and Willow Amos.

Establishing Communication: Daegan Kyl

Entering the Interview Room, I sat down at the table on the opposite side of the man I had asked the SPD LEOs to Arrest and bring to the station the night before. They had removed his tuxedo and replaced it with a standard-issue orange jumpsuit with SPD INMATE written across the back in bold, black letters.

He was no longer smiling.

As usual, there was a row of windows high on the outside wall, allowing sunlight to filter in.

Daegan Kyl stood leaning against the wall with his eyes closed as I entered the room, allowing the sunlight to wash over his face. It was a hot day in Seattle; almost eighty degrees, and yet here we both were, covered from the neck down with uniforms, symbolizing who we each were. Our uniforms, however superficial it seemed, served as a reminder to each of us that we were unlikely to trust the other, and had a generational stain of conflict that was not easily overlooked.

He seemed to enjoy the sunlight; since the room was air-conditioned and lacked any discernible fresh air, it was easy to see why he wanted to squeeze every second out of it before we began.

He opened his eyes and watched me once I had settled in. I had placed my E-File Pad on the table along with a paper folder and then set the E-File Pad to 'record' even though I knew that both the eye in the sky and my uniform and visor would record our interview as well. His eyes followed my movements, but his face didn't betray a hint of emotion. For a man facing the Death Penalty, or Exile at the very least, he gave away no sign of fear. His broad shoulders were resting comfortably against the wall and his arms were crossed. He rested on his right foot with the left knee casually bent.

There were several guards milling around. Two were stationed outside the room and another inside, strategically positioned in the corner near the door and facing Daegan Kyl the entire time.

None of it was necessary, of course. He had been fitted with an RFID-Chip as soon as he was booked, and at the slightest provocation, I could send a bolt of electricity down his spine that was severe enough to stun him into submission while temporarily making it impossible for his lower extremities to carry his weight.

But both Daegan Kyl and I knew that if he wanted to make a run for it, he had probably already had several opportunities and had chosen not to. He was here because he allowed himself to be.

"I trust you slept well?" I asked.

Of course, he didn't. The lodgings here were primitive, at best. But they weren't designed to be accommodating, especially not for a man who had undoubtedly developed a taste for the finer things.

Still, he had been provided with a bed, a shower, edible food, and clean drinking water. It was more than many of the prisons around the globe provided, and, without a doubt, generous enough that many of the world's inhabitants would have begged to trade places.

He shrugged slightly.

"I learned a long time ago to catch your Z's where and when you can. No complaints here. Decent food, too. A little bland, but isn't all cafeteria food?"

Curious, he didn't mention the water pressure.

"This is Investigator Ivan, Washington State, Badge number 9890, establishing a line of communication with a Mr. Daegan Kyl—"

"Daegan Kyl—" he interrupted.

"I'm sorry, what?" I asked.

"Daegan. Day-Gun. Not Duh-Gawn. And it's Kyl—as in Kyle. Not Keel. Daegan Kyl."

He looked at me intently, waiting for me to correct myself.

I started the recorder again.

"This is Investigator Ivan, Washington State, Badge Number 9890, establishing a line of communication with—Day-Gun Kyle—"

He gave me a nod of consent and a grin.

The man was a force to be reckoned with. As a general rule, there was usually a fair bit of intimidation that went along with my job. By the time they ended up in an Interview Room, they were usually a little concerned about how things were not working out very well for them. This was apparently not the case with Mr. Day-Gun Kyle.

I was curious if he always had such a dominant personality or if he was merely putting on some airs and bravado because of where we were. He wasn't aggressive; on the contrary, he was exceedingly polite and well-mannered.

And he wasn't concerned in the least about any of this.

In fact, he still hadn't even questioned why he was here. It was a little strange considering he had been Arrested while at a black-tie event and had been in police custody for almost twelve hours already.

He wasn't angry, scared, or belligerent.

He hadn't even asked for an attorney—which I was certain he had on retainer—and yet he was perfectly content to allow this to unfold as it was.

I wasn't sure what to make of it yet, but his behavior was unusual for the situation he was in.

Interview I: Arlan

I spent most of my interview time with Victims, their families, and everyday Citizens. I followed leads and secured first-hand accounts of events, all with the intent to help solve crimes. The 'Alleged' perpetrators of Crimes seldom agreed to interviews, and interrogations were not mandatory if there was enough forensic and electronic evidence to Convict. They were welcome to confess, and welcome to explain their actions—but it wasn't necessary. Their justifications and excuses for committing Violent Crimes seldom made a difference to anyone forced to listen, and had no bearing on their Sentences.

I sat back in the chair I was occupying, slowly and casually. I folded my hands in my lap, my black gloved fingers interlocking as I stared patiently at him. He met my gaze as best as he could through my visor. It was designed to conceal specific features, such as eye color and shape, both of which could be identifiers of our ethnicity. It was the most common complaint listed regarding our visors; people didn't like not being able to see our eyes and make eye contact. I understood this, of course, and appreciated the intimacy of real Human Contact as well. But when confronting Criminals, the less personal information they could extract from Law Enforcement, the better. I did not want this man to read anything from my demeanor, and anyone with expressive eyes would be read like a poor poker player.

On the other hand, this was a man that had served over ten years in our military. They had counted him among our most elite soldiers. It seemed…cowardly of me to conceal myself from him.

The visors were a necessary evil; we could remove them as we wished while in the company of our Victims or their Bereaved. While confronting men such as this, however, authority and security mattered; our visors also prevented any Bodily Fluids such as blood or spit from making direct contact as well. In most cases, being within spitting distance of any known Criminal was enough to make me use my visor; it was always better to err on the side of caution.

Daegan Kyl didn't seem to mind it, however, but he was a tough character to read. He was by far the most understated personality I'd ever encountered.

He moved away from the wall quietly, pulled the chair out from under the table and sat down opposite me slowly. The man now sitting directly across from me was a mountain, all muscle and mass, with the added advantage of having some Native American, Hawaiian, or possibly Samoan in his genetic coding. His thick eyebrows, shoulder-length dark hair that was tied back in a knot, and his facial hair all seemed very natural with his darker complexion.

He leaned back in his chair and crossed his hands in his lap casually.

"We're here to determine if you're responsible for the murder and burial of four Victims recently discovered," I began.

"Based on what evidence?" he queried.

His voice was deep, refined, and well-spoken.

I'd read his file; he'd never been in any type of trouble with the law, not once. Whatever this guy's game was, I found it difficult to believe he was a Murderer. But it was still entirely possible he was responsible for their burial, and there were far too many unanswered questions to discount anything.

He sat there stoically.

I opened the paper folder. There was a photograph of Arlan, standing alongside his family, all the kids surrounding him, Micah Davidson on one side, and his wife, Caroline, on the other.

I pushed the photograph toward him so he could see it. He leaned forward, studying the people smiling at him.

"Meet Arlan. He was one of your Victims. That's his wife, Caroline, and the manager of his family farm next to him, Micah. Those are all his kids and grandkids. They diagnosed him with terminal cancer right after this was taken. He was reported as a Missing Person a few months ago. We recently located him buried in a field along with three other Victims. The Postmortem Examination listed the Cause of Death as an overdose. Someone administered a lethal dosage of his pain medication to him."

Daegan Kyl looked up at me in surprise.

"I've watched the interviews, I heard the Emergency call sent out by his wife, and I've seen all the surveillance footage. His wife was absolutely devastated by his Disappearance. Pretty soon, I'm going to have to go out there and tell them we've found the man that has been the rock of their family, and that he had been buried in a field and left to rot."

He winced; an odd reaction for the man that I believed had dug the grave himself.

Picking up the photograph, his gaze locked on the image before him.

I watched him closely, looking for any signs of physical change or acknowledgment that he knew where I was going with this. His hands, while subtle, had stopped moving for a moment.

"One of your moving trucks was captured on a surveillance camera exiting the property the graves were found on," I said.

"And? My work trucks are seen all over the state. They're moving trucks," he replied dryly.

"Did the camera happen to capture me as the driver? Do you know how many people drive our trucks? How many employees I have?"

"The footage actually did not show the driver well enough to identify him," I confessed. "But we were able to capture other video footage from the Transportation Department CCTV that shows driving the same truck. So, are you stating on the record that employees use every truck?"

He laughed. "I'm saying that I own a moving company and we have thousands of trucks and over a thousand local employees. More to the point, I'm not even directly involved in running the company anymore, and I don't know who might drive what at this point. But I'm willing to wager that, yes, other people have been driving the truck. It's not even a rig I keep at my house; it stays on the lot with all the others. Sorry, but you're barking up the wrong tree, cowboy. And even if I had driven it, let's be honest—you don't have any way to prove it."

"Well, we do have a solid connection between you and the property—you used to work there, didn't you? And by you, I mean *you, specifically*. Not one of your 'thousand' employees who might have been out joyriding through a graveyard? I'd consider that a pretty solid connection that you were likely the one seen exiting the property in one of your work trucks."

He smiled. "I've worked in a lot of places—you're going to have to be more specific."

"The graves were found on a back part of the property owned by K&H Textiles; you worked for them about twelve years ago if you recall."

He raised an eyebrow, completely unruffled.

"Yeah, I did a construction job for them right before I opened my moving business. As far as I know, the factory shut down, didn't it? And that was a long time ago. I think it took me about six months to finish the job."

He leaned back against his chair and smiled.

"Investigation must not be going so well if I'm your best lead. A short-term construction job from more than a decade ago and one of a thousand possible employees driving one of more than a thousand moving trucks, and now I'm a Serial Killer? I dunno, man, seems pretty thin," he said, shaking his head.

"Maybe. But I'm just getting started," I replied. He was entirely right, of course. I don't know what I was expecting from him, but he was completely at ease so far.

"Apparently, there was a woman working for the Randall's; she was a Hospice Care worker that was being paid to help take care of him during his final few months of life. Her name was Willow Amos. Ever hear of her?"

Daegan Kyl set the photograph back down on the table gently, eyes focused. Nothing gave his reaction away except a slight tightening of his jaw.

"She was on the property at the time of his Disappearance. We're currently investigating her to see how she pulled it off. We believe she had some additional help from another vehicle. Now, it's possible that you were there, in that extra vehicle, and you might have helped to remove Mr. Randall from his home. He was in a wheelchair, and you look like a healthy guy. And, conveniently, you own an entire fleet of moving trucks, don't you? So maybe you were there; maybe you weren't."

He looked me dead in the eye and leaned back against his chair again. I couldn't read his expression. He moved with the finesse of a cat; quiet, subtle, and quick.

Still, he said nothing and gave nothing away.

"So, was one of my company's moving trucks witnessed at this man's house, or was it just some white vehicle that you're *trying* to link to my moving company? Again, I gotta ask, do you actually have *any* proof? Not only of *my* involvement, but anything that links *my* business to your investigation. Because I'm still not seeing anything except hopeful wishes."

He had an easy smile, a high degree of self-confidence, and was comfortable in his own skin. By nature, I was a quiet man, used to long silences and prone to introspection. The man sitting across from me was noticeably different in both demeanor and personality; the kind of man who thought life was meant to be taken in stride. But there was something stealth-like about him; like the assassin you worried about if the lights suddenly went out.

He stared at Arlan's photograph, his eyes sweeping over all the kids and grandkids, before resting on the man's wife.

I had tried to entrap him by stating that the extra vehicle used on the farm to remove Arlan had been from his moving company—a fact that we couldn't confirm either belonged to the Hospice Care facility or the moving company, in truth—but his expression had given away nothing. The white van in the surveillance footage did not have any external markings, and both the moving company and the Hospice Care facility had white vans. And although we had found footage of Daegan Kyl driving his rental truck, Stanton had not found any footage of him behind the wheel of a van.

Additionally, after tracing as much surveillance footage as we had been able to, we had never documented any other vehicles either entering or exiting the factory land. We had set up surveillance of our own directly following the removal of the Victims, but to date, we had not documented one single vehicle either entering or exiting from the two known entrances.

He didn't seem to know as much as I would have expected him to if he were directly involved in the Disappearance of Arlan, either as an organizer or a participant.

I had no idea why this man was sitting in front of me; none of this made any sense.

Interview II: Rebecca

The following day, I tried again, hoping his time spent in his Cell had provided him with enough discomfort to make him reconsider his position.

I sat down opposite Daegan Kyl and pulled out a photograph of Rebecca.

He casually picked up the picture and then held it in his right hand while leaning back against the chair. She had been a pretty girl; petite, long hair, friendly smile. He stared at her face for a moment, so I began to speak again.

"This is Rebecca. She was a college student over at the university. She lived with a roommate and had two parents that had begged her to stay at home until she graduated."

Daegan Kyl was still holding onto the photograph of Rebecca with his right hand, but he took his left and wiped his face in a downward direction, as if to smooth his beard. He cupped his lower jawline area in his hand, thumb on one side and fingers extended across the rest of his face. His elbow rested on the arm of the chair as he sat there staring at her picture.

"This was one of the women buried out in that field," I said. "But I'm sure you knew that already, right?"

I was running out of time to hold him, and I was still not getting anywhere.

"I'm curious about something though, before we get started on Rebecca. I'm wondering why and how you cut out their RFID-Chips? What was the purpose of doing it? How did you even know where they were located, or if they were the old model or the newer one?"

The man sitting across from me had a micro-expression of surprise run fleetingly across his face before returning to its familiar stoicism. I doubted he'd ever even seen an RFID-Chip or had the technology to extract the Chips.

Knowing I was wasting my time and he wouldn't have any answers forthcoming, I moved on.

"Rebecca was also a Lost Treasure."

Daegan Kyl raised an eyebrow, and the hand on his face moved a bit.

"She'll be added to the database once this case is done. Rebecca, although she somehow buried herself out in a cold, dark, empty field, hadn't been Murdered. Her Cause of Death was found to be Suicide."

He looked up at me, and even without the facial program, it was easy to see that his face registered surprise. He really didn't have any idea who these people were or why they were being buried.

I knew people would do something as deplorable as burying the Dead in unmarked graves for money; people had done far worse for financial gain since the dawn of time. But I was having a hard time reconciling that the man in front of me was a guy that could casually go about burying bodies, especially for money that he clearly didn't need. So, if he wasn't doing it for a paycheck, what was he doing it for?

"Aren't you curious about why this young woman killed herself, though? Doesn't it seem like a girl like this would have her entire future ahead of her?"

I took out the mugshot of LeRoy Jones from his Arrest only a few hours earlier and slid it across the table toward him.

Staring at the image, he seemed to pause for a moment, but didn't pick the photograph up.

The way he had looked at him was exactly what I was hoping to see. He knew this man or knew *of* this man. He had recognized him.

He glanced up at me for a quick second and then back at Rebecca's photograph.

"This is LeRoy Jones. LeRoy was that one random chance encounter that this young woman couldn't have possibly imagined happening that changed her life. Rebecca just caught his eye, and it was game over. She didn't know him. She didn't even know he had been watching her. LeRoy Jones brutally Assaulted her. He dragged her into the bushes and Raped her."

Daegan Kyl let out a low sigh, and his hand was now rubbing his bearded jawline absentmindedly.

I leaned forward a little and opened my visor entirely so he could see my eyes. I wanted him to see the truth in my face when I told him the rest. For the first time, we made direct eye contact with no filters. He could see enough of my face that he could identify me if we ever met anywhere else, of this, I was sure. At this moment, though, he wasn't looking at me; he was focused on what I was sharing with him about Rebecca.

"We believe he knocked her unconscious; she had a black eye afterward. LeRoy Jones Raped this young woman, stole her virginity, and left her bloodied and bruise behind a row of bushes not even a quarter of a mile from the campus security building. From there, instead of calling for Emergency Responders, she went to her school counseling office and sought help there. And do you know who she found, Mr. Kyl? She found a student counselor named Willow Amos."

Daegan Kyl's head jerked up, and he stared at me. He was surprised again.

"Apparently, this Willow Amos gal was not only a part-time Hospice Care worker, she was also a part-time student counselor at GSAU. So here we have one woman linked to not one, but two of the Victims that somehow ended up buried in your graveyard. A woman that we know you have a history of visiting and calling on your cell phone. Curious, isn't it?"

He met my stare, so I continued.

"For whatever reason—and I have to tell you, I am absolutely lost as to what this part-time student counselor was thinking—she somehow convinces this poor girl that has just been Raped that she should *not* call the police, that she should *not* go to a hospital to get a medical examination, and she should *not* file a police report. She convinced this distraught Rape Victim to *not* seek help from Law Enforcement or the hospital because she had either talked her into believing that the LEOs were the enemy, or because she had convinced her that if the Rapist were caught, he would be sentenced to Death—and apparently that was too harsh of a sentence for *just a Rape.*"

Daegan Kyl set the photograph of Rebecca down on the table and leaned back into his chair heavily. I could see he was trying to analyze all of it in his head and work through whatever it was he thought he knew versus what I was telling him now.

I continued.

"The situation with Rebecca didn't end there. We know she met with Willow Amos in the campus counseling office directly following the Rape. We know that for whatever reason, Rebecca chose not to seek out the police or go to the hospital. Had she done that, we could have Arrested the man right then; all we had to do was check the security cameras, and we were able to get a positive ID of him. He would have been off the streets that same day. As it stands, because we did not pick him up, we can now confirm that he Raped at least one more woman, but that woman ended up getting Murdered. God only knows what else he has done, because I'm not done investigating him yet and we've already found this much."

Daegan Kyl looked up at me sharply, and after an initial moment of shock, he suddenly looked tired. His shoulders seemed to slump a bit, as if the new information was physically weighing him down.

"So, here's what we think happened at that point. Rebecca did not receive any type of assistance from Willow Amos that day directly following her Rape. She ended up leaving the campus immediately following the event. She had to walk all the way back to her vehicle in the parking lot, which she did in the company of one of the security guards. That security guard has now been identified as a man named Evan Harrison. Evan Harrison worked part-time at the school as a campus security patrolman, attended classes, and was also an employee at the Winter Season Hospice Care facility where he worked with Willow Amos. Guess what he did? He was a driver.

"But it gets better, because as soon as Evan Harrison went back to the campus security office, he deleted the surveillance footage that showed Rebecca getting grabbed and pulled off of the path and into the bushes where she was Raped."

I continued.

"It wasn't common knowledge, but the school had a back-up service that copied and stored all footage automatically. His efforts to conceal the Rape were pointless. But we have his full confession—he was very interested in avoiding as much trouble for himself as he could, and he wasn't nearly as loyal to Willow Amos as she might have expected. So at least now we have confirmed proof that it was intentionally deleted, and that he was linked to Willow Amos. It also supports that Amos was instructing others to do her bidding.

"Here's the last part about Rebecca, and I think we'll stop there for today. We'll meet again tomorrow morning, but for now, I have to go take care of a few more things. But before I go, I want you to have as much information about this girl as I do, so you can really think about what you're trying to take the fall for."

He straightened up in his chair a bit; we had been sitting for quite a while already.

"Rebecca drove herself home. She didn't turn her paintings in to the art show, and she didn't go back to school. Ever. She never stepped foot on the campus again. From what we can see, she went home and stayed there for five days straight. Her roommate said she didn't see her very often, and because she was an artist, she was often closed off for long periods of time and worked odd hours. So, it wasn't strange to her roommate that they hadn't seen one another. No one knew what had happened to her at the university. She spent almost a week by herself without ever talking to anyone directly following her Rape. No one knew what had happened to her at that point except for Willow Amos and the security guard."

I paused for a second because I really wanted all of this to sink in. His eyes were downcast, and I could see him looking at the young woman in the photograph.

"On the fifth day after her Rape, she left her house for the first time; we tracked her car using the mileage system she had in place through her insurance. The only place she went afterward was to the pharmacy. She bought one thing: a Pregnancy test, thanks to the store surveillance cameras and the store purchase tracker. We now know that she was, indeed, Pregnant, although we never found the test itself. We believe it was after she took the Pregnancy test and found out that she was Pregnant that she first tried to kill herself. We found a pair of scissors in her room that had traces of her blood. We believe this is what she used to cut her arm with. The Medical Examiner said it wasn't deep enough to have caused actual damage but had probably bled quite a bit and most likely scared her as much as it hurt. So, she didn't follow through on the other side once she realized it wasn't as easy as she expected it to be."

The man sitting across from me leaned forward a little and covered his face with his hands. I watched as he rubbed his temples, his forehead, and moved his hands over his closed eyelids. He seemed to become increasingly more tense with our talk, but I didn't want to stop yet until I'd told him everything I knew about Rebecca so far. I wanted him to know the full extent of what sort of mess he was in.

He was covering for someone, most likely Willow Amos. Whatever was motivating him to bear the burden of this entirely on his own, it was counterproductive to his own future, and he needed to know that there was nothing to be gained by it. He was trying to take the fall, and even if I couldn't understand why he was willing to do it, I could at least make him recognize that what they were doing wasn't worth protecting—especially not when he was the one that was going to end up paying the ultimate price for it.

"She didn't leave her house after she cut herself, so presumably she just bandaged it up on her own. We know that over those first five or six days that there had been a handful of people that had tried to get in touch with her. The day after she took the Pregnancy test though, Rebecca called Amos. It only lasted for three minutes, so I'm assuming they just set up a time to meet and talk."

Daegan Kyl had been sitting there listening intently, waiting for me to get to the part where she Committed Suicide. He had no idea what that poor girl went through before it got to that point, even still. It seemed almost naïve of him to have been so directly involved and yet not have a clue what was happening around him.

"At that point, we know Rebecca went to a licensed medical doctor that was moonlighting as an Abortionist and got an Abortion. We were able to track her bank and see surveillance of her as she pulled funds from a drive-through ATM. She was alone in the vehicle, and we believe she met with Willow Amos afterward or was otherwise instructed how to have her Abortion done. It was unlikely that she would have driven herself home or elsewhere directly following the Abortion, but her roommate didn't recall when she returned, and couldn't recall if she was home. She did, however, return with her own car at some point."

I took a deep breath.

"So now we have a girl, she had everything going for her, and she ends up getting Raped by this monster in broad daylight. In less than two weeks, her world is upside down. She went to both the security guard and then the school counselor on duty, thinking she would find help. She gets completely betrayed by what they presumably recommended to handle it; being told that social agendas are more important than reporting oneself as a Victim.

"She should have been able to expect some help from the campus security, but instead finds that the security guard is already aware of the Crime, but that he's doing the bidding of the student counselor. She doesn't know what to do or believe; she knows what has happened, but she's being made to feel responsible for protecting her Assailant. Just think about that for a second; she went to them for help, and they made her feel a social responsibility to cover for the man's Violent, Criminal Assault against her that stole her virginity and left her physically, emotionally, and psychologically scarred."

He looked over my head and at the light coming in from the narrow window. Still, he didn't speak.

"She wrote an email to her mother that week letting her know she was fine, just busy with classes. She was supposed to have been one of the featured artists, and yet she never dropped off her artwork. Several people that were working on the art show had reached out to get her paintings. She didn't even read their emails; she had already checked out in her mind, and whatever was going on with her during that time, all we know is that she stayed holed up in her room and isolated from the world."

At the time of her initial investigation when the SPD LEOs had visited her home and done a preliminary walk-through, they had looked through her bedroom, finding the pair of scissors, her laptop, and an unmade bed. Everything else seemed ordinary and in its place; there had been no other technology to go through, nor was anything else found that showed what she had been doing during that time.

I leaned back in my chair and used my right hand to rub my eyes, much like I had seen him do only minutes before. I understood his mood; it was wearing on me, much like I imagined it was on him. It was a lot of information to process; after all, we were summarizing the last two weeks of a young woman's life.

A Life that had ended far too soon, and in a manner that was especially stressful just to recount.

I could see images of her every time I closed my eyes. *Rebecca on the cold, metal table at the Medical Examiner's office, lifeless, still. Rebecca taking money out of her bank; eyes swollen and red from crying, distraught. Rebecca, lying in her room, curled up in a fetal position, hour after hour after hour…*

Rebecca, climbing over the bushes and back onto the trail, dragging her paintings and backpack, shoe missing, stockings torn. The dirt, twigs, and branches clinging to her hair as the camera watched her walk through the campus.

But worse than that, the images of her being unexpectedly pulled from the path from behind; helpless, confused, instantly sensing danger but not being able to see where it was coming from yet or why. Struggling; yelling out in surprise, feeling another person near her, but stronger, angrier, and using their power to control her.

That instant flash of understanding as she realized what was about to happen; when she realized what the man she had been struggling with was trying to do. She would have known she was too small, too weak, too isolated to fight back effectively. He had been hitting her, holding her arms down, pinning her with his body.

And then that awful moment; that moment that could never be taken back, that instant when she realizes not only the physical pain of having been Sexually Assaulted, but that the man on top of her had done it savagely, stealing something from her she had been saving for her husband, for her wedding night. Something sacred that she could never get back; that no one ever had a right to steal from another.

And that pain—that fear of not being able to control one's own physical surroundings, the fear of realizing that she wasn't strong enough to defend herself. The fear of not knowing if he was only going to Rape her, or if it was going to get worse because she had seen his face. That moment when she realized that this man, this Evil, Brutal animal that wouldn't just hurry and finish so she could escape—could decide to End her Life if he wanted, and that any man that would punch and Rape a woman would probably not have too much more difficulty killing her, too.

She would have been praying for it to stop, and yet no one had heard them, no one saved her.

My brain was overwhelmed with images of her, and I tried desperately to do what we had been told to do as part of our training whenever we found ourselves too overwhelmed with the realities of our jobs; I tried to imagine her as I'd also seen her.

I pictured her at her parents' home, laughing with them as they shared a meal together; *Rebecca as she hugged her mother and father goodbye as they helped her move into her new place, her first new apartment all on her own and the excitement and happiness that she must have felt.*

And then I pictured her in the best way I could; how I believed she was most happy and content. I envisioned her up in her loft, her long hair pulled back into a ponytail, a colorful canvas in front of her and the sunlight filling the room. She held a paintbrush in her hand as she worked, surrounded by her paintings, lost in her own world of imagery and beauty, capturing what was in her mind and heart and putting it down onto her canvas in a way that only she could have.

That was the person I needed to remember that I was here for. *The girl who loved to paint.*

But I also needed to remember that she was *'the girl who would never paint again'* for the sake of Justice.

We both sat there, lost in our own thoughts.

This much talk in one day, with this much detail, was hard on the Soul. It wore me down but what I was doing was important. It was the only voice that someone like Rebecca had left; I was the only person with enough power to fight for her, because she could no longer fight for herself.

It didn't matter that she had chosen Suicide; that was a technicality based entirely on the circumstances of her final weeks.

If we did not fight for those that could not fight for themselves—if we did not do everything in our power to rid the world of the Evils that plagued it, to denounce all those who found no moral shame in causing Violence or Harm to others—if we did not do what must be done, we were no better than the animals. Apathy and inaction were the same as granting consent.

I sat up straight in my chair again and collected my wandering thoughts before continuing.

He had been watching me quietly.

"So, her roommate said she heard her around the house on the days of the seventh and eighth, but they didn't talk. She hadn't been there very much because it was nearing the time for Finals Week at school. On the tenth day, the roommate had recalled that Rebecca had left the house because her car wasn't in the parking lot when she returned from her morning classes. We don't know what happened after that point. The last thing we have on record is that her roommate finally realized she hadn't seen her since the day she had heard her in the kitchen. It was because she had been in the kitchen that her roommate had finally figured out that they weren't just missing each other because of their schedules, but that she hadn't returned. Rebecca had a habit that she apparently did as a matter of routine, which was to rinse off her brushes in a container in the sink. She would bring her brushes down, soak them in specific containers depending on what type of paint she was using, and then she would eventually clean them off, return the chemicals to their spot under the sink, and then take her paintbrushes back to her loft where she painted. This time, the roommate realized the paintbrushes had been sitting in the same chemicals for almost a week. As soon as she had thought about it and added up the days, she had hit the Emergency Response button and reported her to Missing Persons."

Daegan Kyl took a deep breath and exhaled slowly.

"I haven't established a timeline beyond that," I said.

"But somehow, that young woman ended up dead and buried in a field, and you're the only link I have to her beyond what role I already know Willow Amos has played."

He looked at me.

"I would really prefer it if you didn't go down for Violence that wasn't of your own doing."

I stared at him for a minute, watching as he looked down at the pictures of Rebecca and LeRoy Jones, a dark scowl across his face.

Interview III: Cut from the Same Cloth

"You and I aren't so very different, you know," Daegan Kyl said.

"Oh, is that so? Enlighten me," I responded.

"It's a dog-eat-dog world out there; you're either the hammer or the nail. It wasn't so long ago that all the LEOs were busy being the scapegoat of the West; beaten down into submission, neutered and kept on such a short leash that your kind may as well have not even bothered to show up for work."

I understood his point, but I wasn't certain where he was going with his assessment or what he hoped to gain by it, so I didn't interfere with his monologue. He hadn't been very willing to talk thus far, so it was interesting that he would choose to begin with a philosophical comparison of our two career choices. Assuming, of course, he was comparing Law Enforcement to being a Soldier rather than being a gravedigger; I would have asked, but it was antagonistic and low-hanging fruit—the kind of snarky comment that one would have expected from the stereotypical donut-eating, overweight Detective frequently depicted on old television programs from the 21st century. The man sitting across from me did not deserve such needless jabs; even if he was a Serial Killer and a gravedigger, he was still a man that owned a massive corporation and had given more than a decade of his life to the service of our nation. That entitled him to a certain level of respect—even if he couldn't provide the same in return.

"Soldiers do the same thing; we all follow someone's orders, right? The difference is in public perception, though. We Soldiers commanded respect, and we never lost it. Even in the darkest chapters of the 21st century, we still held on to our honor and respect from the People. You know the same can't be said of Law Enforcement."

I knew, but everyone knew that much. It was common knowledge.

"You know what one of the greatest differences was? LEOs became braced for impact, while Soldiers caused it. You know what I'm saying? Soldiers were never neutered in the same way that the People had demanded from LEOs. We were always out there shooting, blowing shit up, and storming the castles—taking what we wanted and apologizing to no one—ever.

"LEOs, on the other hand, you guys were basically emasculated, beaten into submission like good dogs. All your cool toys were taken away, and you were told to hold the line rather than advance—even as they took away all the resources you needed to do your jobs right.

"They took more than just the dignity of Law Enforcement; they took your ability to be proactive—to be the source of authority that commanded respect. They stole your ability to do your jobs effectively—and it always left you playing defense rather than offense, making it impossible for you to do the jobs you were being paid to do.

"They said you couldn't be situationally aware, couldn't read the signs because you would be 'profiling', that being proactive only resulted in racism. They denied the evidence supporting reductions of crime and violence through broken window policing, attacked everyone who promoted stricter criminal justice policies, and called for an end to mass incarceration. They even blamed LEOs for juvenile arrests and harsh sentencing, citing that all it accomplished was the school-to-prison pipeline.

"They said you were all too mean and aggressive as they protested 'police brutality' and use of deadly force. They took away your ability to walk the streets with your Billy clubs, carry lethal weapons, and left you holding your…tasers…while the Criminals walked all over you, slaughtering you every chance they could."

He smiled wryly, his voice thick with sarcasm and contempt as he spoke.

"But somewhere deep down inside of the Sheepdog there's still a wild animal. He may be wired for civility better, and he may toe the line so he can engage with the Citizens more professionally, but the Sheepdog is only protective because he chooses to be. In the right situation, those Sheepdogs would turn into ravenous wolves and go for the jugular just like any Combat Soldier. Being told you have to stay on a leash doesn't make you trained, and it certainly doesn't mean there isn't still a primal animal at the end of it. The only thing being house-broken means is that you've learned how to play by the rules so you don't get thumped on the nose with a newspaper. All it takes to see the Sheepdog return to his primal self is for someone to come into your yard and threaten your life or the lives of those whom you're there to protect; they'll see soon enough that it's not just the K9s that have sharp teeth."

Leaning against his chair casually, he put his hands behind the back of his head and laced his fingers together, extending his thick arms into two pointed triangles behind him which deceptively resembled angelic wings.

"All things considered," he continued on, grinning, "I'd still take my LEO Brothers-in-arms over any other demographic in America other than my Fellow Soldiers. I know that when it comes down to it, the good guys are always fighting on the same team—and we are. You might not see it, and you might live in such a dull world of black and white it would make most people go insane, but we're still on the same team—and we *are* Brothers. You just don't know what I know yet, and based on what you can see, you think I'm on the opposite side of your war. Nothing could be further from the truth; I'm not your enemy. There are some terrible people out there still, I'm not disputing that. But I'm not one of them. I'm just a Soldier trying to get through this life with my Soul intact. But you should know—once an Oath-Keeper, always an Oath-Keeper."

I cocked my head a little to the side and furrowed my brows, considering his words. I could see his point more than he could ever really believe, but my job wasn't to coddle the crazy. Nor was it to applaud the Alleged Offenders as they climbed up onto their soapboxes and asked for a spotlight while they unloaded their maniacal justifications for Committing Felonies. I was not obligated to find 'common ground' with him. The man, even if he had once been a Soldier, was sitting across from me because he was connected to the burial of four sets of Human Remains—while I sat opposite him willing to send him to Death Row for having broken the Laws of our Land.

Law Enforcement and US Soldiers may, indeed, be cut from the same cloth, but this man and me were nothing alike, and we were not the same.

I did not mean this to diminish their professions or the importance of what they did; I held a deep and abiding respect for our military professionals and knew what they brought to the table for our nation and Citizenry. But to say we were on an even keel regarding our daily professional experiences was false, and it did a disservice to our national Law Enforcement to proclaim those in our military branches were placed at a higher level of danger or significance just by wearing the uniform—and yet many believed this.

Soldiers might need to 'hold the line' occasionally, but my Brothers and Sisters in Blue had been holding the line every day within our nation since the very first whispers of a New World had been formed. My profession had a proven track record of being an integral component within our society, and they expected us to hold the line so our Fellow Countrymen didn't have to.

We risked danger to ourselves—including the risk of Death itself—every single day when we put on our uniforms and punched the clock. My Brothers and Sisters lost their lives every year, and it was a heartbreaking reality that this risk would never diminish completely. There would always be Peacekeepers who lost their lives in the line of duty.

We were *not* the same.

American Soldiers were only genuinely in direct danger whilst deployed—and there were many career fields and Soldiers who went their entire lives without ever deploying or facing a battlefield. Yes, there were some Combat Soldiers, such as the man sitting across from me, who might have spent more time than average in awful places doing awful things. But for the most part, in times of Peace and within most job descriptions, being a Soldier did not differ from any other job—and was certainly no more high risk. Outside of combat zones, combat MOS's, and specific branches of the military that were more inclined to see and take part in Violence and Warfare, many of the Soldiers he spoke of would never taste blood unless it came from a paper cut, and the only time they risked mortal danger was during field training exercises and weapons qualifications.

When Soldiers returned home after a deployment, they were secure, knowing they were out of Imminent Danger.

My Brothers and Sisters were never afforded such courtesies. Law Enforcement was never granted the peace of mind or security that came with knowing we were removed from the Line of Fire. We knew we could face Ambushes and Attacks merely for wearing a uniform or even parking in front of our own home in a squad car, on duty or not.

We had *always* been At Risk of Ambush, and always At Risk of Death, and perhaps most unsettling, we almost always lost our lives because of the actions of other

Americans. It was far, far worse to know that our lives were being placed into danger at the expense of our Fellow Citizens—and our own neighbors and Countrymen were the ones who were so full of Hate and Desperation that they were willing to Murder us just for doing *a job*.

Our 'Enemies' weren't some unknown demographic on foreign soil that we were told were Evil and must be stopped as they handed us a weapon and told us where to go. We were never given carte blanche to go wipe out anyone—no matter how Violent they were or how much we could identify them as the 'bad guys'. The same Evildoers that went around wreaking havoc in Third World nations had committed the same egregious Acts of Violence and Acts of Terror on US soil, but we were never given the same rights or protocols as our military regarding how to address it.

In matters of Deadly Force, both our actions and consequences were decidedly different—oppositional, even.

Soldiers went overseas, and into the jungles and deserts of the world, knowing why they were there and who their Enemy was—or at least who their Enemy *could* be. They could walk with their hands on their firearms in anticipation of Confrontation, Ambush, and potential Danger. Our Soldiers were told to annihilate the Communists and Oppressors who were Violating Human Rights and slaughtering Innocent Civilians. They were then revered for their efforts as if they were artisans and craftsmen, glorified and exalted for their skill and marksmanship.

We as Law Enforcement weren't allowed to use Deadly Force even when confronted with Evildoers of the same ilk within our communities; we couldn't address their Murderous, Violent, or Psychotic ways directly unless they first placed us into Harm's Way or were a direct threat to other Civilians. Unknown and unquantifiable numbers of lives of both Civilians and Peacekeepers were lost because of these rigid policies.

Under the blanket of our Constitution, even those whom we knew to be foreign terrorists, serial killers, sexual predators, or violent career criminals, were expected to be treated with humane courtesy, captured, and detained without lethal force or loss of life. Soldiers were never accountable for every bullet spent, whereas Peacekeepers were expected to explain and justify every procedural act with minute detail and rigid, by-the-book responses, automatically placed on 'administrative leave' after every shooting, and subjected to internal investigations at will.

Soldiers might be beholden to the rules of the Geneva Convention—or at least had been when the United Nations had been in existence—but we Peacekeepers had been handicapped by legislation designed to cripple us. They wanted to tie our hands and drown us in exhausting paperwork, legal barricades, and accountability standards that placed us at an almost impossible disadvantage for self-defense. The Rules of Engagement were entirely different, as were the consequences.

It couldn't be classified in the same ballpark when Soldiers were shipped off for an all-expense paid trip to another country, given a blueprint outlining what their mission and objective was, told how they were going to achieve said goals, and then provided with every conceivable piece of artillery, top of the line equipment, and the best technology in the world to complete their mission. They were armed with the best of the best, given almost unlimited financial backing from our government, and outfitted with the most elite and advanced arsenal of weapons, protective gear, and array of firepower. They were the most well-equipped Soldiers in the history of Civilization. No matter what point in time one considered, the US military had been a reigning champion on the international circuit. As a First World nation—as *the* First World nation—our Soldiers had been considered the elite simply because we provided them with the most basic of self-defense and tactical gear, and when our troops arrived, the ground shook with the force of our might.

The world knew what we were doing, and we were almost always given the benefit of the doubt and the blessing of Humanity for our efforts to do Good Deeds on behalf of Mankind. Whether it be intervention because Evil was on the rise and advancing, or stepping up to save the world through Humanitarian Aid by providing manpower, resources, and equipment after a natural disaster, US troops and the US government had always been there. America could always be counted on to be where they were needed.

None of that applied to Law Enforcement, nor to the perception of LEOs, and it didn't matter at which point in history one referred to. Soldiers got to play the Heroes on a global scale, even if they were oftentimes demonized by our Enemies and those who bore deep-seated resentment toward the West. And the world fell at their feet because there were none who could compare outside of Western Civilization.

Did they put their noses into places they didn't belong too much? Absolutely. But when they did, at least their government had their back, didn't betray them, and always ensured that they had what they needed to get the job done. They also didn't mess around with their ability to do their jobs effectively or place their lives in unnecessarily compromising positions which could result in adverse consequences or the needless Deaths of Soldiers.

In addition, Soldiers weren't given two sets of rules based on which political party was in power and in charge of them. This had been standard practice for Law Enforcement, however, and the amount of support they received had been largely contingent upon the political party currently in office, creating a compromised system that seldom resulted in a positive work environment for Peacekeepers. This had been prevalent throughout the history of Law Enforcement during the 21st century before the Great Reformation. It was because of this type of hostility that LEOs had needed the protection of unions, knowing that they could count on their Brothers for safety even if they couldn't find the necessary support from their local leaders, Mayors, or Governors.

Our budgets had constantly been under attack and cut by politicians who loathed the badge and had no issue abusing their authority. They had done this even when it resulted in high costs to the American People and countless lives were lost within Law Enforcement due to inadequate Personal Protection Equipment.

Peacekeepers had spent generations struggling for adequate funding. They were incessantly challenged for not having the appropriate gear or Personal Protection Equipment, such as cameras for their uniforms, while simultaneously chastised for having equipment that both the public and politicians branded as 'militarized'. They had to fight for adequate resources to staff Emergency Services and even do crowdsourcing to secure enough funding to supply K9s with Kevlar vests. Major cities had politicians cut their annual budgets for political reasons, endangering both Peacekeepers and Citizens alike. Cities were under-staffed, emergency call centers were over-whelmed, and countless 'non-violent' reports went completely unanswered without investigations due to a continuous lack of resources. Even Rape Kits and other vital lab work went unaddressed due to backlogs and lack of resources, and that didn't even begin to address the bottle-necked backlog of criminal cases that went untried and buried by overwhelmed and underpaid legal professionals in a system being entirely crushed by the sheer volume of crime and violence. Throughout the history of America, there were few systems that were ever as fundamentally underserved and broken as our Criminal Justice system, and that affected every aspect of Law Enforcement.

The US government rarely had the backs of Peacekeepers, especially when political powers chose to place targets on the backs of our LEOs and paint them with broad strokes in the hopes of inciting more resentment as they created an anti-Law Enforcement sentiment throughout the nation. For generations, this was illustrated time and again by the dwindling numbers of Peacekeepers and the inability to drum up new recruits—all of which caused a chain reaction of increased crime and violence with every decreased Police Force.

The US Soldier was glorified as Noble and Heroic, and thanked for their service merely for wearing the uniform wherever they went. Soldiers had their meals paid for by strangers while Peacekeepers were gunned down as they tried to have lunch in their patrol cars. If they were on break, sitting in a restaurant or coffee shop with their colleagues, and they were seen by the Criminal Class to be in a vulnerable enough position for Ambush, they were attacked—gunned down in public without any provocation. Every single year, for absolutely no other reason than because one of our Fellow Countrymen was employed as a member of Law Enforcement and wore the uniform, our Fellow Citizens were murdered in cold blood. Violently. Savagely.

We as a nation celebrated our Soldiers who were Lost during each and every battle through tributes and memorials, while very little recognition was ever provided to the Peacekeepers who paid with their lives, often leaving behind Loved Ones.

All of this was decidedly different than how things were for Law Enforcement within These United States and how it always had been in the past. It went far beyond just how the two were perceived. It was as fundamentally ingrained within the fabric of American culture as any of the core tenets of Americanism; there had always been a negative light cast upon Law Enforcement that was not often present for the Armed Forces. The results of this were evident not only by how Law Enforcement was discussed, but in how it was provided funding and representation as well. Everything related to the core operation of local, state, and federal was dissected and subject to scrutiny, debate, and public opinion.

Even our Oaths were different, with a much higher emphasis placed on the personal Honor and Character of Law Enforcement than the Soldier. We were held to a different level—judged and vilified by very different standards. Whether right or wrong, fair or not, that was just the way it was.

Soldiers not only never faced public outcry for breaking laws or the rules of their enlistment contracts, it was a well-established system which had actually provided the means for the Criminal Class to join the military rather than face criminal prosecution—something that only resulted in a lowering of character and class of military personnel overall and of which would never have been allowed within the ranks of Law Enforcement. Even when members of the military committed crimes, they were censured and punished through their own system of justice—none of which was subject to scrutiny, headlining notoriety, or public vilification like members of Law Enforcement endured.

And finally, to the best of my knowledge, Soldiers hadn't ever been put on Death Row for failing to do their jobs in accordance with the latest policies and public opinion. LEOs, on the other hand, had been subjected to extreme workplace accountability from the point of rigid application processes, job performance, and microscopic public evaluations after anything deemed controversial more than any other profession in the 21st century. When an Officer was determined to have done something inappropriate according to the court of public opinion, his entire life and job performance was placed under a microscope. Every infraction or commendation was thrust into the public eye for judgment as his personal and professional life were torn apart and his future left uncertain, precariously perching on the animus of the Prosecutor's office and the calls for blood in the streets.

As if that weren't enough, Peacekeepers were vilified for the color of their skin, and accused of being racist whenever a controversial case occurred and the Offender was of a different skin color. Law Enforcement, regardless of the personal character of the Peacekeepers, regardless of their own cultural identities or even the color of their skin, were arbitrarily branded as 'White Supremacists' and 'Nationalists' by every disgruntled Citizen looking to cast dispersions—regardless of the truth or realities of such claims. Such attacks against their person were commonplace, even if irrelevant or entirely unfounded. None of this was an issue within our Armed Forces, nor was it a common sentiment, given the diversity within our ranks.

No other profession had demanded so much from its employees yet provided so little in return, and very few had ever asked their employees to sacrifice everything, including their own lives. No other career demanded the Death Penalty for cases in which a professional responded to a situation with a greater use of force than what was determined to have been necessary—as judged by others who were not there, who never wore the badge, who had no comparable training or experience, and who were incapable of relating to the situation with any type of first-hand knowledge or emotional connection. It was an extremely high price to ask someone to pay for something classified as a 'mistake on the job', and yet we had not only expected members of Law Enforcement to pick up the badge as that hung over their heads, we also expected them to lay down their lives for the same job and Citizenry. It was an outrageous, and wholly misguided, expectation to demand, and yet for generations, our nation had demanded it.

There were zero other government professions with that standard of job performance, and yet despite this, we still had brave men and women willing to sign on, choosing to accept all risks and pay whatever costs required of them. In the history of our nation, where countless politicians lined their pockets and broke their promises, where public educators failed to teach our children, and where warmongers in our government risked the lives of our Soldiers in dangerous, unfounded, and costly military ventures, none were ever asked to bear the burden of equal consequence for their disastrous job performance. Only LEOs, only those whom our nation could never survive without, were expected to bear such a weight, and accept such severe consequences for actions frequently done within seconds and while under extreme duress. Nothing compared to what we demanded of our Peacekeepers or expected them to agree to as part of their profession.

Daegan Kyl might have been looking for common ground—a way to create a bridge during our time together to construct the illusion that we were, indeed, on the 'same side' as he had stated. But after watching my Brothers die at the hands of the very Citizens they were Sworn to Protect and Defend for the last three-hundred years, it was not a platform I was quick to share. Nor was I willing to diminish the significant Sacrifices—and willingness to Sacrifice themselves—that my Fellow Law Enforcement Officers had done.

Each of us may have Sworn Oaths for our nation and Citizenry, but the expectations for those Oaths were decidedly different—and one only had to look at the standards and character of each party to see the difference. Our country may have once held Soldiers to a certain standard of professionalism, but it was a bar that had dramatically lowered during the 21st century. Meanwhile, the levels of accountability had only increased and advanced as the nation turned the evaluation of Law Enforcement Officers into a national pastime. Their work performance was evaluated and sensationalized, subjected to national debate for armchair quarterbacking and sanctimonious political controversy.

There may have been a time when the man sitting opposite me might have been something similar to myself, but he was a long way from being the Soldier he once was—and I was nothing like my manacled Brothers from a century ago.

TWENTY-TWO – WILLOW AMOS —ARRESTED

Meeting Willow Amos

The first time I laid eyes on Willow Amos, I had been surprised by her. I don't know what I had expected regarding her personality, but I suppose I had envisioned someone much craftier and snake-like in her demeanor. Caroline Randall had described her as the type of person who was usually in the background, whispering in a person's ear, casting spells and manipulating everyone with a few carefully chosen words or turn of phrase. I had observed her through the SPD surveillance footage following her Arrest after Arlan's Abduction, but she hadn't spoken in those videos. She hadn't even moved other than taking the time to make the phone call to her attorney; she had been frozen like a statue the entire time, making it impossible for anyone to see her true nature.

Now that she'd been Arrested and brought into an Interview Room, I could observe her in person. I had mixed feelings about what I was looking at. She seemed young, sullen, and hostile. She didn't seem like the Criminal sort—she seemed like every other young woman in her mid-twenties or any other young professional.

She didn't seem violent, physically confrontational, or as though she were going to be the next menace to society. I didn't see her as some Criminal Mastermind, the leader of the great anti-American Anarchists club. She was…underwhelming.

Yet here we were—her second Arrest in less than a year, her hands covered in the blood of possibly four Victims.

She sat there, arms folded, brooding, waiting for someone to enter.

She'd had a lucky break with the investigation of Arlan.

It was time to figure out just how much she had gotten away with since then.

Establishing Communication: Willow Amos

At the very least, given her age and the personality that seemed to seep through despite her contrary behavior, I had expected someone with an outgoing personality; someone socially adept and used to being the center of attention. It wasn't just that her appearance was almost waif-like; she had a pixie cut hairstyle and wore street clothes with a color palette that made me question if she was colorblind. Everything about her made her seem like she was just a young and carefree adult—except this one had the behavior of a sewer rat, and the mouth of a sailor.

"I have nothing to say to you."

She stared at me, her arms folded across her chest. Her body posture was as petulant as a child's.

"You don't have to say anything to me at all, but as a reminder, you can still ask to have an attorney present."

She made eye contact with me and scowled.

"And how long are you planning on keeping me here?"

I met her gaze through my visor. It was open to the quarter setting, so my eyes were clear enough for her to see them. Details were still concealed because of the tint, such as my eye color, but they were exposed enough for her to see that she was speaking to an actual Human Being. I didn't think she was ever going to be released back into society again even if she got an attorney, but common sense dictated that this woman was untrustworthy enough I needed to follow protocol.

Even if my lodgings were contained within the Law Enforcement barracks and my transportation was secured in underground, private parking, there were still plenty of cases from the past that had proven that if bad people wanted to get to good ones and cause them Harm and Death that they could always find a way.

"I don't need an attorney; I haven't done anything wrong. It doesn't matter what you attempt to do to me, don't you get it? I'm not making any apologies for anything I've done, and I'm not sorry about any of it. You probably don't have any evidence anyhow—but even if you do, what difference does it make? Do you think you're going to stop us?"

She was staring at me, her body tense as she leaned forward. Her face was contorted into an angry grimace, brows furrowed, openly hostile and aggressive.

I didn't move back, even as she continued to push toward me. I knew her RFID bracelet would prevent her from being able to lunge toward me, and it would halt her in her tracks if she tried. She posed no physical threat, but I didn't understand why she wouldn't stop talking. She knew that anything she volunteered could be used against her during her trial and at her Sentencing; any chance she had of escaping punishment would be squelched if she incriminated herself, and yet she kept talking.

"We can provide you with an attorney. This is your right as an American Citizen. Do you wish to have someone present?" I calmly asked her again.

She let out an angry scream. It wasn't too loud or long, it was just something that expressed her frustration, and I believed it was more about her lack of control over her situation rather than the interview itself. Even still, she was a twenty-seven-year-old woman—a graduate student presumably capable of handling intense medical situations and functioning like a normal, educated, professional adult. Her loud screeching had caused several of the LEOs standing guard to jump. I could imagine the looks on their faces as they turned to look at her through their visors, trying to process why a grown woman was behaving in such an immature manner.

As for my guest, I didn't believe she was concerned about getting caught or being held accountable for her actions in the legal sense as much as it was about her not being able to just get up and leave because she didn't want to be here. She had also made several comments about how she felt about Law Enforcement though, and had entered the room kicking and screaming, screeching at the local SPD LEOs that had Arrested her and brought her in. They appeared unmoved by her behavior, but I had found it moderately childish, not to mention unbecoming.

It seemed misguided. It was no light matter that she had been brought back into the SPD Headquarters regarding these issues or her prior interactions with Arlan. She was here because she was 'Allegedly' helping people Commit Suicide; that was a dangerous discussion to be engaging in with your Fellow Man, and she had not only invited the conversation, she had been advocating on behalf of it.

She was giving them a well-oiled song and dance about how it was 'their right' to choose Death rather than fighting with everything they had to stay Alive. Her sales pitch promoted the idea that it was somehow 'empowering' for them to choose their own path even if that path led them straight into a flatline and the complete forfeiture of all additional days they might have been given. She had even referenced the old 21st century Death Campaign slogan that had been used, which had declared that Ending Life through Suicide or Assisted Suicide was a way for Citizens to 'Die with Dignity'— as if glorifying Death and attempting to create a romantic, idealized, glossy coating over it would altogether diminish the abhorrent finality and horror of it all. Yet despite all of this, she was indignant about being inconvenienced after having been called out about it and Arrested.

It seemed like such a contradiction; was this person an enlightened anarchist that believed in her convictions and was willing to stand by them to the very end regardless of their criminality, or was she an emotionally petulant child that was now throwing a tantrum because she didn't get her way? I didn't agree with her views and knew that what she was doing was contrary to our legal system. I believed her actions to be morally and ethically reprehensible as well; but none of that was relevant to the conversation that I was now attempting to have with her. If she believed in what she was doing, believed it was the right thing to do and stood by those beliefs, then she shouldn't be regressing into this emotionally infantile behavior; she should stand firm and resolute.

She couldn't have it both ways; she couldn't denounce our laws because they were oppositional to her 'values', and disregard all those that she deemed unacceptable, without eventually facing severe consequences for her lawlessness. Likewise, she couldn't make bold declarations about how her views were the only ones that were acceptable, cross significant legal, ethical, and social boundaries by pushing those views onto others, but then follow up with ridiculously childish, entitled, and immature histrionics once she had been caught.

"No, I don't want one of your Big Brother lawyers! What good would it do? They're just more of the same—a bunch of gutless snakes hiding behind masks and pretending to fight for Americans right until the minute they help them get sentenced to Death. You're all the same! So, what does it matter if I have someone here or not? You're just going to make me disappear or kill me anyhow, aren't you? Isn't that how this goes?"

She sat back in her chair and seemed to relax a little. I said nothing.

"I mean, that's what this is, right? The big, grand finale? My Swan Song before I vanish?"

She laughed. It was a little on the fringes of hysteria.

"Don't worry—the people that need to know already know that I'm not there anymore. My life would be over if you let me go anyhow. Do you think they would trust anyone once they've been dragged in here and put face to face with you monsters? Do you think anyone out there would let me within ten feet of them once they knew your robot thugs had picked me up?"

I kept watching her, but she broke eye contact and stared at the end of the wall toward the window. She kept her arms folded across her chest angrily as she slouched in the chair. After a moment, the expression on her face changed, reflecting what was possibly the first genuinely sincere look since we had met. It showed who this woman truly was at her core, beyond her outrage, hate, and frustration. She looked sad, and full of regret. Her shoulders had fallen into a slump that indicated a sense of hopelessness and defeat. It was a look of surrender.

I don't know why, but it made me feel sad as well.

She had thrown her life away. She was young; only twenty-seven. Many people at her age were only just finishing their educations, just starting their careers. They were immersed in idealism, had spent their lives in relative security and ease, having been sheltered within the world of academia. Many, such as herself, had never really been out in the 'real world' yet; they had gone from their childhood homes to universities or trade schools, and then many had moved on to advanced educations such as I had. I understood the naivety regarding world views that she still had; she'd never had the responsibilities that came with adulthood.

She had never known what it was like to be married or a mother that needed to take care of people other than herself. Her entire adult life had been spent in a protected community where ideas and idealism reigned. In her limited experience, everything was black and white; there was no connection to the realities of what it was truly like to live in a world where everything was some shade of grey, all of which were constantly shifting based on new information being processed. In such a world, every new element a person was exposed to was an opportunity to take in new perspectives, gain a deeper, more complex understanding of the intricacies of our society, and at the very least, help reaffirm and expand upon the reasons why the views one held were already in place and the right ones to have. A belief system, when uncontested and which prohibits any conflicting or opposing points of view, could not conceivably allow for the continued development and advancement of oneself. There was no easier way to ensure one's stagnation than to live in an environment that serves as an echo chamber and disallows any outside discourse from occurring.

Many years before the Great Reformation, universities were highly prone to creating a toxic, repressive atmosphere rather than an enlightened one. It didn't seem as though an entire university could recreate such an environment in these modern times, but it was plausible that it could occur on a much smaller scale such as strictly within the healthcare program to which Willow Amos and her cohorts had belonged.

She was sitting here because she believed in her convictions with a childlike wonder that had as much of a grasp on reality as her ability to comprehend that she had gambled in a game that had real life consequences which might destroy her.

She was to be pitied, but she also presented an obvious lesson. This was what happened when idealistic beliefs lead a person to perform acts that violate the law. There will be accountability. We may choose our actions, but not the consequences that follow.

But there was also another lesson to be noted, and this one mattered just as much: This was what happened when people stopped paying attention to the dangerous cancers that were being developed and spread beneath the surface. Such poisonous beliefs were not only capable of undermining a nation and its Citizens, they could spread like wildfire, and if left unchecked, could cause extreme Harm within a nation and to its Citizens.

This woman was not alone in her actions or her beliefs. She was but one domino amid dozens, or hundreds, or thousands—or possibly even millions. Who knew how deeply this cancer had already spread, or how far. This was but one woman in one city in one state—and I had already linked her to two Victims with complete certainty, and an entire network of co-conspirators that had been working alongside her.

Our nation was in trouble; far more trouble than this woman was. She was going to lose her freedom and her Citizenship without question. At the very least, she would be Exiled, but it was much more likely that she would pay with her life. That was the risk she was willing to take, and it was a price she had clearly come to terms with as one she was willing to pay.

But America was unprepared for all of this; whatever was festering beneath the surface was still unknown to the Citizens of our nation, and as such, we were blindly being led to the slaughter by unknown forces that we could not control. There was nothing more dangerous than an ideology that could influence its followers to the point of Murder. Because of this, our nation was under attack. And once again, Americans were not only completely oblivious to it, neither Her Citizens nor Her government understood just how dangerous this cancerous poison already was.

The American People and Willow Amos were examples of the extraordinary price that could be paid because of naivete and idealism—even when unaware of the danger.

Irreconcilable Differences

Willow Amos had spit on me.

Spitting on Law Enforcement had been happening since the earliest days of Peacekeeping. It was one of the more disturbing things that people were known to do when confrontational, disruptive, and aggressive.

That level of disrespect was extremely uncommon, mercifully. We rarely encountered Citizens who would do something so dangerous, but when it occurred, it was usually because they were intoxicated or on drugs. It seemed unimaginable that a Human Being would spit on another, especially for no other reason than because they didn't like them, or 'approve' of them or their profession.

Yet the person sitting across from me, a person that I had never met before this day, a stranger that I had never shared any specific history or grievances, had smugly sat facing me with a scowl on her face and her arms folded across her chest, and then lunged forward and spit on me.

After a while, though, it all blended together. Her tirade might eventually prove useful to the Prosecutor, but it certainly wasn't helping her any. She had a lot to say about a series of social issues, most of which were completely irrelevant to our modern society and laws. But the more she spoke, the more she showcased where her mind had absorbed most of her information and political beliefs, and just from the brief time she rambled, she had made several declarations that indicated she thought she had been Arrested because of her political activities on the university campus.

I knew nothing about her activities there. I knew nothing about most of the people, groups, or social agendas she kept defending. For legal purposes, she had been read her Miranda rights and told numerous times that she did not have to speak. She knew that everything she said was being monitored and recorded, and that she didn't have to speak until she had her attorney beside her. Still, she persisted.

From a professional standpoint, I wanted to tell her to stop talking because she was obviously only making her situation worse—and there was absolutely no doubt about that. She sat there making condescending, blatantly hostile remarks, and all the while she was incriminating herself and fueling her own demise.

I was glad that it was all being recorded.

Grace O'Connor was watching from the other room, and I could see from her expression that she was more than a little taken aback by the woman's behavior.

This was the vague, shady grey stuff in the realm of ideological Terrorism. These weren't Crimes of Passion; they weren't Murdering because they were in love with someone, hated someone, or couldn't have someone.

I hadn't ever worked in the private sector, and I hadn't ever worked in psychology or psychiatry. But I had taken a lot of required classes over the years for my education. They taught us about the importance of 'de-escalation' and learning how to defuse volatile Citizens, such as people who were drunk or on drugs, or those that might suffer from psychological issues. In order to do that, they gave us a comprehensive education regarding the more well-known mental illnesses that we might encounter as Peace Officers. Beyond just being able to assess situations, read people's Body Language, and being trained to look for certain behavioral signs and verbal cues, we were also taught how important it was to understand what our own Body Language and interaction with such people might lead to. We were trained to monitor our own behaviors, aggression, Body Language, and to select our wording carefully.

None of that had ever helped me deal with women better, especially when they were just plain crazy.

There was a certain point when talking to people was a useless endeavor; some people just had too much adrenaline surging through to control themselves, and nothing 'rational' remained. When that happened, it was usually best to extract oneself from the situation and just wait for another time. Sometimes, certain people were so easily triggered that even without provocation they were still impossible to talk to, and that was just the way things were with them. Willow Amos seemed to fit into that category.

I could appreciate that she was 'impassioned', and she believed that her actions were Morally Just. I understood that she believed she was providing a fundamental, ethical Human Right to the people that she helped.

I wasn't so narrow-minded, pragmatic, or strait-laced that I couldn't appreciate that a person had some idealistic notion about people taking their own lives in dramatic tales of lovelorn fantasy or dark, brooding melancholy. I could even see how people had twisted Euthanasia into some romanticized, profound act of heroic valor and independence. It was 'seizing control of one's own destiny' in some grand 'Final Act' in which the brave person declares they have 'chosen to part from this earth on their own terms'.

People were strange; they frequently glorified things that were socially unacceptable or difficult to understand. By design, people were also obstinate, argumentative, and oppositional; it was very appealing to certain personality types to seek anything they believed society was opposed to and cleave to it purely for that reason. There were plenty of people that were exactly like that. They were like toddlers fighting for independence; as soon as they were told something was off-limits or they couldn't do it, that was all they wanted to do more than anything else. Some personality types just wanted to buck the system; they always had, and they always would.

I wasn't saying that was who this woman was, or that was what she was doing; but one thing I was sure about was that she was not capable of being reasoned with, and no amount of time or effort on my end was going to make it worthwhile. I would not risk procedural issues related to her Arrest because of her meltdown. There wasn't a sane person who would look at the manner in which this woman had behaved since entering this room that would lead them to believe that she was of sound mind at this time.

Trying to have a conversation with her, let alone a productive interview, would not happen now; not with her being so agitated. Maybe later, after she cooled down, she would be more reasonable, or at least allow an attorney to be called.

I was tired.

My uniform was covered in saliva by a woman that had called me a 'killer' and a 'savage'; the irony was not lost. Of the two of us, I had not physically touched her—not once—but she had spit Bodily Fluids on me several times throughout her enraged outburst as she had been brought into the Interview Room. She had spit on multiple other LEOs as well.

Her spit—the transmission of any biological substance, whether it be spit, blood, urine, or feces—was not only a Criminal Offense and resulted in Felony Assault charges, it was also a potentially lethal action. She would be tested as part of her Arrest and Detainment processing, and if any of her blood work came back as Positive for any communicable diseases, it would compound her predicament considerably. If it could be proven that she was aware of her status, or there was suitable reason to believe that she should have known, then she would face Attempted Murder charges for each LEO that was spit upon.

If she had documented medical records attesting to her condition, it would serve as evidence against her. If she was infected with a communicable disease, such as HIV/AIDS, Hepatitis C, or a litany of others that were on the list, then she would face a multitude of additional charges. Because every Citizen had healthcare, and because everyone had 100% access to their records, it would be reasonable to presume that she was aware of her condition and would be held accountable for the transmission of her fluids, especially as a healthcare professional.

It didn't matter that the LEOs, including myself, were protected from contact through our uniforms; there was no guarantee that our uniforms would be entirely impenetrable for everything 100% of the time. She had placed us at risk through her actions. It came down to the usual pattern of questioning in which one only had to ask, "Would the LEOs have been at risk of anything at that moment if she had not done what she did?" And if the answer is that the other person's actions created the risk, then the responsibility was there because of their actions. She was going to get charged with Felony Assault as it was, but the outcome of her testing would determine if there would be any further charges.

When there were incurable diseases out there, and Citizens that were willing to endanger us just for doing our jobs, we were fortunate to have the Personal Protective Equipment and security measures that we did. But it was unacceptable behavior, and it was important that we as a society had taken the measures that we had to correct it. No member of Law Enforcement should have to fear for their own safety so much that they are facing dangers from every direction, with all of it being beyond their ability to control.

Ensuring that LEOs were given the best, most advanced safety equipment possible was a good first step, as was making it a federal Felony Assault charge if Citizens used any Bodily Fluids as a weapon against Law Enforcement. But the dangers were still there; the risk of developing something that might end one's life, end their career, affect their families, and unquestionably alter or halt their sexuality and relationships were all very real consequences that Law Enforcement faced every time they encountered dangerous Citizens that did not care about how their behavior could affect others.

The Criminal Class had long since been documented as being the highest demographic of Citizens in the US during the 21st century that were infected with communicable diseases. They were the least likely to seek proper medical care or treatment, the most likely to engage in risk-taking behaviors that resulted in the spread of disease, and the most violently aggressive people for Law Enforcement to work with and physically restrain. The chances for infection through their workplace environment—because of their interaction with the Citizens they were most likely to interact with—were exceptionally high for many LEOs, especially those on the Front Line. It wasn't often that I was placed into a position where I was subjected to such vile, disgusting behavior, and for that, I was grateful.

As with all the other Officers she came into contact with, I would have my Uniform inspected and then have a period of follow-up care monitored over time to ensure that I had not been infected with anything. Obviously, the risks were reduced if Willow Amos checked out clean for her blood work, but there was still a risk if she had been recently infected herself. At any rate, protocol would ensure that both she and each of the Officers affected—including myself—were monitored regularly for the next year.

Given what was at stake for each of us, I hoped for her sake she checked out clean. She was not making any of this any easier on herself.

TWENTY-THREE – AOM — ARRESTED

Rounding Up the Angels

We still needed to connect The Angels of Mercy anarchists to Daegan Kyl; at least one of them had to be in contact with Kyl and arrange for him to transport and then bury the Victims. I was certain that Willow Amos would be the one that served as their communications liaison, and she would be the person who was in contact with Daegan Kyl. I needed to establish that connection; I was certain that Officer Stanton could extract that information through his end.

We had Arrested all the 'Alleged' Angels of Mercy that were known to be employees of the Winter Season Hospice Care facility and students at GSAU. They were taken to the SPD Interrogation Division, awaiting my arrival. Grace O'Connor and I read through their files while we were transported back to SPD. None of the group had any prior criminal records, and none of them had ever been Arrested. We saw nothing unusual to show that they were prone to felonious behavior, and there were no documented issues regarding Violence or abuse throughout their childhoods and educational years. They all had some degree of higher education, and almost all were employees of Winter Season Hospice Care facility. The only connection they seemed to have between them was the link regarding their involvement in this criminal enterprise.

We would conduct our interviews, compile our data, and proceed from there. The only way to know just how deep it went, as well as how far, was to get as much information extracted from them as possible.

One of the typical issues, of course, was that we could not pit them against each other since all were looking at the same levels of Sentencing if it could be proven that they were all complicit. Given that I had not requested Warrants until I had enough evidence to confirm that each was complicit in their roles, I did not foresee any of them ending up with anything less than Exile. If it came to be known that any had directly supplied transportation, information, funding, or medical aid—including medication—to any of my Victims, especially Rebecca and Arlan, they would be Sentenced to Death.

This did not disturb me, and I felt no remorse. They knew the risks; they knew the price. If they had been motivated by their own system of beliefs and values rather than through money, then they also had made the decision that it had been worth the risk despite the consequences if caught. This was the result of freedom of choice; we would all be held accountable for our own actions, with no one forcing our hand. Our deeds determined the nature of our life as well as the path toward our own demise when we chose to cross the line into darkness. Their Victims, especially Katarina and Mariam, were not given that choice. Their Deaths were forced upon them.

In one of the most reprehensible experiences Humanly possible to endure, they had been subjected to unbelievable Pain, Suffering, and Torture during their Final Moments spent on this earth. They were denied the full measure of their lives and the opportunity for a peaceful Death in their winter years.

There would be no sympathy, and there would certainly be no quarter given.

We would use every tool and resource we had, every method of tracking their histories, every technological advantage we owned, and do everything within our power to provide an indisputable, air-tight, forensically, and technologically secure file of evidence. And with this undeniable trail of proof, we would land a Conviction for each, and give them the Sentences that most accurately fit their Crimes.

Should they be fortunate enough to only find themselves Exiled, they should consider themselves very lucky indeed. It would remind them of the purity of our Criminal Justice system, proving that there was no personal emotion involved in their Sentencing.

For this, they should be very grateful. Because without the Sentence Reform Act serving as a neutral guideline, there would be many calls for their Deaths, especially from those who were Left Behind after their Loved Ones had been Murdered through Euthanasia. For all those who had lost someone, nothing short of the Death Penalty would suffice, and they would consider it not just Equal Justice, but *Divine* Justice.

They would be wise to count their blessings and be grateful that they would not be subjected to the same judge, jury, and executioner they had been to those Euthanized while under their care.

Ideology

After conducting a series of interviews, The Angels of Mercy seemed very much like the anarchist group from the 21st century. They seemed to be of the mindset that the 'government' was their enemy, and they did not have an obligation to follow laws they considered to be overreaching or contrary to their values. Such people had existed throughout the history of the nation, and many ideologies motivated them.

Being a law-abiding Citizen was not an 'optional' choice, however. Citizens who chose not to follow the Laws of the Land would ultimately create a nation filled with chaos. A society that disregards any laws they disagree with could only lead to Civil Unrest, Anarchy, and Social Decline.

Murdering for ideological reasons was far more dangerous than an individual acting out a Crime of Passion. Crimes of Passion were easy to recognize, easy to understand, and typically easy to solve. But when Crimes were being Committed for no other reason than to disobey the Laws of the Land because they disagreed with them and refused to obey, it became something more akin to the mentality of terrorism, and terrorists, no matter what their motivation, were dangerous and unpredictable. More importantly, radicalized terrorists had no problem killing Innocent People in order to promote their own agenda and achieve their goals.

There was nothing more dangerous than a man that took action rooted in radicalized beliefs, believing that he was justified in whatever he did because, in *his* mind, it was 'for the betterment of the world'. It was a dangerous system of thought, to not only consider oneself an instrument of change, but to discount the needs of the Whole because of self-righteous personal beliefs. It was also troubling because it implied a certain superiority; the notion that one's own beliefs and opinions were superior to the Laws of the Land was the height of arrogance and required an almost pathologically dangerous ego. It was even more disturbing when one believed that their values should be considered so important that others should be forced to agree and adopt them as their own. It was one thing to hold beliefs that were contrary to popular opinion and even current laws; it was another level altogether when they were building an army of like-minded anarchists to promote their agenda and influence others.

But this was not just one radicalized person following their beliefs as they brazenly justified and committed felonies. It was an entire movement. How many, we did not yet know.

If this was happening here, it could happen elsewhere. That deep, sickening feeling of foreboding had been slowly growing with each additional layer being discovered, and although I had not yet shared it with anyone, I was becoming increasingly disturbed by the direction I believed my investigation was taking. We were on the edge of a dangerous awakening.

This movement could be growing. Years ago, it had been a force to be reckoned with; a movement of Anarchy, Violence, and Activism that had created chaos and an adversarial opposition to their government. Whenever an ideology, no matter if classified as a 'religion' or 'political' in nature, overrode the laws and created Violence, mayhem, and Death, it was a matter of national security to contain.

As much as I could not quantify just how problematic this organization was, I was certain that we were looking at a much larger demographic than I believed anyone within the national Law Enforcement community or any other government agencies were aware of. Extremism, whenever it called upon its followers to take action, was dangerous to Innocent people and the entire nation. America had a long and sordid history of dealing with those who would rather destroy than build, and those who made constant efforts to destroy the Rule of Law and the Constitutional Rights upon which our nation had always existed. Those who would seek to destroy from within were well known and had been identified repeatedly throughout world history.

Ours was not the first nation to undergo a siege of political unrest under the name of 'progression.' History had told the tales of many a nation that had endured painful bouts of ideological terrorism by sects of their Citizens who were disenfranchised, hostile, and willing to do whatever necessary to create the change they wanted to produce. Whenever there were Citizens that believed in their own ideological values more than they believed in the popular beliefs that were supported by the Majority, and backed by the Rule of Law, and as long as they were willing to create change by any means necessary, and regardless of the consequences or collateral damage, every nation and Innocent Citizen would be at risk of Violence and Victimization. When one demographic of a country held more value in their own beliefs and agendas than love for their Fellow Man and national identity, their Fellow Man was at risk of being caught in the crossfire of Domestic Terrorism.

Although it would not pertain directly to this investigation, I could not imagine that our government would not insist on doing additional research and investigative work to uncover exactly what was happening below the surface within our nation. If there was some type of political movement, antigovernmental anarchist sect, or even just a black-market enterprise that was exploiting Human Lives, Trafficking Innocent Citizens, and providing Suicide Assistance, it was going to be a catastrophic revelation for all. It would not reflect well on our government that it had existed to this extent and had not been discovered or contained. This movement was responsible for at least two Crimes Against Humanity already. Left unchecked, it was impossible to say just how dangerous and costly it could become.

PART FIVE

And the Lord said to Moses,
"I will do the very thing you have asked,
because I am pleased with you
and
I know you by name."

Exodus 33:17

TWENTY-FOUR - TWO ICE AGENTS

Governor Interference

I had submitted my briefing to the Chief recently and asked him about how to proceed regarding the property. I had kept him in the loop during this stretch because I realized it was a precarious situation because of the current political climate regarding the Middle East. But when I had asked the Chief about getting the Search Warrants to go over the rest of the property—including the factory itself—the Chief had all but balked at the idea and said that we should be more prudent in the future.

On his advice, I had given him my report and allowed him to forward it to the state Governor. It was not the standard way a Warrant would have been obtained, but I trusted the Chief regarding his caution and additional years of experience. If he believed it would have been erroneous for us to go through traditional means, get a Search Warrant, and then attempt to Arrest both men, I had to believe that he would have done what was best for the case and the Victims, and not just to protect his career.

But within twenty-four hours, he had returned with an answer. The Governor had at least been cognizant of my desire to move with some speed for the Warrants, and I was grateful for that. The news, however, was not in the least what I had hoped, nor expected, to hear.

I also hadn't expected a personal visit for the answers I sought, but by mid-afternoon the next day, the Chief had knocked on the door of the conference room, politely awaiting permission to enter. Given that I was in his building and the door was open, I found it an unnecessary but oddly respectful courtesy. He seemed to be a decent man on many levels, and I appreciated the small things he did.

"I hate to bother you with this, but I have some news that you're not going to like. I'm sorry to bring this to you but I received a response from the Governor."

I raised an eyebrow and motioned for him to take a seat. I had been standing and sorting through some files that I had gathered of all the places where each of the Victims were last seen. I was trying to see if there was any connection regarding their places of Abduction and the roadways, or if any of the locations were conveniently within easy access to the factory land where the gravesites had been found. It seemed to the contrary; they were all in different parts of the Greater Seattle Area, and none were even on the same freeway access point near I-5, well-known for its relation to Sex and Drug Trafficking.

I sat down across from him and gave him my full attention as he began.

"The Governor's office called. He said that he was happy to meet with you, but he wanted it understood that in no manner were the two Foreign Nationals to be arrested or charged with anything. He also stated that it was too premature to get any type of Warrants to search the factory itself or anything else found to be frequented or owned by the two men. He specifically said that just because the land had been used, it did not hold water that the two men were involved at all."

"Are you kidding? Why? Did he say anything else? Did he read my report?" I asked.

I shouldn't have been surprised; I knew it was going to be a political mess, which was why I had taken the time to inform the Chief and create the report. I knew that before we approached a Judge looking for a Warrant, I would need to present my case and ensure that I had the evidence to merit their Arrests. They wouldn't take the Arrest of these two men lightly; I understood the political implications and knew it was a tricky situation.

"Of course he did; he said that it appeared to be coming from a 'point of profiling' and that we therefore 'needed to tread with extreme caution'. He said that the appearance of profiling alone was enough of a reason to run from any notions of obtaining a Warrant until there was something concrete establishing that at least one of the men were directly connected to the site."

I sat there staring at him, dumbstruck.

So that's how we were going to play it? The fear of being regarded as potentially discriminatory against someone of another culture or from another country now meant that they expected us to forego legitimate investigative work? Despite no one beyond the Judge issuing the Warrant even knowing what was being done or why? Really?

I shook my head. It was entirely political.

"Well, you know I supported it before I even sent it out," he continued. "We both knew it was going to be a problem. I didn't think he would give me a formal directive disallowing it, though. He said that you should call him if you wanted to discuss it further, but to understand that he would not change his mind. He said that you needed to be cognizant of the repercussions before proceeding, and that once your full investigation was completed, he wanted to review it."

"So, complete my investigation without actually investigating the land the gravesite is on. Brilliant." I replied.

The Chief leaned back in his chair and folded his arms. He shrugged a bit, and for the first time I realized he was just another man caught in the spoke of a giant machine, just like I was. There was zero reason for any politician to be involved in issuing an Arrest Warrant. The only reason this man's involvement even existed was because I had elected to proceed with extreme caution because of the identities of the two men involved. Had their immigration status as Foreign Nationals and their political identity been anything other than Islamic, I would not have felt the need to 'report in' to the Chief to begin with, nor would I have followed his recommendation to submit my report to the state Governor rather than just going to a judge. By its very nature, I had changed my own protocol because of the political issues presented, which was evidence that our nation still had a substantial problem regarding the public interests of the American People and Islamic Immigration. Concealing their involvement in a Crime—especially *this* Crime against *this* Victim—was only further evidence that Justice was not being served because political interests were more important, including my own.

Had I not been completely convinced that my own career would have faced certain backlash had I gone forward with a Warrant and Public Arrests, I would have proceeded as I normally would have. But because of their status, we were already making concessions again, which was largely why Islam had been proven unfit for Western Cultures to begin with. Although our laws had changed considerably over the last century to help ensure that Justice was based solely on the Crimes and not predicated on the identity of the person behind them, there was still plenty of occasion to see that no system could be entirely air-tight across the board. Because if Justice truly were blind, none of us would have been walking on eggshells about this situation or these Predators; we would have already done what needed to be done and removed these Savages from the streets to ensure they could create no other Victims pending trial.

Nothing about this was right, nor was it acceptable. But I would do as I was being instructed for the time being and proceed with caution until I could gather enough indisputable evidence to ensure these cases were ironclad.

I sighed.

"Yeah, I'm tracking. Of course. Well, we knew it was going to be a mess if it became publicized. I knew before I presented what I knew of the case to you that their identities were going to lead to issues regarding their status."

The Chief gave a weak smile.

"Well, we know what we know. The Governor is just delaying the inevitable, and for all we know he's already discussing it with people at Immigration or higher up the food chain elsewhere. The evidence has already been laid out and we know they would both be facing the Death Penalty based on what you've already gathered. He wasn't disputing the evidence or the legitimacy of their Arrests. He was just doing what all politicians do and trying to put out a fire before it begins by making sure that everything is squared away first."

"Of course, Sir. I understand that. And I agree—if we had been trying to publicize it. But we had made it clear that we wanted it to be low key and were prepared to keep it under wraps. I don't want Katarina's family to know anything about these men until we are certain we can get a Conviction sealed. I don't see any benefit to making this a public case. The instant that the American People hear about this, they are going to be turning this into a national hotbed regarding Middle East Immigration again; you don't have to convince me."

The Chief stood. I followed suit and then shook his extended hand. As I watched him leave, the random realization that we were similar struck me, despite all our differences. It was a basic philosophical idea, really, whether or not morality was complex, there was a basic degree of Good or Evil and right or wrong. Favoring a political agenda over an Arrest Warrant might have been a shade of grey for our Governor, but for the Chief and myself, it was simply a matter of right versus wrong, Justice versus Injustice. We were just two decent men trying to do what was best for our Fellow Man. I understood he was not in a position of authority any more than I was, and we each recognized the delicacy of the situation. I could hardly fault him for it when we both knew it would require finesse.

Nonetheless, there was enough evidence already gathered to have secured both Warrants. Being able to get Warrants to search the rest of the land was vital to the investigation, but being able to bring the two Foreign Nationals in for questioning was also extremely important. It was imperative that the Governor not impede the issuance of the Warrants necessary for their Arrests. Now was not the time to play politics.

The Governor might have the best of intentions, and I would respect his authority for now. But there was no way that this case was going to be brushed under the rug simply because the two men being Accused were part of some huge national political dog and pony show being put on display within our government as an effort to extend 'good will' to the Middle East, especially not at the expense of our own Citizens.

Under no circumstances would I allow what happened to that little girl or her family to be concealed or denied by politicians to advance some international relationship, especially not one that had already burned every bridge within our nation in the past and was heading down familiar paths once again.

I was under no obligation to ensure our nation could build any type of 'peace treaty' with the Middle East. My own political opinions meant nothing in the grand scheme of things, and neither should the Chief's or the Governor's. There shouldn't be a single thought given to the political, ethnic, or immigration status of Known Suspects regarding the issuance of an Arrest Warrant, Charges, or Conviction. That's not how Justice works; that's not how the American legal system was designed, and it's not how it has been practiced. There should not be the slightest bit of political favor or bias granted over their identities. That it had already played a role was very concerning. The Governor should have considered it extremely unethical that he had just told his head of Law Enforcement not to permit a Lead Investigator to proceed with Arrests because of his own political agendas or fears.

America had already traveled this road, and the Citizens had been the ones that had paid the price for it. When agenda matters more than Justice, it's the first clue that something is amiss. Perhaps this Governor needed to take the time to visit the morgue and see what the two Suspects had done to a six-year-old little girl for the last three months of her life before they Murdered her and Stole her future. Afterward, he could then take some time to visit Oscar and Lucia Urakov so he could understand the full weight of what they had done. Like many politicians, he seemed to consider his own plans regarding the 'national agenda' more important than the Innocent Citizens he was elected to represent.

It was a dangerous calculation that relied heavily on the gamble that his Citizens would neither find out, nor find it abhorrent that he would choose his own self-interests over the Rights of one little girl and her family. His actions were wrong across the board; morally, ethically, and legally. But for the time being, I could do nothing about it. I would do what I must do in order to get enough evidence to make their Arrest not only impossible to avoid, but requiring an imminent response. When there was no other choice but to pursue Justice, hopefully this politician would remember the Oath he took to Defend Justice and his constituents above all else.

Two ICE Agents Arrive

The Chief appeared outside the hall area at the entrance of our assigned work section but did not venture in. Instead, he stood in the main hallway and spoke with two men in dark suits. We were in our main conference room, which held a large window in the front. Although we did not have any work product out that would be visible from their position about twenty paces away, it still made me feel as though I were in a fishbowl as they glanced our way, obviously talking about us.

Our workspace was in the back of the building, one section over from the Chief's own office, but distant from all others because of its corner status. This made it necessary for the Chief's 'tour' to be intentional; he would not have brought them there to observe us through our front conference room window had he not been looking for us specifically. We were being shown to the two men as if we were animals in a zoo.

We had been sorting through all the photographs and documents that had been seized from the properties of Daegan Kyl, Willow Amos, and the homes of The Angels of Mercy. We were looking for anything incriminating that displayed premeditation, anything related to their 'ethical code' or agenda, and everything related to their communications with each other. Likewise, Officer Stanton was busy reviewing their social media and technology.

I was still uncertain about the Chief or where he stood, which so far seemed to be right on the fence.

If he had brought them this far down the hallway, however, it had been done with intent. Much like local Law Enforcement, they wore visors that concealed their features. Unlike Law Enforcement, however, they didn't remove them while inside of the SPD building. The message was clear, and everyone that saw them knew who they were and what it was meant to convey: "We are not the same."

It was easy to find that disconcerting; they were protected from being recognized, but everyone else was left bare and exposed. Years back, people had commented that Law Enforcement had worn sunglasses that were reflective, and Citizens had found them exceedingly unapproachable and distrustful. It was Human Nature to want to feel a sense of connection made through establishing genuine eye contact; I responded to their generic blackened external visors negatively as well. By standing there with their visors on even from twenty paces, they could record everything they observed around them. The two were taking stock of their surroundings, and I knew it was likely that we were being recorded as well.

Depending on their clearance levels, anyone unmasked within the SPD had already provided them with a full briefing on who they were, as well as their credentials and basic background information just through their retina scans and facial recognition program. Some agencies and ranks meant they could have used the inter-agency connection program to catalog every person within the entire building already, recorded, downloaded, and preserved for reasons as yet unknown. Even though we were all supposed to be on the same team, that level of unevenness in the playing field was bound to unsettle even the most composed of professionals.

It was my two colleagues that were the ones being placed in a vulnerable position currently; neither Grace O'Connor nor Officer Stanton wore any type of headgear. It wasn't necessary, since neither of their jobs required it, and they typically worked among their own peers. I was the only one covered because of my visor, but I had my eyes exposed, which I knew allowed them to get my professional credentials. They had approached our section of the SPD with a purpose, but their demeanor was not one that showed they had come in peace or with goodwill. The manner in which the taller of the two carried on the conversation with the Chief while the much-shorter second agent continuously looked around told me that the taller one was probably the higher-ranking agent of the pair.

The two men were obviously from some other government agency, the FBI, CIA, or Homeland Security, most likely. It was possible that they were ICE agents since we were working with a case involving the two Foreign Nationals, but it seemed a little strange that they would make a personal visit, and I had good cause to question who they were. They were visiting a Police Department, had entered a private, concealed parking space, and had traveled through security measures that disallowed any Citizen from accessing this portion of the department. They knew they were among hundreds of Law Enforcement Officers, all of whom were working to do their best to help create a safe city for their Fellow Citizens to live. Despite all of this, they did not even lower their visors enough to show their eyes.

There were legitimate reasons for this, of course. Law Enforcement had not been the only leg of the government to take a hit over the years, nor were they the only ones that had faced dark times in the years leading up to the Last Stand. Border Patrol Agents, ICE, and Homeland Security were targeted in droves. There had been several notable Attacks against the FBI in the 20th century, followed by several more in the latter 21st century. But none had compared to the damages that were inflicted on agents that were connected to protecting the US Borders.

All things considered, it was easy to understand why certain agencies, as well as most agents, were secretive and protective of their identities. Especially the older ones, or those that were retired and still remembered what it was like during the years following the Great Reformation; they had lived through the dangers, remembered what it had been like to live with a target on their back, and knew the high cost their jobs could demand. The strain and fear of knowing they were hated and at risk of Violent Attack or Death every time they went out into the general populace was difficult for many agents. In the years leading up to the Last Stand and during the years of the Great Reformation, they were hunted down just like Law Enforcement. For many, the rising Death Counts every year made them question whether or not a job was worth their lives. The sharp decline in staffing showed that for most, putting their lives on the line and living in constant fear of Assault or Death was not worth the risk.

There were thousands of vacancies in agencies that at one time were overflowing with eager Civilians all vying for a chance to join their ranks. The agencies had enough highly qualified applicants they could choose to be selective and hire only the cream of the crop. Even though that was how it was once again, no one would ever forget how it had been during those lean years when no one was certain if America—or any of the West—would survive. During those years, there was a camaraderie among all government employees that was not capable of being breached, and no lines or egos stood between the various government agencies. There were only two groups—those that stood on the side of the Rule of Law and the Constitution, and those that were hellbent on destroying America and butchering Her Citizens.

The feeling deep in my gut was a warning I would do well to heed. It told me that these two men were representing a much greater purpose, and that was to keep tabs on my investigation as it related to the two Foreign Nationals.

I wasn't sure who the men were that were meeting with the Chief, but I believed we would hear more from them later. The two Foreign Nationals were the only part of the investigation that would cause another agency to step up, intervene, take over, or shut us out entirely. I knew they were there because of our investigation simply by the way they had responded to our room as they peered through; their slowed step, the methodical manner in which the secondary man took a visual read of the room while the primary man mirrored my stare—presumably some manner of eye contact underneath his masked face—and had focused on capturing images of each of the figures in the room.

It was standard teamwork that allowed each party to document key factors and record everything; a way to double check a scene through their recorded video footage with two separate points of view that allowed for maximum information processing. I couldn't see any other reason for them to care about what we were doing in our office or who we were; all that I was left with was my own perception, and I believed they were there because someone of a higher rank than us wanted to ensure that the two Foreign Nationals were never linked to the Kidnapping, Sexual Abuse, and Death of one little girl. The two men meeting with the Chief were there as a security measure; they were there to do damage control.

This alone was terrible, and it left me with a new understanding of just how far my government was willing to go to ensure this did not result in any type of negative publicity. It was not only disheartening; it was potentially dangerous. I was jumping the gun on this, and rationally I understood this to be the case.

But the Governor had already shut me down once, and I had been adhering to his demands. Clearly, though, if these men were here to discuss my findings because of my report to the Governor, it had not been remedied simply with my word as a professional. The Governor had reported my case and findings to someone higher than himself, and now it was developing into something beyond even that.

As with everything, I was not positive at this point.

Another thought occurred to me as well, and as much as I hated myself for being so selfish that it was even a consideration, I knew it was a well-grounded reality just as surely as the potential for Injustice existed because of who these two men were. I knew then, with the same clarity and understanding that I was convinced the two Foreign Nationals were Guilty and our government would work to conceal their Guilt, that if I disrupted the outcome of this case that my own career would become nothing more than a pile of tinder set to implode. My career, my reputation, my entire future as I knew it, would all go up in flames if I went against the system.

I looked at Grace O'Connor and then at Officer Stanton. Both were good workers, Good People, and professionals that were dedicated to solving these cases and helping their Bereaved Loved Ones to find answers and Closure. It was one thing for me to go down, but another to take them down with me. I was in dangerous territory. It was not only going to be wise to tread with caution from this point forward, I would need to walk gently on eggshells and leave an exceptionally light paper trail behind me until I had this case entirely resolved. If these two men were here regarding this case and the two Foreign Nationals, then everything we had done until this point and processed through the SPD infrastructure was already being tracked and monitored by them.

If their goal was to continue building these 'relationships' with the Middle East, then their agenda was going to override our work and my determination to investigate, find the culprits responsible, and bring them to Justice. I knew in that moment that from this point forward, we must all tread with extreme caution.

The Chief and the Two ICE Agents

Before long, the Chief and the two men stopped talking about us in the hallway and visited us directly. As soon as the Chief entered the room, I knew that the two men standing behind him were the ones in control. The Chief was merely a figurehead, a talking mouthpiece to keep us in line and let us know that our work was all being done as a 'collective effort'; we were all part of the 'same team' and we should all do well to remember that we were all working together to accomplish the same good work. I knew all the talking points; they hadn't changed in hundreds of years. When they wanted you to shut up and toe the line, there were only so many variations of false flattery they could extend.

"The involvement of the two Foreign Nationals is a complicated facet to your case and now that the Governor has been advised of it, he thought it was prudent to pass the information along to some people over at ICE so they could investigate on their end as well. They were, after all, the ones that allowed the men into our nation and had kept supporting their renewals."

I nodded but said nothing. I noticed that the two men behind the Chief still refused to remove their visors, but I could feel their eyes focused on me like lasers. I could feel both Grace O'Connor and Officer Stanton both staring at me as well.

"Of course," I said. I was careful to keep my tone neutral and professional. Their actions did not surprise me; they had dropped the ball, of course they should want to review the case. It should be done; had they done their due diligence in the first place we wouldn't be here, and Katarina would be home with her parents today.

"So, what exactly will that entail? They'll be meeting with Katarina's parents? The two of you will go over there, offer your condolences, and help them understand how two Foreigners from the only region in the world that the US has maintained a ban that disallows immigration from could not only enter the US but remain in for more than a decade without ever having been properly vetted? Will you be explaining to them that their daughter was Abducted by these two illegal foreigners, kept alive for this whole duration of time while they were terrified and traumatized about what might have happened to her—and that their very worst fears had been completely realized? Are you going to tell them that had you guys done your jobs properly that their little girl might not have been Savagely Brutalized, Raped, Sodomized, and Abused for the last three months of her life before they finally Murdered her?"

The two men stood stoically behind the Chief and stared at me.

"We will not be engaging with any of the Bereaved, nor will we be interfering with your investigation in any manner. We will share none of those details with these Grieving parents, and we expect that neither will you. We've been ordered to be kept in the loop and granted access to your case files, that's all. The Chief has already granted us clearance. If we have questions, we'll be in contact."

The taller man spoke. He had been the one that had watched me the most intently as they had passed in the hallway earlier, while the shorter one had used his time to catalog everything present. The voice modulator in his visor made his words all sound monotone and generic, but even though his words were technically non-threatening, there was no question about the message his brief response had conveyed. I was being instructed to keep every inch of known data about the 'Suspect' or 'Suspects' behind Katarina's Abduction to myself; her parents were not to be given any information about the case, factual or otherwise. They were going to withhold the two men's identities entirely because of who they were, and I was going to allow it to happen. There was no 'or else'; the man wasn't issuing a warning to me or even a threat. He was just telling me how it was, how it was going to be, and that I shouldn't even presume that I was a big enough dog in this fight to consider doing anything otherwise.

I smirked because he didn't even have the professional courtesy to allow his own voice to be filtered through; he wore his visor on the darkest tint and used the generic voice modulator to conceal his own voice. While this was a common enough practice out in the public to avoid being recognized while off-duty, it seemed excessive while in a Police Department among fellow professionals—especially during a speech discussing how we are all 'working together'.

"Excellent. Is there anything else we can help you with?" I asked.

The room was thick with a heavy tension that I knew I was not only probably contributing to but causing. It wasn't merely because of this push of seniority or power being yielded over me. I knew I was good at my job and would get this case resolved in its entirety—and with integrity. The issue was about the abuses of the system that I had never witnessed before now.

These tactics were from a bygone era, where corruption bred corruption, power was used against the American People, and government agencies withheld information and hurt Innocent Citizens for sport. It was a toxin in our system; a poison that was making a statement to the effect that protecting the self-interests of international policies was more important than finding Justice for one little girl, her family, and protecting the American People from the Evils of the World. And if the two men standing in front of me were willing to support those people and that agenda, then they were just as toxic and vile as their employers.

America had already fought one long, grueling, bloody war against these cancerous ideological forces; if we had not learned from it and were still dealing with it, then we were at true risk of losing ourselves permanently. There was no room for back-alley dealings, and no place for government officials that would strive to protect such Evil men or the region that normalized their behavior.

The taller man stepped forward and placed a paper folder on the table that stood between us. He then resumed his position near the Chief, motioning for me to open the file. I flipped open the front page and stared at a photograph of a Deceased man lying on a wooden floor, a bloody, violent mess. His face was beaten beyond recognition and covered in blood. His hands were facing downward in the picture.

"This is one of the men you have alleged is responsible for the Kidnapping, Assault, and Death of your young Victim, Katarina Urakov. This man's name is Fatik

Mahjub Ghazwan. He's been properly ID'd through our Immigration system and his body has already been processed. Because of his non-permanent immigration status and the delicacy of the situation, ICE had already been reviewing this case. We sent a couple of ICE agents to their addresses, and they discovered Ghazwan's body at the home of the second man in your file. However, Khalam Athil Harb was not there. Our men processed the scene, began a search, and could not locate him in the vicinity. ICE confirmed that the second man has left the US and already returned to his native country. We have been informed that he won't be extradited."

I heard a slight gasp from Grace O'Connor, and Officer Stanton shifted uncomfortably in his seat.

"Then why are you even here?" I asked bitterly.

"What's left to investigate or intervene? If you won't extradite him, and since you ensured we couldn't do our jobs and arrest them when we had the opportunity before, what's the point of getting involved now?"

I was angry.

It was all for show anyhow; there wasn't anything to either confirm or deny that the man featured in the photograph before me was one of my Suspects. There wasn't anything to even confirm or deny that the man in the photograph was even Dead; he was a guy in a picture being presented with outdated, antiquated technology in a 2D depiction that wouldn't even fool the average American. I was skeptical enough to even question the intent behind why they had chosen to only print paper photographs. What was it they were attempting to cover up, and why was it so imperative that it didn't make it into any official records—either the SPD's databases, my own, or even those of the two ICE agents standing before me? Why were they trying to keep what had happened to this little girl a secret? Why were they trying to conceal the identities and known information about these two Foreign Nationals?

The photographs did not even prove that they were taken from inside of the factory. We couldn't even verify it was the same building; we hadn't been allowed to search the property yet and had no way of even knowing what the inside of the factory looked like. They had blocked us at every turn, and this was nothing more than throwing us a bone. It was almost laughable to believe that this 'evidence' was being presented as legitimate, considering our own court system had denounced them because of their ability to be altered and faked.

So I was expected to believe—an Investigator with decades of experience and education, in one of the most advanced nations on earth with some of the best technology in the world at our disposal—that ICE, the government agency responsible for securing our borders and keeping our Civilians Safe from Harm, could only take a few grainy photographs to document the Death of a man that they knew to be a danger to the American People? And they wanted me to believe this with no reservation or concern; that the only way to confirm this man's Death was through some low-budget, low-resolution paper photographs that could not be given any real scrutiny. They had covered the man's ears, eyes, and fingerprints. He was covered head to toe with clothing and didn't have a single mole or tattoo visible to link him to any registered person. Every Immigrant, Citizen, dual Citizen, Foreign National, Convicted Criminal, and Tourist was documented through DNA and 3D imaging scans that even catalogued their ears, retinas, and fingerprinting, but they wanted me to believe this was sufficient evidence to confirm their story as gospel. Obviously, they were working hard to cover things up; I just wanted to know why.

I didn't know if they believed we were as gullible and stupid as they thought we were, or if their actions showed they didn't care if we believed them or not. Among the hundreds of government agencies that still existed within our nation, there was still plenty of elitism, power, and corruption. If we were going to be subjected to the abuses of our own government because they were taking over our investigation, monitoring us, and wanted to document our progress because of the intricacies involving Foreign Nationals and a potentially volatile international situation, that was one thing; I wasn't so naïve that I didn't understand the monumental global and political implications of this case.

But the actions by these ICE agents proved they weren't here overseeing this case to ensure that no detail was overlooked, or because of the risks and ramifications it could have. They weren't here to ensure that the investigation led to the successful identification of those responsible for this heinous act and doing everything necessary to secure charges and the deliverance of a fair and just Conviction and Sentence. Their intentions were not about doing everything possible to ensure that Katarina and her family were provided with the Justice that they were entitled to receive, or reassuring the American People that Justice truly was blind and would be delivered no matter who the culpable party was. And now we knew they weren't concerned about ensuring equal measure was meted out for every person who broke our laws and Committed Crimes Against Humanity without exception or regard to race, income, background, political standing, or even Citizenship.

As I looked at the two government agents making their way out of our office and down the hall, I realized that this entire charade didn't have a single purpose that mattered to the Urakov Family or the American People; what they were expecting to be done would in no manner serve in the best interest of Justice for anyone. What they were expecting us to do could only result in negative consequences. There was nothing to be gained by handling this in this manner, in betraying this poor, helpless family after having failed their daughter entirely.

This was political, pure and simple.

Government Accountability for Katarina

The Victimization of Katarina would have a significant impact throughout These United States. The public outrage would be immeasurable. It was highly likely there would be demands for complete travel restrictions to be enforced. There was no excuse for what had happened to this little girl, and she had deserved better. The People would declare that the government had dropped the ball and chosen financial gain and international commerce over the Life of one Innocent Child. The US government already had a lengthy history of sacrificing its Citizens for reasons of gain and profit.

For this reason alone, when they discovered that not only had this poor little girl been Savagely Violated and Murdered, but that her family could never find resolution and comfort through our Criminal Justice system, there would be demands for accountability. Once it became known that the man responsible was from the Middle East and had fled beyond our reach, there would be an incomprehensible backlash from the People.

This had not been the first issue with this tentative union, but it was undoubtedly the most profoundly disturbing and offensive. There would never be a substantial enough apology by the US government to make amends for what had happened to Katarina. It had been entirely preventable.

The US had engaged in trade with the Middle East despite the overwhelming public and political opposition. Instead, even on a restricted trial level, the leadership of the US had allowed temporary Immigration from Middle Eastern nations. Even though this was only related to trade and commerce and not for Permanent Citizenship, and despite all the measures taken to secure proper vetting, a little girl was now Dead.

The American People would not soon forget that two men from an Islamic background had Stalked, Abducted, Sexually Assaulted, Sodomized, Starved, Physically Assaulted, and Murdered a little Catholic girl from a Western European background living in a Western nation. They may as well have bombed another village as they hosted their annual Christmas market; it had been an Act of Terrorism whether the US Government gave it the official name or not. Whether or not they chose to own it, it had been an entire cycle of Terrorism to that little girl, and the American People would never allow their government to hide behind political correctness as they had cowered once before.

There would never be Justice delivered by the leaders of any Islamic nation, and the American People would be foolish to expect this. Nothing from this situation should have ever occurred, had the government adequately protected its Citizens from known Predators as they had pledged to do.

Ultimately, this grievance reflected the failure of the government to abide by its own commitment to honor the Sanctity of Life that our Forefathers had guaranteed, and then our Ancestors had pledged to defend through our Great Reformation. The American People would not respond well to this clear breach of duty, and no amount of Restitution from our leaders would atone for allowing this to occur.

Even the complete cessation of the 'trial' program between the US and the Middle Eastern region would not remedy this. This had been an egregious offense against two entirely undeserving parents of which there could be no true Restitution delivered. But most of all, this had been an Act of the worst degradation; the most heinously tragic exploitation of the most vulnerable of Citizens among us. It had been a Crime Against Humanity, but equally monumental, it had been an endless series of Violent Crimes Against a Child.

Our leaders should tread with caution regarding how much the American People would tolerate for the sake of permitting their elected officials to make decisions on their behalf. They were, after all, only there by the powers *Of* the People, *By* the People, and *For* the People. A failure to uphold the duties and promises of their Oaths would not only lead to their failure to maintain their elected positions as representatives of the People, they might be held Criminally liable if blood was found to be on their hands.

And if the history of These United States was any sort of reference, then it didn't take much to recognize that far too many of our elected officials had not only bathed in the blood of the Innocent once they gained their prized title and position, feasting on their Sacrificial Lambs without care or concern, they had felt no qualms about exploiting the American People even as they climbed their way into power over the broken, bleeding Bodies of our Citizens just to get their start. Here in America, everyone knew; you don't need to fear the Reaper. History had proven you needed to fear your politicians and government.

Planning the Next Move

After the two men from ICE had left our conference room, I took a few moments for myself back in the office. I could see Grace O'Connor and Officer Stanton talking quietly among themselves. It was appropriate that they should do so; their own careers were being placed into the spotlight simply for being part of my team. I had unwittingly placed them into an investigation that could subject them to political persecution, professional sabotage, extortion, and even cause them to face their own moral and ethical dilemmas by forcing them to either stand against our Victim or go along with the pressures being presented by another agency and their own Chief. I was only an Investigator; I had only been called here to find out how four Innocent Citizens had wound up in unmarked graves in a nation that was built on a foundation that instilled the belief that all Human Life had Value.

And yet, here we were. I was dangerously close to risking my career, reputation, and entire future. Two other professionals that had innocently worked alongside me and only wanted to do the right thing for the Victims they were supposed to be fighting for were also being placed at risk now. I knew I couldn't ask them to proceed any further now that I fully understood what was happening.

It wasn't a story that ended well for the hero, and the hero's companions were usually the ones that ended up paying the greatest price. I wasn't prepared to venture down that road with either of my colleagues; they both deserved better than what this case was now dumping into their laps. No matter what I did, I was only going to be responsible for my own actions and fallout; those were the terms I could easily live with. Neither of my trusted companions was going to be sacrificed for this case. They deserved better, and while this case was proving to be a much greater problem than anyone could have possibly anticipated, it shouldn't have ever been a case that could have resulted in anyone having their careers or lives potentially endangered.

I wasn't being melodramatic; we were being placed into a very precarious position, and the power dynamic had established itself just as clearly as the rest of that which had been left unspoken. We had been sent a message that had carried enough weight that the two men had not even needed to utter a single syllable; we were being watched, we were being controlled, and we were being directed. We were to make no aggressive decisions, nor were we to withhold anything. 'Our' investigation was being allowed to continue, but we now had to answer to a higher authority—of which we were not allowed to know anything about, debate, or question.

So, what I knew now was that I needed to be careful and more strategic in the future. In hindsight, I would have just kept quiet about the two Foreign Nationals, thereby preventing the Governor from getting involved. The Chief was right, of course; we had done the right thing professionally. And it had been the *prudent* thing to do. But it had been the wrong decision and course of action if we were serving the needs of our Victim and her parents.

There had been zero way to know that informing the Governor would have resulted in this level of chain reaction, but had I known, I would never have done it. I knew I had made a fundamental mistake on a level of which I was not used to making, and not only were the consequences going to affect the one person we were supposed to be protecting the interests of, it was a price that was going to cast a shadow over her parents, the rest of our Victims, our investigation, and ourselves as well.

We had done it to safeguard our own professional careers so we could know that we had followed protocol every step of the way. The two Foreign Nationals had been a high-risk gamble either way from the very beginning; whether or not we were forthright, we should have anticipated that there would be fallout from some direction. The lesson was well-learned; we had opened the gates with our investigation, and from that we had not only endangered our own careers, we had managed to completely destroy any possibility of straightforward Justice for Katarina and her family.

In this sense, we would have been better off just announcing our case on a national platform and used every known news broadcasting network to inform the public of our findings. I wasn't a stranger to news reporters; I had a few reliable contacts that I trusted. I had done my share of interviews as part of my work. In addition, my teaching and research publications had also put me in the spotlight over the years. Although I was not comfortable exploiting that aspect of my professional life, should I ever require it, I knew I could summon a fair amount of journalistic attention if necessary. They would regard what I was telling them as significant and beyond reproach, as I was considered a credible expert worth listening to.

And without even talking to Grace O'Connor, I knew she had probably done far more interviews and news briefings than I had because of her role in the Victim Advocacy Agency. Between the two of us, we would have been able to get an interview on local channels the same day if we had ever initiated contact, and from there it would have spread like wildfire as national news.

But we didn't; because that's not who we were and that wasn't how it was supposed to be done. It would have created panic and hysteria, it would have been blown up into some type of Serial Killer on the loose, and the Greater Seattle Area would have been living on edge for weeks as we conducted our investigation. We would have both faced an unfathomable amount of professional, political, and even public backlash for it. We would have broken the rules and the law. And no matter how well-meaning our intentions, we would have broken the trust of the public, because Law Enforcement Officers were not meant to be glory-hounds, and we were not supposed to exploit the Dead.

As it stood, no one in the Greater Seattle Area even knew of the gravesite and the four Victims. I was not certain that any of the cases would ever be shared with the public. It was clear that the story of Katarina and the danger that had befallen her would be swept under the rug, hidden away for 'the Greater Good'.

But they would not be able to conceal my investigation entirely. No matter what these men wanted to do, there would have to be a formal resolution for the other

Victims at the very least; the knowledge that there were four Missing Persons cases active in the Greater Seattle Area was already public.

My faith in my government was more than a little shaken, and I had never found myself in this position.

I didn't know who was behind this or how high up it went. It really didn't matter, because the fact that it was happening at all only proved to me that my nation was still under attack from Her Enemies, or She was under attack once again. Someone, somewhere, did not want the fact that these two men were responsible for what had happened to one of our youngest, most Innocent and Vulnerable Citizens to come to light. They were going to extreme measures to ensure that this case was presented as insignificant, irrelevant, and a dead end.

Prudence told me to play nicely with the two gentlemen that had issued direct orders to me regarding how I was to report my findings to them from this point forward. I intended to do so, and would be certain to include them in everything we documented as agreed upon. It did not serve my own best interests to do otherwise. I would play along and allow whatever was happening to continue to play out until time presented an alternative option.

I gained nothing by causing issues, and I still had work to do. As long as I had unanswered questions and my case could not be presented as ironclad in a Court of Law so I could get Convictions for my Victims, I was not going to jeopardize losing my access to their files or my investigation. I needed to remain malleable enough to have unfettered access to every resource I might need. I must tread with caution, maintain composure, and keep my eye on the long-term goal.

Equally important, I needed to ensure that I wasn't removed from my own career and purpose by corrupt actors I could not yet see but now knew could pull strings and control people from behind the scenes. Now that I was aware of these actors, I had even more purpose and questions to consider further down the road. I would not stand for corruption and criminality from within my own government any more than I would from my Fellow Citizens. The same Rule of Law must apply to all, just as the same Rights, Liberties, and Sentencing Laws must.

The nation had sacrificed too much over the centuries to begin backsliding into that disgraceful, sordid past that had been teeming with predatory, self-serving politicians who had used their powers to destroy our nation, reduce our security, and sell us out in systematic betrayals to our enemies. It didn't matter to what extent the corruption, criminality, back-alley deals, or abuse of power existed or to what end. If it existed at all, the American People had an obligation and a right to expose those culpable, pursue Justice to the fullest extent possible in a Court of Law, and expel all the corruption from the ranks as thoroughly as we were capable of doing.

America, for all Her beautiful bounty and lofty dreams, would never be immune from the endless corruption, pollutants, and agenda-driven villains acting in the background. Power had a way of drawing Evil toward it, and the ability to influence, manipulate, and control a nation was one of the most powerful things an Evil person with an agenda could aspire to do. There were still Evil people working within our most important government agencies that were manipulating the system and destroying the faith and trust of the American People. Likewise, it was evident by the two lower-level mystery agents that had arrived that there were plenty of corrupt pawns and Soldiers out there willing to do the dirty work of their Masters, regardless of their oaths or own personal status as American Citizens.

It was beyond comprehension how those that purported to love their native land could do such Evil, unethical, criminal things that undermined our nation and Her Citizens. Anyone that would willfully betray their own Countrymen to further their own political, professional, or national agendas, whether they did so as Citizens, as government employees, or elected officials, was not part of the America that myself or anyone I knew wanted to belong to. Too many Americans had lost their lives because of the ugliness, greed, and Godless cancer of government corruption. I would not bow down to it, nor would I allow it to fester now that I knew it existed.

I knew this much, as a Citizen and a member of Law Enforcement, my Oath to Protect and Defend my nation and Fellow Citizen was always going to be more important than blindly following the lead of higher-ranking government officials.

We The People had an obligation to dig out the disease by the roots.

TWENTY-FIVE — DK — HOLDING CELL

Holding Cell

I decided to meet with Daegan Kyl again briefly before I set out. I wanted him to know that my time spent with Willow Amos had not only been unproductive, it had been extremely costly for both of us.

I realized he was playing it cool with Willow Amos and trying to keep a respectable distance from her, but this wasn't a situation that was going to end well for her without his intervention. I didn't have any confirmation regarding this yet, of course, but I believed she was the missing link that connected him to the case regarding The Angels of Mercy. He had no other connection to them; Officer Stanton had done the interviews as I had requested and none of them even knew his name or of his Existence—save one young guy who recognized the name because of his charity work around the city and state. It seemed clear that Willow Amos was the center of everything regarding how these men got involved. Until otherwise proven, I was going to trust my gut instinct on this one and assume that there was a connection between Willow Amos and Daegan Kyl that just hadn't been formally confirmed, and trust that with that connection he would want to do what he could to help her.

Because I was only planning on meeting him for a few moments, I went directly to his Holding Cell with one of the Officers on duty. It wasn't commonly done, but it was permitted. Generally, it became more about safety, but I wasn't concerned about Daegan Kyl being Violent toward me or anyone else, despite his prior military experience and training.

He was sitting on his single-wide bed writing on a pad of paper, his back against the wall, legs extended. The cots rested on an enormous concrete block that spanned the width of the back wall, leaving two feet of bare concrete for shelving. Aside from that, each room came with a toilet, sink, and a Holy Bible. Anything extra must be requested and justified; superfluous items such as decorations were prohibited. It was a jail Cell for those who had broken the Laws of the Land; creature comforts were as unwarranted as their demands for better entitlements.

As I approached the clear, framed doorway of his cage, he noticed me and stood. It was the first time we were eye to eye. Both of us seemed to tower over the Officer that had escorted me, and as soon as we approached Daegan Kyl's Cell, the Officer straightened his shoulders as if to appear larger, almost as if he were being confronted by a bear in the woods. He was not wrong to do so; although I hadn't read Kyl's military records, I was certain that he could have snapped the smaller Officer like a twig. Luckily for both of us, I did not believe Daegan Kyl had a propensity for Gratuitous Violence, nor did he seem to feel compelled to escape.

I nodded my head toward him in greeting, and he did the same in return. He walked toward the frame of the Holding Cell, folded his arms across his chest and assumed a comfortable standing position with his legs firmly planted in a wide stance opposite me. We each stood a foot from the partition. The Officer that had escorted me down the corridor entered a code on the wall so a small panel could open for the free flow of conversation, and then he left us alone. We watched him walk down to the end of the corridor and strike up a conversation with one of the other guards patrolling the area.

"I wanted you to know that the SPD picked up Willow Amos again yesterday. She's been formally charged already regarding Arlan and is looking at the Death Penalty," I began.

I wasn't so much concerned about relaying the news as I was about watching his reaction. His shoulders seemed to slump a bit, and he exhaled deeply. He then uncrossed his arms and put his hands in his pockets, thumbs remaining out. He grimaced.

I continued. "She was picked up without incident, but as soon as she got here, she began acting out aggressively. She's looking at another handful of charges for Assault, but that's only part of it. By the time I could get in there and meet with her, she'd become something a bit more unbalanced…"

Daegan Kyl remained unmoved.

"Aside from the rampant verbal abuse, emotional outburst, and Physically Attacking a handful of Officers as they tried to get her processed, she then spit on me. Twice."

I wasn't trying to project myself as a victim, and in all honesty, I would rather have not gone down this route for a first choice since it made me look like I couldn't handle a feral cat without complaining. But I needed Daegan Kyl to take the bait and step up to protect Willow Amos. I needed him to get her to cooperate so I could get the answers and information I needed. I was certain that Willow Amos was the head of the snake, so getting it straight from her was going to be the most reliable source.

"So, what do you want me to do about it?" he asked. He wasn't a stupid man; he knew what I was expecting from him.

"I'm giving you a choice. You can either help her so she figures out that it's in her best interest to help herself, or you can do nothing and watch her go down in flames. I guarantee you that Option B is inevitable given her behavior."

He sighed again and briefly used his right hand to rub his forehead and temple.

It appeared this was not the first occasion in which Daegan Kyl had been required to take care of Willow Amos or her messes.

"All right; what do you have in mind? Can I meet with her?" he asked. There was something about the way he spoke of her that was familiar and paternal; he was impatient and tired of his darling little juvenile delinquent and her antics, but still willing to clean up after her.

"I'll arrange it. I'm going to keep at a distance as well. She obviously doesn't respect any of us, but she sees me as the Root of all Evil. That's something that I'm going to be expecting you to correct. I'll arrange for you to have five minutes with her; nothing more, nothing less. You can either get her to cooperate so I can at least try to get her cleared from the Death Penalty, or not. But the only shot she has at getting Exile will depend on whether or not I can clear her of direct association with Arlan, Mariam, and Rebecca. Frankly, I'm not sure if even then they will let her downgrade; she's linked to all of this mess far beyond anyone else—including yourself, and there's not much to convince anyone otherwise. She doesn't have much by way of redeeming qualities, and the worse she looks in her interviews, the more the Judges are going to see her as a problem not worth dealing with."

"I'll talk to her," he said. The tone of his voice confirmed his statement, and the steady eye contact left no doubt.

"I'm not providing much time. I shouldn't be providing any at all. But I need answers, and there's only one thing I can negotiate with in order to get what I need. It's up to her whether her life is worth it, but I'm not interested in wasting any more of my time dealing with her or her petty antics. I hope you can make her understand that, because she won't get the same patience from the Judges."

Daegan Kyl nodded his head.

"I'll get it on the books for later today. I'll let you have the room to yourselves, but keep in mind I'll be monitoring, and it will be recorded as well. I know you're not interested in telling me everything and I'll respect that because it won't make a difference regarding your Conviction. But I hope at some point you decide that I'm a better ally than enemy—because Willow Amos is going to need all the help she can get. I'm not even sure I can keep her free from the Death Penalty; I need more to go on before I can determine that. Make your time count with her."

He nodded his head again. I could see he could understand the urgency in my voice even though I still had my face covered other than my eye visor.

I looked down the hall and motioned for the Officer that I was done with my conversation and then closed my eye visor again. There had been no one else in this corridor between Daegan Kyl's Cell and the locked entrance, but full gear was required.

"I'll meet with you tomorrow afternoon, hopefully after I've had another chance to interview Amos. Get her to talk. There are more than twenty other Suspects out there who are looking for someone to blame, and I'm telling you—no one has as much loyalty from their comrades as they believe they do when Death is on the table."

Daegan Kyl grimaced again, but nodded his head, letting out another long sigh. I wasn't telling him anything he didn't already know.

As I returned to my office area, I wondered if Officer Stanton was any closer to being able to secure Kyl's military records. It was the one area that we had not yet explored, and I felt there was still much about him that I didn't know.

I knew he was connected to Willow Amos, and it was a hopeful shot in the dark that he would have influence over her. I had gone on instinct that he would be able to speak with her.

Hopefully, his military records would shed some light. I was certain that being able to observe their Body Language would reveal at least a little bit of just how intimately they knew each other, although I still wasn't convinced it would be on a romantic or sexual level.

My goal remained the same; the more they talked and told me what I needed to know, the easier it would be to get to the truth. As with most investigations, Citizens could either help or hurt themselves through their contributions. For whatever reason, I was looking at two people who were more determined than the average person to self-destruct—but if I played my cards right, I believed that each would do what they could to help one another.

DK and WA Preparing to Meet

Everything related to the meeting between Willow Amos and Daegan Kyl had to be anticipated beforehand; I could leave nothing to chance. It was important to me to have the scene play out as organically as possible, but I had still weighed out various scenarios and how they would appear based on my influence. If he were in his own clothing, it would appear more suspect to her, as if he might have already betrayed her and was being released. I didn't want to create any type of distrust between them; on the contrary, I wanted them to trust one another to tell the truth. My goal was for Willow Amos to turn to him for guidance.

On the other hand, if Daegan Kyl were not only in a standard-issue government Corrections uniform, having lost his street clothes entirely, it made it appear as though he were just as likely as she was to see long-term consequences for his Crimes. This might motivate her to speak more openly to him, attempt to help him, or at the very least feel compelled to listen to him now that they were both facing the same uncertain and precarious future.

No matter how it worked out, I needed for Willow Amos to understand that without her full cooperation she was undoubtedly looking at the Death Penalty, and I was sure that the only way I was going to get any cooperation from her was through Daegan Kyl. Hell or high water, I was going to get her to work toward her own future freely and of her own accord; it was not Daegan Kyl's job to get Willow Amos to care about her own life or its outcome.

If Daegan Kyl was her weakness, and the only one who was seemingly not her pawn, then she may find it in her best interest to take his instruction so they could help themselves. It seemed clear that no matter how much 'leadership' she held, Daegan Kyl was not to be considered among her ranks. For this reason, I had the impression that if he were under duress, it might be the only means of drawing her out.

It was entirely possible that Daegan Kyl was the only one that could compel her to disclose what she knew in order to protect him from the Death Penalty. One solid truth had always held firm; people might not do much to save themselves, but they would almost inevitably break when it came to protecting their Loved Ones from Danger or Harm. Exploiting their love for one another was a tried-and-true form of psychological torture and manipulation, and it had been working for millennia.

Without having sufficient backstory yet to explain how the two were connected, I couldn't say for sure how far they would go to help one another. But there was something there that Daegan Kyl was already invested in; I could only hope that Willow Amos was equally concerned about protecting him as much as he seemed dedicated to protecting her. With that in mind, I went full in regarding their meeting, and made sure that she could bear witness to the more severe aspect of what 'incarceration' could mean to an individual. The more active her imagination, the more she was convinced Daegan Kyl was suffering, the more likely she was to cooperate.

As with many people, she might not be motivated by self-preservation, but her guilt over how a man such as Daegan Kyl could be brought to his knees, rendered helpless, and have his entire life destroyed might be the proponent that turned the tide. Guilt could very well be the ticket to her compliance—but I based all that on my instincts. I was gambling that her feelings for Daegan Kyl were strong and genuine, and that he meant more to her than the students in her anarchist club.

I watched from the next room as they brought Willow Amos in and seated her on the far side of the table. I wanted her to have a full view of the doorway when Daegan Kyl was brought in; I had instructed the SPD guardsmen to restrain him with a two-foot radius and full restraints for hands and ankles. If Willow Amos could handle watching Daegan Kyl chained up like an Offender bound for Supermax, then I could see just how cold and heartless she really was. This guy was clearly trying to look out for her, but I had yet to see any effort made on her end to help him with anything. She needed to see just how bad things could get for each of them if she didn't start cooperating.

Willow Amos was positioned and left alone in the room again, waiting for Daegan Kyl's arrival. I wanted her to have a few minutes of solitude; it didn't take long for most people to realize they would rather be anywhere else than an Interview Room at a Police Department, and it didn't matter if they were Guilty or Innocent in that respect.

She looked around the room, an expression of bored disdain on her face. She was old enough to have outgrown that petulant teenage entitlement, and yet she still maintained an air of smug superiority. I was becoming familiar enough with her to see that it was always present. She always looked like she had a chip on her shoulder.

Within a few moments, Daegan Kyl was being led down the hallway and brought into the room behind one of the biggest SPD Officers I could arrange. I wanted him dwarfed between a few big SPD guardsmen; the bigger, the better, and all for the sake of appearances. Given Daegan Kyl's stature, it hadn't been an easy audition—but the SPD had not let me down; there were always bigger bullies on the playground.

Along with this, the two guardsmen were in full gear for effect as well. Their batons were out, powerful enough to bring Kyl to his knees with an internal shock that was reminiscent of the cattle prods of yesteryear. Their visors were at full tint, which always seemed a bit menacing to those who had an aversion or disdain for Law Enforcement because they couldn't see their faces or eyes. Most little kids looked at them and thought they were almost like the robotic versions that patrolled neighborhoods; when they were raised by parents who taught them that Law Enforcement was there to help and not to hurt, it was amazing how well they responded to them.

It was all about the conditioning and psychological issues one held; for children who had no reason to believe LEOs were something to be feared, they neither found them intimidating, nor potentially dangerous. To them, they were robotic transformers with cool sunglasses and armor just like the Knights of the Round Table. For those who regarded LEOs as dangerous, Violent, or 'power-hungry', all they could see was oversized, militarized, faceless predators with seemingly unlimited government power.

After having interviewed Willow Amos, I knew this was what she saw—and all she saw.

The reality was that the only person in this entire scenario that had exhibited any type of aggressive, Violent, or potentially lethal behavior was Willow Amos, but I knew there was no way that she would ever see it from that perspective.

There was something else to consider, and that was the overall training that both Willow Amos and Daegan Kyl had each received in their past. It was inevitable for Daegan Kyl to have gained substantial self-defense training along with tactical and weapons training as a Soldier, so if Willow Amos could think things through rationally, she shouldn't genuinely fall for the game of shadows I was trying to pull over. Not only was Daegan Kyl not in any genuine Danger or Risk for Harm, it wasn't even a scare tactic for any rational Human Being considering the legal confines we as Law Enforcement were bound by. Willow Amos should be able to defend herself since self-defense training was a mandatory series of courses in every US public school, and had been for the last century. And because she was female, she would have spent additional time in training with an emphasis spent on self-defense against male Assailants that could have physically overpowered her more easily because of their size and strength.

The bottom line was that my 'plan' was manipulative, but completely transparent if she could be reasonable. If she could see that Daegan Kyl was not in any real Danger, the entire plan of using this situation as a bargaining chip was out the window. What I was banking on was that she would not respond like a logical Human Being; I was counting on the same emotional response she had displayed in our first interview—all emotion and minimal critical thinking. Call it a play on sexism, but I had every intent of using her emotions against her. Between the guilt, the sympathy, the inherently protective desire to save her friend, and all of it being done with an emotional response on hyper-drive—I was going to use every tool in the toolbox to get this 'leader of the revolution' to crack within minutes.

And I sincerely hoped for both of their sake that they cooperated; their very lives depended upon it. The time for covering for Murderers and playing American Anarchist was over. We had four Citizens who had lost their lives somehow, and each of their families needed answers if they had any expectation of ever gaining any Closure. Willow Amos was the key to all of it.

The look on her face was priceless; she didn't even know that we had already picked up Daegan Kyl or that we knew anything about him. As much as she had played things cool in the video from the Randall residence before, and as crazy as she had seemed in my first interview with her, nothing had prepared me for how she responded when she realized that Daegan Kyl had been Arrested along with the rest of them.

In a split second, I watched her face turn from surprise to guilt and shame before finally resting on the genuine emotion she was feeling: remorse. Her eyes had welled up with tears. This girl deeply cared about the man entering the room.

I had leverage.

DK and WA Meeting

I watched as the two guardsmen seated Daegan Kyl opposite Willow and secured his wrists to the tabletop, and then his ankle shackles to a lock below. It was done electronically, but the sound was loud as it echoed through the small space with high ceilings.

"Don't freak out," Daegan Kyl said.

That's all it took; Willow Amos, the leader of the American Anarchists Revolution—the crazed, hysterical sociopath determined to 'bring down the man'—started to cry like a child.

Whatever their relationship was, there was no longer any question about it; Daegan Kyl was her kryptonite.

She tried to reach across the table to touch his hand as it rested near the other. They were both fastened and then secured to the table and could not be touched directly because of the security settings that restricted his movement. As soon as she reached her hand forward, it gave her a bit of a jolt and she yanked her hand away instinctively. Only the guardsmen, while wearing their protective gear, could touch Daegan Kyl directly when his perimeter settings were activated. It was the same as that which had been used on Willow Amos at our first interview, but today I had allowed hers to remain off. I wanted her to see that Daegan Kyl could, and would, suffer the same fate, and there would not be any special leniency for him, regardless of how superficial his role in her 'cause' had been.

Not being able to touch him seemed to matter. She held her hand where it undoubtedly still had the traces of a minor rug burn from the shock she received, and I watched as her eyes filled up with tears again. She put her head into her hands and her shoulders fell.

"It's ok," he said softly. "I'm fine. Don't cry. It's all going to be alright. Look at me." He leaned his body forward and I could see he wanted to comfort her, but he knew he couldn't.

He spoke with a bit more urgency and directed her to look at him again.

Wiping her eyes with her hands, she looked up. Her face told a story of such powerlessness and guilt that it was clear she genuinely cared about him.

"I'm so sorry, Daeg—" she began.

"Shh! Stop!" he said forcefully. "I mean it! We don't have time for any of that. I only have a few minutes and I'm lucky to have that long. You need to listen to me, and you need to follow every single word of what I say. Do you understand me?"

Willow Amos nodded her head. Tears were still falling down her cheeks.

"Pay attention. This is no longer a game; do you understand me? This is no longer about whatever you believe you need to do or why. It doesn't matter whether you think you've been doing the right thing or that your principles are worth fighting for. I've already told you about that and I've told you I support your choices. But this isn't a game anymore. I should never have let you get this deep into this. I should have put a stop to it long before it ever got to this point. But this is where we are now, and the consequences are here. You made that choice when you did what you wanted rather than what was legal."

She opened her mouth and started to respond—showing that her passion for her cause was still just below the surface.

"No! Enough! We don't have time to argue about any of this anymore. I don't know how long I have or if I'll be allowed to see you again. You know that this is going to be a brief window before you are charged, given a trial, and then Convicted. Don't even delude yourself into thinking they won't find you Guilty—you all are. *Every single one of you is going to be found Guilty.* We don't have time to argue about any of it. There's only one thing that matters—and that is you telling the Investigator everything you can about Jones so you can save your own ass. Do you understand me? Tell him whatever you know about Jones, or you are going to be charged with *Murder*. Am I getting through to you?" He spewed the words at her, his Body Language telling her just how angry he was by the way he leaned toward her as he threw the words out, his patience completely gone.

Daegan Kyl was fuming. He wasted no time in ensuring that she had a full understanding of how things stood, and I appreciated that; he was holding true to his word.

She stared at him, her eyes big and round, and she nodded. She seemed surprised by how angry he was, and it left me with the impression that he was more paternal toward her than anything else. His opinion mattered. His *wrath* mattered. She didn't want to disappoint him, and she was now doing so in spades. It was like watching a little girl get chastised by her father; she was willing to do whatever he wanted just so he would love her again.

"Listen to me. Whatever you thought you were doing; *it's done*. Do you hear me? Done! The only thing that matters is that you tell the Investigator everything he wants to know. Hold nothing back. Tell him anything he asks, so they hold Jones accountable. You have one fight—do you understand me? One fight, and one mission. You are looking at the *Death Penalty*. Your one job is to make sure you tell that Investigator everything you know so you can get downgraded to Exile. Do you understand? This is no longer a game, Willow. I mean it. Your political goals or agendas no longer matter. You did what you could—and I get it. I understand why you needed to do it. But this is no longer about that; you gambled, and you lost. And now there is only one thing you can do, and *I swear to God, Willow...you better do exactly what I'm telling you to do because I will never forgive you for dragging me into this mess if you don't at least try to get yourself out of the Death Penalty.*"

His words were spoken so low that I almost missed them, but their impact was priceless. She had clearly never heard him speak to her with such force, and its impact was powerful.

She nodded her head quickly in agreement and started to cry again, letting loose a loud sob.

She burst out, "I'm sorry!"

I messaged the two guardsmen in the room that it was time to remove Daegan Kyl. Within a few seconds, they had him freed from the table, loosened his shackles once again so he could walk easier, and started him toward the door.

Willow Amos was crying and trying to stand up. A third guardsman stood near her with his hand on her shoulder, firmly suggesting she remain seated while they removed Kyl from the room.

As he neared the door and the guardsmen waited for it to open, he turned his head back toward her.

"I promised him, Willow! Don't you let me down!"

Willow shook her head again, let out another loud sob, and jerked her shoulder away from the guardsmen.

The door closed behind Daegan Kyl and his two escorts, leaving Willow Amos in the room alone aside from the guard who retreated into the nearest corner to await further instruction.

I watched her for a second as she put her hands over her face again and her body moved with racking sobs.

She loved him.

Whatever their relationship, whatever it was that connected them, it was clear that they loved one another and wanted to protect each other.

I instructed the guardsmen to return Willow Amos to her Holding Cell once again.

Officer Stanton and I replayed their conversation, concentrating on that last phrase spoken by Daegan Kyl as he left the room. We didn't know what it meant or who the man mentioned was that Daegan Kyl had promised something to.

But Willow Amos did, and it mattered to her. Whatever Daegan Kyl had meant by his final comment, it had struck a nerve with Willow. The entire conversation had been effective in the sense that it had showed a pre-existing relationship between them on a deeply personal level for the courts. But it also verified that Daegan Kyl knew about what Willow Amos had been doing, but that he himself wasn't directly involved in any of it as I had expected. His words hadn't been coded with anything; there had been no double-meanings or secret sentences out of place. On the surface, it was just an older man lecturing a younger person, criticizing them a bit but also instructing them how to make amends for their misdeeds.

It presented as a very straight-forward conversation; he blamed 'Jones', though he didn't actually say his first name, unfortunately. He wanted Willow Amos to tell me everything and save herself. It was all very cut and dry; I could only hope that she was going to heed his advice, and sooner rather than later.

I returned to my office to gather my things before heading back to the barracks so I could get some dinner and hopefully a decent night's sleep.

DK—Military Report

We had finally received a copy of Daegan Kyl's military records from more than a decade earlier. As expected, it provided an insufficient amount of information and a lot of blacked out pages; it appeared Daegan Kyl had been among those Army Rangers who spent more time in the shadows than the public view, and Uncle Sam intended to keep it that way even from us. There were more pages redacted than visible, but his Physical Fitness tests, along with other testing, all showed a remarkable Soldier with no trouble advancing within his career.

And yet at the peak of his game, the man had left the Armed Forces, left an impressive rank and pay grade behind, and set out into the world. For a man who seemed on the fast track for higher leadership and a lifetime career, it made little sense. His Psychological Evaluations all showed a well-adjusted Soldier with no underlying issues or Combat-related PTSD. His team had been well-established since his early years, and he was in peak physical condition with many of the highest marks among his peers. A lifetime spent in the Armed Forces seemed like it would be a fulfilling and gratifying career for a man such as himself. It wasn't as if it were a career solely for meatheads; he had been among the elite within our entire military system, a place well-known for exacting the highest of standards across the board.

His file showed he had more weapons training and combat experience than probably every Officer in the building combined, discounting the Officers that were retired military or prior service. That he could probably kill any of us but chose not to was part of his charm; it made me curious as to why he was wearing an orange uniform instead of one just like mine.

I had originally believed that anyone that would be immersed in this type of back-alley, seedy environment would have a lengthy history of social and criminal problems along with a lack of compassion and low regard for Humanity. Not only did this man not fit any of my preconceived ideas, I was concerned that I was missing something about him I should be able to understand. Everything indicated that something was amiss here; that this man I had Arrested and interviewed already was just not the kind of man that should be here. It made me doubt what I was doing, and that was something that I hadn't ever done before in an investigation.

Something didn't add up. This man was no killer. According to his records, he was a national hero, and had plenty of medals to prove it.

DK—Interview IV: LeRoy Jones

"The last time we met, you seemed surprised that LeRoy Jones was connected to Rebecca's case. I'm not sure what I need to do to make you understand how important your testimony is on this subject, but right now the Death of Rebecca is being connected to Willow Amos directly. She's the last known person to have any type of contact with her. There are phone records between them. I have surveillance footage proving that she was in her office building, and I have documentation that they had met. Within moments of being Raped she had sought the help of a counselor, but she never received support or guidance."

I looked at him, and his steady gaze told me he was standing by his previous position.

"Look, I get that you obviously intend to defend Amos; I just don't get why. So let me tell you how it is from my perspective. This young woman went to the office to get some rather urgent help directly following her Rape. Someone advised her to keep the information to herself and not report the Assault. This resulted in a spiraling effect that ultimately led to her inability to control her own situation effectively. We can go back and forth as to whether or not you believe that advice from Willow Amos would have had a direct impact on her decisions or not, but ultimately what it comes down to is whether or not you are going to face Exile for the rest of your life just to protect someone who knowingly Concealed the Rape of a young woman. By covering for this Rapist, she allowed a man whom she obviously knew to be a dangerous Predator to roam the streets freely until he eventually Raped and Murdered his next Victim. Her actions protected a Brutal, Sadistic Serial Rapist—a man whom she knew personally and was willing to sacrifice the Innocence and lives of her Fellow Citizens over, and now you're protecting her. I'm just having a hard time understanding why you'd be willing to lose everything to continue to keep the secrets of such a selfish person when she clearly has no problem throwing you to the wolves for it."

Daegan Kyl raised his eyebrow, choosing to retreat into his now familiar coat of armor, brooding, self-contained. I knew he was processing everything I said and carefully examining my words and Body Language; just because he barely spoke didn't mean he wasn't weighing all the information being presented to him with critical precision. On the contrary, I measured my own words to project only the fact-pattern I wanted him to have and nothing more. I fully believed he could discern my own Body Language and words, both spoken and withheld. He was a shrewd entrepreneur and a prior Combat Soldier with a history of discreet missions in his resume. Surely those experiences also required some interpersonal skills. He might be emotionally involved regarding Willow Amos, but something about the way he always listened to me so intently made me believe we were constantly in the middle of a game of chess.

He sighed deeply, and folding his hands behind the back of his head, interlocked his fingers. His reclined position allowed him to look upward, and I could see him staring up at the line in the wall where it intersected with the ceiling directly above the window. He was weighing things out, but there was something about the way he seemed to focus that struck me as being tenser than he had been previously. If he were half as smart as I believed him to be, he would try to figure out how to extract himself from this whole mess and put as much blame as possible on LeRoy Jones. But he wasn't your average man, aside from there being very little about this case that could be described as 'average' anyhow.

"I don't know the man personally; I never met him at all. But I saw him a time or two when I would go check up on Willow," he began.

I interjected, "Just to be clear, we're talking about LeRoy Jones? The Suspect in question regarding the Alleged Rapes of Rebecca Summers and Mariam Pembrook, for whom he is also the Suspected Murderer?"

He lowered his head and stared at me, "Yes, the same."

He raised his eyebrow again rather condescendingly and then continued.

"I didn't know who he was, and I never knew his name. I don't know why or how he knows Willow Amos or how well they know each other. I haven't ever had a conversation with her about the man or any of the events surrounding my Arrest, so I have nothing to base anything on regarding what her involvement might be or to what extent. All I can say is that I would visit her occasionally and there were a few times when I saw him there. But she always had people around; she was a student and was always around other students. It wasn't uncommon to see her with people—especially men—whenever I saw her," he said.

"And when you would visit her, this was usually where? And how often would you say this occurred?" I asked.

He shrugged.

"We were both busy people. I didn't see her very often, once or twice a month, usually. Not as much as I should have, clearly," he muttered. His tone was bitter, almost a growl. His downcast eyes spoke of guilt, remorse.

"Do you have any reason to believe the two of them were romantically or sexually involved?" I asked him. I thought the question might make him angry, but I was trying to understand the nature of his relationship with Willow Amos, and it still seemed too complex to rule out jealousy.

He let out a short laugh, a snort.

"I'm not sure if there's ever been a man she's ever been in a relationship with—sexual or otherwise..." he replied. "She's never been driven by common, base desires. I'm afraid you're going to have to work harder than that."

I found my frustration growing; he had the home court advantage and was throwing it in my face. He was still being derisive, despite understanding the gravity of the situation; almost unable to abstain from his arrogant nature enough to remember that he was supposed to be at least pretending to show contrition. I wasn't here to waste my time with him. If he wanted to hang with the rest of them, so be it.

Sensing my frustration—presumably—he sat up straighter and ran his hand through his hair.

"Look. You're going about this all wrong. You're trying to think of Willow as being some type of college girl who got caught up with the wrong kind of guy or like she's some sort of petty thug. That's not who she is, that's all. She's a smart girl; probably one of the smartest you'll ever meet, and she's a freethinker. I can't tell you what she was doing with him because I wasn't there; it would appear that I didn't know as much about her or what she has been doing as I thought I did. But I'll tell ya what—I can promise you that the next time I talk to her, I'm going to find out what exactly she was thinking. Because I'm not going down for some two-bit scumbag Rapist, and I don't owe anyone anything. I don't know why she would cover for a guy like that or even why she knows someone like him. Clearly, we both have some questions for her."

He leaned back in his chair again, still looking at me to see if I understood he wasn't trying to cover for the actions of LeRoy Jones directly. It seemed that Daegan Kyl was as much of a victim of circumstance as possible, given the information presented. It didn't explain everything, but he didn't seem to be intentionally trying to conceal the Human Remains of Innocent Victims.

"We still have a lot of unanswered questions," I said.

"So do I," he responded.

He shrugged.

"I don't understand why a man like you would be caught up in any of this. Even if you found yourself mixed up in a situation outside of your own knowledge regarding LeRoy Jones, I still don't have any answers for Katarina Urakov or Arlan Randall."

He shrugged again.

I sighed and then stood up.

"Failing to help me will not help either of you. LeRoy Jones will hang himself, but for a guy who seems to do all of this because of a woman, you sure seem to be better at digging holes than digging yourself out of them."

It was truly, without a doubt, one of the absolute worst, dumbest things I think I'd ever said in my entire life, and I immediately wished I could take it back.

He looked up at me, the faintest curve of his mouth peering out from his bearded face, his dark eyes fixed on mine from below his heavy brows. At least he found it amusing.

"We all have burdens to bear," he said.

I nodded my head slowly, not sure what he meant. Maybe it was a dig about my investigation not progressing well. It had many facets. I wasn't happy with the rate the layers were being unraveled.

He gave a curt nod in my direction, and I pushed the slight indentation on the side of my visor that closed it instantaneously, eliminating his ability to see my eyes any further. I motioned to the guard that I was done and made my way to the door. Daegan Kyl stood, and the two Officers placed him back into the shackles and handcuffs for transport, choosing caution over the misguided and overconfident notion that just because there were four guards within ten feet that they could have kept him contained.

Of all the Citizens I had watched go through the same process, it never seemed quite right to see Daegan Kyl experience it. As much as he was a somewhat reserved individual, he also had an often quietly patronizing demeanor. But even with these two personalities seemingly at odds with one another, there wasn't anything about him I had observed thus far that was anything less than honorable, let alone cruel.

He was always courteous to the SPD Officers, demonstrating patience with them as they applied restraints that were little less than the bondage of slaves, and even appeared to provide a subtle subservience on their behalf to ensure they were neither intimidated nor prone to provocation and aggressive bravado. I imagined he had spent much of his adulthood in competition with most of the men he encountered, such was the way of the male ego. Many would see a man of his stature and strength and respond with their own male pride prickling, consciously or not.

I had a difficult time reconciling the Criminal treatment with the man; it didn't match the man I sensed him to be at his core. None of his past, including his childhood, military service, or prior work history, showed that he was anything other than an upstanding guy who had lived a successful life until the point he ended up here. The current situation didn't support the probability of this man being Guilty of anything Criminal, least of all Violent Crimes; there was nothing that would lead anyone to believe this man could even behave in such a monstrous way. He was a man with an impressive legacy of positive and productive contributions to society; he was extremely well known, and he would probably have countless character witnesses at his disposal to validate his integrity and support his reputation as a Good Man. They would have declared that anything contrary to that would have undoubtedly been questioned as being the exception, not the norm. It was an implausible leap to imagine this man was even capable of such ugliness—especially regarding poor little Katarina.

I still had a lot of questions about who the man was, who Willow Amos was to him, and why he would go to such lengths to help her. The goal was to investigate and garner conclusive evidence; I was not such a fool as to immediately believe in his Innocence, but my goal was always going to be to get to the truth, and I was willing to think outside of the box and employ every resource available in order to do so.

I had been mulling over the idea of having Daegan Kyl meet with Willow Amos so he could ask her some questions; either that or I could place him in a Holding Cell next to LeRoy Jones. But now that I knew for certain that LeRoy Jones would have recognized him, it was unlikely that we could have used him to extract information. I knew that Daegan Kyl had not been lying about Jones by his reaction; he hadn't realized the women had been Physically Harmed or the circumstances surrounding their Deaths. He hadn't understood the role that Willow Amos had played in their Final Moments, but he knew she had lied to him about it. It seemed to me as though he himself might have been betrayed by her; he may have Disposed of their Remains with the understanding that he had been doing it to help her—not realizing she was doing it to help someone else. That would explain a lot regarding his negative reaction to LeRoy

Jones, and it would also account for why he had been so willing to speak with Willow Amos to try to get some answers of his own.

I was not trying to pin anything onto anyone—including Willow Amos—or have them held accountable for anything beyond that which they were personally responsible for causing. My intent was to learn the truth, and if this man was willing to help me on that path as an effort to spare another, then it only spoke more to my original assessment of his character than against it. There was no harm in giving him the opportunity to do what he could. And should the truth result in Willow Amos being cleared of any direct involvement in either Deaths, she would have much to be grateful to Daegan Kyl for.

No Known Motive

As I had told myself many times before, being able to read people was a gift, as was having an innate understanding about what motivated people's actions. It was a common perception within the world of Law Enforcement that Detectives and Investigators often had something resembling a sixth sense about things related to Crime and Criminals. With each investigation, their intuition and ability to read faces and Body Language became more fully honed.

Over time, technology made the procedural aspect of Detective work infinitely easier, more scientific, and incontrovertible. But it was still the Human component that steered the ship, determining which leads to pursue, and relying on our knowledge, experience, training, and yes, gut instinct, in order to get our investigations solved.

I found it a little disconcerting how Daegan Kyl had apparently distanced himself emotionally from the work he engaged in. He seemed to compartmentalize his own role while disconnecting it from the Violence and Criminality of those whom he worked for. It was this or a simple lack of conscience, and sometimes as he spoke, it was difficult to determine which it was. I couldn't prove at this point or understand why, but he was lying to me. I wasn't sure what he was hiding, but I knew I was still missing something. He had helped a lot with the information about Willow Amos, what he knew about The Angels of Mercy, and he had even offered some explanations about the two Foreign Nationals that made enough sense to pass muster. But it still just wasn't right.

It wasn't that I thought he was intentionally trying to play me or lie to me. I think he had genuinely attempted to explain things as best as he could with the information he had knowledge of. He didn't hold back his contempt of LeRoy Jones, and he had seemed genuinely interested in ensuring that he had been removed from the streets and would be Charged, Convicted, and Sentenced to Death. Whether or not he had known him personally or known of his role regarding Rebecca and Mariam, there was clearly no love lost between them. In fact, out of everything we had discussed, LeRoy Jones was the one issue that seemed to evoke strong negative emotions, especially anger and disgust.

I didn't know why he would be in the muck with people that were not of his background and held oppositional values and views from what he seemed to hold. He was an ex-Soldier, a capitalist, a wealthy man, and until his recent Arrest, had never been found to have broken any laws. And yet he was aligned with this strange group of individuals that were touting anti-American beliefs, had facilitated a litany of Felony Offenses, and felt entirely justified in doing so.

I decided to do something a little different just to follow my hunch. It wasn't that Daegan Kyl had intentionally failed to answer any of my questions or explain anything; he had done everything as requested. But I couldn't shake the feeling that he had carefully sculpted what information he had conveyed through concealing important details and not objecting to any of my assumptions.

He had done this by allowing me to believe he was an Angel of Mercy. And yet, his interviews were the only ones completely lacking in any of the tired lines that all the rest had offered up. Willow Amos herself had blasted me thoroughly with a string of Abuses and anti-LEO rhetoric. She had declared that her government was no better than Nazi's from World War Two. Daegan Kyl had never said a word about anything that conveyed the sentiments of their movement. In fact, much of what he had said to her in their meeting seemed to indicate that he had tolerated her beliefs and the corresponding actions she had taken because he had been supporting her personally, not whatever it was that she had been up to.

I made a note to ask Officer Stanton to re-interview all of The Angels of Mercy again. I wanted him to insert a few notable mentions of Daegan Kyl. If he was working within The Angels of Mercy, his name would have been known either as leadership or as one of their 'comrades'. Surely, if he were involved in their movement, he would have been known to at least some of them, especially as he knew Willow Amos personally. It would be beneficial to know what the other Suspects thought of him.

Also, I didn't know if there were other Citizens that had fallen Victim to their agenda, or if there were other Human Remains buried elsewhere. I had no reason to believe that there were more burials, but I had no reason to doubt that there might not be. I would ask Officer Stanton to explore what they knew about the burial process itself, and if they knew who was responsible for handling them. My guess was that they didn't have a clue who was doing it.

The more I thought about it, the more I believed that Willow Amos was Daegan Kyl's *only* connection to this Criminal band of miscreants, and he himself wasn't involved in this ideology at all. I bet that none of those malleable little pawns had even known this man, not by face or name. Who knew if they had ever questioned what happened to the Victims after they were Deceased, but I was willing to bet they hadn't known it was Daegan Kyl that was burying them.

Even then, if I could establish that his involvement was solely related to Willow Amos, it still needed to be explained. He was, what? Fifteen years older than her, and probably twenty years older than the rest of them. I pictured her in my head—goofy-looking, skinny, and with a personality that was 100% political zeal. Their personalities were completely contradictory to one another; he was cool and composed, almost fatherly, and she was a wild, impassioned activist with an overly dramatic, entitled personality. It made little sense to imagine them romantically involved, and that was outside of the age-gap.

But that didn't mean there wasn't some other type of relationship. He wasn't related to her biologically; that would have come up in their files after their Arrests. I wanted to understand why Daegan Kyl felt this compulsion to do her bidding like all the rest.

And on that note, what was it about her that made all these crazy young men bend over backwards for her? There were several females Arrested from her 'club', but there were over twenty young men between the ages of twenty and thirty, all from her campus. Were they just drawn to the anarchist world she illustrated, or was she actually that convincing of a leader of this movement? Something drew them to her. And a forty-two-year-old man that was fifteen years older than her was trying to take the blame for her involvement so she wouldn't get any type of punishment that would exceed Reform. We had to know why.

There were still some gaps in the Investigation, though, and I still felt it was linked to the information that Daegan Kyl had chosen not to disclose.

He had taken the position that he was unaware of the Victims until they called him to Dispose of their Remains. This may have been the case, but it would have been near impossible to convince anyone of this selective knowledge and involvement given that he had been directly tied to all four Victims by their burials.

Since the little girl, Katarina, had not been a Victim of The Angels of Mercy, but had been Abducted and held captive by the two Foreign Nationals, her case was entirely separate and disconnected. We had found no connection between the two Foreign Nationals and either Willow Amos or The Angels of Mercy yet. Daegan Kyl was essentially caught in the middle of two separate groups of people that were both Causing Harm and Death to Citizens, and he was the only one.

He had failed to report the people to Law Enforcement and had also knowingly concealed evidence of Human Remains by choosing to dispose of their bodies when called upon to do so. Regardless of his own participation or level of intimate contact he had with any of these poor Victims, he had still made the choice to conceal the Crimes of those complicit.

If he had known that the two Foreign Nationals had Abducted the little girl Katarina and failed to inform Law Enforcement so they could have potentially rescued her and saved her life, then he was partially responsible for everything that had happened to her—including her Death. In which case, concealing her Remains was an effort on his end to hide his own role in it. That was something that might result in the Death Penalty if it could be verified. But Daegan Kyl would have us believe he had no knowledge of their Disappearances, no reason to suspect that the men he had once worked for would have played any role in the Abduction of Katarina, and that he had no sign that Katarina was being held by them.

Somehow, though, that little girl had still ended up being buried by him, and with one Foreign National dead and the other having fled the country, it was going to be extremely difficult for him to clear his own name. For as much as Daegan Kyl had shared with me and attempted to clarify his own limited role in things, there were still so many questions, loose ends, and unexplained pieces that it was becoming increasingly clear that he was holding back so he didn't incriminate other people. He was intentionally omitting information to keep directing the blame toward himself, which was also still an effort to protect someone. I was sure it was Willow Amos. We just needed to understand why.

TWENTY-SIX – FINDING ANSWERS

Results of Search Warrant: Willow Amos

When we conducted the Search of Willow Amos' house and office, the Front-Line Officers had located some belongings that were later confirmed to have been the property of Rebecca Summers. I had no idea how they got there, but apparently Willow Amos had buried some artwork and a purse belonging to Rebecca Summers in her garage. Within the purse had been several prescription pill bottles—anti-Depression pills and some type of Oxycodone—the exact types that had been reflected on her toxicology report weeks earlier.

The pills had been filled at a local pharmacy, and the name of the prescribing Doctor had been listed. From that, Stanton had done a comprehensive background check of the Doctor, finding enough evidence to support that her office might be conducting illegal Abortions.

This evidence allowed us to apply for a Search Warrant, and the Arrest Warrants were quick to follow.

Results of Search Warrant: LeRoy Jones

Our search of the small studio apartment rented out by LeRoy Jones had yielded little results. However, hidden away in one of the ventilation shafts, two pairs of female panties were located, along with a large, serrated hunting knife.

Testing confirmed that DNA found on each of the articles of clothing belonged to Rebecca Summers and Mariam Pembrook. Semen was also detected on both panties. The first pair, confirmed to belong to Mariam Pembrook, had been bled-soaked. The blood, once tested, was proven to be that of Mariam Pembrook.

Blood was also present on the serrated knife, as if it had been wiped off before being put away, but without any genuine effort to clean the evidence. Testing confirmed two separate samples were present; one was a match to Mariam Pembrook, the second belonged to LeRoy Jones.

Arrest of the Doctor

The Abortion Doctor's home and office were approved for Search Warrants and all related materials pertaining to her work, Abortion enterprise, and medical care were seized. The Warrant for her clinic pertained to everything on-site and included all staff. Working in a clinic where Abortions were occurring was cause enough for Arrest and typically Conviction, and so each of her employees were also Arrested.

Just as having an Abortion when it was illegal was a choice, so too was working in a clinic that carried out Abortions. One did not have to hold the scalpel in order to Commit the Act; blood was on their hands just by letting it occur. Failing to report Abortions was Criminal and would not be disregarded by our Courts. Not one person working in her clinics would be exonerated, and each would face life-altering consequences, as they should.

There would be close to a dozen Arrests tonight from my calculations of the clinic and a quick review of their employment records. The SPD S.W.A.T. had conducted simultaneous raids at both locations, and already had the Abortion doctor in custody. Her husband was also taken in for questioning. While this was a good night for ridding our nation of a large criminal network, it also left a dark shadow over the Greater Seattle Area and dampened my spirits considerably.

There was no denying that it was a large group of people that would have their lives destroyed, and their actions would undoubtedly impact dozens or maybe even hundreds more. And all for something that never needed to be done because there were numerous alternatives legally and freely available.

It was a difficult reality of our modern times; our population numbers and cultural emphasis on the Sanctity of Human Life made Abortion a contemptable means of Ending a Viable Pregnancy. Science and technology had made it entirely unnecessary, and for these reasons, those who chose to venture down this path were committing Crimes Against Humanity. Although this would not be carried out by my own team, the investigation of this Doctor and her clinic would eventually reveal the identities of many other patients who had used her services, and all would be prosecuted in due course. Those that chose to live by the sword would die by the sword.

Something Missing with The Angels of Mercy

Something wasn't adding up about The Angels of Mercy or Willow Amos, and it had been weighing on me for quite a while.

They weren't doing anything illegal.

There was one set of Human Remains that they had been responsible for burying that we were aware of, and that was Arlan.

They were claiming to be responsible for having 'assisted' Mr. Randall with his Passing because they had supported the position that he had held regarding Assisted-Suicide. We could also place Willow Amos, along with two of her henchmen, directly at the scene, and each of them was building a strong case against themselves without me having to do any of the work myself.

But that was it; that was the problem. There was an entire 'club' working within the university campus, with half of them also working at the Winter Season Hospice Care facility. Over fifteen of the students in the healthcare program at the university were employed at least part-time at the Hospice Care facility with her. She was a graduate student at her school, was obviously regarded as their 'leader', and had at least influenced them enough to help take responsibility for the Death of at least one man.

And that was the problem, right there. We had a young woman who was working on a graduate program in nursing. She was highly educated and capable, and she was already working professionally within the healthcare field. But just as her other cohorts were doing, she had taken a low-pay, low-skill job at an elder-home facility doing work that a person with a one-year community college certificate could do.

It made little sense.

The only reason I could see any of them choosing to work there legitimately was that it was part of their educational requirements. The problem with that was that there was so much of a variety within the education levels of the students; although many of them were freshmen and sophomores, there were also older, more advanced students and several that were in the same graduate program as Willow Amos.

It made the legitimacy of their 'having to have a job and work as some type of intern' less credible, and it made the graduate students even less plausible for taking on positions that were clearly below their pay grade.

Nonetheless, for the sake of being thorough, I would have Officer Stanton check with the educational program requirements for all the students to see if they had mandatory internships or the like. I would also have him see what he could find out about their hiring process and see if anything jumped out regarding how it came to be that so many of the students had gained employment there.

Who knew what they had been doing or getting away with. I was cautious about proceeding down this road, but my worst fear would be to question other healthcare facilities or elder-care homes and discover a similar trend. The possibilities were endless in that regard, and the more I realized how expansive their feeding grounds could have been, the more nervous I became. There could be doctored records and cases of

Missing Persons across the state, with terminal and elderly patients having Disappeared from elder care and hospice care facilities all over. With so many of our elders on their own, it would be far too easy for them to Vanish without anyone ever noticing, especially if their records could be altered.

All that aside, we were still looking at a major elephant in the room. We had a fair number of young students that were all making the same political declarations as had been commonly heard during the 21st century. They protested Law Enforcement, our government, and what they considered to be fascism and a restriction on their 'freedom to choose' what happened to their Physical Autonomy. They advocated support of Euthanasia, Suicide, and Assisted-Suicide. They had sworn their allegiance to both Willow Amos and their group, The Angels of Mercy. But we did not have any tangible evidence that they were culpable of committing any sort of Crimes…because we had no Victims.

Not long before, I had believed that discovering four Deceased Victims was such an extremely rare find I thought it had topped any tragedy in the last century. But now…I was worried that we were on the brink of something much worse and we just didn't know it yet. *What sort of anarchist's club, intent on breaking the laws and starting a revolution, didn't break any laws or commit any of the Crimes Against Humanity they were promoting?*

DK—Final Interviews: Choices

While meeting with Daegan Kyl once more, I summarized how I was intending to use the information I had about him to push for the Death Penalty. I wanted to give him some time to weigh things out.

I knew he was covering for Willow Amos. He still wouldn't explain his relationship with her, but I knew she was the whole reason he was continuing to play this charade with me.

I didn't believe Daegan Kyl was directly responsible for causing any of their Deaths, and I had no intention of seeking the Death Penalty for him when so far, the only thing I could prove was his pure stupidity and willingness to take a bullet for someone else.

Daegan Kyl's ignorance of the four Victims and what had happened to them was his saving grace, and he didn't even realize it. He was helping himself escape Capital Punishment by exposing his own Innocence. As much as he might have been trying to keep a stoic front, he had revealed much more than he knew already.

He stared at the wall behind me, but his mind was miles and miles away. His hand went back up to his bearded jawline, and he rubbed it thoughtfully, slowly. He was caught between a rock and a hard place, and there was no way for him to extract himself. He was trapped, and he knew it. The only question left was whether he was going to allow his association with Willow Amos to take him down, and if he was prepared to go down for the Deaths of four Innocent Victims that he knew he had not Caused any Harm to. It was hard to imagine that it was worth the consequences I was placing in front of him.

He would still be Exiled; he was still complicit, and he had still been involved to some extent.

Exile was not Death; he could still have some semblance of a life and a chance. But Death? Who was worth dying for? Who was worth protecting so much that not only would he allow himself to be sent to Death Row, but his Crimes and reputation would be publicized, and his name utterly decimated throughout the nation?

His legacy, his family name, and his entire existence would forever be tainted by the stain of his Crimes, with every detail available to anyone that ever mentioned his name or searched for it in any type of database. What could make it worthwhile to carry the legacy of having Raped and Murdered two women, and kept a little six-year-old girl as a Sexual Captive for over three months? Not to mention being held responsible for at least the Assisted-Suicide or Murder of an old man—a former Marine who had served his country honorably just as he had? It was bad enough to be considered a gravedigger, but to be considered a Sexual Deviant, a Serial Killer, and a Sexual Predator of Children was unfathomable. Who would allow their reputation to bear such a stain?

Surely, he would not continue with this charade. No matter what his role, he did not deserve such a fate when he was clearly not a Murderer.

I stood up. I had done sufficient damage and left him with plenty to consider. The one thing that was always profoundly effective on the Criminal Mind was the sheer absence of everything, and I intended to ensure that my guest Daegan Kyl had absolutely nothing to do except sit in his Cell and examine his life.

"I'll let you take some time to think things over. I'll be working on finalizing everything for each of your Victims with their families in the meantime. Let the guards know and they'll message me when you're ready; I'll be around."

Daegan Kyl didn't move; he just stayed motionless, staring at the wall. I knew that his mind was going through the dozen steps that occurred all leading up to this point in his life when he found himself sitting in a Holding Cell and facing the Death Penalty.

He wasn't angry. In fact, the only thing that struck me was that he seemed resigned to his fate; he knew he would have to talk at least a little in order to have a fighting chance.

I made my way toward the door.

From behind, Daegan Kyl finally spoke.

"So, if I tell you what I know, then what?" he asked.

"Then we talk. If I can use your information, and if it can exonerate you entirely, then the Death Penalty would be removed. You'd just be looking at Exile. As I said when we first spoke; I'm after the truth. Ultimately, that's all I want."

I knew he had a lot to consider. I didn't intend to pressure him, and I wasn't chasing a confession based on duress. I was more than happy to help him try to save himself and lessen his own punishment if he was willing to do what must be done. I had no interest in sending an Innocent man to Death Row; I served Justice, and it must be delivered fairly and in equal measure to the Crime.

The man sitting in front of me was not afraid of dying, and he wasn't afraid of the Death Penalty.

He sighed. It was the heavy sigh of a man that had made peace with his troubles.

"All right," he said, surrendering. "But I really don't know as much as you think I do."

I made my way back to the chair opposite him.

Maybe he was afraid of something after all.

Daegan Kyl, Soldier

"I served for ten years. I had every intention of being a Lifer, but Uncle Sam made it clear that it wasn't going to happen."

Daegan Kyl leaned back in his chair and put his arms behind his head, fingers woven together and locking them into place. It made his biceps look like overripe watermelons as they strained against the fabric of his Corrections jumpsuit. He would have been a prime candidate for any Super Soldier program, and I wondered if there wasn't some secret vault out there somewhere with a stash of his DNA currently being used as part of a recipe for disaster.

"So, what happened?" I asked. I knew the gist of it, but I wanted to hear his version. I had a feeling that it would be a little more insightful regarding how he came to be here today.

He sneered.

"My government isn't worth the price of my soul; that's what happened. You've read my file; surely you've received a copy by now."

"I have, actually. But you know it doesn't tell me anything too out of the ordinary. Certainly nothing that would explain why a dedicated Soldier would forfeit his career and then end up here. I'm not in the field of 'investigative guesswork' and your file wasn't that telling."

He raised an eyebrow and almost seemed amused.

"I was deployed, as you know. I was with a team of men that I had worked with many times before. I trusted them, and they trusted me."

He looked me in the eye. "I'm sure you know what that means, having people trust you when they don't have any other reason to do so beyond that you work together. They aren't your family, but they rely on you. They believe you won't steer them wrong."

I nodded my head in agreement.

"So, there we were, in another shithole sandbox, American Soldiers fighting someone else's battle in yet another war that wasn't worth the loss of life—for reasons that weren't worth the time it took to explain. And all to produce results that wouldn't last longer than a hot second the instant our troops hit the bricks, and the US stepped back again—"

He straightened himself up, dropped his hands to his lap, and rested his arms on the armrests of the chair.

"Doing exactly what Soldiers have been doing since the dawn of man—following orders and losing their lives for one of the three basic reasons that I think accounts for pretty much everything we've ever done: to Conquer, Rescue, or Defend.

"We go places we have no right to go to and fight to conquer, advancing ourselves or our interests and taking shit that isn't ours, but we want anyway. We go fight to save foreigners from themselves or other oppressors because we think we're the Saviors of the World, or we fight to defend and keep what is ours or under our protection.

"I can't think of much that we've done that hasn't been for one of those reasons when it all comes down to it—and of those three reasons, the only one that is even worthy of asking a Soldier to lay down his life would be for the protection and security of his own nation, family, and freedom. Anything else, I've come to realize, is just a bunch of snake oil being peddled to the Soldiers with some good PR work so they'll do what they are being told to do without question—and willingly pay with their blood if necessary—all to advance some government agenda."

He leaned back in his chair, his monologue over and the fine print pertaining to his views regarding our government's use of our military conveyed to his satisfaction.

"Did you ever serve?" he asked.

I shook my head 'no'; it wasn't a question I normally encountered—I seldom received questions at all. It was against protocol to answer, but I wasn't concerned about the rules with this man. If he had known anything about what it meant to be an Investigator, he would have been able to do the math and known how many years of education and training I had been required to do before starting my career. We were of comparable age and had both chosen difficult paths straight out of high school. It was a legitimate question, however, because I could have served in the Armed Forces for a period of time before becoming an Investigator. But it would have been impossible to have reached my current rank and position at this point had I done so.

I wasn't defensive about his question or any potential judgment behind it, although I knew full well that there were plenty of men out there who looked down their noses with thinly veiled contempt at other men who hadn't served at least once in their lifetime. Whether they considered it to be a rite of passage for young men, or a necessary aspect for any Citizen who considered himself to be a Patriot, many Soldiers believed that military training, experience, and commitment was an integral part of Citizenry. Given the number of nations that have required conscription for their Citizens, it wasn't entirely biased or without merit.

I wondered if he had asked so he could establish the universally accepted connection of brotherhood between military members, or if it was merely to know if he needed to use a more generalized dialogue and layman's terms.

Trying to search out commonalities so people could relate to one another was an important tool for building trust and communication; he was a smart guy, and if he was familiar with certain psychological concepts, he could certainly manipulate a conversation, my emotions, my perceptions, and my impression of him easily enough with the right tools. Knowing that two people both understood a lifestyle that was typically regarded as an exclusive brotherhood could be a powerful asset—or weapon.

"Well, anyhow, I'm sure you've put in plenty of time here with subordinates."

He looked around the room and out the hallway window. There were LEOs everywhere, and most of them were Front-Line street Officers. He was right in the context that I technically 'outranked' them, and he was right about having had many people rely on me—and usually strangers. He was even making a fair comparison between his elite band of Soldiers and the unique prestige that came with my own career. But Daegan Kyl had that familiar pride and sense of comradery that came from being prior service and one of the more elite brands of US Soldier; it came to the surface almost immediately once he started talking, but that was something that our personalities seemed to process differently altogether. He had the type of pride that came with permanent ownership over having taken part in something that was akin to a private fraternity, something that, because I worked independently as an Investigator I had never quite achieved. What I found interesting about it, though, was how it was still clearly a source of pride despite having left his chosen career voluntarily.

"So, I had this buddy I'd known since the beginning. We had the same type of personality, which, believe it or not, was really laid back compared to the rest of the men we were with. Neither of us were slackers; we knew how to get the job done and we took our work and training seriously. But we could also keep some perspective about it while a lot of the other guys were losing their heads every time they messed up or didn't do as well as they wanted. I think it helped that both of us were big guys and the physical fitness stuff was easy for us most of the time. At any rate, we got along well from the start.

"They see two big guys like us and they pit us against one another—or the two big guys would instinctively have some of that competitive spirit. We just didn't have it; we worked well together, and I think we were alike enough that we knew we were stronger as a team than as competitors. He was a Good Man."

Daegan Kyl looked at me for a second and then looked out the window.

"His name was William. William Amos."

There was a long stretch of silence that I felt no compulsion to interrupt or break. I knew that Daegan Kyl would tell his story in due time.

"We'd served together for the first ten years of our career; we were both going to stay in for as long as they would have us. We had everything we needed; the training, the adventure, the travel, and important top-secret missions…Hell, we even had the girls. We always had plenty of fun between missions and for a couple of guys in their twenties, it was a good life. We got along well and for a long time, everything was golden.

"Eventually, we ended up on another mission right before the start of our eleventh year. Everything went wrong. Shit just hit the fan, and everything changed."

I could see Daegan Kyl was in the middle of a thousand-yard stare and knew he was no longer on the same continent, or even in the same decade.

Suddenly, he snapped himself back and looked at me.

"There isn't much to tell, actually. We were somewhere we shouldn't have been, doing work for our government that we should never have been asked or expected to do—and too many of our guys didn't make it home. Will Amos was one of them."

He shrugged nonchalantly.

It wasn't believable.

I kept watching him but said nothing; I was trying to get the story out and confronting him with his obvious attempts to minimize what was at the core of the story would not help.

He sat silently for another moment, looking out the window again with that famous thousand-yard stare.

"We were Soldiers doing what we were being paid to do. And I swear to God, had my government honored the deal we had made with them—had they only even *attempted* to live up to the bullshit they had been spewing at all of us throughout our entire lives, I would still be there doing exactly what I should have been doing. But they didn't, and so I'm not."

I watched him as he displayed the first physical signs of discomfort and uneasiness.

"We were dying; it was an ambush. There wasn't supposed to be anyone around for miles; we had our orders and knew what we were supposed to do, and it was supposed to be a simple job."

I knew what his last assignment had been and where; it was in his file. Whether or not he felt he was being discreet was immaterial; he had no obligation to do so at my expense because I had obtained his records already. Anything that I wasn't allowed to know would have been omitted or redacted already. Since the details and location of his last mission had been included with little fare, I was left to assume it hadn't been that important for the grand scheme of things. Then again, it might just have been because of the age of the events as well. At any rate, I was certain that he probably hadn't discussed anything related to his past military service with anyone other than perhaps Willow Amos, so maybe it was just instilled in him to be secretive and vague.

"It wasn't that they had sent us there to do the mission. I didn't care about that or the consequences. They trained us to do a specific job, and we were all prepared to do it. But we were ambushed, and we took heavy casualties as a result.

"But even that wasn't the problem. Every single one of us was willing to die over there; we were prepared to die for the security of our nation and for the safety of our Fellow Citizens. It was a risk we had all been willing to take and an Oath we had been committed to defend. Dying wasn't the problem, and it wasn't Will's problem either.

"The problem—in case my file doesn't say it clearly enough—was that they just left our men over there. They wouldn't allow us to go back and retrieve their Remains. They cited it was just 'too dangerous', that the area was crawling with hostiles, that the feral savages had already swept through the land, and that according to their satellite imagery, they had already seized hold of our men, stripped them of their weapons and gear, and had dragged them naked through the area in celebration. We hadn't left any men alive that we knew of, but when we had to leave, we had no idea that we were taking hits from so many directions at the same time. Had we known we were leaving our Brothers there, that they had been ambushed and cut off from us as we brought up the rear, we would never have kept going. But we didn't know, and our spotters on the other end never once radioed to tell us. They let our Brothers fall, and they chose not to tell us. They said they didn't have a choice, but there is *always* a choice. And they followed whoever was handing down the orders from an office somewhere rather than someone with boots on the ground and a rifle in their hands. And our men died there. William died there.

"Yeah, I dunno, man. I just couldn't get over it. I couldn't keep fighting for a government that would hurt their own in such a way. First, they didn't provide proper warning about the potential for ambush, then they didn't tell us while we were close enough to help that our own men were under attack more so than we knew, and then we found out that they knew about the risks ahead of time but never told us.

"But the worst part—the very worst part—was that they allowed those savages to keep our Brothers' Remains. The same shit we'd been dealing with for the last fifteen-hundred years. The exact same shit! We weren't allowed to retrieve them or even fight back against it. Our own government allowed those third world inbred savages to desecrate our American Citizens. And not just any Citizens—they allowed them to desecrate the Physical Remains of the bravest men our nation has ever seen. Her own Soldiers, men that had already promised to sacrifice everything if they needed to. But even that wasn't enough because they just left them there. They left them on foreign soil—in a shithole sandbox filled with illiterate, violent, disease-ridden savages that hate our nation and hate the West—and they left our boys to die there and have their bodies destroyed by them.

"I just can't get over that. That's not the country I want to die for; those aren't the politicians that I'm willing to sacrifice my own life for. And that's not the America or the American values that either my Founding Fathers or The Watchers On The Wall believed in. My Brothers should never have been left there. I don't care what it would have taken; my nation does not leave Soldiers behind, and neither do our troops."

He sighed deeply, and his hands were finally still.

"But that's what we did. And apparently that's *who we are*."

His words hung in the air, but the true weight was witnessed by the manner in which his shoulders seemed to sag as he sat there staring out the window.

He was telling me the story about how he came to arrive here, stemming from a situation that had transformed his entire life and perception more than a decade earlier and many thousands of miles away. His journey had not just begun because he had decided to cross some legal or ethical line over a girl in recent months, as one might have guessed. Given that so many others had ventured into the realm of Euthanasia through Willow Amos as she lured them into The Angels of Mercy philosophy, it had been a natural assumption the same tactics had enticed Daegan Kyl. I had originally felt some misgivings regarding his motives for helping Willow Amos because it had made no sense to me initially. He had been so much older than the rest of the young men following her lead that it seemed unlikely that the ideological propaganda had manipulated him. He hadn't seemed like a man that would be easily led by anyone, and he hadn't ever presented as someone with a weak moral constitution or penchant for Crime. But until now, it had been the only possible connection.

"I couldn't do anything about it. Not then, and not now. But there was one thing that I was expected to do once I returned home stateside. Will didn't have any family other than his little sister, and after his Death, she had become an orphan. Their parents had been dead for a few years already, but because Will had been a legal adult, he had been allowed to take care of her. After his Death, she was on her own. The military had provided her with Will's standard issue Death package, and she had been eligible for the federal compensation funds as well. So, she had plenty of financial security for the future, but she was still a minor and too young to be out on her own.

"The State of Washington made her a Ward of the Court and she was placed into foster care until her twentieth birthday, putting all her assets into a trust that she couldn't access until her release from the system as an adult. I had already known her, of course, and had met his parents a few times as well before their car accident. Willow had asked me if I would try to get custody of her, but there was no way that they were going to grant legal custody of a fifteen-year-old girl to some random guy. The best I could do was stick around Washington, keep an eye on her, help her get through the five years she was legally a Ward of the State and living in situations beyond her control, and help her in any manner I could. So that's what I did.

"That's it. That's all the connection there is. He got screwed over by his own government, and now his little sister is all grown up and making her own decisions. She went through almost ten different foster homes over that five-year period, getting passed around from stranger to stranger, forced to live in homes that never seemed to offer enough love or attention and always seemed too impersonal for her to ever find comfortable. I can't even imagine how it must have been; by that point, I was the only source of familiarity to her, and I just couldn't imagine leaving her to deal with it alone while I left on more deployments.

"I was tired anyway. No matter what I did, I just couldn't reconcile what my government had done to us during that last deployment. I wasn't looking for a reason to get out of the military; I thought I would be in there for as long as they would have me. Honestly, I thought that all of our issues with sketchy, corrupt politicians were over; I was a firm believer in The Watchers On The Wall and all the changes our nation made during the Great Reformation. Hell, I still believe the Last Stand and the Reformation were the only things that saved our nation and Citizens. But I don't believe we changed D.C. enough. I don't know if it *can* be changed. Maybe evil will always win. Maybe we just need to keep fooling ourselves so we can get through this lifetime and feel like we're making a difference. I don't know anymore. But I know one thing for sure—We the People have short memories, and it doesn't take much for corruption and evil to regain power.

"I just know that I'm not going to die defending a nation being run by politicians who are as corrupt and hypocritical as they have revealed themselves to be. No nation that declares they believe in the Sanctity of Human Life is going to leave our own Soldiers on foreign soil or let them die in such a heinous way. No politicians that dare tell the American People they're fighting on behalf of the Citizens of These United

States and for our nation are going to turn around and ignore the cries for help from our own Soldiers when they're being attacked and butchered by our enemies. D.C. didn't just leave our guys there; they left them there when they knew that there were still Soldiers in the area that could have gone back and helped them. They knew that they were under heavy attack. They left them there to die because they didn't value their lives enough to risk losing more Soldiers trying to rescue them—and then they really showed us how little they valued them by refusing to let us go back and retrieve their Remains.

"It wasn't just inexcusable, it was criminal. No leader with a genuine love of America, Her Citizens, or our national security would ever just sacrifice our Soldiers in such a manner. It's beyond reprehensible; it's disgraceful. Things like that shouldn't be happening in our world; not anymore. We scraped that level of sludge and slime from our politicians more than a century ago and there should be no way it could ever be allowed to happen again. Only anti-American traitors would sanction such actions, and that's not a government I trust."

The whole time he had been talking, he had been focused on me, compelling me to understand his position. It wasn't difficult to see. I understood his disillusionment.

His version was a lot more detailed and personal than his records, of course. It explained everything. He felt paternal toward Willow Amos; he did what he did because he was protecting her. *Everything*, it seemed, was because he was trying to protect her—in this case, *from herself*. I might not have had all the answers yet, but I did at least understand his motivation for why he was here. She was the key to solving the cases, but he was the key to getting to her.

I stood up, holding his file in my left hand, and gave a slight nod in his direction to let him know we were done for the time being.

I said nothing else, and neither did he. They would return him to his Holding Cell, and I was sure he knew I would be in touch again soon enough.

After I left, I found myself contemplating the man and his words.

Beyond Innocence or Guilt, it all came down to acknowledging one simple truth.

It was difficult not to respect a man such as Daegan Kyl.

TWENTY-SEVEN – THE RIDE SOUTH

The Trinity Triangle

    The walk between the HQ building and the GSA Incarceration Unit was the distance of about a block. It was possible to travel through an underground tunnel passageway that linked the two parking lots and walk the distance, eliminating the need for top-side travel. The two departments were also linked to the GSA Courthouse where all Criminal trials were held, creating a third path which completed an underground triangle of usable underground space within the Criminal Justice sector of the city.
    The triangle was open in the center with a wide walking trail on the outward side of each section, which led to their respective parking garages. The system was known as the Trinity Trail and was a popular space for employees within all three buildings. It was a fitness trail designed for bikes and runners. Within the triangle was an arboretum; a garden filled with natural light let in through reflective passageways woven into the architectural design with intricate precision and finesse. It was not the only one of its kind in America, but it was among the best. The natural brightness of the garden was a place of solace and refuge for those who worked within the field of Criminal Justice, especially those who spent their days wearing tinted external helmets for the sake of safety. It was a place of tranquility for many, away from any of the noise experienced above ground, and without any of the risks because access was restricted to employees within the field of Criminal Justice.
    I strolled between the two buildings and enjoyed the quiet scenery. It was still early enough in the day for full daylight within the arboretum and the area was only being used by a few others; two women ran together past me, different heights and shapes but obviously female beneath their required Physical Training uniforms. Their hair was tightly bound within their Kev-Tek, and they secured their air packs along their backs, allowing them to get the highest quality of airflow and ventilation beneath their visors. Even though they were safe to run without their visors while underground, it was not uncommon to see them opt for full concealment. Most believed it was better to know their running speed and endurance with their full gear on. After all, when they were topside and out on the streets, they would be wearing their external helmets and full gear. They trained as they needed to perform.

I could not remember the last time I had seen a female member of Law Enforcement able to run freely throughout a public park, but then, it had been dangerous for women for so many decades that many had refrained from doing it altogether.

I had been a young boy when I first began seeing women run for fitness outdoors; I remembered it well because I had been playing football in the park with my brothers, and they had stopped in their tracks when a group of girls had run past. There had been three of them, all with their hair in ponytails; two of them had been wearing shorts with their t-shirts, and one had even worn a tank top. They had recognized my two oldest brothers—the twins—probably from school. I remember the way the girl in the tank-top had turned around, running backward for a moment, waving, and smiling at my brothers as her ponytail bounced around. I remember at the time just being surprised; caught off guard because it was a fresh experience—a vision of something never before seen.

It took me many years to realize that what I had observed was a sign of the changing times; a moment captured in my own history of the world as I knew it—the birth of our nation after a period of tyranny and fear. The next time I thought about it was while I was in college. I had traveled on foot between buildings, as was often my habit, but on that hot, sunny day I had stopped to buy a cold drink from one of the vendors. I remember standing there, taking a few minutes to pause and enjoy the day. The campus was beautiful, a combination of modern and 21st century architecture; a juxtaposition of everything new with remnants of a world in which windows and doorways still had to be opened and closed manually. And as I stood there, enjoying my drink, I remember noticing that there had been students everywhere, walking, sitting, and enjoying their day. The campus had been filled with single young women, smiling, laughing, their hair down, uncovered, and even their legs and arms entirely bare.

What I remember the most was that there was no fear; the women were not overdressed, and none of them had short hair or head covering caps. Women had worn their hair as short as the men so they could avoid having it used against them; men had targeted it for nefarious purposes for generations. Hair-pulling and grabbing rendered women helpless, but they had also been targeted because of its beauty. By the end, between the shapeless clothing and the short hair, it had been difficult to tell many of the women apart from the men—which, of course, was the point.

It was common for both sexes to walk around with cameras attached to their clothing, but women were usually the only ones inclined to wear them attached to their hair coverings, especially if they were extremely short or petite. They connected the cameras to a cloud and recorded everything off-site; it had become the primary deterrent for Sexual Misconduct and Rape during the mid-21st century. Likewise, it had been because of False Allegations that men had worn cameras for their own protection as well. As with most things, however, the statement by the women was extremely vocal and meant to be outspoken, thus making the headgear and cameras a loud show of defiance: "I will not be your Victim, but know that if you were to try, your face has already been documented, and you will be Captured should any Harm befall me."

That was what it had been like, growing up in a culture where Citizens were pitted against one another, the seeds of distrust having been sewn so deeply that no one felt safe. The division of the American People had been incomprehensible; everyone had been afraid of one another, afraid of being the subject of yet another 'Random' Act of Violence at the hands of their Fellow Citizen.

Women had been afraid of men, especially strangers. They were afraid of relationships, of being subjected to Domestic Violence, of becoming yet another statistic of a woman Beaten, Stabbed, Shot, Strangled, or Bludgeoned to Death at the hands of her spouse or the male figure in her life. The average Citizen was afraid of walking down city streets for fear of Random Assault, Robbery, Drive-by, or Random Physical Attack by some gang or pack of Savage Thugs looking for an easy, presumably defenseless target. Citizens were afraid to pump their fuel for fear of their vehicles being stolen, their belongings taken from unlocked cars, or carjackings, which inevitably endangered their small children strapped down into car-seats in the back.

They were afraid to go into the gas stations to pay, afraid of the risks of Armed Robberies or credit card theft. There were countless events that should have been routine and mundane, but because of the fear of Violence, had become terrifying. Even random shootings in the parking lot were a bleak reminder of how fragile and precarious living within urban areas could be. When the mentality of criminals meant that it was easier to shoot someone in a home invasion or carjacking rather than deal with them alive, the average Citizen began to fear even the most basic of tasks. When Crime and Violence rates escalated, everything became high risk if it involved being out on the streets, especially at night.

Larger gatherings and massive parking lots could mean car explosions by gangs of roving Criminals, Terrorists, or Anti-Nationalists focusing on property damage and chaos. Aggravating this problem, Citizens were prohibited from being armed in arenas, stadiums, concerts, and fairgrounds. This had effectively turned them into sitting ducks, both within the buildings as well as during their walks to and from their vehicles.

Disarming Citizens who were legally trained and qualified to carry firearms also led to further problems during times of crisis. Innumerable situations occurred where lives could have been saved had the Citizens been able to keep themselves armed while in public settings but were prevented from doing so by bad policies. People that could have helped were rendered powerless, and whether it was a giant stadium or shopping area under attack by armed Terrorists, or a lone female Raped and Murdered as she attempted to run through her local city park, the Violence was so extreme that it had caught the entire nation in a cycle of fear, self-containment, and helplessness. With all the odds stacked against them for being able to live normal lives free of Violence, women covered themselves, disguised their beauty, cut their hair, and hid their figures as much as possible just to offset the risks.

It was a testament to the changing times to have actual memories from both worlds; I never forgot how appreciative I should be for the world I now had. We had fallen into such disrepair and a state of desperation that it had served as a powerful reminder of how quickly things could change if the balance of Good and Evil shifted once again. As I watched the two women running into the distance, I imagined a time when all women—including members of Law Enforcement—could move freely about in public spaces throughout the nation without cameras, companions, check-ins, GPS trackers, and RFID-Chipping, as many were still prone to do out of an abundance of caution.

There was minimal threat anymore, and women were safe, overall. But the lessons from the past were not easily forgotten, and even though our Crime and Violence rates were lower than ever before, it was hard to shake off the fear that had once controlled almost every Citizen and their actions.

Women no longer had an unspoken dress code; they wore reasonably form-fitting clothing and showed bare parts of their arms and legs routinely now. It was a choice to dress modestly, not a necessity as it had been a mere fifty years before. That was a huge distinction to be made. But as long as women were still conducting their physical fitness under such conditions—below ground, covered head to toe, hair, and physical features concealed—America was still not fully repaired. We may well be in the time known as the Final Wave of the Great Reformation, but we were still not as we should have been entirely. Perhaps this was because we as Law Enforcement were still wearing Kev-Tek and visors, or because our women were still being self-protective.

But maybe it was just because somehow, despite all that we had done, we still had two Deceased Rape Victims and a dead little girl that had been Abducted and Sexually Assaulted for the last several months of her young life. Perhaps, no matter how advanced we had become—we just weren't better yet. We still hadn't figured out how to eradicate the Evil within men before they committed Acts of Violence—especially against our most vulnerable Citizens.

Seeing women pretending not to be women was a disservice to all involved; it represented a society immersed in Fear and Demons—a nation built, destroyed, and rebuilt again with the Blood of Innocent Citizens and Violence. It meant we were persistently haunted and forced to live in a state of fear that we had not learned to overcome. It meant we still had a culture where men were hurting women and little girls, despite all we had done to prevent it from happening, and all our efforts to rid our nation of its Predatory Offenders.

No matter what we did, there were always more men doing Evil things; it was a war we couldn't get ahead of and never would, at least not until we could anticipate their propensity for Violence, and either Exile or Destroy them before they had the opportunity to Cause the Harm we knew was Imminent.

No matter how many Good Men were out there trying to do the right thing, their goodness was always going to be overshadowed by those who embraced the Evil in their hearts. As long as we were in a battle against Evil Men, our women and girls could never be themselves, and there would always be those who were distrustful and wary of men, regardless of their character or actions.

If only Americans had seen that in the decades before the Great Reformation—it was easy to imagine how many Innocent Women and young Girls would have been saved had their Fellow Citizens only chosen to stand up for them back then.

All it would have taken was for them to recognize that those who were Evil and living among them were Irreconcilably Broken and would never be capable of functioning within our society without Causing Harm to others.

If only our Citizens had realized that; millions of Innocent Lives would have been saved.

It had taken so long—far too long—for us to realize it back then.

And here we were…barely pulling out of it, operating in recovery mode just as our Ancestors had in the years after each of our World Wars. It was taking so long for us to rebuild ourselves, to remember what it meant to be alive, to be free, and to be an American. Our spirits had been broken not only because of the Violence in our communities and the overwhelming fear it created, but also because we had endured endless years of indifference to our cries by our government. Just as we had watched our rights slowly being eroded away over the generations, healing and regaining our strength would also be a generational process.

It did not take long to arrive back at the parking garage area next to the SPD Headquarters building, and I made my way to my vehicle easily enough.

All things considered equal, even as I contemplated such thoughts on my way back to the barracks for the evening, I realized that the older I grew and the more cases I worked on, the more cautious I became—not less so. One would imagine that after years of seeing productive, successful, and secure Law Enforcement in action that I would have more faith and trust in the security and stability of my nation than most other Citizens. But as I considered everything I was now questioning, I had to acknowledge that I wasn't as confident as I once was. Just as how women had kept their hair short with the illusion it was making them safer, so too did I feel our government had been playing on the innocence and trust of the American People—even now. And as I watched all the buildings pass by on my way home, I realized it was all just an illusion of safety, even in these modern times.

Riding Down to the Factory

After seeing Daegan Kyl at his Holding Cell and then making my way back to the office, I drove over to the barracks, preparing to settle in for the night. But my head was filled with too much to contend with while cooped up in a compact unit during one of the most pleasant evenings I had observed in Seattle so far, so I took my bike out for a ride along the I-5 corridor.

I hadn't gone for a single ride since my arrival over two months earlier, and as soon as I hit the freeway, I felt my mood lighten almost instantaneously.

I wasn't sure where I was going—just riding south to get out of the city for a while. It didn't take me but a few miles to realize I did have a plan. I was going back down to the factory—although I probably wouldn't cross the property line…

I needed to see it.

I needed to see what they didn't want me to know about.

The Line Between Good and Evil

I thought about Daegan Kyl as I rode south. Traffic was minimal because of the late hour and mid-weekday, and the freeway was almost deserted. Daegan Kyl was a complex individual, and I had found his behavior regarding this case to be out of alignment with almost every other facet of his character and personality that had been revealed thus far. It was a testament to the beliefs and principles outlined by The Watchers On The Wall during the latter half of the 21st century. The complexity of our character and all that we were capable of contributing through our individualism was a priceless principle of the Ripple Effect. It had been a cornerstone of the new American foundation, as it was restructured during the Great Reformation regarding the importance of appreciating how multi-faceted each Human Being and Citizen was within our society.

Daegan Kyl was a man with a lengthy military career, a leader, and as a professional Soldier, he had been a fighter and a killer. But he was also an entrepreneur, a businessman, and a man that had learned to navigate the perils of being a socialite bachelor thrust into the spotlight, handed unlimited income and prestige, and—according to the Seattle newspapers—hailed as one of Seattle's finest men.

His decision to enlist in the military as soon as he had been legally allowed to was dedication that I could appreciate given I had pursued Law Enforcement with much the same zeal. But then, when his impression of it had changed, he left it, choosing to take a risk rather than to dwell in the mire, even though it meant ending the career he had worked so hard for and had initially wanted to stay in until retirement forced him out. By his own admission, he left because of his own disillusionment, not because of his inability to do the job he had signed up for. And while one could consider that to be the behavior of someone who lacked the resolve to follow through on a commitment, what it had demonstrated to me was that his conviction for his country and Constitution was greater than his need to serve with blind submission. He longed for a greater purpose; he followed only truth and integrity, and when his own government had failed to provide it, he refused to recognize that he owed them any allegiance.

This was how it would be for many Americans. It was why half of the American People had fallen out of love with the notion of nobility within Law Enforcement during the 21st century; there had been too many cases of flawed men wearing the uniform, and for those who were determined to destroy the public perception of Law Enforcement, focusing on corruption and brutality had been the way.

The media had concentrated solely on the rare cases of LEOs who had behaved without Honor or Valor, those who had Exploited, Terrorized, Victimized, and Brutalized the Citizenry they had been trained and paid to Protect. The stories of fallen and disgraced Peacekeepers had been fuel for those who desired to create disharmony and mistrust between Law Enforcement and the communities they served. They exploited the cases that vilified the men and women in blue, feeding off their dishonor and shameful actions like parasitic vultures feasting on disease as it rotted the flesh and destroyed all the healthy tissue along with it.

By launching hysteria about how one bad apple was proof that Law Enforcement was entirely contaminated, they spread both the fear and the false belief that it was already an epidemic that must be defunded and dismantled, or the nation would never heal. Such protests and vitriol had proven disastrous for the reputation of the Rule of Law and those who represented it.

Luckily for most, myself included, we could understand that while there were men who wore the badge that should not—whether it was because of their temperament or propensity for Violence or corruption—most Peacekeepers did their jobs honorably and with the best of intentions. Even still, it was impossible to deny that there were those who should never have become Law Enforcement Officers, and as with any profession, there would always be cases of poor performance and ill-behaving employees.

Had Daegan Kyl known what he did for our government, had he been able to confirm the callous disregard for Human Life he later experienced first-hand as a Soldier, he would probably have never offered himself into their service to begin with. But that was how our culture had always been. Our government and society had always been good at selling public service; we took pride in promoting those who served our nation, and we did so because we knew the sacrifices they were expected to make. It was somewhat idealistic, promises of heroism and opportunities to work as cogs in a wheel to implement, build, and advance democracy, justice, and equality for all. It was a familiar story, and in that regard, my idealism at twenty had been parallel to Daegan Kyl's.

The only difference I could see was that it took me longer to be confronted with the bleak reality of Humanity. After years of working within Law Enforcement, I now knew that not all men who worked in noble professions were legitimately noble in either character or deed. He had borne witness to things that had transformed his views before I had, but ultimately, we had each arrived with a much greater understanding of such things as we grew and matured within our careers. I could only presume it meant that he had been exposed to more unfortunate situations and greater corruption along the way. I knew I should be grateful that I had survived as long as I had before I discovered that there were still those among us who were unworthy of their titles and the power they had been given.

My disillusionment had not affected me in the same way, of this I was certain—and perhaps that was one of the most obvious differences between the two of us. He had changed course, removing himself from what he considered to be a racket being sold under false pretenses.

I still believed in the system; I just believed that it was the responsibility of those who were Good among us to do everything within our power to ensure that the Evil was gutted from our nation in its entirety, and if we failed to do it, we were no better than the vermin we knew to be leaving a stain on our world. It was simplistic to believe that if each of us did not rise to the occasion and do all that we could to prevent Evil from spreading that others would do it for us while we passively lived our lives in the fray. More so than that, it was selfish and unworthy of us.

I could no more keep my counteractions to myself when combating the Evil among us than I could have prevented myself from pursuing the one I loved had there been any sort of obstacle placed between us designed to hinder our union. The compulsion to do that which was Good and Right was only rivaled within me with the inherent desire to both love and protect my fellow Human Beings and those whom I was intimately connected to. My existence could be stripped away from every accomplishment, personal achievement, label, and badge of honor or familial connection, and as long as I died as honorably as I had lived, giving all that I had to give to better serve my Fellow Countrymen and Protect them from any Evil, Peril, or Harm that I could, I would consider it to have been a Life Worth Living.

I believed that this philosophical set of values was not just my own, but that of most of Humanity, and it did not vary due to age, sex, socio-economic position and class standing, or based on the esteem of others. I believed this to be a core element of what it meant to be Human. I had witnessed it innumerable times. The desire in me to stand up for what was Pure and Right was built within me by Divine and Inherent Design and was the same fundamental desire that was found within most of us. I believed that when it came time to choose, by and large, we were still mostly driven to *be good* and *do good* rather than not.

This wasn't the case for everyone, and I must admit that sometimes I worried the tables had shifted too far toward Evil for Good to Prevail in the grand scheme of things. Far too many of the Good ones were taken because of Violence, and every time this happened the scales tipped just a little more in favor of Evil. As much as I wished for myself to be more optimistic, it was almost impossible to retain such Innocence or hope as a baseline because I was almost entirely working within the darkest examples of what Humanity could produce. I knew all too well just how freely Evil walked among us, and how easily it conquered. I knew that there were many occasions when those among us were trying desperately to walk the straight and narrow but were pulled over to the Criminal side just because of the lack of opportunity to break free.

Daegan Kyl wasn't so different from many who had become embittered and disillusioned with his career or the government. His story was not an unfamiliar one, nor was it even extreme. It was always unfortunate, however, whenever our military or Law Enforcement lost Good Men. The world needed as many Good people as it could muster just to keep the Evil at bay and help keep the scales tipped in the right direction.

The Benefits of a Team

By the time I reached the cut-off road for the factory, I had all but decided that I was going to investigate the building and surrounding areas regardless of the two ICE agents or their 'warning'. I couldn't do it immediately—I wasn't even wearing my uniform, and I wasn't in an SPD Cruiser—had I done it, I may as well have been Breaking and Entering. But that didn't mean I couldn't come back again—in uniform and with my badge. It was, after all, still part of an active investigation. The two men that had arrived at the SPD HQ might well have been working for ICE, but their orders had come from the Governor—he was the one responsible for the hard block on progress, and that was something I just wasn't sure I was prepared to accept. It was a gross overreach of his authority, especially since he wouldn't have even known about the case had I not initiated contact by keeping the Chief apprised of my investigation to begin with.

I wasn't ready to throw in the towel just because I'd been handed orders from any number of people or other agencies that had absolutely zero right to dictate the course of my investigation or how I chose to proceed.

Parking at the edge of the main dirt road that led to the back way of the factory where the white truck had been spotted leaving, I weighed things out and gave in. I had wanted to investigate the building from the start; there was no point denying it or failing to do it. Had this been any other case, had I not been met with obstruction, it would have been done already.

I took out my phone and sent a quick message to Officer Stanton—not actually expecting an answer this late at night but half anticipating that I would—asking him if he knew if ICE had sealed the factory up or not. He responded immediately, forwarding some Aerial shots dated within the week that showed a massive metal building with very little surrounding it beyond a large parking lot. I scrolled through the satellite images from various angles, trying to see if there were any tags or tape marking the windows or doors, but found nothing. Had ICE seized the property, there probably would have been something present. Given that the images were about a week old, I couldn't be certain for sure that there wouldn't be something upon my arrival on site, but for now, it looked like every other abandoned building from the 21st century.

I sent him a quick note thanking him, told him to have a good night, and that I would probably be in tomorrow afternoon—all without telling him exactly what I had planned. Sometimes less information was better, especially when transmitted via technology.

Officer Stanton was proving to be the lone Officer that might change my mind regarding the advantages of having a team. His ability to work independently and proactively pursue potential leads and links within our investigation made me realize how advantageous it was to have a few extra hands out there, building our case independently in ways that I personally found mundane. His work was not only going to create a solid foundation based on concrete facts and connections, it would also cement all the intangibles that could not easily be proven because of their circumstantial nature, such as explaining motive.

Over the years, I had worked with dozens of Research Specialists, but there was something about the sincere love of both technology and research that made Officer Stanton's work superior to any I'd ever known. He brought a certain level of skill and finesse to his profession that made it seem more of an art than the labor-intensive procedure that most would find burdensome. The more leads we developed, the more evident it became that it was an exceptionally complex case, but we were making progress. This wasn't because of the legwork on my end; many of the breaks we were getting were because of the extensive amount of leads that Officer Stanton was putting together through his research.

The work that Grace O'Connor and I did out in the field was important in the sense that it enabled us to meet with the Bereaved and learn about our Victims on a personal level. We could also assess a great deal through examining those we encountered, discerning their Body Language and non-verbal cues, and paying close attention to clues in their tone and verbiage. It would probably never be possible to do investigations solely from behind a desk or through technology, especially given that our investigations were still being conducted by Human Beings and with Human Beings as our subjects. Nonetheless, between the advanced craftsmanship and forensic advancements within the Medical Examiner's office and the work Officer Stanton was doing, it was clear to me that the team I had been provided to work with was a team of remarkable quality.

I was becoming more and more grateful to have the support team that I did to assist me with this case. I knew now more than ever that I could not have gotten this far without each of them and their contributions. I wondered sometimes if the American People ever gave pause to consider just how fortunate they were to have the help and service provided to them through their Fellow Citizens. It was likely that most never even thought about such jobs or professionals until the time came that they needed them, and even then, they were so overwhelmed with their Grief that they never really considered who was out there working tirelessly on their behalf to find Justice for their Loved Ones. Having witnessed, and relied on, the outstanding work from countless professionals behind the scenes, I was in a unique position.

I made a mental note to put Stanton up for a recommendation once we'd completed our investigation. His file should reflect how important his work had been for this case and how hard he had worked over our months together. I was a strong Investigator on my own and I knew it; but this case had demonstrated time and again that no matter what our task or who we were, as Human Beings we were only made stronger, smarter, and better when we joined one another and worked together collectively.

With my plan in place, I took a last look down the dirt road, checked the sun as it lowered, and made my way back toward the northbound freeway and the barracks.

Thoughts on Grace

As I made my way back from the road just beyond the factory, the sun was fading against the beautiful backdrop of the Pacific Northwest, and the sky was a clear, pale blue. I took a moment to appreciate how deserted the area was, the lack of traffic this far outside of the city, and how quiet everything seemed. I was surrounded by evergreens as far as the eye could see, and other than the freeway, for once there wasn't concrete anywhere in sight. The mountains always cleared my head and my heart, and I'd always enjoyed hiking whenever I could—something of a Washington State rite of passage for many of us that we carried our entire lives. Having let another summer pass without spending time in the Cascades due to work, I realized this was the closest I'd been to the mountains and forest since the summer before.

I would never be one of those who ultimately settled down in a large metropolis—especially not somewhere like the Greater Seattle Area where more than a million Citizens lived and worked surrounded by concrete. The idea of it killed my soul and my spirit.

I imagined I would eventually end up in a much smaller area once I was finally done with my time as an Investigator. I hadn't put too much thought into it—beyond likely staying in Washington State so I could remain close to my family and possibly the family of my future wife. I had always appreciated how my older brothers and younger sister could live near one another and our parents. It seemed the most ideal way to raise a family.

Even if my future wife believed that the Greater Seattle Area was where we should raise our future children, I wasn't sure it was a game plan I could ever get on board with. Aside from knowing that the chances for Random Acts of Violence were infinitely greater in larger geographic zones, deep in my heart, I longed for something much more akin to what I had found Arlan and Micah Davidson doing; somewhere with plenty of space and greenery. Somewhere better for kids; a chance for animals, space to run, and plenty of room to grow within their own community.

I found my thoughts turning to the woman I had been working alongside for over two months already. I could picture her clearly in my head despite not even having seen her all week, and only having corresponded with her via email and phone. She had been busy doing things for the families, and since I had been preoccupied with interviews, there hadn't been much room for crossover in our schedules. I wondered if she had given any thought to having a family, or if she was dedicated to her career so exclusively that motherhood was not something she desired. Although it was far more common to find women who embraced the traditional roles rather than being solely professional, I knew well enough that every woman was different, and all held their own secret desires of the heart.

I wondered if she had thought about me over our time apart—ever—but then chastised myself for my arrogance. Nothing in her behavior had indicated that she was even remotely interested—unless one counted random looks thrown my way whenever we were occupying the same space, or the occasional blush or smile that seemed exclusively for me. Still…There seemed to be something there…Or at least I hoped it wasn't all in my imagination.

Our work was a terrible place to meet people—friends or otherwise. It was already an atmosphere that typically carried a heavy veil of secrecy, privacy, and discretion because of our safety protocols. Even though she as an employee of the VAA wasn't beholden to the same restrictions as myself or the local SPD Officers, it didn't make it any easier or more balanced given that I knew both what she looked like and her real name.

She knew next to nothing about me—as was the point of our balaclava's, visors, Badge IDs, and all the rest of the heavy cover applied to ensure it kept us safe as we conducted our duties.

It was hard to get to know someone when they hadn't even seen you outside of the same uniform day after day, when they had never seen your smile, and when they weren't even legally allowed to know your real name.

I was being foolish—foolishly naïve if I thought it could be any other way, too. It reminded me of Sampson and Delilah and what happened when a man placed his trust too quickly into the hands of a woman simply because he desires her. We were a long way away from being able to share such intimate details, and as much as I enjoyed her company, I knew it was foolhardy to imagine being able to overlook protective protocols just to feel closer to her.

But still…I wanted to.

I was surprised by how much.

I wanted to see her again; I wanted to talk more with her about things that were completely unrelated to our work. I wanted to laugh with her—of all the things that I missed while I was on assignment, it was the ability to spend time with my friends and family, being able to relax and laugh. It was always difficult to live in a constant state of transition and surrounded by strangers; work consumed us, and while we were still around other Human Beings, it was not the same as being around people we knew well and loved. And though I was often in locations long enough to develop solid professional contacts—of which I had gained many over the years all over the US—they were still not to be confused with personal ones, and the relationships never managed to grow beyond a professional capacity in most cases.

Yes… I missed laughing. I missed being around people and simply enjoying myself. This had been a trying last few months, even as we were making good progress.

I tried to think about why things were rubbing me differently this time, but all I could see were images of the pretty girl with the red hair and the green eyes as she stared at me from across the conference room table.

It had been a long time since I'd dated anyone—since before the last case in New York…or was it before the Sex Trafficking case in Nevada? I was having a hard time even remembering the last girlfriend; she hadn't lasted very long. She had been a much more hands-on type of woman—not the kind that would have survived military deployments without someone there to warm her bed, let alone waiting around for some guy while he was off saving the world voluntarily.

Maybe it really was getting time for me to settle down. I had been doing this for years—far longer than most Investigators made it as a single stint without a break. I knew, as long as I carried on, nothing would change, either. I would never meet a girl, never get married, never buy a house, never settle down and give my parents those grandbabies my mother now mentioned every time I was over.

I felt an unfamiliar sensation gnawing at me, making me wonder how much of this was more causally linked to the woman with the green eyes rather than my own restlessness.

I had finally asked Stanton a while back if he knew if she was married since she didn't wear a ring, and he'd shared that she had never been. He told me she lived locally and had been with her agency for about fifteen years, putting her roughly around my age if she began after college. I didn't ask him how he had come by the information, and I didn't ask him anything else, but he mentioned they had worked on more than a dozen cases together over the years, and he knew the Chief thought highly of her. It was, it seemed, his seal of approval, and I had found myself glad he was far too young to entertain dating her himself. Still, I was grateful for the information, as it had at least freed my mind to roam every now and again.

I looked out at the water now visible on my left, realizing I had spent the entire ride back north to Seattle thinking about her. I tried to recall the upcoming schedule, wondering when I might see her again. I had reports to write, interviews to conduct, various points to review…Nothing concrete that would place me at our shared office space, and besides all that, I did not know when she would be there.

There weren't very many occasions when I could return to the barracks early enough to still see the sunlight shimmering on the water, but for once I wasn't pressed for time or too exhausted from the day to appreciate how beautiful it was in Seattle. I knew the view from the apartment would be worth its weight in gold. The deep blue of Puget Sound sparkled, a shimmering sheen of colors blasting through my visor and reminding me of just how quickly time had passed as summer faded.

After over two full months working in Seattle and alongside Grace O'Connor, though, there was one thing I was certain of. I had no idea how to cross over from colleagues to something more—or even remotely how to get started.

The I-5 Corridor

    I had almost reached the exit for the barracks and found that my mood had lightened significantly just by being able to get out and go for a ride. Summer was fading already—always too brief in the Pacific Northwest as it was—and I had worked straight through it. The case had consumed my thoughts and my time, and I realized I hadn't even checked in with my folks in several weeks. I knew my father understood such things as a professional, but my mother always liked to keep tabs on her youngest son as all mothers did. The fact that I was over forty hardly mattered to her; all she saw was a dangerous line of work and the bloody history of my profession. I made a mental note to send out an email or maybe even phone home if I made it back before the sun set.

    I signaled and slowed for my exit, fully enjoying the last taste of freedom before I returned to the barracks, the weight of my uniform, and what came next. Now that I had gone riding for a few hours, cleared my head, entertained and processed some things that had been clouding my thoughts, I felt infinitely more comfortable with where things were settling. Having decided to go back to the factory on my own—even if it was without legal authorization—was not something I took lightly, but I found myself completely at peace as I made my way back to my temporary home.

    Seattle had its perks, and the sparkling water was probably the best one. It was called the Emerald City for a reason, and the sunsets during this summer—the ones that I had been fortunate enough to catch on the rare evenings when I had been back in the high rise early enough to see them—had been spectacular. Seattle had come a long way from the garbage-ridden streets filled with homeless vagabonds and hypodermic needles.

    Less than a century before, Seattle had been so overrun with Crime and Violence that the government had declared a state of emergency for the entire Greater Seattle Area. In those decades before the Great Reformation, all Blue Zones had been deemed too dangerous for any law-abiding Citizens or tourism, and Seattle had been among the worst. Decades of poor 'leadership' had resulted in the once beautiful city becoming little more than a war zone; the travel bans implemented by our government had been the same for Seattle as they had been for Mexico and countless other Third World nations that were considered so savage that neither the government nor their people could be trusted to hold the Sanctity of Human Life in high regard.

    It would never have changed or improved without the Great Reformation. Sometimes it was necessary for a city—or a nation—to be burned to the ground before it could be rebuilt. Seattle had been nothing more than a poisonous tree, producing the same putrid toxin that had spread from I-5 all the way from Canada to Mexico. The entire West Coast had become nothing more than a cesspool during the 21st century. Flames…Waves…it didn't matter what destroyed the region; something had needed to be done. America had been long-overdue for a reset, and whether it came by way of fire, earthquake, tsunami, or Civil War, the West Coast had needed to be cleansed. An earthquake leaving deep chasms in the ground, swallowing Seattle whole, or giant tsunami waves could have done wonders. I could imagine all the receding waves dragging the hypodermic needles back out to sea.

But none of that happened. Americans had been waiting for a miracle, or Divine intervention, that had never come. They had spent decades in silence, watching their nation consumed from within, quietly praying for something—anything—to rise and help them regain control over the mess they had been trying to survive in. No one had come; nothing had magically swept in to save them. All the signs of chaos and moral degradation had not resulted in the Second Coming of Christ; the End Times had never arrived, despite all the misery and suffering.

The streets of Seattle had been crawling with Vermin, Disease, Filth, Drugs, and Violence for so long no one had even remembered they had once known it as the City of Emeralds. The only thing that ever shined in Seattle was the metal on illegal guns being used by countless Violent Criminals right before they claimed another life. The only blessing about it was that by the time Americans were gearing up for the Last Stand, there hadn't been any Innocent Citizens still living in Seattle or anywhere along the I-5 corridor. All who had longed for a decent quality of life had fled long before it was known as the 'Hypodermic Highway'.

Others called it the 'West Coast Track', usually condensed to 'the Track'—a befitting name for a place that got its origins because it was part of a freeway system used to conduct mass trafficking of both humans and drugs. Over the decades, 'the Track' came to include all manner of Crime and Violence, with heavy use of the entire corridor for deviant, criminal activity. In the early years, the three West Coast states had attempted to curb and control the influx of destruction being paraded from one end of the nation to the other. But by then, policies had been implemented that had restricted Law Enforcement to such an extent that they could do little to prevent the destruction being done. The entire corridor, from Mexico to Canada, eventually fell to Criminals, and open trafficking occurred with virtually no pushback by politicians or other government agencies.

Law Enforcement—especially the State Patrol agencies of California, Oregon, and Washington—had taken such extreme hits to their numbers because of the Violence that by the mid-21st century, there were no longer any State Patrol agencies working the freeway system. Gangs, turf wars, Drug and Sex Traffickers, and illegal aliens from Mexico were so prevalent along the I-5 corridor that the entire system was declared part of the Blue Zone, and a comprehensive travel ban was placed on it advising that no American Citizens travel within twenty miles of the Corridor.

The Mexi-Can Corridor Ban was the official travel ban implemented by the US government in 2051 and was one of the first official markers of the Last Stand. It was an absurdity that there was any need for it, and perhaps even more of an absurdity that there were places in America that were deemed so unsafe that American Citizens could not travel. It became a national crisis.

The only thing that prevented America from devolving into an abyss of Violence and Criminality was the Rule of Law and those working within Law Enforcement who were willing to put their own lives on the line to prevent the Criminal Class from consuming our nation entirely. However, with little government assistance, they had no way to regain control of the region.

It was only after The Last Stand and the onset of the Great Reformation, led by an epic purge of Criminals through the Sentence Reform Act, that the I-5 corridor and the three coastal states were reclaimed and made safe once more.

TWENTY-EIGHT – AOM — AFTER ARREST

An Angel of Mercy Confesses

Many members of The Angels of Mercy had willfully confessed to the ideological values of their 'cause'. They acknowledged sharing propaganda and providing resources and information to people interested in Ending their own Lives. This included offering services to help facilitate the removal of Physical Remains to an 'unknown location' for burial. The purpose in providing burial services was monetary; it was intended to enable the Bereaved family members to collect the financial compensation package following the Death of a Citizen, even if it took years to collect.

One young man, having confessed to being the driver that had picked up Arlan from his home in a Winter Season After-Care van, was facing the Death Penalty because he had stated that he had personally been present and had helped facilitate the injection of drugs that had been given 'to help that old man end his life'.

I had intentionally zeroed in on the young man because he had seemed like a newer recruit. He stated that he, along with six others, had assisted in the removal of Arlan from his home.

His newness to The Angels of Mercy organization had benefited us regarding his willingness to save his own skin, and his youth had made him especially vulnerable to both the threat of the Death Penalty and a life in Exile.

His fear became a useful tool for us, and it was undoubtedly the worst-case scenario that Willow Amos or any of her other cohorts wanted to see brought to fruition.

He had been a student at the same university that each of them attended. Like everyone else on the list, he had direct ties to both the healthcare program and Willow Amos. He had begun school a year ago and was only now entering his twenty-first birthday. It was an unfortunate situation that they had reached out to him and several of the others who were almost as young; it seemed even more predatory that they weren't solely focusing on potential Victims, but also preying on other impressionable, malleable young Citizens that were easy to manipulate into doing their bidding.

The poor young man had sat in the Interview Room with me and wept like a baby, asking if he could have his parents with him. As was the law, I invited him to contact his parents and ask them to help him obtain a private attorney before we proceeded. He seemed grateful for the opportunity to speak with familiar people he knew to be working in his best interest and out of love for him.

The legal age of adulthood was twenty. It was the much-anticipated arrival of a Citizen's young life; the final seconds ticking by until the exact moment of their birth into this world precisely twenty years before. It was a major life transition, the shedding of all things childish and a newfound freedom and responsibility as a worthwhile, independent member of society. For many, it was a rite of passage that no other could compare to; it was hope, trepidation, and pure, untainted optimism. It was the biggest celebration of a young adult's life and was usually a treasured memory for most youth.

The young man sitting in front of me had not seemed like an adult. Nor was he a Citizen that could cherish reaching his age of maturity, because that had been the day when he had first been invited to attend a 'meeting at the university' during which he had first been introduced to his new 'friends'. Less than six months later, he had been Arrested along with the rest of them.

His story was not uncommon. At some point during their statements, each of them had said the same thing: they had been welcomed into the fold, and the existing members had made them feel valued and important. The older members of this diabolical organization had filled their heads with idealistic nonsense about starting a counter-revolution and restoring the Rights to all Citizens equally, but there had been something far more insidious about what they had done.

Out of everyone, including Willow Amos, the youngest member of their group had been the only one that had confessed to being linked to the death of Arlan Randall by name. But by his confession, we had secured the names and identities of the other six who had helped facilitate Arlan's death. He had been the only one facing the Death Penalty until he had caved and shared all that he could remember about the day of Arlan's Disappearance and all those who had been present.

He had been a pawn, and he had been terrified.

It was probably one of the most disturbing ways I'd witnessed people exploit other people, and it drew my ire that this one young man was going to pay with his life for things that far more than seven of them had participated in.

Along with this was the disturbing reality that the Seattle Police Department had been oblivious not only to their criminal activities, but their very existence as a group.

The Watchers On The Wall Speech: Civil War

Fellow Americans,

Our nation has been engaged in a period of history unlike any other. Families are estranged, our communities and states are divided, and our elected officials are vying for power and control with such Violent ferocity and hate-filled rhetoric that we are coming apart at the seams.

The time is upon us when we must ask ourselves who we are as a collective nation, and what it means to each of us to be American. We have been told in the past by one of our greatest Presidents that a house divided against itself cannot stand; a man who was himself forced to contend with a conflicted nation divided both by the existing way of life at the time, and the vision of a very different future moving forward. He carved a path that would strive to reunite the differences in values and opinion and help both sides to remember that despite our differences, we are all still Americans. Despite his efforts, his Fellow Americans chose war. They chose Bloodshed, Violence, Pain, and Suffering.

We ask you now, Fellow Countrymen, at what point do your values and opinions become important enough to assert that they are the only ones permissible? At what point do we, as Americans, draw the line and decide that our way is the only acceptable way and that we must reign, or else?

We as a nation know the true cost of Civil War.

Our own Civil War was a war that claimed many lives.

Many thousands of Good Men died on the battlefields; their blood seeped into our American soil as our Ancestors watched their Fellow Countrymen bleed out from horrific injuries while the battles raged on. The very land upon which this nation was built has known the history of the boots of Soldiers marching across it, trenches dug deep within Her soil to protect Her sons from Attack, and then dug into again to Bury those Fallen.

And when it was all said and done, when it was finally over—the stronger half prevailed, and a newly defined nation was reborn.

But we did not get to that point without great sacrifice or consequence.

The Civil War did not end without significant cost and trauma to our nation, or our government. Our husbands, fathers, sons, and brothers were sacrificed on the altar of political and moral victory and domination.

Over six hundred and twenty-two thousand of our Fellow Countrymen Lost their Lives because of the Civil War, and although the North prevailed, they paid heavily for that victory, losing over three hundred and sixty thousand of our bravest men.

The Empty Spaces you are surrounded by are reserved for their memory and legacy. They serve as a reminder that America exists today without the presence of the lineage being carried through from the lives of over six hundred and twenty-two thousand American men who died fighting for a war that *never needed to occur.*

America was forever changed because of that war within our own borders, and those changes were evident from the instant the lines were drawn and the first drop of blood was spilled. The fabric of our nation was torn asunder from the moment when every mother and wife hugged their husbands fiercely, crying as they left and fearing they would never return. It unraveled thread by thread as mothers struggled to come to terms with watching their young sons eagerly embrace the opportunity for danger and bravery, while they themselves only yearned to hold them close and keep them safely in their arms as they once had.

Were we able to ask, we would find that the women and children who were Left Behind held very similar points of view no matter which side they represented; and none of them would have declared it was a cause worth sacrificing their Loved One to. Were we to ask, we would find that their Tears, their Grief, and the Ripple Effect of Suffering and Sorrow they endured both in the years of war, and following it, was too great a price to pay. For the women and children whose husbands, fathers, brothers, and sons never returned, the toll their government and Fellow Countrymen asked them to pay was both Unfair and Unjust; it was a price that no American should ever be called upon to pay again.

Every life that was lost during the Civil War was an American whose life was cut short. All that they could have become, all that they could have contributed to our world, was lost because of their Death.

They paid the ultimate price in a war against their own countrymen, and We The People can never reconcile with that fact.

No American life should ever be Stolen from another American; it is a Wrongful Death, an egregious Injustice, and a Crime Against Humanity itself.

We are One People, or we are Lost.

Our Ancestors believed that the only solution for the division within their country was to be resolved through an Act of War, and they picked up arms against one another. They chose Violence, Bloodshed, Death, and Physical Force to end the contentious climate rather than other means. Our Ancestors used base, Human Nature to resolve an issue, and our government leaders used our Fellow Citizens as disposable collateral damage to win.

But the Civil War was not about which side could produce the greatest strength or power; it was a battle of values, ideological beliefs, and the power *to control the future of our nation*.

It was a battle not merely about policy, but rather the ideological differences of two opposing demographics; *one content with the way things were, while another clamored to create change.*

And here we are again, Fellow Citizens. We now stand at the precipice within this great nation, determined to wage war within our own borders and between ourselves for a second time, and all because we cannot pause long enough to listen or understand the other side.

We are faced with the uncertainty of our future as a nation and a people once more; a house divided against itself not merely in one conflicted matter, but in virtually every matter of social, cultural, moral, religious, and political relevance. Never has our nation undergone such a transformation into such oppositional political and social extremes. It is a polarization of values that will never find room for tolerance, acceptance, and co-existence unless each side makes a conscious effort to do so.

And once again, one side is forcefully pushing their agenda for control and change upon the other, citing that their way is the *only* way, and demanding the other concede in all matters.

It could be said that one side is clinging to the past and trying to preserve all that once was, *but who are we as a nation and a People* if we do not hold fast to our national identity, our roots and heritage, our ancestry and lineage, our Founding Fathers and their Vision, and our Constitution and Bill of Rights?

The preservation of America must be prioritized, and our national identity as a People must be allowed to continue without fear of recrimination, ridicule, blame, and contempt.

Fellow Americans, we do not wish for another Civil War to occur on our own soil. The Sanctity of Human Life is far more precious than any calls for War could justify, and we refuse to accept that War within our own borders is the only way our two sides can come to terms with the contrasting views and dominion over the governance of this great nation.

But let it be known under no uncertain terms that if those who oppose us continue to escalate in Violence and Deed, in Corruption and Terrorism, in the agenda to release more Violent Predators back onto the streets of our nation, and in their blatant disregard for the Sanctity of Human Life through their Un-Godly promotion of Abortion, Suicide, and Euthanasia, no true American will be left with any other choice except to choose Civil War

We as a People cannot stand idly by as we watch our Citizens Lose their Lives through Unconscionable and Unjust Acts of Violence. Every day, more Innocent American Lives are Lost because of Unnecessary Death, many of which are entirely preventable. It is a travesty for our nation as we watch our numbers decrease and the rows of Empty Spaces fill with the Memories of all who should still be here among us but are not. We have already lost too many Loved Ones who have paid with their lives because of a broken and corrupt Criminal Justice system. It is a system beyond repair, one which not only fails to place value on Human Life, but is steadfast in its determination to obliterate any form of accountability or consequence.

A Crime Against Humanity is a Crime Against Ourselves.

The time has come when all true Americans must decide if they are going to stand on the side of Goodness, on the side which honors the Sanctity of Human Life, and stand with all who are willing to become a voice for the Victims and the Preservation of our national identity as an American People. For one thing is entirely certain; if we do not rise collectively together, we shall surely fall one by one, and Crime and Violence will be the only tangible reality left for the America we once knew.

    The Watchers On The Wall
    On this date, the one-hundredth twenty-third day
    In the Year of our Lord, 2050

PART SIX

"Do not fear, for I have redeemed you;
I have summoned you by name; you are mine."

Isaiah 43:1

TWENTY-NINE – THE FACTORY

The Factory Parking Lot

    I pulled into the factory parking lot; it was an enormous space that had once held hundreds of petrol-based vehicles, and probably a great deal of them had been the oversized diesel trucks with eighteen wheels that had been used to transport goods back in the day. There weren't many places with such excessive space surrounding the buildings, specifically just for employment. Between the vast majority of Citizens being able to work from home and the lack of storefronts because of online shopping, there had been little demand for oversized buildings or massive parking garages and lots.

    The rise in Terrorism and Violent Crime had led to abrupt decreases in public recreational activities, and even after Crime had been drastically reduced following the Great Reformation, things hadn't returned to how they had been before. The probability of Attacks and Assaults had been too high for too long; no one had found public outings to be worth the risk to life and limb.

    The last time I had seen public parking lots this big had been surrounding those old-style shopping centers that had been called 'malls', where there had been hundreds of stores consolidated under one roof. Mass shootings had made those a thing of the past, and with the same merchandise available online able to be delivered from secure, unmanned warehouses by use of self-navigating drones, the risk to Human Life had been drastically reduced and the malls rendered obsolete. In most cases, the parking lots in such urban locations had either been converted into housing units, or the areas underwent purposeful rehabilitation of the ecosystem for habitat restoration.

    After the National Population Decrease because of the Sentence Reform Act, America had found that urban areas had experienced the most significant decline in overall population. Between those Exiled and given the Death Penalty, most cities had been reduced by half, leaving plenty of space for housing and recreational facilities with sufficient security. There was also a concentrated effort to create green space, resulting in a healthy return to conditions before industrial advancements and population growth had led to the environmental concerns that had plagued the 21st century. Clearing our nation of those who could never be rehabilitated or live among us peacefully had cleansed our nation of more than just the threat and fear of Violence and Death; it had led to beautification projects and the self-healing of our nation and planet.

Touring the Factory

    I approached the end of the building; it was a monstrosity of another time in history—ugly, massive, austere. The metal siding was covered in copper and burnt red due to rust, windows were broken, and the raw edges of exposed glass posed a constant danger to any person or animal that approached during hours of darkness. They had paved much of the parking lot area with black asphalt, although it had long since faded into a dull, cracked, grey because of the oxidation of the materials over time.

    I walked around mounds of crushed glass covering the cracked pavement, stepping carefully over piles of abandoned metal building materials, rotten pieces of plywood that had once covered the dilapidated windows, and stacks of wooden pallets once used to transport materials. There were a half dozen oversized rolling doors running the length of the loading docks that were securely locked down into thick, bolted rings cemented into the ground.

    Making my way to one end of the factory, I navigated through the debris as I searched for an access point that wouldn't prove too difficult. I finally settled on a metal door down at the corner. The constant rain had faded the once bright red paint and replaced every dent, ding, and scratch with rust. Someone had put an oversized chain around the door frame and locked it with a deadbolt after having run it through a pipe that was coming from the building and disappeared into the ground. I assumed the two ICE agents had done this to secure the building after they had discovered the mysterious 'body' of one of the Foreign Nationals. If they were to be believed, according to the two ICE agents, the other owner fled the country. If that were true, the ICE agents and their Crime Scene Investigators would have been the last people here.

    The chain was a weak attempt to secure an old building that likely needed to be officially condemned—and now probably would be if the state were to seize hold of it. Condemned or not, if there had been a man Murdered here—even if he was illegally within our borders and a Foreign National—it was a Crime Scene. That was, of course, aside from whatever I was potentially going to find that could have been linked to Katarina or Daegan Kyl. Anything related to either of them would only reaffirm that this entire building should have been locked down from the beginning and processed thoroughly by our Crime Scene Investigators. We had the best technology, forensics, and even Cadaver dogs; God only knew what we could find if given access.

    Another wave of frustration rolled over me as I considered the state of things, so I pushed everything to the corner of my mind. I reminded myself that I was still here, and at the very least, still doing what I could to get a proper overview of what may lie beyond. Whether or not the Governor had intended it, he had interfered with a formal investigation, and had issued an ultimatum that I could only presume he knew was an unethical breach of conduct—aside from being illegal and a violation of his Oath of office. He could not claim ignorance as it was a well-established federal law that was taught from the very earliest years of Civics in our education system. His authority did not extend to me or anything I investigated; all investigations were beyond the realm of any Governorship.

As a courtesy, I had included him in my progress, and respected his wishes for the time being. Having first been intrigued by his response after our initial contact, I had done nothing directly oppositional to him. But after the two ICE agents had conveniently appeared to put their boot on my throat, I was more committed than ever to gain a broader understanding of both this factory and the Governor who had attempted to pull rank on me for reasons as yet unknown. What was clear, however, was that when a Governor abused his power by attempting to create some warped amalgamation of shared investigatory powers between himself, ICE, and my own independent investigatory team, he was doing it for personal reasons that he believed were worth the possible backlash. I intended to find out why.

The chain was rusted and probably decades older than me, but its unwillingness to give was a credit to its solid construction. I turned my attention instead to the door itself in the hopes that it had not aged well because of the weather. The handle was strong, and still firmly connected to the metal plate beneath it, but the bolts that secured the frame to the metal door had rusted all the way through, giving me an idea. After some searching through the piles of debris around the doorway, I found a metal rod about four feet in length and thin enough to fit into the handle space. I braced my boot against the wall next to the door and applied what I hoped to be sufficient leverage and force to release the handle from its rusted casing.

Within seconds, the door handle gave way, sending me flying backward and struggling to catch my balance as a thunderous cacophony of noise broke out all around. The metal rod hit the wall before swinging wildly out into the piles of metal scraps, clanging into everything along the way, while the door handle slammed forcefully against the concrete below. Its hollow vibrations resembled the shrill ringing of a bell, and then, mercifully, the heavy chain followed, each link dropping pound by pound, smashing into one another like gold coins being emptied from a pirate's treasure chest. The sound ricocheted throughout the open valley, and I looked around sheepishly as if someone had flipped on a light switch and found my hand caught in a cookie jar.

From somewhere in the distance, a dog barked in response to the noise, shaking me out of my moment of awkward clumsiness and drawing attention to the fact that I was in a very isolated area. It was more than a little unsettling considering I was only about fifteen minutes from some of the busiest working districts in the Greater Seattle Area and surrounded by over a million people.

Despite its proximity to the thriving metropolis surrounding it, the isolated factory served as a bitter reminder of the transformation of industry. Just as the Industrial Revolution had turned this into a prosperous location at one time, the tech industry had eradicated it for more sophisticated and environmental alternatives, leaving everything to rust, rot, and deteriorate in its own time and unbeknownst to anyone save the birds and whatever wildlife remained.

No one ever asks what becomes of ancient artifacts until there's money to be made from them, granting them significance once again. I wondered if the factory had ever created anything of importance, or if it was just as so many other buildings were, outdated and unworthy of modernization.

I opened the door wide and peered into the vast emptiness within, trying to see down the long hallway before me by utilizing the brightness of the day. It would instantly become dark if the door shut behind me, so I took a moment to look around for something to ensure that the heavy door remained open before finally just bending over and moving a pile of the chain toward the edge of the door. The weight of it was sufficient, but it was slow progress and required several long motions back and forth as I shifted the yards of heavy metal chain from the doorway to the outside edge, where the door could be left open as much as possible. By the end, I was convinced that as far as good plans went, there could have been better, but at least it had no chance of accidentally slamming shut and scaring the bejeezus out of me.

The hallway seemed to span the length of the building and there didn't appear to be many doors branching off its sides. Directly inside the entrance was another set of heavy double doors. A wall plaque identified it as a stairwell leading both up toward the second and third floors, and down to the basement. I knew I would explore the entire building by the end, so I made my way past it, intending to review the first floor, then the basement, then go up to the second, and finally the top floor. With that plan in mind, I turned on the external LED lighting attached to my visor, the two on my chest plate, and then took out an additional small flashlight I had as well. The light faded quickly the further I traveled away from the doorframe.

Various rodents scurried about the dusty floors, kept in constant company with the insects. A dead rat was covered in maggots, but it was nothing compared to the endless cobwebs and spiders covering the hallways and corners of every room I explored. I wasn't squeamish by nature, but I was certainly no fan of spiders and was glad for my impenetrable uniform—especially around my ankles, sleeves, and collar. My balaclava and visor would keep my head and neck safe even if something dropped on me from above, and for that, I was extremely grateful.

It was a filthy place, somehow made worse by the darkness and silence. After venturing through every room on the ground floor, I came to a hallway at the opposite end of where I had entered the building and was met with a large set of metal double doors. There was a faded sign next to the door frame stating I could proceed to the second floor or basement.

It was an immense building, and between the sounds of creaking, plastic flapping in the breeze, and disease-ridden vermin scurrying about, I was suitably on edge. By the time I had reached the bottom step of the staircase, it was necessary to turn on the additional tiny LED lights connected to my helmet as well. For added light, I turned on the LED's used by my visor for reading and writing, and then did a quick check to ensure that every light I could use was set to the highest power available. It wasn't usual to see all the lights activated, but when used in a group, they provided substantial lighting and were intended to ensure that all Law Enforcement could keep their hands free. It also helped ensure there was adequate lighting as the cameras recorded events during the hours of darkness

The basement was musty, dark, dusty, and smelled of garbage and sewage. It seemed to follow the same blueprint pattern as the main floor, with two corridors that seemed to run the length of the factory and connected at each end, making a large U-shaped hallway with rooms on either side. Despite the space, the hallways didn't seem to lead to many doorways or side rooms; there were a few electrical rooms, a room for water tanks that even had some laundry facilities, and then a large room filled with furnaces and boiler equipment for the heating. Nothing seemed out of the ordinary, and I believed everything would have aligned with the standard blueprints for buildings such as this. I wasn't sure what I was looking for, but everything seemed normal and as it should be.

Although it didn't seem necessary, I took the time to make my way through the entire boiler room. It was at the far end of the basement and at the furthermost corner away from the staircase. I imagined that had any of the equipment been operational that this would have been done by design to decrease the output of noise traveling from it. This would have been the heart of any enormous building, generating all heat, electricity, and eventually, most similar rooms incorporated their wireless technology and any environmental equipment, including solar or energy assistance. It was the hub of the factory operations and had probably been a noisy environment to work in back in the day when everything was up and running. Today, however, it was just another dark, miserable room filled with oversized pieces of machinery reeking of excrement.

I could not wait to be done and proceed back up to the second floor.

I made my way to the end of the room before I found it; the space that I had been expecting to find but had dreaded knowing existed. It was as I expected—worse than I could have imagined...worse than any Crime Scene I had ever before been a part of.

No.

To say it was a Crime Scene was to make it as though it were a place where a singular, tragic event had taken place, and I did not believe that to be the case in this situation. This was the place where they had kept her; it was the place where two Evil men had held a young girl against her will, against all hope of escape or comfort, and for the vilest of imaginable reasons.

It was not a Crime Scene. It was a prison.

It was the place where she had been kept, and the place where she had Suffered.

It was a place where Evil men had done Evil deeds, and where Innocence had been Stolen.

It was a place where everything had eventually been Taken from her, including her life.

I had found it, and it was of no surprise that it had been deep in the ground.

Monsters always lived in the dark.

The Third Floor

After touring the basement, ground floor, and second floor, I made my way up the stairs to the third floor. I had gone through a half dozen rooms, taken photographs of various oddities I encountered—such as furniture having been arranged in such a manner as to show recent usage—and was almost done with a complete sweep of the building. The last door at the end, provided it mirrored the ones below it on the second and ground floor, would have been lined with large glass windows and office equipment. The two rooms below had been overflowing with desks, chairs, and machinery—everything having been left to rot after the factory had closed its doors.

I believed I had already found what I was looking for in the basement, and anything else would have been unexpected. The factory had done nothing out of the ordinary, nor had the two men in charge done anything within the building—beyond the basement—that would have drawn unnecessary attention or criticism to them. With that in mind, I opened the door of the last room casually, already prepared to find nothing more beyond duplicate rooms in a similar state of disrepair.

The door seemed to stick, though, and it took a few hard pushes with my shoulder before I could get it dislodged. After giving it a final shove, I felt the door break free from its hold as my body jolted forward, propelled by the motion of the door.

Instantly, a searing pain registered from deep within—and then nothing.

Meeting the Governor

I opened my eyes slowly; my head was pounding, and I could feel the wetness of blood on the back of my scalp. My helmet, visor, and balaclava had all been removed. There was some type of laceration on the back of my head. The blood covering the floor I had been lying on only moments before confirmed it.

I could feel the sting of air as it made contact with the open wound, but without my visor, I had no way of assessing how bad the physical damage was. I was concerned about the blood loss, but more concerning was the intense throbbing in my head and the fact that I had blacked out because of it.

I didn't see what had hit me—but as I struggled to sit up on the rough wooden floor, there were quite a few loose 2x4s lying around. There was a good chance that one of them had been the culprit. The only question was who had been holding it and where they had come from.

My eyes were straining against the brightness of the room, struggling to adjust to the pulsating pain coming from behind my eyes. The glaring blaze of the summer sun was streaming in through the oversized windows lining the entire length of the capacious forty-foot room.

I could see a pair of boots standing about ten paces ahead. They were government issued.

I strained my neck upward, holding the back of my head with my left hand. He had really done a number on me; my eyes still had trouble focusing and I couldn't think of a time when I'd had such a headache in my life. My position on the floor left me staring toward both external walls, forcing me to look up and directly into the sun resting high in the sky.

The room was lined with rustic wood on the walls, and the floor was made from old hardwood; on a typical grey Seattle day, it would have made this room feel cold and drafty due to its size. But on a day like today, with both outside walls lined with twelve-foot-tall windows, the blue skies and the bright sunshine flooded the entire space from corner to corner.

The factory was so old that none of the windows had security tinting to them, leading me to believe they were probably just the standard double-pane variety from the 21st century. The room was filled with old, dusty air; further proof that the windows did not contain any of the technology that had revolutionized the window industry in the last fifty years. Had the windows been the modern industry standard, they would have been regulating air quality through built-in ventilation panels, filtering out any pollutants and replacing it with clean air.

Western Washington had struggles with mold, moss, and even rust because of the moisture and salty sea air coming in from the Pacific Ocean and Puget Sound. It did not, as a general rule, need to worry about the heat temperatures rising above ninety most summers. Had it been more of a factor, it seemed likely that the architect that had designed this room might have reconsidered the two eastern-facing walls. As it was, the room was being consumed by the heat of the day as the unholy brightness of the foreign object in the sky pierced my eyes with its intensity.

I pulled myself up into a sitting position and propped myself against the wall. The doorway where I had been Ambushed was directly to my right.

I sat there for a minute, assessing my surroundings and the damage I could feel to the back of my head. I wasn't in a hurry to engage with the man in the boots; I knew he would wait. I probably wasn't the first man he'd seen trying to recover from one of his attacks.

Besides, there wasn't much cause for concern about the ICE agent trying to kill me; if he had wanted me dead, he would have done it already and I would never have seen it coming.

From across the room, I heard a distinctly familiar voice speak.

"I'm just not sure what we need to do to make things clearer," he said.

I'd heard that voice before; I knew I had. It was familiar, but between my skull feeling like it had been cracked open with a sledgehammer, and the brightness making it impossible for me to regain focus, I was having a hard time opening my eyes enough to see the man standing near the windows.

Warning bells were going off inside my head. I was vulnerable, exposed, and unable to call for back-up. I couldn't even defend myself properly while in a sitting position, but I wasn't sure I was able to stand just yet.

All I wanted was to get my visor back on so I could use the tint darkening to shield my eyes from the glare of the sun. My head was screaming.

The visor could have assessed my damage, but it was also used to alert local Law Enforcement and any necessary responding Emergency Medical Technicians as well, so I didn't think I would be getting it back anytime soon.

I pulled my right hand free from my glove and rubbed my face, closing my eyes briefly and pressing on the bridge of my nose to see if it helped moderate the pain. It didn't seem to make a difference. I couldn't think of anything else I could do beyond just trying to remain awake until I was free to leave.

I reached down and removed my other glove. It had gotten bloody when I used it to feel the backside of my head right after I had regained consciousness. I could tell I had lost quite a bit of blood just based on how much had smeared all over my work glove; they were designed to be water-resistant and had a chemical cover on them as well, but I could feel the moisture on my fingertips. I folded the glove in half and used it to apply pressure against the wound. It was an awkward angle to reach, so I pulled my leg up to prop my arm in place for stability.

As I adjusted myself and tried to get a solid grasp on my surroundings, I tried to recall where I knew that voice from. And then suddenly it hit me.

It was the Governor. *The* Governor. The most powerful man in the state of Washington, taking time out of his busy schedule just to come here and kick my ass. I was touched.

I knew I had recognized it.

I squinted my eyes and tried to look up in his direction. He was standing directly between two of the windows, and even though I tried to shield my eyes with my hand like a visor, the glare of the sun was still just too much.

There was movement to my right.

I tried to turn my head, realizing that both ICE agents had been standing in the room the entire time. I hadn't even noticed the second man, and he was only a few feet away.

He was immediately recognizable despite his full uniform and headgear. I estimated him to be about 5'5" or maybe 5'6"; an unfortunate height for any man, but somehow made worse by those who insisted on over-inflating their chests and swaggering around with their arms cocked and loaded with their fists clenched. His height and naturally thick build gave him the appearance of a bulldog; short legged and abnormally muscular.

Although he had not spoken during our first encounter, his distinct physical attributes had made him unmistakable. When the two men had come into our meeting room with the Chief, I had originally thought that they were partners, as was common practice for most government agencies and members of Law Enforcement. Even though the taller one hadn't impressed me much through his decision to keep his face and voice entirely concealed, I had just assumed he had been the more dominant of the two because he had taken point. Now I was just left with the impression that the two were nothing more than hired guns, and Fido here was exactly what he appeared to be: the knee-breaker.

"That's quite the arm you've got there, Slugger. You sure you're not in the wrong business? Maybe you should play baseball instead." I said to the guy on my right.

The little bulldog had attacked me with a ferocity that was far more aggressive than the situation warranted; something drove that level of animus and I was pretty sure it wasn't all because he didn't want me to do my job. He had taken joy in his use of excessive force; a dangerous precedent to set as a man working within the field of Criminal Justice to be sure, but even more disturbing knowing it had been against another Officer of the Law.

"I bet baseball would pay more than this racket does," I stated.

My eyes were finally focusing better, and I was able to look around the room at all three of the men. The one that had given me orders back at HQ was leaning against an abandoned table casually. He was holding my visor and cracked helmet. That my helmet had cracked—made from a combination of lightweight, durable Kevlar, Gore-Tex, and special polymer-based mixes—was a pretty good sign of just how hard the bulldog had struck me. My bleeding head and throbbing brain were clues I was going to need an Emergency Room visit and a head scan afterward.

The guy had cracked *my military grade helmet*.

I wasn't going to forget I owed him one.

"Is there something I can help you with, Governor?" I asked.

The first agent stood up a little straighter as he realized I had recognized his boss. I thought that had been the entire point of his boss being here; I was *supposed* to recognize him and tremble in fear. Why would the guy think I *wouldn't* recognize him? He was an elected official. Apparently, a total scumbag Criminal, but an elected official, nonetheless. His face and videos were plastered everywhere—it made little sense for his minion to expect his identity to remain unknown.

I found it a little unsettling that this was the caliber of intellect our government had allowed in; I was a little embarrassed for him, being as dense as he was. I mean, I was sitting here with a cracked skull, a possible concussion, a pounding headache, and three potential Killers surrounding me and yet I still figured out that the Governor wanted to be recognized. How many bad guys does one have to watch in the movies to understand that being able to show one's enemies just how tough they are is a key factor in Criminal Mastermind 101?

I was not thinking clearly yet; my ability to maintain focus was becoming a concern. I felt like my brain was processing information in disjointed increments of incomplete, pointless nonsense.

The Governor began walking slowly toward me. I was certain his Number One would not let him get close enough that I could spring up and snap his neck if the opportunity presented itself, but I tried to compose myself anyhow.

I had to be honest though, the bulldog had bested me this round; I had not anticipated any manner of Attack or Ambush, nor did I have any memory of seeing or sensing anyone present as I had entered the room. He had stood within a few feet of me during those few seconds when I had crossed the threshold and struck me from the side, connecting with the back of my skull so effectively that I wouldn't have had any defense even if I had been concerned about danger and had expected to encounter it. That had never happened to me before, and I'd had my fair share of encounters with those willing to use Deadly Force to secure their own freedom and avoid Arrest. I found it troubling that I'd allowed him to get the drop on me, but perhaps even more bothersome was the knowledge that he could have Ended my Life and I would never have seen it coming. It was a sobering thought.

I didn't see myself jumping up and taking on these two well-trained government agents in some heroic, epic battle of Good versus Evil anytime soon. I knew I was going to need stitches, but I would have traded a pint of blood right then just for a couple of aspirin and a pair of sunglasses. The first ICE agent didn't have any genuine cause for concern regarding the safety of the Governor; by his choosing to be here, he must have known that he would not be at risk of Harm. Men in power were used to setting the scene and controlling people; they rarely faced situations they didn't anticipate the outcome or couldn't dictate the terms of.

"You do remember meeting these two gentlemen, do you not? They met with your Chief, and I believe they made it clear that this case would not be resolved through you. Was this not the impression you were given?"

Was this guy really being patronizing toward me? He realized everything he was saying was illegal, right? Clearly, he just didn't care, which either meant that he didn't care that I heard it because he didn't view me as any sort of threat to his agenda…or he was just giving the classic Evil Overlord speech before he killed me and dumped me into a shallow grave somewhere—and probably nearby would be my guess.

"Yeah, I got the memo," I replied. "Let's just say I'm a little slow, though. Why don't you explain to me why you're trying to cover up the Murder of a little girl? You know what they did to her, right? What happened to her?"

He stopped walking once he was about five or six paces away from me. His first henchman brought over an old wooden desk chair and set it down next to him, taking the time to sweep the dust off with his gloved hand. He was a well-trained lapdog, no doubt about it.

The Governor looked down at the seat for a second and then sat down, leaning forward so his elbows rested on his knees and his hands were positioned in front of his chin area, one hand over the other in the shape of a fist. It was an arrogant pose to strike; the air was filled with rancid entitlement and the smug elitism of the wealthy politician. This was exactly what Americans had gotten rid of with the Great Reformation; this was what they had worked so hard and risked so much to eradicate from their nation. Men like this—supposedly representing the American People while covertly working against them for their own personal gain…I knew how this story ended, and it wasn't in this man's favor.

"Mr. Mackay, I am fully aware of what the two men in question were responsible for doing. I know exactly who they were, what they did, and how they got away with it."

I looked up at him, staring long and hard into his dark eyes. Shark eyes.

"Don't be so surprised, Mr. Mackay. Of course, I know who you are. I know everything about you. I know your entire family," he said.

It did not surprise me he knew who I was; when two ICE agents show up at your work and tell you to stop investigating a Murder, chances are it's an order from some source of corrupt power. I already knew the Governor had refused to let me get a Search Warrant for this place; why wouldn't he have secured my identity as well?

I just took it for granted that he wouldn't care enough about me to think it was a worthwhile threat. I was only one guy. I didn't have enough political or professional power to pose a genuine threat to this man. I didn't have a wife or kids he could use as leverage, either. My family wasn't in the city, and although they were all hard-working professionals, none of them worked in fields that this man would consider influential or potentially risky to his agenda. I didn't even see any of my siblings or parents enough that an investigation by this man would present the illusion that we were a close-knit family—although we were, and I would not soon forget that he was making a bold threat against them.

"So how can I be of service, Sir? What exactly do you want from me?" I asked, dryly.

The comment about my family had not gone unnoticed, but I wasn't giving anything away to this man. A man with something to lose can be manipulated and threatened. It was exactly why our identities were *supposed* to be Concealed and Protected. My family wasn't supposed to become leverage just because of a job I did *for a paycheck*. Apparently, this 'political leader' had missed that history lesson.

The Governor smiled.

"My man said you were a smart one."

I raised an eyebrow and looked over his shoulder at his Number One.

"I knew we had a connection from the moment we met," I said. I watched him visibly tense throughout his shoulders and his hand grip my helmet tighter. He had a short fuse. Good. Because one of these days I believed I was going to meet both men again, and it wouldn't start with me jumping them from behind. I was sure they had just been following orders, but what kind of men would do such a cowardly Assault, really? Pathetic.

"So, what do you want? I have things to do," I repeated, looking back at the Governor.

"I want you to drop the investigation."

"Can't do it. What else ya got?" I replied.

"Yes, you *can,* and you *will,*" he said. His voice was a little more forceful this time. He didn't have a long fuse either, apparently.

"Look," I started. "I don't care about your political games with the jihadis. I thought I already made that clear to *'your man'*, but I'll speak slowly and go over it all again for you. I'm not interested in messing up your political games with the Middle East, and I'm certainly not concerned about your obvious political aspirations or ladder-climbing."

The Governor tensed his body and seemed to freeze. I couldn't tell if he was getting irritated by what I said or because I had said it in front of his men, but I continued anyway.

"So do what you need to do. I know I'm at a dead end with the two Foreign Nationals—you already screwed me out of my chance to capture them, and if the other guy really has fled the country, then there isn't much left for us to talk about. So, I'm not sure what all this is about or why it even matters anymore. As far as my investigation goes, the two Foreign Nationals are just a blip on the radar. Or didn't you realize that my case was a lot bigger than just them?"

The pain in my head was resulting in my own lack of patience, and I was growing tired of the game. I could feel every heartbeat as the blood pulsated through my skull; I was thirsty too. Sitting around in a dirty building flooded with sunshine as the summer temperatures rose wasn't how I had intended to spend my day.

"The problem, Mr. Mackay, is that I'm not asking you to just end your investigation regarding the two 'Foreign Nationals', as you called them. You need to drop everything involving the man you have being held downtown right now."

"Wait, what? I'm confused. Are you talking about Daegan Kyl?" I asked.

Why would this man care about him?

"Are you really this obtuse? I've read your records. You have an impressive background. Is it really so difficult for you to understand this?" He looked down at me with a patronizing look on his face.

"Why don't we just assume I am. If you want something from me, you're going to have to spell it out," I growled.

My legs were pulled up, and I had my left arm thrown over my knee while my right hand rubbed my temple. The only thing I wanted was for this pathetic excuse of a Human Being to leave already and take his cohorts with him. I couldn't get any medication until I got back to the SPD Cruiser, and I couldn't check my head or vitals until I had my visor back on or I used the generic spare that could be found in the Cruiser. There had been international treaties established in less time than what this guy was taking to get to the point.

He sighed deeply and motioned for his Number One to bring me my visor and helmet. The agent stood in front of me with his arms extended, holding the two items directly in front of him. His own face was covered entirely, of course, although I could feel his eyes on me.

It was hard to respect a man that considered himself an agent of the law but chose to align himself not only with the corrupt politician next to him, but who also chose to keep his helmet on after unmasking another. It was weak; nothing more than cheap theatrics and an unnecessary display of power. I remembered he had even used his generic voice modifier when he had been at the SPD. The irony of his hypocrisy wasn't lost to me. Unmasking and naming an Investigator while he hid behind his security shields as a plush federal agent moonlighting as someone's unethical lapdog was shameful.

I took my visor and helmet from him and set them down next to me. I could have activated the Distress signal now that my uniform was linked to my visor again, but what would have been the point? They would be gone by the time help arrived, and even then, the man was the *Governor* of the State of Washington; any Responding Officers would initially trust him, and any Citizens that heard about it would buy whatever lies he told them. From the look on the Governor's face, he knew I wasn't going to activate it already, which was probably why he sent his bodyguard over with it. He hadn't been testing me; he had been proving his dominance.

The Governor motioned for both of his men to go over by the door. His Number One began to object, presumably because I was such a threat, and the Governor waved him off dismissively. The two little dogs moved toward the door, obedient and well-trained even as they both kept looking in my direction from behind their security visors. I was beginning to understand why some Citizens found the blank mannequin molds tedious.

"How's your head?" the Governor asked. Ah, good cop/bad cop. I knew this one.

"I'll be fine. You should really tell your minions that Assaulting a Peacekeeper with Intent to Harm is a Punishable Offense. I'm pretty sure knocking me out would be enough to make him lose his pretty little uniform and get an orange one instead—at least until he was set loose in the wild or paid his full dues with his Final Breath."

"Yeah, I think he enjoyed that. You must have made quite a first impression," he replied. "No worries, though; I'll handle it."

"You know he could have just used his taser on me," I said. Hitting me with a 2x4 just to contain me was more than a little obnoxious; it was entirely unnecessary. Overlooking the obvious—that we were supposed to be on the same team, for starters—he had enough weapons in his arsenal that resorting to a piece of lumber was just...*uncivilized*.

The Governor nodded, running his hand through his hair. He was the consummate politician; well-groomed, smooth, and an easy smile. He had won the state in a landslide.

I pictured him playing in the backyard with his socialite wife and his three little kids. Daughters.

"You get that these men were not only responsible for kidnapping Katarina from outside of her church, but that they kept her here, in *this* building, for over *three* months, don't you?" I asked. For the first time since our meeting, I spoke without the slightest hint of sarcasm or anger.

He nodded.

"Because I'd like to understand why you're asking me to conceal not only what they did to her, but another man's involvement as well. Have you seen where they kept her?" I asked.

He nodded again.

I hadn't seen or heard them arrive, so it was entirely possible he had been here before I had done my tour of the building. I was assuming he had flown in on a gyrocopter; it would have been virtually silent, and if he had landed on the back side of the building or the rooftop, I wouldn't have known he had arrived until it was too late. I didn't know if he had been tracking me, but it stood to reason that if he had, and I had deliberately disobeyed his orders by entering the factory, that he would have shown up to put me in my place.

I expected he had been tracking me. Gyrocopters were the fastest method of independent travel, seating up to six and able to be flown by any licensed driver in bursts of up to four-hundred miles between refueling. I remembered the Governor had been licensed, and was an avid flyer, from the same campaign videos I had recalled seeing his family.

I was going to have to go through the SPD Cruiser, my uniform, and anything else with Officer Stanton to figure out how he had been tracking me. But that was later.

For now, I wanted to know if he had personally gone down into that room and seen where she had been kept, and how. The man was a father. I wanted to know how he could expect me to do what he was asking when he knew what had happened to her, and what they had done.

"I've been here before. I've seen the room. I was here when they took the photographs you were given."

Well, that was surprising.

"This is bigger than you understand, Mackay. I realize that you're an Officer of the Law and this seems like it's cut and dried to you, but it's not. I know you just want to 'catch the bad guy', and I can appreciate that. But this isn't going to be that kind of case, and you don't get to be that kind of hero. This isn't something that can be won; not here, not in a Court of Law, and not with an investigation. You're not going to catch your bad guy this time because no one is going to let it happen."

I stared at him.

He was making the same speech that the Chief had made earlier, trying to make it seem as if his hands were tied, and all of this was being done beyond his control and over his head. Both the Governor and the Chief had more political and professional clout than I did, and yet amazingly, no one could do anything in this situation, and everyone was just another spoke in the wheel.

I didn't buy it.

"Suppose that you're right," I said. "Suppose that nothing gets done. Suppose that I just go about my business, work out the rest of my case, and figure out how to remove Daegan Kyl from the equation. One—why would I do that when I can prove he was involved—and two, why would it matter? Why does he matter? What do you care? He has nothing to do with your *quest for peace* in the Middle East."

The Governor raised his eyebrows and tilted his head as if to mull over my comment and the illusion that I had any semblance of a choice in how this situation played out. I had to appreciate his self-assurance that everything was completely under his domain. Perhaps it was. But at the very least, I deserved some answers.

"I like you, Mackay. You're a fighter; I appreciate that. And you're clearly one of the good guys; I get that about you. It's honorable; I've always been a big fan of the Boys in Blue, so let me help you work this one out so you can understand it a little better."

The Governor stood, and taking hold of the old wooden chair, flipped it around so he could sit on it backwards with his legs open on either side. He rested his arms along the back of the chair and gave me an earnest smile. He really did have an affable personality; I would never have imagined he was capable of such subterfuge and unscrupulous behavior. Then again, he had that easy-going personality reminiscent of a sociopath too; arrogant and determined, but adept at social games and giving the appearance of fitting into society. The guy had the textbook identity of a high-functioning Serial Killer, and the more he smiled at me, the more I wondered what he was hiding behind that pretty family of his.

"You're going to drop this entire case because Daegan Kyl hasn't done anything wrong, and you're not going to destroy his life just to have at least one guy to blame for what happened to that little girl."

I laughed.

"And you know this how? If you actually have some evidence that will clear the guy, why am I here at all? Why didn't you just give it to me?" I asked him.

"What are you even *doing* here, Governor?" My words came out with more contempt than I intended, but the man was being intentionally cryptic.

"Please, call me Miller," he replied cordially.

I sat up straighter, slowly moving my head from side to side.

"Thanks, but I'll pass. Are we about done here?"

He smiled at me, tapping the top of his chair with his fingers.

"Not quite," he responded.

"Just a few more minutes of your time if you don't mind. Let me ask you about Daegan Kyl. You've had him in your care for what, about a week now? And how's that going for you?" he asked.

"Has he said anything to you yet? A confession? An explanation for how he came to be on the property or how he knew about the Victims?"

How he was staring at me told me everything I needed to know about what he was asking; he already knew that Daegan Kyl hadn't confessed anything, and that I was still shooting in the dark with him. He probably knew that despite ample circumstantial evidence gathered through Officer Stanton's efforts, and some indirect connections, that I had nothing substantial enough to incriminate Kyl. I doubted I could secure a Conviction for his Exile, let alone for the Death Penalty. I didn't even have a motive yet—and in all honesty, I had more doubts about his Guilt than I had of his Innocence.

But if the Governor knew all that, then why had he just left him there for a week?

Maybe it was because he was determined to distract us while he moved his foreigners out of sight. I reminded myself to give it further consideration and returned my focus to the man sitting across from me. My head was still screaming, but the throbbing in my temples was diminishing. I still wasn't operating up to code, though; now was not the time for serious critical thinking.

"I imagine that you're pretty good at your job. I followed your work in New York on your last case, and I know you made quite the name for yourself with that Nevada sex-trafficking one. I know you don't trust me, but I'm trying to help you—just like I was when I sent those two down to HQ and let you know about the two Foreign Nationals. You don't have to trust me; but you do need to believe me. And I'm counting on you to go talk to Mr. Kyl as soon as we're done here."

He was a smooth speaker. I was halfway convinced that he meant well just because he was selling me such a convincing sales pitch.

And I had every intention of going and speaking with Mr. Kyl the instant I was done here. It would be worth hearing about how a man such as Daegan Kyl managed to have the Governor of Washington going to such extremes to vouch for him.

"So, here's what you need to know, and then we can wrap things up here. You're going to let Mr. Kyl out—and not 'at some point'—you're going to release him *today*. I'll have my—what did you call them? Minions?—check up on it to make sure it's done. So don't test me on this one; I want him released today."

He raised his eyebrows as if to confirm an answer from me, so I obliged, giving him a slightly patronizing nod of consent.

"And I'm sorry—I truly can't help you any further with the two foreigners. My men were telling you the truth about them and there's nothing more we can do about it at this point. But I'll do you a solid and let you know that Daegan Kyl has the answers that you're looking for. You were wrong about him being responsible, but you weren't wrong about him being involved. He buried that little girl, and I'm sure he'll tell you what you need to know. I'm not sure why he did it or why he got involved; I can only tell you we know for certain that he was indeed here at one point and had removed her Remains himself. He wasn't the cause of her death, however, nor was he responsible for anything else…*untoward*. I doubt very much he even knew about her existence until after her death; I rather doubt that he would have allowed it. But that's just my opinion; you'll have to get confirmation from him when you speak."

"But he knew the two men?" I asked. I could take his information with a grain of salt, but it wouldn't hurt to hear all of it, anyway. He was here for a reason; he had intercepted me for a purpose.

"Oh, yes, he knew them. But it wasn't on friendly terms, as you would imagine. I rather believe that he is a lot like you, actually; one of those insufferably good men always trying to do the right thing. You're rarely wrong, Mr. Mackay, but regarding Daegan Kyl, you have missed the mark by a mile."

"Why are you trying to clear him?" I was right to be skeptical; the man had not given me cause not to be suspicious. Just because the Governor said he was being helpful did not mean he was doing so because he was just altruistic; I imagined he seldom granted any 'favors' without exacting his weight in gold in exchange, and I had no desire to be indebted to him.

"Because the man is *Innocent*, Mr. Mackay, and contrary to whatever you believe me capable of, I will not allow you to send an Innocent man to Death Row nor have him Banished. You're going to have to understand the man a little better to know why he's just sitting there allowing you to railroad him, I'm afraid. But let me make it clear, Officer. Daegan Kyl will not take the fall for what these two men did, nor will I allow him to take the blame for someone else's misdeeds. The man will not be turned into an example just so the American People can have someone to crucify. I'm very sorry, but the story of Katarina ends here. What happened to her was a tragic tale, but it is not something that the American People are ever going to hear about."

"But he didn't just bury Katarina—even if what you're saying is true—he was still responsible for the other three Victims. I know you understand this. So, explain to me why you're so quick to vindicate this man and assume he's Innocent when you're not even clearing him of everything. Just because he wasn't involved with the events surrounding Katarina, it doesn't mean he wasn't liable for the other three Victims at least in some capacity."

I was growing increasingly frustrated with the game; he was determined to use me to clear the man when we were already looking at two men that had successfully avoided Justice as a direct result of his actions, and yet he still wasn't clarifying anything with actual evidence.

"Mr. Mackay, your investigation isn't complete yet, but you don't have nearly as much information as you believe you do. There are those who are responsible for a great many tragedies, but this man is not one of them and you're not going to destroy his life by smearing his good name prematurely. You need to rest on this. I've been exceptionally patient with you, and I've taken the time to explain things to you far beyond what I should have to. I'm telling you; Daegan Kyl is not going to be your poster boy for your next headline."

His eyes never wavered. Did he actually believe I was in this for a *headline*?

"On whose authority do you intend to conceal what happened to her?" I asked him.

It seemed incredulous that he would presume to conceal not just the evidence regarding the two Foreign Nationals, but also that of my only other Suspect. And he was *still* my only other Suspect until he had been legitimately cleared of all wrongdoing. And then on top of all that, the Governor was intending to completely sweep this little girl's entire life under the rug as well, as if it mattered so little that she did not deserve the Justice of having her story accounted for and known to the nation.

That's not how things were done. We didn't conceal evidence, and there was no way in hell I was going to hide the horrific circumstances of her Disappearance, Captivity, and Death all to appease some politician—no matter who he was, or what he threatened me with.

"Mr. Mackay, everyone reports to someone."

He sighed, and then stood up, using one arm to set the chair off to the side. Turning back toward me, he put his hands into the pants pockets of his expensive dark-blue suit, leaving his thumbs out.

"This isn't a discussion, and it's not negotiable. Release the man today. You've taken enough of his time, and I've wasted enough of mine. If you want to ask him any further questions, do it as soon as you return; he may even tell you the truth. But release him."

He seemed very used to getting his own way.

He looked at his watch; a shiny monstrosity from a bygone era when men used such ornaments as decorative displays of their obvious financial prosperity and stellar accomplishments. Peacocking; the epitome of success. Any doubts about his mode of transportation were gone; I was certain there was an oversized, shiny gyrocopter just outside the window now. Nothing but the best for good ole Miller.

I put my hands on the ground, trying to keep steady as I pushed myself up into a standing position. My head was still a wreck, and for a moment, the room was spinning.

I must have winced because the Governor approached me, placed his hand on my arm and turned me around; I could only presume he was looking at my injury.

Odd.

"You'll be fine; but yes, probably a few stitches. You'll have to forgive my man; I don't think he's very fond of you, but let's hope he's just not that good at communicating. You have my word I'll address things with him."

I snorted. The last thing I needed was this guy fighting my battles for me. There was something extremely off-putting about how he operated. Knowing that this man had ordered the Assault but then approached me with a tender touch and a sincere, compassionate interest in my well-being was like having a lover beat you and then do your triage; it was psychologically perplexing and distorted the Victim's perception and emotions. Besides, I wanted to be in this man's debt about as much as I wanted to go have a beer with his bulldog.

He was a strange one.

He patted me on the arm and began walking toward the door on the far wall.

"Go speak with Daegan Kyl, Mr. Mackay, and then release him. You're welcome to address everything you need to regarding your other three Victims and however they came to be; you won't have any opposition from anywhere else. But there will not be the slightest stain on the man's record or reputation. He's a heavily decorated Combat Soldier with an exemplary record; I will not have you besmirching his good name any more than you already have. I'll address having his Arrest Records expunged entirely; you're welcome to inform him that there won't be a single document linking him to any of this, and his record will be just as it was before his Arrest. You can tell him you made a mistake—or you can shift the blame onto another; I really don't care. But please be so good as to let the man know that his reputation and history within our military will remain entirely untarnished."

He looked at me, taking a long moment to compose himself before continuing.

"I'm sure you understand how important one's honor is," he stated.

Of course I did. But this man was sitting on a pile of dead bodies; any connection to his 'honor' was probably buried somewhere between two Rape Victims, an Abortion, the Overdose of a Former Marine, and the Kidnapping and roughly one hundred days of Sexual Assault and Sodomy of a five-year-old little girl. His 'honor' wasn't what I had been focusing on.

The Governor looked at me.

"The man was named Seattle's Most Eligible Bachelor three years running. He's one of the most prominent self-made men in our state," he shared. He sounded as though he *admired* him.

"Oh, well then; of course, he must be Innocent. Because rich, well-known, prominent men could never be responsible for Committing Crimes or doing anything unethical. Thanks for clearing that up for me; I'll get right on it, boss."

My sarcasm was ignored, but he sighed deeply and then took a moment to measure his words and reaction by straightening his fire-engine red tie. He was the epitome of the patriotic politician, right down to the little US Flag pendant attached to his lapel.

I watched him as he stood in front of me; his face a blank slate, revealing nothing. Miller Reed was a man that seemed to control his emotions well, maintaining his stoic composure with the precision of a well-oiled machine after years of practice. Were it not for the tightly clenched jaw and his muscle twitching below his ear, I might have believed that I didn't get under his skin.

Quiet men were often the most deceptively intelligent and cruel; this man knew how to project exactly the right personality to his constituents in order to put them at ease and trust him, but I wondered which of his personalities was most often on display behind closed doors. Did the women in his life receive the light-hearted, graciously smiling, and effervescent man shaking hands and kissing babies? Or did they most often find themselves subjected to the man standing in front of me—the cold, distant, merciless man manipulating the Justice system and making thinly veiled threats?

"Complete your investigation and do what you must. You're welcome to tack Katarina's Death onto another case file for the sake of Closure, but it's probably for the best if you just orchestrate it as an unfortunate Accident. She wandered away, got lost, drowned in a creek that swept her away—you know the type. Something tragic but non-Violent and without any boogie men in the background to account for. Tell her parents whatever you need to, but keep her story quiet. There's no need to make a production out of having found her; there's been enough time since her Disappearance that no one out there is still thinking about the case. It's sad, but you know it's true. Let her remain yesterday's news; just put it to rest quietly with her parents and let it go," he continued.

He paused at the door frame and turned toward me.

"Spare them; you and I both know it's not a story that any parent ever needs to hear. It won't bring her back, and it would destroy them. They're good people; I know you realize this."

I nodded my head. It was true. I had already shared the worst imaginable news. There was nothing to be gained by telling them how much worse it had been. Despite having been to the morgue and having heard every sad infliction she had experienced, I had mentioned none of the worst details. Simply knowing that she had Passed Away had been enough, and if I were honest, agreeing to keep the circumstances of her last few months and the manner of her Death a secret was something I could live with. I would not wish any parent the knowledge or vision of what Katarina's Final Moments had been like.

He tapped the door frame a couple of times quickly; the same pattern he had done on the back of his chair earlier, and then rounded the corner.

Just before he disappeared, he ducked his head back into the room.

"Oh, and Joshua—" he said.

"Let's make sure that the rest of your team understands everything—but not a word about my involvement, understood?"

I stopped in my tracks and stared at him. Seriously?

I sighed, shaking my head slightly.

He smiled, tapped the doorframe again, and disappeared.

I leaned over and picked up my helmet and visor, feeling my head pound the instant I bent downward. It took me a minute, but I realized I had also been missing my Kev-Tek balaclava that was worn underneath my visor. My guess was that once he had detached my visor from it, he had probably just yanked it over my head and then thrown it out of the way. I began looking around the floor, and eventually found it about ten paces away from where I had fallen, over by where the bulldog had been standing.

As soon as I picked it up, I could feel the wetness where my head had bled after being struck. It had been flipped inside out when they had pulled it over my head, leaving more of my blood all over the floor. Contaminating potential Crime Scenes with my own bloody DNA was an amateur move, giving me yet another reason to be irritated by the two renegade agents.

All I wanted was to set the Cruiser to autopilot and take a nap, but I knew I was going to have to stay awake and go back to the office. With any luck, Grace O'Connor would be there, and I could turn things over to her for a while.

But my day wasn't going to end early just because I might have a little swelling on the brain, a concussion, or could be bleeding out like a stuck pig; not today. My new boss had given me a set of instructions, and a deadline.

Provided I didn't pass out on the way back to HQ and die, I was planning on speaking with Daegan Kyl once I got my head patched up.

If I was going to have to release him, I intended to make the most of the remaining time I had to get some actual answers from him before I set him loose.

THIRTY – AFTER THE FACTORY

Grace's Office

    I wore my visor back into the office and carried my Kev-Tek helmet discreetly when I returned. The black balaclava I wore underneath my helmet covered my head and neckline, and my visor concealed my face. There was no outward sign that anything was amiss, which was my goal. I had to pass through the entire front section of the building before I got back to the hive that had been assigned to us.
    We were in a secluded part of the building clear in the back, which had made it good for us in matters of privacy. But it was also the furthest away from the main entrance, and although there were other access points, I had only used the front ones because of their proximity to the elevators and underground parking. If I were to use another route, it would have been immediately suspicious and noticeable.
    The surveillance monitoring system would have also flagged it as a variation should anyone ever review the cameras, and I didn't want any unnecessary attention, even down the road. As long as I kept my visor on, my head and face would be entirely concealed, and no one would notice my damaged helmet if I just carried it. I had a spare one back at the barracks and could replace it later. Because it was still early in the afternoon, however, it was necessary for me to have one in my possession for the return trip to the office; I wouldn't have been out in the city without it. I had considered swinging by the barracks to replace the helmet and change out of my bloody clothing first, but given the head injury and pain, I decided to err on the side of caution.
    I went straight to our communal office space and was glad to see that Grace O'Connor was already there. She was sitting at her desk when I entered. She had smiled when she had first seen me, but then her smile had changed into an expression of confusion when I motioned for her to remain seated and then closed her office door behind me. There was a small window by her door, and after setting my helmet down on the loveseat on the opposite wall, I took a quick moment and pushed the button on the control box to blacken the window and lock the door as she watched.
    My helmet had cracked along the back side almost directly down the middle section at least once, but I hadn't examined either the outer helmet or the visor itself beyond that first cursory view in the factory. Once I had returned to the SPD Cruiser, the only thing I had wanted to do was close my eyes and rest, but knowing that a concussion was likely, I had opted to drive myself back to HQ without using the

autopilot feature. It had kept me awake and alert, navigating the roads, but it hadn't provided me with an opportunity to examine either my gear or my head.

I removed my visor carefully. Since the right side of my face was also hurting, I guessed I had probably been struck from behind, and probably hit my head or side of my face on the ground when I landed. I couldn't recall anything; the memory of that first five or ten minutes after regaining consciousness was blurry.

I removed my gloves and tossed them down onto the couch. Underneath the visor, I still had the Kev-Tek balaclava on. I removed it as well. Although it was considered soft body armor and the fabric moved freely, it still had a bit of additional weight from the jawline down to its base where it rested along my shoulders. It provided full ballistic protection for my entire head and neck, widening slightly as it formed around my trapezoids. The collar of my uniform fit around it snugly and required the top six inches of my uniform to be unfastened before the balaclava could be pulled free and removed.

Once I'd loosened my uniform, I set to work, lifting the neck portion of the balaclava from its position. It had a self-fastening magnet along the left side that went from the bottom of my ear down, and I eagerly unfastened it so I could then pull the entire head-covering over my head. It was heat-regulated, fire retardant, and had the same chemical weapons protection as my uniforms, and usually I could wear it comfortably with no issues—even sleep in it. But my head was still throbbing and not only was the weight of it pressing on my skull, the blood on the back of my head was sticking to both my hair and the balaclava.

All I wanted was to strip my gear off, get rid of the blood-soaked clothing, and take a hot shower. The stickiness of the drying blood had traveled all the way down the back of my head and neck. My undershirt was glued to my back where the blood had dried. I could feel my neck and shoulders aching just as much as my head did. As flippant as I had been about the injury and blood loss back at the factory, I knew I had been hit hard, and it probably needed to get professionally checked out. It was, after all, a head injury. I had lost consciousness for an unknown period and there must have been some type of metal nail or something that had made contact with my head to explain the gash I'd received.

I was facing the couch as I moved to take my balaclava off. I heard an audible gasp from her as I pulled it over my head, exposing the blood and wound. It took me a minute to remove it entirely, but I tossed it onto the couch as soon as it was free from my head. Before I could even turn around, I heard her get up from her desk and walk toward me. Her hands were reaching up to the back of my head within seconds, trying to assess the damage.

"What happened?!" she asked. I could tell by her tone she was both shocked and concerned, but I didn't really want to give her cause for worry.

I turned around, standing only a foot or so away from her.

I felt her eyes upon me, taking in whatever injuries she could see that I had not yet been able to assess. When she was done, it seemed as though our eyes met for a long moment before she looked away, seemingly a little caught off guard. I wondered if the damage was so serious it had left her queasy, but as the heat moved to her cheeks, I realized it wasn't about the injuries at all but about whatever she had been thinking. I must have looked different from what she had thought I might look like. She'd never actually seen my face before; she'd only seen my eyes without my visor occasionally. If I hadn't been hurting so much right then, I might have found it amusing; it was just one of the disadvantages of the job when one had to be in full uniform all the time.

She composed herself and focused on my injuries, moving her gaze to the right side of my face, and then moved her hands gently over each of the trouble spots she could see, telling me I was only marginally dinged up but that the wound in the back would need stitches. I asked her if I could use the mirror in her bathroom. She nodded, and I moved over to the far side of her small office and then went through the automated door once the sensor activated. Her bathroom was a replica of the one in my office and included a shower and a large mirror over the sink.

She came and stood in the doorway as I took my first good look at myself. The right side of my face was swollen and bruised, confirming that I must have landed hard when I fell. It was likely made from the impact of the visor smashing against my face as my helmet hit the floor. It would explain why it was the whole cheekbone and eye area. The weight of my head crashing against the visor as I hit the floor would have been a hard hit. Still, the helmet had probably saved my life. God only knew what damage would have been done by the bulldog had I not been wearing my protective gear.

I pushed around on my face with my fingers to see if it felt like anything was broken, but it only seemed as though it was some heavy impact bruising. Most of the pain was still coming from the back of my head.

She watched me in the mirror, waiting for me to explain myself. I looked at her through my reflection and said, "I met the Governor."

She opened her mouth as if to speak, her eyes rolling up slightly as she processed the information and considered the implications.

After assessing my head and seeing that the blood was everywhere, she instructed me to remove the jacket of my uniform. I was happy to comply, and grateful I could turn the reins over to someone else. I could feel my neck and shoulders getting sorer by the minute as I unfastened the front and then used my arms to pull it off. It wasn't usually that heavy even though it had the Kev-Tek lining, but I struggled with it as my neck and shoulders ached. She helped pull the sleeves down and then left to put it on the couch. I stood and looked at the plain white t-shirt I wore underneath, turning to see what I could. There was still wet blood seeping down through the midsection of my back, so I pulled my shirt off as well.

She had been standing in the doorway waiting for me to finish. She then took my t-shirt and set it on the couch with the rest of my stuff.

Moving into the bathroom, she retrieved a hand-mirror from a drawer, and then held it up for me so I could assess the cut myself.

After looking at it more closely, I could see it was about a four-inch vertical gash along the back of my head. Judging by the amount of blood caked on my hair and the back of my uniform, it had bled a fair amount before subsiding.

I watched her as she readied the space to help clean the blood from my body.

She motioned for me to have a seat on the closed lid of the toilet, and I obliged. She was too short to do a full assessment of me as I stood, since she couldn't see the top of my head, and I was happy to hand things over to her while I sat for a moment.

Rummaging around, she turned on the hot water, removed a few towels and washcloths from the cupboard next to the sink, and then placed one of the largest towels onto the heating rack on the wall, turning it on to warm. Then, wetting a towel with hot water, she rang it out and approached, motioning for me to turn slightly and face the mirror so she could begin cleaning up the back of my head. I watched her work in the mirror, quietly removing the dried blood from along my neck.

My head was still throbbing. I asked her if she had any medicine in her first aid kit, and then took a few migraine pills with a cup of water after she handed them to me. She turned the light down to a low setting, assuming correctly that the brightness wasn't helping my head any, and I felt myself finally able to relax a bit.

I told her about the Governor and the two ICE agents, and how the shorter one had landed the blow from behind me when I entered the room. She nodded but did not speak.

Finding the sink too far away to be useful for the job at hand, she leaned over toward the shower, and turned the water on just enough to get a steady stream falling. There was a pile of white towels of various sizes on a shelf above the toilet, and she took one down, used it, then another, discarding them on the shower floor.

The sound of the water, combined with her touch, was too soothing of a distraction, and I relaxed, the adrenalin finally abating. For just one long, blissful moment, I allowed myself to sit there with my eyes shut while she went about her work. I felt her hand rest on my shoulder from time to time as she held the wet washcloths up against the back of my head, letting the heat from the water do most of the work to remove the blood from my hair. She wrung out the hot water from a towel, placing it across my shoulders afterward. The heat was a Godsend against my aching muscles. She continued this process, and in between, wiped away the blood from my head, neck, and back.

I leaned back against her a little, using her as a prop of sorts to stay upright. I could feel her hands moving across my skin and hair, her subtle touches light and conscientiously tender. The heat from her body warmed my bare back as I leaned against her, and for just those few perfect moments as she tended to my care, as I felt her hands moving along the back of my hair, I relaxed entirely.

I opened my eyes only after she placed the warm, dry towel from the towel rack around my shoulders and shut off the water. Sadly, both were signs that I could not remain as I was and drift off to sleep, but instead must rise and carry on.

I looked at her in the mirror, still standing behind me, her hand resting on my left shoulder, and felt overwhelmed with gratitude for her presence. I'd been angry—rage-filled—earlier; full of bitterness over the situation. But I felt as though I had regrouped, as if I had a clearer perspective, as if the Attack hadn't been as personal as it had been, and now I could do what must be done to ensure it was resolved objectively, and without personal emotion involved. She had soothed my spirit.

I smiled at her, and without even caring how it may have looked, placed my hand over hers, capturing it as it rested against my chest for a moment. She smiled back at me through the mirror, and then I stood, exhaling deeply. Would that I could, instead of leaving the softness of her touch and the safety and warmth she created, I would have stayed.

I still couldn't believe the Governor of the State of Washington had sanctioned a federal agent to whack a member of Law Enforcement with a 2x4; this wasn't New York City in the 1970s, after all. And despite that certain level of arrogant animus I had picked up on during their visit here at HQ the first go round, I had actually thought most of us had some professional courtesy, and I don't know, respect for Human Life if nothing else.

There wasn't much that could be done to close the wound since my hair surrounded it. It needed some glue, or stitches, or it was going to leave an ugly, gaping scar right in the back of my head. Although I was reluctant to spend the time doing it—especially since I still had to go see Daegan Kyl—I was going to have to go down to the Urgent Care department that was within the building. It was a small facility, but it was available on a walk-in basis for the SPD Officers in the event of an emergency.

The standard protocol had changed in the years leading up to the Great Reformation; years of Peacekeepers being Assaulted and Attacked while seeking emergency treatment at local hospitals—especially in situations where the streets were being overrun with Violence during riots—had led to the demand for more protection. They faced so many risks while seeking emergency services that additional levels of protection had always been required. Emergency rooms were chaotic and frequently lacked privacy, causing further issues for both the Peacekeepers and their families. Attacks against them resulting in hospitalization required armed security to be posted in their rooms, leaving everyone little better than sitting ducks with minimal defense.

There had also been enough occasions to demonstrate that anytime groups of LEOs were gathered in one location—even within a hospital setting while offering support for a fallen Brother—they had been subjected to Random Attacks against them. During those tumultuous years leading up to the Great Reformation, too many families had been subjected to aggressive protesters and media antagonists as the Loved Ones tried to see their Wounded or Fallen Officers. The only viable solution to the constant additional strain, requirement of resources, and Targeted Assaults and provocation against them had been to establish small Urgent Care units within the Police Departments. For minor cases like this, I appreciated the convenience.

Grace O'Connor had tended to my wounds the best she could, and for that, I was grateful. The bleeding had stopped, and although the cut was long and moderately deep, I had serious misgivings about being able to go to any medical facility without it being reported back to the SPD Chief. Grace, ever the voice of reason, reminded me I had lost consciousness and still had a pounding headache. Like it or not, I needed to be looked at. She said we could work out the lie for the Chief later; for now, we should make sure I was stable. I knew I was going to have to waste the time at the Urgent Care before moving on to the SPD jail and addressing the Daegan Kyl issue.

I had no choice but to put my bloody t-shirt back on, and then follow it up with my uniform jacket and balaclava. I made my way back out into the main office area and got dressed again. She had folded my clothes neatly on the couch, which seemed an odd thing to do for some bloody pieces, but I found it mildly amusing and representative of the caregiver she seemed to be.

As I got dressed, she stood leaning against her desk, listening to me talk about my encounter with the men at the factory. I summarized it as best as I could, and then told her we'd need to discuss Daegan Kyl a bit more with Officer Stanton. I then asked her if she would contact him so he could meet us. I would return to her office after my trip to Urgent Care.

I strapped my balaclava and visor back on so I could get ready to leave. Now that I knew that the Governor already knew who I was, knew my real name and presumably everything about my personal life, it might have seemed irrelevant to conceal my face anymore. But I had no reason to know or trust that the men working within the walls of the SPD were trustworthy. He had, after all, just used two federal agents to 'deliver a message'; it stood to reason that his political influence extended to the SPD as well.

She asked me if I wanted her to go with me down to Urgent Care as I made my way to her door, but it didn't seem necessary, knowing how the healthcare process worked. As much as I would have welcomed the company, I told her it was probably not a very good use of her time. I gave her a big smile before my visor covered my face, thanked her for taking care of me, and told her I'd see her soon. I didn't expect it would take very long unless there were other LEOs already down there.

With that, I motioned I was going to leave my helmet in her office, put my gloves back on, and released the lock on her door. I was feeling much better by the time I made my way down to the Urgent Care department.

I thought about the woman that had just given me some much-needed TLC.

I couldn't be sure, and I knew I was terribly out of practice with this sort of thing, but I was almost certain that I had not only caught Grace O'Connor looking at me when I had removed my shirt, but that she had actually blushed. I thought about the way her eyes had watched me, seeing the way her cheeks had turned pink as she stared at me while we stood there.

There was something about the idea of her finding me pleasing enough to make her blush that I rather liked, and despite everything, it lightened my mood considerably.

Leveling the Playing Field

The entire ride back to the SPD HQ, I had been going over the issue with the Governor, the ICE agents, and Daegan Kyl. There was no easy fix for any of it, especially if I was going to play by the rules. But that wasn't my intention. I was going to employ the skills of my premium Research and Investigation Officer to do some deep, deep undercover work. Officer Stanton was going to find out who the two ICE agents really were. My hands might be tied for the moment, but they would be held accountable for their misdeeds by the time I was done in Seattle.

It would mark the first time I'd ever intentionally or knowingly broken my Code of Ethics and the Oath I'd taken as a member of Law Enforcement. It would also mark the first time I'd ever recruited another person and asked them to break their own Code of Ethics or professional Code of Conduct. But we were at a point where we needed to know; it was the only way I could hope to ensure the safety of my colleagues. I had to know what we were up against.

If I couldn't confirm their identities, they might as well be ghosts. I wasn't going to allow my team to be targeted, threatened, and potentially Victimized by some unknown agents who were clearly working on the side for the Governor. I had no way of knowing just how much they were abusing their professional positions and authority on behalf of the Governor's agenda, but I knew they were already crossing a myriad of ethical, professional, and moral lines—and the instant it became Violent it became personal.

I wasn't going to allow anyone else to be placed in danger or risk something happening to them, only to realize that I should have planned ahead and secured their identities when I had the chance. I had to know—and if Officer Stanton wasn't willing to do it for me, hopefully he would at least direct me how to use the government agency inter-connectivity system to access the ICE records. I wasn't even sure if it could be done, but I had to ask Stanton just to know what we could do.

They might have had the upper hand thus far—and the little bulldog might have completely blindsided me and drawn first blood. But only a pair of fools would believe that just because their boss was protected, could manipulate cases at will, and get away with making threats that they themselves were protected simply by proximity.

If there was one thing I had learned from the era before the Great Reformation, it was that the Rule of Law and Rules of Engagement were only as good as those who elected to follow them. When your enemies refused to play by the rules, follow the law, or conduct the rules of engagement with honor, everything changed for everyone.

Only fools believed one could continue along the same path, use the same strategies, and prevail once their opponent had revealed just how far they were willing to go in order to secure the win. Now that I knew what sort of war games we were playing, I would not be caught off-guard again. My life would not be so easily Sacrificed, and my nation would not be given to the wolves again without a fight.

Protecting the Team

Both Grace O'Connor and Officer Stanton still had their own personal offices within the SPD network and had been time-sharing between their own respective spaces and other professional duties. The Chief had assigned them to my case and services, but they were each still part of their own departments and had other obligations to delegate and contend with. I knew I had been fortunate with how much work they had each applied toward my investigation thus far, but it was also unfair of me to presume they would always be available when I needed them.

I wasn't entirely convinced I could trust the SPD Chief. For now, I was just going to play my cards close to my chest, assume the worst until I could prove otherwise, and volunteer only the bare minimum. I didn't owe him anything, nor was I obligated to keep him informed about my case or progress. Just because he had invited me in and provided me with a workspace didn't make me beholden or accountable to him in any manner. I didn't know how close his connection was to the Governor. I didn't have any way to know whether or not the two were in regular communication or had been working together.

Logically, it made little sense for the Chief to have called me here to investigate the four Victims if he was working in collusion to conceal the Crimes or Criminals involved. But I had heard his own words mirrored in the Governor's speech, and whether it was just because of their generic excuses, or because they were both working on the same side, I couldn't be sure. The only reasonable solution was to keep a respectable distance until I could know for certain where he stood.

For now, I was going a bit rogue, and I was going to do whatever was necessary to ensure the security of both Grace O'Connor and Officer Stanton, neither of whom deserved to be Targeted or Terrorized in any manner. I sincerely prayed for the Governor's sake—not to mention his faithful dogs—that neither of them dared approach or lay hands on my colleagues. The very idea of that short little bulldog of his even stepping into the same room as Grace O'Connor made my blood boil.

Not being able to warn them or protect them was not an option. They both needed to know how far things had escalated so they could be prepared, and I believed they each had a right to know the risks involved. Their safety was far more important than any 'warning' issued by Miller Reed, and I would no more withhold any known information about the risk of potential danger than I would want them to remain working on the case if they wished to withdraw.

The Governor might believe that being a political representative for the Citizens gave him some type of ultimate authority over the individual. He also seemed to have this misguided notion that his political title, and the professional prestige and authority he held through it, were also an insurance policy for his own protection. He believed, as so many hundreds, possibly even thousands, of politicians before him had believed, that he was untouchable and above the law. Nothing could have been further from the truth on either count.

His position did not grant him unlimited power or authority in the least; it was actually far more restrictive than permissive. To be in politics meant constant scrutiny and minimal privacy. It meant the risk of all one's dirty little secrets being revealed, and a permanent spotlight with laser focus at all times. There was no freedom of anonymity for those who spent their lives in the public arena, and the Governor had made this choice when he decided to go into politics. As a result, he was under enormous pressure to succeed. Failure, and damage to his reputation for poor decisions or scandal, mattered a great deal to him. It had to. That wasn't power; that was living in a cage—a very public, very open, very exposed cage.

The American People had done their best to eliminate such issues and games for those whom we hired to represent and lead us, but it had taken a thorough transformation and the establishment of significant changes to our government in order to secure its success. Term limits negated any risk of overuse and abuse of power. Transparency laws removed all back-alley dealings. Restrictions on lobbying, donations, and corporate interference prevented any bought-and-paid-for votes. And severe Sentencing consequences were set in place to offset any criminal activity conducted during one's time in office. If this Governor believed he held anything resembling genuine power over me or my team, he had seriously missed some key parts during his Civics and History lessons. I'd been raised to believe that the bigger they were, the harder they fell.

Even though the VAA was not technically a branch of Law Enforcement, they worked directly with Victims of Violent Crime, and there was no way to guarantee that they would not encounter dangerous persons out in the field. Firearm training had been required for field agents, just the same as if they were members of Law Enforcement or Investigators.

I was comfortable enough with my colleagues to ask that they each carry their side-arms for the time being even if they were only planning on working in the office. I wouldn't be able to monitor Grace O'Connor in particular, and I knew she would be out in the field working with the Loved Ones of our Victims routinely. Officer Stanton was probably not as high of a risk for a random Ambush, but I believed he was at greater risk because of the content of his work and what he might access. There would not be any fool-proof way to ensure their safety entirely, but at least by being well-informed and vigilant, we could reduce the risk.

My concern was that the Governor couldn't control his bulldog as much as he thought he could. Any government agent willing to go off the reservation for dirty dealings, who could Inflict Violence against another government employee with such callous disregard for the Sanctity of Human Life and the Rule of Law, could not be trusted. I doubted the Governor realized the quality of the man he had working for him, but I knew exactly what sort of man he was. No matter how this case played out, there would be a day of reckoning for the Governor and his two hired thugs. Until then, however, I needed to ensure that my team was safe, and in order to do that, we needed to be prepared and protected.

After Urgent Care

After spending an hour in the SPD Urgent Care Unit and getting cleared for work, I had gone back upstairs to speak with Officer Stanton and Grace O'Connor before I headed back over to the Incarceration Unit. Despite my headache, I had tried to put some thought into the matter of whether or not to release him, and I wanted to get their final input before making my decision. I had asked Grace O'Connor to catch Officer Stanton up on everything while I was getting my head looked at.

I now had stitches going down the backside of my head. I had been greeted with a warm homecoming upon my return to the office and my neatly sutured gift from the bulldog was met with an impressed whistle from Stanton.

Grace O'Connor did not say a word as she spun me around to check out the freshly stitched 'seam' I had running down the center of my scalp, but her slight shake of the head, pursed lips, and raised eyebrow had reminded me whole-heartedly of my mother after every single mishap and dumb move I'd ever made as a kid. She might not have claimed the glory outright, but I knew as soon as I walked in with my discharge paperwork telling me to take it easy for the next week that the game point had gone to her; the scar line in a space that required twenty-two stitches would have left an unsightly—perhaps even disturbing—vertical half-smile from the top of my scalp almost down to the neck.

Officer Stanton's clenched jaw line as he met my gaze over Grace O'Connor's head provided me with all the answers I needed before I even had to ask him for his help. Although he had responded casually with his whistle, I had no doubt that he had refrained from expressing his contempt for the man's cowardly actions because of the presence of our female companion. Most men would have probably shared the same sentiment; any with honor, of course.

As our lovely colleague fussed over my injuries, taking a moment to look over the deepening of the bruising on my eye and cheekbone, Officer Stanton leaned against the desk flipping a stylus through his fingers absent-mindedly. We stood there in silence as she finished her examination, allowing her the small favor of providing me care, since it seemed to please her to do so. I knew from the look he gave me he was on board with addressing the two ICE agents on another platform through our own means at a later date. He understood what we were up against and would not play by the rules if it put us not only at a disadvantage, but also at risk.

Grace's touch was soft, and I couldn't help but notice how tenderly and instinctively nurturing she was. But my mind was distracted by what was looming ahead of us, and I desperately wanted to speak to Daegan Kyl and resolve my lingering questions.

We settled down for a brief talk before we unanimously decided to release Daegan Kyl for the time being. The situation didn't bear weight in the legal setting; we would never have been able to justify to a Court of Law why we elected to release him, and it would never have been sanctioned. From the lawful position of authority in which we were supposedly trying to uphold Justice, we had enough to hold him and charge him already; we wouldn't have kept him for a week otherwise. But there wasn't much point in doing it if the Governor was only going to intervene on his behalf, pull strings, edit his Criminal Record, and then clear him anyhow.

Aside from that, ultimately what we needed to do was much larger than just one man—and if we ended up getting benched by those with higher political influence than we could deflect, we were going to lose everything, including any opportunities to bring Justice to our other Victims down the road. We had to be smart about things, and the only way we could do that was to choose our battles carefully. In the end, we decided we couldn't win this round, and with each of us in agreement, I made arrangements to have Daegan Kyl released.

Afterward, with each of them left to carry on their own tasks in the morning, we said our goodbyes and closed the shop for the day. I was still battling a headache; more of a dull throb and a sore neck by that point, but still enough to cause a general sense of discomfort and make me want to lie down. The evening was already upon us, and the trek back and forth from the jailhouse wasn't a walk I relished making, so I drove. As much as I needed to speak with him of many more things, the day was fading already, and I was too tired to contend with the Governor again before I had recouped entirely. I intended to offset my long day by having a quick conversation with my Primary Suspect before I cut him loose; I was not expecting it to be our last.

THIRTY-ONE – END OF DAY

A Lesser Man

I thought about the Governor the whole time as I traveled to release Daegan Kyl from his Cell. I knew that the Governor's intention was to silence me. He had displayed just enough force and power to allow me to understand what he was capable of without disabling me or restricting my ability to do my work effectively. Only by doing my job, and finalizing the case, could he ensure it was resolved to his satisfaction. He wanted to bury everything unsavory regarding the two Foreign Nationals, however necessary.

I posed a threat because I had done nothing that could have been used as leverage. Because of this, the Governor had found it necessary to go above and beyond; thus our meeting at the factory. They had done what they could to prevent me from speaking out. However, I had not had my family directly threatened, been issued Death threats, or been aggressively accosted in such a way that my Death had been imminent. Compared to what other LEOs had endured throughout history, I had been relatively safe despite their demands.

Had they truly wanted to silence me and prevent me from speaking out, my life would have been forfeit. My vehicle would have been bombed, or I would have met with some previously undiagnosed mysterious 'ailment' or 'depression' that would have resulted in my untimely 'Suicide'. Obviously, they had not considered me much of a threat at all, given that the Governor had stopped after only one Physical Assault and conversation; he clearly believed his minor efforts and threats carried enough weight that I would take them seriously enough to comply.

And that was the important part.

I had not wanted to risk everything in pursuit of one investigation; I had a Calling. I could not hope to fulfill my own important work if I were sidelined because of one failed case where I had refused to understand the stakes or allowed my ego to overwhelm me. I was not so sanctimonious that I believed it was imperative that I must be 'right'; I could set aside my own personal pride to keep my focus on what truly mattered. I was self-aware enough to realize that it was the wounded pride of a man and his masculinity that had been caught off guard in that factory by those men, and their Assault against me had been both physical and psychological.

One had physically 'bested' me by attacking me, immediately shifting the power dynamic out of my favor. The Governor had then followed this act of aggression with a non-verbal message—one that I had not failed to catch—by showing me just how easily he could have me killed without me ever seeing it coming. He had also asserted his dominance by telling me not only what he expected, but by informing me about what I was going to do, as if it were already set in stone, and he knew I would comply.

It had been a great show of force in that regard, and for a lesser man, it might have been very problematic. Lesser men—men who lacked self-discernment and self-control—would have taken his actions and words as a direct confrontation, and they would have likely responded with equal aggression and show of force; it was how little men with small minds settled their differences and vied for power and supremacy over one another. Such men, when confronted with a bold show of bravado and muscle-flexing, were prone to over-reacting; they would have immediately regained consciousness as I had, assessed the situation, and then responded with a barrage of verbal challenges and threats—usually followed by direct physical provocation, and Assaults. They would have felt cornered, outnumbered, and attacked. Feeling vulnerable and threatened would have been the very worst reactions during those precarious moments; those emotional responses would never have helped the situation, de-escalated things rather than escalated them, or helped to improve their chances of walking out of there alive.

What would have also become clear was that I was not so mild-mannered that I would passively allow myself to be overrun because of an authoritative abuse of power; I was not willing to kowtow to anyone solely out of my respect and regard for the Rule of Law and the 'chain of command'. I knew I was secure within my profession because I was beholden to no state politician or department head. Not even the Attorney General could prevent me from fulfilling the duties within my independent investigations, and they had no power over me, nor could they compel me to do anything. Additionally, I could not be reprimanded, demoted, or forced to endure other acts of retribution as payback for any of the findings within my investigations. My strength came from the People, who, as a unified Citizenry, had granted me authority. It did not come from politicians, or those who ruled with power and had a history of abusing it.

I might have lacked the docile compliance the Governor had expected, but my self-control should have made it clear that I possessed an adequate understanding of the necessity for subtle nuances within professional and social games. I knew what I was up against. I knew the power he had, and now that he had displayed such Violence and Aggression toward me, I knew how far he was willing to go to win—or at least knew that I should not expect such an enemy to draw an arbitrary line at Murder when he was obviously capable and able to Commit other Crimes and Acts of Violence. It was a fair warning, and I took it to heart.

The outcome of this case mattered to him. He was concerned about the truth of the circumstances being known. He had tipped his hand in that regard; I might not yet understand why it mattered so much, but I knew that it was something he wanted kept secret. For whatever reason, he was trying to keep one of the worst cases of Sexual Assault, Physical Abuse, and Crimes Against Humanity from becoming known to the American People.

Federal law allowed for all known criminal cases and Acts of Violence against Citizens to be transparent and known to the Citizens of These United States. The Governor did not have the authority to prevent the information from being shared with the general public; nor did he have the right or authority to prevent me from issuing a full report upon its completion. A full report that would, and should, be shared with The People.

There was something important behind his threats. He hadn't prevented me from advancing in this case because of Daegan Kyl—although he had used it as an excuse—and he hadn't cared one iota about the other three Victims that had been found. This was about Katarina, and the fact that there were two Foreign Nationals responsible for everything. Whether it was specifically about Immigration and open borders, or the future of foreign policies with the Middle East, remained to be seen. It was entirely probable that it was specifically because these Crimes Against Humanity had been done to a young girl, involved Pedophilia, and her Assailants were from an Islamic nation.

If knowledge was power, then not knowing important information was just as dangerous as knowing too much. I had to discover the reasons this man was so dedicated to concealing the truth; I had to know what was not only worth dishonoring the life and legacy of that little girl but was worth his taking such drastic measures to ensure the truth remained hidden. By refusing to let the nation know what had befallen her, he was denying the Citizens a proper chance to Grieve.

His actions dishonored every sacrifice our Ancestors had made throughout the Last Stand and the Great Reformation as they carved their way into a new age within our country. They had fought to protect our Citizens and fought for their Right to be Recognized and Honored as Victims of Violence. Their Voices were *entitled* to be heard. His actions were a flagrant disregard for the Laws of the Land and the Rights of the Victims and their Bereaved. There had to be a reason he would do so much to prevent the Life and Death of Katarina from being known.

I would not pretend to be any more of a man than I was, but in this game of cat and mouse, it seemed important that I continue to underplay my hand and maintain the position that I believed myself to be inferior to the Governor. As long as he believed he was in control, and that I was in full compliance with his commands, he would not overreact. It was imperative that I continue my investigation and gather as much evidence as I could to understand the root of the Governor's actions and motivations. I needed for the Governor to believe wholeheartedly that I had taken his warning to heart and was going to obey his orders dutifully. This was the safest way to proceed for now, and it would not cost me anything except pride if he initiated contact again and expected me to pay homage. His displays of weakness and poor conduct had given me some important leads; I just had to figure out what it all meant, and what he was so afraid of.

For the time being, I could relinquish control. I could play his game. I could allow him to believe he was still setting the rules. If he needed to believe that I was a weak man who was willing to follow orders just because I was in fear for my life, it could only work in my favor.

The Governor had made several critical errors, however, and I had full faith that in due time he would come to realize it.

For him to believe that he could manipulate any Sworn Officer into doing his bidding without any type of question or pushback was a serious mischaracterization of who and what Peacekeepers were. Such men were willing to sacrifice their lives on behalf of the Citizens they represented if they were called upon to do so. They were willing to work a job that required them to dedicate their lives to the safety and well-being of complete strangers. They had to be willing to die on their behalf, to place their lives in danger to save them from perilous situations and Violence, to leave their Loved Ones Behind, their children as orphans and their spouses as widows if need be. It was absurd of him to believe that any Peacekeeper would bend to his will out of fear for his own life.

His second mistake was in believing that I, as an Investigator, was not equally willing to lose my life in the Line of Duty just as any of my Fellow Brothers and Sisters were. My rank and title did not change the fact that I was still a Peacekeeper through and through, and I would never have put on the badge if I wasn't prepared to lose everything for the sake of my Fellow Citizen or my nation.

But perhaps his greatest mistake was simply in underestimating me as an individual. I was slow to anger, but I possessed an abundance of patience as an Investigator. I was used to investing time into building my cases and digging for the truth in order to get the Convictions I needed. I was inclined to play the long game rather than seek immediate gratification. He was a fool to believe his authority was threatening enough to win. We were just getting started.

Aside from that, underestimating a man's sense of Honor, his desire to lead a Righteous Life, and his dedication to doing the Honorable thing was a mistake that would prove costly in the end. If I was not willing to fight for Katarina, who could?

Release from Custody

Daegan Kyl was sitting in his jail Cell reading when I arrived. He slowly put the book down as I appeared in front of the clear cage that held him. I told the two guards I wanted the aisle to myself, and then we both watched silently until they disappeared through the secure door at the end of the hallway. He was the only one in the section, and I had established that I didn't want our meeting recorded when I came in.

Once we were alone, I disconnected and removed my helmet, setting it on the floor next to my feet. At this point, he could see my entire face exposed through the balaclava, and while I was certain he was wondering what I was doing, he did not speak. I gingerly removed my last layer of head covering, allowing him to not only see who I was entirely, but see the handiwork I was now sporting thanks to his guardian angel. He didn't register any emotion, but he took his time assessing my bruised face.

But that wasn't the part I was most interested in having him see; I wanted him to take a good, long look at the back side of my head. It wasn't for sympathy—it was for leverage. He needed to know who had his back, and what sort of game he was in. He needed to see what they were willing to do to one of their own, just to conceal what had happened to one little girl. He needed to see it—because if they were willing to do this to me, they were undoubtedly willing to do much worse to him, to Willow Amos, or to anyone else they considered a threat to their agenda.

I unfastened my jacket, letting it fall to the floor, and tossed my gloves down as well. And then I turned around, allowing him to see my still bloodied white t-shirt and my stitched-up scalp. When I turned back toward him again, he crossed his arms across his chest and stood in a wide-legged pose.

"Looks like someone got the drop on you," he said. His lips curled in disdain; I knew he wouldn't be impressed.

"Apparently you've got friends in higher places than you've mentioned," I responded.

He raised his eyebrows and looked me in the eye.

"Not my style, bud, sorry."

He rubbed his hand across his jaw, propping his elbow in his other hand and casually assessing the situation in his mind.

"It was the Governor, actually," I replied. "Apparently he's a big fan of yours; I guess you're a big shot bachelor out there?"

He nodded his head slowly, trying to think things through.

I smirked.

"He had a couple of fellas from ICE standing guard. I went to the factory. I didn't even know they were there."

I reached up and rubbed my forehead for a minute; the hallway lights were brutally bright, and I was ready for a hot shower and sleep.

"He hit me with a 2x4 from behind, I think. I hit my face on the way down," I explained.

"I don't know how long I was out, but when I came to, the Governor was there, singing your praises and telling me to release you. So here I am."

He cocked his head to the right and squinted his eyes a bit, considering my words.

"So, you take orders from the Governor?" he asked. His voice was skeptical.

"No, I don't. But apparently, he's going to make sure that your good name isn't besmirched at all, and I have a case to solve. I'm not sure what's going on yet—and you haven't really been very helpful, so there's not much point in arguing, is there?"

I leaned down and picked up my gloves and began redressing. The pressure was worse when I leaned forward, and I winced.

"Well, I appreciate your kindness, but I think I'll pass," he stated.

I paused for a second as I pulled my glove on, processing his words, before I let out a little laugh and shook my head. I reached down for my jacket and started with my right arm first, speaking to him as I dressed.

"Look, Mr. Kyl. I don't know what you have going on—I haven't gotten it all figured out yet. But the Governor has already put up some roadblocks regarding the two Foreign Nationals, and for whatever reason, now he's focused on making sure that you're off-limits. I don't know exactly why that is right now, and I'm honestly not even sure if *you* do—" I said, looking at him. My tone was measured, but impatient and tired, as was I.

"He says you're Innocent—that you're not responsible for anything to do with anything related to Katarina and that I was done with my investigation as far as you or they are concerned."

I reached down for my balaclava and visor, putting them on slowly and carefully as I moved the fabric around my stitches.

"I have four Victims out there that you and I both know you buried. I don't know why—and I don't know who for. But I know you were there—I know you're linked to both Willow Amos and the Foreign Nationals, and I know you're protecting all of them; I just don't know why yet.

"But I don't have the time to deal with whatever you have going on with this man—a man who has violated his Oath of Office. I can promise that he'll get his due, and so will his little guard dogs. But that's not happening today. Because for now, he wins—and that means *you* win.

"So take it up with him; do whatever you want. I'm not going to risk my entire investigation just to keep you locked up for now—and as much as he made it clear to me he meant what he said, I'm also not going to risk endangering my team just to win the battle today."

I met his gaze and hoped my point was driven home.

"I've issued your release. I can't do anything about Willow Amos at this point. Your friend didn't seem to care too much about her, so she's staying here. I get you intend to protect her, but maybe you can do more out there than inside. At any rate, the Governor said to cut you loose, so I am. He wanted me to make sure you knew that all records of your Arrest and involvement will be erased."

I gave him a brief salute with two fingers on my right hand and prepared to close my visor before leaving.

He was almost snarling at me, and I understood exactly why. Neither of us was happy with the Governor's involvement. He wasn't playing with honor—and for men such as us, we didn't mind an uphill battle—but for God's sake, it must be done with honor.

And yet here we had a game-changer—a puppet master controlling our lives from beyond, pulling our strings with no regard for what we were trying to do. Each of us had our own purpose for being here, and a code by which we lived, and the Governor's interference was decidedly contrary to how we had been handling things. I could appreciate Daegan Kyl's position—even his anger.

"They'll be back as soon as I leave to get you out-processed and then you'll be free to go."

He stood there with his usual stoic expression, but his jaw was tightly clenched, and his nostrils flared.

I watched him as he closed his eyes for a moment, let out a sigh, and slowly shook his head. It was an odd response after informing someone that they were being cleared of all charges and released. Even if what the Governor had said was true, Daegan Kyl still held some degree of responsibility for things, and his release was not in the best interest of Justice. But at that moment I was tired, and it was time to throw in the towel.

"Wait," he said.

"The answers are in the factory. 1300. Tomorrow."

I looked at him for a moment, weighing my options, and then gave a quick nod of consent before closing my visor.

I felt my anger and frustration subsiding a bit as I walked back down the hall and then headed home. I hadn't genuinely considered Daegan Kyl to be a cold-blooded Murderer, but he had been in bed with some very shady people for quite some time and none of it made any sense. All I had needed in order to clear his name or prove his guilt had been more information—information that he could have shared with me, and yet he had withheld. I knew he was protecting Willow Amos, and I understood why. But taking the fall for her without even fully understanding what had motivated her to protect a Murderer hadn't redeemed him in my eyes. It had made him another one of her pawns, and I didn't understand why he couldn't see that. Aside from that, none of it cleared him for his role in the Abduction, Captivity, and Death of Katarina, nor did it explain why he had buried each of the Victims. He still had a lot to account for before I would consider him 'Innocent' of the events for which he was deeply immersed.

It hadn't been wrong to Arrest him; it was wrong for him to be released.

But I would meet with him tomorrow at the factory, hear what he had to say, and go from there.

And when this was all said and done, I was going to finish my dealings with the Governor and his two lapdogs.

For tonight, mercifully, I was finally going to be able to remove all my gear and blood-soaked clothes, take a hot shower, eat something, and sleep. Tomorrow would be here soon enough.

Back at the Barracks

It had been a long day, and by the time I arrived back at the barracks, it was all I could do to make my way from the underground parking garage and up the elevator. I was starving, but I knew it would take at least a half an hour for a hot meal to arrive from the cafeteria. It was already after eight. A hot shower and meal would put me past nine; normally reasonable, but I was exhausted, and my body felt it needed to rest and recharge more than it needed refueling.

It seemed, however, by some divine mercy that I would be given just the slightest of reprieves. As soon as I entered the small apartment, the delicious aroma of grilling steak filled my nostrils as the sweet sound of sizzling left me salivating. I rounded the corner of the entry, dropping my broken helmet on the hall bench. At that moment it wouldn't have mattered if it had been the Governor himself grilling dinner for me as my last meal; I would have gladly surrendered, provided he fed me first.

It was not the Governor, however—it was Grace O'Connor. She was standing in the small kitchen, removing baked potatoes from the oven, and placing them on a tray.

I peeled off my balaclava and dropped it on the bench next to my visor and helmet. As tired as I was, it overwhelmed me with gratitude to see her. I didn't know by what sorcery she had arrived within my borrowed dwelling unit, but I was exceedingly grateful to see her there.

She smiled at me, blushing sweetly.

"I just thought you could use a little help tonight," she said.

In her mind, she might have seemed too forward—but clearly not enough to permit her from taking charge, and for that, I was feeling very blessed.

"Stanton helped me," she explained.

I smiled. I was exhausted, but I was truly, genuinely glad to see her there.

She nodded her head toward the small dining table, motioning for me to go seat myself. I did, gladly, noting that she had put on the adjustable light to a very dim setting, and had been using only the lowest console lighting beneath the kitchen cabinetry to cook as well. She had been thinking about my headache, I realized.

Still, despite it not being mood lighting, it made for a much more intimate atmosphere, and it was hard not to stare at her as she brought a plateful of hot food to me.

The table had been set with a side salad, French bread, water, and even some butter and sour cream for my baked potato. She had planned it out well and had obviously had time to prepare everything while I had gone over to release Daegan Kyl.

My plate had a fat, juicy steak grilled to perfection, a side of steaming corn and an oversized baker which she had split and mashed into consumable pieces. I couldn't help but smile as she placed it in front of me, and for the first time in many hours, I had completely stopped thinking about how much my head was throbbing. I hadn't cooked since arriving, having only had the cafeteria send up meals. Although they were generally hot and decently appetizing, it was nowhere near comparable to the feast currently in front of me.

    She had returned from the kitchen a second time with a chilled mug and a bottled beer. I was feeling very blessed.

Sleep

    I ate my fill, talking quietly with Grace O'Connor of things we had yet to unravel. When I was done, she instructed me to go shower and then sleep. Motioning to the paperwork given to me by the Urgent Care medical staff, she reminded me I had been instructed to take things easy for two full weeks and to have someone monitor my behavior for the first twenty-four hours.

    I was more than happy to turn things over to her capable hands, and with a full belly I lumbered off to take a blissfully hot shower before changing into a fresh white t-shirt and drawstring plaid pajama bottoms. I carefully dried my short hair off with a towel after having washed it free of the dried blood and then went back out into the living room where she was sitting.

    She motioned for me to come over to her so she could take a last look at my head, and I obliged, opting to sit on the floor before her so she could see the backside from an overhead view. I sat in front of her, feeling the warmth from her legs on either side of me as she slid her hands through my hair, checking the stitches to make sure I didn't disrupt anything in the shower. The couch was situated in such a manner that it was possible to see out the sliding glass door that led to the small balcony, and I could see the lights from the city glowing in the distance. But it was seeing our reflections in the glass that caught my eye, and I found myself watching her image. I was sitting below her, between her thighs, and as I watched her reflection, I longed to turn around, climb to my knees in front of her so I was on her level, and kiss her.

    Before I could explore this new line of imagery, she patted me on the shoulders, dismissing me and interrupting my ill-timed thoughts, and once again I was reminded of how exhausted I was. I climbed to my feet, stretched, and looked at the pile of resources she'd gathered to help her pass the night.

    She had found some extra blankets and a pillow from one of the closets and had placed them at one end of the couch. The couch, being a very generic, austere fixture, was designed to endure a high turn-over of short-term—typically male—Officers and Investigators. It didn't seem as though she were in for a very comfortable night.

    I asked her if she'd rather have my bed, but she declined, insisting that I needed to get quality sleep and she was intending on keeping an eye on me anyhow.

    She motioned toward her travel bag and the files she had been reviewing while I had showered and told me she would be fine. I looked once more toward the cold, uncomfortable couch with the almost pleather covering and then remembered an extra comforter I had noticed in the bedroom closet.

    I motioned for her to follow me, and then I led her back into the only bedroom of the unit where we ransacked the walk-in closet together. We stood side by side, previewing the extra storage items that the housekeeping department kept on hand for their guests. Together, we grabbed several more pillows and then found the extra thick comforter I had recalled seeing when I had placed my extra uniforms there weeks earlier.

As with most of the things in the one-bedroom apartment, the colors were dark and plain; grey on one side and black on the other, matching the black bedding. Alongside the light-grey paint on the walls and my black uniforms, the entire unit was masculine through and through. She was a stark contrast to the cold, dull space with her red hair and pale skin. Even her clothing—some kind of soft, pink fabric designed for cozy nights indoors—was strangely out of place against the hyper-masculine room.

I followed her back out into the living room as she carried two large pillows, listening to her as she laughed about the unnecessary work I was doing.

We put the extra comforter down on the couch for a few more layers of distance between the hard pleather couch fabric and the blankets she would sleep under, making a decent-enough bed for at least a little sleep. She thanked me for my help, noted that it was already after ten—although I had to admit I had barely noticed, not even remembering how tired I had been earlier—and then she chased me off to my own bed.

I went—almost reluctantly—as she told me she would check on me and then listened to her instructions about trying to sleep on my side or stomach as the paperwork had outlined. As much as I had been slow to get there, as soon as I climbed in between the sheets, I felt my body melt into a state of relaxation.

She stood near the doorway, turning the hall light down until it was almost off. I motioned for her to come closer and sit by me on the edge of the bed. After she had taken a seat on top of the covers alongside my chest, I reached out my hand, taking hers and just holding it for a moment.

Yawning, I thanked her; nothing could quite tell her how grateful I was, but as I met her gaze, I hoped she understood. I knew she was a caregiver; most within the VAA were. But I was forever in her debt—as well as Officer Stanton's—for stepping in tonight and doing such a thoughtful thing for me. We hadn't worked together for long, and it was undoubtedly unorthodox for most professionals to do so much, even for those whom they considered to be part of their own team.

Securing access to my dwelling unit wouldn't have required a great deal of work for Stanton, but it would have required some time, so I was grateful the two of them had made the effort. Grace had mentioned that she had left Officer Stanton to it while she had gone to the store to pick up the items through the drive-through and that he had completed the access authorization process by the time she had arrived.

I found my eyes growing heavy and closed them for a second, still feeling her hand resting on my own. The last thing I remembered was the delicate touch of a woman's hand on the top of my head as her fingers ran gently through my hair.

THIRTY-TWO – WAKING AFTER THE FACTORY

Waking After the Factory Visit

    The room was dark when I awoke, and it took a moment to realize there was daylight poking through the slits in the blinds. I had never changed the setting of the tint on the windows since my arrival; I hadn't taken any days off yet and hadn't ever slept later than seven. Today, however, it seemed much later than that, and I wondered how I had managed to sleep so late despite having a normally predisposed tendency to be an early riser.

    I sat upright facing away from the window in the small, drab bedroom, and stared at the digital clock next to the door frame leading to the main living area. Ten thirty-seven. I felt my eyebrows raise involuntarily and yawned. All things considered, I felt much better. My head wasn't pounding from the headache that had plagued me all evening, the back of my head wasn't causing any discomfort, and even my body seemed to be well-rested and nourished thanks to the hearty meal I had consumed directly before falling asleep. My body had obviously rejected the idea of waking as early as usual, and since I had never needed to set an alarm, there hadn't been one to wake me before I was ready to rise.

    I rubbed my jawline, feeling the roughness of my unshaven face, and debated whether or not it was worth the effort. Most of the time, I kept myself clean-shaven because it wasn't as abrasive against the headgear I was almost always wearing. This was especially true during the summer months when I was a lot less inclined to use the cooling system within my uniform unless it was over eighty; I usually weathered the heat well enough, but when it got too hot, my face would get itchy with a beard. Today, for now, I preferred to save myself time and work. I didn't need a shower since I'd had one directly before bed, so it seemed clear I was getting a free pass for the day all around. The message was to take things easy, and that's what I intended to do; there wasn't anything too pressing other than my intention to meet Daegan Kyl at the factory at 1300.

    I listened for a second to see if I could hear Grace out in the other room but heard nothing. Standing slowly, I motioned for the monitor to activate and then turned it to one of the local Seattle news channels for the day's headlines, and then readied myself for the day. She had tidied up the living room, folded up her bedding, cleaned up the kitchen, and even put away all the dishes from the night before. Looking around, aside from the comforter and pillows that needed to be returned to my bedroom closet, the abysmal apartment looked exactly as it had before her arrival; bland, sterile, and as grey as Seattle most of the year. Somehow, though, even as it had only returned to exactly as it was before, it seemed just a tad quieter than I'd previously noticed.

I waited for a cup of coffee to percolate and read the note left for me on the wall monitor. She had handwritten it rather than typed it, and for some reason, it warmed my heart to see something personalized. I was finding myself drawn to her a bit more than I had anticipated and was a little embarrassed about how pleased I had been to find her here the night before. It wasn't just that she was pretty, or even that she was kind and obviously a very bright woman; I couldn't quite identify what it was about her I was so smitten by, but if I were honest, I just had to acknowledge that I was.

I enjoyed working with her—with both of them. There were quite a few things about my time with her that made me appreciate her more than I usually valued my VAA's. I liked knowing that she was out there, that she got what we were doing and that she wasn't afraid of the trouble we were looking at. I appreciated that she was always on point, that she always brought her 'A' game. I liked the fact that she seemed taken with me, as quiet and seemingly shy as she was at times. I felt we were well-matched in temperament, and that we both seemed to be bad at expressing ourselves despite our obvious professionalism; we were equal doses of intellectual, career-oriented, and socially awkward. And it had warmed me to my core that she had blushed when I had arrived home last night, bashful and second-guessing her decision. But, oh, how I adored that she had still been assertive enough to come here.

With all that swirling around in my head, I found myself in a strangely good mood, and after eating some breakfast and taking the time to enjoy a cup of coffee, I eventually headed out so I could make my way down the I-5 corridor to get to the factory by 1300. Her note had been brief. She had stayed until morning and touched base with Stanton; they weren't going to expect me to check in until after I had met up with Daegan Kyl. She said that I seemed to have slept well, and that Stanton had told her he was going to track both the SPD Cruiser and my uniform just in case anything else happened.

It was deceptively cold once I hit the underground parking garage; I had expected it to be a cool autumn day in a region known for its damp climate, but it was cold enough I contemplated going back inside for my overcoat. I wasn't a big fan of wearing it while in uniform because of its weight and the additional strains on my maneuverability, so I measured its advantages as I walked and found it not worth the effort.

I left the underground garage and passed the security checkpoint. As I entered the city traffic, there was a low-level fog present. It was severe enough to hinder driving, resulting in everyone shuffling along below the required speed limits. There were not many autopiloted vehicles that were capable of speeding since the sensors prohibited them as a default setting. Not that it mattered; most people no longer drove their own vehicles enough to have a natural connection to the road anymore, happily handing over yet another task for the machines to do on their behalf. As a result, the traffic carried through the downtown area at a snail's pace while I got held up by every red light, pedestrian, and loading zone imaginable before finally accessing a south-bound freeway entrance.

Thoughts on the Governor

As I made my way to the factory to meet with Daegan Kyl, I found my thoughts wandering back to the lingering images of the pretty girl from the night before. I had been granted a brief reprieve, but I knew there was much to be done and I still had far more questions than answers. Almost entirely uncharacteristically of myself, I found it difficult to stop my mind from replaying certain moments; my colleague was a distraction I'd never before encountered through work, and although I wasn't opposed to where my thoughts naturally went, I knew that it could not have been at a worse time. I consciously had to push thoughts of her aside and redirect my brain to something more constructive so my travel time was not wasted. It was, after looking out the window and backward into my mind's eye, a challenge which I sadly accepted and knew to be necessary.

Begrudgingly, I chose to consider all the possible explanations I could to try and gain some type of understanding as to why the Governor had chosen to take the path that he had regarding Katarina and Daegan Kyl. He could have remained entirely on the sidelines, but instead he chose to interfere, thereby impeding my progress from the very first point of contact we foolishly established with him. I reflected on my own decision to consult first with the Chief and then with the Governor after I took the Chief's advice. It was easy to recognize that I could have avoided many of these issues had I just pursued the case on my own and not involved anyone—including the Chief. In that respect, I had brought about my own difficulties. Nonetheless, I had reached out to the Chief, and had followed his recommendation to run it up the chain of command.

The Governor's approach had been appropriate, initially, even if I disagreed. Logically, it made sense to tread with caution; even I had understood the significance of the Suspects and how it could play out once their identities became known. But it was the wide, pendulous swing in the Governor's actions after his first contact that was worth noting. His first efforts were to present himself as a moderate, law-abiding leader, grateful to have been apprised of the situation and able to contribute his own assessment. He had been nothing more than a concerned government leader making a recommendation regarding how to proceed with the case so it would inflict minimal damage and harm to the family involved and to our local Citizenry. He had played above the belt and by the rules; his 'recommendation' was soundly outlined and justified so succinctly, and with such deft professionalism, that it was almost forgivable that he had issued a directive rather than just supplied his 'esteemed opinion'.

But it did not take long before his gloves had come off and I was introduced to the more ruthless side of the man, and it was worth taking some time to analyze why that came to be. What had been so provocative that he had reacted with such a powerful display of force in such a brief burst of time? Was it merely that I had persisted? Was there something in the manner in which the Chief had responded to him after receiving orders not to proceed any further that he had interpreted as threatening? Had he somehow ascertained that I had a professional history of 'always getting my man' and he, therefore, felt the need to provide 'oversight' to my investigation as an assurance against my success? What, precisely, was it that had resulted in the escalation from a politely worded Cease and Desist to an on-site visit by his two henchmen?

I had to assume it was not about me, my professional experience or expertise on the matter, and nor would it be related to my newly created team. I was trained to look at the evidence presented and to explore every consideration with a critical mind and objectivity, but there was nothing to indicate that the Governor's actions were anything personal.

For too many years, our states had been paid for by the most powerful among the elite and the top echelons of society. The highest bidder with the most influential power and ability to either grant favors or destroy futures had been steering both policy and policymakers for generations. After the Last Stand and throughout the years of the Great Reformation, countless laws and policies had been implemented, revised, and abolished all with the Will of the People in mind. No government entity, elected official, or representative would be granted absolute power over any agency whose primary purpose was national security, public safety, and the prevention of Criminal activity or the prevention of Crimes Against Humanity. Government oversight was an integral part of every agency and branch of government, but anything related to the well-being of the People of These United States was a matter of public record and required absolute transparency. For these reasons, any direct effort made by government officials within the State of Washington that might move to impair, impede, or restrict my ability to carry out my investigation was emphatically against federal laws.

No matter how this man had dressed up his initial 'recommendation' to drop my investigation or to circumvent any developments thereafter, his actions were in defiance with my authority as an Independent Investigator. I was responsible for solving the mysteries behind four Crimes Against Humanity; there was no higher authority in the nation than the People of These United States, and I was accountable only to them. The Citizens could call into question any federal mandate of suppression and would require accountability; for a Governor to believe that he had the authority or power to interfere with my investigation—let alone prohibit it—was extremely arrogant and foolish. Despite this, he had done precisely that, and had believed he had the might and muscle to follow through. He had done all of this from his very first response and had been defiantly oppositional to what he knew to be the Laws of the Land. His actions since that point had only become progressively more aggressive and Criminal, making it appallingly clear that he unequivocally believed himself to be Above the Law.

I didn't have any difficulty understanding this or even believing it. There were many out there in positions of authority who incessantly stood on the threshold of Abuse of Power and walked the line routinely. It was, despite all that our nation had gone through in the last century, still a persistent problem that many were aware of, but had great difficulty openly acknowledging because of how it could negatively impact another man's reputation and honor. Unfortunately, however, the only thing this did was exacerbate the issue as the national standards for ethical and moral behavior gradually began to decline among our political leaders yet again. The Governor was not alone in his ambition, desire for power, or even in how emboldened his behavior was. I feared it was more widespread than people realized, and it deeply troubled me just how far he and others like him might be willing to go just to impose their will upon the People they were elected to represent.

But those matters were a different discussion for a different day. For now, the only aspect I needed to focus on was who the Governor was, and how much I needed to be concerned about his behavior and actions so I could assess the level of risk involved to myself and my team. In order to know how to proceed with my dealings with him and best determine how to address our interactions, I needed to understand exactly who the man was, what his motivations and possible gains could be regarding this case, and exactly how dangerous he could be based on what his motivations were.

It was frequently said that the greatest man to fear was the one with nothing left to lose, but I disagreed. I had always found that the most unpredictable, ruthless, and unexpectedly Violent among us were the ones who had built empires and were willing to do anything necessary to ensure their position at the top remained uncompromised. The most reckless, dangerous man in the room was the one with the most to lose and the power to conceal his Crimes. That made the Governor of the State of Washington a very formidable enemy indeed. The fact that he was supposed to be representative of the People, and someone that Investigators and Law Enforcement should have been able to call upon for assistance, made his corruption even more problematic and concerning.

Perhaps, in the most gracious of possibilities, he could have done it with some sense of altruism. It was a stretch; it would have meant that he was selflessly placing the needs of the nation above his own, and it was difficult not to believe that his actions were not done in an effort to benefit politicians more than the common man. But perhaps in some skewed sense of logic, the man believed that Threats and Violence were acceptable terms if it ultimately served the best interests of the 'Greater Good', and perhaps he genuinely believed that lying to the People was what was best for them.

He may have done it to spare our Citizenry what he considered to be an egregious attack against our society by the two Foreign Nationals; the Crimes they committed against one of our most Innocent and Vulnerable was beyond anything I had ever investigated. The nation would erupt in demands for Justice and full retribution without exception. As thin of a motive as it was, any politician would know that this case would cause the Citizens of this country to explode once the news was made public. By the time the Medical Examiner released the Postmortem Examination Report that outlined the exact Harm that had been done to her frail little body, the entire nation would be on fire. Any Governor would be guarded and cautious in how they addressed such a case, especially if the Alleged Offenders were not brought to Justice or accounted for.

Perhaps his sole motive had been to conceal the depravity of the nature of their Crimes, thereby preventing the spread of concern over the possibility that such Crimes were occurring within the State of Washington. It was entirely possible—plausible even—that he had acted in such a manner in an effort to prevent fearmongering and mob-vengeance from forming. Such action was morally wrong in the sense that he had broken laws through his effort to conceal Crimes and Criminality from his Constituents, but there were probably many among his kind who lived in fear of how their state was viewed on the national level, and sadly, probably many politicians who lived unscrupulous double-lives and committed many travesties against the American People, just as there always had been.

Another possibility—which was undoubtedly the most likely and realistic—was that he had done everything he could as a means of protecting himself. The People held politicians, and expected them to be held, fully accountable for their actions. In an age of transparency and accountability, the American People were not only well-informed and involved regarding the state statistics for Crime and Violence, they were dedicated to monitoring the state of the nation and ensuring that our Citizens were safe and accounted for.

A well-informed Citizenry was not likely to let the devious or morally corrupt dealings being done by an immoral politician slide for very long once his misdeeds became known. He was just as likely to be brought down through the next election cycle for failing to keep the Crime and Violence rates low as he would have been if exposed for any type of corruption. His record for ensuring public safety for the American People mattered above all else when it came time for re-election. An ambitious man would go to great lengths to ensure that those numbers reflected a successful legacy. He would not survive a re-election without it, and any further political ambition would have been eradicated. It was extremely likely that his actions had been done in some manner to create a pathway toward his future political aspirations, although it was a dangerous gamble should his misconduct ever be brought to light.

The slightest misstep in his plan, even the most questionable besmirchment of his name or reputation, could result in the end of his political career. It was a dangerous precedent he was setting, attempting to control events behind the curtains, hiding Violent activities and Predators from the People whom he had been entrusted to represent. Were his scheming and actions to be discovered—whether by Law Enforcement, investigative journalists, or anyone within the general public, he would have become the spotlight of an intense investigation and faced significant Criminal charges.

There was another possibility, and it rang true if one took the nature of a man into account. If he were a truly ambitious politician, time would be at the forefront of his mind, and would play a key role in his political aspirations. There were term limits imposed on virtually every elected position. Men either went up, or out, in the political arena. If the Governor was willing to violate the Rule of Law in order to cover up for Crimes and heinous Acts of Violence, he may be far more driven than imagined, and it would not be wise to underestimate him—now, or in the future.

For an ambitious politician, being a Governor was only a stepping-stone. If he had intentions to continue to work within American politics, his Governorship was only a brief layover on his way up the ladder—but climbing such a ladder was fiercely competitive. A man would do well to make a name for himself and ensure his passage into the next level. Perhaps he was working on ways to bring Washington State into more power, or to put the Greater Seattle Area on the map as one of the most relevant and authoritative regions in the nation. The West Coast was a vital component to the import/export industry, among other things, and if there was a Governor driven to conduct backroom dealings for nefarious reasons, there was no telling what lengths he would go to in order to advance his agendas. Concealing some Criminal activity—especially if it meant securing decent relations with the Middle East or helping to advance new Immigration policies for his own regional political aspirations—could be a small price to pay.

No matter how it worked out with the Governor, I was not going to let it rest until there was a full and complete reckoning over his actions. The American People, Katarina, and her parents, deserved nothing less.

I didn't care what his motivations were at the end of the day. He was corrupt. He was a shady, Violent man who had exploited our system, crossed countless lines, and failed to protect the American People from two known Predators. There would be accountability for that, someday, somehow. I would make sure of it.

THIRTY-THREE – IN THE BASEMENT

A Conversation at the Factory: 1300

At last I arrived at the factory, the heavy traffic only allowing me to arrive minutes before 1300. I parked the SPD Cruiser alongside an unfamiliar vehicle that I presumed belonged to Daegan Kyl. It was a newer model, very sleek and powerful; exactly the type of vehicle that one would have expected an eligible, wealthy bachelor to have. It still seemed peculiar to me that a man such as he should have found himself entangled in the mess he was in, and as I looked at the sharp lines of the gorgeous racer as I walked past it, I wondered how any man could forfeit his entire self-made life solely to protect someone whom he by all rights had no legal obligation to protect.

His accomplishments, in the eyes of the world, had made him into something of a dark horse; a true testament to the power of the American Dream for all those who worked diligently to create it. For many, his elevation in station was a marker of his tenacity and hard work. It made him far more worthy of both respect and admiration than those who inherited wealth rather than forging their own way toward its creation. America had always embraced the soul of the entrepreneur. They would find the circumstances of today regarding Daegan Kyl to be perplexing—as did I.

Still, I understood honor, and I understood promises.

But at what point could Daegan Kyl draw a line regarding the pledge he had made to his friend and fellow Soldier?

Surely William Amos could not have expected his friend and military brother to have continued to care for his sister after she had reached adulthood; at least not once she had chosen to make her way down such a dark road. No friendship should ever result in one having to sacrifice one's own reputation, honor, integrity, or legal standing. That wasn't friendship, and I had a difficult time imagining that William Amos would have expected Daegan Kyl to have carried it along as far as he had. At some point, Daegan Kyl had lost his clarity and allowed his sense of camaraderie and brotherhood to dominate instead of common sense. Willow Amos herself should have put an end to Daegan Kyl's involvement in her life. That she hadn't only spoke to just how selfish she was.

I looked up at the wall of windows on the 3rd floor, recalling my last visit within. It was still fresh enough to serve as a reminder that my own life could have been ended abruptly, and that before it had happened, I had been caught completely unaware. We had a sensor within our visors that could detect movement through infrared heat signals, but at the time, I had not activated the program because I had made the erroneous miscalculation that I had been on my own within the building. I did not wish to repeat my mistake again, nor did I want to walk into a new trap. Prudence dictated that I do everything within my power to behave responsibly, so I activated the highest levels of protection available within my uniform. If I were struck again, it would send a signal back to the HQ for reinforcements, supplying them with my coordinates. I also found it reassuring to know that Stanton was actively tracking my movement in real time.

I walked to the end of the building, intending to use the same entrance I had on my previous visit. As I rounded the corner, I was met with Daegan Kyl leaning against the wall, patiently waiting for me. He gave me a bit of a weak smile, extended his right hand, and we shook briefly.

He looked none the worse for wear after a week in the SPD jailhouse, but then it was hardly common for anyone to complain of mistreatment while incarcerated in a jail Cell in the greatest nation on earth. Our worst Cells used for housing the most vile and Evil among us were still far better than most daily living conditions around the world; it was all perspective. Entitlement fed dissatisfaction and complaints; those who had genuinely known suffering knew what it meant to do without, and knew what deplorable conditions truly were. For many, an American jail Cell would be a haven: a private space with temperature control, regular meals, a warm bed, and even healthcare and dental. A man such as Daegan Kyl, having spent years in the military and undergone top secret deployments, would have undoubtedly encountered many rough living situations; his time at the SPD was probably mild by comparison, with his greatest threat being boredom.

I'd only ever seen him in formal evening wear and the orange jail uniform, so it seemed strange to see him before me wearing contemporary fashionable clothing, much like the rest of America and those in Western nations. He was not dressed very well to go traipsing about in the factory among the dirt, dust, cobwebs, and muck, but he would survive.

So, I paid no mind to his buttoned-up vest, wide-legged trousers, bulky overcoat, and the newsboy cap that was such high fashion these days. As with most men not in uniform who followed the trends, he was more reminiscent of the early 20th century English aristocracy than a man recently incarcerated and staring down the barrel of the Death Penalty. Compared to my own timeless Law Enforcement uniform, he appeared very sophisticated and put-together.

The day was cool, even for late autumn in Seattle. As was to be expected, it was barely fifty degrees, and the greyness of the day left little by way of natural daylight once we were inside. I knew we would be going to the basement and there wouldn't be any natural light anyhow, but I didn't appreciate how much light we lost just by stepping through the doorway as we started down the long hallway.

Daegan Kyl pulled a small flashlight from the inside pocket of his overcoat and turned it on. I followed suit by turning on the two LED flashlights on my chest plate, and then the one on my visor as well. After glancing over and giving a slight nod of approval over the additional lighting, he began to walk slowly through the debris at our feet, keeping his flashlight focused on the walkway before us. Occasionally, we would hear the familiar scurrying of the rats, but no other noise could be heard.

"Are you going to record?" he asked.

It was the first time either of us had spoken.

I shook my head. It didn't matter; as far as his involvement went, the case was closed.

"There's nothing you could say that would change the dynamics of the case at this point—unless you'd prefer it?" I looked at him, waiting for his reply.

He shook his head.

"No, I'm just here for your understanding of the situation, that's all. It's the least I can do."

I nodded slowly, unsure what he was driving at. By all accounts, he was going to walk away a free man. The truth would have nothing to do with it. He was going to be immune from consequence because of his connections and identity. Whatever the 'truth' was had no meaning or relevance at all.

That was the privilege of the elite within our society, apparently; two sets of tax laws, ethical principles, and criminal prosecution from an adjustable Rule of Law—all based on class, social status, income bracket, and connections. Those in the ruling class had protected him even though he had not desired it nor expected it; they protected those whom they considered to be their own even when it was unrequested and unwanted. It wasn't the version of my country I wished for, nor was it that way for most; but clearly there were those among us who believed this was the way it ought to be since it seemed to have always been, and no one had ever put an end to it.

He continued. His deep voice was a sharp contrast to the silence surrounding us, despite his attempt to speak softly.

"I met the two men that owned this building during the year after I had first left the military, which I'm sure you probably know. I didn't really know what I was going to do with my future; I didn't have much by way of skill or education beyond what I had picked up along the way. My file probably shared the specifics, so I'll spare you. But I enlisted just as soon as I was legally able. I couldn't wait to start my new life and career. I mean, I was amped for it; it was exactly what I had been born to do.

"I don't know how much my file shares, so please just let me know if anything gets redundant for you," he continued.

I remained silent, nodded my acknowledgment, and allowed for him to continue when he was ready.

"My records may not reflect who I am adequately, but it's important, I think—at least to me—that we each come to terms with our own history in order to best understand how we each can serve to make our own mark on the world in our own time. If one is to believe in The Watchers On The Wall and all they stood for, then we must also believe that who we are as unique individuals matters a great deal. Do you agree?"

He glanced over at me, and I took a moment to look up from the hallway floor to meet his eyes and contemplate his question.

Of course, we were all part of our own familial history; but how did that affect what we were here doing today, I wondered.

He continued.

"My family predates the Great Reformation, as most do. My lineage is Alaskan. My very-great grandfather arrived here in America back in the day and then went with thousands of other men from Washington State all the way up to Alaska during the years of the Klondike Gold Rush. Few people can say they can trace their lineage back that far, but our bloodline truly began at that point.

"My great-grandfather—however many 'greats' it goes back, of course—chased the dreams of getting rich just like so many thousands of other men during those early days. He was a textbook prospector, truth be told. He left his parents' farm in South Dakota to go to Alaska at the onset of the gold rush.

"Through his journal, however, we were able to verify that his father and mother were both immigrants from 'the Old Country'—but we can't be certain which 'old country' they meant. His name was spelled a bit differently on a few of the Alaskan records, but that could be because the men in Alaska during that time period were not the most educated or concerned with accuracy. For that reason, I haven't found anything to lead me any closer to identifying which 'old country' either his father or mother hailed from—or their parents.

"I'll take comfort in what I can verify though—no thanks to the destruction of 2048, of course. Like so many other families, I couldn't research my family lineage because of the bombings. I can no longer trace my lineage or entry into These United States. The documentation of my family rested in the immigration records of the mid-1800s that were stored on Ellis Island. But if you remember your history, you'll recall that the records were destroyed by all the domestic terrorism of the 2040s. You remember the Great Riots that took place in all the major cities right before the Sentence Reform Act was passed? Well, they say that's when Ellis Island was bombed—along with a whole slew of other places. And if you remember from your history classes, they managed to destroy pretty much all of the historic documents. Anyway, they're gone forever. And really, I totally get what their goal was—I understand they were trying to destroy all records of immigration, and that's why they bombed the places that they did. But all they really managed to do was prevent a lot of genealogy from being known and passed down for millions of Americans. I mean, really, the idea that everyone would be 'equal Citizens' if there were no way of cataloguing Citizenship was just kinda asinine. But I suppose they were anarchists and terrorists for a reason, and no one ever said they had to be bright in order to blow shit up, right?"

He paused for a moment, looked briefly at me, and then took his flashlight and slowly moved it all along the left wall, then over the ceiling to the right. Although they were mostly bare other than the occasional cobwebs or darkened smear of dirt, toward the end of the beam of light, there was a collection of metal squares jutting out from near the end of the hall.

The building was enormous by modern standards; to my knowledge, there had been nothing constructed of its size in at least the last fifty years. There had been nothing created—not for work nor for pleasure—that would have required such an expanse of space. The danger to the American People all having gathered in one place would have made it both a foolish and unnecessary risk to Human Life; no employer or recreation provider would have willingly placed so many Citizens directly into Harm's way, especially with such seemingly endless hallways and virtually no safety measures provided.

I tried to imagine a world where architects had designed buildings with no thought in mind about how to protect people from rapid gun fire and Molotov cocktail bombs. The endless space offered few side doors to escape through, and to my knowledge, there weren't any barricades built in that would close sections if a threat were detected or reported. The hallway was a slaughterhouse waiting to happen; it was probably for the best that the business had shut down. It would have required an extremely expensive renovation in order to get it up to Domestic Terrorism regulations.

He moved his flashlight back down toward the flooring ahead of us and began moving forward once again, continuing with his story.

"So, my family tends to do what so many other American families have done since the days leading up to the Last Stand, and we just claim our history as far back as we are able to confirm, leaving it at that. I know I'm very fortunate to be able to verify as much as I have been able to, and it grants much peace of mind to know that my ancestry is as true as Native as one could ever hope. My bloodline might have originated in some old European country—Germany, or possibly Italy—I may never know, since those lines have been entirely severed.

"But I know for certain that part of my lineage is derived from Alaskan Natives. My family line has persevered through the generations, and from our bloodline, we have created an intergenerational Alaskan legacy. My point, you'll see, is that I am a true-born American to my very core—a Patriot to my nation, and more than just a Soldier who has taken an Oath, I'm an American who has lived my life in accordance with the Rights and Liberties that only my Heavenly Father and Founding Fathers could have guaranteed were mine by Divine Right."

He was an eloquent speaker, and I was content to listen to him as we slowly walked along.

"Watch your step—" he said and waved his slender flashlight a bit to show the rotting remains of a dead rat to the left of my foot. I gave a curt nod in acknowledgement and waited for him to continue his story. I wasn't sure how it applied, but I knew where we were going and why, and was oddly grateful for the diversion his talking provided.

"My great-grandfather Melnyk made his way north with some hundred-thousand other brave men, and even some women, as they all dreamt of striking it rich from the bounty of the lands. There is substantial historical documentation and recorded history of Alaska and the epic gold rushes our nation experienced. But there isn't much out there that documents the individuals who were part of it. Most Americans may never even know they had an Ancestor that took part in such a journey and time.

"Out of the many thousands of prospectors, most did not get rich, and many others died. Some, however, gave up on the hunt for gold while still electing to remain in Alaska to build their lives and futures. They were the backbone of the boomtowns, and many became wealthy just because they had the good sense to become shopkeepers and saloon owners.

"My great-grandfather's journal proved priceless for securing our heritage as US Citizens since it predates the gold rush entirely. I'm fortunate enough to know that my family was part of the initial immigration stories thanks to his entries talking about the 'old country'. As much as I would like to know where our family began, at least I know my Ancestors came here to build new lives and to become part of the new country. It's a rare legacy to hold, and one of which I remain very proud. I know I'm part of a select handful of Americans who can not only confirm their roots are tied to an American heritage almost from the earliest years of settlement, but that my bloodline became joined with the Natives of the great Alaskan Wilderness, twice blessing me with a connection to this land that few others can still lay claim to."

We reached the end of the long hallway; the metal boxes situated on the wall appeared to contain first aid supplies. I hadn't stopped to read the stickers posted alongside the boxes the first time I had passed this way, but I did so now. There were gas masks, air purifiers, a first aid kit, and directives on cleaning out chemicals from the eyes, nose, and mouth if contaminated. A small, red fire alarm was situated next to some sort of fire axe.

Given how many Acts of Violence there had been in the 21st century, I couldn't believe there was an actual box built into the wall that contained an enormous red axe, and the only thing preventing anyone from accessing it was a willingness to break the glass and take it. I wondered how many Innocent Citizens had lost their lives because of such random attacks; workplace violence had been extremely high back then, especially in factories. It was ironic that such a weapon would be here. Politicians had worked so hard to deny Citizens their Second Amendment Rights, but they had failed to address the hundreds of thousands who had been 'randomly' attacked with machetes, kitchen knives, and other sharp weapons plainly left out in the open for the taking.

It had only been a few moments of walking, but it had been made into a much more interesting experience than my first solo trip because of Daegan Kyl's conversation, and I had barely noticed our surroundings. It was a strange topic, but he was an extremely captivating storyteller. I had hardly noticed where we were, or what we were doing, and was surprised to find myself so willfully distracted by his ancestral account.

I knew after we walked the length of the second hallway that we would descend into the basement where a little girl had been savagely violated as a matter of routine. But for the next several moments, I allowed myself the experience of being transported back in time and nodded toward Daegan Kyl to continue his story.

"Our records show Melnyk arrived in 1896; the first big year of the Klondike Gold Rush. He stayed near Bonanza Creek—it was in Yukon Territory—for just over a year, just one man among many thousands, all buying into the gold rush hype, hoping to strike it rich. He said in his journal that he was 'going to use his body to toil under the sun either on the farm or in the bed of a creek searching for gold, so he might as well invest into his dreams while he was still of sound enough health to grant him the freedom to choose'. Although there wasn't any direct mention of his father or grandfather openly disapproving of his actions by leaving their homestead, he said that his mother had told him to 'be sure to return before his father lost his strength to manage the lands'. There weren't any records dated beyond 1912, so I can't be certain about whatever happened to those whom he left behind, but we know that he never again left Alaska after the gold rush years.

"He stayed in the Bonanza Creek area for several months, and then right before 1897, he made the move further north and holed up in the thriving boomtown of Dawson City. He talked about the makeshift boom towns frequently because he used them as landmarks for his travels during those days; some were pretty shady little shantytowns, high in crime and violence and low in respectability.

"He would make little mentions of any noteworthy tales of success by the other men he encountered, and he would outline his plans and ideas. It was clear he was using the journal more as a milestone marker than a diary.

"You'd find it interesting to read about how he referenced his time spent in Dawson City. There were about thirty-thousand people when he arrived, he said. A thriving city that had blown up almost overnight. What I remember the most was that he said that the North-west Mounted Police—a Canadian policing system—were well-known for maintaining law and order despite the huge influx of populations and the geographical regions they policed. He told of how little crime there was despite the high population and lack of women. He said it was a 'credit to all Canadian Law Enforcement to bear witness to how well-done their efforts were considering that most of the American men living within the Yukon Territory were frustrated, cold, hungry, subsisting on hopes and dreams, and had sacrificed both civility and women in order to embark on such a journey'—"

He stopped walking and looked directly at me, causing me to stop walking as well.

"He had great respect for Law Enforcement; I always appreciated that. I'm not sure how many other accounts there have been about the gold rush era by the men that lived in those days as prospectors, but I was always very proud not only to have been from such a lineage and among those who could boast a direct claim, but also that he had obviously been such a genuinely decent man. I remember first reading his journal as a young boy, and could imagine the Canadian Mounties in their uniforms, keeping all the rowdy American men in line. It set quite a high standard for Law Enforcement and taught me well from a young age that good men were made better by their respect for those who kept the law and were the Peacekeepers among us."

I raised an eyebrow, impressed. He couldn't see it, of course, since my visor was still down. But I appreciated his comment.

I gave another curt nod of the head and pushed on, giving his back a slight double-tap as I walked past him. In another world, I believed he and I could have gotten along very well; may have even been friends. We would have engaged in some interesting discussions.

We were almost at the end of the hallway, and I could see the giant metal doorframe looming ahead of us. It was an ugly building—an ugly metal monstrosity from a time in history where most things had been ugly—and the boiler room itself was grim and dark. More than anything else, I hated where it led, and hated what lay beyond the doors ahead of us.

Maybe Daegan Kyl understood the need for a distraction better than I realized. I certainly recognized that I appreciated his words more than I could have anticipated, but as I walked slowly toward the heavy, creaking metal slabs hanging in front of us, everything else faded away as I remembered what I had seen not long ago. The oversized doors were the sole objects separating us from what lay beyond, and as I slowly followed him through, I found myself grateful for the efforts he had made to transport us to another place and time. Anything would have been better than what we were now doomed to discuss. The entire purpose for our being here was the absolute last thing I wanted to remember, let alone hash out one Violent Act at a time, and I imagined that having been cleared of the Crime, he would have felt the same. Nonetheless, we pushed on.

The Basement

We reached the end of the hallway and stood before the double metal doors. I knew what I had observed during my first visit, and what sort of prison lay beyond. Not long before, the Governor of Washington State had spoken on behalf of the man standing next to me, asserting that he had not participated in the brutalization against young Katarina Urakov. Along with this, Daegan Kyl himself had declared his own innocence, although he had never disputed that he was responsible for burying her and the three other Victims.

Both of these facts may well have been true, but as an Investigator, I needed more to go on in order to believe the words each man spoke. Neither had provided me with any type of explanation regarding how Daegan Kyl had come to be in the factory after so many years, how he had ended up with the Remains of little Katarina, or why he had chosen to bury her in an unmarked grave rather than report her Death to the proper authorities—even anonymously. Additionally, I had never been granted any type of explanation as to why the Governor knew of these events, could attest to Daegan Kyl's innocence, or why he had worked on his behalf to clear his name. Even though none of these answers would change the circumstances or lead to Criminal accountability for Daegan Kyl or the two Foreign Nationals, I was still searching for the truth—even if I was going to be prohibited from putting it into my Final Report.

It may have been a stretch or blind optimism, but I was hoping Daegan Kyl was sincere in his desire to help fill in the details.

We had paused momentarily before entering, but I now found myself pushing through the doors and leading the way, eager to get it over with. I did not have any daughters of my own, but it did not matter; all I could see was someone's daughter, someone's little girl. What they had done to her was beyond a national tragedy; it was an act of savage barbarism that should have only resulted in their Deaths. There should not have been any other outcome—and the more I learned of the case, the harder my feelings on the matter became.

It was partially why the Victims of Homicide had taken center-stage during the years of the Last Stand and Great Reformation. The American People needed to know precisely what manner of Savagery and Violence was being inflicted upon the Innocent Citizens of our nation. They needed to see it clearly outlined so they could imagine how the Final Hours and Final Moments of each Victim had been lived—and what specific acts of gory, traumatizing, bloody Violence were responsible for stealing their Last Breath from their bodies and Ending their Lives. It was for these reasons that every Victim of Homicide was named from coast to coast, and why it was passed into law that Autopsy Reports would be made public and stored in a national database. Medical Examiners became an integral part of the Sentence Reform Act, giving testimony as to the consequences of Violent Crime throughout These United States.

And here we were.

I needed to see it again. I needed to hear what this man knew and why. And if he were, indeed, innocent of all wrongdoing, I needed to hear it so I could rid myself of the contempt in my heart for him. We were Investigators and Peacekeepers. We were supposed to be neutral and objective. We were also expected to be compassionate and regard each Victim as a Sacred Human Being. It was a fine line, balancing our emotions and keeping them in check. As professionals, we needed to be emotionally detached so we could do our jobs effectively, but as Human Beings, it was virtually impossible not to internalize all that we saw and were subjected to while out in the field.

I needed this man to be cleared of all wrongdoing because I needed a win. I needed for my instincts about him to be proven right, for him to be the kind of man my gut and years of experience still said he was. I needed for him to be a source of information and help rather than a Suspect. And perhaps more than all of that, I needed for this little girl to have known at least one Final Moment of kindness and compassion from someone rather than just the sheer obscenity of Pain and Suffering I believed she endured in the last months of her life. I was searching for a miracle.

We walked along the center of the room, each taking slow, measured steps. I had entered ahead of him, but as we walked, he took the lead as he had in the hallway. The sides of the rooms were lined with enormous metal machinery, all covered in protruding pipes, hoses, and temperature gauges. The room hadn't been operational in years, and everything was heavily layered in dust and cobwebs. There were no windows or other artificial sources of light, so the only light visible illuminated from our own slight offerings. It was not enough to remove the vast darkness surrounding us.

"I came through here," he began.

"They had called me to do a job the same year I got out of the military, which I'm sure you already know. It was a short job, all things considered. They were only looking for one man, and I didn't have anyone else working for me at the time. They told me they needed a private dwelling space that was separate from all the other offices so they could host the occasional meeting or provide a private living space for themselves as CEOs.

"It never occurred to me that they were here illegally or that they would be doing anything they weren't authorized to do. I was paid with a paycheck directly from the company—as I'm sure you are aware. All they wanted was a private apartment built. They said that they selected this location because it was far enough removed from the business area and office space that no one else would try to access it or use it for their own purposes.

"I told them that having any type of dwelling space near the boiler room was a terrible idea; that they would be much better off having it on the 3rd floor so they could have light and plenty of space. I told them just to post a notice that the designated living space was off-limits to all employees, but they stated it might cause issues with zoning if anyone knew it existed. I had to agree with that one, but since it wasn't technically a permanent dwelling and since the entire building already had bathrooms and similar kitchenettes, it wasn't like I was going to be building anything that wasn't already available on every floor and accessible to every employee. But I had persisted with the recommendation for the 3rd floor location and gave them some basic information about how they could create an access point that could only be used by those with access codes, cards, or even a scanned retina or thumbprint. I tried to convince them that the 3rd floor would provide more light, space, and the ability to control noise, but they wouldn't hear of it.

"And then I made my final case—that being next to the boiler room in a basement was going to amplify the noise so drastically that it would be impossible to sleep or use the space constructively. I told them that even if they couldn't hear footsteps and noise from the rooms overhead, they would still be bombarded with the heavy noise from the boiler room itself. They suggested 'soundproofing' the boiler room, but you can see how large of a space this is. The obvious solution was to add soundproofing to the apartment. I know now that I was a complete fool. I was dumb and naïve, and I walked straight into it. I never even questioned whether it would be used for anything nefarious. Not at any point in the last decade has it ever even entered my mind one time that the rooms I had built for them were being used for anything unscrupulous, let alone pure evil. I gave them exactly what they wanted, and I swallowed their lies whole."

He shook his head, grimacing. He was disgusted with himself.

His face was pained, covered in guilt and anger.

With his eyebrows furrowed together and his jaw clenched, I watched as his disgust and contempt for the situation turned into rage directed against the two men. He had been played for a fool, and his actions had resulted in pain for another person—an innocent child.

Everything about his demeanor attested to his truthfulness, including the increasing aggression in his tone and wording as he continued.

"They said it needed to have some built-in structures as furniture because they didn't want to be bothered with shopping or things aging or breaking apart. So, when I designed the space, I created some cement seating, the table, and countertop, and in the bedroom area, I created the concrete foundation that the mattress rested on. I used the same design to create the slab of concrete for the couch area—which they specified should be adequate to host one of them as a sleeping space. I designed the bathroom in the same manner; a basic shower, toilet, and sink area that would be functional rather than aesthetic. I remember telling them it was very much in the style of how our prisons were, immovable pieces with minimal appeal but long-term sustainability. They had laughed and said function was always more important than the space being 'pretty'—that they were only 'a couple of single men without families'…"

His voice faded away as his eyes looked off into the distance, recalling the details of the conversation. Then, shaking his head, he cleared his throat and pointed toward the end of the room where the entrance to the 'apartment' stood.

It was down a set of stairs with a green handrail. Daegan Kyl nodded toward it and said the space they had selected had once been the primary operations area for all the maintenance. He said that while he had customized the walls and everything within the apartment, the size and shape had been dictated by the original structure of the building itself. He recalled how the two men that had hired him had specified that the square footage would be more than adequate to meet their needs. He believed it had been just under four-hundred square feet. It wasn't a large space, but for a one-bedroom unit, it was serviceable.

We reached the front door. There was a lock box off to the left, but it had been smashed open. It had been rendered useless without electricity.

For the first time since meeting him, I saw him hesitate as he reached up to grab the door handle, pausing mid-air and then lowering his arm again. I didn't know what he was struggling with, but he took a deep breath and straightened his shoulders broadly; a self-defense mechanism all done in a sharp second as demons waged war inside his head. The man had engaged in open warfare with foreign enemies but did not want to open a door.

I was beginning to understand the man better.

I took the time to raise my visor; I was not recording anything, and although the night vision had helped lighten the space considerably, it had kept me separate from the man standing next to me. We were in this together at this point; he needed to see that.

I gave him a quick pat on the back, and he nodded his head.

The door was heavy; three-inch solid steel with a sizable deadbolt resting within. I pulled it open and held it as Daegan Kyl walked through into the small main living area of the apartment.

The first time I visited, I had noted that the door had a powerful hinge that forced it to spring back into a closed position. I did not want the noise to be too startling, so I held the door wide, and controlled the speed as it closed.

I hadn't planned on asking—nor did I believe I needed to—but Daegan Kyl volunteered the information anyhow, denying all responsibility or knowledge of the condition of the door.

Someone—presumably the two men responsible for the atrocities that had been committed within this room—had placed an inside screen door against the metal. It was made of metal but covered in sharp, jagged edges, all jutting out. Its intent was clear; the room was soundproof but the door that Daegan Kyl had built was only a three-inch piece of metal. It was the easiest—and likely only—place where a captive could have escaped or possibly banged against the metal loudly enough to be heard from the outside. The two men had devised a makeshift screen that prohibited anyone from the inside from being able to touch the smooth metal lining of the original door. They had covered it with pieces of pointed, sharp metal. It looked like an instrument of torture. Anyone that attempted to press up against it would have been cut and sliced in dozens of locations. The danger and threat it presented was undeniable. It was a monstrous piece of work and a very prominent aspect of an otherwise almost barren room. Understandably, Daegan Kyl did not want to be associated with it, or what it represented.

We stood there for a moment, looking around. It was a bleak place made worse by the dull lighting and shadows cast on the walls. The main room had a concrete rectangle shape serving as a couch area. It held some type of foam mattress; dirty, dusty, and covered in a few mangy blankets. Fleas or lice had been a possibility at one point, though after months of isolation in the dark, it was probably no longer an issue. Still, neither of us ventured near the couch; there was no need.

Two cement blocks extended from the walls for seating with the table surface raised higher between them, followed by the kitchen area that held a refrigerator, stove, sink, and a wall of cabinets overhead. At one point, the kitchen had been in new condition, with decent mid-level appliances and cabinets. Now it was all covered in dirt and crusted old food scraps; a testament to the quality of life for anyone within this space. There were boxes of processed foods still sitting in bags at the end of the counter; whether they were there because they hadn't been put away or because that was where a little girl could reach them to feed herself would remain forever unknown.

Stepping through a doorway area, we entered a small section that divided the bedroom space from the bathroom, each having been supplied with their own doorway next to one another. The bathroom was small and virtually empty. I had noticed a brush and a few hair ties when I was first there, and I was certain the brush and toothbrush resting on the counter by the sink would each be found to contain the DNA of Katarina; but we knew this to be true already, and frankly, the idea of rounding up the few personal effects of the poor little girl was too heart-wrenching to contend with. It would have served no purpose, and would that I could, I would just as readily have torched the entire building and watched this hellish prison burn to the ground.

We went into the bedroom. It was nothing more than a separate, smaller room. There were no windows and the only item to be found was the concrete block off to one end large enough to hold the queen-size mattress that had been placed upon it. Like the other sleeping area, it was covered in dirty old blankets and pillows.

It was a filthy dwelling that would have been considered uninhabitable for any American family. It should have been condemned and burned to the ground like something out of the era of the Black Plague. Instead, it had been used as a sex dungeon for two Foreign Criminals so they could Abuse a little girl until she eventually died.

I felt deep anger rise inside of me.

None of this should have ever happened.

We were both quiet, lost in the darkness of our thoughts. Neither of us were fathers, but we were Protectors by nature and instinct. This could have been anyone's little girl, and she had been subjected to unspeakable horror.

What she must have felt.

What she must have prayed for.

Finally, he spoke.

He stood next to me, hands in the pockets of his overcoat. He had shut off his flashlight and put it away; there wasn't much to see and there was enough light from my own devices. But it was more personal than that, I thought. He didn't want to see anything in more detail; his mind was reliving it enough.

"They called me here that day out of the blue. I hadn't heard from them or spoken to them since the end of the job more than a decade ago. I couldn't even remember who they were or the man's name; all I heard on the other end of the phone was a thick accent and broken English as a strange voice asked me to come and see him. I had to clarify the man's name three times before he finally made sense and was able to explain that I had been the one that had worked on the 'factory house'—that's what he called it, the 'factory house'. So, then I figured out who he was and was able to ask him what exactly he wanted.

"And that was when he told me he needed me to come here to the factory. He said he had a problem with the 'factory house' and needed my help. So, I checked my schedule, called my Assistant, and drove out. I had been working on the main site for my company that day and as you know, I had one of the company's moving trucks kept available for my own use. I didn't want to drive my car out here because as you know, the roads are a mess and it's pretty low to the ground."

"And you had been using the moving truck as you worked with Willow Amos, correct?" I interjected. I wasn't going to let him off entirely; he was still accountable for his actions related to Willow Amos.

He looked at me, slightly raising an eyebrow. "Yeah—same truck."

"So, then what?" I asked. No point in getting off-topic.

"So, I drove down to the factory and parked next to another vehicle that was there—some type of sedan. I'd never seen it before, haven't seen it since. I hadn't been to the factory or the building site I had worked on—this place—since I completed the job. I hadn't kept in contact with either of the men that had been running it. I would have needed to look up the name of the company on an old tax return before I would have even remembered it. I hadn't 'colluded' with either of them; they were strangers then, and they were strangers at the point last May when I arrived back at the building for the first time in over a decade."

I nodded. I believed him.

"But you admit you had been on the property before May—recently even. Just not near the factory." I said slowly. I wasn't trying to trap him. I just wanted clarification about what he was, and was not, claiming responsibility for. Someone had buried all four of the Victims on the property; if he was going to accept responsibility for every burial, it confirmed that he was directly connected to each case, Victim, and because of Katarina, the factory itself.

"Yes—I had been on the property. I had worked for almost six months converting this space into an apartment and I had spent long days here during that time. I knew from the time that I spent working here that the factory only took up a small portion of the overall property.

"But it was after working for a few weeks that one of the men approached me while I was working and asked me if I could start putting in more hours so I could get it done faster. I explained to him I was only one guy, and I could only do so much in a single day. He offered to increase my pay and give me a big bonus if I could get it done ahead of schedule. I told him I could hire a few extra workers, but he told me he didn't want the extra people on the payroll. So, I told him I could only do so much work as long as I had to commute all the way back to the base. At the time, I was renting a small place just outside of the main gate at JBLM—you know the area? It's always been so thick with traffic; it was just eating up my days with that drive.

"So, the guy—I think he must have been the Senior CEO, but who knows—they weren't very forthcoming with the information, you know? Anyhow, he told me to stop by his office the next day before I left work, and he would have a solution worked out. So, the next night, after I had wrapped things up, I went to his office on the 3rd floor—and I remember it was late enough that everyone had already left, and the factory had shut down for the night. Anyhow, he was busy talking on the phone. He waved me inside, and I remember just standing there covered in dust and dirt, thinking I didn't want to track it in all over his shiny little office. So, I stood there waiting for his phone call to end—all in Arabic, of course, and believe it or not I had never picked it up during any of my deployments. Never bothered taking the time to do one of the language courses and they never made me, so it never happened. Besides, I wasn't there to communicate; I was there to kill the Terrorists before they killed me or my brothers. If I was close enough to have a conversation with an Arab, it was only for a minute before I cut his vocal cords. It was always such an ugly language, anyway; to this day when I have to listen to it, I'm always reminded of the stench of every sandbox I ever had to waste time in, and every time I hear the call to prayer I'm reminded why those 7th century religious zealots need to be kept in their hellhole countries.

"That I even took the job from them in the first place should show you just how pissed off I was at my own side; there's never been any love lost between me and the fanatics out there destroying the Third World.

"Anyhow, so the guy finished his phone call, handed me a wad of money, and told me to go rent an RV for six months. He handed me a piece of paper that had a property description and told me not to park it anywhere close to the factory itself or visible to the workers, and just stay on site. So, I did. I rented a small RV that met my needs, drove around the property 'til I found a spot I liked, and then set up camp.

"I picked a spot right near the water. I had a gorgeous view of Puget Sound, and it was far enough away from the freeway and the factory to obliterate any noise. There were acres of forested land behind the field I was parked in, a long beach area in front of the high grass, and you could hear seagulls and the sound of the waves all day long. Puget Sound was a sparkling paradise; it was an oasis after my time spent overseas surrounded by the noise of war. By the end of the second week on the job, the guy had asked me to only work during the night because I was working in the same space as the regular factory workers, and they didn't appreciate the mess or noise—or so he said. At any rate—he wanted me to work during the nights only; that left all day to hang out on the beach and listen to the sound of the waves.

"It was my first big job after I had gotten out of the military. I'd spent most of the ten years before in some type of transitionary situation or another. Most of it was spent in hostile territory, and I know that when I left, I was still extremely angry about how the government had mistreated my Fellow Soldiers.

"The time spent working on this space—being out there in that field every day and just learning how to be my own man again…It was therapy to me. I was trying to figure out who I was without being a soldier. I'd spent my entire adult life working and living under the framework that was outlined by my government; I needed that chapter afterward to decompress and re-establish myself as a regular civilian.

"I had fond memories of the place where I had set up my temporary living conditions. I had grown to be content there during those months…" His voice faded and he looked around the room.

"I'm sorry to see that this was what it had all been done for… I'm sorry that the memories I once held fondly had become part of this…"

"So, the place on the property that you had selected to place everyone—" I began.

"Was the place where I had spent my time when I worked here. It was a beautiful spot. I just thought—if you must be buried …It should be in a beautiful place…"

He looked down.

"I spent my entire career pushing back against evil and violence—fighting against the oppressors and even the ideas that could destroy everything that was so glorious about our own Western Values.….And all the while there was such ugliness still happening right here at home. Who knew there were so many ugly people left in our world?"

We stared at one another; an honest, vulnerable moment where two men striving to be good let down their armor and dared to acknowledge the overwhelming futility of the world we lived in. The vulnerability didn't come from admitting that there was Evil, or that Good Men were necessary in order to fight against it. It came from recognizing that we both understood the odds were stacked against us, that they were stacked against all good Human Beings. Deep down, we were afraid we were never going to be able to tip the odds in our favor or prevail. What was terrifying was knowing that even with Good Men such as us out there earnestly fighting the good fight, we were still facing insurmountable odds, and those who worked on the side of Evil never seemed to tire of the relentless Tragedy and Suffering they created.

This was a man who was struggling to understand how something that he had created could have been used as a weapon to inflict the most hostile, degrading, and disgustingly Inhumane mistreatment against an Innocent Child. He was drowning in shame over a situation that he had no earthly right to bear the responsibility for or feel any guilt over, and yet he did.

I was finally becoming more aware of just exactly who Daegan Kyl truly was. He hadn't asked me here just to clear his name. Whether he was aware of it or not, whether he fully understood it or not, he had brought me here because he had needed to tell his story. He had needed to explain himself to someone, to share with someone the reasons for how all of this had come to be; how he had come to know this building and these men, how he had come to find the little girl, and even how he had found himself alone in a field with four sets of Human Remains. He had brought me here because he needed to bare his soul.

He was seeking forgiveness and redemption. He wanted someone to hold him liable, to tell him he somehow should have known or guessed. I think he believed that because he had spent so much time in the Middle East and had known their ways that he should have anticipated what the two Foreign Nationals might have been planning. He believed that because he had known enough about Sharia Law, their Human Rights Violations and Crimes Against Women and young girls, that he should have seen the signs. In his mind, perhaps, he believed that because he had gained this knowledge by experiencing it first-hand rather than having read about it in history books like most Americans growing up in the years after the Great Reformation and the end of Immigration, that his radar should have somehow gone off and served as a warning. Ultimately, he believed that 'he should have known'.

It was all false, of course. It was his nobility getting the best of him. His emotions were overriding the facts of the case, at least regarding Katarina and the two Foreign Nationals. Even if he had suspected something and reported it, there was little chance it would have been taken seriously back then. Bearing in mind that the two Foreign Nationals had been using Visas that had been cleared, the Immigration Officer might have taken a cursory glance at the case and then dismissed it. It was even possible that Daegan Kyl would have been quietly accused of 'profiling', and they would have taken his complaint and tossed it the moment he vacated the building.

I was not the person he needed redemption from; I wasn't sure if such a person existed, but I knew it was not me. He hadn't done anything wrong in this regard in my humble opinion; he could not have known what was yet to be. No one could have anticipated what their intentions were at the time. Was it perhaps a little unorthodox that he had been asked to do the work after-hours? Perhaps. But they had presented legitimate reasons for everything, and by his own description, he had explained that his work had been messy and full of dust and debris. The workspace had not been ventilated, and there were other factory workers that spent their shifts laboring in the boiler room; trying to work around another construction job that created plumes of dust and noise would have been problematic enough that it would have seemed a reasonable request to have Daegan Kyl work only while the factory was closed.

Everything he had shared with me gave credibility to how he had come to be involved but only on the fringes. It was clear from the way he recalled the events that he had been an unwilling and unknowing accomplice to their nefarious plans. I wasn't sure that I had ever considered the possibility that he had been directly related to the Abduction or Death of Katarina, but after hearing his testimony, I was more certain than ever that there wouldn't be a Judge in our nation that would have held him accountable for anything premeditated. What remained to be understood, however, was how he had come back to this place and ended up being the last person known to have any contact with the little girl.

He nodded his head in the direction of the queen bed and then pointed to the space between the end of the bed and the wall.

"I found her there, lying in the corner all by herself," he said, his voice so soft I could barely hear.

"She was so small."

I looked at the cold, hard, concrete floor between the end of the bed and the wall, imagining the little girl that had been left there to die alone.

Beside me, the man who had lived the life of a warrior stood silent, his eyes full of tears, grieving for a young girl that he had never known.

Upon Finding Katarina

"Start at the beginning," I said. "What happened when you arrived at the factory?"

I hoped that by giving him an opportunity to regroup and start thinking about the steps that had occurred before he entered the apartment, he would have a moment to compose himself and we could get through it easier. I was ready to leave this room, the apartment, and the factory itself—but it was important to him we were here.

He took a deep breath and wiped his eyes with his thumb and forefinger, then looked up toward the ceiling for a moment before exhaling slowly.

"I pulled up alongside some kind of sedan; I hadn't really paid close attention to what it was. I could see some lights on inside the building, so I just went around to the same door we entered through and made my way up that first flight of stairs to the second floor. I knew that back in the day the CEO offices had been on the top floor, but the lights had all been coming from one of the rooms on the corner of the second floor. I wasn't that familiar with the place, so I just went toward the obvious direction and then I heard two men arguing—in Arabic, of course. So, I assumed it was the same two guys. I shouted out to them, letting them know I was there.

"There were a few more little comments back and forth, and then one of the men came out from the room and smiled at me, saying, 'Welcome! Welcome!' like we were old friends. It had been over a decade, and honestly, I couldn't really remember what either of them had looked like. I was assuming they were the same two guys—they were both from the Middle East somewhere, both spoke Arabic as their native language, and both were about average in every way, which is exactly what I can remember from before.

"So, the guy motions for me to follow him into the room—one of the big office areas, only it's obvious that it's been gutted for inventory, covered in dust and hadn't been in use for a long time. I didn't know how long it had been since the factory was operational, but I was pretty sure it had been a few years, and I didn't even know anyone was still using the space. If I had known..." his voice trailed off again.

"If you had known, you wouldn't have used the land over by the water to bury the other three Victims?" I asked.

He looked at me and nodded.

"I didn't know they were still around. I hadn't been at the factory itself, but I remembered reading an article about the factory shutting down, but I couldn't recall the year it happened. I didn't think it mattered much—only that it wasn't operational anymore. I assumed that no factory meant no one working on site anymore—and obviously no CEOs. Why the hell those two men were even still in the country was a mystery—they shouldn't have even been here or allowed to stay," he said bitterly.

I agreed, of course, and nodded my head. "You're absolutely right about that one. They weren't supposed to be here. They were both here illegally—they had expired work Visas and should have been ejected the instant this factory closed its doors. Immigration dropped the ball on this one."

He looked at me, his eyes angry and filled with the need to blame someone other than himself. I waited for him to continue.

"So, I followed the guy into the room. The other one, the one he had been fighting with, was sitting on a couch. He didn't smile at me, didn't stand up or offer to shake my hand. Made zero effort to be polite or civilized. It was obvious that he didn't want me here and they had been fighting. So, I ignored the guy that was sitting over on the couch and had turned to look at the man that had called me here. He was still smiling at me—that same shit-smile that made me positive that he shouldn't be trusted, and I remember looking at him and being even more apprehensive about the situation because of how sketchy he was.

"I wasn't concerned about myself, of course. I was carrying; I usually do. But you know I'm also plenty capable of taking care of myself. They were situated on either side of where I was standing, and I remember thinking that I didn't like that. But I just stood there and waited for the guy to explain himself and let me know why he had called me there.

"And then as soon as he started talking to me the other guy interrupted him again, and his tone made it clear he was warning him—arguing with him against telling me anything, so then I was *really* curious. The first guy—I'm pretty sure he was the one I had dealt with all those years before, the one that had set me up with the RV—he just put his hand up in the air to silence the second guy, smiled at me again, and then started to talk about how he had 'a slight problem' he wanted me to take care of. And I remember thinking, 'This is the guy in charge of everything, and he has done some pretty bad shit in his day'. I could just see it in his eyes and in the way he had silenced the other guy; he was not one to be messed around with and the other guy knew it, because he kept quiet after that."

He sighed deeply and ran his hand across his bearded face.

I said nothing, waiting quietly for him to continue. It was a small room with stale air, musty and dark. I longed to leave it and never return, and I never intended to. There was nothing more to be done here; it was a tomb.

"He said he had a 'little problem' that he needed me to 'dispose of' for him. He said they were planning on leaving the country and returning home.

"I didn't know what he meant, but his tone was...not just cryptic, it was condescending. He was smiling the whole time, like he was trying to be friend—but all the while he had this snide little arrogance—like he was laughing at the situation, and I didn't deserve to be treated with the respect he was trying to pretend he had for me.

He had been looking at me while he explained himself, and I could sort of understand what he meant. I imagined most self-respecting Human Beings were capable of picking up on enough social cues they would be able to tell when someone was being condescending toward them, and it would probably rub them the wrong way once they did. For a man such as Daegan Kyl, it was probably even harder to choke down.

"So, as he was explaining how he was planning on leaving in a few hours, the other guy started talking in Arabic again. I remember he had flashed him a vicious look that let me know they were involved in something serious. I remember thinking that the guy was bad news, and I didn't want to get involved at all—that I needed to get the hell out of there.

"Anyhow, so the guy tells me, 'Just go to the apartment, you'll see.' I'm thinking he's asked me there because he knows what my business is, so I start to hand him a card, telling him that he can call to make arrangements—I can help him set it up—that I didn't have to do it myself because I had staff and cleaning crews that could handle it.

"And then the guy laughed at me, and waved his hand, telling me to put it away. I could feel myself getting more and more irritated. But then he suddenly stops laughing and gets completely serious—just flips a switch and becomes cold. So, then he's staring me down, and he says, 'No. You will go down there and clean up the mess. You will dispose of everything as needed. You will make sure this is done. Only you. You will do this now—or I will make one phone call before I leave so they will know what secrets you keep over by the water. Understand?' And then I knew he had been watching me."

His jaw was clenched tightly, and I could see his entire frame grow rigid as he recalled the conversation.

"They knew what I had done. They knew about the other burials, and they were blackmailing me with it. I didn't say anything else to them. I just nodded my head and left the room. I was angry. And probably part of me was worried about someone else knowing about the burials. But mostly, I was just pissed that some raghead motherfucker was going to threaten me, and he thought I was just going to jump.

"But I needed a minute to think; I needed to process what I knew about the guys and the situation. Make sure I knew what it was that I was working with before I did anything reactionary, you know? I could see they had been gathering up their stuff, there were a few duffel bags on the floor. But they were still packing up paperwork, so I didn't think they were quite ready to go yet. So, I just went downstairs to check on things and see what he was so worried about. The lights were still on at the time, and I took the elevator down. I came straight here.

"It was a little different than when I had worked on it. The metal door was propped open. I had been the one who ordered and installed that door. They said they were planning on storing payroll and other stuff in the apartment, so it made sense to have that extra security. But as soon as I got close enough to see the place, I could see the inside screen was there, which was *not* something I had made or installed."

He took a deep breath, but it didn't help much. The more he shared, the more strained his tone became.

"I noticed right away that the screen door—if you could call it that—was installed backwards, and it was on the inside of the unit rather than outside of the main door. And that's when I realized that there was something really bad going on inside and I knew I didn't want to keep going forward. I could feel the panic—and feel my anger over being involved in any of this. Everything seemed beyond my control, and there were certain external factors that were suddenly controlling my life—Willow and her bullshit, and now this guy. So, I was raging angry at that minute. I didn't want to get involved in anything beyond that door—I knew that much.

"And then I heard it, the faintest little cough in the world. There was someone inside—someone that didn't sound like they were doing too well. And all my fears and anger just vanished—all I could think about was opening that screen door so I could get inside.

"I just grabbed the biggest, heaviest hunk of metal I could find—some type of piping that was about the length of a baseball bat, and I went to the control box and just started wailing on it. I had installed it; I had built the metal casing around it. I knew it was wired into the wall, but I also knew the wall was only concrete. I hit the control box directly. It took me a few good hits. And I remember calling out to whoever was in there to hold on and that I was there to help. That I would be inside in just a minute, and I could help them. I remember feeling so scared in that moment. I panicked because I could still hear that little wheezing cough in my head. I was terrified that the door I was trying to unseal meant exactly what I feared it meant."

He paused, looked at me, and said, "I swear, I don't think I've ever been that scared or panicked in my entire life. I was hitting that wall with everything I had and all I can remember thinking is 'someone is in there; someone needs help *right now*'."

He looked around the room, his face grimacing in disgust again.

"I smashed the control box. It deactivated the bolts when it lost its connection. I couldn't really see the inside of the screen door until I reached over and pulled it open, and it sliced my hand a bit. And that's when it all began to sink in—what this place was, what I was going to find. I didn't know how many girls I would find—or their ages—but I knew I would find at least one girl or woman, probably more. And I knew exactly who those men were and what they were at that minute.

"But I wasn't thinking about the men—I was just trying to get to the bedroom so I could get to whoever was back there. She had sounded so weak; her cough had been really raspy—wheezing.

"The lights were on everywhere, but you know there's no heat. Those assholes never made me do anything to put any type of heating system in here. It was in the basement so it wouldn't have ever gotten hot in the summer, but it sure as hell would have gotten cold. And even though it was May, it was still cold down here—it was probably never warmer than fifty.

"I'll never forget it. I'll never be able to block it out. I came into this room and saw her immediately. She was so tiny…"

He looked down at the ground where he said she had been lying, his mind a million miles away.

"She was curled up in the fetal position. Her hair was blond, but I couldn't see her face because she was kind of hiding under her little arm. She was barefoot. Dirty. In a dress. God, she was so skinny. Such a tiny little girl, barely moving."

He put his hand up to his mouth again, covering it and then rubbing his hand across his beard. It was an absent-minded gesture, but it was also a defense mechanism he used often when his mind was provoked by something particularly emotional; I doubted he realized it.

He cleared his throat, took a deep breath, and continued.

"I must have made a noise; I reacted somehow, and she looked up at me from behind her arm. She had these big blue eyes poking out at me from behind her messy hair. It was all I could see for a second—those big blue eyes and how afraid they were.

"I moved slowly toward her, had my arms up so she could see them, and I was talking to her. I kept my voice low, tried to be gentle. I told her I wasn't going to hurt her, that I was there to help her, and I was going to take her far away from there. I asked her if she wanted to see her mommy and daddy again and I told her I was there to help her so I could take her home."

He looked at me then, his eyes filled with tears once more.

"And that was it. She opened her arms so I could pick her up, and I could see just how much effort that took for her. She was covered in bruises. She had blood all over her legs and her dress; she was bruised all over—even her face. But she let me pick her up—after what those men had done to her—for however long they had kept her and hurt her. She let me pick her up."

He shook his head, blinking back the tears as they spilled over onto his cheeks. His jaw clenched, and he looked up at the ceiling again for a second.

"I'll just never get it. I'll never understand how there can be such evil, sick people in the world."

He sighed, letting the air out slowly, measured, composing himself.

"I sat down with her on the bed and put her across my lap. She was cold; she was lethargic, barely moving, and had significant wheezing. I knew they had been Sexually Assaulting her—I didn't know how long they'd had her, but it looked like a while. She was filthy, her hair was matted, and she was malnourished and underweight. And she was clearly very sick from vitamin deficiency, lack of sunlight, lack of fresh air—all the cold temperatures. She was sick. But she had been beaten severely, and I think that was the final push that her poor little body couldn't handle. She had blood all down the insides of her legs; I don't know if it was from just being raped or if they had sodomized her, but I didn't see any visible cuts on her legs or thighs, so it had to be from that.

"I took off my jacket and put it over her. It was May and early evening, but we'd still had some rain and it was still cool enough in the evening to need some type of jacket. So, I took mine off slowly—still holding her, and she was kind of dozing off on my lap a bit. And as I covered her up, that's when I realized she was really near the end. I think the wheezing was from broken ribs or a punctured lung; it was a sound I heard during some of our heavy combat; it wasn't the same as the sound of a chest cold or even pneumonia. She seemed to struggle to breathe.

"I thought about trying to leave—to drive out of there. But I didn't think they would just let me walk out with her, and I didn't think she was going to survive a drive."

He looked over at me, eyes still full of tears.

"I knew she was going to die. I think she had been put through enough. Her little body was done with the abuse.

"I just held her. I wrapped her up in my jacket, I wrapped my arms around her and tried to get her warm—I didn't want to hurt her by holding her too tight because her breathing was getting so much worse, but I didn't want her to die alone either. I wanted her to know someone was there; that someone was protecting her."

His lips trembled and his voice cracked as he spoke, and then his hand moved to cover his mouth again. He blinked as the tears fell, and all the while he stared at the bed with a million-mile stare that kept him locked in his memories.

"That was it. She died. She died while I held her less than ten minutes after I picked her up. She only looked at me twice—once when I told her I was going to help her when she was on the floor right before I picked her up, and then a second time after I put my coat over her. I had been looking down at her, had moved her hair away from her face, and she looked up at me. She had reached her little hand up toward my beard and had put her hand on my face. I took her hand and pulled her close. She closed her eyes and a few minutes later, she was dead.

"I sat here, in this filthy, cold room with that poor little girl and listened to her as she struggled through her Final Moments and took her Final Breath—listened to her wheezing, struggling to breathe, too weak to even fight for her own life anymore. Her skin was cold, she was frail, and she was covered in so many bruises you could see that it wasn't all from one beating; they had been doing it for a long time. And I sat there with her—helpless—with no other noise to be heard except the sound of her trying to breathe—until even that sound disappeared.

"And then I stayed there for a minute or two, just trying to process what was happening. It wasn't long—because of the sadness I was feeling—the shock of what I had just witnessed was wearing off, and it was quickly replaced with anger. I wasn't going to let those two men get away with this.

"I set her down on the bed. I didn't want to leave her there, but I had to go back upstairs and make sure they didn't get away. I had to try to stop them. I left her there, and I went back upstairs."

After Losing Katarina

"I got back to the room, and both men were still there. The first guy actually smiled at me—and before I could even think twice about what I was doing, I punched him square in the face, wiping his smug smile off with as much force as I could muster. It knocked him to the ground and as soon as I did it the second guy jumped up from the couch and started running toward me, screaming at me in Arabic the whole way. He jumped on me, and we scrapped a bit. I got a few punches in, but he just kept grabbing hold of my clothes and tugging at me, not really trying to fight but still being a pain in the ass. I finally pushed him away, and was about to punch him again, and out of nowhere, the first guy just shot him. Shot him right in the side of the head, a foot away from me.

"That's all it took to see the dynamics change; I put my hands up right where I was. He was standing in front of me with a gun pointed at my face; sometimes you gotta know the odds. I was already on my knees after the guy had wrestled with me and knocked us both off balance, so any physical advantage I had over the guy was lost. I had my firearm, but it was holstered in my backside because I didn't want them to know I had it when I first arrived. So, for the moment, I was at a disadvantage.

"But the guy didn't want to kill me—he wanted me to clean up his mess. So, he stood there for a minute, rubbed his jaw where I had nailed him, and then gave me that shit-eating smirk again. He looked around the room and told me I was now in it as deep as he was. He pointed to my hand that had been bleeding from where I cut it on the screen downstairs. He was right; my blood was all over at that point. It was in the apartment, it was on the stairs, and it was all over his office, and even on his buddy. I'd even held the little girl and sat on the bed with her; I probably had hair and fibers—not to mention my blood—all over the whole place. He had laughed at me because he knew I was screwed unless I cleaned it all up and did his dirty work for him. He knew he had the power to secure my help at that point.

"So, there I was, on my knees, a dead guy on the floor in front of me covered in my blood, a dead little girl in the basement that had been beaten, Sexually Assaulted, and starved to Death, and I had literally zero chance of explaining my innocence—especially since I had built that damn dungeon to begin with.

"The guy made the choice simple for me. He looked around the room, had a good laugh at my expense, picked up his duffel bag and briefcase, and then shocked the hell out of me with the taser setting."

Daegan Kyl looked at me, full of contempt over the whole thing.

"When I came to, everything was the same. The guy was still dead on the floor and the little girl was still downstairs. There wasn't much I could do at that point except try to clean up the wreckage.

"I used the guy's white shirt to wipe down the blood spots, wiped off his hands since he had grabbed me, wiped off his face where he had pushed his greasy head up onto my chest and I pushed him away with my hands, and then I wiped down the only piece of furniture—the desk—that I knew I had touched.

"I then backtracked my steps, wiped down the handle on the doors and stairwell railing, took the elevator ride so I could wipe the button, and eventually cleaned up the metal post I had used to smash the control box in the basement, all my blood splatters from the screen door, and called it good. I knew there was a minimal chance of ever being able to conceal my involvement if you guys were called in; between the Investigators and the forensic technology, there was almost no chance of my not having been identified as soon as an investigation started. It was a lost cause; I was surprised it took as long as it did to have my name brought into it. I was even more surprised it came from all of Willow's shit instead of from this case."

I raised an eyebrow; he had a point. With that much DNA left around, he should have been ID'd easily enough.

Without any further discussion, the time had arrived for us to depart from this abysmal place and make the ascent back out toward light, fresh air, and life again. I took the lead after glancing over and seeing the way his eyes had rested on the bed once again and left him on his own to collect himself. Whether he wanted to say a silent prayer, or simply come to terms with his experience, he seemed to want to remain for a moment on his own, and so I left him to it. As I walked out, I heard him click the light on his small flashlight, but he did not move around nor follow me.

I found myself saddened by the weight of it all; he was a man haunted by his own thoughts and the images that were stuck replaying in his head. Outward expressions of emotion or sentiment regarding matters held dearly to his heart did not seem likely to occur. But the depth of his capacity to love and grieve seemed to be underestimated, not to mention the depth of loyalty he had demonstrated toward his 'brother' William. Everything he was as a man was exemplified and reflected through his actions for anyone who chose to look below the surface.

His introspective demeanor and personal integrity had even been present in how he had chosen to address his Arrest and incarceration. He had not made any grand declarations or pledges about his Innocence. He had not made loud or aggressive demands for an attorney, even though he had been entitled to have one, and could have afforded the best our nation had to offer. Even as I had interviewed him and railroaded him about the Victims, he had not trivialized anything about the investigation, no matter how off-target my line of questioning had been. Above all else, he had not disparaged any of the Victims or the events surrounding their deaths even as he rebuked any responsibility.

Before long, he was on my heels, and we left the small 'apartment' at a leisurely pace. The silence surrounded us as we walked along through the boiler room and then ascended the stairwell, each lost in our own thoughts.

As we returned to the main level and traversed the dark hallways toward the exit, the only sound we heard was that of our heavy boots meeting the concrete floors and brushing through random debris.

But even as we walked in complete silence, with every step I felt the Evil fall away from my shoulders, and my confidence return as I thought about all the work that was yet to be done.

I had entered the building with a set of beliefs that all seemed to show that the man accompanying me had been part of a criminal enterprise that had been terrorizing our local Citizenry, but nothing could have been further from the truth. Instead, I had gained a more comprehensive understanding of who he was as a Human Being, and the man walking alongside me had revealed more about himself than he probably realized. It was clear that he had a lengthy history of hard living through his time as a Soldier, but perhaps what was most unexpected was gaining an understanding that he was no stranger to the depths of Human Suffering.

The burden he carried was heavy; he had witnessed several events that would have left a substantial impact on anyone, and he had carried it all in silence. He had also experienced years of close combat fighting within war zones and had known both danger and fear intimately. There were few men of our day that had lived lives where Civility and Peace had been replaced with Brutality and Bloodshed. But he had embraced the opportunity to join our Armed Forces, even knowing where it could lead. He had chosen to become a Soldier and had taken an Oath to Protect and Defend our nation from our enemies. Such an Oath was never taken lightly, and it did not end just because the Soldier stopped receiving a paycheck. He had the mentality of a Soldier and the heart of a Protector; it was as deeply rooted within his Being as any character trait could be within a man.

Despite these aspects of his professional career and personality, he had found himself engulfed in the seedy underbelly of a subculture that neither one of us had known about prior to our recent introduction, and he had been tested in a multitude of ways. He could have handled the events regarding his Ward, Willow Amos, in a much different manner; he could have abandoned her or hung her out to dry by turning her in. Despite the potential repercussions, he chose to help her, siding with loyalty and respect for her own beliefs over his blind obedience to the law. Whether I or anyone else agreed with his decisions—especially since he had clearly been manipulated and used at the time unbeknownst to himself—he had still made his decisions based on what he considered to be honor-bound obligations.

Even now, as we reached a new understanding between one another and found ourselves at a place of agreement, he kept his emotions in check and played his cards close to his chest. He could have expressed even the slightest hint of selfish gratitude over knowing that he was being cleared of all wrongdoing and spared any potential legal punishment—but he wasn't capable of it. His life, freedom, and future were all secured. No further action against him would be taken by me or any other agency. He had narrowly escaped an almost certain Death Sentence—and yet he could not escape the disquietude that enveloped him.

There was much more work to be done, and many more questions to be answered. It seemed that Daegan Kyl had dodged a bullet but was still intertwined in my investigation too far to withdraw without seeing it through to the end. I still had to work out how to resolve the other cases and Willow Amos. Daegan Kyl was not going to stand by and watch her get sentenced without a challenge or response. Aside from that, the Governor might have absolved this man of his sins, but he was not ready to forgive himself.

THIRTY-FOUR – EMERGING FROM THE DARKNESS

The Walk Back Outside

As we walked outside once more and slowly made our way toward our vehicles, I brought up how curious it was that the Governor had interjected himself into the case so deeply when I still hadn't been able to form a clear connection between him and Daegan Kyl. We hadn't even been able to find a connection between the Governor and the two Foreign Nationals. Even with all our legwork, interviews, and the research Officer Stanton was doing, we still hadn't figured out how the Governor had even known about what had happened at the factory, or Daegan Kyl's involvement. But after speaking directly with him, he obviously knew at least some version of the events.

I told Daegan Kyl about my interaction the day before with the Governor, going into more detail than I had at his Holding Cell. I told him how the Governor had informed me that he knew him to be innocent of any wrongdoing, that he didn't believe he had anything to do with the events that had transpired over the last months of Katarina's life, or that he believed him to even be capable of it. I also mentioned how he had seemingly known that he was responsible for the burials, including Katarina's, but that he had made it very clear that he would not be held accountable even for that part of things.

There was no connection to explain how a man such as himself could have known about the events involving the two Foreign Nationals, nor how he could have known about Daegan Kyl's Arrest, let alone how he could have been so adamant that I had 'missed the mark by a mile' regarding his character and involvement.

I told him about how he had alluded to being answerable to someone else—some unknown higher authority or puppet master. I had inferred from his comments that he was going to have to explain himself to someone if he didn't get me to do exactly what I was supposed to do. We discussed what we knew for certain, and what we could only speculate about. We agreed that the Governor seemed like he knew too much to not have been personally involved with the two Foreign Nationals somehow. The only explanation for how he would know the two men directly came from Detective Jarrett, and I shared with Daegan Kyl how he had said that there were 'powerful men' out there who would End his Life to prevent him from talking, and how he had referenced the words 'plaything' and 'playpen'. It certainly seemed to indicate that there was some type of pedophilia ring. But if that were the case, then everything pointed to the Governor himself not only being aware of it, but directly involved. No other explanations made sense for why he would have worked so relentlessly to impede my investigation, conceal the two Sexual Predators, and demand I omit the truth from my Final Report. It had to be for his own agenda or self-protection.

"It almost makes you wonder how much the Governor knew about this case and when exactly. It's a little curious that the Governor worked so hard to protect you, don't you think?" I asked him.

He nodded, following my train of thought.

"Yeah—there's something there. I'm not sure what it is, but I know he wasn't doing it to do me any favors. What was it he told you? I'm one of the most 'eligible bachelors in Seattle and a war hero'? So that's why I should have gotten off the hook for a possible double-Murder here and another three Victims buried across the field? That's a pretty lucky break for me then, huh? The Governor has your back just to clear your name, so he doesn't look like he's been hobnobbing with the riffraff. Guess I got lucky your buddies Arrested me at his party," he scoffed.

"I don't understand." I said, confused.

The SPD Officers had only told me that when they went to serve him his Warrant and Arrest him that he had been at a party. Given that he had been Arrested while in a tuxedo, that had made sense. No one mentioned whose party it was, and I never thought to ask.

He laughed.

"Um, yeah, it was at the Governor's Ball. Your guys just rolled up like it was all by design. I wasn't even planning on going at first. I just received the invitation one day; I'd never been invited before, although I knew it was an annual event. I figured it was just one of those things that happened when you got to a certain level on the social scale, you know? I'm pretty bad with that type of stuff; I've spent a lot more time eating MREs than I have sitting at fancy tables wondering which spoon to use. It all seems like a lot of hoopla over nothing, really. But I had the invitation, and it seemed like a pretty nice way to spend the night. I'd just met this gorgeous woman. I figured if she had a reason to get dolled up, it would make for a good time, you know? Women like that sort of thing and I figured what the hell."

He shrugged his shoulders and gave a sheepish laugh.

"I never even got to meet the guy though; we had just arrived at the Governor's mansion when your boys showed up. They caught up with me before I even went inside; I'd just had my car taken by the valet and was starting to walk up the stairs when two of your undercover guys approached me and asked me for a 'word'. They were both wearing suits at least, but I told my date to go ahead inside, and I'd meet her there by the bar—because there's always a bar, and where else was I going to tell her to go wait for me, right? So, then we walked down the driveway out of range of the guests, and they told me they were placing me under arrest. They had another two guys waiting somewhere in an unmarked cruiser just like the one you drive, and they just pulled up alongside us and asked me to climb in, so I did. That was it; I rode down to the Headquarters building with four of your local guys and then met you. I've never even seen the Governor in real life; it would have been the first time I'd even been in the same room as him."

He shrugged his shoulders again; not being able to meet the Governor wasn't something he was losing sleep over.

"I wasn't that surprised. Like I said, I was kind of expecting it. But I didn't think it would happen in a public place like that—I figured it would probably happen at my business or house at some point. But not as I was heading into a party. They didn't handcuff me, and they weren't jerks about it or anything, and it wasn't like they made a big public scene. I didn't think anyone had even noticed, but maybe someone told the Governor about it. But I doubt the guy even knew who was on his guest list; I doubt he knew anything about me personally before that night."

He stopped walking and looked at me.

"But seriously, next time, let's at least try to work it out so I don't end up ditching my date without any warning and having my car left in a parking lot somewhere. You can't even imagine the nasty messages I had waiting for me from that woman once I finally got home," he said.

"I mean, I've done some shitty things in the past, but I've never just left a woman high and dry like that. She was probably the most beautiful woman in that place, too. Gorgeous red dress—and I just left her sitting at a bar—she didn't even have a ride home. Think about that. Not cool."

I had to agree.

He had a valid point—not that any Police Department was going to give two bits about him or his date; he was being brought in for his connection to four sets of Human Remains that had been linked to him. But all things aside, it hadn't been the most decent way a man could have handled things on a date with a woman, and it probably wasn't quite his usual style. All of it was news to me, however; the SPD Officers hadn't mentioned anything about it, nor had they explained any of the specifics.

Still, they knew they were going to Arrest him; they could have just told him he was going to need to arrange another ride home for her, suggested that she hold on to his car keys, or one of them could have at least found the girl and let her know once they had him in the Squad car securely. He was dressed in a tuxedo, and they had already seen his date; they knew what she looked like and it would have taken a few moments of their time. It defied logic and reflected poorly on them. However, it wasn't their duty; it was just something that could have been done as a courtesy.

"Ahhh…" I started. "Well, I apologize. They could have handled that with a little more tact and some better social skills, obviously. I wasn't aware of that. Hopefully, your date was at least a little forgiving once you got out and called her, but I suppose after a week that probably didn't happen, huh?" I asked.

He laughed, "Ah, yeah—I'm pretty sure no amount of flowers were going to set that one back on track, but I did at least try; and no, not with the truth. Pretty bad first date though. She's probably still shredding me over it."

He grinned, and I had to chuckle; no matter how rich or good-looking a guy was, he always ended up in the doghouse. We shared a moment of levity, and for a second, we both forgot where we were and what we were doing.

"So anyhow," he continued, "I never met the guy—the Governor, I mean, and I have no idea why he tried to intervene. I thought about it though, and the only thing I came up with was that he might have followed the lead after my car was left sitting in the parking lot after the party—wherever it was. The ball was at the Governor's mansion, but I'm sure they had to take the cars off-site somewhere to park them. Maybe they contacted his office or something and asked about me not picking it up. I had the ticket in my tux, but they had my keys. Maybe he found out about the arrest through that, and then he started digging around. I don't know, but it seems like that's the most likely connection. It's all I could come up with anyhow."

We both knew there was more to the story than what was being presented, but now that I understood just how entrenched Daegan Kyl had been in the situation with both the Foreign Nationals and the Final Moments of Katarina's life—along with the heavy trail of DNA that would have proven his involvement and all but guaranteed the Death Penalty for him based on the evidence we could have obtained—we were both on the same page regarding its full implication.

For reasons as yet unknown, the Governor had intervened on the pretext of helping Daegan Kyl. His true motives were not yet understood, and if we considered what we already knew, we would come to the conclusion that seemed most obvious; we were never supposed to understand it any better. The Governor had his own agenda in the works, and he needed to conceal the actions of the two Foreign Nationals.

It was only by lucky chance that Daegan Kyl was involved enough that the Governor wanted to ensure he was cleared of any association; his goal was to conceal the Crimes against Katarina in their entirety—he wanted a complete blackout of her Abduction and Captivity by the two Foreign Nationals. Daegan Kyl had been caught in the crossfire, and the Governor was willing to do whatever necessary to make this case disappear.

"So how did you get your car back after you got out?" I asked. It still didn't make any sense; he had it now—he had driven it here to meet me.

"Dunno, man. I got back home to my place after I was released, and it was sitting in the driveway. My housekeeper said she found the keys in the mailbox next to the front door. I have no idea; there wasn't a note, and she didn't see anyone drop it off—but she comes and goes as she needs to and doesn't live on-site, so who knows when they did it. She doesn't have to stay very long or do very much work when I'm not around and she hadn't seen me or any signs of me in a week. Damn woman, I could have been lying in a gutter somewhere and all she would have done was keep changing out the flowers and putting a new dinner in the fridge every night for me."

"Women," he said.

I had to laugh again.

We didn't deserve any of them, and they most certainly didn't deserve us.

Final Conversation at the Factory

We stood by our vehicles, wrapping up our conversation before we parted ways and went about the rest of our day. As if by unspoken agreement, neither of us mentioned the basement nor the events that had occurred down there. God willing, we would never have to venture through those doors ever again. Now that I had a full background on how he had come to find Katarina, the case seemed to gain substantial traction, and I felt I understood many of the things that had not seemed to make sense.

He hadn't said anything about how he had buried her, but I didn't feel it was necessary to dredge it up just to get a firsthand account. I could picture him in my mind's eye well enough and knowing how he had attempted to clean up the 3rd floor and then retraced his steps, it seemed clear how he had gone about doing it.

All I needed to think about was the image I had in my head of him picking her up and then cradling her small frame in his arms as her Life Force slowly left her body. The imagery of her taking her Last Breath whilst cradled in his arms as he tried to hold her tenderly, without causing her any more physical pain, was unbearably bittersweet. It tore at my heart when I recalled it, and I doubted I would ever escape the imagery entirely.

I imagined he would have returned down to the basement after he had regained consciousness, and then attempted to clean up his DNA and any other signs of his presence. He had stated that he had placed her gently onto the bed upon her Death, and then he had returned upstairs where he had fought with the two men. From there, it was easy to imagine that he later returned, picked Katarina up from the bed, and carried her lifeless, fragile body back out into the boiler room, up the stairs, down the length of that endless corridor, and then placed her inside of the moving truck he said he had been driving. He would have placed her into the front seat rather than the back of the truck, and though it was heartbreaking to consider, he would have driven from the factory to the edge of the field next to the water with her lifeless form next to him.

He would have placed Katarina in the same location as the others even though he didn't know her, know who she was, or know why she was there. He would have buried her because it would have been the natural progression for the situation, and the only way he could have taken care of everything without forfeiting his own future and life. I believed each of us would have likely handled it with that same degree of self-preservation.

I glanced over at my companion as I shut down all the LED lights on my uniform and watched as he turned his head toward the skies and took a deep breath, exhaling slowly.

He then turned and looked at me, tipping his finger toward his cap and then started off toward his vehicle.

I nodded in return, making my way toward the SPD Cruiser.

He reached the door of his low sports car and then turned to me and asked, "What would happen next—if I were to leave? If I ended up in Alaska? Would they seize my assets, or would you have the power to direct everything toward anyone specifically?"

I paused for a moment and considered what he was asking; it wasn't usually black and white, but in his case, it wouldn't be an easy solution.

"Taking into consideration that the Governor won't allow you to be charged and that he intends to fight any criminal action on your behalf, I doubt you'll be going anywhere or losing anything—"

I held my hand up just as he responded, knowing it was now only a battle of wills and his own autonomy being debated.

"Your assets would normally be frozen—they would be frozen at the onset of any Felony charges or any that met the standard for Crimes Against Humanity. They would be inaccessible for everything except your own private legal representation. But you weren't charged—and won't be charged—with anything. The Governor said he cleaned out any records that might have been there, and I believe he'll monitor us to ensure this goes through as he demands. But that's a different issue altogether," I continued.

"Normally your assets would remain frozen until Conviction, at which point they would be seized, cataloged, liquidated, and then go through a final court order for redistribution. Depending on the charges, if you were to have been found responsible for one or all four of the Victims, they would have divided your assets between the Bereaved as best determined by the case and each circumstance. From what I have seen, they most likely would have only been able to prove a substantial enough case to merit restitution for the Urakov family, which I doubt you would have objected to anyhow. But I think the Urakov's would have refused any payment, even if they knew the full story. I might be wrong, but I don't get that impression from them; they would consider it blood money and reject it."

He winced; his assets and net worth had been acquired through hard work and accumulated over time, and his intentions had been pure. He had hoped for a better response.

"In the event that would occur, the state would probably just add it to the coffers; the vast majority of Crimes Against Humanity are done by the dregs of society, so most of the Victim Compensation Fund is taxpayer funded and follows the set minimums. Most of the cases where the Convicted Offenders have assets worth seizing are done through Crimes of Passion, and something like 80% of the cases are from one family member to another, so their 'assets' are just being left to the remaining family members afterward. But there are still the random Acts of Terrorism, mass shootings, and other events where substantial sums of private assets have been seized and then allocated among the Surviving Victims or their Bereaved; it's not the standard, especially not for someone of your status, but it has happened in the past.

"At any rate, there are enough programs and under-privileged cases within the Victim Advocacy Agency and the Crime Victim Compensation Fund that all your resources would be put to good use and would have ultimately ended up in the hands of other families who were suffering because of other Acts of Violence. The state has never had any problems spending money, especially if it isn't their own."

He nodded his head slowly, but still dissatisfied with the answer.

"I don't have the means or the resources to either lay claim to your assets nor to charge you, Convict you, or Sentence you to Exile. I can pretty much guarantee that Willow Amos is going to face Exile and she'll get deported over the next month or two—and she'll probably go along with a lot of others by the time my full investigation is complete. LeRoy Jones is a dead man walking, and good riddance. But my hands are tied with you, and it doesn't matter how altruistic you intend to be. The two men who deserved to get the worst punishments we could deliver have somehow managed to escape any Justice at all, so in the grand scheme of things, I can't say I'm bothered by knowing that at least you're not going to be forced to pay for their Crimes.

"You have a clean slate here. I'm not saying that what you did over on the other side of this property was how I would have done it or that I might not have still been able to pursue some legal action against you. On its own, it's probably enough to secure Exile. But I wouldn't pursue anything regarding Katarina even if I didn't have any orders coming down on me about it, and I really hope you get why that is and learn to accept it. I get why you think you need to stick by Willow Amos too, and it's commendable. But it's wrong—and I can't help but think even her own brother would be telling you that too.

"But I'll tell you something else, and you can do with this what you will. I can't advocate for Banishment for you, and I don't think I would even if I could figure out how to make it happen. And I don't want you to lose your money; I don't know what your total net worth is, but I can guarantee that you can do better with it than the state could. And if you really want to do something to help that little girl's family, then you need to figure out how to do it yourself, and you need to be here to do it. They aren't getting any Justice otherwise."

He clenched his jaw again and sighed heavily.

"If you intend to protect Willow Amos, you can't let her go to Alaska alone. It's hell on earth. It's the worst possible place a person could find themselves surrounded by the worst possible scumbags Humanity can produce. She wouldn't stand a chance there; they'd destroy everything good and decent about her—let alone innocent. They would make her pray for Death—and Death would be better than life out there with them.

"So, if you really want to do the right thing, figure out how to get your affairs in order, figure out how to make amends with the Urakov's if you feel it's necessary, sort out how to protect your finances for a while, and then try to figure out how you can get to Alaska.

"But she's not getting out of the mess she created, and I wouldn't even try and help you with that one. So, if you're really going to see it through with her, then you should know what kind of place she's going into because if she can't even figure out how to function here, there's no way she's going to survive there."

With that, I nodded in his direction again and closed my visor, masking my eyes and creating a barrier between the outside world and myself as a member of Law Enforcement once more.

Daegan Kyl tapped the top of his car with the palm of his hand and then opened his car door and climbed inside.

I followed him out of the parking lot and back onto the freeway before his high-powered machine disappeared out of range while I meandered back toward HQ, lost in my own thoughts. I didn't know how he intended to pull it off, but I believed he would choose to go to Alaska right alongside Willow Amos.

Whatever else could be said of him, he was a man who did what he believed to be right. It was unfortunate that Willow Amos was held in such high esteem by him; I doubted she would even comprehend, let alone appreciate, the sacrifice.

PART SEVEN

Whoever conceals their sins does not prosper,
but the one who confesses and renounces them finds mercy.

Proverbs 28:13

THIRTY-FIVE — KU — 4

The Bearer of Bad News

Now that I had a fully comprehensive report on everything that had happened to little Katarina Urakov after her Abduction, I was left with more information and imagery than I could have ever imagined. I felt confident that I had garnered as much evidence possible forensically, and that the ME had done his best to make the case airtight regardless of the opposition we had encountered, and despite the efforts to destroy and conceal the truth. I also felt comfortable that Daegan Kyl had provided me with as thorough of a recount as I was ever going to receive, and that what had happened to Katarina was a case I could close out knowing we had done our best to discover the truth and document everything thoroughly.

But I did not want to divulge any further details to Katarina's parents, even though I knew they would always be left with unanswered questions. God Help Me, I could not be the one who turned their Tragedy into a nightmare any greater than it already was. I could not bear the notion that either of little Katarina's parents would be provided with the full description and report regarding what their sweet little child had endured. Would that I could, I would have taken their heartache and borne it myself.

What she had endured until her Death was something that would create an immeasurable depth of Grief within the Souls of each of her parents; a Grief so profound it was likely that neither would have ever been able to recover fully—not that anyone ever recovers wholly and permanently after having been touched by Loss and Grief.

Even so, I could not be the person who broke through that safety wall and destroyed any remaining measure of faith or hope that either could retain. God Help Me, but I could not let the tragedy of Katarina result in the complete annihilation of her entire family, and it surely would have. Her mother, for certain, would never have recovered had she known. She was already there, standing on the edge of faith and reason; it would not take much for her to fall over the edge, and somehow, I could just sense that it would be a wall she would never again climb over if she went. And if she were to know how it had truly been—and for how long her daughter had Survived and Suffered before finally Surrendering—I did not believe that Lucya Urakov would ever again try to rejoin the living. It would have been her final descent, and I could not have blamed her for it.

As an Investigator, I had the right to employ discretionary measures regarding how much information I shared. I believed that most of the Bereaved had a right to know what Harm had befallen their Loved One, especially if it was because of Intentional Harm and resulted from a Crime Against Humanity. This line of thinking was in alignment with the philosophies of The Watchers On The Wall, and it had been a catalyst for them, helping them pave the way for our national Reformation. They had used the realities and horrors of the Violence caused by the Criminal Class of the 21st century to expose just how devastatingly negative they were to our society. It had been a remarkably effective campaign strategy. By showcasing the Evil that men committed within our own nation and against our own Citizens, they had proven that Evil begets Evil, and we ultimately only had two choices: To Submit To It, or Rise Against It.

I had applauded their efforts and philosophies my entire life, and throughout my education and career. I knew that reading Postmortem Examination Reports was a hardship that the average American did not want to ever be exposed to or made to endure. I knew it was precisely for this reason—that desire to keep oneself separate and distant from the savagery of our world—that it was imperative for them to take the time and do the work. I knew that only by seeing the photographs, by reading the reports, and hearing the comprehensive descriptions of wounds and damage done to their Fellow Man's Physical Form that it would be possible for the average American Citizen to truly grasp the horror of Violence being caused. I understood the amount of descriptive information necessary for the average American to realize that even though they might be free of such associations today, that there was no guarantee that it would not be them or their Loved One Tomorrow.

I believed it was not only the right of the Bereaved to have complete access to case evidence gathered by Law Enforcement, but that it was also the responsibility of every government agency to disclose all relevant information to them as a matter of principle. There must be complete government transparency if any government is going to exist within a society and make declarations about being in service to The People. If they are going to profess to be representatives of The People, to have the best interest of The People at heart, and to be the elected officials who were being paid—and well-compensated at that—to represent the needs of the many, then they should have a lengthy track record of Honorable Conduct across the board.

That being said, after years of working within my industry, I had to recognize that if there was a clear line distinguishing Good from Evil, and Government versus Citizen, my entire line of work was caught in some type of purgatory, because I could no more walk among the Citizens than I could proclaim myself a government official. I was of both worlds, and yet neither. I was beholden and accountable to everyone, but I was also exempt from obligation to all parties; I had no direct duty except to follow the truth, expose Evil wherever I might find it, and root it out from our society entirely.

This made my Code of Conduct particularly difficult as it pertained to the Urakov's, because what I desired to do was in direct contradiction to what I believed ethically ought to be done. I should not have the luxury of deciding how to process information based on my feelings, nor should I have different sets of standards for each case.

If I were to process this case with the same equity I delivered to others, then my emotional connection or desire to protect the Urakov's would not alter my actions. Therefore, my perception regarding the strength of their marriage would be irrelevant. The capacity for Oscar Urakov to lay blame at his wife's feet or to forgive her was irrelevant. Clearing Lucya Urakov of any parental negligence, even in hushed whispers, was also not my responsibility. Trying to convince Lucya that it could have been anyone's child, all in an effort to keep her state of mental health from deteriorating, was also not my duty.

Professionally, it wasn't my job to provide comfort, or to even care how the Bereaved processed their Grief. But on a personal level, as a Human Being and their Fellow Citizen, I wanted to do all I could to diminish their pain. Not only to ease their suffering, but because I knew that broken people were a hardship for any society to contend with, and the world was always made better if we could help our Fellow Man heal and overcome their trials.

None of that mattered, in the grand scheme of things, because the only thing that counted was the undeniable reality that their daughter was Gone, and now they knew for certain that she was not only Deceased but that she had been Murdered.

I couldn't tell them anything beyond any of that; I didn't want to.

God Help Me, but I could not put that family through any more than they had already endured.

How We Had Failed Katarina and Her Family

I found it necessary to reconcile my professional standards with the reality that there would be no Closure for Katarina's family. Her mother and father would spend the rest of their lives knowing that Justice had not been served, and the Criminal Justice system had failed to provide them the relief they had sought. They would never be given the full truth of what had happened to their daughter, and though I had tried to give them Peace and Closure, I knew that the lack of information and details would only leave them confused, disappointed, and angry.

It would go down as a travesty, the worst of my career. There was nothing that I could have done to change the outcome, no matter how much I wished we could have done things differently. Sometimes, unfortunately, no matter how much work is invested in a case, it just doesn't resolve itself in a way that provides any consolation or peace. This was an Injustice through and through—not just against Katarina, a helpless, beautiful little girl, but also against her parents, who deserved better.

It sorrowed me that I could not do more to prevent this outcome from transpiring as it did. My report, however, would not be crafted as the Governor had instructed me to write it. It would reflect the breakdown of events and outline the issues that had been presented in this case.

The best I could hope for was that it would shed new light on an old issue. America had a lengthy history of foreign persons, non-Citizens, who were not only in our nation illegally, but on US soil despite being Violent Offenders. Foreign Predators had always been here, among us, Committing Crimes and Acts of Violence against our Citizenry. On many occasions, the lax Criminal Justice system allowed for Offenders to be released pending trial, only to find that the 'Alleged Offenders' had fled the US and returned to their homelands, escaping Justice entirely. None of this was new to America; it was just a story that was no longer as common as it had been in previous centuries.

In this case, however, the injustice was even worse. Extradition would not happen, even if we could demonstrate with clear, unquestionable proof that the man that had fled back to his country of origin was responsible.

So here we were, unable to deliver any sense of Justice to the poor parents that had lost their daughter not just once, but twice. At least when she had Vanished, they had held out some measure of hope for her return; they could entertain the faintest glimmer of fantasy that she had not Disappeared because she was being Hurt, but because she had been wanted by a family that had been unable to have children of their own. It seemed like a foolish trick of the mind, but there were many parents that had admitted that after their children had Gone Missing, they had secretly harbored that same hope just so they could find some degree of solace and pretend that their precious child wasn't Suffering instead. It was probably Human Nature to hold out for hope, at least a little, and who could ever begrudge the parent of a Missing Child for trying to survive the emotional trauma of their situation by any means necessary when the alternative meant facing unfathomable Grief?

I imagined, had I asked Grace O'Connor what she knew of the subject, she would probably tell me that parents employed this strategy as a coping mechanism so they could endure the horrifying realities of their situation. She would say that it helped them cope with the gravity and desperation of their child's well-being and odds of survival. That they told themselves these little stories so their minds did not stray to where they would naturally go; a place where, as adults, they knew just what depraved, mercenary acts their Fellow Man was ultimately capable, and of which their beloved, innocent child was most likely being subjected to.

Katarina's parents had not been allowed to maintain that illusion of their daughter being safe, because I had shown up on their doorstep and destroyed their reality yet again.

I had not caused Katarina's Death. I had not failed to protect her from being Abducted, and I had not failed to find her while she was still Alive. But there would always be that little voice inside of my head that said, *'If only they had contacted me right after she had Gone Missing. If only they hadn't waited so long before they called for an Investigator.'* I would never know what might have been different *had they only called for my help*. The Seattle Police Department had been granted over three months to find her, save her, and return her back home safely to her parents. And had they only called for additional help, they might have been able to.

The Death of Katarina's Killer—the vague, unnamed man I accredited her Abduction and Death to—meant that there would be no genuine sense of Justice for her parents. They would find no solace in knowing that the man being held responsible for the Death of their daughter was already Deceased. It meant that there would be no Closure for them as they proceeded through a Trial and Sentencing. They would never have the opportunity to address their child's killer in a Court of Law, staring him in the eyes as they explained what his actions had resulted in. There would never be a chance for them to make the man who Murdered their daughter see the Pain and Devastation his actions caused them. And they would never find peace in the knowledge that at least he was trapped behind bars until his Execution.

It was difficult to consider a dead Killer as having served any sense of actual Justice if they died before spending even a day in prison. If 'Justice' meant being Apprehended, Convicted, and found Guilty of a Crime, then those steps must be provided in order to gain some sort of Closure for the families to Grieve. How could one consider it Justice if the killer died without having served a single day of punishment for his crimes?

There would never be an apology to Katarina's parents or the American People by the US government. Even if they accepted accountability and the truth were known, nothing our government could do would make amends for things, because it had been entirely preventable. They had willfully chosen to put American lives in danger by engaging in high-risk immigration policies from those whom they knew were from a region with contrary values and beliefs. Even though this practice was only newly being allowed again, and even though it was only supposed to be for trade and commerce and not for permanent Citizenship, and despite all the measures taken to secure proper vetting and public reassurances that all would be well, a little girl was now Dead.

THIRTY-SIX — WA — CONFESSION

Getting Willow to Talk

Three days after seeing Daegan Kyl at the factory and hearing his account of the events that had transpired there months earlier, I met with him in the parking lot of his business. I was having a difficult time making progress with Willow Amos, and I needed to close out my case with her full confession.

"I'd recommend that you go meet with the girl and get her to talk to me. I need to put an end to this little three-ring circus she's been building and close out these other cases. If I can't get to the root of this little side-project she's been running, and if she doesn't confess regarding the entire specifics about Arlan and Rebecca, I'm going to have a hard time trying to sell that either of them were done by their own free will and without any pressure. Right now, between her version and the swill coming out of LeRoy Jones' mouth, he's doing everything he can to convince us he didn't act alone.

"She's responsible for concealing the bodies of two Victims—you get that, right? A Rape Victim followed by the Abduction, Rape, and Murder of Mariam, and I know you are aware of the grimness of the cases. She might not have known anything about Mariam until it was too late, but you understand that she not only played a pivotal role in covering up for him, she then dragged you into it."

The man nodded his head in understanding.

"I'll arrange it so she can have another visit from you. Just go to the SPD jailhouse tomorrow afternoon and I'll make sure they can sign you through." I instructed him.

"What exactly do you need?" he asked.

"Well, everything you can get her to tell me. Anything she knows about LeRoy Jones, how she came to know him, how he came to be involved with her little club since she obviously didn't meet him on the campus like she did everyone else, and how everything unfolded between them. I have almost nothing to explain how this one random guy ended up being a Rapist and a Murderer but then managed to get this rogue college campus vigilante group to clean up after him—but clearly, they did. Willow Amos holds the key; she knows the truth about him, why he did it, why she covered for him and helped him, and—God forbid—whether or not there are any other Victims out there.

"I'm sure you want to understand it, too. She had you doing her dirty work for her as well, didn't she? Did you expect to be cleaning up dead bodies for a Predator like him when you agreed to help her? I somehow doubt it."

He stared back at me, one eyebrow raised, a smirk on his face.

"Obviously not," he replied dryly.

"Well, here's your chance. I need answers. I don't understand why she did what she did to help him, and she won't talk to me, even though I can't help her unless she does. I can't find any links between them, and this LeRoy character has been off-grid his entire adult life. I can't see his juvenile records because they're sealed and apparently the guy hasn't ever had a real job or paid any taxes; how he's lived so far under the radar I have no idea, but it doesn't give me much to go on."

"I'd like some answers about him, too. Do you know if she has an attorney?" he asked. He hadn't spoken to her since the brief meeting I had allowed between them before his release.

"She does, but I don't know if she's been meeting with him; I know she had someone at one point she called after her initial Arrest at the Randall farm. Since then, I'm not sure and I'd have to have my guy go through the records at the jailhouse to see if she's had phone calls or visitors. But to my knowledge, she hasn't ever requested someone from the state although she is entitled to; she doesn't have to use her own guy unless she wants to," I replied.

"Wouldn't her own attorney be better? Should I send someone over?" he asked.

"That's up to you. They all go through the same levels of education somewhere. But she's entitled to a state-funded defense attorney just the same as you were; it's not income-based—that would be discriminatory. Neither of you can be penalized and forced to pay for your own representation just because you can afford it, especially not when someone like LeRoy Jones will get all the free legal counsel he'll need throughout the process. Neither of you should be required to use your life's savings just to get fair representation—especially if you end up nickel-and-diming it or trying to cut corners just to afford it. But it's up to you; you're not going to have to take out a second mortgage just to have someone defend her. Ask her about her attorney—send her one of your own if you prefer, or let me know and I'll send someone over from the state.

"She should probably have someone there for our next interview or to oversee any type of confession she might submit. I need to get as much information as I can from her—not only to help with clearing both of you regarding LeRoy Jones, but also because I have to get this Angel of Mercy thing under control before I can finish this.

"She isn't out of the woods yet. Just because she's not being put up for the Death Penalty doesn't mean they couldn't still push for it—especially if they can link her to anything that shows that she knew about things ahead of time. I'm not making any promises where she's concerned, but if you genuinely want to help her, you need to get her to talk to me. Get her any attorney you think can help her best and meet with her tomorrow so she knows what's going on."

If she knew Jones had a history of Rape or prior Victims and concealed it, she could face more trouble.

"Also, her assets are probably frozen or about to be frozen—and soon they'll be seized altogether after her trial. So, if you intend to have her get some legal representation of her own accord, then she needs to get her forms filled out. They already sent over the packet outlining everything, but my guy said nothing had been returned. She's been formally Charged now and there's not much chance she'll avoid Conviction."

He nodded his head again, and I continued, "She had quite a bit, didn't she? Pretty sure I saw it was assets from her parents after their Deaths and then her brother as well, right? Because he was killed in a Combat Zone?"

I knew it was a touchy subject, but he needed to understand that she had thrown her whole life away—a good life at that. She was obviously intelligent, highly educated, and hadn't needed to worry about any of the usual money woes that plagued much of the world.

He needed to know that she had been granted everything necessary to build a strong foundation and a good life for herself and had thrown it all away. More importantly, she was still happy enough to drag him along with her; it would be good for him to see exactly what it meant to go from wealth and privilege to incarceration, destitution, and soon enough, the ultimate punishment—that of losing one's nation and Fellow Countrymen.

He scowled, but then raised his eyebrows and sighed heavily.

I knew he would go speak with her, do what must be done, do whatever he could to help the girl.

It was like watching someone keep going back to an abusive lover, the manipulation, the denial, the inexplicable submission, the incessant Abuse and Misuse of a Human Being.

I desperately wished I could understand the hold she had over him, but I still just couldn't see it. I prayed, for his sake, that she was aware of what she was doing and wouldn't do anything that would become too injurious to him. Out of everything she had been responsible for, I did not want Daegan Kyl to pay for her Crimes and decisions. She was already getting away with more than she deserved.

Interview I: Regarding Arlan Randall

"Please state your name for the record," I began.

"Willow Gloria Amos."

"Do you know of a man by the name of Arlan Randall?"

"Yes," she replied.

"Please tell me about your relationship."

She sighed, leaned forward, and propped her head into her left hand with her arm resting on the table. She stared at me, tired, listless, but not disengaged.

This wasn't about a lack of accountability or denial of her involvement; she just can't stand to be controlled by any type of authority figure.

"Arlan was a Citizen that I had met as part of my part-time employment with the Winter Season Hospice Care facility. He was a terminal patient dying a slow Death because of Cancer. He exhibited signs of extreme physical distress and frequently mentioned praying for Death to come quickly. He was the classic example of why Citizens such as The Angels of Mercy believe what we believe and why we so strongly advocate for the Right To Choose for all those who wish to End their own Lives.

"Mr. Randall had been suffering extensively by the time that I started working for him, providing End-of-Life Hospice care services on his family farm. I worked shifts along with six other regular staff workers and provided around-the-clock medical care for Mr. Randall. We were all employed by the Winter Season Hospice Care facility, including several drivers responsible for providing medical transportation."

"Do you recall how long you worked at the Randall residence?" I asked.

"Not long; a few weeks. About six. I'm sure you can check the records at Winter Season for the exact dates; I can't remember for sure."

I nodded. We knew the answer already; it was just under five weeks. But I was curious how close her attention to detail had been regarding her time spent caring for Mr. Randall. She had, after all, intentionally enticed him to End his own Life and orchestrated the events that had led to his Disappearance. I suppose I was just wondering how important she had regarded her time with him.

It was a shame that someone who had worked so diligently to End someone's Life and deprive them of their Final Moments couldn't even remember how much time she had spent around her target or invested in his demise. There was no question that Arlan's family remembered every treasured moment, event, and holiday they had been fortunate enough to share with him; in the end, being remembered was one of the most important aspects of our time here. To be remembered, loved, and missed through Grief was a sign of a life well-lived.

"Please tell me about Mr. Daegan Kyl's relationship with Arlan and how it came to be that he was responsible for his burial after his Death."

"Mr. Kyl had been contacted by me not too long before the situation unfolded with Rebecca and Mariam. I had contacted him because I was concerned I was going to get into legal trouble because of my involvement with The Angels of Mercy and the death of Arlan.

"Mr. Kyl did not know who Mr. Randall was and had never met him or heard about him while he was still alive, to the best of my knowledge. They were strangers. The only reason Mr. Kyl got involved in anything involving Mr. Randall was because of his connection and loyalty to me. Mr. Kyl did not have any contact with Mr. Randall until after his Death."

"Why did you contact Mr. Kyl?"

"I had been working with Mr. Randall at his farm for a while. He had stated that he wanted to leave the farm but was unable to do so on his own because of his physical limitations and pain. He was in a wheelchair and was taking a large amount of morphine just to get through his days. He was in constant pain and unable to move around on his own and could not drive anymore. He could have used autopilot, but he couldn't have gotten himself to his vehicle or physically climbed into any vehicle on his own. He asked me for my help to leave the farm."

I watched her face carefully, looking for anything resembling a conscience, but found nothing. Her words had been so artfully and carefully selected that it was almost poetic. It wasn't that anything she was saying was untrue; it was what she wasn't saying that stood out. She was carefully constructing a scene in which she felt a moral and humanitarian obligation to help Mr. Randall; he was in *such dire need of assistance* that she felt as though she could not refuse him. It was well-crafted.

What was missing was the part about how she had nursed him while repeatedly whispering sweet nothings in his ear about how she could 'help him' End his Pain and Physical Suffering, and all he had to do was ask for her help. She failed to mention that he only asked her to help because he already knew she was willing to break the federal laws and the Sanctity of Life Oath—not to mention her Hippocratic Oath—to help him End his Life, despite it being a Crime Against Humanity for her to do so.

She was drawing a compelling line regarding intent. A lack of conscious intent would reduce her culpability and would ultimately translate into the difference between Exile and the Death Penalty.

I wasn't sure if she was smart enough to know how to walk this legal line or if she had been coached by her legal representation either before or after her arrest, but she was doing an admirable job. She was rehearsed, well-prepared, and factual—even as she mustered some hard-won tears to emphasize how much she had cared about the man and was therefore 'conflicted' about her decision to help him.

But in the end, as she narrated how she felt she 'had no other choice' but to help him leave his home and take enough of his medication to 'put an end to his suffering', I had to applaud her efforts. Every time she gave testimony, she created a portrait of innocence, selflessness, and even painted herself as a victim at times.

Perhaps the most important benefit to these shams she was attempting to pass off as 'confessions' was that she was demonstrating one truly noble and selfless act throughout every single statement she made. She did everything in her power to exonerate Daegan Kyl and cleanse him of all wrongdoing, accountability, and knowledge every single time.

I wasn't convinced she had a heart or a conscience; I found her to be too smart for her own good and as manipulative as Satan in the Garden of Eden. But somewhere deep down inside that black soul of hers, she genuinely seemed to care enough about Daegan Kyl to not want him to end up paying for her Crimes.

It seemed evident that he had been manipulated six ways to Sunday and the Panel of Judges would see that. Although I didn't think it would matter, it was my hope that after Daegan Kyl himself had seen and read her sworn statements that he, too, would at least recognize this. He was still planning on following her to Alaska; the least I could hope for is that he did so with a full understanding of who she was and what she had put him through for her own benefit. He would still be loyal to her—of this, I was certain—but better to be a well-informed fool than a blind one.

"So how did he leave the farm?" I asked.

"I contacted several men I knew who could assist; they worked part time at the Winter Season Hospice Care Facility with me."

"And were these men also involved in The Angels of Mercy?" I asked. She wouldn't give an inch unless she had to.

"Yes."

"Do you know their names?"

"I can't remember."

"Did you help anyone get hired at the Winter Season Hospice Care Facility, and if so, were any of the men who assisted you with Arlan Randall among those you helped gain employment?" I asked.

"I have suggested to the Human Resources department at Winter Season that they could always look for good employees through the nursing program on campus, but I wouldn't be able to tell you if they ever did that or hired anyone, so the answer to your second question would also be unknown."

"To the best of your recollection?" I asked sarcastically.

"To the best of my recollection," she replied.

We continued in this manner for a few more rounds, always back and forth, always just evasive enough to avoid anything self-incriminatory and almost always vague or forgetful when it came to remembering dates, times, or names.

She was there, but she couldn't remember when. She had spoken to him about options, but she didn't physically help him leave the farm. She had been Arrested, and she didn't know what happened afterward. She believed in the ideologies of Assisted-Suicide, but she hadn't directly contributed toward the Suicide of anyone, including Arlan.

"When you were Arrested and taken into one of the Interview Rooms, you were offered an attorney, correct?"

"Yes."

"But you didn't accept one," I stated. It was a fact, not a question.

"No."

"May I ask why not?"

"I didn't feel I needed one," she replied innocently. "I had done nothing wrong."

"But you consulted another attorney, did you not? You called an attorney while you were inside the Interview Room." More facts: I just wanted to hear her reasoning.

"Yes…" she said slowly. There was a slight inflection in her voice; a question rising at the end of her brief answer—just barely pronounced enough to remind me that she genuinely believed herself superior to Law Enforcement and that my clumsy, leading questions were no match for her dazzling intellect.

"You called a law firm by the name of Karl and Radcliffe, didn't you?"

She nodded her head.

"Please answer with a verbal response, Ms. Amos, for the record," I reminded her.

"Yes."

"And how was this law firm known to you?" I asked.

"They are the law firm that I have on retainer," she replied.

"And how long have you kept this law firm on retainer?"

"A few years; I'd have to research for an exact date," she responded. Her voice was curt. This was not a line of questioning she wanted to address.

"You inherited a substantial amount of money and assets because of the untimely Death of your parents when you were a minor, did you not?" I asked, probing deeper.

"Yes."

"But because you were still underage, that was all structured through attorneys and set up in trust for you. Is that correct?"

"Yes."

"And who established that for you? Was it all set in place by your parents, or did someone intervene after their Deaths?"

She sat up straighter, her back as solid as a plank of wood, her eyes glowering and her mouth tense. The emotional response was much more pronounced when someone was discussing the Deceased members of her own family; the Death of Arlan was met with indifference—a game from which she was being inconvenienced. The Deaths of her own parents and brother were apparently off-limits and met with swift hostility as her hackles raised in self-defense.

She might not have been a sociopath, but she was damaged; she wasn't someone that I would have wanted to hand out lectures on the Value of Human Life. It was like asking an atheist to assess how much stock someone should put into their faith or church; they were hardly a source of knowledge to be trusted if they couldn't even understand why such issues had value to begin with. Likewise, if one couldn't appreciate how precious life truly was—especially if they were so wounded from their own experiences with loss and unaddressed Grief—were they truly the best source for evaluating whether or not life was worth savoring even if already in Hospice and terminal?

The very thought of this fragile little girl whispering to tired old men that it was ok to surrender to the pain and sacrifice their Final Moments on this earth was extremely depressing to me. She was advising those who had lived more than three times her length of life about matters of Life and Death—having never been married, having never had children of her own, having never even been in love before. She was advising the elderly and infirm to sacrifice what little time they had left and surrender to the Great Unknown when she herself had never known how precious the Value of Human Life was, having only experienced Grief, suffering, loss, loneliness, and Death herself. It was deeply troubling to realize, and for the first time I saw what compelled Daegan Kyl to continue to save her from herself; if he didn't do it, no one would.

"My brother took care of everything. He was a legal adult at the time of their Deaths. He inherited everything. He set up the trust fund for me that was made available upon my Twentieth Birthdate."

"And he did this in such a manner that he included provisions for his own assets, including his Death Compensation through the military and his portion of assets from your parents as well? To the best of your knowledge?" I asked.

"Yes; it was all established through the trust fund. He was required to have everything in place as an active-duty soldier, especially since he had legal custody of me and deployed into combat zones," she stated.

She still spoke matter-of-factly, but her voice was filled with a quiet sadness that was hard to miss. She didn't want to talk about him. She didn't want to talk about her parents either, but perhaps because her brother's Death was so much more recent, or maybe because she had been closer to him or loved him more, he was the one she didn't want to share with me. He was hers to treasure; I had no right to her memories.

"Just a few more questions, Ms. Amos," I said. I had lost my taste for this entire sordid ordeal already; I just wanted it over and done with. There would be no winners here; not today, not tomorrow, not at the end of this case—not ever.

"Was the law firm Karl and Radcliffe the firm that was hired by your brother to tend to the trust fund and address all of your financial needs?" I asked.

I already knew the answer and already knew why they weren't. But I had to have it on record, and she had to answer the question in the only way she honestly could.

"No," she responded.

"What was the name of that law firm if you can recall? And do you still retain their services?"

"They were known by the name of Powers and Gore back then. I think they are Powers, Gore, and Levin now. They have a new partner."

"And you still retain their services to oversee your assets?" I asked.

She nodded, "Yes."

"So why then, may I ask, do you have the other law firm on retainer?"

She looked at me without flinching, and said, "Because they're criminal defense attorneys."

The room fell silent as I considered her answer. I already knew; Officer Stanton had researched the phone call and then researched the law firm. It didn't take long to see she already had a private criminal attorney that was known to her, although I hadn't known any of the specifics. I certainly wouldn't have imagined she had kept them on retainer for 'a few years'–and I knew just as well as she did it made her look more guilty because of it.

Normal, law-abiding people rarely had criminal defense attorneys on retainer—certainly not for years. Criminals had criminal defense attorneys; even then, most of the time, they didn't retain their services until after they had been caught or Arrested for 'Alleged' criminal activity.

Young women were even less likely to keep criminal defense attorneys on retainer. And Willow Amos was hardly an average young woman, making her situation even more intriguing. She was a hard-working graduate student specializing in a difficult advanced program, and a wealthy trust fund recipient to boot.

There wasn't anything left to say; she wouldn't explain it any further and anything she said would most likely be incriminating.

The damage was done just because the information was out there. The prosecutors could take it further if they could, but I doubted it would happen.

She had the funds to retain any attorneys she wanted; she was independently wealthy and could easily have said it was a matter of caution. Really, she could have just said she retained them because of her association with LeRoy Jones and how she had wanted to ask them private questions about him because he worried her so much. It was just as valid of a reason as anything associated with The Angels of Mercy and would create enough doubt to allow her to wiggle free from self-incrimination.

For now, it was enough.

We were both tired; I felt it and I could see it in her eyes. Today had been harder to contend with; it was a difficult, tedious process.

I asked her to go through the closing statement once again for the record, and as I listened to her recite the words, I found myself wishing that neither she nor Daegan Kyl had ever entered my line of fire.

I would never understand how seemingly good people always managed to find themselves neck deep in situations that obliterated their entire histories of good behavior and replaced them with life-altering consequences that invariably destroyed everything.

Maybe we were all just one person, one relationship away from losing it all.

"I, Willow Gloria Amos, swear these statements to be true and factual to the best of my knowledge. The statements made within this interview were voluntary and of my own accord and made without duress. These statements were made with my own words and under penalty of law."

Interview II: Regarding Rebecca Summers

"Please state your name for the record."

"Willow Gloria Amos."

"Ms. Amos, do you know of a woman by the name of Rebecca Summers?"

"Yes."

"Please tell me about her and your experiences with her."

"On the date in question, a young woman entered the Healthcare and Counseling Office at the Greater Seattle Area University building where I was working part time. She appeared disheveled and emotionally erratic and stated that she had been Raped on campus only moments before. I contacted the Security Guard and the two of us attempted to render aid to the woman whom I now know was Rebecca Summers.

"When the Security Guard reviewed the tape that revealed a Physical Encounter as she was pulled from the main path, I recognized the man in the video as LeRoy Jones. I grew concerned about my involvement because I knew that if LeRoy Jones were arrested that he would have a great deal of personal information about me and the work I was doing with The Angels of Mercy. They would have asked why he was on the college campus, and I knew it was because he had been to visit me. I did not consider LeRoy Jones to be an intelligent man, and although I was loyal to him, I did not trust that he would be as loyal to me or even understand why he would need to be discreet and keep my involvement out of anything if he were questioned.

"I worked with the Security Guard, a man whom I knew to be loyal to The Angels of Mercy, and directed him to conceal the video surveillance to hide the identity of LeRoy Jones."

"Do you know the name of the security guard?" I asked.

"Evan Harrison."

"Thank you, please continue."

"I convinced the woman, Rebecca Summers, not to pursue further action, either medically or through Law Enforcement. I employed unethical practices in order to shame her into silence, including references to make her question how she would be perceived once it was known she had been a Victim of Rape. I placed the life and death of a fellow citizen in her hands because if convicted, LeRoy Jones would have been sentenced to Death. I infused enough shame to make her believe no Rape was comparable to the price of a Human Life, and by reporting the man she was condemning him to die. I intimated that if she were a Good Human Being and Christian, then she should be focused on Forgiveness rather than Retribution, and that blood would be on her hands if she caused another Human Being to be Murdered for his Crimes."

"Can you please describe the events regarding any continuation of contact with Rebecca Summers?"

"I attempted to remain in contact with Rebecca Summers and contacted her several times in the days and weeks that followed. I deeply regretted my behavior and the manner in which I had conducted myself. I do not believe that I would have handled it the same way had it been any other man than LeRoy Jones and I was not only protective of him enough that I did not want to see him Arrested, Convicted, and Put to Death, but I was also deeply ashamed because I knew I had done it partly to ensure that my connection to him would not be discovered. I knew my actions were morally wrong and contemptuous, but I had done it to protect the Greater Good of what I believed The Angels of Mercy were doing, and I did not want anyone to find out about the network. Concealing one Rape that I justified could not even be proven was a small sacrifice for the Greater Good.

"Rebecca Summers contacted me after a period of time and told me she was pregnant. I knew then that it would not be as easy to resolve the matter as I had hoped. I had not seen LeRoy Jones, nor heard from him, since the day that he had been on campus and she had made Rape Allegations against him.

"Upon hearing from her that she had confirmed a pregnancy, I arranged for her to meet with a third person to have a Medical Examination. This person was a licensed medical practitioner whom I knew to be supportive of The Angels of Mercy and believed in the same philosophies. I did not go with Rebecca Summers to the appointment, I did not take part in the appointment in any manner, and I was not privy to the circumstances of the appointment. I heard nothing about the appointment either beforehand or afterward. I did not fund any services provided, nor did I have direct contact with the Medical Practitioner or speak to the Medical Practitioner about Willow Amos."

Once again, her answers were neatly outlined, well-rehearsed, and eloquently skirted the law and accountability. And while they may have implied she had some reckoning of the events that transpired or might have known, there was no way to prove she knew what would happen.

She was both fluent and adept in the art of manipulation and wordplay; I wondered how much coaching she had received over the years from her attorneys or if she really was just as smart as she seemed.

"Please state for the record the specifics regarding the Abduction and Disappearance of Mariam Pembrook," I said, shifting gears. There wasn't any point in trying to trap her; she was well-trained and sharp. She would not easily be tripped up.

"During this period, I was also aware that there was a woman that had been listed as a Missing Person who had a direct connection to the university. She was an Adjunct Professor on campus, but I did not know her personally and had never met her. Her name was Mariam Pembrook. She had reportedly been abducted after doing her grocery shopping.

"I had no reason to believe there was any type of direct connection to my own life or to anyone within it. I did not know that LeRoy Jones was the Alleged Suspect depicted in the surveillance footage I had observed through local news and in still frame notices that had been posted throughout the campus. The footage was too grainy for me to clearly identify him, and at the time I did not have the slightest suspicion of his involvement."

She looked out the window toward the dark grey sky. Her shoulders seemed to fall forward as if a heavy weight bearing down on her suddenly overwhelmed her. She was a slight figure; small-boned but lacking any obvious femininity to speak of. She always looked gaunt, under-fed, and stricken with the same pasty pallor that so many in the Greater Seattle Area were known to have.

"I'm tired. Can we take a break? Can we just do this another time?" she asked.

She did look tired; it was that same fatigue I'd seen many times in here before, and usually hit after hours of grueling interrogation much like this. It was a mental fatigue that came from no longer being able to just go home, put your feet up, and relax. It came from knowing that your life was no longer yours to control, your bed was no longer available for a long nap on a wet, chilly day, and that your time was no longer yours to prioritize.

It was the fatigue of being powerless, of being rendered insignificant, and then finally grasping the full magnitude of what that meant. It stemmed from mental exhaustion and the depression which follows as one comes to terms with exactly what it means to be incarcerated. For many, it was the moment of reckoning as they began that long march toward Death Row.

As a medical professional, Willow Amos should have recognized it for what it was. Even though it was slightly less familiar in the Criminal Justice system, the sentiment was still the same. After all, her own colleagues had coined the grossly Inhumane term for it themselves. In a manner of speaking, she was showing the first signs of 'circling the drain'.

Interview III: 2nd Interview Regarding Rebecca Summers

"Let's begin with your final communication with Rebecca Summers," I began.

"The last time I heard from Rebecca Summers was the day of her Death. She contacted me and asked if she could see me. She told me she wanted to thank me for my help and guidance. I asked her where she was, and she said that she was sitting in the little park area that was connected to her apartment. She had walked over, but she said that I could just pull into the parking lot.

"I didn't have much time before I had to be to work, but I thought I should see her because I hadn't checked in on her since her visit to the Medical Practitioner. It was a very warm day for late spring, and I thought everything was fine because she was sitting in the park.

"When I arrived, she was sitting at a picnic table and was facing a forested area at the edge of the park. It was not a very big location and to my knowledge, it didn't have any CCTV cameras. She was sitting there with a cold drink, some pastels, and a sketchpad. There was also a small plastic bag next to her that was about eighteen inches in length and size, that appeared to be flat or empty. I thought everything was fine; I thought *she* was fine.

"I was only there for a few moments before it became clear that something was wrong. She greeted me and asked me to sit down, and then she said she wanted to thank me for all my help. She said that I had been 'instrumental in helping her make the right choice'. I thought it was in relation to her decision not to proceed with rape charges or perhaps because of her visit to the Medical Practitioner.

"Within a moment, she suddenly started laughing and then she put down her sketchbook. She said she had painted something for me. She said she was supposed to have been a 'great artist' and she was supposed to have had her first 'big show' recently. She said it was supposed to have been 'the show that launched her career'. And then she handed me the plastic bag, and when I took it, I could feel it had a piece of canvas inside; it was about 12x12 in diameter. I was flattered; I told her she didn't have to do anything for me but was grateful. And I remember feeling nervous about it because her laugh had been just a little strange; a little too high. But I'd never heard her laugh before, so I couldn't tell for sure.

"I looked at the picture she had drawn, and it was a picture of what appeared to be Mary and the baby Jesus. It followed one of the old paintings—I don't know which one—but one where the 'Virgin Mother' gives birth to the baby. I knew she was an artist, but I'd never seen her work. But this wasn't meant for anyone else; she had drawn this for me. The painting had the baby all torn up into fragments—it was torn apart and had hanging pieces of flesh at the limbs. It was grotesque; it was a butchered baby."

She paused in her story for the first time, taking a moment to look out toward the endless grey sky as she delved deeper into her mind's eye. Her recounting of the events was haunting; it was far worse than I had imagined and shed a dark light on just how fragile Rebecca had been at the time. How Willow Amos was not drowning in her own feelings of guilt and responsibility was bizarre; she seemed to compartmentalize her emotions better than anyone I'd ever encountered.

I wondered how much of that had been developed as coping mechanisms to help her navigate the lengthy series of different foster homes she had been placed in throughout the last five years of her childhood. We all developed different ways to cope with the stressors in our lives, and she had been handed many at a very impressionable age.

Before long, Willow Amos began again. Her voice was soft, but emotionless. She did not make eye contact with me, but continued to stare vaguely out the window.

"And then I knew something wasn't right. She wasn't right. Her eyes were weird and out of focus, and she wasn't laughing anymore. She told me that it was all my fault. She told me that I ruined her life. She told me that he had raped her, and I had protected him instead, and I would go to hell for it.

"And then she fell to the ground, just crumpled over like she was drunk and fell from the bench to the grass below her. She was moving her head around and I dropped the painting and rushed over to her as soon as it happened. She said that he destroyed her body, that she killed her baby because of me, and that he left her stained forever. She said I stole her future, and she hoped I would die for it. She said her God was a wrathful God, and she didn't forgive me.

"And then she began to shake, and white foam came out of her mouth. I panicked. I didn't know what to do. I picked her up and tried to carry her to my car. I didn't know I could be as strong as I was. But I was sincerely trying to save her life at that point.

"I knew she had taken some type of pills or poison and thought they could pump her stomach if I got her to the hospital. So, I picked her up and half-carried, half-dragged her to my car, which was only a few steps away. I was able to put her into the backseat and I ran back and grabbed my own purse and the stuff she had brought with her. I didn't know what she had in her purse or the lunch bag she had brought, but I thought maybe she had the pills she had taken, and they would be able to look. Sometimes they can decide whether it's better to pump the stomach or not based on the type of pills or chemicals they ingested; I wanted to make sure they had them if they were on her. I wasn't really slowing down to think things through, but my brain was telling me to grab the bags, so I did.

"I didn't stop to look through the bags when I ran back to the table; I just grabbed everything. I threw everything into the back seat with her and rolled her onto her side. When I started to drive away, she was still breathing.

"I started driving to the GSA Hospital, which I knew was the closest. She stopped breathing within a few minutes, and I knew she was dead."

She stopped talking again, still trapped in her mind's eye and focusing on the window.

I didn't push her or rush her; she would continue when she was ready.

After several moments of silence in the room, she finally continued.

"I just didn't know what to do. At that point, I just had no earthly idea what I was supposed to do anymore.

"I didn't know how everything had spiraled out of control so fast like that. I kept driving around the back streets, trying to compose my thoughts, and trying to figure out what to do. After probably fifteen or twenty minutes, I finally just drove her to my house and parked in my garage so I could think.

"I sat in the garage for a few minutes once I'd parked and shut the door behind me before I got out. Once I left the car, I kinda walked around for a few minutes and then I opened the back door on the driver's seat, leaned over her as she lay there with the white foam still covering her mouth, with her eyes still open...And I grabbed her purse and the other bag that she had; the one that was a regular brown lunch bag. I knew the other plastic bag was just covering the painting; there hadn't been anything else in it I had seen. If she had any pills, they had to be in the other bag or her purse.

"So, I looked through her bag and found a bottle of Oxycodone that had a prescription amount of one-hundred-twenty pills. I recognized the name on the bottle as the name of the Medical Practitioner that I had given her the contact information to. I don't know why she issued her the pills or why she gave her so many. I didn't contact her to find out. I didn't contact anyone.

"I was late for work already, but I didn't realize it until I had calmed myself down. I was still in my garage, but after I looked at the pills, I started pacing around in the front of my car and trying to figure out how to handle things. I called my work and told them something had made me feel suddenly ill, and I thought it was food poisoning and I wasn't going to be able to make it in. I wasn't ever absent, so they were concerned, but believed me and told me not to worry.

"I had to figure out what to do. She had overdosed on pills that she shouldn't have had from a doctor that I had sent her to where she had gotten an illegal abortion. She blamed me.

"My only choice was to conceal her death and hide her body, so I tried to figure out how to do it. Normally I would have called LeRoy Jones to help me, but I didn't want him to know that I knew what he had done or know that I had covered for him. I did not trust him to have that information about me and I did not feel safe with the idea of LeRoy Jones knowing that I knew he had raped and physically struck a woman. I felt as though I would be in greater danger if he knew I was aware of his crimes or if he thought I had surveillance footage of it even though I had deleted it. I was afraid of what he might be capable of doing.

"I took all the material items from the back seat and hid them throughout my garage. I hid the sketchbook and pastels, her purse, the bottle of pills, and that awful painting in different places around my garage until they could be disposed of properly.

"I covered her with a blanket and left her in the back seat of my car and then went into my house through the garage door and into the kitchen. I remained in my home like that for the rest of the day until after it was dark. The days were growing longer already, so it was probably at least after seven p.m.

"I still didn't know what to do or who to call. This was not something that anyone that I knew through The Angels of Mercy could explain, and the only person who knew anything about it was the Security Guard that had helped me. I was worried if I reached out to him he would blame me and say that it was outside the realm of The Angels of Mercy or might even report me to Law Enforcement."

She finally took a moment to pause from her story and then glanced my way. I knew she wasn't a big fan of mine, and she didn't want to be here. I was probably not one of the people she would have ever wanted to share her story with, but at least she was getting through it.

There wasn't supposed to be any room for compassion; it was all supposed to be done entirely by the books. I knew that there would be plenty of people on both sides of this case—half wanting her dead and half wanting to at least show enough mercy to only sentence her to Exile. For once, I was glad that it was not up to me. Her confessions were incriminatory, but they had not led her to the steps of the gallows just yet.

"After many, many hours of contemplation, I felt I had no choice but to contact LeRoy Jones and tell him I needed him to help me. LeRoy Jones responded he would meet me at nine p.m.

"I made arrangements to meet him in a location that I knew well and knew was not somewhere that was monitored by any type of CCTV or live patrolling by Law Enforcement because it was private land.

"The location that I had chosen to meet with LeRoy Jones was the personal property of Daegan Kyl. I was planning on meeting him by the Moving Trucks and Storage Units. On the far side of the property, Mr. Kyl had his second business; the maid-cleaning business.

"I knew the area well and had spent many hours there because I had known Mr. Kyl since before he had launched his business enterprises. I had worked in both areas of his business casually while I was an undergraduate in school, and because of the personal connection between myself and Mr. Kyl, I had always had access to the businesses and facilities.

"There have been times when I have used the facilities and Mr. Kyl's rental trucks for my own purposes after hours and without his consent or knowledge.

"Mr. Kyl did not know that I had arranged to meet LeRoy Jones on the property. He was not aware of the meeting before the meeting took place and he did not know it happened afterward."

"That's a good place to stop if you would like to," I said.

She nodded her head, and for a split second I thought I saw something flash deep within her eyes that almost seemed like fear. She had looked scared for a split second, and then it was gone and replaced with what appeared to be a look of relief—but that, too, disappeared in a heartbeat as she regrouped and regained her composure.

She had been doing a tremendous job talking about all of this; none of it had been easy, and I knew she was not the heartless monster I had previously believed her to be.

She was a young, dumb, idealistic kid who seemed to be more emotionally damaged than most. She had lost everyone in her family that should have been there for her, and while she had gained the support and even some mentorship and familial connection from Daegan Kyl, she had still spent five long years being shuffled around from stranger to stranger without a home to call her own. She had lost a lot over the years; it had been a system that had always been known to be difficult to navigate, and statistics continued to prove that the odds of children evolving into high-functioning adults after experiencing time within the system were slim. The fact that she had not only survived but gone on to obtain an advanced degree, hold down steady employment, and appeared to be as functional as she was would have been considered miraculous by most.

All things considered, she was foolishly naïve despite her experiences. She was too emotional for her own good, and despite being highly educated, it was clear that she lacked even the most basic coping skills or stress management. None of those issues were likely her fault; she would need to grow a little longer in the tooth before earning those traits on her own.

I watched her shuffle back to her Holding Cell as she walked between two oversized SPD Officers. Most of the time she walked quietly but with her head held high, defiant, and proud to the bitter end. But tonight, she carried herself differently; her head was down, shoulders still defeated, and she was moving more slowly.

She was sad.

She walked like she knew she was beaten, like the truth of the situation was written on the walls, and as if the past that had brought her to this moment in her life had finally gotten the best of her.

I intended to finish my line of questioning tomorrow, and at least the additional strain from these interviews would be over.

As she disappeared around the corner, I made a mental note to send Daegan Kyl a message telling him he should plan a visit for tomorrow evening. I could arrange it so she could see him for a while; it wouldn't hurt the SPD any, but it would probably go a long way toward helping her adjust.

I packed up my stuff and got ready to head back to the barracks. It had been another long day.

It occurred to me as I walked down the hallway toward the exit that she could have been playing me just like everyone else, but it didn't seem very likely. There was nothing to gain by it.

She was no longer the fiery little hellion that had first met me inside that Interview Room; it was so noticeable that even I could see it.

I didn't know her well enough to know how she would behave down the line, but there were many who simply could not handle being incarcerated, even if it was only for a short duration, as were most criminal cases. It seemed unlikely that she would be

Suicidal, but I understood that she obviously had no issues with those who chose to Commit Suicide and she believed it to be a matter of choice.

That gave me a little perspective on the situation and what was possible; especially since she was such an emotional person. If she didn't feel any semblance of hope—if she believed she would confess but still face the Death Penalty, or perhaps even if she knew the outcome was going to be Exile—the consequences may end up being too great for her to endure.

It was all speculation on my end, but I would contact Daegan Kyl nonetheless and I would let her know I was going to authorize the visit. Perhaps if she at least had something to look forward to, it would help her transition better.

Soon enough she would be out and free once again; if freedom meant anything, it was better to have it in the wilds of Alaska than to be in a cage here.

Statement I: Regarding The Angels of Mercy

I, Willow Gloria Amos, do hereby provide this statement as my sworn testimony regarding all allegations and formal charges issued against me in relation to The Angels of Mercy:

I.

During the first year of my enrollment at the Greater Seattle Area University, I began to examine materials available through the library system pertaining to the progressive ideological beliefs of the American People from before the Great Reformation and the Last Stand. I did this freely of my own accord, for my own interests, through the free use of educational materials available through the university library system, and in due accordance with my First Amendment Rights as a Natural Born Citizen of These United States.

My personal educational endeavors pertained to the health and well-being of all Natural Born United States Citizens and were the beginning steps toward an advanced education degree in Healthcare, although when I began reading and growing in my knowledge I was only an undergraduate and taking traditional, standard courses. My long-term goals were to become a Healthcare Professional. Throughout my formative years, I began to develop a worldview that was contrary to the traditional national views that were established as part of the public education system during my primary educational years.

My interest in broadening my knowledge of national matters grew exponentially upon learning of the Death of my Beloved Brother, William Ronald Amos, who was Killed during a Combat Mission on Foreign Soil and whose Physical Remains were not returned to These United States for proper care and Memorialization. As his only Sister, as the Primary Head of Household because of our parents having already Passed Away, and as his Bereaved Surviving Family Member, I developed serious misgivings and questions related to my government, the national policies which were in effect at the time and remain in effect to this day, and how those policies did not seem in accordance with the practices experienced with my own Loved One.

These experiences became the cornerstone of my developing interest in my research and formative views, and once I became an adult and a university student, I began to examine these issues with comprehensive dedication.

II.

I spent four years as an undergraduate student at the Greater Seattle Area University and then almost two complete years as a graduate student working on an advanced degree in Healthcare.

During these years I started a movement among my Fellow Nursing Students to increase their knowledge regarding the national policies for Healthcare and the Sanctity of Human Life so that they might form their own opinions as to what concepts such as 'free will' and 'autonomy' meant for the Individual.

I did knowingly promote the 'progressive' ideology from the era before the Great Reformation in which Individual Americans could legally Commit Suicide, End their own Lives through Euthanasia, and petition for qualified medical assistance through Physician-Assisted Suicides. I explored the subject and prior laws regarding the 'Right To Die' policies within our nation and in various states.

I also studied laws related to the Act of Abortion, the history of Abortion in relation to laws, policies, the Supreme Court Case of Roe vs. Wade, and the series of national and Supreme Court cases that served as the End of Legalized Abortion throughout America. This included laws regarding the Criminalization of Any Physicians, Healthcare Professionals, or Individual Citizenry who Sanctioned, Funded, Assisted, or Performed the Act of Abortion. I examined all available materials related to law, medical information, policies, statistics, population decline, and the advancement of scientific Alternatives which ultimately made the need for Abortions because of Unwanted Pregnancy obsolete.

I introduced such information, theories, and perspectives to many of my peers and Fellow Nursing Students hoping to influence and sculpt their opinions on such subjects. My intention was to increase the chances for national changes to the laws through the increased public awareness of such subjects, and the overall transformation of beliefs within the Healthcare profession nation-wide. I did so willingly and of my own free will.

III.

During my graduate years at the Greater Seattle Area University, I did knowingly create an informal network of my Fellow Citizens and Fellow Nursing Students who were like-minded and dedicated to the advancement of the same ideological causes as myself. We did knowingly conspire to infiltrate various Hospice Care facilities, educate our Fellow Citizens about End Of Life possibilities, and provide them with the knowledge and support they needed in order to make informed, personalized decisions for themselves, their own Quality of Life, and their own choice regarding the Right To Die.

This loosely connected group of Individuals came to be known as The Angels of Mercy, a name that was bequeathed to us because of its historic significance within our own American History and as part of a collective world society.

I do solemnly swear that I never caused the Death of, nor assisted in any End-Of-Life Measures directly. I supplied no one with medication, injected no one directly, and never purchased nor provided the funding or resources which were used to End Human Life. This includes any payment for Abortion, help for performing Abortions, or as the Primary Healthcare Professional that Induced or Performed any Abortions. Nor did I provide any transportation to or from said events directly.

I swear these statements to be true to the best of my knowledge, signed in the presence of an authorized witness, and made of my own accord and without duress.

Willow Gloria Amos

Interview IV: Regarding LeRoy Jones

"Please state your name for the record," I began.

"Willow Gloria Amos," she responded.

"Do you know a man by the name of LeRoy Jones?"

"Yes."

"Please tell me about your relationship with him."

"Regarding the events surrounding the man known as LeRoy Jones, middle name unknown, I did willfully take part in the concealment of Crimes on his behalf and for my own personal reasons," she responded.

"Why don't you start at the beginning?" I asked.

She nodded, looking at me. Gone was the melodrama, gone was the anger. She sat calmly and without a hint of emotion.

"I first met LeRoy Jones as a foster care child, having been placed into the Care of the State upon the Death of my only living Family Member, William Amos, who was Killed In Combat on Foreign Soil during my fifteenth year.

"My underage status and lack of extended family left to care for me resulted in my needing to become a Ward of the State and placed into a series of foster homes. During these years, I traveled from home to home and family to family until I finally reached the Age of Maturity at the end of my Nineteenth year and the moment of my Twentieth Birthdate.

"I met LeRoy Jones while living in the third to the last foster home and we developed a friendship. He was a foster child who had spent most of his life within the State Care because of a Deceased Father and an Incarcerated Mother who was undergoing Rehabilitation at the State Correctional Facility. She had been Incarcerated a multitude of times for petty Crimes and was consistently sent for Rehabilitation and Advancement in Education and Training programs. LeRoy Jones was one of four siblings who were shifted around throughout the foster care system and seldom kept together. He and I found a friendship and shared commonality because of our lack of parents and siblings, and we grew to rely on one another over time."

"And what was the nature of your relationship with LeRoy Jones?"

"Our relationship was never romantic, and we never cohabitated outside of our formative years as foster children. I did hear from LeRoy Jones occasionally during the years while I was in college, but contact was sporadic and so irregular that it would sometimes be a full year between communication. He seemed to be transient, did not go to college after Aging-Out of the foster care system on his Twentieth Birthdate, and suffered from persistent joblessness and lack of income. I was usually contacted when he needed help, and I usually gave him money so he could pay for food, shelter, and other necessities.

"I did not share his world with him; he ventured into mine at his convenience and when he needed help. I accepted the terms of our friendship as such. I maintained a telephone number as a point of contact for him and, occasionally, he also supplied me with an address. On almost every encounter between us, he reached out to me, and it was almost always by arriving unannounced at my place of employment."

"And this was at the Greater Seattle Area University campus? In the counseling and healthcare center?" I followed up.

"Yes."

"What was LeRoy Jones' connection to the 'Angels of Mercy'—or was there one?" I asked.

"Occasionally, I would ask LeRoy Jones to do various jobs for me regarding work I did as part of my involvement with The Angels of Mercy. I paid him for these services, and he did not ask nor care about the specifics. He was not an Angel of Mercy and did not subscribe to the same political ideologies as myself or the other people in my circle. He was virtually unknown to any of The Angels of Mercy and to my knowledge did not have any prior or existing relationships with any of the members of The Angels of Mercy."

"Did he ever take part in any of your meetings, lectures, or events? Was he ever involved in any activities, legal or otherwise, that also included other Angels?"

"To the best of my knowledge, there was only one Angel of Mercy that knew about him or had seen him was someone whom I worked closely with regularly. This was also a person whom I had shared an experience with regarding Rebecca. He was the security guard at the GSAU campus building where I worked."

"Note for the record that Ms. Amos is referencing one of the Victims located at the gravesite, Rebecca Summers. Also, for the record, Ms. Amos, could you please state the name of the security guard you are referring to if you know his name?"

"The security guard's name was Evan Harrison. LeRoy Jones was known to the security guard named Evan Harrison at the Greater Seattle Area University because Evan Harrison worked within the same building as me and was a close associate within The Angels of Mercy network. I worked with Evan Harrison almost every shift I worked at GSAU and knew him very well through our networking as Angels of Mercy.

"Other than Evan Harrison, I do not believe that any other Angel of Mercy knew who LeRoy Jones was, had ever met him directly, knew of my connection to him, or had spoken to or worked directly with him."

"Do you have anything else to add regarding your personal relationship with LeRoy Jones and the reasons for your association with him at this time?"

She shook her head 'no' and then clarified verbally that she did not.

I nodded my head in acknowledgment and asked her to verify her statement for the record as per policy.

"*I, Willow Gloria Amos, swear these statements to be true and factual to the best of my knowledge. The statements made within this interview were voluntary and of my own accord and made without duress. These statements were made with my own words and under penalty of law.*"

One down, another handful to go.

THIRTY-SEVEN — WA — STATEMENT

Compromise and Results

Willow Amos looked better this afternoon than she had the night before when we had parted. After I had watched her walk with such solemnity back toward her Cell, I had continued to mull things over. My intention had been to reach out to Daegan Kyl and make arrangements with him so he would know I felt a visit would be in order in the next twenty-four hours, but I had continued to have that undefined nagging feeling as I began my trek back to the barracks, so I decided not to wait before taking action.

I sent word to the SPD jailhouse to have her brought down to their communication center so I could speak directly with her via telephone. It wasn't that I didn't trust that they would have relayed a message, but it was important that I knew it was done. If they would have forgotten, put it off for later and then had a shift change, or if they had dismissed it as insignificant or non-urgent until the morning, and then something had happened to her, I would have taken it very personally—and I know that Daegan Kyl would have as well. My instincts were intuitive enough that I trusted them and usually followed the warnings I received, and last night she had seemed dejected enough I wanted to err on the side of caution.

After she returned my call, I had simply told her she had done a tremendous job recounting the events, and that I realized it had been a difficult process. I wanted her to know that we were almost through it and that I had been in regular communication with Daegan Kyl and had been keeping him apprised of our progress. She thanked me and then I asked her if she would like to have him visit tomorrow evening after our interview time. She had seemed almost choked up as she blurted out 'Yes!' and it was then that I knew my instincts had been accurate.

I was rewarded for my efforts with another statement; possibly the most enlightening received, and without a doubt the most incriminating across the board.

Statement II: Regarding The Night in Question

I, Willow Gloria Amos, do hereby provide this statement as my sworn testimony regarding all allegations and formal charges issued against me in relation to *the night in question*:

On the night in question, I met with LeRoy Jones in a heavily wooded area of the property. I attempted to explain to him that I had a situation regarding something that involved him, and I needed his assistance to handle it. I explained to him that I had the Physical Remains of Rebecca in the back seat of my car and that I was aware of what had transpired between them on campus. I told him I needed his help.

LeRoy Jones did not respond as I had expected, although I had always known him to be a person with a terrible temper and a very short fuse. He responded with aggression and told me he already had his own problems. He said that I could help him right then and he would help me take care of 'my problem' if I helped him take care of his. I didn't know what he was talking about, but then he showed me the Deceased body of Mariam Pembrook. That was when I knew I had made a terrible mistake in trying to keep him from being held responsible for the Rape of Rebecca Summers and I knew I was responsible for what had happened to Mariam Pembrook because I didn't stop him when I could have by turning him in.

He told me I had to help him because they were my problem now too. He said I could help him bury their bodies right there, right then. I argued with him and told him he couldn't, that it wasn't a suitable place, and then he told me he knew the land belonged to my 'rich uncle' and I could do 'whatever I wanted there, and no one would ever know'.

I tried to argue with him about it, and that was when he struck me. He punched me in the face with his right fist, knocking me down into the dirt and the weeds. I was a little dazed for a second, but I stood up. As soon as I did, he came at me again, pushed me up against the side of my car and had his hands around my throat, choking me. I couldn't breathe and I was desperately trying to push him away by putting my hands on his face. This only made him angrier, and he grabbed me by my hair and slammed my head against the car repeatedly. He then grabbed me by the throat again and threw me against the car, which then caused me to fall to the ground. I tried to crawl away from him toward the back of the car, but he was behind me before I got more than a few steps. He yanked my head back and told me, 'You're lucky I still think of you like a little sister or I would slit your throat right now, you selfish bitch.'

And then he let go of my hair, which flung my head forward once again. I tried to move away from him while I was still on my hands and knees, so he kicked me in my stomach, and then kicked me again on my shoulder and side of the head. I curled myself up and tried to catch my breath.

He then walked away, back to his truck, and began pulling something long and bulky from the back. I didn't know it yet because it was dark, but it was the body of

Mariam Pembrook. I remember how it sounded when her body fell to the hard ground; he had wrapped her body in a blanket, and I could see her light-colored hair fall out.

He then walked back over to me and told me to 'clean this shit up and he better never hear another word about it.'

He spat on me and told me I was 'lucky I was such a frigid bitch' and then said that 'this better never come back on me because you know I know where you live and who your rich uncle is'.

And then he started his truck and left. His truck tires had caused gravel and dirt from the field to spray all over behind the truck, landing all over Mariam Pembrook's body and pelting me with small rocks and piles of dirt as well.

And then I cried.

My throat hurt where he had squeezed it, my stomach hurt where he had kicked me, and my head had gotten beaten against the side of the car on the right side several times and then kicked by his foot later because I had been facing the other direction each time, so it all landed on the right side of my head.

But I was alive.

I was terrified that he would come back. No one knew where I was, no one knew what was happening, and if he had killed me, no one would have known why I had disappeared or what had happened to me.

I knew I had crossed many lines and was in serious trouble. But I was terrified that LeRoy Jones would return, and I desperately wanted to leave. I was almost as afraid of what he would do if I just called the Police and stayed there. But I was afraid that I would get blamed for their deaths, and I didn't want to go to jail or get the Death Penalty, and I was afraid that LeRoy Jones could still hurt me or Mr. Kyl.

Daegan Kyl was not actually my family, but he was all I had left. He had promised my brother to look after me if anything happened to him, and when my brother was killed in Combat, Mr. Kyl had stepped in to do exactly that. I didn't want him to get into any type of trouble or get blamed for anything. I couldn't bury their bodies on his land and risk him getting blamed for their deaths if they were ever discovered.

I was also afraid that LeRoy Jones would try to do something violent to Mr. Kyl. Even though I knew he could defend himself since he was an ex-Soldier, I knew that LeRoy Jones would do something sneaky, and that Mr. Kyl wouldn't know he had been targeted.

I didn't know what to do, but I was deathly afraid of being caught out there alone and that LeRoy Jones would return.

So, I did the only thing I could think of and I called Mr. Kyl.

Regarding the Arrival of Mr. Daegan Kyl:

Mr. Kyl arrived at the site on his property after I called him and told him I had to meet him urgently because of an emergency. I told him not to ask any questions.

Before he arrived, I had taken the time to clean myself up and straighten my hair so it did not look like I had been Assaulted in any manner. I covered up my throat area where I had been nearly suffocated to Death by LeRoy Jones.

The next day, I could see significant bruising all the way around the front and sides of my throat. I also had a significant knot on the side of my head, a bruise on the side of my jawline from his boot, and a giant bruise on my right shoulder from getting kicked by LeRoy Jones. My stomach and ribs were also bruised. I did not seek medical attention. I found it necessary to wear sufficient clothing to conceal all physical marks until they had disappeared.

I did not want Mr. Kyl to know anything about the events between LeRoy Jones and myself because I believed Mr. Kyl would have gone after him if he knew he had done anything to harm me.

Before he arrived, I removed the body of Rebecca Summers from the back seat of my car and laid her alongside the body of Mariam Pembrook. I placed the covers over each of them and attempted to secure the blankets around them as best as I could. I covered both of their heads and faces with the blankets. I did not look at the body of Mariam Pembrook, nor did I want to. To the best of my knowledge, Mr. Kyl did not look directly at either of the Victims either.

Mr. Kyl frequently drove one of the moving trucks from his business. When he arrived, he was driving his little sports car.

I told him I needed his help with the disposal of two bodies. I told him I had no right to ask for his help, but I desperately needed it. I told him he could not ask me anything more beyond that because I did not want him to be incriminated. I told him I would never ask him for his help again, but that it was necessary, and I had no choice. I told him I could not do it without his help.

Mr. Kyl assessed the scene and did not ask any questions. I do not know how much he observed, but he did not question anything, just as I had asked.

Mr. Kyl went to his business and parked his company car. He returned with one of his moving trucks.

Mr. Kyl told me that I needed to leave and that he would take care of everything and so I did. I knew he was angry; I knew he had questions he wanted to ask, and I knew he wanted answers. Most of all, I knew he was disappointed in me and that he was only helping me because of the promise he had made to my brother. I knew he was ashamed of my actions and that he believed my brother would have been too. He probably regretted helping me and he probably resented that he felt obligated to do it. Despite all of that, he helped me, and he did it so I wouldn't get into any trouble.

Mr. Kyl never asked me any further questions about that night, nor did he ever bring it up again.

I swear these statements to be true to the best of my knowledge, signed in the presence of an authorized witness, and made of my own accord and without duress.

Willow Gloria Amos

Statement III: Regarding Relationship to DK

I, Willow Gloria Amos, do hereby provide this statement as my sworn testimony regarding all allegations and formal charges issued against me regarding my personal relationship to Mr. Daegan Kyl:

The location where I met LeRoy Jones was private land owned by another man that I knew, Daegan Kyl. I had known Mr. Kyl since my brother first introduced us when I was a young girl. He was a soldier who had worked with my brother for almost ten years before my brother was killed in Combat. I am not related to Mr. Kyl biologically. We do not, and have never, been engaged in an intimate sexual or romantic relationship. I regard him to be 'my family' and I believe he has always tried to be a good substitute brother to me since my own brother died.

The land was his personal property and was next to the acreage where he had a local business, which included Moving Trucks and Storage Units. In a nearby location that was also connected to his land, he had another business for Professional Cleaning Services.

I knew the area well and had spent many hours there. I had known Mr. Kyl since before he launched his business enterprises. I have always had access to the businesses and facilities because of my personal relationship with Mr. Kyl.

There have been times when I have used the facilities and Mr. Kyl's rental trucks for my own purposes after hours and without his consent or knowledge.

Mr. Kyl did not know I had ever used his property outside of his knowledge or without his consent. He did not know that I had arranged to meet LeRoy Jones on the property. He was not aware of the meeting before the meeting took place.

I swear these statements to be true to the best of my knowledge, signed in the presence of an authorized witness, and made of my own accord and without duress.

Willow Gloria Amos

Statement IV: Regarding DK & AOM

I, Willow Gloria Amos, do hereby provide this statement as my sworn testimony regarding all allegations and formal charges issued against me in relation to Mr. Daegan Kyl and The Angels of Mercy:

Regarding Mr. Daegan Kyl and his Knowledge of Angels of Mercy:

To my knowledge, Mr. Kyl has never engaged in illegal activities of his own volition or because he held any personal connection to The Angels of Mercy aside from his association with me. He did not render aid to me regarding the Burials of any Victims out of any association or support toward The Angels of Mercy; everything he was involved in was directly because of me, for me, and because of my involvement.

Mr. Kyl was familiar with my work with The Angels of Mercy and that I held a firm conviction in the progressive political and humanitarian ideological values of The Angels of Mercy. He knew that there were those among my group who held what he considered to be 'radicalized' views that were contrary to the national federal laws. I do not believe that Mr. Kyl would have ever been involved in any of the Crimes or Acts of Violence described within these statements were it not because of his associations with me and his desire to protect me from negative situations and consequences, including those I have caused or contributed to myself.

To my knowledge, Mr. Kyl did not, and never has, subscribed to the ideological values outlined by The Angels of Mercy, and has never participated in any of their events, networking, or activism. To the best of my knowledge, Mr. Kyl has never associated with The Angels of Mercy, enabled them to conduct nefarious or illegal dealings, nor provided the means of rendering aid to anyone for illegal purposes.

I swear these statements to be true to the best of my knowledge, signed in the presence of an authorized witness, and made of my own accord and without duress.

Willow Gloria Amos

Statement V: Regarding DK & LJ

I, Willow Gloria Amos, do hereby provide this statement as my sworn testimony regarding all allegations and formal charges issued against me in relation to Mr. Daegan Kyl and Mr. LeRoy Jones:

I. Regarding History Between Mr. Daegan Kyl and Mr. LeRoy Jones

Mr. Kyl did not know LeRoy Jones personally, nor did he know him by name. To my knowledge, there was only one occasion where Mr. Kyl and LeRoy Jones had ever interacted or had seen one another in person. This occurred during one specific occasion sometime last year, when Mr. Kyl had come to my place of employment on the university campus to pick me up so we could go have lunch together. We did not see one another very often, as we were both very busy.

During this visit, Mr. Kyl arrived just as LeRoy Jones was leaving.

When these two men encountered one another, Mr. Kyl had asked me who the man was as he was leaving my office.

I had explained to him he was another person who I had met and lived with when I was in foster care years earlier.

The two never spoke, and I did not introduce the two of them. To the best of my recollection, I did not even mention LeRoy Jones by name. I do not believe that Mr. Kyl would have approved of LeRoy Jones either by character or temperament, and I did not believe he would have wanted him to be around me.

To the best of my knowledge, this was the only interaction between the two men that there has ever been.

I believe that if Mr. Kyl had been informed of this situation and the actions of LeRoy Jones, especially the physical Violence done against me, he would have reacted with extreme anger and would have hunted LeRoy Jones down. I was afraid he would get into a Violent altercation with him on my behalf and then he would get into trouble, so I never told him. To this day, I have never discussed LeRoy Jones with Mr. Kyl or shared my experiences with him.

I have never had a conversation regarding my history with LeRoy Jones with Mr. Kyl, explained to him about my fear of his temper or his behavioral issues, or told him anything personal about my past experiences or knowledge of Mr. LeRoy Jones. I have never explained to Mr. Kyl that although I have known Mr. LeRoy Jones since I was an underage minor that I have never trusted him or felt safe around him, nor had I ever given Mr. Kyl the information he would have needed to know how dangerous I believed Mr. LeRoy Jones could be.

I swear these statements to be true to the best of my knowledge, signed in the presence of an authorized witness, and made of my own accord and without duress.

Willow Gloria Amos

Statement VI: Regarding DK, RS, MP

I, Willow Gloria Amos, do hereby provide this statement as my sworn testimony regarding all allegations and formal charges issued against me in relation to *Mr. Daegan Kyl*:

I. Regarding Mr. Kyl and Knowledge of Rebecca and Mariam:

Mr. Kyl did not know that the Deaths of Rebecca Summers and Mariam Pembrook were because of the Intentional Infliction of Violence, that the two women had been subjected to any Physical Injury or Harm, or that they had been Victims of Crimes Against Humanity.

Mr. Kyl did not have any knowledge that either woman had sustained injuries to their Physical Remains, that they had been subjected to Rape, or that Mariam Pembrook had been the Victim of an Abduction, Rape, and Murder.

Mr. Kyl never knew that when he helped me in the matter of Rebecca Summers and Mariam Pembrook that he was doing so because of the violence caused by LeRoy Jones.

I do not believe that had he known he was doing something because of the violent actions of another Human Being against two Innocent Citizens that he would have done anything or had any type of involvement. I believe that he would have reported LeRoy Jones to Law Enforcement immediately if he had known that either woman had suffered harm or injury at the hands of LeRoy Jones.

Mr. Kyl did not assist me with the Burials of the Physical Remains of Rebecca Summers and Mariam Pembrook because he believed that there was a third-party involved, that he was concealing any Violent Crimes or Acts of Violence, or because he believed I had committed Acts of Violence.

II. Regarding Mr. Kyl and Motives for Rendering Aid:

Regarding the night in question, Mr. Kyl conducted a series of events that were illegal and unethical. I believe he conducted these events specifically to protect me and for no other reason.

Mr. Kyl assisted me solely because I misled him and made him believe I had been involved in work with The Angels of Mercy and that the two women were subjects of Assisted-Suicides. I intentionally misled him into believing that I was placed in an emergency situation and desperately needed his help, but solely because of my work with The Angels of Mercy.

Mr. Kyl rendered aid to me because he believed he was protecting me because of what he considered to be my 'ideological naivety and extremism'. He believed I was young, impressionable, and had 'gotten in over my head'. At the time of our encounter regarding the night of Rebecca Summers and Mariam Pembrook, he believed that The

Angels of Mercy were responsible for the events that led to my desperate call to him. He had no knowledge that it had anything to do with LeRoy Jones or that there was violence involved. I do not believe the thought had even entered his mind that there could have been different circumstances, or that LeRoy Jones was involved.

It is my belief that Mr. Kyl helped me on the night in question because he believed that if he did not that I would end up going to jail and then either Exiled or given the Death Penalty because of my involvement with The Angels of Mercy.

Everything that Mr. Kyl has done regarding these matters was done as an effort to protect me and based on misinformation caused by me as an intentional effort to manipulate him in order to get the help I required. I exploited his good will and the knowledge that he would do what I needed him to do if he believed he needed to do it in order to help me and prevent me from getting into serious legal or criminal trouble.

III. Regarding Mr. Kyl and his Actions:

Mr. Kyl was not directly involved in causing physical harm or violence against any citizen of These United States to the best of my knowledge, nor did he intend to Cause Harm to anyone.

Mr. Kyl was not directly responsible for concealing any Acts of Violence, nor did he believe he had been doing so. He did nothing in relation to the Physical Remains of any known Citizen that was not done under the premise that they were Assisted-Suicides brought about by The Angels of Mercy and that the circumstances surrounding their Deaths were of their own volition and free will and by their own hand.

I swear these statements to be true to the best of my knowledge, signed in the presence of an authorized witness, and made of my own accord and without duress.

Willow Gloria Amos

Interview VII: Regarding RFID-Chip Removal

"Ms. Amos, there's one area that we haven't discussed yet. Each of the Victims had their RFID-Chips removed from their hands. This was done with intent; presumably to help conceal the Deceased Remains. Three of the four Victims that were buried in that field were adults, and each of them had been cut on their right hand where their RFID-Chips had been located. Their Chips were missing."

Willow Amos stared at me, a look of disgust passing across her face. It caused me to wonder if she had been the one who removed them.

"They couldn't be found," she said in a low tone.

"Who couldn't be found?" I asked. I thought she meant the Victims, but clarification was necessary.

"Any of them. They had to be disposed of. Their Chips would have revealed where they were. They had to be removed."

"The Victims?" I asked again. I needed her to specify what she was saying for the record.

"The Victims were tagged like cattle—just like you've tagged me now. Even if our government has tried to sell the Chipping as something that is 'for the greater good', it's still just putting us all into some mass inventory classification system. The AOM would never stand to keep any of our tags active. We've been removing our tags for a long time—I knew how to do it. I had to do it or each of them would be found," she stated.

"So, you did this yourself? All three Victims had their RFID-Chips removed after they were Deceased. Are you saying that you alone removed their Chips?"

She darted her eyes, but then shook her head 'yes'.

It seemed as though it were only a half-truth; knowing that Arlan had been buried at a different time than the two women—as well as Katarina, and now knowing what had happened to the two women before they were buried, it seemed unlikely that she was responsible for the removal of Arlan's Chip.

It probably wasn't an answer that would ever be forthcoming with any degree of conclusive proof. My best guess was that she was responsible for the two women and had likely done what needed to be done before Daegan Kyl had arrived. She had, after all, just stayed at the location after LeRoy Jones vacated the area.

But something told me that she wasn't directly responsible for Arlan—that it had probably been some other Angel of Mercy. It also seemed possible that she had never done it herself before the two women—it would explain the look of disgust that had flashed across her face as she remembered the event.

It was one thing to promote Death, quite another to touch a Deceased Human Being and then desecrate their body. Even if it was to conceal a Crime or promote one's agenda—it was still a Deceased Human Body, and for many, it would be a squeamish undertaking no matter how devout their ideological values.

"How and where did you learn how to find the Chips?" I asked her.

"It's just something that I heard about," she answered.

"What did you do with the Chips?" I followed up, knowing it was probably a lost cause.

"I just threw them away. I flushed them down a toilet."

Smart. Water would cause the damage, but the sewer system would eliminate any chance of ever finding any of them—even if it wasn't the truth, it was an effective, irrefutable lie.

"And you removed the Chip from Arlan as well—even though he was buried much earlier, and you had nothing to do with his Disappearance or the events surrounding his Death?"

"Yes. Because I was responsible for ensuring he got buried."

It was like swimming upstream the whole way, relentlessly.

"Who put you in charge?"

"What do you mean?"

"Who decided it was your task to bury Arlan if you weren't responsible for causing his Death or even his Disappearance?" I asked, growing impatient. I already knew that Daegan Kyl had buried Arlan's Physical Remains—and I knew he had done so in order to help Willow Amos.

But who had tasked Willow Amos with the Disposal of Arlan? I was under the impression that she was at the top of her little group of anarchists—but if she wasn't, then who was?

She shook her head, disputing both my line of questioning and my question.

"No one put me in charge; I tasked myself with it after learning of the circumstances regarding Arlan. That's it. Anything else?" she asked, obstinate until the bitter end.

She would never say or admit to anything that might lead to the incrimination of her cohorts, showing that at least she held something resembling loyalty. She was crafty—too smart for her own good, too intelligent to be caught in contradictions and confessions. One thing was for sure, Daegan Kyl had not undersold her when he stated she was one of the smartest people he had encountered. I didn't think I'd ever interviewed or questioned anyone who was so dedicated to evading the truth that they never once slipped up or did anything that was self-incriminating, at least to some extent. Every word uttered by Willow Amos was carefully measured and weighed; she was meticulously well-prepared.

PART EIGHT

Therefore we do not lose heart,
but though our outer man is decaying,
yet our inner man is being renewed day by day.
For momentary, light affliction is producing for us
an eternal weight of glory far beyond all comparison,
while we look not at the things which are seen,
but at the things which are not seen;
for the things which are seen are temporal,
but the things which are not seen are eternal.

2 Corinthians 4:16-18

THIRTY-EIGHT – CR —2— DEATH NOTIFICATION

Arlan—Why He Left

We were preparing to deliver the Notification of Death to Caroline Randall. Even though quite some time had passed since she had last been with her husband, I did not enter the Notification process lightly.

She knew he had been terminally ill, and that he had been close to Death before his Disappearance. She had mentioned that she knew it was likely that he had already passed away during his absence. But there was a difference between speculation and proof.

I rather thought her ignorance had at least allowed her to get used to his absence, to learn what it meant to stand on her own, to spend her days and nights learning how to get by without him there, without hearing his voice or seeing him in the next room every time she turned around. Maybe not knowing all this time had allowed her the time she needed to begin the Grieving process by degrees.

Yes, he had Disappeared suddenly, but she had not been left with the sudden bolt of shock she would have been if he had Passed Away in front of her. She would have been left with only the overwhelming finality of his Death after he had drawn his Final Breath. Confirmation of a Loved One's Death was proof of Death's permanence—a truth that was powerful enough to knock the wind out of someone if their love was deep enough.

Maybe Arlan had understood this and realized that although his wife was strong in her own way, he didn't believe she was strong enough at that point to handle the impact of his Death, especially not directly in her presence. Maybe he worried she couldn't bear the instant shock of it, or maybe he felt the shock of seeing it happen would have been too hard on her physical body or heart. We knew nothing about Caroline Randall's own health concerns, and she was just as elderly as her husband; it was entirely possible that he knew the stress of the situation would be too difficult for her to endure and he wanted to decrease the risks to her own health.

It was all speculation, of course; but Caroline Randall had been placed in a unique position of limbo. The Missing Person status was considerably different from that of a Grieving widow.

His Disappearance would have provided the tools she needed so that she could learn to adapt to the idea of his permanent absence—and all the while she would still be holding onto the hope that she might still be able to see him. Consciously or not, she would have begun to get used to a new way of living and going through her days without him present, but she would have still been protected from the full weight of the truth behind his absence. She would have grown used to him being gone and removed from her daily life long before she would have learned of his Death, thus providing a valuable defense mechanism and a layer of protection insulating her from the pain she would have felt upon seeing him draw his Final Breath.

We were trained to look for motives behind Crimes, and motives were oftentimes obvious when one had enough information at their disposal. But it was a difficult subject to incorporate into meaningful interview questions because the Loved Ones were so Grief-stricken and hyper-sensitive to the situation unfolding around them. We were being asked to investigate and explore the reasons Citizens chose to Commit Suicide and provide reasonable answers for emotional issues they were experiencing. Often, we were expected to come up with ideas even when friends and family had not known any reasons or observed any signs ahead of time.

Sometimes those answers just weren't forthcoming.

Maybe it went against his nature to End his own Life, but it was certainly within his character to save his beloved wife and Loved Ones from ever experiencing any type of hardship or suffering. He knew she had been extremely devoted to him during those final months as his health had deteriorated, and he was fully aware that his own physical pain was causing a great deal of emotional suffering for everyone else as they watched his health decline. As they had reported, he was in full control of his faculties, and as Caroline Randall had emphasized; he had been a strong, proud man his entire life. It would have been a tremendous test of his own endurance and even his ego to experience the loss of health, mobility, strength, and physical stamina that had once been central to his identity.

But perhaps what Arlan had dreaded losing more than his own health and mortality was watching the toll his illness had taken on his beloved Bride, and above all else, he wanted her to be happy once again.

It was out of character for a man such as Arlan to choose to Commit Suicide, especially if he knew it was illegal. It was also highly unlikely that he would have taken the route of an Assisted-Suicide; to do so would have required engaging others in his plans and forced them to become Criminals themselves. The odds of a man like him doing all that seemed slim.

But it seemed entirely within his character as a man, a husband, a father, and a Marine to do all that he could to protect those whom he loved and shield them from anything tragic in life—including his own Death. In that regard, his Disappearance and Death were not acts which defied the man's character but exemplified it. He was a man of action. What greater action was there than orchestrating one's own Disappearance and setting the terms of one's own Death?

Confirmation of Nefarious Misdeeds

I intended to provide Caroline Randall with the truth she needed so we could obtain the Justice everyone deserved. She didn't know she had been right about Willow Amos and the other Hospice workers yet, but she deserved to know. Her instincts about evil intentions by the Hospice workers, Willow Amos in particular, had been wholly accurate, to her credit. She had been unable to act on them, however, because Arlan Randall had prevented her from doing so.

While it may take her some time to come to terms with the realization that Arlan had utilized their services himself, it was important that she understand that he may have been of sound mind, but he may also have been influenced by heavy medications or pain levels. Just because he allowed this to occur didn't mean he was capable of consent.

I hoped Caroline Randall would be satisfied knowing that the people who had hurt her husband and deprived her of her Final Days with him would never steal those moments from anyone else ever again. These 'Angels of Mercy' were never going to be able to entice, scam, or lure any other Innocent Victims.

The Bereaved Suffered enough in countless ways after the Death of a Loved One. These extenuating circumstances would exasperate Caroline's ability to process the Death of her husband and would undoubtedly unsettle whatever little peace of mind she had managed to acquire.

In the meantime, we would continue to process the evidence as we acquired it, utilize every resource we could to secure the truth and any impending Convictions, and do what we could to build the case substantially enough to assuage the heart and mind of those Left Behind by Arlan's Passing.

Upon Learning of Her Husband's Death

Caroline Randall would learn soon enough of her husband's Death. I wished I could delay it forever so she could continue to exist within the safe cocoon she had constructed around herself that was insulating her from the rest of the world. I had already put it off though, choosing to bide my time a little beforehand so that I could ensure that I knew enough information to provide suitable answers regarding the circumstances surrounding his Death. But no matter how long I delayed, eventually she would have to be told, and I knew that when that happened, it would change everything for her once again.

It had been a seemingly beautiful life she had shared with her husband; it was understandable that she would prefer to linger in a state of fragile uncertainty rather than have the finality of facts and truth squelching any lingering possibilities. She had been loved; she had been the love of someone's life, and she had lived the life as someone's lover and best friend that many dreamed about and longed for, but never found.

Confirmation of his Death would be different from her belief that he was simply 'Missing'; it would be the last page of a story that had finally drawn to a close and from which there could be no re-writing ever done again. Death was the ultimate division between hope and truth revealed, and for many, living with hope was more important than ever being given the answers.

Still, she would need to come to terms with the reality that he had *chosen* to End his Life in this way.

Proof of his Passing meant that their time had finally come to an end, that he would not be returning, and that he had not been able to pass through this life without her in his Final Moments.

I would make sure that Grace O'Connor, as well as Micah Davidson, were both there to help her process the news. But I hoped that she would also find peace by the end of this Investigation, no matter what the outcome.

The man had been a beloved Citizen. He had been a Loving Husband, Father, Friend, Employer, and an Upstanding Community Member. No matter what else had occurred or what came to be of his Final Moments, the man had earned the right to be Remembered and Memorialized as the man that he was, not just who he became during the final few moments or hours of his life.

Ultimately, Caroline Randall was going to be Grieving over the loss of her husband; she would finally have Closure. It was entirely possible that she would end up angry over this situation and even at her husband specifically. She had unequivocally stated that she had wanted to be there during his Final Breath, and he had robbed her of that time.

But none of it had been her decision, and everything pointed to Arlan having acted of his own accord, and carried out his own Final Wishes in the manner he felt most befitting. I was not the one with a body riddled with cancer and living with unimaginable pain, and neither was Caroline Randall. We could rail against the heavens over this, but when it all came down to it, there was only one truth that would be known at the end of this investigation, and perhaps it was the only truth that mattered. Arlan had Departed from this earth, and he was going to be missed.

Death Notification

Grace O'Connor and Micah Davidson sat on either side of Caroline Randall. They had done so as casually as possible, but I realized it was intentional so they could be there to provide her with physical and emotional support once I had shared my news with her regarding the Death of her husband.

"Caroline, I'm sorry to have to return here without good news, but this is an official Notification from the State of Washington and the Seattle Police Department that your husband, Mr. Arlan Randall, has been confirmed Deceased by the Seattle Medical Examiner's Office. The Seattle Police Department can confirm that the Remains of your husband have been located, and the Seattle Medical Examiner has verified his identity. We can confirm that he Passed Away shortly after he was last here at the farm. Please accept my condolences on behalf of the State of Washington and the Seattle Police Department."

"Well...How did it happen?"

She was baffled.

I had not only informed her we had found her husband's Remains and that he was, indeed, Deceased, but that they had confirmed it had been through an Overdose and an Assisted-Suicide.

More than anything else, the woman just wanted some answers.

I explained briefly that his Physical Remains had been found on private land that was owned by a local Seattle business. I kept the specifics out of it in relation to the state of his Physical Remains and Decomposition. It was unnecessary information and did not add to the facts. I also refrained from mentioning that there were other Human Remains located there as well.

I told her they had determined through his Posthumous Medical Examination that he had Died because of an overwhelming level of opioids within his system, and that it had been ruled an Assisted-Suicide. I explained to her that even though we had cause to believe that he had sanctioned the usage of the additional levels of Morphine to be administered into his system and that we believed he had intended to Take his own Life, that because it was an Assisted-Suicide it was still classified as Homicide.

She put her hand up in the air toward me as if to say, 'Stop; no more'. I looked at Grace O'Connor and then Micah Davidson, pausing in my script. As with every Notification, it was important that I understand the details of each investigation, especially the relevant aspects of the Victims Medical Examination and Cause of Death. This ensured competency, and enabled me to not only articulate the facts as I gave the Notification, but also to answer any of their questions without needing to fumble through my reports.

For those who were left with lingering questions or who needed more time to process things before hearing such details, the Medical Examination reports were available to view. They were a matter of public record and meant to draw attention to the heinous nature of all Homicides. Should Caroline Randall or Micah Davidson wish to explore the contents of Arlan's Examination in further detail, she would be provided with the appropriate information upon request through the VAA. After my work was finalized, the case would be entered into the national database for the preservation of records.

But she wasn't asking me to pause in my information-sharing so she could understand the contents of the Medical Examination.

Death by Assisted-Suicide was the one thing she had been adamant about; she did not believe that her husband would have ever left her before he had to. She had refused to even entertain the idea that Suicide or an Assisted-Suicide was a possibility, and that had been based not only because she didn't believe he would ever willingly leave her but also because of his religious convictions.

She didn't fully understand what it meant for someone to be in that much pain. His decision had nothing to do with whether or not he had loved her or 'loved her enough' to stay. Nor did it reflect on his spiritual beliefs, in my opinion, but that was something she would have to sort out between herself and her spiritual leadership.

The man had been in excruciating pain. He had reached the point where he knew it was too much to bear; he knew he had an insignificant quality of life remaining. The choice he had made had been simple enough, and based on his own reasons. It was going to be difficult for his wife to understand, and that was reasonable.

What was going to be even more difficult was for her to come to terms with it because of how it related to the Winter Season Hospice Care facility, the woman whom she believed to be responsible for his Disappearance, and now a confirmation that the words Willow Amos had been whispering into her husband's ear had been worse than she could have ever imagined. She had cause to be angry and to struggle with this revelation.

Grace O'Connor would ensure that the Victim Advocates would address these concerns by helping them secure the Grief Counselors and other After-Life services that could be utilized to help people sort through their conflicts with the Death of a Loved One—especially for those who were Grieving over someone that had chosen to Commit Suicide. She was going to be struggling with the idea that her husband had wanted to End his own Life.

Of course, she had known it would happen. Somewhere deep inside of her, she had known that his Death was only a matter of time.

The time that he had been gone had been quiet, to be sure. But while he was gone—until the moment that I had uttered the words that finalized everything and removed all doubt or hope—she might have deluded herself into believing that he had left her to seek some experimental treatment and hadn't wanted to trouble her about it, or he had just gone away as he had during all the years he had been a Marine, when he would be absent and she would miss him, but she knew he would eventually return home to her.

Until I had spoken, there had been hope.

Until I had entered the home I had been warmly welcomed into and destroyed her last moments of innocence, she had lived within a comfortable bubble of familiarity and security. She had remained in a carefully constructed reality that she had honored by staying in the home that she had built with her husband. She had been able to quietly move through her days, function, and pray—keeping faith and hope even when her mind told her differently.

But my words had finalized everything, and now she knew.

"He was my world," she whispered.

The room fell silent as she looked out the window.

THIRTY-NINE - CONVICTIONS

Life Evaluations: LJ, Rebecca, and Mariam

LeRoy Jones would be tried for the Rape and Physical Assaults of both women. He would face additional charges for the Stalking, Abduction, and Murder of Mariam.

Trial preparation for LeRoy Jones would include a Life Evaluation. This evaluation was a mandatory part of every Criminal Trial and was done for every 'Alleged' Offender and for each individual Victim they created. It was an assessment that was frequently used to identify the failures of the lawbreakers and illustrate how their damaged, fractured issues spilled over and caused a negative, costly impact on the Innocent. They had been done as a matter of routine since the Great Reformation began and had been instrumental in illustrating just how problematic the Criminal Class was to a civilized nation trying to live in peace. After reviewing the reports, it was difficult not to see that the Criminal Class was financially parasitic and costly to society. It was a harsh reality that rang true around the world and throughout time.

Their overwhelming criminal backgrounds were almost exclusively filled with Violence and Assaults against their Fellow Americans, and as the reports were completed and compiled, it became evident that America was under Assault by a demographic that contributed very little beyond the negativity they created. The data spoke for itself; the same tired story was showcased repeatedly: lack of education, lack of any type of school graduation or certification, lack of adult skills or knowledge that made them capable of being hired for anything beyond basic labor and minimum-skills professions, and a lack of employment or taxes paid into the system. The Criminal Class was living on the fringes of a different society. It was not something that could be attributed solely to those that were living in poverty because not all those who lived in poverty were devoid of the morality, ethics, or respect for the law that the Criminal Class was.

They were a part of the nation. Everything they failed to do were things that the vast majority of Americans managed to do successfully as a matter of routine. The results could not be reduced to arbitrary findings such as poverty, lack of opportunity, and lack of equality. Ultimately, it came down to a lack of interest in being part of the Collective Whole, and sometimes, a complete rejection and refusal of it. No matter what the reasoning behind it, no matter how it was justified or attempted to justify, the evaluation reports produced millions of undeniable examples of Career Criminals that habitually failed to progress, assimilate, follow the Rule of Law, and lead productive lives.

Because every Victim would have their own lives processed as well, it only further highlighted just how troublesome and useless most of the Criminal Class were in comparison. After reviewing the life of LeRoy Jones and comparing it to those of Rebecca and Mariam, it left no question as to the true Measure of the Man that had Wrongfully Stolen the lives of two of America's most beautiful Souls. He had claimed the lives of two women who had their entire futures ahead of them. They had been beautiful, healthy, involved, creative, loving, and had contributed to making the world a better place through their passions and Callings. They had been loved and wanted. They had been valued.

And a man who had done nothing for our nation, who had never paid taxes, who had never held a functioning job, had never gone to college, trade school, or learned a useful skill, a man who had a history riddled with evidence that he had failed to integrate and improve over the years, had removed them from our world without any regard for the Sanctity of their lives. He was a man with clear signs throughout his past that indicated he would someday escalate in his Criminality and Violence. It should not have come as any surprise when eventually he did just that. Had anyone paid attention, it was entirely predictable.

The cost had been the lives of Rebecca and Mariam.

And like so many millions upon millions of other Victims who had lost their lives at the hands of Violent Predators, the trade-off had not been equal in measure or value. We had failed to read the signs regarding LeRoy Jones, failed to conduct the appropriate Assessments and take the necessary actions afterward. The final cost for this had been paid for in the blood of two Human Beings. It was an exceptionally high price to pay.

Convictions

For his Crimes Against Humanity in the cases of Rebecca Summers and Mariam Pembrook, LeRoy Jones had been Convicted of Rape and Murder in the First Degree. He was Sentenced to Death.

For their role in the case of Arlan Randall, the seven Angels of Mercy who had confessed to their involvement in the Abduction and Death of Arlan Randall were Convicted of Crimes Against Humanity. They were Convicted of a litany of charges, including Abduction, the illegal administration of an opioid, unlawful practices of medical practitioners, and medical malpractice under medical supervision. They were found to be Guilty of Providing the physical means by which the other person attempts or commits suicide, and Participating in a physical act by which another other person attempts or commits suicide. Finally, the seven were Convicted of Murder in the First Degree, citing premeditation and predatory behavior toward a debilitated, elderly Victim receiving Hospice Care as aggravating factors.

In addition, as with all the remaining Angels of Mercy, they were Convicted of unlawful use of psychological pressure and the use of actual or ostensible religious, political, social, philosophical or other principles.

The seven original Angels of Mercy were Sentenced to Death.

All remaining Angels of Mercy were Sentenced to Exile, as there was no direct evidence linking them to Deceased Human Remains, and no solid connections could be found between them and any of the four Victims.

As expected, though likely not appreciated, especially by the parents of Rebecca Summers, Willow Amos was Convicted of a multitude of crimes, but saved from the Death Penalty. She had made an art out of skirting just enough involvement to be held personally accountable. Willow Amos had dodged bullets left and right throughout this entire case, but it did not make her any less culpable in my eyes.

She had been incarcerated following Arlan's Disappearance, and it was during this period in time that the Medical Examiner had traced his Time of Death. Our technology wasn't precise, but it was accurate enough that it was beyond reproach in a Court of Law. If the official Time of Death timestamp exonerated her from liability because she had been Arrested and Incarcerated during that window of time, then she was either extremely lucky or extremely ruthless.

Evan Harrison, the security guard who had taken Rebecca Summers to Willow Amos, failed to report a Sexual Assault on campus, and then deleted the security footage, was Convicted of his crimes.

The Abortion doctor, along with more than a dozen other medical practitioners working in her office, were Convicted and Sentenced to Death.

And finally, although there was still much that had never been discovered, Detective Jarrett had been Convicted of several Crimes for his involvement in concealing official documents and files within the SPD, along with various financial crimes.

FORTY – CASE CLOSURE

Final Case Summary

It was done.

Although I could not say that the entire case had been completed to my satisfaction, it had been resolved to the best of my ability given the obstruction I had faced.

We had taken four sets of Human Remains that had been found lying within the ground in an isolated, dark, forgotten field to decompose, and removed them from their primitive graves so they might be provided the Memorials each had been entitled to. They had been placed there in the hopes of being destroyed through the Decomposition process after each of them had Disappeared. We had found them, removed them, secured their Remains, and given them back their Identities and Dignity.

We had provided the means for each of their Physical Remains to be reviewed by qualified Medical Examiners who had then pored over their bodies, isolated and identified every Injury and Wound that each Victim had experienced prior to their Deaths, and enabled the Courts to fully see the tragedy and horror of the circumstances surrounding each of their Final Moments.

We had done what we could to bring Honor to the lives that had been Stolen.

We had brought Justice to the Predators that were culpable. We had proven their responsibility, confirmed their involvement, and used that information to render Convictions.

We had secured Victim Compensation Funding for the Bereaved, allowing them to take care of their Loved One's Physical Remains, immortalizing them through the process of Memorialized Gemstones. In addition, each of the Bereaved families and other persons that had been adversely affected by their Deaths had been financially compensated for their losses as per the federal mandate.

We had done everything possible within our power to deliver the best measure of Justice given the circumstances and limitations.

But it wasn't enough.

I was entirely dissatisfied with the overall outcome. There were not only loose ends still unaddressed, there were also severe issues within the entire process that had led me to experience some grave concerns over what had been left remaining unsaid and undone at the end of our official investigation. There were still too many unanswered questions.

Above all, what had been the outcome regarding the Governor and his unethical henchmen had left me extremely troubled. I had not appreciated their behavior or threats regarding myself or my colleagues, certainly. But their behavior had gone far beyond the Governor's inappropriate actions, abuse of power, and blatant threats against us and our safety; they had desecrated the Rule of Law in its entirety, and such actions had no place within any civilized society.

Who were we, as a People, if those we elected and appointed to our most select and important positions were working against us rather than for us? We were only as good as the sum of our parts, and when we had Criminals working within the highest echelons of our government, abusing their power and position to commit nefarious misdeeds and conduct dirty dealings behind closed doors unbeknownst to the American People, we were little more than fools and pawns if we failed to fully investigate, expose, and address the disease once it had been revealed.

For many years during the 21st century, the American People had been little more than sheep, blindly following whatever directives came from their government regardless of consequence to themselves or their nation. And it had almost cost us everything.

Any demographic that is blindly willing to trust another source who professes to advocate on their behalf or swears they are representing their 'best interests' without questioning their intentions or ulterior motives should not be surprised when they are exploited and deceived. Citizens should always hold a healthy and active distrust of their government.

If our government leaders can work corrupt dealings behind our backs that harm our own Citizens with impunity, how could our nation continue to thrive without further damage to our Constitution, our way of Life, and the very Citizens such leaders were sworn to uphold, defend, and represent?

The same applied to the two men that were working within the ICE agency. They were Agents of the Law, Sworn to Protect, Preserve, and Defend the Sanctity of Human Life. If nothing else, they were responsible for upholding the most basic tenets of their Oath, and they had failed to do so in a multitude of ways.

Such actions could not be left ignored or overlooked. The obligation they held to uphold the Rule of Law and the societal standards of our time were greater than that of the average person among us; they were members of Law Enforcement. The standard of measurement was higher for them because of the career paths they had chosen, not lower. If it came to be known that men representing either our government or our Law Enforcement were working secretly to subvert the Rule of Law, conceal evidence, and waylay the truth instead of exposing it, the nation would be up in arms over it.

I could not speak for those who had labored alongside me, but I was far from settled regarding this case or the outcome for each of the key players responsible.

There would come a time when appropriate and fitting punishments might be served for all who needed it, but that time had not yet come.

With the full weight still resting upon my shoulders, I knew it was necessary to acknowledge that our Criminal Justice system, along with the current Laws of the Land and policies being implemented regarding certain political issues, had failed the Victims of this case and the true deliverance of Justice. The Innocent had not been vindicated, and those responsible had neither been exposed nor held accountable; it was the worst example of how flawed our Criminal Justice system still was, and I was appalled by it.

I did not have the solutions worked out, but I knew this was not how this should be resolved. In my heart, I knew this to be a moral and ethical outrage, and I struggled with what it could mean for the future of my country. I worried about what else might be happening throughout my nation that was unreported and as yet unknown. It felt heavy on my heart and mind—a nagging sense of impending doom as if everything was about to change.

I knew, despite everything that had been neatly summarized on my reports, that this case had not found any legitimate 'Closure'. It had done the exact opposite; it had opened my eyes to an entirely new world of subversive corruption that could be more extensive and powerful than I could ever have imagined.

I knew Katarina was not the only Victim out there.

It was impossible to know how severe the issue was in these modern times, or how many little girls were out there that we might not even know were Missing, had not been searching for, and may never find.

My heart was heavy because, for the first time in my career, I felt powerless. I now understood that Evil could win no matter how hard we all worked against it. The world was full of corruption, and little girls were never going to be completely safe from Evil men—especially if their own government refused to protect them.

Thoughts on Mariam and Rebecca

The loss of both Mariam and Rebecca would create a long-lasting Ripple Effect that would endure for generations and would impact countless lives. Mariam's absence would be felt by too many to count, but none more deeply than within the lives of her husband and children.

Each of their lives had been granted a finite period of time here on this earth and within our nation as our Fellow Citizens. Individually, they were little more than a speck of sand in the grand scheme of things and represented only a sliver of time within the sum totality of all that had been ordained by God. Arlan had been gifted with the most time, but even he had been delivered into the loving hands of his Heavenly Father after being alive just under a mere thirty thousand days. It was not much time, despite all who may claim he had lived a long and fruitful life.

And then to consider the rest; two women who were cut down in the very prime of their lives. They could have each lived decades more, both borne many more children—become mothers and grandmothers, lived to share their lives, hearts, and wisdom with hundreds or even thousands of our Fellow Citizens.

It did not escape me that Rebecca was a Lost Treasure and her Loss to the world would forever leave a blank space. Rebecca's Death would mean that we would never know who she could have become, what she could have accomplished or created, or what impact she might have had on the world.

The Loss of all Human Life was tragic in its most basic simplicity, but to lose those who have been identified as Lost Treasures left a stain on our world that could never be explained or otherwise filled. There were Empty Spaces throughout our collective history because of such Lost Souls; their talent made them significant enough to be Set Apart and Treasured differently than all others, but their Loss was what immortalized them with endless Sorrow. Such was already the case of many artists, writers, and musicians—the troubled Souls that could not reconcile with the pain in their conflicted hearts.

No greater example of this could be found than Vincent van Gogh, who Died by his own hand at only thirty-seven years of age. He had but a brief lifetime on this earth, amounting to only *thirteen thousand six-hundred days*. The world had lost too many of our most important and gifted Human Beings because of their struggles and mental health issues; we had been surrendering our own to the darkness within since the beginning of time, and it was always at a tragic price.

I did not want for her story to remain untold, nor did I want her beauty as a Human Being to be overshadowed or lost because of the circumstances of her Death.

Would that I could, I would bring honor to each of these Treasured Souls, both in their lives and to the Final Moments of their Last Breath. I would tell their stories and share their Value to the world without ever finding it necessary to disclose one ounce of ugliness or bitterness; I would wipe the slate clean and let no hint of impropriety or disgrace touch their Legacies. I would do this regardless of the evidence I had been able to confirm along the way; I would let go of everything just to allow their memories to live on with no distraction or the pain such distractions might cause. *Would that I could.*

I understood Rebecca's choices even if I did not agree with them and wished she had chosen differently. She had felt *trapped* and there had been no one there to help her through it. It was a situation that merited anger, and I was slow to forget that Willow Amos was at the root of it. Rebecca was Dead because the person that had been capable of helping her had not done so, and as a result, she had become overwhelmed with the bleak ugliness and sheer helplessness of things. And instead of being able to reconcile her situation with some manner of peace, instead of being able to come to terms with things and find out what her options had been, she had chosen to End her own Life. That level of tragedy was inexcusable, and I laid it entirely at the feet of Willow Amos.

But what rested at the feet of Willow Amos did not end there, because she had a day of reckoning coming to her regarding Mariam as well.

Willow Amos had a lot to be accountable for.

Thoughts on Katarina

My anger didn't end with Rebecca and Miriam.

More than all else, I always drifted back to poor little Katarina.

What would it take to turn the tides so that no American Citizen could ever overlook or justify the ugliness that existed both within our own borders and around the world? Countless nations and cultures had mistreated women throughout history, including those throughout the West. Even regions that were governed with the expressed recognition of Human Rights and Dignity for All Mankind had appalling statistics. Our collective history was riddled with Missing Children. Our nation had *always* known the horror of Missing and Exploited women and children. We knew the weight of empty graves and tiny bones, of Stolen Lives and Stolen Futures.

It was a wonder that all Peacekeepers were not drunkards and addicts. How had they rested when there were *hundreds of thousands per year* that resulted in tragedy? How had they survived their jobs when so much of it resulted in Sorrow and Failure—when the bleakness of it all and the harsh realities meant far more negative outcomes than positive ones?

I was angered by the actions of those two vile men, and all I wanted was to avenge dear Katarina and *butcher them* with as much pain as I could physically muster.

I did not seek forgiveness or Closure for her or for her family; I sought Vengeance—bloody, angry, savage, slow, agonizingly torturous Violence. I sought the ultimate punishment—an eternal damnation—but only after experiencing as much Physical Pain and Harm as could be created for them during their Final Hours alive.

And I knew it would never happen like that.

I knew that pain would never be given in equal measure.

The Good among us would never allow it, no matter how worthy or deserving, and no matter how vicious or Evil the two Predators had been to that little girl.

And this was my point of contention—all those who professed to being 'Good' while making declarations that capital punishment was morally wrong or against God. Where were they when it mattered? What had they done to protect the Innocent?

Where were the millions of men who professed to be among the good and honorable of our nation? Where were the men who were considered law-abiding, noble, patriotic, and composed of integrity and impeccable character?

How many of our 'brave and heroic men' of yesteryear had stood by while the Good and Innocent suffered, expecting the Criminal Justice system to resolve everything? How many had borne witness to its historic and lengthy track record of failed accountability and the deliverance of Equitable and Morally Just Verdicts and Consequences?

At least I had tried to engage in the fight; it was more than most had done.

Victims themselves had spoken out long before there had ever been a national outcry for the creation of a Victim Advocacy Agency; they had left a trail of blood behind them that led from Crime Scenes to Courthouse steps.

The halls of every courthouse in our nation could be sealed shut and filled entirely on the lost blood from Victims who should never have been created, and who were never provided Fair Justice from our government. The courtrooms were submerged in the blood caused by the Violent; the walls and floors were stained red from the voiceless Victims who had depended on the Law of Man to fight for all those who could not fight for themselves.

The blood was thick, and there were many who were drowning in it. Our nation had been overrun with the apathy of 'Good Men' who either remained willfully ignorant so they could avoid accountability, or who lived lives of apathetic indifference—leaving it all at the feet of Lady Justice and washing their hands of the social burden.

The time for Good Men to stand idly by and let the Rule of Law dictate the cost of Human Life and Consequences for its Loss was over; it *had* to be over. We could no longer afford to let policies protect Evil from the Deliverance of Justice. No Good Man should ever watch Violence ensue and not intervene.

One could not be both a Good Man and a Spectator; if any American Man proclaimed himself to be a Patriot and a man worthy of respect, he had an inherent obligation and moral calling to intervene and render aid on behalf of the Weak, Vulnerable, and Powerless. It was the Good among us that had been Silent too long, and our most vulnerable who had paid the price for this.

The Weight of it All

It seemed a long battle.

My Brothers and Sisters had been there beside me the whole time; they had struggled as I had struggled, surrendered when it became too difficult, drank when it became too overwhelming, and even Ended their own Lives when they could take no more.

It was Hydra, the never-ending battle between Good and Evil as we fought to restore the Tree of Life and protect it against all who would poison it. It was an exhausting task, trying to hold Evil at bay.

It required constant vigilance to continuously thwart its advances, and I could feel how it wore at my Soul, weighing me down and leaving me to wonder if it was all worth the trouble when it seemed overwhelmingly hopeless to prevail against.

It was mentally and physically draining work, trying to keep the peace in a world hellbent on self-destruction and chaos.

It was easy to understand how Law Enforcement had dwindled to the insignificant numbers they had in the years leading up to the Last Stand. We invested so much of ourselves, our time, and our energy, all done to stave off the ugliness that lie just beyond the door, all so we could keep the wolves at bay for just a little while longer.

We kept trying—I kept trying—but no matter where I turned, there was always more. It tore at my chest like a piece of sap pulls from a tree, covering everything, staining, ripping, and damaging all it comes into contact with. My heart felt as though it had strips missing from it; chunks of my own history, the places I had been, the people I had shared my days and nights with, the Pain I had caused through my Notifications.

My lifetime could be defined by those missing strips. They had been peeled away, piece by piece, and strewn about the nation, left with families that were not my own. I was, after all, just someone that had met them as I was passing through; we shared a moment, a chapter in time, and usually only the worst of all memories—the ones that most wanted only to forget. I was a mere snippet in their lives, the person who had entered their world for reasons beyond their control, never considered anything more than a temporary figure with an expiration date.

But for me, every new place had become another stamp in my passport, a photo album filled with memories of strangers who had never intended to include me beyond what was required, and yet I had been allowed into their lives as intimately as any family member could be. It wasn't a natural connection, it wasn't welcomed, but it was necessary. The true cost was in the residual effect—that was the part that I never anticipated or realized—how much it would weigh on my Soul over the years.

What was difficult was knowing that even though I had left their homes, left their hometowns, and left their lives entirely, that I still retained the memories I had developed while I was there. I may have only been there briefly, and I may have even tried to maintain a respectable distance, but it was an impossible situation to invest that much time into the lives of strangers and then leave it all behind once it was time to move on. In this regard, I knew that my own life and career had mirrored how children in foster care had felt; they, too, had been strangers in a strange land, and had felt their lives intercept with other people's lives in the same way, except with no choice or voice in the matter.

We Humans might be capable of being nomadic, and we may have the internal social abilities to interact and adapt to our surroundings, but we weren't supposed to drift through our lives with such restlessness that we engaged, and then disengaged, with our Fellow Man without ever forming roots or becoming stationary at some point. We weren't supposed to connect and disconnect with people so routinely that it left a trail of broken, jagged experiences and memories. We all needed to belong, to feel a sense of community.

The benefits of a nomadic lifestyle were illusionary. After enough years of watching how other people stayed in one place and planted roots while I drifted from location to location, it became noticeably more pronounced; people were building lives while I was merely drifting between them, temporary, transient, rootless. It was inevitable that all the traveling would eventually take its toll, even on the most restless spirit, no matter how powerful their wanderlust.

It had begun to create an impact within me once I recognized it for what it was—once I understood the cup was continuously getting drained, but it was never getting replenished. Without a deeply grounded sense of self, without a strong and enduring connection to my own heritage and people, I feared the personal consequences if I continued on this path indefinitely. I worried all that would remain was a hollow career consisting of unsettling memories featuring the worst of humanity, and the shell of the man I used to be.

Nonetheless, there had begun a deep stirring within me to find something different, something that fed my Soul. I felt that the older I got, the more I was searching for something on the horizon, a lighthouse to guide me home, lighting the way back toward something of substance rather than more of the same as I waited for the next reason to leave.

The memories of my cases were not memories one wanted to hold on to; they were all made from the time I had to be in other people's lives and homes for reasons that were not legitimate. I carried no treasured memories of those broken chapters; they were filled with Pain, Emptiness, Sorrow, and Anger. Every Human emotion was always present—even Love—but none of it related to me, my life, or who I was. I had only been an observer of the Human Condition, not a participant.

We, the Peacekeepers, kept sweeping up the messes, kept clearing the streets of the most vile and reprehensible, Godless, Soulless, Evil animals imaginable, and they just kept resurfacing—some the same, some new. We kept doing our part, and yet somehow, between the failures of our society, the failures in our system of Sentencing and Punishment, the failures in nurturing, and the absolute failures of our government each and every time they provided too light of a Punishment when presented with one of these predatory criminals, it was never enough.

We kept pushing that rock up the mountain, even knowing the struggle and odds.

We were like Sisyphus, condemned to the same fate without having deserved any part of it, yet destined to continue rolling the giant boulder up the steep hill. We worked tirelessly, never quitting, never surrendering, and never accepting defeat. Despite our efforts, once we finally reach the summit, our only reward was to watch the boulder roll down to the bottom again, waiting for us to take our place behind it once more so we could begin all over again in a never-ending cycle of fruitless labors and hopeless dreams of progress. That was the weight of a career in Law Enforcement; that was the true price of job security. Knowing I was needed meant no one would ever be truly safe.

FORTY-ONE - SENTENCING

Final Stages

There would be no tribute for the Damned. Not for The Angels of Mercy Convicted of helping facilitate Arlan's Death, not for LeRoy Jones after his involvement in the Rape of Rebecca and the Abduction, Rape, and then Brutal Murder of Mariam, and not for the Abortion doctor and her associates.

There would be no Funerals, no Memorial Services, no Obituaries. There would be no options between Cremation or Memorialization, they would not be converted into Memorial gemstones, nor would there be a State-funded Grievance Stipend for the remaining family members of the Convicted. Once they had passed beyond Sentencing and received the Death Penalty, the courtesies ended.

This was, of course, of their own doing. No one had forced them to choose lives of Crime, and they were provided the same Free Will that every other law-abiding Citizen had been granted from Birth.

There would be a reckoning for each of the days Stolen from their Victims.

There would be no sympathy or Compassion applied toward LeRoy Jones after the Heinous Acts he Committed. He would be provided with a much more Merciful and Swift Death than most would agree he had earned—and it was a Tragedy that it would come as quickly and easily for him as it would.

He, along with The Angels of Mercy and the group of Abortionists, would spend their Last Moments in isolation, silence, and reflection. If they were capable of feeling remorse or regret, they could make their peace within this time, though it would fall on deaf ears. There would be no 'last meals', no 'Last Rights', and no one would be there to listen to any 'Last Words'. This was the essence of non-Existence; for those who demonstrated a lack of Humanity should not expect to receive any.

It was precisely as it should be. The Angels of Mercy might have felt they had helped people ease into death, but in the eyes of the Courts, murder was murder. The system would see no distinction between their actions and those of LeRoy Jones or the group of Abortionists.

Those who committed Murder were all the same at the time of their Sentencing, and only Death would suffice. There was no place for redemption or forgiveness for those who had willfully Stolen the life of another.

No, they would find no sympathy from anyone. There would be none to Grieve their Loss, none to Mourn their passing. In that final second of last drawn breath, the world was better for it.

AOM—Window of Time

The Death Penalty was final, and it was not negotiable.

After Sentencing, there would only be a thirty-day window for other Investigators to extract any additional information they could before their Execution. There would be no extensions provided. Investigators and Prosecutors would not have any leeway regarding either time or incentives to bargain with. They could not offer better deals in exchange for information rendered.

Anything the Convicted Offenders failed to share would die with them. The Citizens had spoken long ago and declared that there would be no further concessions or bargains provided to Convicted Offenders for any information they might have. They were much more likely to lie, exaggerate, and withhold relevant details just so they could stall or otherwise profit through deals and perks.

It was imperative that I do everything possible to learn more about this group of anarchists and see exactly how widespread and toxic their message was. It was equally important that my predecessors do everything they could to interrogate the Suspects and Convicted Offenders in an effort to garner any information they could from them before it was too late. My worst thought was that there were not just a few more groups such as this, but that there were many. It was entirely possible that they existed in every major city across our nation. I wasn't a conspiracy theorist; I was a realist. These people, with their rabid ideology and willingness to break the law as they saw fit in order to 'help' those whom they believed needed their assistance, were a menace to society. An underground movement of lawless dissidents willing to help people End their own Lives could affect thousands of Innocent Victims with potentially millions of Bereaved and Loved Ones left in their wake, and that made them extremely dangerous.

There was one key difference I noticed regarding these 'Angels' and I hoped it was because this movement wasn't as big or as advanced as I knew it could be. Everything prior to the Last Stand and the Great Reformation had been done with bells and whistles; they had prided themselves on being the most aggressive, outspoken, proactive demographic in America. There had been protests, marches, sit-ins, boycotts, and riots. As things escalated in the years before the Last Stand, they had become more disruptive in their tactics, even causing Violence and Deaths. It was as if 'the Squeaky Wheel gets the Grease' was their unwritten mantra; their behavior had always been predicated on being the most vocal and demanding in order to command as much attention as possible so they could force their will upon everyone else.

But these people were not doing that. Instead, they were extremely quiet. They were protected, organized, and strategically placed in order to seek those that they wanted to influence. It was a quiet movement, carefully designed with access to potential targets being central to their progress. Unlike the 21st century, where one only had to look at various Citizens and one could identify their political beliefs by the manner in which they dressed and looked, these Citizens had never drawn any type of negative attention to themselves. They weren't out there demanding changes, projecting their beliefs onto the general public, or standing on street corners waving flyers around. To my knowledge, no one was openly advocating for any type of reform regarding Suicide, Abortion, or Euthanasia. Our nation was of one collective identity, and everyone agreed on our national policies. Except—clearly, we weren't. If this group was only one sect, and if, Heaven Forbid, there were many such groups, our nation was actually in the midst of a very discreet, quiet movement of dissidents that were not only of a different social mentality, they were already advancing their cause through criminal services being rendered. Tracking such a movement would be difficult if they continued to be this understated.

This level of secrecy was profoundly more disconcerting than the openly hostile anarchists and dissidents that had plagued the mid-21st century and the years leading up to the Last Stand. Their solidarity, as well as their ability to maintain their discretion while advancing their cause and actively taking Human Life, struck me as disturbingly calculated. I was left with an ominous feeling whenever I considered how much I did not yet know about who they were—or how many of them were out there.

The Execution of LeRoy Jones

LeRoy Jones had been Executed.
I didn't watch. I didn't need to or care to.
But I was glad it was finally done.
It wasn't enough, but it was something.

Rebecca's life would be remembered. Her Death, although listed as Suicide, was not going to define who she was. Her parents had deserved to know the truth of what had befallen their daughter. They had deserved to know that she had not given up on her life for any reasons due to them, or even her own struggles. Her Death had been the result of many falling Dominoes, and I wanted them to understand this so they could mourn her loss and gain honest Closure.

Mariam, too, could now rest in peace. It was important to imagine that if Mariam could look beyond the veil, at least she would know that the Savage Animal that had Murdered her, and ripped apart her entire family and community, had been neutralized.

She would know that her Death had not been in vain; we had ensured that No Other Victims would ever lose their chance to live and thrive because of a weak Criminal Justice system. It was more than families Left Behind over the generations had been left with, and although it was not enough, it was at least something.

Nothing, unfortunately, would ever replace the Empty Spaces that had once been filled by Mariam, however.

The Execution of The Angels of Mercy

The seven Angels of Mercy that had driven the van, loaded Arlan, and removed him from his home for the last time had been Convicted. Their Sentences had been carried out soon after Conviction, as expected.

They had offered up very little by way of information about where Arlan had been killed, who had administered the drugs, how they had removed his RFID-Chip, how they transported him to the gravesite, or who had buried him.

Arlan's wheelchair had been recovered at the Winter Season Hospice Care facility. It had been placed into a storage room with other broken and defective medical equipment was kept and identified by its registration number. There were dozens of other wheelchairs and seemingly functional pieces of medical equipment that were currently being analyzed and traced back to their respective owners to ensure there were no others who had fallen prey to the Angels or died under mysterious circumstances.

They had never referred directly to Daegan Kyl or another person as being the one responsible for the burial of Arlan Randall. They had taken their stories with them to their deaths. I imagined we would never know the specifics regarding what role each individual had played. Still, they had confessed enough about themselves and their comrades to secure their Convictions and Sentences. Most of them had left heartfelt messages of regret for their families.

The consequences for their naïve belief in her had been the loss of their own lives; a price they might have been willing to make, but one that their own family, friends, and Loved Ones would undoubtedly have wished they had avoided. Our nation had lost more than just Arlan by the spread of that toxic ideology; they had lost many young men and women who were now going to see their entire lives and futures cut short because of it.

Willow Amos had encouraged them to become Criminals, idealizing and romanticizing what it meant to be part of a fringe movement that was dedicated to 'changing the world'. They were, indeed, accountable for their own role in every activity they took part in and every Criminal Act they were responsible for. They were even responsible for their own sheer stupidity and gullibility. Nonetheless, they were young and impressionable, and it was my contention that she knew they were easy targets.

Somewhere out there, seven sets of parents had said goodbye to their college students knowing that they were going to face execution for their Crimes Against Humanity regarding their participation in the Death of Arlan Randall. They had sent them off to college to help them gain an education, never knowing that there was a toxic poison hidden below the surface in the powerful messaging they were being exposed to.

The Watchers On The Wall Speech: Crossroads

Fellow Americans,

We come to you today with heavy hearts. Although we wish for it to be very different than it is, there is little point in denying the current state of the nation or the unbearable weight of the problems contained within.

We are no longer at a point where we can speak of matters as we 'wish' for them to be; we have passed that window of time and must now make the concerted effort to either create the changes that we long to see in our country, or we must accept the state of the nation as it is, and henceforth submit to every abysmal, immeasurable dysfunction and misdeed.

When the writing is on the wall, only those who are willfully ignorant and intentionally in denial refuse to admit it. It has now reached the point of necessity when all good, law-abiding Citizens must take a full and careful measure of the state of the nation in which they are living. We must engage in a fully-comprehensive evaluation of all relevant social issues, the Criminal Justice system, and its heavy toll on our society. We must address the persistent, undeniable social decline of our Citizenry through the degradation of our moral and ethical standards.

This evaluation must be done with the same level of candid thoroughness one should use when contemplating whom to choose from among us to represent the American People through our election process, and should be done without bias or ill-will. Every Citizen should spend time in thoughtful contemplation and with a sincere heart, weighing all evidence one considers to be relevant for their evaluation. It will only be through such inward self-reflection that the truth of the matter will be manifested to each of us with each conclusion being entirely subjective and uniquely our own. There are no right or wrong answers to these questions. We ask only that Citizens address these issues to the best of their ability and with their own personal beliefs, standards, and desires in mind.

Is this the America that our Founding Fathers dreamed of, and imagined would exist in the future? Is the America we are living in today the best version of America that we can achieve? And is this the America that we wish to pass on to our Children and our future generations?

Is this truly "the Greatest Nation on Earth" anymore? Or has America deteriorated into such a cesspool of Savagery, Violence, and Lawlessness that we can no longer distinguish ourselves from other Third World nations?

America has no room for Citizens who believe in the principles currently being promoted by our lawless government. Every Citizen is at risk because of the policies set forth by the current regime, and those who support this administration are betraying the American People and the very foundations upon which this nation was built. All those who stand on the side of the Savage Predators, the Sex Offenders, the Career Criminals, and the Illegal Invaders have made the choice to stand against their own

Countrymen, and the security of their nation. They have chosen to defend the worst among us at the expense of our Children and our most Vulnerable Citizens. We must ask ourselves if they are the types of neighbors and Citizens we are willing to continue sharing our nation with.

America is standing at the crossroads. How we proceed will determine the trajectory of our future, and the state of the nation that we will leave for our Children and future generations.

No matter how we choose to present these facts and circumstances, there are several truths which will remain undeniable and unavoidable. If Americans are going to prevail, we can no longer be a nation of pacifists, naysayers, or truth-deniers; we must come to terms with the reality in which we live.

If we choose to take the path of conscious denial, we risk everything. The restoration of our faith and values is already predicted to be a brutal upward battle because we have taken the path of least resistance for too long already. Continuing to deny the existence of our problems and their sources will only hurt us further and hinder our ability to self-correct before it's too late.

Whether we choose to act or not, we are making a choice. Apathy, inaction, avoidance, or denial, by hell or highwater, all will still create and produce results, and those results will create change.

Inaction is a choice, and no one that chooses to remain silent today should have any illusions or expectations regarding what sort of reaction their apathetic indifference will cause tomorrow.

We must acknowledge that we are no longer safe among our own Fellow Man. The bitter reality is that we never were. But we are no longer living in a time where we can afford to live with naivety, optimism, and delusional denial about this subject.

There is no middle ground anymore, and no one can choose neutrality. Failing to choose to fight for one's nation and future is choosing to submit to tyranny and die.

It is the slow hemorrhage as one watches first his neighbors bleed out, then his family, and then finally, himself.

The Wolf is at the door.

Those who make deals with criminals and corrupt politicians will reap the costs soon enough. But is it fair to expect equal consequences by those that are loyal to our Constitution, the Rule of Law, and our Heavenly Father?

Those who wish to dismantle the foundation of our nation have worked diligently for decades doing everything within their power to deconstruct all that our Founding Fathers and our Framers envisioned and created. Their agenda is the antithesis of what America was intended to be. Our Founding Fathers created this nation not only for themselves, or based on what type of world they themselves wished to live in, but for The People, and for every American that would follow them, reaping the endless bounty and protections that their hard work and determination brought to fruition.

We have endured years of Civil Unrest and the intentional disruption of peace throughout our country by those who intend only to destroy all that we are. For too long, the American People have quietly watched as violent predators tore apart our nation, murdered our Innocent, and targeted our Law Enforcement. We have watched as they clogged our Criminal Justice system with perpetual criminality and recidivism at our expense. We have sacrificed our privacy and freedom in order to establish extreme laws to curb such lawlessness and destruction. These laws are only necessary because of those who cannot, and will not, abide by the Rule of Law and the social rules of civility upon which every civilized nation and People exist.

It has never been the intention, nor the Will of the People—the rightful Patriots and ancestors of this great nation that adhere to the principles of our Founding Fathers—to evoke political strife, disharmony, or a Second Civil War. The People of These United States have demonstrated long-standing positions of patience, tolerance, and self-control regarding the continuous, unyielding deterioration of the nation they hold so dear.

Only through the unified rising of our individual voices will we begin to implement the changes necessary for our nation to prevail against these dark forces which seek to destroy us from within. Every voice counts, including the Victims who have been silenced forever due to the Violence inflicted upon them by their Fellow Citizen.

The time for apathy is no more. The time for action, accountability, and justice is upon us. Let no man ever find cause to reflect upon his time granted here on earth and second-guess his own indecisiveness or lack of action. God has not only provided each of us with the unalienable right to self-protection, He has commanded that we Love our Neighbor as Ourselves. This means we have a duty to Protect and Defend the Sanctity of Human Life.

We have an inherent obligation to protect those who cannot protect themselves.

We are Mortal Beings with a Divine Purpose. Let no man squander the Time and Gifts he has been granted only by the Grace of God. Take up arms, my Fellow Citizens. The time to reclaim our nation is upon us.

The Watchers On The Wall
On this date, the Fourth of July
In the Year of our Lord, 2051

PART NINE

Do not take revenge, my dear friends,
but leave room for God's wrath,
for it is written:
"It is mine to avenge; I will repay," says the Lord.

Romans 12:19

FORTY-TWO – PLAN FOR DEPORTATION

Plan for Deportation

It finally came to me how we would ensure that Daegan Kyl could get to Alaska and past the Alask-Can border and security system. We were going to add him to the same Transport headed for Alaska that Willow Amos would be traveling on. It was the only way we could guarantee we could get him there without being apprehended or screened. It was also the only way we could ensure that he would arrive at the same time or before Willow Amos did, not to mention in the same location.

I spent some time with Officer Stanton and went over my idea as we reviewed the potential flaws and ways it could all go horribly wrong. There was some risk, but ultimately, if we planned it out well, timed everything impeccably, and made absolutely zero miscalculations, there was a fairly good chance that we could pull it off without ending up incarcerated and Exiled ourselves. And like all good criminal plans, it couldn't be carried out solo, no matter how great the criminal mastermind believed himself to be.

I had to solicit the assistance of Grace, Officer Stanton, and even Daegan Kyl himself in order to bring our plan to fruition. At the end of the day, we would only be as successful with it as we could strategize and work well together; the slightest unforeseen variable or case of cold feet would put a wrench in the plan just as surely as if one of us submitted a report to the 'appropriate authorities' before we even got it underway. Ironically, we had to be as 'thick as thieves' if we were going to succeed, and despite three of us working within Law Enforcement and none of us being Convicted Criminals, if anything went wrong, we were all going to be at risk of serious, life-altering consequences.

I discussed this extensively with each of my colleagues and with Daegan Kyl, and did so separately. They needed to know the risks involved; my colleagues especially needed to understand and accept that they could lose everything if our plan failed.

Even Daegan Kyl would have faced certain negative consequences if my plan was unsuccessful. As it stood, our intention was to get him to Alaska at the same time and place as Willow Amos—otherwise, it made little sense for him to be there. For safety reasons, it was imperative that he arrive at the same destination as Willow Amos; she would be extremely vulnerable from the moment of her arrival, so his being there by her side was of vital importance. If our plan fell through and he was Convicted, he would have been Sentenced and Exiled as much as another thirty days out; a lot could happen during those thirty days, and he might have forfeited everything for a girl who was already Dead. It was a grim worst-case scenario, but he needed to understand it.

If we didn't plan out the travel timing, we had no way to guarantee he would arrive at the same date or time as Willow Amos. The Transports did not establish their final destination coordinates until the moment of flight. They could end up at one of three Drop-off Zones from Patos Island; the only way to know which one she would get dropped off at—and do so at the same time so he could protect her—was to be on the same flight. Of course, he could still get dropped off at any location and then scour the countryside looking for her; it would be much easier if he had a map and knew the other locations as well—both of which could be addressed in some capacity before he arrived. But how long would that take before he found her? And what would have happened to her before that time? The risk was far too great to leave to chance.

And finally, a Conviction meant the loss of all personal assets—something we could avoid if he went there voluntarily and didn't get caught. He was going of his own accord; there was no reason that he should lose everything and never return. As long as he went there willingly and as a law-abiding Citizen, he could return whenever he felt compelled to. He didn't really have a plan beyond going there—and he and I hadn't discussed things to that extent. But should he ever want to come back—and if he could figure out how to get out of Alaska, which was unquestionably going to be far more difficult than our getting him in—he could legally return at any point. Should he end up doing so, having his financial assets, his business, and everything else intact from his 'old life' would have been to his advantage. He might not be thinking that far ahead now, but at some point, he would. Alaska was no place for old men.

For Officer Stanton, Grace O'Connor, and myself, the risks meant considerably more. It meant risking the end of our careers—the end of our lives as we knew them to be. It meant Sacrificing all the years of our educational endeavors and hard work, our goals and aspirations, and forfeiting every accomplishment, promotion, and advancement in our careers. To be found Aiding and Abetting someone in such a manner was an extreme risk to take and could result in the highest levels of loss for each of us. We would be risking the loss of our families, our homes, our financial stability, our reputations, and even our futures—all to end up Exiled and in the very place we had spent our entire careers sending Convicted Offenders.

For any member of government or Law Enforcement to end up in the wilds of Alaska was rare, but it was also exceedingly high-risk for them if they did. There was a reason they didn't place Convicted Peacekeepers among the general population in traditional prisons during the 21st century; it meant a Bloody, Violent Death. But our government no longer had such reservations. Convicted Criminals were all the same, and they only came in three varieties: Deserving solely of the Death Penalty, Able to be Rehabilitated, Or Incapable of change but not Violent enough to have merited a Death Sentence. For those falling into the third category, no matter what their Crimes, they all shared the same Sentence resulting in Loss of Country and Citizenship. For anyone who ended up Exiled, the US government had already washed their hands of them; they didn't care who they mingled with, or what happened to them anymore—they were non-Citizens and no longer the problem of the US government or The People.

Everyone had to be fully aware of the risk and the consequences. Each of them had to know what was at stake if it backfired, if they were betrayed by anyone from within, or if we messed things up. We all had to decide for ourselves—with no harm, no foul if we weren't comfortable, didn't feel it was worth the risk, or didn't want to follow through. It wasn't, after all, anything that we ourselves stood to benefit from; we were doing it for no other reason than to provide a man with the means to travel into uncharted territory through illicit channels. It was a phenomenal risk for reasons that were wholly unnecessary and unrelated to our own personal lives; no one would have passed judgment had any of us declined.

But that did not happen.

I wasn't sure if I was relieved about everything once we'd finalized our plans. We had set everything in motion and were left only with tying up loose ends before the final date—with Daegan Kyl tying up more than anyone else. It was all established for the same time and date as Willow Amos' departure from the WA-SET facility on Patos Island, and all things considered, it was a flawless plan. Once we knew when she would be shipped out, we could then set things in motion. Until then, all that was left to do was wait. For Daegan Kyl, it meant preparing to leave his own country for an indefinite period of time, setting out into the Great Unknown.

We sorted out the intricacies while Daegan Kyl put his affairs in order and each of my colleagues finalized the specific elements of the plan for which they were responsible.

Afterward, all that was left to do was wait.

Thoughts on Willow Amos

I wasn't sure how I felt about Willow Amos getting off so easily, or why it seemed to bother me as much as it did that she was. It seemed unfair, in the grand scheme of things, that by her own admission she had done some horrific things to her Fellow Man and yet had faced nothing worse for her punishment than Exile. I found it difficult to align my sense of Justice with the impact her actions had on Arlan, Rebecca, and then Mariam. She had set a Ripple Effect in motion that would ricochet throughout entire families for generations to come, and yet she still failed to even consider herself responsible for causing any of the Harm directly.

I could see it from a multitude of perspectives, but I just couldn't reconcile myself to the idea that she should have things as easily as she was going to. Easily, in the sense, that she was going to be allowed to live, allowed to live beyond a cage, allowed to roam free over millions of acres of wilderness where she could build a manageable, even decent, future for herself. A future that would be better and easier because Daegan Kyl would be by her side—another aspect of Willow Amos and her 'punishment' that I wasn't sure I agreed with or considered 'fair' compared to her Crimes.

Perhaps I wouldn't have felt so bitterly about it had she either seemed more remorseful or if her actions had not resulted in such deeply layered elements of Harm to so many of her Victims. She had caused so much damage, even if it was inadvertent, and she hadn't intended for anything to be done with malice. Rebecca had deserved a better turn of Justice, and yet there hadn't been one. Mariam had then suffered as a direct consequence of Willow Amos failing to address Rebecca's Rape. Perhaps she hadn't intended for those events to occur, and perhaps she hadn't meant for everything to spiral out of control as it had. And maybe it wouldn't have been so bad if she had even demonstrated the slightest bit of growth or comprehension regarding the political and social views—her 'values'—that had led to their Loss of Life, but she hadn't even seemed phased by why her views were so dangerous both to our society and everyone affected by them. And then finally, maybe I would have been a bit more inclined to be patient with her if she was at least a decent Human Being, but she had done absolutely nothing to redeem herself or make it understandable why Daegan Kyl would defend her.

I wasn't even sure why we were fighting so hard to help Daegan Kyl when he had still tried to conceal four sets of Human Remains—even if he had done so for completely altruistic reasons.

I wasn't sure why I was trying to help anything happen that could benefit Willow Amos. I still couldn't understand why Daegan Kyl was completely willing to destroy his own life to protect her. She was neither likable nor trustworthy; my first impression of her had been that of an uncivilized shrew behaving like a petulant, entitled, hysterical she-devil, and it would take something akin to a miracle before I believed that first impression was erroneous or mischaracterized.

I wasn't one to carry personal grudges, but it was not easily forgotten that the woman had *spit* on me and a half dozen other members of Law Enforcement—a move that was punishable by Death if her spittle, blood, or any other bodily fluids had been found to be tainted with anything potentially deadly. One did not easily forget those who endangered their lives, and while I was apparently willing enough to help Daegan Kyl Commit Felonies just to protect her, I was no more trusting of her today than I had been before.

I understood she believed in what she had been doing; I truly appreciated her devotion to her beliefs and her willingness to fight for them when she felt it necessary. I could even appreciate that she was willingly breaking the laws because she felt they were archaic, unfair, and a violation of individual autonomy and free will.

I could even appreciate that she was still young, still stupid in a thousand ways, and so short-sighted and possibly emotionally damaged that she lacked the ability to navigate our world as a normal, high-functioning adult like the rest of us. I genuinely understood how the Deaths of her parents at such an impressionable age, followed by the even more devastating Loss of her brother—which actually seemed to be more influential and scarring—could cause enough issues with Grief and Loss that she would have struggled in some very compelling ways throughout the rest of her teenage years.

I could appreciate all of that—just as I was certain the Panel of Judges and the Victim Advocates could address those factors and take them into account—but it still did not eradicate the aspect of self-accountability that made her responsible for the choices she made. There must still be a day of reckoning for all the damage she had done, and she had caused a lot. She had hurt a shocking number of people through her selfishness and her carelessness.

Yes, Arlan had approved of what she had assisted him to do. And despite her involvement, they had held others accountable for their direct role in Arlan's Death. They were young, dumb kids who had gone off to college as their parents had wanted them to do, but then had fallen prey to the manipulation of others. They had all been easily influenced, impressionable, and gullible—over-eager to fit in and believe in something more substantial than the traditional values they had been taught at home. They had gotten tangled up with the pseudo-progressive political agendas being pushed through an echo-chamber of influencers, who had exploited them and essentially compelled them to do their bidding. Her ability to preach to those kids and manipulate them had effectively ended their lives, whether by the Death Penalty or Exile, and yet she herself had avoided taking any actual responsibility for her role in it. It was reprehensible, and I still didn't know how she had pulled it off.

I wasn't sure how I felt about that, even now.

And I realized—it was a moral issue. It was a question of principle and a question of ethical standards and honor. I realized that the others who took the fall were just as deep in the muck with her, and they should have been punished alongside her for their Crimes. But should she have skated while others were Sentenced to Death?

I didn't know, and that was just one of the lingering questions and doubts I still had about her. I couldn't profess to be enough of a scholar on any of these subjects; I didn't know where to draw the line, where the line should have been drawn, or where accountability ended and Humanitarianism began. I was a member of Law Enforcement, a Peacekeeper, and an Investigator. My job only began when Crimes had been Committed, and only Crimes Against Humanity. I only investigated Crimes in which my Fellow Man had been Physically Harmed and subjected to Human Rights Violations, and Malicious Intent was frequently a central component determining whether or not anyone would be held accountable.

I couldn't control the outcome from the trials or dictate the terms of Sentencing. I couldn't even guarantee Convictions would occur. They could find her to be 'Criminally Insane', or even just so severely emotionally damaged because of the Deaths of her entire immediate family that she wouldn't be held criminally liable at all. And all of that was entirely beyond my expertise, training, and power to control. Such things, I believed, were a heavy weight to bear, and I shifted in my thoughts and feelings on the matters far too much to entertain the idea that I should be given the ability to pass judgment regarding her or her actions.

None of that was part of my job description, and for that, I was grateful.

But somewhere in there, we had to have room for Humanity to make Human mistakes. We had to make room for forgiveness, for repentance, for redemption, and room for personal growth.

Was any of this worth losing a potentially valuable Citizen over? An entire group of them? And if our society were slightly different, if people had the Free Will to choose their own fate and actions without any legal conflict, would any of these Citizens even be likened to the real Criminals that I dealt with in every other case?

Or was this a miscarriage of Justice because there were Victims created by this group of misguided, dangerous youth and by only facing Exile they were getting away with Murder?

I should have been following the letter of the law; there was no room for emotion, and no one cared about sad childhood stories when they were going around Murdering people. The laws were there to be upheld; if we didn't like the laws, we knew how to change them. By those definitions, she was, at the very least, Guilty of Conspiring to Commit Murder—provided they could prove it.

But out of all that she had done, and all that she was going to get away with, the part that truly nagged at my Soul was how she had mistreated Rebecca that day of her Rape. If all else could be overlooked and forgiven, how she had worked so hard to protect LeRoy Jones at Rebecca's expense was the real tragedy. That was where I think the true Willow Amos revealed herself, and that's the person who I thought was now laughing all the way to the bank.

That was the side of Willow Amos that I wasn't sure Daegan Kyl understood was still a very prevalent part of her personality and character. I was worried Daegan Kyl was unwittingly sacrificing his entire life to help and protect her, and all the while, he would probably never understand that there was a monster lurking just below the surface. I believed there was something within Willow Amos that was so exceptionally selfish, self-serving, and cold-hearted that she would cut his throat while he slept if it resulted in her getting what she wanted.

But trying to warn another person about the character of someone they were about to climb into bed with was always a fool's errand, and it didn't matter if it was about a romance or a business deal. We do it anyhow, usually, and we do it as a testament of the love and respect we bear for the person whom we are trying to warn. We issue such warnings, hoping our message will help them make sound choices sufficient to bypass some potentially serious mistakes which could lead to permanent damage and scarring. We do it even when we know it is unwelcome information, an unwanted opinion, and in spite of the fact that when we do it, there is an almost infinitesimal chance of it being well-received.

What a mess we creatures were when it came down to our interactions with others. This was never clearer than with Daegan Kyl and Willow Amos. They could each be classified as either monumentally selfless, self-sacrificing, and loyal—or they could be wholly negative, in which case they were both displaying equal measures of self-destruction and codependence. It was either a testament of their love for one another or it was a toxic relationship built on guilt and misguided loyalty and honor.

His relationship with her was as grounded in cement as any I'd ever seen, and I did not believe that anything I or anyone else said would alter that. I firmly believed that whether or not we helped him, he would be there—and he would go regardless of the consequences, expense, or the price he would ultimately wind up paying if he were caught.

He had the facts. I'd let him read all the case files, her statements, and the interviews. He knew where the evidence stood with Arlan, Rebecca, and Mariam. He had been brought into this case because he had been accused of being at the root of everything—and she had caused all of it. If this were my brother, I would have already told him to consider her Exile to be a Gift so he could freely escape. I would have issued the warning without delay or minced words. I would probably have done everything within my power to help him break free while the rest of my family helped—because that's what family does.

And because that's what family does, I decided to just keep my mouth shut and my opinions to myself about Willow Amos; because he was a grown man, he had all the information I could provide about who and what she was, and I could only presume he knew what he was doing.

Maybe she was toxic; maybe she would be the end of him.

But then, perhaps, maybe she just needed a fighting chance to grow up, to gain some maturity, and to have a fresh start with someone whom she knew loved her and knew how to handle her.

I hoped she was already fully aware of just how much the man had done for her, and that she would always take that into consideration regarding her treatment of him. As long as she knew he was a Good Man, maybe it would all work out.

Well, that, and for him to remember to pack some hollow-tipped silver bullets and a wooden stake. At the very least, a few venom-extraction kits.

Alaska, Utopia Realized

Alaska had once been a majestic place; a stronghold in the West that held treasures unlike any other state. It was plentiful in wildlife, gold, and oil. Its beauty generated significant tourism.

Its remarkable size had made it a tremendous land of untapped potential, but the isolation and segregation from the rest of the nation meant the state and its Citizens were forced to sustain themselves with limited opportunities in only a handful of cities, or submit to a slower, harder way of life in more rural areas.

Still, despite these disadvantages, Alaska had somehow thrived. As with any geographic region that was prone to long, cold winters and a difficult northern climate, the people learned to adapt to the frigid temperatures, endless hours of darkness, and hindersome inclement weather conditions. The combination of snow, ice, short days, and endless darkness was a union that a statistically low percentage of Americans could endure, but for those that did, they were quick to counter that the freedom of lifestyle, outdoor activities, and the never-ending beauty of the rugged landscape was well worth it. They were not only content to live in the northernmost state; they were grateful that they were among the select few that made Alaska their home and valued that it was unlike any other state in the Union.

The Alaskans came in two forms: native or transplant. The Native Alaskans were the original inhabitants of the Alaskan frontier before the American settlers arrived in pursuit of gold and glory. As generations passed, both demographics survived and flourished, each adapting to the other and finding mutual respect through their shared love of the unchanged landscape surrounding them.

The Native Alaskans were a protected demographic and struggled to preserve their heritage and their unique and separate identity from the rest of the Americans. They frequently lived in isolated villages and communities and clung to their traditional values and way of life. In one of the few uncontested positive actions conducted by the US government, they allowed their Native Alaskan populations in the north to live their lives with complete freedom from the pressures to conform to the White Man's world, and to their credit, they honored that pledge almost beyond reproach for many generations. Even as the White American population grew within Alaska and the two demographics found it necessary to interact with one another, they did so amicably. This was because of the Native Alaskans continued separatism and the White Americans respectful distance, choosing to never encroach on their lands or disturb their way of life. As with all Native Americans, the US government had provided designated lands for the Alaskan Natives, and within those boundaries, they lived as separate but equal US Citizens.

The rest of America, including the government, was mostly indifferent to the happenings of the North, affording their inhabitants to lead lives of independence and self-sufficiency that often supported more traditional values such as homesteading, hunting, fishing, and trapping. There were cities within the state that were as equally advanced and focused on urban lifestyles, professional development, and progressive worldly achievement; but even then, because of all the factors that made Alaska the truly last wild frontier in America, there was still an undeniable connection to the unwavering formidable Human Spirit found within the Alaskan Citizen.

And so Alaska had thrived, despite its harsh climate and isolation. Many would say that their separation from the rest of the US had worked to their advantage, since they were never historically linked to any of the national problems that had plagued the rest of the country during the mid-21st century in the years leading up to the Last Stand. Their isolation had kept them far from the toxins of the political and social climate, and their low Crime Rates, Conservative values and lifestyles, and willingness to live in hard conditions had built up their endurance and stamina like no other state could. The Alaskans were tough, patriotic, and independent.

But their low-population, remote location, and excessive geographic size were eventually proven to cause their unfortunate downfall. The rural landscape that had once been largely ignored by the American Citizenry and their government ended up being the spotlight of the nation in the years leading up to the Last Stand, and the Alaskan people were soon to be taught a lesson about sacrifice that they could never forget. The US government, likewise, had demonstrated to the world yet again that when America wanted something, America got it.

It created bad blood when the state of Alaska was chosen to be the future home of all those that were to be Exiled. Citizens had burned their cities to the ground in protest when the Sentence Reform Act passed into law, but that was to be expected. Government officials had done everything they could to cause political obstruction and dissension within the nation, but that came as no surprise, either. Those that opposed the Sentence Reform Act had become increasingly more Violent, leading many to believe that Civil War was not only inevitable, it was long overdue. Just as some had consistently chosen to stand alongside the Criminal Class and defended what they considered to be 'violations of their Human Rights', the American People were dedicated to removing all those that had chosen Violence and Criminality over the Rule of Law.

It placed political representatives within Alaska into a difficult position. They supported the national reforms being implemented, but they faced negative consequences no matter what they did. If they agreed to the reform with Alaska as the chosen Relocation Zone and allowed their state to become the dumping ground for the Criminal Class, they would have been overthrown. It would have been considered a betrayal. Likewise, they were also supposed to be the last line of defense against the rest of the nation regarding Eminent Domain. They could not vote against the Reform measures that were imperative if America was to survive, but they could not condone forcing the Alaskan Citizens to leave their homes through the induction of Eminent Domain. It was a conundrum for all involved, and the nation was in conflict.

The lower forty-eight states were losing their battle with lax policies. Crime and Violence were happening at unprecedented levels. There were thousands of Violent Deaths every day with no chance of it abating, and Law Enforcement had stopped functioning in every major city.

The animals were controlling the zoo.

It wasn't a difficult premise to understand; if consequences were not severe enough to stop Crime and Violence effectively, the problem would only continue to escalate. Without penalties and consequences harsh enough to pose as a sufficient deterrent for people to compel them to abide by the Laws of the Land, Crime and Violence would continue to rise. If the problems could not be prevented, then something had to be done to address the fallout from Violent Criminality. They had to be cordoned off and removed from the rest of society entirely. Something had to be done, or America was going to be lost forever—one violent, savage Death at a time. If the problem was not corrected before there were no longer enough good people left to fight back, there would be no recovery.

The Alaskan Citizens understood this. There were many of their brave men and women that had volunteered in militias, and many thousands more that had willingly signed off on their homes for fair housing prices and relocated to carefully selected Safe Zones that were secured by Conservative Leaders and Law Enforcement. But there were still many, many Citizens that refused to move, and declared that they would take up arms against their own government if forced to leave their homes. The government had obliged, but they had not submitted to their demands; the time for compromise and appeasement had long since passed. America would not have ended up here had Her Citizens not surrendered so much to grant concessions to a party that had been hellbent on destroying their nation in the first place.

There was but one small blessing to be found in these last days before the Sentence Reform Act began their first Drops into the Alaskan wilderness. The Native Alaskans had all but disappeared from the timeline and were no longer a registered demographic. Sparse populations, low birth rates, and long histories of shared bloodlines had led to a steady decline of Native populations over the centuries. The Natives of America had always held the highest morbidity rates of US Citizenry, and between alcoholism, Violence, vehicle accidents, and a myriad of issues related to health and poverty, almost all Native American tribes had become nothing more than a chapter in history. They had documented the Suicide rates among the Native Americans and the Alaskan Natives as the highest demographic in our nation for countless decades. As with every other Native American tribe in the United States, it was only a matter of time before the populations would decline into extinction; they had never truly stood a chance.

The one minor consolation was that the Native Alaskans did not have to watch their homeland get destroyed as their government desecrated it by turning it into a dumping ground. They would not understand that their Fellow Citizens were only doing what England had done long before by attempting to remove their most unsavory Criminal Class and separating them from the rest of their Citizenry to save the collective whole. All they would have seen was betrayal, as did many others.

The seizing of Alaska and the Sentence Reform Act that led to the Exile of so many American Citizens was controversial for both sides of the aisle, but it was a necessary evil. The desire to preserve Alaska was largely based on the sentimental attachment and emotional responses that the beauty of Alaska presented; it wasn't a logical argument. Alaska was the only place that the US could reasonably use as a separate society within their own borders that had the necessary square miles, separation from the general Citizenry, and ability to control its borders effectively. If America was to survive, Alaska had to be sacrificed. The needs of the many had to outweigh the wants of the few. There was simply no compelling argument that could be made to protect Alaska from being sacrificed for the Greater Good, and no alternative that would suffice.

And here we were, decades after the Sentence Reform Act, a state repurposed for a country that was still in its fledgling stages after undergoing the most expansive transformation in history.

Alaska had become exactly what one could have expected with no form of governance or the Rule of Law. They had turned one of the most majestic places on earth into a contaminated wasteland in a matter of decades. Alaska was no longer simply the 'Last Frontier'. It was a wild, lawless place filled with Violent, ruthless Predators living with no semblance of law or order. Throughout American history, there had been many Citizens who had called for less Law Enforcement, more leniency for Criminals, and an end to mass incarceration.

Alaska was the answer to their demands; it resulted from the lack of accountability and an end to the Rule of Law that they were so inherently opposed to.

It was not the Utopian Dream that they may have expected it to be, but it was a very clear affirmation of what America had been turning into before the Last Stand and the Great Reformation. It was the closest thing to hell on earth that America had ever known.

Alaska had become exactly what one could expect from Mankind when all the rules and social protocols were thrown out the window and pure primalism remained. It was a dog-eat-dog world, where even within a place comprising solely of Predators, there was still a ranking system in which the weak became prey to the more savage of their kind. None were free from victimization in a world where power, dominance, and Violence were the only systems of order; there was one rule, and one rule only—learn to survive and be prepared to do anything necessary in order to do so.

This was what they had wanted, after all. The Criminals were no longer 'unjustly persecuted', there was no 'police brutality' or 'profiling', and no one was being incarcerated in ways that were deemed 'excessive' or 'discriminatory'.

Alaska was the Socialist Utopian Society that Citizens had fought for America to become. Everything within the borders of this vast no-man's-land was done under the principles and policies that had been heavily fought for in the decades leading up to the Last Stand during the 21st century. They had secured their own nation-state within Alaska, and as one could have expected, it was a dangerous, horrifying world for all who ended up there.

Three Drop-Zones

There were only three designated Drop-Zones that were used by Washington State to discard their Exiled Ex-Citizens, and each of them left a lot to be desired. Two had been selected because they were National Forests, already government land that would not have required any negotiations for terms or Eminent Domain seizures. The first was the Gates of the Arctic National Park, and the second was Denali National Park. The third location selected to be a Drop-Zone was Nome, Alaska and the region surrounding it.

None of them were ideal places to live for most people, and without the securities and amenities provided by the lower forty-eight, they were considered among the worst travel destinations an American could ever end up. Given the incalculable Crime, Violence, and Death rates, most of the nations in the West were inclined to agree.

The Gates of the Arctic National Park was the most northern part of Alaska where Convicted Offenders could be Dropped and would have been the most rugged and unyielding to endure. The area was a difficult one to navigate. Because no roads or hiking trails had ever been established, it was rough terrain to trek even for experienced people in peak physical condition. Although it was pristine and undeniably beautiful, it was also extremely dangerous because of the elements, which were given to frequent summer rainstorms and temperatures of seventy-below in its harshest winters. It was an acceptable Drop-Zone for late September, which was where we were now, but anyone that attempted to live in this region year-round would need to be far better prepared than they would initially be after being Dropped-Off there through a Transport, especially if it were already late fall.

The Gates of the Arctic Drop-Zone was so far north already that it was foolish for anyone to proceed further north; it was wild country, with hundreds upon hundreds of miles of nothingness except freezing temperatures, wild animals, and relentless winters. To our knowledge, there were no encampments north of the Drop-Zone, and satellite imagery only rarely detected the odd, random Convicted Criminal that clearly held survival skills and knew he was better off on his own than among his own kind.

Nome, Alaska, was not likely to offer anything better, especially just at the onset of winter. What remained of the small ocean-side town was now overrun with ruffians the likes of which had never been seen in Alaska, even during the years of the Gold Rush. Satellite imagery had shown that most of the town had been decimated in a multitude of fires over the years, and without the resources, dedicated manpower, and general inclination to improve anything, nothing had ever been rebuilt. The leftover lumber—along with anything else usable—had been burned during the harsh winters, and now the entire region was a barren wasteland that provided only enough shelter for those who were dominant enough to secure it and keep it. Out of the three places,

Nome was reputed to be the worst psychologically because it had been the singular Drop-Zone that reminded their New Arrivals of all they had sacrificed and lost. Although it couldn't be proven with any true empirical data, it was widely theorized that Nome had the highest Suicide rates of the three.

Neither the Gates of the Arctic nor Nome could boast of an ample supply of geographical and environmental resources that could help sustain life for anyone; there simply wasn't enough available that could provide for a community with no outside resources being flown, trucked, or boated in. They wouldn't have known how to use the land or the sea to forage, fish, hunt, or survive; the bounty that was available was wasted on them. I doubted that even the most rugged, experienced outdoorsman would have been able to build a sustainable long-term existence for himself given the tools at hand—and that was based on a premise where the people one was surrounded by were like-minded and friendly instead of bands of rogue cut-throats ready to steal and kill just to take whatever they could.

The days of self-sustaining Native Alaskans had passed with the last of their kind, returning to earth as entire cultures faded away into oblivion; those who inhabited their lands now were nothing of their character or heritage, and they certainly possessed nothing of their strength, beauty, endurance, or the inter-generational cultural knowledge and skills that would have been required to live prosperously in such unforgiving terrain

The best choice out of the three would have been near Denali National Forest, located in the interior and much further south than the other two locations. Only the Denali National Forest had both geographical advantages and a more temperate climate. The other two locations were brutally harsh environments—if the Convicted Offenders didn't kill them, then the elements would.

If anyone ventured north within Denali, they could expect to have over three hundred miles of rough travel between themselves and the next nearest Drop-Zone. It might not have seemed like much, but traversing over three hundred miles on foot through the Alaskan wilds would have been a difficult—near impossible—journey, even if they chose to embark during the brief Alaskan summer months after the snows had departed.

With hundreds of miles between each of the Drop-Zones, it was highly improbable that there was any communication or travel between the three known areas with dense populations of Exiled Ex-Citizens. They had no means of transportation between the Zones, no electricity or plumbing, and no known methods of communication. Each location was rural, isolated, and cut-off from the rest of the world in every capacity. It was impossible to gauge how many of those living in Exile perished every year, but with no form of proper healthcare, medication, winterization, or even people living among them with an advanced knowledge of wild plants, it was undoubtedly extremely high. Beyond just a broken bone or an infection resulting in Death, the slightest epidemic could wipe out thousands. Perhaps the only true mercy was that those who were Exiled were almost always sterilized, so at least they were not dragging future generations of traumatized children into the hostile world they were condemned to live in.

If Daegan Kyl and Willow Amos could land at the third location within Denali National Forest, there were plenty of forested lands, water, firewood, wildlife, and shelter opportunities. If they stayed near a water source but far away from the hordes, they could get by without too much discomfort once they were established and had their basic needs taken care of. It was possible to find old cabins as well; many shelters had been built in the past within the remote locations, and then abandoned as their owners either died or vacated the region after the Great Reformation, leaving their homesteads intact with many of their earthly possessions still usable and available for the taking.

The Denali National Forest was over six million acres of wilderness. It provided them with everything they needed to survive on their own within the wild—but it also provided them with safety and security because they could venture far away from the rest of the population. There would be risks taken at every turn, and with the Drop-Zones, it was a fight for survival from the moment they disembarked. But should they escape with their health and their lives after that first test, they might even learn to love certain aspects of their new world. It would never be easy there, but it was not a land that had ever been an easy lifestyle for anyone; perhaps it was not intended to be so. But they could survive—and thrive—if they had the right start, the right state of mind, and enough frame of reference to know what they needed to do to achieve maximum success. Daegan Kyl was likely one of the best men to attempt such a transition and prevail.

There was a genuine, quantifiable chance for them in the Denali National Forest. The Gates of the Arctic and Nome had both been carefully chosen precisely to limit those odds from ever being in the favor of Convicted Offenders.

Additionally, one of the best-kept secrets about Alaska, and something that we had determined was largely unknown and unaddressed by those Exiled, was in regard to pre-existing housing. Ironically, there were outrageously extravagant mansions located along ski-resorts—all sitting empty and unused. They had been abandoned after the Sentence Reform Act, left on their own to gather dust and weather the storms in isolated grandeur. Solar panels, alternative energy, water wells, composting toilets, and septic tanks had all existed long before the Sentence Reform Act, and while there may never be another opportunity for a true connection or reconnection with the contiguous states, for the right person or people, they could still build a good home and life if they were first willing to travel to find the most ideal environment to begin again.

For those who were willing to envision a new life for themselves—regardless of the circumstances that had led to the new lands they were forced to contend with—Alaska was still a majestic wonderland that held unlimited potential for those brave enough to discover it. Yes—it would have been primitive, wild, and untamed; but in the right location and for the right people, it wouldn't have been any different than it had been for the original homesteaders, trappers, and vibrant figures throughout America's glorious past.

All of this was negotiable, and nothing was ever set in stone; there were hundreds of thousands of Exiled men and women who were living in encampments among the worst of environments—truly deplorable Third World conditions—and all they had to do was decide to venture beyond the areas of the Drop-Zones and find their own private world. It was likely a terrifying prospect, leaving the group of people who you had embarked on a new journey with, and some people just couldn't be alone. They would rather suffer with a crowd than be content in isolation.

I rather felt it was more reflective of the quality of Humanity that ended up in such places to begin with; they were often the underachievers and degenerates that hadn't ever blended in with traditional society. Those who could build, create, work, and advance our society were not usually among those who ended up Cast Out; those Exiled were dysfunctional within our nation and were content to be equally dysfunctional in their new world.

When all was said and done, the differences between the three locations were monumental, and their chances for survival and success rested heavily on whichever place they were slotted to go. It seemed imperative to me that Daegan Kyl and Willow Amos ended up in the only one of the three that could provide them with a fighting chance—and Stanton and I had to figure out a way to ensure that we could get them there.

It appeared we were looking at very bleak projections without this level of intervention.

Preparing Daegan Kyl for Alaska

Because Daegan Kyl had time to prepare for his trip to Alaska, he had the unique advantage that would have been unheard of for any other Convicted Offender to have before their Banishment.

There wasn't much I could volunteer to provide as a warning about what conditions he would encounter once he hit the ground on the other side; my own knowledge was more limited than one would believe, but there wasn't much information that had been gathered over the years. As students, we were all taught the same basic truths about what sort of place it was, and anything I had learned along the way during my career was limited to post-dated information and theories rather than current facts.

The government hadn't compiled a significant amount of data in recent years; seemingly because the subject had not been deemed worthy of the effort or the funding that would have been required to investigate. I'd never been given any type of explanation related to the reasons behind why there was a complete lack of credible, current evidence documenting the circumstances on the ground, but no better explanation came to mind when I considered everything. My guess was that it lost its importance because no one there was classified as a Citizen of These United States anymore, and as such, they ceased to be worth consideration or investment of time and resources.

Daegan Kyl could get ahead of the curve by using his freedom to his advantage before his flight to Alaska. All things considered, if Daegan Kyl were to spend some time researching the information about the history of Alaska in the years leading up to the Sentence Reform Act, then he would be entering the situation with a more comprehensive background than most. Being able to research and gather documents and materials related to the geography and terrain would provide him with a far better advantage than others who had been Exiled.

I could only presume that his time spent in the military, especially given how much of it had been spent in combat zones, would serve in his favor. It was another major distinction that I was certain would set him apart from the vast majority of those who had gone before him, and it stood to reason that any survival skills, fighting and self-defense, and other training he had received involving the importance of a clear psychological outlook and level head would all prove instrumental in his success.

Researching the transformation of Alaska, as it shifted from one of our most glorious states to the place where we dumped our worst Predators, would have allowed him to gather knowledge on what sort of Convicted Offenders would have been Sentenced there rather than issued the Death Penalty or Reform. The better prepared he could be regarding the Violent Offenders he may encounter, the better off he would be. Many people didn't realize just how shockingly Violent and cruel their Fellow Man was capable of being, and as a result, they were never prepared for the quality of people they encountered after their Banishment. At least we knew that Daegan Kyl had experienced plenty of darkness in the past, and would be better able to handle it than most.

He had time to discover relevant information related to all the Drop-Zones—not just the three that were designated for the State of Washington to use, but for each of the other regions that had specific Drop-Zones established for their Offenders. By knowing where these Zones were, he could know which areas to seek or avoid. The locations were common knowledge, just as most other information regarding how Alaska used to be prior to the Sentence Reform Act. The reason for this was simple; it wouldn't have mattered to most people, and most American Citizens didn't care enough about the subject to make the acquisition of information a threat. The entire state of Alaska had become a dead zone to the world, as had other designated Drop-Zones for different nations.

As far as the US government went, everything that had been left in Alaska by the Citizens who had migrated south to the lower forty-eight had been discarded. The US government would not go back into Alaska to reclaim abandoned buildings and outdated products, and there wasn't anything worthwhile regarding natural resources that they couldn't get elsewhere. The US had written the state of Alaska off, leaving everything west of the Alask-Can Border Wall fair game for anyone who wanted to use it—and could keep hold of it, given what owning anything of value could mean when surrounded by such circumstances.

For someone such as Daegan Kyl, it was a blessing. He had a substantial amount of time to take advantage of learning what he could about the region and what had been there before the transformation. More so than that, he could download, print, and store the information he could acquire so he could take it with him when he left, since he was planning on traveling with some supplies. He couldn't take a lot—and I had told him that there were flaws in our plan that could result in difficulties or even an entire collapse of everything we anticipated. But Officer Stanton had done the research on the Transportation Hub and one of the things he had discovered had proven to be of significant advantage to Daegan Kyl as he made his preparations.

Officer Stanton had decided to invest some time learning what he could about the convoys that hauled the Ex-Citizens from Washington State to their final Drop-Zone. He wasn't sure if it would yield anything of value, but it was important for us to at least explore as much as we could to avoid walking into any traps. I could see a hundred scenarios where we could be caught. It was left primarily up to Officer Stanton as our most advanced IT guy. He alone could do the research, hack the system, and figure out how to pull it off.

As such, I played out every potential move with Stanton, and we did everything to resolve any variables. We had a little over thirty days total from the time of the charges for their trials to the point of Sentencing, and then up to thirty days from their Conviction to their Sentences needing to be carried out as per the federal laws. It wasn't much of a window to come up with a foolproof plan given the level of research that both Officer Stanton and Daegan Kyl needed to carry out their plans flawlessly, but it was the best we had to work with.

I had also told him to gather information regarding where known hotels, lodgings, timeshares, hunting lodges that were listed as rentals, and any other types of buildings that would have large stocks of resources at their disposal. Such places were loaded with beds, bedding, toiletries, kitchen supplies, and various other commodities that would have been left behind by Citizens who had vacated once the Sentence Reform Act had commenced.

There were endless places throughout the State of Alaska that had been known for travel and tourism, but most Convicted Offenders were unaware of just how much of an emphasis there had always been on the tourism industry along with all outdoor recreation. The sporting industry, including kayaking, boating, white-water rafting, and fishing, had all resulted in a state-wide investment of small businesses that had emphasized outdoor recreational opportunities for traveling tourists. This wasn't limited to the water sports, as there was also a plethora of similar businesses which concentrated on hunting wild game. Others were dedicated to outdoor hiking, climbing, and backcountry backpacking expeditions. These adventure-type businesses were important to know about and have a general idea of locations on the map, because when they abandoned everything and relocated, they had been notorious about leaving their inventory and personal effects behind.

At one point, there had been a national discussion regarding it because it had allowed the Exiled to gain access to an arsenal of assets that they would not otherwise have had access to. This had been concerning to many of the Citizens in the lower forty-eight. For those who were Citizens leaving Alaska, however, it wasn't worth the extra work and headache to transport everything back down to the lower forty-eight and to their newly selected relocation states. They had all received fair compensation and replacement of their business ventures, so they had felt little compulsion to tack on unnecessary work and expense.

Many felt they had sacrificed enough. Their homes, businesses, assets, and plans had been cast aside in order to allow for the worst Offenders among the American Citizenry to invade the lands they had loved and nurtured. But for the most part, they had welcomed the opportunity because they understood that their small sacrifice would lead to a nation-wide transformation for the Greater Good. They knew it would ultimately benefit everyone, especially their own children and future generations.

They had left their homes so that every American could have a brighter future for themselves and their children; they had left the lands they loved so the rest of the nation could sleep in peace once again.

What they had so selflessly surrendered had been invaluable to every Citizen in the lower forty-eight states.

Now, after all this time, it would also be invaluable to Daegan Kyl.

The Transport Station Plan

It had been necessary to meet with Stanton one final time to get everything in order and finalized for the Transport. We were holed up in his office down the hall from my own, studying everything we could find about Patos Island, the Transport Holding Cells, and how the entire system operated.

Our plans were pretty solid, and we had gone through every scenario we could imagine in anticipation of anything that could go wrong. Most of it came down to Stanton, though, regarding whether or not he could successfully access the right places at the right time.

He was going to have to hack into the system, figure out which of the Transport Holding Cells was empty so Daegan Kyl could use it to travel in, then open the door of that unit—and only that unit—and then close it behind him. It didn't seem like much, but he had to do in the five-minute window available before the monitors would kick on. Along with the timing being near perfect, he had to monitor it after the flight landed at the Drop-Off Zone to ensure that Daegan Kyl's door opened and released him as well. Since it wasn't a Cell that was expected to be in use, we had no way of knowing if all the doors opened or not. If it didn't open automatically with all the rest, he would need to do it manually, and time it with all the others. And after all of that—he had to cover his tracks by concealing any footprints that anyone had been there or done anything, and at the very least, ensure that if it showed that someone had hacked the system that it didn't reveal what they had done. We were counting on him to do a great deal of technical work—under extreme pressure and with intricate, precise timing. He would have to do it at great personal risk to his own future and without a practice run.

It was a lot to ask.

Despite this, he didn't have any reservations about doing it.

"So, once they arrive at the Transport Station, they won't have any further contact with each other until they arrive at their final destination, correct?" he asked.

I turned his attention to the screen with the blueprints so I could explain it to him.

The cameras were positioned to grant an aerial view of the island and were controlled by satellite. I navigated the angle so he could see the Holding Facility more clearly.

"Do you see how it's shaped like a hexagon? Each of the sides holds five Cells. The center of the Hexagon is an open-air space they use while they wait for their Transport date. Both ends of the Holding Cells can open; they're called 'Tunnels'. Once a day, each of the sections of the Hexagon will open up into the center area so the Convicted Offenders can spend a bit of time outside. The timers are set at random intervals to off-set anyone trying to log the time for opportunities to escape or signal each other. The Convicted Offenders are never put into the Holding Cells at the same time, and they have no way of knowing how long they will be there. They don't share the same space outside, and they can't communicate or see any other COs while they are there. The walls are reinforced and soundproof; the only thing they can ever hear is a slight noise from other doors opening and closing if they are near theirs."

Officer Stanton studied the map of Patos Island and the locations of the Holding Cells. Everything we did would matter; where we landed, how long we remained on the island, and how quickly we left the location after the Transport began its flight north would come into play.

"So, there's four Transports that are stationed there permanently, and then there are four refueling stations with enough landing space to support one at a time, right?" He pointed to the diagram as he talked, noting that it was a well-made structure and clarified that the dimensions were the exact specifications for what was lawfully required to provide as housing and transport for all inmates without an extra inch to spare.

"Exactly," I replied. "The Cells have ventilation and climate control through the top; they're metal containers although they're insulated well enough. They're typically only in them for a week or less. Each Cell has an iron-framed bed with a mattress and bedding that is affixed to the frame, and a metal-framed toilet and sink that have functioning water access and waste evac which detaches from the external wall on the Cell."

One thing Stanton and I had discussed was the time it took for the Transport to fire up and get ready to go. If we were going to time it so that Daegan Kyl could be put onto the Transport directly, we had to be there at precisely the time it took for the Quad-blade—the rotary system that powered the Transport—to affix itself to the Hexagon before taking flight.

It took about five minutes for the Transport to be locked, disengaged from the plumbing, and secured to the Quad-blade when it was ready for travel. Both the toilet and sink would work for six hours during flight; the toilet converted to compost with an air-evac system, and the water system had a surplus tank, so anyone traveling still had access to both since travel time depended on the Drop Zone.

The Transports were one of the best travel systems out there; it allowed for the safe, efficient transport of often extremely dangerous Predators without ever requiring any live supervision or contact. Throughout the history of this great nation, there had been thousands of Corrections Officers, Bailiffs, and Peacekeepers Murdered by Convicts trying to escape. Traveling was always a high-risk time because it had the weakest security measures and was often seen as a prime time to escape. As a result, the Corrections Officers that transported Convicts to and from prisons from county jails and courthouses had greater exposure to Injury and Death.

We logged into the system using my credentials and watched the Patos Island live feed for the Transport that was engaged for a new Drop. He needed to see how intricate the system was for surveillance and get a feel for where the cameras were located.

"The worst-case scenario from a technical standpoint pertains to accessing these cameras. I will need to block their view so Kyl can be loaded without it being captured on video. I'm going to try and block them with a loop, but if anything goes wrong, I'll have to knock them all off-line and let those in surveillance think it's some sort of technical issue. That should buy enough time, and as long as I get them back up within a half an hour or so, they probably won't consider it significant enough to investigate further."

"What do you need to know or have access to before you'd be able to see what would work?" I asked him. We would only get one shot at this, and if we were caught on camera, it would be game over.

"I'm going to need to hack into the system to see how many cameras they have running, what the system is, if they are all connected or separate, and what I'll have to do to control the ones we need to control," he said matter-of-factly and then laughed.

"Don't worry; this isn't nearly as intimidating for me as it is for you. This is a government system, after all. Not only do I work on them all the time, I know what their weaknesses are. This isn't nearly as difficult of a system as your average department store online, believe it or not. Most of the nation doesn't even know this system exists because they don't know or care about Patos Island. Our government isn't worried about hackers—they know the island is as good of a fortress as Alcatraz but even colder and more isolated. Out of all the systems to break into, this is not one I have any doubts about," he said.

"So, you're confident, then?" I asked, with some skepticism. He hadn't ever let me down, but we had a lot riding on it being foolproof.

"Yeah—I'm not worried about it. I'm going to get this all worked out and I'll probably make a looping program, so they won't even know it's had any issues. Do you mind if I log into this again so I can watch another flight take-off? If I can record it, then I can just make a looping program and then there won't be such a tight time frame for when the cameras have to be out and back again."

I shook my head; if he wanted to re-watch the flights—or do anything else—to help him learn how to do what he needed to do, it didn't matter to me. His knowledge was far more expansive than my own and I was grateful that even though I wasn't tech-savvy, I did at least understand his tentative plan. I trusted him and his skill; it was only the possible incarceration and Exile we faced that made me overly cautious and feeling as though every step needed to be triple-checked. I wrote down my information for him so he could log in again and then motioned for him to look at the Quad-blade Transport vehicle that was getting ready to load the Convicted Offenders.

The Quad-blade was a standardized transport vehicle designed for carrying the Hexagon Hives. It was completely automated and self-contained. Much like cargo ships, it was a machine designed to carry heavy loads. The Holding Cell Hives were 8x8x4. The Quad-blade was an enormous engine with a magnetic underground surface designed to hover over the Holding Cell Hives and secure a connection which then enabled large, metal brackets to fasten to sections of the Holding Cells. Once secured, the Quad-blade would lift the entire Holding Cell and begin the flight to its designated Drop-Off point.

This one was slotted to arrive at the Gates of the Arctic National Park; I felt sorry for the degenerates that were located within, knowing the odds were stacked against them entirely. Given that it was already late September, I think I might have preferred a quick Death. It was an easy reminder for both me and Officer Stanton to do everything within our power to ensure that when Daegan Kyl headed out, that their Transport was bound only for the Denali Drop-Zone. Stanton watched the Quad-blade connect to the Holding Cell Hive and begin its flight.

For a while longer, we worked together, going over everything we had been able to get our hands on and running various plays just to see how things panned out.

We got along well, and I was glad to see him have an opportunity to not only illustrate just how gifted he was, but that he embraced a challenge. As with most technical jobs, he often worked independently and had to rely on his own expertise to navigate trouble spots.

After a while, I could see the wheels turning in his head as he worked out various aspects of the task at hand, so I gave him a pat on the back and thanked him, leaving him lost in thought. Stanton was proof that genius was not reserved solely for the arts.

Awaiting Deportation Dates

The departure dates for Willow Amos and The Angels of Mercy who were being Exiled rather than sent to Death Row were not set in stone, nor were they able to be for the time being. I had been trying to work with Officer Stanton to prepare for the interception at the Transport Hub, but it would be difficult to do until we had a definitive date handed down to us from the courthouse, at least for Willow Amos.

Grace was told by one of the Prosecutors that they were going to have all The Angels of Mercy transported at the same date and time, but it was highly unusual to see that happen, so we were both suitably skeptical about it without seeing it in writing. All things considered, however, if they decided that shipping all The Angels of Mercy in the same trip was a plan they could agree on—regardless of their reasoning behind it—at least then we would know we had a specific time frame to work with.

The dates were only tentative because they were maximum times allotted for Trials and Sentences, not minimums. Their Sentences needed to be carried out within thirty days.

Exile was a kindness I still wasn't convinced Willow Amos deserved. She should have considered herself extremely lucky for it because out of everything that had transpired, what she had caused Caroline Randall to go through on an emotional level was beyond acceptable. Having spent time with her…I was still deeply conflicted about who she was and what she was responsible for causing—and I wasn't sure she was worthy of the Redemption being granted to her by the Randall family.

Had she not been there working directly with Arlan, he might never have felt the compulsion to Take his own Life; he might have Passed Away in his wife's arms, having drawn his Final Breath surrounded by his Loved Ones, his wife and children, and his dear friend Micah Davidson, knowing that everything was going to be alright, feeling safe and loved.

As it was, we would never know the circumstances of his Death because no one was willing to share them. His Final Moments were Lost for all time; no one had spoken up or shared the events, where they took place, how it occurred, or when precisely it happened. There would be no full Closure provided to the Randall family either; it was yet another example of the arrogance and selfishness of those who believed they had the authority to steal both Time and Life from other Human Beings. They felt no obligation to divulge the truth of their wrongdoing, and they felt no remorse for having done what they did.

Willow Amos would certainly lose both her inheritance from her parents and her brother. She would also likely face the loss of her Citizenship, Deportation, and Permanent Exile. But no matter the results of her Trial, it still would not replace all that she had Wrongfully Stolen from her Fellow Man.

FORTY-THREE – EXILE

Marking the Date

It did not take long before the Final Sentences were issued, and the results were sent to us. Willow Amos, along with The Angels of Mercy who were not Sentenced to Death, as well as Detective Jarrett, the local SPD Detective from the Missing Persons Division, had all been Sentenced to Exile as expected. The date of Exile had been determined and posted, and the countdown was on.

The cases were closed on my end. It was purely a courtesy and a matter of standard notification that I was being informed of the departure time of those who had been Sentenced to Exile.

Perhaps by watching, it would remind me that sometimes the Suffering of Human Existence was worse than an easy, quick execution, and it could still serve equal Justice.

I felt I needed to watch the closing process of their Exile this time, and not merely because we were orchestrating an additional piece of cargo independently. I knew that by watching I would at least feel as though they would still be given a Just Sentence even if they were not Executed.

I had never been to any of the Exile Transport Stations within the US, nor had I ever been to Alaska. But I had read and learned about each and how things were conducted throughout the process.

I never watched Executions or the Drops. I found both to be a bit too distasteful.

I knew they were necessary, and I genuinely believed they were a vital groundwork for our society to sustain itself. But I did not need a connection between seeing their Executions and the deliverance of Justice. As long as I knew it was being done, I was content.

On that note, however, I felt a significant level of anger whenever I thought about the man that had fled our nation and was now living a life of ease and freedom in the Middle East with no fear of Punishment. He was never far from my thoughts.

For now, I would have to placate myself with the results and carry on with the other leads and ideas that I had considered over the months. I felt a sinking suspicion The Angels of Mercy were still a factor; I just wasn't sure on what scale.

Standard Policy Measures for Exile Drop-Off's

For many, Exile was too kind a Sentence. But if the Crimes they had been Convicted of had not merited the Death Penalty, it was the only alternative. For those that could not be redeemed through 'rehabilitation', for those that lacked a moral and ethical conscience, and for those that were simply 'broken' beyond repair, such as Pedophiles, there were no other viable solutions.

Prisons were not worth the effort. At the beginning of the Last Stand, a series of orchestrated attacks were carried out by an unknown terrorist group in Washington State. Over a dozen prisons had been decimated, with more than a million estimated Criminals killed in the bombings. Later, as the bombings began to spread from state to state, the nation learned that a group of Citizens known only as The Watchers On The Wall were behind the attacks. And although there were many who denounced the violence, and despite the government launching a relentless investigation to hunt down all potential members of what they classified as 'the worst Domestic Terrorists in the history of our nation', the group only gained more support and influence as the years passed.

It seemed that to most Americans, the prison system was an archaic way of addressing our problems with Career Criminals. Citizens were tired of prison guards dying at the hands of Evil Predators. They were also tired of footing the bill to keep incurable offenders with a thirst for violence contained.

Trillions of dollars had been wasted in the past toward policing, trials, containment, and 'rehabilitation'. Statistically, it was almost always a useless endeavor given the recidivism rates. Exile, as difficult as it was to accept, was the only solution that protected the American People.

By the end of the Last Stand, most prisons throughout the nation had been destroyed—along with the majority of their inhabitants. The People had never rebuilt, instead embracing the Sentence Reform Act and reducing all Convictions to either the Death Penalty, Exile, or Reform.

The Sentence Reform Act created an entirely new system of Criminal Justice, including the standard procedures carried out after Sentencing. One significant change involved the creation of the Victim Advocacy Agency, which then provided Victim Advocates to assist the Bereaved during any of the Executions or Drop-Offs they wished to observe. This helped the families understand what was happening in real time.

The presence of Victim Advocates also ensured that if anyone needed additional support services, the Advocates could provide them. Grieving people were often prone to self-isolation and withdrawal from social events, but studies had shown that in such times, most Citizens were grateful for the assistance after-the-fact even when they were initially opposed to it.

They were authorized to provide services at the private home of the Victim or one of the homes of the Bereaved. They could also secure a private viewing within one of the conference rooms at the Victim Advocacy Agency.

It was not uncommon to have someone on site that was trained to work within Anger Management; there were many Citizens—usually the men and most often the fathers—that responded with extremely volatile anger. We knew the root of it was a sense of hopelessness, frustration, and a lack of control over the situation that had resulted in their precious Loved One being Hurt by another, and their inability to prevent it.

The Execution of LeRoy Jones was the only true semblance of Justice that I could say was genuinely delivered. It was a Drop-Off that left me feeling more than a little flat regarding its productivity. It felt as though we had missed the mark despite how many Convicted Offenders we had secured; it was a feeling of emptiness and lingering inefficacy that I could not shake.

WA-SET: The Washington State Exile Transport Station

The WA-SET was located on Patos Island, which was the Northwestern-most point in Washington State. It was a small island of only two hundred acres of land, and until it was repurposed as a Transport hub by the federal government during the Great Reformation, it had been owned by the Bureau of Land Management and unused other than as a tourist spot. Because of its location, rough shoreline, and inability to be accessed by anything other than aircraft or boat, it had proven ideal for the small holding facility and flight station. There were a few high-security detainment buildings and four flight stations for the Exile Transport vehicles to land and refuel. It was not much, but it was everything necessary.

It was a two-hour flight from the Washington State Exile Transport Station to the Drop-Zone located within the Denali National Park and Preserve in Alaska. There was usually one flight done per week according to the national registry; as could be expected, other places such as Los Angeles and New York City still had enough Criminal Activity to merit a daily charter. Those flights were typically also conducted through the Washington State Exile Transport Station as a refueling station for the last leg of the trip.

In the days or weeks leading up to their Exile, Convicts would receive zero Human interaction. They were in a place of transition between two worlds. One could classify it as Purgatory, but after entering true Exile, most would then declare that being in the relative security and isolation of detainment on Patos Island was much more welcome.

Nonetheless, per our laws, they could be held in the Exile Transport Stations up to thirty days. This could be because of inclement weather prohibiting flight, legal delays, or simply waiting for more Convicted Offenders to be added to the roster before a flight.

How they chose to spend their time there, waiting for one chapter of their miserable life to end before the next could begin I could only imagine. It was not intended to serve as part of their Sentence, although being in solitary confinement was considered cruel and unusual punishment to some. Instead, it was expected to be a time of reflection and self-examination. For many, it was merely a time of mental and emotional preparation as they said goodbye to their old lives and attempted to come to grips with what lay beyond.

I imagined it was difficult to endure no matter how many days it lasted; the anticipation of Death and fear of the unknown would monopolize their thoughts, and isolation would only exacerbate those troublesome worries. They were, after all, being ejected from their country by their own Countrymen and cast out into the world just as had been done in the earliest of Biblical times. Such was the price of Evil and Sin.

FORTY-FOUR - DEPORTATION

Transportation Hub Deportation: Phase I

We met Daegan Kyl at the Moving Men & Maids building, parking in the back when we arrived. We were slotted to meet him at 1530 and had planned our exit time for 1600. This would provide us with exactly two hours of flight time to arrive at the Washington State Transport Hub. Daegan Kyl had stated it would be a one-hour and fifty-minute trip from Seattle to the island hub in his gyrocopter.

The timing was important.

We could not arrive with too much time to spare because it was an unmanned station. It didn't have any personnel on site, but that didn't mean it couldn't have reinforcements if necessary. As long as we were in and out within that time frame, we wouldn't have any type of interaction, nor would we need to explain ourselves to anyone.

There were some basic security measures around the perimeter, but because it was already on a small island and was in a part of the state that guaranteed cold waters year-round, there had been little need for heightened security. No one would normally ever venture out to the island; it could only be accessed by an ocean-worthy vessel or by aircraft, and anyone that happened upon it was soon to have an unexpected welcome party by government officials. Aside from that, there were barricades in place around the island itself that made it almost impenetrable, along with various warning signs. Most people knew where the Transport hubs were and knew well enough to leave them alone.

Daegan Kyl pulled into the parking space alongside us moments after we arrived, climbed out of his sleek sports car, and shook my hand as I approached. He reached back inside, leaned across the seat, and grabbed a slim rectangle file box before shutting the car door behind him. Grace walked around from her side of the vehicle and extended her hand. They shook warmly and then Daegan Kyl handed the file box to her; she would oversee his paperwork, ensure that the appropriate people were doing as directed, and maintain a firm hold on everything while he was gone.

He was dressed more casually than I'd ever seen him. He wore black combat boots, fatigues with ample pockets along the pant legs, a couple of layers of shirts, and had a balaclava wrapped around his neck much in the same manner I was certain he had worn it while deployed in the past. Attached to his waistline were several key items carefully selected for their use, including a long hunting blade on his left and a semiautomatic handgun in a holster on his right. He and I had never discussed his carrying firearms but there didn't seem to be much harm in his having them; he was going there of his own free will, and it wasn't against the law for any law-abiding Citizen to have whatever firearms he thought practical.

From the trunk, he pulled a large hiking backpack in hunter green that was probably loaded down so heavily it would have toppled Grace over had she tried to carry it. The lower portion had two sleeping bags secured across the bottom, and I recognized a waterproof bag I knew to contain a lightweight two-man tent designed for four seasons and rough terrain. There were various other attachments secured along the outside and I imagined the contents of his bag were not only top of the line, but all quality tested. Only provisions of the highest necessity would have been included, with each having been selected by a man who had a history of knowing about such things.

He also extracted a long hunting rifle with a high-powered scope; it was a beautiful piece of machinery and I sincerely hoped he would only need it for food, but we both understood why it mattered. He handed the rifle to me, and we loaded everything into Grace's personal SUV for the ride to the airfield. Daegan Kyl climbed casually into the backseat, tapped my shoulder from behind, and then handed me his car keys.

"Take care of her for me. She needs to be driven fast enough to make you nervous at least once a week," he said.

From the corner of my eye, I saw Grace smile briefly. I gave a curt nod and put his keys in my pocket for safekeeping. For obvious reasons, I was out of uniform and dressed in civilian clothing, just a pair of jeans and leather jacket, and as I looked over at Grace, I realized she was also wearing casual clothes, though still more stylish than myself. I realized it was the first time that each of us had been dressed in such a manner at the same time. We looked like three average Americans going out for a nice afternoon drive. Yep, that was us, just out for a casual, informal drive through Seattle; a government agent and a Peacekeeper about to Commit a mountain of Felonies and a gravedigger that no one would allow onto the Naughty List.

What we were about to do was insanity.

It was unnecessarily dangerous—unquestionably foolish—and professionally catastrophic if we were found out.

We were helping a man—an extremely wealthy, healthy, Good Man with a good life—throw away everything just to do what he believed to be the 'right thing'. We were helping him abandon society and replace it with the most Violent and uncivilized animals on our planet—the very dregs of society that we had determined to be so unworthy of us we had literally rounded them up and thrown them out of our own lands rather than risk having to subject ourselves to them or what they might do. And this man was diving head-first into the lion's den—and all to protect a young woman who had taken advantage of him and almost cost him his life on many occasions.

I folded down the visor in front of the windshield of the SUV and looked at Daegan Kyl through its mirror. He was calmly shining up a pair of sunglasses on the front of his t-shirt as if we were going for a day at the beach instead of the edge of Hades.

"Are you sure about this? Absolutely sure?" I asked. "We can still figure out another way—"

He looked back at me, leaned forward a bit, and patted my left shoulder as if to provide some comfort, and then leaned back again.

Looking back at me through the mirror, he said, "You know I can take care of myself up there. For me, it's just a homecoming; my Ancestors were living off the land before those savages ever got ahold of it." He nodded his head toward Grace, who briefly made eye contact through the console mirror and nodded.

"But, man, we all know that Willow doesn't stand a chance. She might put on a tough image, but she's just a fragile little kid on the inside—and when I look at her, that's all I'll ever see with her."

He smiled—the first time I think I'd ever seen him really smile, happy and unabashedly, completely disarming his naturally intimidating demeanor.

"She was starting kindergarten the first time I ever saw her—it was the same week that I first met William's family after boot camp. She was just this ugly little kid with her front tooth missing, a big ole pile of messy hair sticking out all over the place, and she was all elbows and knees. But William loved her, and she loved him..."

He paused, then looked at me, resigned, that all-too-familiar sadness in his eyes I'd seen a thousand times before—the weight of having loved.

"He was the brother we shared between us, and he's the brother that will always live on as long as we honor our love for him. He made me promise to take care of her."

He looked out the window as he continued, "I know I didn't get her into the mess she's in; but I didn't do enough to keep her out of it either. I know the role I played in it. And but for the Grace of God go I, because you and I both know I should have been on that Transport anyhow."

He grimaced.

"I have to go up there. I can't protect her from down here. Just keep an eye on my car while I'm gone."

I smiled slightly and took a deep breath.

That was it, then.

We had just about reached the last leg of our trip; a gyrocopter that was fueled up and ready to go on a small airfield just south of the city—barely a mile from the factory. It was probably the same factory that the remaining Foreign National, Ghazwan, had used to leave the US and head out to international waters before catching his return flight home.

I wasn't satisfied with any of this, even still. I was a man who believed in the letter of the law, but this wasn't Justice.

Willow Amos might have needed some reprogramming. She definitely needed extensive counseling and some Grief therapy to help her address the Deaths of her family since they had all Died in such quick succession of one another. And there wasn't any question in my mind that she needed to learn some coping strategies for stress and her emotions. But did she deserve Exile? The same place where we sent Pedophiles, Domestic Abusers, and Violent Offenders with low-impulse control only one act away from Claiming a Human Life?

I just had a hard time with it, even now. She made a series of bad choices. She was obviously influenced by everything she had read; she was guilty of being impressionable and even influential—but was she a Criminal? Was she deserving of so harsh a punishment with no redemption?

I had known much worse cases that had only resulted in Reform and Training; they had been given some fairly long sentences that had required extensive counseling, education, and training before they could be released, but they had still avoided Exile.

The part that I was so conflicted about was the message her Exile sent. They had determined that because of her political beliefs she was a dangerous person to have roaming the streets of our nation. They had elected to eliminate the threat entirely—despite only being able to draw upon the same information and evidence that I had garnered and submitted from my investigation. It had been suppression—however they wanted to classify it; she had been Sentenced not based on the facts, but on the potential threat she posed. Our collective history throughout the world had been riddled with such cases of information control conducted by the People and their government, and none of it had ended well. I didn't agree with her, but did we, as a nation, fear the other side so extensively that we must eradicate anyone whom we deemed to be a threat merely for speaking their version of how they wished the world to be? Had we really come that far full circle once again since the early 21st century? If that was the primary reason for sending this woman into Exile, then it appeared to be so.

It was difficult to swallow, but it would have been impossible to prove as well.

I just couldn't see this as Justice—not for Willow Amos, and not for Daegan Kyl.

What did our nation stand to gain by losing two such highly intelligent, productive Citizens? They were both single, able to produce children, and capable of contributing to our society in meaningful ways for many years to come. Was that not what we were supposed to be emphasizing?

And I understood all the conflicts involved; I understood no one realized Daegan Kyl was sacrificing himself because of this, nor were they expecting him to. I realized that they would have condemned his bold move to follow her there—and they would have penalized us for helping. But was not the fact that he was willing to go up there, sacrifice his entire world and security just to help her and protect her, part of what illustrated just how important each of them was to one another? Was that not proof of at least a modicum of value?

The vast majority of those who were ever incarcerated or Sentenced to Exile were unwanted—the riffraff and piranhas of society—unloved and unwelcome by virtually everyone. No one missed them, or noticed they were gone, other than through the decrease in Crime statistics, and for that, we were grateful. She was not unloved, nor unwanted. She certainly wasn't riff-raff, nor was she a piranha within our society.

We were losing a lot by losing them, that was all.

And no matter how we dressed it up, it still seemed like she was being made into an example more than anything else.

When I considered everything—the Foreign National that got off entirely free with no punishment, the most despicable, shady, corrupt Governor in probably the last hundred years, not to mention the paid-for shills doing his dirty work while hiding behind their badges—were her actions so terrible in comparison that this was what passed for Justice?

I wasn't sure.

The gyrocopter was ready and waiting for us when we pulled alongside it. Daegan Kyl had asked if I wanted the pilot to stay and man the craft himself for us, but I thought it was more prudent if I did it myself so there weren't as many witnesses.

With a hefty cash payment for the pilot to thank him for his time, Daegan Kyl sent him on his way, and we got loaded. Daegan Kyl sat in front with me, and Grace took the back seat alongside his hiking gear and rifle.

Like many Americans, I chose to fly myself whenever possible, and although I was a little unfamiliar with this particular model, I was comfortable enough in no time. Once we were on our way, I radioed Officer Stanton and let him know our ETA. He would be an integral part of our plan once we reached our destination. He would need to keep things timed almost to the minute in order to pull this off.

Within moments, we were flying through clouds and leaving the Emerald City behind us. As we flew out over Puget Sound, I took a moment to look at the man sitting alongside me. Both he and Grace were staring peacefully out their windows and watching the city fade away as it was replaced with sparkling blue waters. I thought about the sort of man he was and realized why I was doing this despite the risks to my own career. I knew it was the least I could do, and I felt a better man myself because of it.

He was undoubtedly one of the most relentless, unflinching, driven men I'd ever come across. He was also one of the most honorable and loyal. Would that we could all someday become the full weight and measure of the man sitting next to me; what a nation that would be.

In a different time and place, I had no doubt he and I would have been friends, and part of me wished that it could have been so.

Transportation Hub Deportation: Phase II

The time passed quickly. We had traveled as easily as old companions; the conversation was engaging, intimate, and even joyous at times as we laughed comfortably while sharing stories from our lives. We kept things light, overall.

The RFID-Chip was important for several reasons, and we had to consider every aspect of it within our plan. Primarily, no one else in Alaska that had been sent there as part of a Criminal Conviction still had an RFID-Chip that was active. They had been Cast Out of America; they were no longer US Citizens and were no longer able to claim Citizenship or any of the Rights therein. Likewise, the American People and the US government had no legal or ethical right to keep track of those who were Exiled; it violated their Human Rights to be tracked or monitored by the US government or any government agency.

Daegan Kyl was not an Ex-Citizen. As a member of the US military, Daegan Kyl had been Chipped, and it could still be activated even though he was no longer Active Duty.

This meant that his RFID-Chip could still be used to track and locate him. Had he been in any other location, he could have had limited communication through solar-powered devices, but the entire Alaskan region was under a communications blackout zone. Because of this, the only thing even the most highly advanced technology in his toolbox could do was send out a distress signal which would hopefully include his coordinates as well. But we would have no guarantees regarding any of that until it was tested, and if he were to lose his ability to charge things, if he lost them, or if they were damaged, then it would all be useless. It was for these reasons that his being Chipped was a blessing in disguise; all it required was for Officer Stanton to hack into the database and create a bridge, allowing him to continue to monitor him off-site and undetected.

Willow Amos was no longer Chipped, and we would not be able to track her vitals or whereabouts. We assumed if something happened to her, he would want to return home to Washington. But he had not even allowed us to entertain the conversation, and so we hadn't. To my knowledge, he had no game plan regarding his return trip home.

We arrived at Patos Island all too soon, and after confirming with Stanton that we were good to set down, I landed the gyrocopter on the rocky terrain about thirty feet away from the side of the Transport that Stanton had cleared for us to place Daegan Kyl inside of. It was down on the far end, listed as Unit 29.

The three of us exited the gyrocopter and Daegan Kyl pulled out his heavy backpack and rifle from the back seat where they had been situated next to Grace on the flight over.

He slung the pack over his left shoulder with ease and then attached his rifle for the journey. I watched as he pulled out a multi-point sling and then expertly secure his tactical firearm to it in two locations so it hung loosely across the expanse of his chest. I was familiar with the style of sling he was using and knew it would make it easy for him to either maneuver it to his backside for safe travel or to use its quick release feature if necessary. He was smart to keep his hands free to move around, and I imagined his training would immediately begin to show itself from the very first moments of landing on the other side.

Grace slammed the door of the gyrocopter behind him, and he reached over fondly and patted her on the back as thanks before the two of them began walking toward me around the front. He had a warmth within his personality that made him extremely affable; a gentle giant that was a contrast to the temperament most would expect a man like him to have. I had no doubt that he was all of those men; the lover, the friend, the Protector, and the skull-crusher. Most of us were capable of much more than we realized; only conflict and hardship tended to reveal the fullest extent of all we were capable of being. Daegan Kyl had just lived his life in such a manner that his various alter-personalities were more prominently featured and able to be observed. For now, he was just a Good Man saying goodbye to some friends as he left on a backpacking or hunting excursion. I hoped for his sake that on the other side, the Combat Soldier would be ready to go.

We stood there for a moment, checked our time with Officer Stanton, and then Daegan Kyl leaned over and gave Grace a warm bear hug, leaving me with a twinge of jealousy as I watched him pull her into his arms and hold her tightly against him—something I had never done nor would have attempted to do. She was almost hidden against him, her head barely reaching his chest, and I wondered if he wasn't more to her liking in some regards, as I was certain he was to most. He was certainly more light-hearted by nature; even as we stood here and he was the one leaving, he was still the happiest among us. And then, as soon as I had the thought, I felt guilty; he was leaving our country and the last two minutes on American soil, he had wanted to hug a pretty girl and consider himself among friends. But I had turned it into some machismo cock-fight between two stallions rather than seeing it for what it was, which I believed was simply a final act of Humanity as a man issued his goodbyes to the only people who knew what fate had befallen him and why.

Eventually he released her from his hold, and she fell back away from him, looking at me with a flushed face and a strange look that I couldn't readily identify. He turned toward me and gave me a nod, showing he was ready. I checked the time again, and we began walking toward the Transport, leaving Grace on her own by the door of the gyrocopter. We only had a ten-minute window from the moment we landed to the time the motorized engine would fire up and begin its pre-programmed flight deep into what was once the Denali National Forest.

We were within ten feet of the Transport when the door suddenly began to open, each of our steps taking us closer as the door widened, matching our pace.

The time was upon us.

Overhead, the engines began to fire up, officially starting the countdown for its ascent and Daegan Kyl's last chance to back out.

But of course, we knew he would do no such thing; Willow Amos was within another one of these containers, although we could not tell which one it was. Stanton had confirmed she was on it by double-checking the manifest earlier; it would have been equally disastrous if we had sent him out on a Transport prematurely while she sat in a Holding Cell somewhere waiting for a different Transport going to a different location.

But they were both here today, now only separated by some thick metal walls and one long, lonely flight before they would be reunited.

They were all on board; every last one of The Angels of Mercy.

I had been surprised that this had been the recommendation by the Panel of Judges, but now I was beginning to see what they had intended. They had all arrived at this point in time by their working together; they could all see the end together as well.

Only Willow Amos stood a chance on the other side, of this I was certain.

Daegan Kyl turned his head upward toward the skies as if to give his consent for a fair flight; it was predictably overcast, but the wind was minimal. The Transports were one of the safest modes of travel anyhow; he would have less risk for a crash than I would on the return flight home.

I wondered if our paths would ever cross again. Logically, it seemed unlikely, and yet I found it improbable that we would not.

Still...He was a fool to go, and I was a fool for helping him do it—and yet here we were.

I gave a curt nod of the head, bidding him to gain entry while the door was open; the clock was ticking and the ever-increasing noise from the propellers gave fair warning our grace period was ending.

He clasped my hand, and then pulled me toward himself, the traditional bear hug of a man of many layers. I knew he was aware of my skepticism and reservation. He knew what risks we had taken; he understood we had done it for him and not for her. Nevertheless, he was grateful, and he did not have any trouble expressing it. It was a goodbye, but it was also an acknowledgment of mutual respect, trust, and gratitude.

I appreciated it. I'd never been that good at expressing my own emotions, though I did believe I was capable of deep and abiding ones, especially loyalty.

He was a Good Man, and I was sorry to see him go.

The noise grew louder, drowning out any chance for conversation, and with a quick nod of his head, he turned and ran into the doorway of the Transport Cell just as it began to close.

He was fearless.

I watched the door seal itself shut, and the Transport began to rise. Officer Stanton had timed it perfectly; it was a flawless transfer and just like that he was gone.

I watched the Transport gain in elevation, grappling with the events that had transpired around this case; there were so very many ugly things we had borne witness to. There had been so much suffering.

The Injustice was insurmountable and continued to weigh heavily on me.

I had struggled more with this case than ever before, and God Help Me, ever would again.

I watched the Transport as it rose above me, drowning in the overwhelming noise and trying to compose myself before I returned to the gyrocopter. I found myself irrationally choked up over all of it in a single instant; rage, resentment, bitterness, sorrow, guilt—all the worst emotions I was capable of feeling swelling up inside of me just below the surface, threatening to spill over, to boil over like molten lava unleashed at long last, explosive, and unable to be contained any longer, destroying everything in its path.

This wasn't how things were supposed to be. This wasn't how cases were supposed to end. The good guys were supposed to win; they weren't supposed to make giant heroic sacrifices time and again, to always miss out on their happy endings, to never get to experience the joy of a silver lining. There was supposed to be something worth hoping for—a belief that everything will work out in due course, that the bad guy will get what he has coming to him, and that Justice and Goodness will prevail in the end. That's what was supposed to happen—and yet it never happened anymore—the Death Toll just kept on rising, the Evil among us continued to thrive and get away with it, and Innocent Citizens continued to pay the heaviest of prices, and for what?

What was left? Love? Loyalty? Forgiveness?

None of that would bring any of the Victims back that were created, at least in some part, by the people who were now on their own one-way ticket to Hell.

And nothing would justify why a man such as Daegan Kyl should have been on it in any capacity—not through a Sentencing and definitely not because I had Committed a handful of Felonies for the first time in my life just to make it happen.

None of this made any sense, and I knew in that instant more than I'd ever been certain of anything else in my life that there was no Justice to be found on this earth. Maybe in Heaven—maybe God Himself could sort it all out and set things straight—but none of that was ever going to happen here on earth, not when it came to Crime and Violence, and not when it came to the Punishment of Evil.

I turned my attention from the Transport rising in the sky and looked back at the woman standing next to the gyrocopter. She had returned to the driver's side and had been holding the smooth door open, ready to climb in and step past my seat and over to the other side in case we needed to leave quickly. She knew we were running out of time, but she had waited in the distance patiently.

The way she studied me told me she understood that she knew why I struggled. It was as if she knew this weighed on me like a crisis of conscience rather than merely the weight of having broken the very laws I was sworn to uphold. She looked at me as if she understood the fear I tried to keep well below the surface, the fear that I was losing the war.

I turned and began moving toward her—away from Death, away from the anger, away from the Injustice and Violence that had been caused by all those who were now fading away—putting a distance between myself and every negative, despicable act they had promoted and proselytized. Their actions had caused themselves no harm, but they had cost others everything.

I looked at the woman standing in front of me, her bright eyes staring at me with a now-familiar worried look—the look of someone who knows you, knows your moods, and knows when you are hurting. She saw it all on my face—I knew she read it in my Body Language, in my walk, and in the words I could not manage to say. It was sheer hopelessness, tearing away at me from the inside, destroying my faith in Mankind, in my work, in my belief that we could somehow continue to make a difference if we only kept trying. That somehow, if we all just continued to try harder, to do better, that somehow it would all be enough in the end, that Goodness and Justice would prevail and that mercifully, finally, the Darkness and Evil would fade away.

She saw it all in my face and her compassion was blinding.

But I didn't want her pity; I didn't want her to fix me.

I wanted her to want me—to be near me, to want to be close to me as much as I wanted to be close to her—to leave all this behind and go somewhere so we could be alone together. Somewhere where we could put all of this out of our minds, consume one another, replenish our Souls with enough Goodness and Love to replace all that we had lost over the years by constantly being surrounded by the worst of Humanity.

She straightened herself, let the door she was holding fall shut, and held her arm up, her hand extended toward me, beckoning me to come to her. It was all the prompting I needed.

I covered the remaining distance between us before losing myself to her entirely, pulling her near, pulling her inward, close to me, desperately. Our lips met as I held her close, my hands gripped her neck as my fingers got tangled in her hair, cupping her face, feeling the softness of her skin, the longing in her body as she leaned into me with as much hunger as I felt for her. I felt her arms circle my neck as everything else faded into oblivion until there was nothing beyond the feel of her breath—her lips—her tongue against mine.

The sound of the propellers were slowly fading away in the background and I knew that we only had a few moments in which to get ourselves back into the air and headed back toward home—but I would have sacrificed everything—surrendered it all, just to have one more moment standing there submerged in the sensations of desire, compassion, hunger, and love I felt radiating from her and enveloping me just then. She had wrapped herself around me as if I had been away on an arduous journey and had finally at long last returned home. I had never, in all my days, either been wanted nor felt such wanting, ever before.

Standing there with her, I found myself pouring everything I was feeling during those moments into that unexpected kiss—as if we had been living in famine and then suddenly there was a bountiful feast before us. Kissing her was the only thing that made any sense anymore; it was an irrefutable necessity—a compulsion.

That moment shared between us was the only thing that I knew—on a purely primal level, *to the very core of my Being*—to be an absolute truth in a world where I was drowning in conflict and incessantly shifting variables. For the rest of my days, I knew I would never forget how desperately glad she had made me feel just to be Alive and to know she was standing by my side. Would that I could, I would be there still.

268th DOY, 1700 Hours: Return from Patos Island

On the 268th Day of the Year, after we returned to the SPD Headquarters building, Stanton told us that the Chief had offered us the use of his conference room. It was slightly larger and had more comfortable furniture. Our plan had been worked out as best as we had been able, and we believed that we had not overlooked anything. But as soon as Stanton relayed the message to us, we realized we had forgotten one key consideration: We hadn't anticipated that the Chief would watch the Drop-Off—and if he did, he was sure to notice that Daegan Kyl was there when he shouldn't have been.

I exchanged looks with Stanton and Grace as we all realized we had overlooked something that should have been obvious to all of us. There wasn't any reason to presume that either Stanton or Grace would have had any greater intimate knowledge of the Chief's habits than I would, despite them both having had prior experience working with him.

I had reported nothing further to the Chief about the Governor or the case after the initial findings that had led to his involvement, but that hadn't been because I was reluctant, it was because there had been nothing else to report. After the Governor had made his feelings known during our interaction at the factory, I had opted to refrain from 'updating' the Chief about him any further. It hadn't been for lack of trust on my account though; I just hadn't seen any purpose in dragging him into it any further.

It hadn't occurred to me that the Chief would have taken part in the viewing of the Drop-Off because it wasn't characteristic of any Chiefs to do so. They were administrative in their daily work, overseeing the sum of the parts rather than participating in the daily grind of the parts themselves. It was likely that he had read my Final Report as I sent it out because it was customary to include the local Chiefs in the briefing, but it came as a surprise that he would have taken the time to watch the Drop.

In hindsight, we probably should have calculated the possibility into the equation at least—or I should have at any rate, if only because the investigation had resulted in the Governor himself getting involved. But now that it was done—and we were surely going to be found out—I couldn't think of a single polite way to either extract ourselves from viewing the Drop-Off from the Chief's conference room, nor explain how come Daegan Kyl was there when he shouldn't have been.

It appeared that it would be time to pay the piper. We had been so careful and methodical; we had pored over every conceivable problem with the cameras, the security, the Transport doors, and the timing. It was more than a little ironic that we had completely forgotten the *human* element.

268th DOY, 1800 Hours: Waiting

I sat in the conference room at the SPD Headquarters alongside the Chief, Officer Stanton, and Grace. Stanton logged us into a secure channel so we could watch the final chapter of our case unfold together.

It was a somber event, and it wasn't usually something I preferred to do in a group setting. The entire process of the Transport and Drop-off was further evidence of how any society could deteriorate and be flawed no matter how many other positives existed. They served as a reminder that there was no 'utopian society', that even when everything within the social, political, and legal climate of a nation was being done successfully, that even when poverty was minimal and morale and prosperity was high, that there would always be a piece of our culture and Humanity that was incapable of coexisting appropriately among the rest of us.

They made me sad.

They reminded me of all the Lost Potential, the Lost Time, the Lost Skills and Assets, and the Lost Love our world endures. Whatever had led these people down the paths they were on, they had all arrived there by their own doing. But I was not such a monster that I could not see that they were often among the most damaged among us—even as our society flourished, there were those who were just different, outsiders.

The original idea had been to create another world where they could all blend in with their own kind. They could go somewhere and build a new nation, a place where they could be themselves, live their lives as they saw fit, face no legal prosecution or social persecution, and all coexist with like-minded individuals who held similar views. That had been the intent. The reality had fallen far short of that, and with no influence from the lower forty-eight. What it had revealed was that we as Human Beings were territorial, divisive, and self-inclusive; that we always had been, and that we always would be. Their infighting had proven it.

The Drops were hard to watch.

They were hard to watch alone. Watching them with a group was never easier; if anything, it only made them worse, and harder to stomach.

I had seen others host parties when they had brought down big Offenders, especially Pedophiles. I could recall one time when there was an entire office filled with LEOs. They had celebrated together as the live feed of their Pedophile ring had been Transported and Released all at one time. They had slaughtered a multitude of them within moments of being released at the Drop-point. As I watched the LEOs that day, I recalled being saddened by how much joy they had received by it. Their responses had been entirely understandable and would have been shared by millions of other Americans on any given day. But it was hard to watch my Fellow Officers resort to such common behaviors and emotions. We were Set Apart. Our behavior should always be exemplary, and our personal feelings objective in the eyes of the public. No matter how embittered we might be at times, it should never carry over into our professional lives.

Still, I fully believed in Exile. I believed it was the only solution, and without it, only Death would suffice. If the choices were between Punishments that fell short of Exile or Death, and Exile were no longer an option, I would choose Death over anything lesser. It was what our society required in order to sustain the Greater Good, and I would always stand on the side of the Innocent. On the same note, I could recall an untold number of times when the friends and family of Victims of such Crimes had told me that neither Exile, nor the Death Penalty, assuaged their bitterness, and they envied those on the ground in Alaska that could do what they themselves wished they could do, especially since there would be no legal consequences. I understood this as well.

It was heartbreaking that Evil held so much power over us, including its ability to affect the good within us in the name of righteousness.

"Was everyone notified?" I asked.

Arlan's family, including Micah Davidson, would be allowed clearance to watch the Transport and Drop-off. It wasn't much Closure for Arlan's wife Caroline; she had lost her husband in such a manner that it would quite possibly always be an open wound. Whatever time she might have had with him, whether it had been days or weeks, had been lost to her because of the interference of The Angels of Mercy. They may have felt they were being helpful or had done what they believed to have been 'the right thing', but it had deprived the woman and the rest of Arlan's family of their opportunity to be with him during his Final Moments. Such a loss of time would undoubtedly leave an impact; it was even likely that Caroline Randall bore some resentment for her own husband for his having left her in such a manner. Watching The Angels of Mercy pay for their deplorable actions was a small consolation indeed, but at least it was some sense of Closure, and it was more than many received, including Katarina's parents. Hopefully Micah Davidson could help Caroline Randall with both their business and her Grief. He had been an invaluable asset to her husband and, as he had said, he had become an extended part of his family. His wife and children were lucky to have him there as they all processed their Grief and mourned his Loss.

"As far as I know, Arlan's family intends to watch. They have the information and I've heard from their Advocate that they wanted them to be there to help them go through the process and just see how it goes in case anyone needs any help." Grace said.

"Did your people go over with them what to expect?" I asked her.

She nodded her head; it was not the first time she and others within the VAA had prepped the Bereaved Citizenry for either Drops or Executions.

"Did they make it clear that it is a live-feed and there is no censorship?" She nodded her head again, and I continued.

"Did they warn them it could be Violent and that we have no way of controlling what happens once we release them?"

Grace nodded for the third time, raising her eyebrow a bit; her look silently told me to relax—everything was under control. She tolerated my line of questions because she understood the source of my nerves—and it wasn't because I was concerned about her or her subordinate's ability to do their jobs effectively. My mind kept going over everything that was at stake, and while I was normally a level-headed, rational person, I grew more agitated about the proceeding Drop not only because of Daegan Kyl being exposed but also because I didn't want to see him, or Willow Amos, injured or killed. I couldn't imagine what the man would do if something happened to her after everything he had done for her thus far.

Likewise, I could still appreciate that it was a video feed for the Victims and their Bereaved. Our jobs were expected to be done on behalf of the Victims, not those who caused their Deaths, and we were expected to be loyal to them, their memories, and those whom they had Left Behind. Whatever came to those who had violated the Laws of the Land, harmed or defiled our Citizenry, or committed other egregious Crimes that resulted in their Exile, was not only outside of our accepted range of concern or care, it would have been perceived as a betrayal by many of the families we were supposed to be fighting for.

"Have you received any standing orders for a new assignment yet?" the Chief asked, making small talk.

Grace looked up from her screen and directed her gaze toward me. Everyone else in the room was stationed in the Greater Seattle Area, but as soon as the Drop was complete, I was planning on heading out. Technically, my assignment had ended once my Final Reports were filed, and that could be up to thirty days after the last secured Conviction and Sentence. I had wanted to follow this one through to the end, and now Daegan Kyl's Drop had cemented the difference between a desire to see complete Closure and the necessity to finalize it.

"No, not yet. I was just in contact with the Chief in Olympia, though, and I told him he could expect me to report in within the next week. I don't think there was anything pressing; he didn't have any pending cases, so I was planning on taking the long weekend once I got back."

"Well, that's good; you've earned it."

I nodded.

"So, you're usually working out of Olympia, then? That's where you live?" Grace asked. It was funny how little we knew of one another.

I nodded again. "Yeah, it's been my home station my entire career."

"So then, if you moved, you would just transfer your POC to wherever you go? You don't have to live in Olympia for your job?" she asked.

"Yep, pretty much. I just stayed in that area because my parents and extended family are near there."

"So, you'd be open to relocating to the SPD then; I'll get right on that!" the Chief said.

We all laughed, and suddenly the mood lightened considerably. It was a moment of levity for all of us after a long, emotionally exhausting journey.

We talked for a while about our favorite places to visit around the nation, and places that we had an interest in exploring. With each of us historically logging in an excess of work hours—especially during active cases—vacationing and travel time could not be pursued except in short bursts.

I was still at a point where immersion within my work was the only thing I had ever prioritized other than my family. It went without saying, but our preoccupation and over-emphasis on professional development rather than creating and building personal relationships and having children was partly to blame for why our Western population numbers had depleted so severely in the 21st century to begin with.

Pulling myself back from my dark reflections, I considered how pleasant it was to pass the time and discuss such things as I imagined most normal work environments did. We were always so tight-lipped and conscientious about our personal lives it was enjoyable to sit around getting to know one another better. Being among such good company, it was almost possible to forget why we were all there.

268th DOY, 1900 Hours: The Chief's Daughters

The time passed quickly with our conversation. We ordered a light evening meal to be delivered, and as we grazed, we discussed our favorite places to eat. I'd done the most traveling through work, but I had clearly not spent a lot of time exploring the cities I'd worked in. Compared to the Chief and Grace, I'd seen the most airports but had only seen a few of our national monuments despite having been to some cities more than a dozen times. Even Officer Stanton had gone to what remained of the Statue of Liberty as a tourist, but I'd only ever seen her from Police Headquarters, barracks, and Crime Scenes. Everyone agreed that if they ever planned another vacation, they'd invite me so I could see how the other half lived.

It was a nice way to spend the evening, and it was a good send-off for me. I'd spent over three months working daily in the most intimate of circumstances, and I had known nothing beyond their basic personality traits and impeccable professionalism. I learned that the Chief had been married for over forty years and had four single adult daughters as well as two fourteen-year-old twin girls. Six daughters. It was hard to imagine the weathered man with the booming voice standing before me constantly being surrounded by daughters and called 'Daddy', but he assured us he was entirely wrapped around their fingers, especially his eldest daughter, whom he had referred to as the 'game-changer' in his life, the one that 'had turned the boy into a man.'

And then, just because we 'had the time', the Chief opened his screen and showed me a handful of family photos. After showing them to me individually, the Chief brought up the photographs to the 3D hologram version so Stanton and Grace could see them as well, and noted that the two daughters in the middle were both within a few years of Stanton's age while the older two were closer to my age.

Like himself, his wife and daughters were tall. The whole family was bronze-skinned and dark-haired. He then did as all proud fathers are prone to do and gave us a glowing review of all their accomplishments and personalities as he pointed them out from their pictures, naming them as he went.

He patted me on the back as he closed out the screen and told me he'd be happy to take me home to meet the family anytime, telling me that his 'princess', the eldest, would give me 'a run for my money' in the education department, having just completed her PhD in Criminal Psychology.

It appeared he was giving me a very high compliment indeed by subtly hinting that he thought I was good enough for one of his beloved daughters. It was flattering, and I was, after all, single and well into that time when most people were settling down and starting families. I'd never had one of the Police Chiefs suggest that I come home for dinner just so he could showcase his daughters, and had it not been for Grace sitting there I might have been more receptive to the idea. Having the Chief of the SPD as a father-in-law wouldn't be the worst thing in the world either; at least I knew he would approve of me should things ever get serious.

I had noticed that Grace had said nothing about the entire exchange, but she had quietly stolen little looks while he had shared his photos. Maybe she didn't approve of this millennia-old practice of matchmaking, but I was rather hoping it was more personal than that, and that perhaps, just maybe, she was a little jealous.

My mind flashed back to the kiss we had shared only hours before, and I realized I wasn't really single anymore after all; at least not if she would have me. Like most men, I could be fairly obtuse when it came to relationships and picking up on signals, but the kiss we had shared—however ill-timed it may have been on my account—had told me everything I had needed to know to secure my standing with her. I had conveyed my feelings for her, and at the very least, now she knew where I stood.

And as charming and attractive as the Chief's daughters might have seemed, I wasn't the type to jump from vine to vine, always chasing the next big thing. I was loyal to a fault, and although I had never truly tested it, I seemed very akin to my own father who had spent his entire life knowing that all that he was—and was capable of being—was made better because of the love of his wife. It seemed, at least to me, that I was just another man waiting to find the right woman with whom to build my future.

I was, however, historically legendary for being clueless about women in this regard. Like my brothers, I had never wanted for attention thanks to our dad passing along some decent height and a full head of hair. But unlike my brothers, I had always been too much of an introvert to make use of it; even in high school, I knew what I wanted to do and knew it was a highly competitive field that would require my full concentration and commitment if I were to make my way through it. While they were all playing sports and dating the cheerleaders, I was in JROTC, reading about US History for pleasure, and learning everything I could about Criminal Investigation.

I'd just never invested that much time into my own personal relationships. I had never had more than a handful of relatively short-term girlfriends that inevitably ended up breaking things off with me in much the same way: great guy, too much travel, too much work, not enough time, or attention. But maybe it was something that a woman working within my same profession would understand. It was food for thought. At any rate, I had found myself thinking of Grace more than I would have imagined possible, and knew it meant something more—something worth investing the time in to explore, assuming she felt the same, which I believed she did.

She looked my way, and finding my gaze fixed on her, she blushed prettily. I gave her a smile and a wink; a moment shared between the two of us, and then returned my attention back to the food on my plate. The Chief's daughter might have been physically appealing, but it was in that overdone sort of way; too much of everything, too over-emphasized, too obvious. The kind of woman that knew she was beautiful and capitalized off it, spending all of her time focused on looking good. I was glad to hear she was smart as well, but as I drifted between the two women being presented, Grace and her under-stated kindness and natural beauty would win my heart every day over the other type.

I snuck another look over at her, thinking of how she had kissed me back as we stood by the gyrocopter, and felt a strange stirring deep within me. She didn't just make me desire her; she made me desire to be a better man for her, to be *enough*. She made me want to do everything in my power to please her and make her happy, as if her opinion of me mattered so greatly that I now wanted to ensure that I was standing in the light that seemed to emanate from her. I was still exploring how and what that could mean, but I had a feeling I knew, even if I didn't have any prior experience with it.

And as if that weren't enough, there was just something about her freckles.

268th DOY, 1900 Hours: The Man in The Mirror

The Chief remarked that he was going to take a moment to check in with the wife before the Transport landed. I watched as he stood, cleared up his table space where he had been eating, and then tossed his food materials in the garbage on his way out the door.

I took my last few bites and then did the same, exiting through the big double doors of the conference room. My head was full as I considered everything as of late, especially Grace and Daegan Kyl. I earnestly just desired for this whole evening to be over. The idea of what was yet to come left me with a knot in my stomach that I didn't appreciate. Knowing was almost worse than not knowing, but not quite. I was at least prepared and had the knots that I did because I knew what was about to unfold. For many, the shock of everything was difficult to bear, and even when they knew it was a fully merited Punishment, it still struck a chord within their most basic levels of Humanity to watch how the worst among us responded to crisis.

I made my way to the men's restroom at the end of the corridor, skipping the private pair that were attached to the conference room so I could stretch my legs and walk down the hallway for a moment. I needed to wash my hands and clear my thoughts. Once I entered the restroom, however, I found it strangely quiet—too quiet. I washed my hands, rinsed my mouth, and then turned the water to cold, watching as it ran into the drain.

My mind drifted to the man I had sent out on the Transport; something that still weighed on my conscience because I knew in my heart it was the wrong thing to do and I wasn't a man who was used to doing the wrong thing. I considered what I knew about other Drops I'd seen, the Brutality, the Violence, the Bloodshed. I could see it in a flash across my eyes even when they were closed, even as I stared down into the rushing water as it landed against the bottom of the sink. I knew what he was going to be facing soon enough, and it wore on me that I had been so permissive with my willingness to help him.

He should never have gone there; not for *her*. Not after what she had done. She *deserved* to be there. I wasn't so sure he did. If I knew nothing else about her, knowing how she had responded to Rebecca after her Rape would have been sufficient enough to cause the contempt I felt for her and for me to pass the judgment that she belonged in Alaska—that it was a worthwhile and fair Punishment. She had been Sentenced to Exile because our nation was better off without her or the poison she had created within our borders.

But he didn't deserve it; he didn't deserve to lose everything just to be there because of some promise he had made to an old military buddy. I just couldn't reconcile that anyone would have expected him to take things as far as he did to look out for her. But it was not up to me to judge what merited Honor to another man; all I could do was respect it, and either accept it or reject it. I had chosen to accept it, and that had made it almost an obligation on my end to do what I could to render aid as he tried to fulfill what he considered to be his duty. I couldn't explain my actions any other way—why I had felt such a powerful compulsion to help him even when it went against the rules and laws that I had spent my entire adult life upholding. I didn't understand why I had helped him—and that was part of the problem.

I looked hard at the man in the mirror before me. I would be weighed and measured. Had I done the right thing? Had I done the actions that I was willing to take to the altar and defend? I didn't know. I was still so internally conflicted over it that it shifted from moment to moment, and that was part of my problem with it.

I wrestled with the images of other Drops going through my head once again and checked the watch on my arm, noting the time. I took another moment to look at myself in the mirror, splashed some cold water against my face, gave it a good moment under the cold of my hands while I collected myself, and then made my Peace with it. It was done now, at any rate; I had no choice but to accept it and whatever consequences emerged.

I dried my face off and stared back at the man watching me. He'd never given me cause to feel ashamed before, but I realized what I was struggling with was difficult to process because I was entirely unaccustomed to it. I felt the burden of Shame and Guilt wash over me like a wave of water crashing against the shore, creeping up along my chest, crawling through me like a piece of paper singed by fire and spreading. I felt it grow in power, creeping through my arms, around my chest, a blast of heat scorching through me and threatening to close my airwaves. The man in the mirror scowled at me, smirking at my weakness. I felt as though God had left the room, leaving me alone in the cold and silence.

I had sent an Innocent man to his Death.

The man in the mirror smirked; my Soul had a stain on it as toxic as mold growing in the dark.

I felt like I couldn't breathe.

I threw the towel I had used to dry my face into the trash bin and quickly left the room, welcoming the warm yellow lighting that stood in sharp contrast to the sterile fluorescent ones in the empty marble restroom.

I stood there for a moment, calming my heart, and then I walked, checking my timestamp once again to see how much time remained before the Transport was slotted to land. I stared at the walls of the hallway, at the carpet, out the windows of the high-rise I stood in, all done to calm myself and the anxiety I could feel emerging just below the surface. It was alien to me; there were few actions I had ever taken that were questionable, but suddenly I found myself surrounded by indicators that only served as proof that I had failed everyone in this case and that nothing had been adequately resolved.

Very little Justice had been done for any of my Victims or their Loved Ones—the results had been no better than the majority of cases from a century before. If Justice was the purpose of my job, then I had failed entirely. If I was only here to investigate and find the truth, well, I hadn't even managed to do that—there were still countless aspects involving Willow Amos, The Angels of Mercy, the two Foreign Nationals, Detective Jarrett, and even the Governor that had all Died out with this investigation completely unresolved.

This case was not a *victory*; it was a failure to produce adequate Justice for anyone—*especially* Katarina and her parents. And on top of that, I had just sent a man to his almost certain demise—and for what? For *her*? For a woman such as she? For a woman that had done *all that*?

I looked toward the conference room, thought of how hard the two people inside had worked on this case and knew that they believed we had done what we could. We had discovered the answers we could, we had solved the mystery behind their Deaths, we had found the reasons behind how they had each ended up in their unmarked graves, hidden away from the world. None of them considered this case to be a failure.

I calmed myself.

I pictured her red hair, the curls. The curve of her neck. Her smile. The freckles that graced her body. The curve of her hand as it rested in my own while we flew home. The way she looked at me like I was the only man in the world.

I breathed. Deeply.

The world slowed once more.

I took a few minutes to get my bearings once again, weighed it all out and spent a bit of time turning things over into God's care. I left the main hallway and returned to the conference room. Grace and Stanton were both casually sitting in their own spaces, she over on the couch reading, and he spread out over the far end of the conference table. She had immediately looked up as I entered the room and smiled, and I had noticed that I had sought her eyes out first, as had become a matter of course. She stared at me a little longer than usual, but I did my best to appear light-hearted.

I looked over at Stanton as I sat down. He had been reading a manual that I recognized immediately as being one of the Investigatory ones; for him to have it meant he was not only in school, but in his final year as well.

I asked him about it and was surprised by the answer. I welcomed where the conversation led us.

Officer Stanton was close to graduating from school and would soon become an Investigator in his own right. Soon enough, he would be doing the same job as mine, traveling, and handling cases on his own.

I wondered if Stanton would ask Grace to join his team, and I hoped not. I had considered creating my own team just to keep both by my side, but I hadn't felt it was my place to request someone choose such a difficult path. But now that I knew Stanton had aspirations in alignment with my own, I wondered if he had weighed out the pros and cons of having his own team.

I had once considered asking Grace, but I didn't think she would want to travel or do the full-time work as the VAA required within an investigative team even if she wanted to be with me. It would have been a lateral move career-wise and stifled her opportunities for growth within her agency. Aside from that, I think she would have preferred to be the homing beacon, keeping the light on, even if it meant not being able to see me very often. It was, I believed, the role most women would have chosen; to be the warmth and the light at the end of the road, the place to come home to, the creator and holder of the hearth for the one they loved. Should it ever come to it, I would ask and offer, and do her bidding; but at the end of the day, I had to concede that my work would always compel me to leave, while hers would always require her to stay.

We passed the time talking Stanton's education and future career as an Investigator at length, and as much as I believed he would be a stellar addition to the field, I also knew that he was so advanced with his research and technology skills that it would be difficult to see him lose some of that ability once he spent most of his time doing legwork, meeting with people, and doing interviews. On the other hand, he was far more advanced and educated in those fields than any Investigator I knew, so it would only add to his skill set and make him an even more desirable Investigator with a Specialty that would serve him well.

He was exemplary at his job, and I was glad to see that he accepted my praise with a big smile; he was still young enough to appreciate the odd show of support for his choices, but he reminded me a lot of myself. He obviously had a lot of determination and dedication to continue pursuing and advancing his education, and I told him as much. It was well-earned praise; I had often found myself impressed by the man's mastery of his craft, and I'd never met anyone that worked so proactively with such a unique ability to anticipate what might be needed or where research could yield successful results. I had thought it was because he was so efficient at being a Researcher, but what was clear now was that he was already of the mindset of an Investigator, serving as further proof that he was going to be amazing at it.

We chatted some more, compared notes about our education and the long journey it took to be to the point he was finally at, and waited for the Quad-blade to reach its destination.

The Chief returned from his phone call, grabbed himself a fresh cup of coffee, and joined us as we watched the notification begin to play, letting us know it was almost time.

FORTY-FIVE - TIMESTAMP 1-8

Timestamp: 1

The notification system flashed at timed intervals across the screens to let any viewers know the Quad-blade had reached its destination and was powering down to land.

It didn't take long before things became more serious again, and we watched as the automated technology within the Quad-blade itself processed its Final Destination Coordinates alerting its human spectators watching from afar that it had reached the Drop-zone and was initiating landing procedures.

I reminded both Grace and Stanton once again that the Drops could be unpredictable, and although they might not watch very many of them, they were not something one could easily forget. They needed to be prepared that they could be violent.

The atmosphere in the room had shifted, and I hoped the Victim Advocates Grace had selected to work with the families of our Victims were among the more compassionate representatives, because this was often a trying experience for many of them. It was a culmination of their most negative emotions all being brought to attention at the same time. For many, it provided a sense of Closure once it had been watched, but for others, it left them only with a sense of Bitterness, Anger, and Regret. Frequently, they wished for the Death Penalty and had considered the Crimes against their Loved Ones to be deserving of it; they were then left with a sense of Injustice even after they could observe the Drop-Off.

The satellite system tracking the Quad-blade from overhead showed a wide expanse of the Alaskan wilderness below. The Transport had been flying over a heavily treed area and was descending.

The location of the southernmost Drop-Zone had been selected over fifty years earlier. Unlike the first two Drop-Zones, the location had been selected despite its proximity to Anchorage. Both Anchorage and Fairbanks—the two most highly populated cities in Alaska at the time—had been cleared from regular Civilians since the early days of the Great Reformation directly following the Sentence Reform Act.

The Drop-Zone was a dense forest with a natural hilltop area that had been cleared of all trees and paved. The concrete was now weather-worn and had faded to a light, washed out dirty grey, and the cracks were bursting with overgrown weeds. The hilltop was a carefully selected location for Drops, insulated from attack by natural barriers as any good fortress required. The landing area rested upon a steep incline from every direction, with jagged rocks on the eastern side that would have been difficult to climb up or down, and footing mistakes were likely to lead to injury, broken bones, or Death. The top of the hill was approximately the size of a football field and was mostly covered in grass and small vegetation. It was a high enough elevation that it appeared as if it had dramatic Drop-offs from every direction, often worrying New Arrivals about how they were expected to descend once they arrived.

They had good cause to worry. For those that had an opportunity to look at their maps, they would see that there was nothing except harsh wilderness to the north, and their only hope of traveling out of the National Forest toward a known city meant a southern descent and travel direction. Trapped by the difficult terrain to the north, a jagged cliff with whitewater rapids at the bottom on the west, another cliff to the east—the only logical course of descent was the southern hill.

For most of the New Arrivals, they would not have taken the time to explore their maps while in transit, believing they had plenty of time once they landed and got their bearings. Then, in the first few moments after exiting the Transport, they would usually look around, often deciding to venture to the edges of each side before making the choice as to which direction they would set out in. Only by walking toward the edges of the landing pad on all sides could one see the impossibility of their situation in its entirety.

From the north, the incline was the most gradual, but it was the longest route to the top, taking almost imperceptible steps for over a quarter of a mile before it was necessary to put noticeable effort into the climb. Then, near the top, there was a sudden shift in the grading, and it became necessary to use switch-backing measures.

If one were to seek the shelter of the forest after fleeing the hilltop, the dense blanket of trees at the base of the hill was the most feasible chance for success, but the descent down to its shelter was almost as exhausting as its ascent, with neither option providing quick or easy relief.

It was not used as a route toward the hilltop because of the difficulty of the terrain. One had to wade through a thick forest of thorny overgrowth, hacking their way through the clinging vines that choked the trees and fettered forest floor with overgrown brambles in order to find a pathway to begin an ascent. The forest offered minimal comfort along the way, and even in the peak summer months it was cold, filled with insects, and impenetrable to the heat or light of the sun. Only after they left the shelter of the trees would they begin their ascent to the hilltop, and while speed increased once the forest faded, it was a long journey to the peak. Anyone that used this as a pathway toward the summit would be left exposed to all elements, especially the wind and rain, making it a brutal and lengthy ascent. Worse than the sudden shift of inclement weather, however, was the lack of shelter or coverage from prying eyes; there wasn't a prayer for secrecy or discretion—if someone were to climb the north side of the hill, they would be plainly visible and therefore entirely exposed during daylight hours.

The west side could not be traversed because a wide creek ran alongside the bottom of the steep, rocky terrain. It flowed from the forest to the north, too wide and dangerous for anyone to navigate until approximately a mile beyond the southern slope of the landing pad. The creek was filled with whitewater rapids, large boulders, and irregular, broken, craggy rocks that were sharp enough to slice soft skin to shreds. During the springtime, it doubled in size and was prone to flooding because of the glacier run-offs. But during the rest of the year, it became a manageable source of water that could be crossed in several locations within a few miles downstream. The sheer cliffside and craggy rocks jutting high above the creek made it impossible to scale without climbing gear.

The most disturbing aspect of the entire location was not the geography itself, despite how disheartening it may have seemed. The worst part was still yet to come and was all but unknown and unconsidered by most of the New Arrivals. Once they landed and the Transport was back in the air, they were so preoccupied with trying to navigate the terrain and their impending descent that they seldom questioned what might be waiting for them down at the bottom, through the trees, or beyond that which their eyes could see. They never paused to consider that they might be safer at the top with only one decent path of egress, which they could fortify with sufficient preparation and pre-planning; that was, until it was too late—and it was always too late.

In the early years, the government had attempted to put a reinforced security fence around the Drop-Zone to prevent the Exiled from breaching the landing area. It hadn't lasted long, however, because the Convicts had torn the fence down and used the metal sections to build shelters in the surrounding trees. It had been deemed too high-risk to attempt to rebuild, and after the first Drop resulted in the Quad-blade being overrun, the government only sent unmanned Transport Vehicles, refusing to risk Human Life just to do the Drops. Over time, encampments grew near each of the Drop-Zones, allowing for Convicts to reach the Transport landing areas—and New Arrivals—in short order after each Drop.

I watched as the Quad-blade set down on the concrete slab as it had done a thousand times before. The engine and blades were all affixed to the top half of the Transport Vehicle and were unable to be reached by anyone without climbing tools or some type of ladder. Even if they could get to the top, there was no point.

The top section was a solid piece of metal construction; as an unmanned drone, there was only some internal hardware, the solarized motor that received its power through the material of the drone itself, and the four rotors attached to the corners. Its smooth surface made it completely useless and impenetrable to attack. I knew from studying their advancements over the years that even if one were to crash, the technology, wiring, and cameras could be destroyed through detonation from their homing station. They were meant to be used long-term and were indestructible in their simplicity, but they were also easily deactivated if anyone wanted to use them for nefarious purposes.

Even though they were unmanned, a live feed could still monitor them during missions. The best part about them would be their use as living quarters if the metal shipping containers could be turned upright after a crash. Considering they had a bunk with a mattress and were well-insulated, compared to the great outdoors, they would provide substantial shelter if available.

For ourselves, the live-camera feed was an integral part of Stanton's plan; he needed to be able to view the Drop because if, for some reason, Daegan Kyl's compartment didn't open, he would need to open it immediately while the Transport was still stationed on the ground. Glancing over at Stanton, he was discreetly sitting with his laptop open, and although I couldn't see what he was doing, I knew he had hacked the system, and it was open and ready to go if he needed to intervene.

As soon as the Quad-blade landed, the doors opened simultaneously, and at the same speed. It was a beautifully uniform process. One could almost believe it was an intentional act, meant to teach one final lesson to the Ex-Citizens within the Transport. Each of the Convicts was now expected to leave the enclosure, thereby shedding their Final Moments connected to their US Citizenry. The doors opened simultaneously because they were all considered equal in the deliverance of Justice through the Criminal Justice system. For their Crimes Against Humanity, their Sentence was meted out in exactly the same measure regardless of their individualism. Criminality resulted in Punishment, and they were all equal in the consequences for their choices.

Even Daegan Kyl's Holding Cell had opened, alleviating any last concerns either myself or Stanton had experienced, and securing that we had succeeded in our mission. I stole a furtive glance at the Chief to see if he had noticed him, and was relieved to see that he was reading some paperwork while calmly sipping his coffee. He didn't seem to be providing his full attention to the screens.

I returned my attention to the events about to unfold. This was where it usually began to get ugly.

Alaska was a no-fly zone. This meant that any aircraft in the Drop-Zone areas were undoubtedly Transports carrying more New Arrivals. Although the Transports weren't extremely noisy, they could be heard from enough of a distance as to provide some warning to those on the ground that another Drop was about to take place. The Drops were set at random times and followed no specific pattern; this was intended to off-set the chances for problems with the Convicts on the ground.

The idea was to prevent New Arrivals from being swarmed upon their release. It was also meant to thwart any efforts by the Convicts to destroy or detain the Transports themselves. There had never been any aircraft struck down, but there was no guarantee that those in Exile might not have the resources, skills, or technology to create some type of projectile that was capable of making catastrophic contact with anything flying overhead.

Time was not working in favor of those that were being transported and Sentenced to the next chapter of their lives. They did not have any idea what was awaiting them on the other side. Many people in the past had made comments that

Exile seemed more terrifying than Death. There were also some Convicted Offenders that had been given Exile as their Sentence but had asked for Execution instead. For some, even if they themselves had been found Guilty of lawlessness, the idea of living in a land devoid of any regulated system of government or system of Law and Order was too much to bear.

The Convicted Offenders that were about to disembark from the Transport Vehicle were soon to find out what they were made of, and whether or not they still believed that their choices to break the laws were worth the price of the Sentence they were willing to risk.

Timestamp: 2

I glanced over at the Chief, watching nervously as he observed the scene unfolding on the giant screens in front of us. I noted that neither Grace nor Stanton dared look his way.

"Well, Stanton, the doors all seemed to open just fine; don't you think you should exit the program now and just enjoy the show with the rest of us?" he asked.

Stanton and Grace both dropped their jaws in a mutually stunned expression of bewilderment and shame; I imagined neither was used to being caught breaking the rules.

I was by no means a rule-breaker, but somehow, I wasn't surprised the Chief had caught us—nor was I surprised by his knowledge. I supposed it was a credit to his role; if he didn't know what was going on under his own roof, who knew what could happen. I imagined as a father to six daughters that there wasn't much that escaped his watchful eye.

The Chief gave me a cockeyed look over the edges of his glasses, took another sip of his coffee, and returned his attention to the big screen. The look was all he needed to say; we had gotten away with it for no other reason than because he had allowed it to happen. For all our efforts, conspiring, planning, and subterfuge, the only reason we were sitting here tonight—and Daegan Kyl was about to fight for survival alongside Willow Amos—was because the Chief had allowed it to occur and hadn't reported us any further. Without him saying anything directly, he had acknowledged that even if he did not necessarily support our plan—or outright condemn our actions—he had at least understood both why Daegan Kyl had done what he had chosen to do, and why we had chosen to help him. The message was also perfectly clear, however, that we would never do anything like it again.

Timestamp: 3

It began as it always did. As soon as the Transport was within earshot of the inhabitants, the Convicts emerged from the tree line in droves, running frantically toward the landing site. They did their best to make their way up the hillside in the hopes of reaching the summit while the Transport was still grounded.

Although they were able to advance the moment they heard the Transport, it was not an easy ascent to the top. Nonetheless, they tried; they always tried. Hundreds of them began tearing through one another, pushing, and clawing their way up through the rugged terrain.

For many, the Transport was their only means of escape, and every time one landed, it was another chance to try and hitch a ride back toward civilization undetected. The logistics of it didn't matter; they didn't care that it would be heading straight back into the Holding Cells of Patos Island. The only thing that mattered was their dedication to trying, and whatever measure of hope it delivered for them to do so. Those were the good ones. Others intended to do much worse.

At the top of the hill, the satellites were monitoring the Transport. They used both infrared heat signals and live video feeds, ensuring that none remained in the Holding Cells by the time the Transport lifted off once more.

Grace had leaned forward in her chair and put her hand up to her mouth. She had noticed all the random people trying to move up the hillside quickly enough to catch up to the Transport before it lifted off again.

Calling them 'people' was a stretch, however, as their time in Alaska had undoubtedly eaten away at whatever humanity they had. Many referred to those exiled as 'Ex-Citizens', believing them to still be more human than animal. But Alaska had no place for such sentiments, and most who tried to humanize the Convicted seldom had a true inkling of either their Crimes or the conditions that the Alaskan wilderness brought out.

Such labels were an understatement to anyone who had witnessed the events broadcast through these Drops, though; they knew the truth of what these people were, and what they had become over time. Formal titles, names, protocols, and societal mores all seemed to lose value and meaning within this place. We could be certain that those on the ground were not addressing one another as Inmates or Felons, although there was a good chance there were gangs who operated much as they did in prison settings.

As Law Enforcement, we were trained to call them 'the Exiled', the 'Banished', or 'Convicted Offenders'.

Despite these labels and degrees of criminality, there were those who resided in Exile even without having broken any laws. Some were fundamentally broken inside and were simply incapable of living a normal life within a civilized society. Such persons, usually Pedophiles or other sexual deviants, may not have committed serious crimes that had led to the creation of Victims, but left unchecked, knew the probability existed that their behavior would escalate. They were not fit to live in society and posed a danger to Innocent Citizenry. For these reasons, some had willfully chosen Exile, knowing that to stay would have potentially meant Violent Crimes and the Death Penalty down the road. Still others had been 'Red-Flagged', and because of their behavior and tendencies, were Sentenced and Relocated before their behavior escalated. This was what should have been assigned to LeRoy Jones had he not somehow managed to slip through the cracks. Additionally, there were those who chose to live in Alaska purely because they had a distaste for the government and regarded the wilds of Alaska as the last true refuge for those who wanted to live as free men.

The conditions were very similar to the prisons of the past. After they'd been in Alaska for a while, all who managed to remain alive were either made into more hardened Predators or weaker Prey. Most only survived because they became the worst possible version of themselves, tapping into pure primal, animal instinct as they fought to stay alive. They became something far more than just 'Ex-Citizens' after everything they endured. They were Survivors—almost cavemen—primitive men leading primitive lives with primitive and limited resources. But they were also plagued with a constant onslaught of brutality caused by brutal savages, and with that dynamic included, they had to be considered Survivors.

The worst among them were in a different breed, however, and it was this demographic that always posed the greatest threat to New Arrivals. They were commonly referred to as 'Wildmen' because, after enough time living in the Alaskan wilderness, that's what they became. They were almost entirely bearded, with at least shoulder-length hair, and most were seen wearing at least some clothing made of animal pelts, fur, and leather. They were known to use animal bones and teeth as weapons and tools. They fashioned shelters out of trees they felled themselves with primitive axes, and managed to fish, hunt, and even trap animals. The smart ones that either possessed such skills or learned to adapt to their surroundings often disappeared into the great unknown, choosing to take their chances in the wilderness rather than risk their lives trying to exist within the violent encampments. The majority, however, stayed near the Drop-Zones, and in the hierarchy of this cold, unforgiving new world, the Wildmen were at the top.

The primitive campsites and villages were frequently overwhelmed with predatory, savage violence, and constant bloodshed of alpha males all vying for leadership and domination. In this brave new world, those with skills and strength survived, while others learned the hard way that everything, especially protection and vital resources, came at a price.

Timestamp: 4

The satellites picked up the scans of the New Arrivals as they began exiting their Holding Cells. They edged out with caution. They were uncertain, hesitant. They likely would have had more confidence if they had known beforehand that they had traveled with many familiar faces, and their deportation was a collective experience, just as being part of The Angels of Mercy had been.

Several minutes passed, and more than half of the metal Holding Cells still contained the Convicted Offenders that refused to leave voluntarily.

They were afraid.

They were *always* afraid.

It was a rebirth; they had no idea what to expect, and the fear was overwhelming.

For those that maintained a more reserved course of action and stayed near their Holding Cell, they watched as their fellow traveling companions ventured out. The hexagon shape of the Quad-blade meant that there were Convicted Criminals being released in every direction from the top of the hill. Since there were five Holding Cells per side, as soon as the doors were raised, they would have been able to see that they were not alone.

The entire Transport had been reserved for those Convicted because of my investigation, which meant that each of the Holding Cells had contained an Angel of Mercy—and they had all been traveling alongside those whom they were likely to have known rather than strangers. It may not have seemed like much, but to these Convicted Criminals, it had probably been one of the highlights of their young lives to exit the Holding Cell and see familiar faces in such an unfamiliar space and time.

None of them were habitual offenders, let alone 'Hardened Criminals'. Only a few were over the age of thirty and there was a good chance that some of them were still virgins, having only just left their parents' home and gone away to college in recent years. Everything about this experience would have been a shocking transition from one life to another, and had their actions been anything other than Assisted Suicide and Abortion, I would have felt more compassion or tried for Rehabilitation just so our nation didn't lose such young Citizens.

It was a shame to lose Citizens who clearly had potential and no prior criminal tendencies. Seeing how afraid they were now only reaffirmed that, and I was forced to remind myself that it was not my place to pass Sentences any more than their actions and decisions had been my responsibility. They had made their choices; we were here because they believed in what they had done, and that could not be undone no matter how afraid they seemed at this moment.

Recognizing one another once they had left the confines of the Transport had given them more security. They moved around the perimeter of the Quad-blade with more confidence, rounding each section as they sought out their companions. As they gained numbers, they all gathered on the southern side.

Most were already wearing the small backpacks they had each been given before they departed. I was glad to see it, because they were filled with supplies that were worth more than their weight in gold, and once the Transport lifted off, if they didn't have it in their possession, they would lose it.

The backpacks consisted mostly of a months' worth of dehydrated rations and hydration packets, a set of camping cookware and reusable water canteen, a selection of medical supplies, a package of fire-starting tools, a sleeping bag, a two-man all-weather tent and tarp, a compass and waterproof map of Alaska, and a Holy Bible. It wasn't much, but it was a start. Within an additional generic package, there were usually some candles, sewing needles and thread, a length of thin rope and a few hooks, and other assorted oddities for their use. Most Americans would say it was better than what many of them deserved; others would say it was a Death Sentence.

The backpacks were standard in their quality and there was nothing exceptional about them specifically or the contents they carried. Everything provided to them were products and resources that would have been available to them to purchase in a thriving capitalist society for their recreational activities at any point.

But things were different now. The supplies that they were given were their final lifeline from a nation that they no longer belonged to. They were now the most valuable commodities in their possession. They were reminders of a different world and a past life, forever lost to each of them. Every item contained within their backpack served as a stark contrast to what they were now capable of obtaining, achieving, and producing on their own. And precisely for these reasons, their backpacks now made each of them a target.

One of the females had cut a piece of the thin rope she had found within her backpack, using it to tie her long hair out of her eyes and into a ponytail. She should have just cut her hair off before the lice and ticks made it necessary, but she would learn such things over time. For now, at least she appeared to be trying.

A handful of brave men and women ventured out twenty to thirty feet toward the south, hoping to reach the edge of the landing area where they could better assess their surroundings. They were given a full panoramic view of the area, but it would require an assessment from every vantage point to see their best chances for a descent.

From the center of the hilltop where the convoy was positioned, it would have appeared like there was a sharp decline from every direction. The only way to assess their surroundings was to head toward the outer edges of the launch pad and see what lay beyond. It was only by exceedingly poor luck that the only men who were brave enough to move more than twenty feet from the Transport had selected the southern direction to investigate first, placing them in the most dangerous position of all.

From the most Western-facing side of the Hexagon, Daegan Kyl had emerged first of the five, followed by Willow Amos and three others. He had his backpack strapped on over his broad shoulders, and then secured the shoulder harnesses with a strap belted snugly across his wide chest. A third belt with thick pads lined the backside of his hips and then thinned out before latching firmly around his waistline. I could see the muzzle of his rifle sticking out from the top of his backpack; I doubted anyone in the Transport would have known what it was or recognized it as the powerful asset it would prove to be, but there was no question that the men ascending the hill would—and they would do anything within their power to get a hold of it. His sidearm, I assumed, was locked and loaded beneath his loose shirt—at least I prayed it was. I didn't want him to need it, but I wanted him to have it ready to go if he did.

I felt a deep sense of regret surge through me as I realized how little I had shared with him about where he was going or what could be found there.

I should have prepared him more for what to expect.

As soon as Willow Amos saw him, she ran to him, throwing her arms around him with all her might and bursting into him like a waterfall crashing onto the rocks below. The force of her body leaping against him pushed him back a full step and caused him to teeter as he tried to steady himself. Under normal circumstances, I doubted her slight frame would have even caused him to budge, but because of the heaviness of his backpack already creating an imbalance in weight distribution, he was forced to plant himself against her assault. I felt a sense of foreboding as I realized the assets he had packed for the journey were not only going to be a nuisance against the onslaught of any attack, they were also going to be highly prized among men who would do anything to get what they wanted. For the second time in only a moment I realized I had failed to properly prepare Daegan Kyl or even provide suitable warning.

She dropped to her feet and stared up at him with a wide smile and big round eyes. I wondered if she would ever grow to understand or appreciate the price he had paid to be there. All she seemed to realize was that he had told her not to worry the last time they had been together, and he had ensured that she didn't. The magnitude of it seemed lost on her, although at least she seemed extremely happy to see him there.

One of the men that had paused near Daegan Kyl when Willow Amos ran toward him was familiar to me. I recalled who he was after a second.

He was the man that had once been known as SPD Detective Jarrett, but was now only able to be referred to as 'Ex-Citizen'; nameless, jobless, homeless, and without a country to call his own. He had been stripped of his rank, his badge, his anonymity, and his future. It was highly unlikely that his previous profession would be concealed for long if the thirty people surrounding him knew who he was and what he had done. This was not the place to adhere to loyalties; it was now wholly and unequivocally about Survival. As such, any prior connection to one another was not going to carry significant value unless it came in the currency of how each of them could benefit from one another. They would have no such loyalties toward Detective Jarrett, and once it became clear that information was power, and could be leveraged for an ounce of security, food, or protection, his life was forfeit. They were all at risk, but Detective Jarrett was at much greater risk than the rest. This was no place for an ex-member of Law Enforcement.

We watched as the group convened around the southern side of the Transport. It was readily apparent that they were infinitely more comfortable within their new surroundings now that they had noticed so many of their friends, colleagues, classmates, and comrades all around them. It was the first time many of them had seen or spoken to one another in almost a month, and for most of them they had not even caught a glimpse of each other while Incarcerated, or throughout their Trials, Convictions, or Sentencing. They had thought they were alone, and most likely had *felt* alone, until this point in time. They had been cut off from all that they had known, removed from their schools, homes, and workplaces, and kept in solitary confinement throughout their entire experience within the Criminal Justice system. And yet somehow, here they all were, reunited, experiencing this new chapter together, and at the very least, being able to share their emotional journey. It must have been very comforting for them.

And while it was entirely possible that some of them were angry, bitter, and resentful about their cases, holding either their country or their Fellow Countrymen at fault, it seemed as though for the most part they were simply happy to know that they were no longer on their own. Whatever price they had paid, at least they were not paying it alone anymore. For many, that knowledge was worth every sacrifice that had been made, and it gave them the strength they needed to keep moving forward, even if they were still terrified.

Because they were huddled so close to the Quad-blade, none of the group of people standing there watching could hear any of the Wildmen that were slowly making their way up the southern side of the hill. They could not see the giant encampment off to the south, and probably believed they were just facing a battle against the elements. There was nothing to be done about it; they were enjoying what would surely be their last few comfortable moments given the seriousness of the situation, and for many, their guard had been lowered immeasurably because they believed themselves to be at least among the familiar faces of their comrades.

They had no way to know that it was little more than the calm before the storm. From the safety and security of our comfortable conference room, we watched as the droves of our most reprehensible discarded society members scurried up the hill like the disease-ridden cockroaches they were, knowing all the while we were helpless to warn the New Arrivals what was coming for them.

Timestamp: 5

Within a few moments, the screens would be full of chaos. I knew from prior experiences that it was about to become impossible to track everyone's movements at the same time, and we would miss significant portions of what was about to unfold. It would be necessary to replay footage through the Transport cameras and the satellite imaging later if we had a desire to catalog everything. I hoped that vacating the landing zone and finding shelter in the woods as quickly as possible was Daegan Kyl's primary objective.

I knew what was just beyond the edge, and it was approaching relentlessly. Masses of the worst types of savages would soon be upon them, and before long there would be hundreds of Human Beings filling our screens; it would be exceedingly difficult to keep track of the two of them unless they could escape undetected before all hell broke loose.

Although there were men and women that had made their way out toward the end of the landing field on the southern side, they were only beginning to get close enough to pick up on the noise being produced by the horde that traveled just beyond. It seemed as though they were aware of some rumbling, but they must have been accrediting it to the Transport that was now firing itself up to prepare for its return to Patos Island.

The Quad-blade rose from the landing pad, slowly at first, and almost undetected other than the sound of the engines powering up more. Some of the New Arrivals had noticed the change in noise, and turning to look at the Transport, displayed looks of fear and confusion. They may not have understood that their Holding Cells were only temporary lodgings until that moment, thinking that the metal containers were going to be left for them to use as long-term shelters. When they realized they were only being dropped off and would not have any type of shelter once the Transport left, the full magnitude of the situation struck them.

The Transport had reached its full power reserves required for lift-off. As it did, the magnetic connection between the outside edges of the Holding Cells and the top engine section of the Transport disengaged. We watched as the center of the enormous hexagon lifted itself higher and higher while the outside edges were still touching the ground. It created an incline; subtle at first, but then gaining in steepness.

It wasn't losing power; it was intentional. As the Quad-blade rose into the sky, the central parts of the Holding Cells were positioned directly in the middle area underneath the major engine component. With every foot gained in elevation, the Quad-blade rose and took the metal Holding Cells with it, causing the external ends of the Holding Cells to remain on the ground but with such an increase in the vertical incline that most began to realize it was intended to remove any stragglers attempting to remain inside of the Transport. The ride was over; it was time to let go.

The effects of the gain in elevation toward the center meant the angle continued to increase in sharpness as the Quad-blade continued to rise. The result was unavoidable;

any remaining Convicted Offenders had no choice but to exit. There was nothing within the Cells for them to hold on to for very long, and the angle became gradually steeper with each passing second. Within a moment, each of the Holding Cells was at a forty-five-degree angle, and several Angels of Mercy that had been too terrified to leave their Cells could be seen sliding onto the cement below. The Transport was now gaining momentum and was lifting higher and higher.

One final Convicted Offender had been forced to drop after dangling from the edge, refusing to let go. I heard Grace gasp, but he had only fallen a few feet. It was unlikely that it would be the worst tragedy of this Drop. From another Holding Cell a lonely backpack slid out and fell to the ground. A girl ran over to it and hurriedly put it on over her shoulders before rushing back toward the rest of the group. The Quad-blade would make its return flight home inverted in this manner, each of the external doors at the ends of the Holding Cells open and every container at a completely vertical position. It disallowed anyone from clinging to the massive carrier for long, and guaranteed certain death if they eventually did fall. The Transports that entered Alaska were one-way flights only.

This alone was enough to make many of The Angels of Mercy panic once again, and any of the comfort or serenity they had gained by seeing their fellow comrades dissipated as they each processed what being Exiled meant. They were on their own; they had no shelter, no family, very little by way of resources, and they had no special training, skills, or experience to guide them. All they had was themselves, a small backpack of supplies with a finite shelf life, and the other people from the Transport Drop. It was late September in Alaska; millions of acres of what had once been national forest surrounded them, and winter would set in long before they could find or build suitable lodgings.

It wasn't Exile; it was a Death Sentence.

If they had only understood in that moment that it was all about to become much, much worse, it would probably have led to many choosing to jump to their Deaths from the rocky cliffside just to spare themselves all that was about to unfold. If they had not been so naïve, so willing to make excuses for the common criminal who willfully embraced lawlessness and disregarded the Human Rights and social courtesies of his Fellow Citizen, they might have been more prepared for what was now only moments away from occurring.

But that wasn't the case, and they were woefully ill-prepared and ill-equipped to handle the realities that were now at their doorstep.

The Transport was now high enough in elevation that none of the New Arrivals could reach up and touch it anymore. The noise was at its highest peak. The hydraulics that reduced the outer rim of the Holding Cells were now fully extended, and the Cells were completely vertical. Many of the New Arrivals retreated beneath the Transport lines and stared up into the empty chasm of blackness above; perhaps willing the metal contraption to disengage and flatten them instantly so they could be spared what was to come.

Willow Amos was standing next to Daegan Kyl, and soon enough, the remaining Angels of Mercy had retreated further and further, now able to walk fully upright under the giant clearing where there had once been Holding Cells. The Quad-blade was gaining momentum slowly and was still overhead, but it was twenty feet above them, and would soon be gone entirely. They were on their own.

The noise was deafening as the Quad-blade powered up for one last burst required before it could level off at the designated traveling elevation; it was often a noise that was made louder by heavy winds as it competed against the elements, and Alaska was frequently windier than the Transport Station at Patos Island. Between the wind, the additional noise of the hydraulics, and the Transport powering up, the noise was thunderous.

The first time these Ex-Citizens had heard all of this, they would have been on the inside of the Holding Cells already and the engine would have been fired up before it landed over them. They would have heard the noises as the machinery latched on at various locking points in addition to hearing the plumbing disengage, but it wouldn't have been as loud within the Holding Cells since they were built with noise-reduction materials already intended to prevent communication between the Convicted Offenders. By comparison, the experience of watching the Transport lift-off must have seemed very different and much more dramatic.

Had their circumstances been even marginally different, they might have appreciated what a wonder the Transport actually was; it was a feat of engineering genius and another credit to what we Americans were capable of creating and doing when we put our minds to it. It wasn't solely used for the Transport of Convicted Offenders; it was used to transport a variety of other things as well. Farmers used them to transport livestock such as cows, sheep, horses, and pigs. Hospitals and Emergency Responders used them to transport emergency aid facilities. They were used as portable lodgings to zones hit by natural disasters and were even used as emergency evacuation Transports in times of crisis. Corporations had been notorious for using them to transport goods until the government intervened and established human-worker protection measures so they couldn't cut out all human labor just to create a higher profit margin. Nonetheless, for some situations, especially those that posed a danger to the Sanctity of Human Life, the Transports were a Godsend.

The cargo containers were easily transported and could be used as lodging for Combat Soldiers. They were durable enough to last for decades, capable of bearing weight so they were able to be buried for foxholes if necessary, and the military had containers capable of withstanding even the most dastardly of attack methods. When properly prepared, the containers were virtually indestructible and had provided shelter for countless Soldiers against primitive bullets, firebombs, Molotov cocktails, and other rudimentary attacks. They were self-contained for ventilation and capable of withstanding the most advanced high explosive anti-tank (HEAT) rounds, and even thermobaric warheads.

It was highly unlikely that the cargo containers these Ex-Citizens had been transported in were of the same quality as those used by our Soldiers, however. The government wouldn't waste the resources on Ex-Citizens, nor would they allow such important machinery to wind up in the hands of those whom they considered to be Enemies of the People.

My thoughts returned to The Angels of Mercy, now gathering beneath the Transport, and talking among themselves. From a distance, the sound of the approaching men filled the air with a menacing war cry.

Timestamp: 6

Despite the roaring noise, it didn't seem to register with any of the New Arrivals that the sound was coming from over the side of the hill rather than the wind or the noise of the Quad-blade propellers. The wind was raging and howling atop the plateau, and night was falling quickly. When the sounds of their own questions and mounting hysteria created more chaos and fear, some of the more dominant personalities began to emerge and take charge, stepping forward into roles of leadership. They urged everyone to quiet down so they could do a more comprehensive assessment of the situation.

The New Arrivals made a concerted effort to rationalize their senses as they acclimated to their surroundings. They tried to quiet and calm one another so they could process the noises they were hearing over the deafening sound of the engines overhead. Within a moment, it finally hit them full force, as many of them recognized it as the sound of men approaching from a distance.

It was at this point that Daegan Kyl began making strategic moves, and it was evident by his actions that he was now switching gears as his combat training and instincts kicked in. He placed his arm possessively across the front of Willow Amos. Without turning away from the crowd, he began to slowly take measured steps backward toward the north side of the landing area. Although he must have realized that there were 'others' making their way up to their location, his behavior indicated that for the time being, he was regarding the New Arrivals as their most immediate potential threat. He had no intention of being in a large group of people, regardless if they were known to Willow Amos or not; he knew the power of mobs, especially when panic and violence set in.

It was a risky move, however. Even though they were doing it incrementally and trying not to draw any attention their way, they were still separating themselves from any protection a group might have offered.

Daegan Kyl would have realized that the group was an easy target if none of them posed a threat to whoever was approaching. They were all sitting ducks if they continued to stay on the top of the plateau with no known way down, places to hide, or ability to get weapons. They needed to figure out how to get off that ridge—and they needed to do it as quickly as possible.

Daegan Kyl was the only man who seemed to truly understand this and behave accordingly. Willow Amos was a dutiful little soldier and followed his lead entirely.

Unfortunately for the New Arrivals, the strongest leaders among them were likely those who had been brave enough to venture out toward the southern edge of the hillside. Watching them all from a multitude of aerial shots, it seemed clear that most of The Angels of Mercy were terrified, frozen with fear and confusion. Their youth and lack of life experience was quickly proving to be a disadvantage to them. Despite their role in their anarchist group, none of them were street smart or tough in the ways that would best serve them now. They had no comprehension of what lie just on the other side of that embankment, and they weren't capable of imagining how shockingly Violent complete strangers were about to be—or that it would all be directed toward them even though they had done nothing to deserve it. That was the downfall of living in a highly civilized society where your Fellow Man was too polite and kind; all instinct for survival diminished through generations of peace.

Daegan Kyl understood the gravity of the situation, as could be seen by the way he had first reached for his side-arm, hesitated, and then removed his large hunting knife from its sheath instead. He stood poised, confident, and well-versed in the art of war.

He may not have been able to see how many were coming, but he knew his ears had not been playing tricks on him. His behavior indicated that he probably understood that there would be a significant number of them from the sound of their rallying cry.

Following orders, Willow Amos began scouring the ground for anything capable of delivering a heavy blow or keeping attackers at bay.

Daegan Kyl was the only person I wanted to ensure remained unharmed.

I was tense as I focused on the screens. I put my hand over my mouth, rubbed the stubble on my face, folded my arm across my chest, and tried to focus on the facts.

Just breathe. This man could handle things. Stop internalizing everything.

We all make choices.

My legs were firmly planted, and my entire body felt taut with the anticipation of all that could go wrong. The tension in the room was palpable, and I wondered how much of it was because of my own heightened anxiety and feelings of misgivings.

From my right I could suddenly feel the warmth of another body standing near mine, and I realized Grace had discreetly moved from one of the couches and was now standing near me. She was close enough to feel along my entire right side; her thigh pressed into leg, her waistline along my hip, and her arm was curved around my back as it rested along the built-in shelf I had been leaning against. She was close enough I could feel the warmth radiating from her body, smell the sweetness of her shampoo, and feel the pressure as her flesh pressed against mine.

I didn't know what manner of voodoo magic she applied, but it proved to be one of the most soothing, strangely hypnotic instances of transformation I'd ever experienced. Whether it was the sensuality of her physical closeness, the assertiveness of her actions, the power behind the psychology of physical contact as an intent to comfort, or she just intended to jar me out of my focused stress by redirecting my thoughts toward sex, it was pure sorcery. Her intuition was astoundingly accurate and the manner in which she had melted tenderly into the space beside me had been so subtle I had barely noticed that both my body and my mind had shifted gears without being compelled to. Both my heart rate and my agitation had decreased, and the tenseness of my body had all but disappeared as I felt the warmth from her frame meld into my own.

She was clearly a witch.

I put my arm around her backside and gave her a very discreet hug as a thank you, and then returned my attention back toward the screen. It might have been marginally inappropriate for our professional situation, but no one was paying attention to us.

I needed to know that Daegan Kyl could take care of himself and what was yet to come. I knew he had the military background, and his physical size would work in his favor, but I desperately needed to see this end with no harm coming to him.

Although I knew he had travelled with a side-arm and a rifle that would undoubtedly prove useful both in his current plight and in the future, he would have been foolish to have used either of them. Even if he had a hearty supply of ammunition contained within his backpack or on his person, it was highly unlikely he would be able to secure more, even if they traveled extensively and made their way through all homesteads and urban areas they could. Firearms and ammunition had been one of the few things the government had worked diligently to ensure had been removed from the region.

This meant every bullet needed to count, and every time either firearm was used, it had to be absolutely necessary. He was smart to be cautious with his finite resources, but there was an additional reason it had been wiser for him to ignore his most obvious weapons of self-defense—the odds were stacked against him.

The instant he fired off a round, it would have sent an echo through the valley that would have been immediately recognized by thousands of Wildmen. Most of them would have gladly risked death in a consolidated attack against whoever held the firearm just to have the chance of scoring it. The Wildmen would have stormed the landing area and killed everyone in their path until they were face to face with the person pointing a firearm at them.

Daegan Kyl might have been able to fire off a handful of shots before they swarmed him like a hive of angry hornets, and it was entirely probable that he would have been able to kill a half dozen or more before he lost control. But before long he would have been outnumbered; they would have killed him and Raped Willow Amos—and it would have all played out exactly as it had for everyone else.

No, if Daegan Kyl intended to have a fighting chance for himself and his ward, he would need to continue doing things with the same caution and level of training that had helped him survive every other combat mission. He was right to be cautious; it was one of the indications he might have a genuine chance of surviving this ordeal and making it out alive at some point.

From the distance, the noise of the Wildmen increased from a dull roar to a thunderous battle cry as the Transport finally disappeared entirely from all sight and sound. This time, no one thought it was just the wind playing tricks on their minds; they knew they were under attack.

Timestamp: 7

We watched as the Exiled dregs of Humanity finally began reaching the top of the hill and waited for them to pore over like the horde of soulless zombies they were. If the New Arrivals were surrounded, any effort to stave off an attack would have been moot. The Wildmen could gain the upper hand simply by outnumbering the New Arrivals.

For some, it would have been their first effort to climb to the top after a Drop; for others it could have been their hundredth. The older the Exiled man, the more likely he was extremely dangerous. Preying on the weak was one of the easiest means of survival. At one point, every single Wildman had once been among those freshly Dropped from the Transport and left alone and afraid atop the desolate landscape. At one time, they had been the ones who had been Convicted, Sentenced, and purged from their own country.

There were many occasions when the Transports had already departed by the time anyone from below was able to reach the top, especially in the winter months when it was all but impossible to trudge through the snow over such a long distance quickly and easily. There were still other prizes worth fighting for. Even though the Wildmen knew the Quad-blade had already departed, they pushed themselves toward the summit. They charged onward up the southern slope toward the peak, exerting themselves beyond calculation just so they could crest the summit before any of their competition from below arrived ahead of them. They knew what lay at the top was more valuable than just an opportunity to return to Civilization, and it was infinitely more attainable if they were willing to fight for it.

Had they taken the time to stop and think, they would have realized they probably had more in common with the New Arrivals than differences; but this wasn't about finding 'common ground'. The men living in the wilds of Alaska didn't care about building a new world or improving their community by adding more skilled people to it. This was about survival—pure, predatory survival—and *he who had more* had a better chance at it than *he who had less*. It was that simple. They had no desire to humanize the New Arrivals; this was not the time nor the place to espouse virtues of Humanity and lectures about co-existence.

Nothing could have prepared the New Arrivals for what they were about to observe and experience. Even if they had been told, they probably wouldn't have accepted it. Everything the youthful idealists believed about Human Beings being capable of living in peace without Violence as they worked together in some socialist utopian society was about to be decimated by the wild savages approaching them.

Every Drop-off guaranteed two things to the men below: women and fresh backpack supplies. Greed and desperation triggered a ferocious response, and Violence quickly followed. The New Arrivals were incapable of comprehending how little value their lives held now, but they would see soon enough.

Timestamp: 8

The Angels of Mercy had instinctively drawn closer to one another, huddling together for both security and strength. It had been a wise strategic move, driven by their most base instincts. Despite none of them having had any prior military or Law Enforcement experience, aside from Daegan Kyl and Detective Jarrett, they had done as much as they could, given the options. Proving this point even further, many of them furtively searched the ground for rocks and sticks, taking the time to secure their backpacks so they could free their hands for self-defense if necessary.

They had spotted Willow Amos retreating further north, and they all moved toward her. Daegan Kyl needed to distance himself from them. He could not hope to defend them and protect Willow Amos at the same time, and while he might deflect attention away from himself and his ward, he was a sitting duck by remaining in the crowd.

Most had not known Daegan Kyl or seen him in person, according to our investigation. All they saw in that moment was an Alpha-male whom they were more than ready to trust with their lives and defense, approved on sight just because of his proximity to Willow Amos and his sheer masculinity and size. She had been a leader; these had been her soldiers. They now looked to her for guidance, circling around her in a tight-knit group.

They were uncertain about what was happening.

But we knew.

It was always the same.

Their confusion and fear began to mount, and any comfort they had derived from their heartfelt reunion upon landing was fleeting as they realized they were potentially facing severe danger unlike anything they had ever known before. They stood transfixed as the men that had slowly meandered out toward the southern edges and peered over suddenly turned full force and began running back toward them.

We watched in silence as the first of the Wildmen began to appear. Within seconds of one another, the Wildmen surged over the hill, piling over one another to be among the first to reach the New Arrivals.

The Wildmen could see the New Arrivals all huddled into a mass in the distance, and the high-pitched screams of the women told them everything they wanted to know about who would be found among them. They charged forward, some with wooden clubs, others with spears, all racing to get to the finish line while the pickings were still available. There was an unspoken rule about damaging the women, and as some men raised their bows and arrows, they took their time selecting their targets before allowing their arrows to sail. The sound of women screaming was music to their ears and provided them with all the incentive they needed to attack.

The New Arrivals that had ventured out toward the edges of the landing were now in a full-blown panic, able to see the approaching horde for the first time. They scrambled backward, tripping over themselves as they tried to sprint back to the protection of their peers.

One of the New Arrivals tripped over a branch, stumbling forward clumsily before finally landing on the ground and sliding several feet on his hands, forearms, and knees. Another man that had been running more slowly behind him attempted to reach down and help him up while simultaneously looking backward in fear. Upon seeing the hordes of Wildmen finally reaching the summit only twenty or thirty feet behind him, he dropped the man's arm, surrendered any good intentions, and began running back toward the protection of the convoy once again. The man on the ground scrambled to his feet, doing his best to reach the group before the horde caught up to him.

In the distance we could hear The Angels of Mercy scream. From somewhere near the edge of the hilltop, an arrow made its way into the back leg of the overweight young man that had tried to help his fallen companion, and as it pierced the back of his thigh, he immediately sank to the ground. Before the other man could reach him, a second arrow lodged itself in the back of the husky one's skull.

The man with the skinned-up shins and forearms registered complete shock on his face as he watched the arrows strike from behind, and before he had even passed the fallen corpse of his companion, another arrow hit him squarely between the shoulder blades, and he, too, fell to the ground. As his body landed with a 'thud', it was almost immediately pounced upon by the swarm of Wildmen. Without a twinge of conscience, they began tearing away at his clothing, grabbing his backpack, and removing his shoes and everything else separating his now Deceased Remains from returning to the earth where he lay. We watched in horror as they moved from the first man to the second, stripping him bare next. I didn't say anything, but had this Drop been during the long winter months, it was likely that the men would have become a source of food as well.

Within another minute, the Wildmen had pressed on, and as complete chaos broke out among the New Arrivals, the Wildmen seized hold of the situation and claimed it to their advantage. The Angels of Mercy broke rank and began running solo, making it a game of cat and mouse for the Wildmen as the sounds of screaming filled the air.

Grace had looked away in disgust the instant the first arrow made contact, but every man in the room stood transfixed at the sheer primal horror unfolding before our eyes. I kept my gaze affixed to the location where Daegan Kyl and Willow Amos were located so I would not lose them, and pulled Grace close. She didn't have to watch, but she didn't have to be alone, either. Our Humanity was all that separated us from what we were witnessing.

These men were desperate; they had regressed into this condition because their need for survival was more powerful than their need for Law and Order. Although I had never said it aloud, I firmly believed that in the right circumstances, we were all capable of doing what was so shockingly unfolding before our eyes.

The true moment of panic for the New Arrivals had occurred when they realized that there was nowhere to go; they were bombarded with a wall of Wildmen running toward them. And then there they were, left to face an armed, desperate mob of men who were charging at them for unknown reasons but with undeniably Evil intent.

The Wildmen may have been using primitive weapons, but they were still weapons. Weapons—even simple rocks—could be used as a form of attack, and even one well-placed rock to the skull could result in death or permanent disability. The Angels of Mercy, having once denounced Law Enforcement persistently over the use of deadly force, and fought against every offensive and defensive measure they were known to use, were now face to face with an angry onslaught of maniacal strangers who were determined to attack them even though they were both helpless and harmless.

It must have occurred to them somewhere in their mind that these were people that had once been Citizens of These United States. But the savages running toward them now were nothing like the civilized men they had always known, and nothing in their soft lives could have prepared them for such ruthlessness.

FORTY-SIX - TIMESTAMP 9-15

Timestamp: 9

The New Arrivals were now among those that had shared their same values; they were among their Fellow Ex-Citizens, people that were just like themselves, having chosen criminality rather than simply obeying the Laws of the Land. There were countless Ex-Citizens now living in Alaska that had willingly chosen Exile because of their political beliefs, who believed that Human Beings should be able to End Lives through Suicide, Abortion, and Euthanasia without consequence.

They were surrounded by everyone that shared their sentiments regarding the pressures of a law-abiding society, who rejected the steep demands of living within a culture that believed in the good of the whole more than the needs and whims of the individual. They were among all those that had gambled and lost, waged war with their government, refused to comply and conform, and had chosen to do as they pleased regardless of the legality.

It should have been a homecoming; a true meeting of the minds. The New Arrivals were among like-minded individuals at long last. These were their comrades, another group who believed the government was their enemy, who shared their anti-Law Enforcement sentiments.

So why had they been so afraid?

I knew the answer, and while part of me was deeply disturbed by what I was watching unfold, I also understood that life was full of choices, and any man worth his weight in salt should have enough integrity to hold firm to his convictions.

There was great irony to be found within this situation, and it was not something I ever failed to forget, even as I felt sorry for those who were about to become Victims in their own right.

Timestamp: 10

  The battle for survival over possessions, Human Life, and the end of Innocence began with a flurry of Violent Attacks, the grabbing of backpacks, the handmade weapons made from sticks, rocks, animal bones and teeth, and the primal response that happened when the only law of the land became Survival of the Fittest.

  They tore at their clothing, stole their shoes and coats, and pulled their backpacks from their bodies. The Have Nots easily overpowered the Haves, and those that had done without for so long demonstrated that they would go to any lengths just to get the barest of necessities whenever opportunity presented itself. There was no room for compassion, Humanity, sharing, or morality; there was only survival, and those that had less did not usually survive for long.

  The men that had raced up the hill may have been wild animals, but they were also Survivors; they were the ones that understood that in order to last in a world where there were no rules, one must be prepared to do whatever must be done. There was nothing to stop them. Just as those that were willing to take what they wanted knew it, so, too, did the New Arrivals realize almost instantaneously that there was no one to call, and no one would be coming to their aid. The world of Emergency Response was gone.

  And then the final part that always occurred in some capacity or another whether there were women or not. In a land where men had committed 90% of the Crime and Violence, those that were Exiled were almost exclusively male. More priceless than all the backpacks, food rations, winter boots, or hydration packets, were females.

  The women were swarmed by the men ascending the hill, none of them even remotely strong enough to fight back against their attackers, though they tried. They never seemed to understand that Rape was a way of life for the savage animal; the only thing throughout history that had ever prevented women from being Sexually Assaulted at whim was the presence of Good Men. They alone were responsible for creating societies in which women were respected, revered, exalted, and provided with equality. Without them, only primal instinct and power prevailed.

  The New Arrivals were outnumbered 30 to 1 easily, and none of them were known to be trained in any form of self-defense or any type of martial arts beyond the basic courses required in all public schools. It was not enough, however, to protect themselves against hordes of filthy men who were all capable and willing to rape and participate in gang rapes.

  The lack of weapons and recent self-defense training was a combination that would be to the detriment of every young woman on the plateau.

  Female New Arrivals would get used to it soon enough—or they would find a way to End their Lives. For the women, Alaska was made infinitely more dangerous not because of the carnivorous animals, but because of the men.

  On many occasions, the female New Arrivals were savaged right on the landing site, but for this Drop, the Wildmen were forced to contend with a full Transport, and they had no clear way of knowing if any of them posed a legitimate threat. The Wildmen did not have an easy victory this time as a few of the men were brave enough to try and help the women. There was not much of a physical challenge to be found; men that had been living off the lands in the Alaskan wilderness were easily able to overpower the soft urbanites that had spent their entire lives living in relative ease in a First World nation.

Several of the men from the Transport were so effeminate that they, too, became targets for the men; homosexuality was not uncommon, nor a socially condemnable offense. The long nights and winters made all manner of companionship both desired and required. Unfortunately for many of the New Arrivals, however, it also meant delicate men were subjugated and often claimed as prizes regardless of their personal sexual preferences. Sexual conquest and gratification were driving components among the more primitive Wildmen, and standards were low.

The females were always the most prized, and they were ranked on value based on their looks much as they always had been throughout the history of the world. But in the wild, when there were no social constraints, laws, or Human Rights, and when everyone understood that there would be no consequences for their actions, Rape was as commonplace as consensual sex and Murder—all of which was as free-flowing as the blood of the weak.

There was more fighting between the Wildmen as they fought for ownership over the best women; getting a good woman as a captive was frequently worth the risk of dying, and these women were all young—under thirty, in a state of shock, meek, and helpless. We watched as the New Arrivals struggled against their Assailants, fought to hold on to their backpacks, and gave everything within themselves as they attempted to preserve their sexual autonomy, none of which would have been possible for any of them to hold on to for long. It was a brutal display of depredation by the heathen marauders that valued nothing and feared no one.

It could not be considered much of a battle when one side was outnumbered, unprepared, untrained, and inherently weaker than the other. They had been fish in a barrel, there for the taking, and the Wildmen had been doing the exact same thing after every Drop for a very long time already.

The New Arrivals had scattered as soon as they saw the Wildmen emerge over the hilltop. They had scrambled to find something to protect themselves, and desperately searched for some means to help them escape the impending doom coming for them. Many ran away from the battle, racing toward the northern edge of the plateau, half-running, half-sliding down the back hill, eventually finding safety once they reached the woods. Chivalry was for the brave and foolish. Sometimes it was smarter to assess the odds, be grateful you were not a woman, and live to fight another day. Such urbanites were no heroes; they were college kids from a comfortable world filled with soft-handed lifestyles and First World amenities.

When it came down to it, the men were ill-equipped to handle the environment on their own, let alone play the role of valiant knight for the females they had arrived with. Had the females spent any time considering things, it was highly improbable that any of them had expected much from the men by way of protection. And in the end, when it came time to stay and help the women or flee, the most cowardly among them had run for their lives when they knew there was no hope for survival otherwise.

Even though they had spent their lives disparaging the 'harsh' Criminal Justice system of America as being too severe and unjust for the Criminal Class, they opted for self-preservation over gallantry every single time. The realities of Crime and Violence were far more brutal and threatening once they were in the muck themselves.

Timestamp: 11

Daegan Kyl had pulled Willow Amos quickly and quietly toward the back of the group the instant he had set eyes on the approaching horde cresting the side of the hill. He grabbed her by her arm and immediately put her behind him while he backed away from the group and distanced himself from the impending Assault.

The Wildmen ascending the hill had come from the southern side, and based on that, we could see Daegan Kyl trying to figure out his route of egress from the backside of the hill without being able to see what lay beyond the edge. It was a dangerous gamble to put himself and his ward into a corner without knowing the odds; he was smart enough to know that it could have been a sheer cliff from every direction except the one they had all ascended. Logically, he had to know it to be a strong possibility—why else had they all come from the same direction rather than circling them? He continued to back away from the crowd, his dominant hand extended as he held his hunting knife, shielding Willow Amos safely behind him with his other arm. She complied without question.

Everything the New Arrivals had tried to do by staying grouped together instantaneously vanished as panic set in. The Wildmen were forced to signal out specific prey and then pursue; the New Arrivals had scattered, losing all protection from being near one another or working as a cohesive unit for defense. Now, they scurried around toward the east, west, and northern sides of the plateau, as far and fast as they could manage, with no other goal than to escape the threat quickly coming at them from the south. They had nothing but blind chance and luck. For many, their gravest fears were realized as they hit the sheer drops from the cliffside and knew as the Wildmen zeroed in on them that escape was a lost cause.

One female, a dark-haired girl with her hair in a pixie cut, tall and rail-thin, found herself at the edge, caught herself just in time, and then turned around to retreat only to find herself surrounded by the foulest men she had probably ever encountered. Her choices may have been slight, but she still had a choice. And so, she chose, opting for one final glorious swan dive into the rocks and creek bed below. She knew Death would be the end result. It was a fifty- or sixty-foot drop at the very least; too far to survive, too narrow of a passage of water to have been anything more than a creek, leaving Death as the only certainty. She knew what her fate would be otherwise, and with perhaps one of the most graceful examples of free will, she looked at the men, looked over the edge once more, and then leapt with all her might. It was a moment that caught me so off-guard I held my breath, strangely awed by the power of her decision.

Daegan Kyl and Willow Amos had been noticed by the Wildmen at long last, and they were being targeted by some that appeared to be among the largest and most rabid. Some just had a love for Violence and enjoyed the sport of it; they assessed Daegan Kyl and found him enough of a threat to be a worthy challenge. Willow Amos, having been standing behind Daegan Kyl, moved herself slightly so they were back-to-back.

They needed to secure some type of weapon for Willow Amos to use.

There were plenty of homemade weapons lying around, discarded, forgotten, and lost as the Wildmen carried out their raid, but none close enough for either to grab. They continued to retreat away from the men, backing slowly as Daegan Kyl held his arms up, knife poised, ready for combat.

The men were smiling, embracing the challenge. You could almost see the wheels turning as they imagined the goods they could get if they could take everything from Daegan Kyl's dead corpse—fresh clothes, a shiny new blade, and a backpack loaded with potential, considerably larger than the others.

Off to the left, the larger man noticed one of the females still putting up a good fight and defending herself. Her shirt had been ripped open, exposing a plain bra underneath. It revealed enough flesh to make the two men redirect their attention away from Daegan Kyl and focus on the man trying to pin the girl to the ground.

The larger man—the one that had been smiling at Daegan Kyl—picked up a rock from the ground and struck the would-be Rapist over the head with it, bashing the front of his skull in, and causing blood and grey matter to fly out and land all over the girl below. She screamed, and upon his instant death, tried to push him off so she could escape. This was not to be her fate, however, as the large man grabbed her by the hair violently and began trying to drag her away from the area.

The other man had no intention of losing her to the first man—even if that first man had been the one to kill her would-be Rapist. The two men began fighting. The larger of the Wildmen was doing his best against the second man, but struggled, refusing to lose hold of his prize. He had her restrained tightly against him, her hair wrapped around his hand. She was forced down into a kneeling position as he fought off the advances of the second man, her shirt still hanging open where it had been torn. She struggled against his every move, desperately working to free her hair from his hand by using all her strength to pry his fingers loose, but nothing was working.

The girl was finally dragged around and pulled to her feet by the Wildman. She was facing Willow Amos, and she cried out to her, begging, and pleading with her to help.

Willow Amos grabbed Daegan Kyl's arm to get his attention; he had been focused on attackers approaching from the other side, but he glanced over at the girl Willow Amos was motioning to. He couldn't do much against two hardened warriors while trying to protect one girl and free another. Nonetheless, he did his best to intervene.

He made eye contact with the girl and her eyes acknowledged his presence; she knew he was going to help her.

Within another moment, the second Wildman lunged at the one holding her hair.

The man jumped out of the way to avoid the sharpened spear, not realizing he had pulled the girl directly into his path. The long blade plunged into the girl's back, piercing through her front side enough to show the tip protruding from the breast area above her bra. The shock on her face registered with pain. She tried to look downward, quickly succumbing to her injury. She fell limp to the ground, landing on her knees.

The first man that had been holding her by the back of her hair felt the tug on his arm as the weight of her body plummeted forward, and as he looked back to see what it was, he realized the second man had pierced his prize, destroying any chance for either of them to have her. He let go of her hair instantly, and her body fell forward onto the ground.

Daegan Kyl and Willow Amos stood transfixed; it had happened in a flash of time—before he could reach her, before he could help her, before he could intervene. He had watched her expression change from relief when she knew he was coming to help her, to instant pain and shock when she was pierced from behind. She had died staring at him; he was the last person she had made eye contact with.

These were the men who had only been Exiled; they weren't even Convicted Rapists or Murderers—all of whom would have been Executed. These weren't even supposed to have been the worst Criminals within our nation.

Nearby, another Wildman slashed through a much smaller man with a long, handmade blade somehow fashioned out of scrap metal and a wooden handle. The skinny man fell to the ground, the large man-made machete still stuck in his head. Having secured his prize, he grabbed a brown-haired girl by her hair and began dragging her back through the crowd toward the southern slope, pulling her aggressively by the arm as she tried to resist at every turn.

She tried to grab hold of a different Wildman that was in the fold, causing the man to see the young woman clinging to him. In a second, he had grabbed the slender woman by her arm. In a single motion, the man that had been pulling her toward the edge of the landing site turned around to see why she had stopped moving and was met with the axe of the second man crashing into his skull. As he fell over, the woman screamed. The second Wildman, now having secured the young woman for his own, grabbed her by her long hair as she attempted to flee, smashed his fist into her face, and then caught her limp body as she fell, throwing her over his shoulder and descending the edge of the grassy hill.

Daegan Kyl and Willow Amos had almost cleared the field; they were near the edge. She reached down and grabbed not only a handmade blade from the head of a dead man, but also several other handmade bags, a belt, and what appeared to be a bow and arrow that had been over his shoulder. Daegan Kyl stood guard in a defensive position, watching the swarms of people around him and glancing down occasionally to watch Willow Amos as she shifted the dead man around and robbed him of all his earthly possessions. It was impossible to see what she had managed to take from the corpse, but in a land where every provision was an asset, nothing could be left behind.

When she was done, the two began to ease slowly away from the crowd with their backs toward one another. Willow Amos held tight to the long blade, holding it as she would a sword. She held another blade in her other hand, no more than eight inches long at best; another trophy from the corpse that would serve them well if they managed to escape the hillside.

A man noticed Daegan Kyl and looked away, but then his face shot back toward him once he noticed the oversized man was trying to shield a much smaller female behind him.

Daegan Kyl himself was a towering 6'4", well above average and easily able to hold his own against any of the Wildmen. But even a beast of a man like Daegan Kyl would be overwhelmed by a large group, and Willow Amos, although by no means an attractive or feminine woman in any normal situation, was still alive and able to be used for sex—and that was all that was required for the Wildman to consider her a prize worth potentially losing his life for.

The Wildman lunged toward Daegan Kyl, trying to force him to lose his footing, probably hoping the weight of his pack would destabilize him and give the Wildman a much-needed advantage. The man clawed at Daegan Kyl, grabbing hold of his shoulder, trying to land any blows he could.

The two men fought, almost equal in size and build, the Wildman covered in fur scraps with long hair and a full beard contrasting sharply against the man who was still dressed in contemporary, fashionable clothing. Daegan Kyl had been well-trained in hand-to-hand combat and was capable of giving what he got. But he was also trying to be discreet and handle his opponent without straying too far away from his companion.

Switching his hunting knife into his less dominant hand, Daegan Kyl tried to shove the Wildman backward, away from him. The heavy layers of fur worn by the Wildman seemed to be protecting him from serious injury. Despite his knife being ineffective against the thick layers of fur, he managed to get several well-placed hard punches that landed along the barbarian's ribs, with a few more undercuts to his jaw.

The Wildman was not going down without a fight, though, and he was hungry for a good brawl if it ended with a young woman as his trophy.

The Wildman freed his right arm and pushing his furs aside, pulled a long, homemade sword from the leather band tied around his middle. He struggled to lift the unruly blade up, but the act of doing so had uncovered his entire waist area.

His fur open and his body exposed, Daegan Kyl switched his hunting blade back to his other hand and thrust it into the Wildman's midsection, right below his ribcage. The man immediately froze, dropped his weapon, and clutched his middle before falling to the ground.

From somewhere beside me I could hear Grace let out a gasp.

Daegan Kyl, the man that had not been incriminated in any manner for having caused Harm to a single Victim, a man that had not been determined to have shed one ounce of blood on US soil, had just stabbed a man in self-defense while trying to protect Willow Amos from the unimaginable.

The calm, confident actions in which Daegan Kyl had responded only served as evidence to support that taking Human Life during combat was nothing unfamiliar to him.

They did not have long to waste; the hills were still flooded with Wildmen.

Just as she had done before, Willow Amos reached down around the man that had fallen, and picked the long sword up from the ground. From there, she took everything of value from his person.

Daegan Kyl wiped the man's blood from his blade along his sleeve.

Looking around one last time from their hilltop vantage point, they backed another twenty yards down the hill toward the north discreetly, still positioned defensively to guard one another's backs. Before long, they were out of sight and earshot of the landing entirely.

They raced down the rest of the slope as it leveled out, finally reaching the woods, and disappeared beyond our sight.

Timestamp: 12

Eventually, the New Arrivals were defeated; some dead, some dying, some merely rendered unconscious. Not all the New Arrivals had been subjected to the initial attack, and some had escaped entirely, including Daegan Kyl and Willow Amos. By the end, most of the women had been dragged off by groups of rogue men, kicking and screaming. Others were knocked unconscious and carried over the shoulder of their captor, some bound by the hands and led with a rope around their necks.

We knew—from what little research that had been done—the women were usually bought and sold, used, traded for supplies, and forced to endure endless Sexual Assaults. It was unimaginable, but it should not have been surprising. This had been a successful hunt for the Wildmen; they had even collected a handful of soft, young men. Tonight, there would be much to celebrate.

The women who were already living among the men in the encampment were quick to turn a blind eye to the heinous vulgarity and abuses directed at the most innocent among them. Years of Sexual Assault and powerlessness had made them grateful to decrease their own risk for such events whenever possible, even if it came at the expense of newer, fresher meat. It was a land where being considered elderly, ugly, or undesirable seldom offered protection from Rapists; the shortage of women made *any* option a viable option. The only reprieve against the Sexual Abuse was directly following Drops carrying New Arrivals. Shameful or not, they were grateful for the respite.

The wilderness destroyed Humanity incrementally, even for those who still clung to a world they once remembered. The new realities they were required to adapt to in order to survive served as yet another reminder that we were all just one horrific experience, or period of hardship, away from losing ourselves and the person we believed ourselves to be. I did not begrudge any of the women who had already been living in that environment their role in such events, nor blame them for finding relief when they could—even when they knew it came at someone else's expense.

Any Soldier would speak of his desire for a clean Death by the hand of a worthy opponent; no one ever speaks of the slow Death brought about by the scars caused by Sexual Predators and a lifetime of victimization. Women were always classified as Survivors for enduring what they have been subjected to at the hands of men; they should have been regarded as Warriors, for any that could carry on after all they had survived were, without a doubt, the most valiant among us.

I would have gone down fighting before I was ever led down a hill in chains to be passed around from vermin to vermin. Anyone who could truly condemn Suicide had never lived in the worst conditions Humanity could create. It may not be morally right, it may not be honorable, and it may indeed be selfish to do it, but I would fall on my own sword before letting any of those men do to me what they were doing—and I would End the Life of the woman I loved, or my mother, or the life of my sweet sister—before allowing them to be taken.

In a land devoid of laws, there was no metric defining what was lawful or unlawful. All that remained was one's internal moral code, and for many, it was defunct. They had only ended up in such a world because of their refusal to abide by the Laws of the Land of These United States.

Exile was the consequence of their choices.

Still, it was difficult to believe that any of these New Arrivals were deserving of so harsh a fate, especially the young women and what the future likely had in store for them.

Timestamp: 13

It had been the most shocking Drop I'd ever experienced, and by the silence in the room, I was not the only one that thought so.

They had secured at least twenty new backpacks, give or take, and at least seven or eight new women had survived.

As the satellite pulled to a higher camera angle, hundreds of men and women could be seen throughout their encampment. They danced and celebrated around blazing bonfires. It was a victorious night, with a substantial pay-out for their labors.

At the top of the hillside lay the freshly Deceased remains of at least a handful of Angels of Mercy, struck down within moments of their arrival. Along with the Deceased New Arrivals lay at least a dozen Wildmen, almost guaranteed to have been killed by their own kind in attempts to get possession of either women or the new backpacks.

Before long, more roving Wildmen would return to the hilltop to loot the remains of the Deceased, stripping their clothing from their naked corpses, clearing them of all their earthly possessions, taking anything of value, and using whatever they did not want for either trade or as currency—often to buy sex from another Wildman's captive. There were reports that nothing was wasted, especially during the winter Drops. Though unconfirmed, cannibalism was not unheard of when the snows grew deep and hunting became too difficult for men that had always looked for the easy way out.

There had been surveillance footage that showed the Wildmen had secured the means to create various types of fermented liquors, and there were plenty of wild plants such as marijuana and mushrooms to keep them entertained long into the night, especially with new women.

Back in America, a small handful of Citizens still advocated on behalf of those Exiled. They protested their Banishments, referred to their deportations as 'violations of Human Rights', and believed they were only committing crimes because of various economic and societal disadvantages. They believed them to be victims of circumstance and deserving of second chances.

Soon enough, each one of these New Arrivals would be forced to evaluate their new world and contrast it to the one they surrendered. And when one took away all the elitism, sanctimonious lectures, and moral superiority, all that would be left was their desire for self-preservation.

This was the world without the Rule of Law.

This was what it truly meant to live in a society where there were no social constraints keeping Human Beings in line, and no fear of consequences to prevent people from doing as they pleased. Their lawlessness, Violence, and aggression reflected their true nature and morality; what was being illustrated was the stark reality of primal nature without the self-deception of civility and optimism influencing our beliefs.

This was what it meant to live in a society where there were no heroes, and no one to call when you were facing Dangerous, Evil, Violent Predators.

A world without heroes was a world without hope. A world without Law and Order was not a world worth trying to survive in.

It was a costly lesson for many people.

Timestamp: 14

In perhaps the only true deliverance of Justice, the Citizens of These United States had discarded the worst among them and thrown them to the wolves with the same remarkable cold indifference, callousness, and lack of compassion that the Convicted Offenders had typically shown to their own Victims.

Were their Crimes worth this punishment? It wasn't my place to say—and I challenged anyone who said it was theirs. The only thing that mattered was that there were laws which were intended to be followed, and consequences for breaking them. The Angels of Mercy had made their choice. The question wasn't about whether the laws were right or wrong, just or unjust, fair or unfair. The Laws of the Land had been approved by the Citizens. We were either a nation of laws, or a Godless, lawless society; we did not have the choice as individuals to decide which laws were worth following and which we chose to cast aside.

The Angels of Mercy had discovered that they couldn't start a revolution with a smoldering ember and then not expect to pay the price of admission once they had been found responsible. If they wanted to change the laws, they first needed to change society—and ultimately it required ideas and values that would improve the nation, not worsen it. All this had proven to me was that these people were not what I wanted my nation to be made of, and while I was quite willing to acknowledge that there were endless variations in the shades of grey, Citizens were still either fundamentally Good or fundamentally Evil. And those who were Evil were unfit—and undeserving—to live among us.

If there were any doubts as to how 'fair' that might seem, we only had to refer to the young women that had lost their lives at the hands of such Evil Predators. One of them had taken a swan dive to her Death rather than submit to their vile Assault—but these were supposed to be Exiled Ex-Citizens who hadn't even been Convicted of Rape or Murder. The actions by the Wildmen that had attacked the New Arrivals had all been conducted by lesser-Convictions, the supposedly 'non-violent' Offenders of These United States.

How could one possibly expect our weakest, most vulnerable, and Innocent Citizens to co-exist with such putrid, broken vermin? I could no more understand how any of these Angels of Mercy had promoted their ideological values than I could fathom how their like-minded 'comrades' from generations past had pushed for 'Criminal Justice Reform' that only weakened the laws and benefited the Criminal Class. It was a dangerous platform that had repeatedly proven to defile the Sanctity of Human Life and caused the unequivocally unnecessary Brutal Violence, Raping, and Murdering of millions of our Fellow Citizens throughout the history of These United States.

I would let a million Angels of Mercy die just as they did today if it meant our nation was free of the toxic anti-humanitarianism that ripped apart our fundamental Right To Life and ability to live as free Americans safely within our nation. These people hadn't promoted 'free will'—they had promoted the Right To Die. Everything they promoted resulted in the End-of-Life campaign; that's not how we would ever glorify the Divine Gift we had been given, and without being able to exemplify how special and unique each Human Life truly was, how could we ever hope to create and sustain a culture in which all Human Life was considered Sacred and worth Protecting? How could one profess to love Humanity if one were constantly promoting ways to end it and trying to project it as 'free will'? There was nothing less free than being dead, and yet everything these people had done had been with the intent to End Human Life.

The Deaths we had observed today were tragic. Watching any Human Being suffer needlessly—especially at the hands of our Fellow Man—was always difficult. It was an awful thing to recognize, knowing that the young women they had dragged off were going to be Raped repeatedly and treated with appalling disregard.

But were their lives any more valuable than that of Katarina? Arlan? Rebecca? Mariam? Had they contributed more to society—would their contributions have been any more meaningful? Who among us could dictate the value, or lack of value, of another Human Being's life? Who among us then could decide when it should end or how?

No, I was not immune to the philosophical debate of it all, and I would not profess to being firmly planted on either side of the debate entirely. It was far too complex for a simple man such as me.

The one thing I knew for certain was that our nation needed the Rule of Law, and without it…We would be exactly like what we had just observed, and that was not a world I wanted to live in.

I wanted to live in Peace, Safety, and Security. I wanted my Loved Ones to be able to sleep at night and know that they were safe.

And I wanted them to know that even if we couldn't keep the nation entirely free of Violence that there were men such as myself out there keeping the wolves at bay. Even if we couldn't ensure that every Evildoer and savage animal was caught before they ever Caused Harm, we were doing our best. And with our current laws, there was no question that statistically, every American was infinitely safer than at any other point in history.

Maybe we couldn't ever put an end to all of it, but we could set the odds in our favor by establishing effective laws designed to protect the Citizens rather than the Violent Offenders.

Maybe it wasn't ever going to be possible to eradicate Evil entirely.

I could accept that—but only if I knew we were always going to continue doing everything we could to fight against it.

It was not a battle, but a war—and it was a war that could never be fought alone. Peacekeepers, lawmakers, and Soldiers were the only true hope for ever maintaining a safe, non-violent society, and firm Criminal Justice was the only proven deterrent for preventing Crime and Acts of Violence. Out of all the components—free Citizens, a government which served the People, lawmakers, and Peacekeepers, the one element that was guaranteed to improve society was the absence of known criminals. They were the only unnecessary demographic. They were the part of our world that always made everything worse, not better, no matter where they were. And if we already knew and understood this, why was there any debate about why they should be allowed among us when we knew they only brought pain and suffering?

Timestamp: 15

I stood up and stretched; the video would be over any time, and it had been a long day.

"Wait!" It was Grace.

I looked up at her. She was pointing toward the camera, one hand over her mouth again.

I looked toward the screen and noticed the satellite had been moving toward the hilltop once more. Two people had been quietly making their way back up to the landing site from the northern side. It was Daegan Kyl and Willow Amos.

Smart.

I was genuinely surprised to see them again, but it was something that had I considered it, I would have expected from Daegan Kyl. His experiences within the military would have taught him to seize any opportunities that presented themselves and to take advantage of every resource available. They must have hidden in the woods, waiting quietly until they were certain everyone was gone. Given their proximity to the encampment, they might have been close enough to hear all the revelries, even if they couldn't see over the southern slope.

It was getting dark, and their movements were becoming more difficult to see. But they traveled well together, only carrying weapons. The rest of the gear they had collected had been left somewhere in the wooded area.

They crouched low, keeping near the ground so no one in the community could spot them down at the bottom of the hill. They stopped by the man Daegan Kyl had stabbed. We watched as he felt his neck to see if he could feel a pulse, and then hung his head a little as he motioned to Willow that he had not survived.

Willow was unmoved. The man had, after all, intended to kill Daegan Kyl and Rape her.

She bent toward the man and began taking off his fur coat. He had a long jacket that had been stitched together with strips of leather at the sleeves. When secured with the belt, it would fit Daegan Kyl well, keeping him warm at least until they got their bearings. Seeing what she was doing, he reluctantly helped her roll the man over so they could remove it.

They found several additional bags connected to the belt he wore that held up his makeshift pants and took those as well. The man had made leather shin-guards that were tied on with long leather straps around his lower legs. It took a moment, but she left nothing to waste, gaining materials that could be used for a multitude of things down the road.

Willow's light clothing began to glow more against the darkening sky. Daegan Kyl, noticing this, searched through the bodies until he found another Wildman with a fur coat like the one he had just acquired. He motioned for Willow to cover herself with it as he quietly and efficiently ransacked the man's clothing and then took the large leather bag that had been lying next to him. It was clearly almost a foot too long for her, but it would do for now. Even though it was only late September, they were still in Alaska, and the seasons would change soon enough. The long fur coat would provide warmth, cover, and extra material for them down the road.

We watched as they looted the remains of each of the bodies that had fallen on the hilltop, checking the pulses of each of them as they proceeded. One of the Wildmen seemed to still be alive, and in a bizarre moment of Humanity, we watched Willow Amos use some of her nursing skills to bandage a man's apparently broken wrist while Daegan Kyl applied pressure to a knife wound in his shoulder before they used the jacket from one of the Deceased as a bandage and wrap for his wound.

It was only after looking closer did I realize the Deceased man they had removed the jacket from was Detective Jarrett. It was just as well that he had been taken out of his misery right at the beginning. Aside from it being a terrifying environment for most Citizens, he would have been targeted mercilessly as soon as any of the New Arrivals let it be known that he was a former Peacekeeper. The other New Arrivals might not have done anything too Violent toward him, but the hordes of Wildmen would have destroyed him—and it would have been done slowly and painfully. He wouldn't have had a prayer before someone had sold him out; he would have been blackmailed and extorted at the very least, and would have felt vulnerable, afraid, and paranoid until the bitter end.

They found several backpacks that had been concealed by fallen Wildmen. A pretty blonde had gotten stabbed and had bled out not five feet away from the group of men that had all Died fighting each other over her.

Willow Amos had paused over her body for a moment, and even in the dusk, it was easy to see by her emotions that she was saddened by her Death more so than any other. She held the petite blonde girl's hand for a moment, kissed her friend goodbye, and then took her shoes and socks from her body.

Daegan Kyl had watched in silence; all other bodies had been looted for their valuables. The blonde girl had a pair of shoes that would be necessary for Willow Amos down the road; this was their reality.

In another surprising act of unexpected compassion, Willow Amos seemed to express both Sorrow and Remorse over the condition of her comrade and friend. Her shoulders were bent forward and shook slightly as she cried. The full measure of her actions that had let each of her companions to this point had at long last set in as she realized how much each of them could eventually be forced to pay.

Watching her, Daegan Kyl then looked over in the direction of the encampment and seemed to sense it was time to go.

He moved toward Willow Amos, wrapped several bags of newly gained loot over her shoulders, wiped a tear away with the backside of his hand, and made a motion for her to be quiet by placing a finger to his lips.

She nodded her head and began creeping back down the north side of the hill, back toward the woods.

Daegan Kyl bent down and picked up the slight frame of the little blonde woman, cradled her in his arms as if he were carrying a small child off to bed, and followed Willow Amos back down the hill toward the woods.

We watched them until they faded back into the trees again, this time for good.

The live feed ended, and the room became completely silent.

Although we could never know, we understood; the gravedigger would bury another Victim tonight.

PART TEN

The purposes of a person's heart are deep waters,
but one who has insight draws them out.

Proverbs 20:5

FORTY-SEVEN – AFTER A CASE IS CLOSED

Traveling by Train

Anytime I accepted a case on the East Coast, I didn't mind the flight out because time was of the essence, and I understood that. But on the route home, I could secure some downtime, and the old, noisy trains made of sweat and steel were my guilty pleasure. There was a phenomenal transcontinental bullet train, but I preferred to take one of the antiquated ones. Although it took some extra time, it was a wonderful system of travel, allowing me to appreciate just how diverse and beautiful our countryside truly was. There was something to be said for slowing down and going back to the days of Sunday drives.

They reminded me of the history of our nation, the hard-won labors, and ambitions of men long before my own birth. The construction of the transcontinental railway had been a time when the entire nation had rallied together and followed the news of advancement and achievement. It had united us under one glorious, lofty goal of progress and pride—very similar to other points in history where we all celebrated the positives rather than focused on the negatives, such as when we as Americans had put our men on the moon. It exemplified times of prosperity and national pride, and reminded me of Fourth of July parades, fireworks displays, and days spent at the local county fairs.

I loved to see and imagine bygone days when our nation had been united under one flag, collectively dreaming together of ways to build a better future rather than being divided. It was a more optimistic way to think of my nation, of who we were as a People, and to concentrate on all that brought us together rather than that which kept us from connecting with those whom we disagreed. Our diversity had often made co-existence difficult, and we lived like a dysfunctional couple needing divorce, creating wreckage, damage, and chaos in our wake. For too much of our nation's history, our Citizens had lived under dueling political parties and identity politics, allowing our differences to divide us rather than remind us we were still one national community.

The trains helped me forget about all that; they reminded me instead of one of the chapters in history where we had gainful employment for all walks of life, and we were a nation dedicated to recovering after our Civil War. It had been a time when we had worked together to build something tremendous for our future, knowing that, as Americans, we would all benefit from our efforts. We knew then, no matter what our race or background, that our contributions were important; that our blood, sweat, and tears would be poured into each railway tie that was laid on the ground at our feet. We The People knew that only by our own willingness to commit to the task at hand that we would see the fruits of our labor become something awe-inspiring and nationally transformative. Our ancestors knew that only by the Will of God could we create something so dramatically progressive that it could alter our entire way of life, forever transforming and improving our previous existence. The building of the railroad was a tremendous feat of accomplishment for our country.

They had manipulated us into believing that times of war and crisis were the only things that unified the People. I was willing to concede that to some extent, however, it was true. The airplanes that crashed into the two towers in New York City on September 11, 2001, were a testament to how well we could unite under tragedy, how we could all set aside our differences and come together to help fight for each other and one common goal—and against one common enemy.

But we as a People could also come together for things that were positive and good as well; it was why we took pride in the landmarks that graced our cities. It was why Seattle prized the Space Needle during the years it had stood before it was destroyed, as well as the Eiffel Tower and the Statue of Liberty. Before the Terrorists had decimated them, they had been iconic landmarks that had represented our countries. They were symbols of prosperity and unity; symbols that had united our nations and Citizens.

Our People had united during 'world expos'. For generations, we had shared our national pride during the events known as the Olympics, where our countries would all meet together in harmony to compete against one another in hundreds of athletic events. It was important to remember the things that showed us what we had in common rather than what divided us and kept us from all being Human together.

I loved ending my cases with the train rides for these reasons and more. It was probably the main reason I preferred working cases on the East Coast rather than the West, but if I were honest with myself, I knew it was more than just that. Working cases on the East Coast meant that all the horrors I was constantly knee deep in were all in larger cities, areas that had always had worse Crime than the smaller, more rural places. It meant that the Hate and the Violence were still exactly where they had always been. If it was confined to the East Coast and the larger cities like those in southern California, at least I knew it was far away from where I lived.

It meant that the Hate and Rage that could destroy a nation was far away from my parents, my siblings and their spouses, their children, and everyone else that we loved. As long as I knew I had to travel far distances to do my job, it meant that the ugliness was not in my backyard, that my Loved Ones were safe from Harm, that the wolf was not at the door.

I wanted things to stay as they were, for time to stop during this period in history, and for Crime rates to remain low. I wanted my nation to stay as it was rather than decline into chaos and fear again. I wanted for Americans to live in a place and time when virtually everyone was safe, where children could play outside until the streetlights came on without fear or supervision; where little girls could practice riding their bikes in church parking lots and didn't have to worry about being Abducted and then Suffer unimaginably before eventually Dying.

Would that I could, I would halt time before the world shifted for the worse once again. Only those who grew up when we were allowed to be children first and High-Risk Victims second could know what it meant to feel truly safe. If I could, I would wish for the means to show everyone what such a world could be like if we would only do what must be done to obtain it. I knew—just as so many others who were raised in times and places of safety and low Crime rates—that it was possible that we could live in peace together. We could provide good lives and futures to all our children and Loved Ones if we only worked together to keep the wolves at bay and ensure that the savages among us were contained and eradicated.

More than anything, I wished I could impart to my Fellow Citizens how important it was that we Protect the Innocent and the Weak rather than subscribing to the disturbingly misguided and ill-formed beliefs that we should focus on the Rights of Violent Predators. If it were possible, I would show them the world I had seen, the broken hearts I had been exposed to, the hundreds of weeping mothers and fathers, brothers and sisters, husbands and wives, and the cries of the children who had all lost their Loved One because of Acts of Violence.

I would do everything possible to help my Fellow Man understand just how unfair the Losses were to our society, how unfair it was that we allowed such Predators the opportunities we did when we knew who and what they were. We knew what the signs were and knew if we did nothing, it was only a matter of time before they acted on their compulsions. I would eradicate the poison that I felt growing just below the surface, and I would unite my country against the one true common enemy we had—that of Evil, and those who would choose to live by it rather than by all that was Good.

But that was all beyond my skill and scope of influence.

All that I could do was my job, to do my best within each case, provide a voice for my Victims, and hopefully deliver Justice on their behalf. The best I could hope for was to find the responsible party for their Death, gather the evidence necessary to Convict, and do everything within my power to ensure that Violent Predators could never walk the streets of my nation again or claim another life through their actions.

I was only one man. But I did, at least, find peace in knowing that there were many others just like me out there. I could take time away from work, not to mention sleep at night, knowing confidently that there were many Peacekeepers out there who lived and breathed their duties and their Oath to Protect and Defend the Sanctity of Human Life just as I did.

The Call from the Chief

I carried my two bags out into the parking garage to my bike in preparation for the ride home. I fit one inside the locked box attached to the rear and strapped the other down on the seat behind me. Since I had only been a few hours from home I had traveled light and had sent a third duffle bag back home internally through the SPD. It was dry tonight and I intended to ride home, although it was considerably cooler now than when I had arrived more than three months earlier.

I intended to let my local Chief in Olympia know I was going to take the time off when I checked in with him. I hadn't seen my parents for several months despite only being a few hours away. My parents were expecting me for dinner Sunday night which gave me plenty of time to get back home and settled. Life had continued on without me in my absence, but I had missed them and was looking forward to seeing everyone again. It had been a long case.

If traffic was reasonable, I could be home by dusk.

My phone vibrated in my front pocket. Pulling it free, I saw it was the Chief. Answering the call, I heard the Chief asking if I was on the freeway yet.

"No Sir," I responded. "Just leaving the home garage."

"Well, don't get too comfortable. I'm sending you an address. I'll be waiting."

The call ended abruptly, but immediately buzzed again with a text. The GPS brought up a location along Puget Sound. With southbound traffic, I could be there in about twenty minutes. Not knowing why the Chief was out in the field, I couldn't imagine what he needed from me. But at least I was still moving in the direction of home.

The Designated Location

The sun was setting. My twenty-minute drive was closer to an hour due to everyone trying to return home after a workday.

Pulling off the freeway and finding my way along an old, paved road, I was in an unfamiliar area in an older part of Seattle. I passed run-down buildings and factories with broken windows and industrial smokestacks. I crossed train tracks and followed the navigation onto a dirt road. I wasn't one to spook easily, but this was not the type of place a solitary Peacekeeper should be wandering, especially without a uniform and security visor while on a civilian motorcycle.

The sun finally fell behind the darkening land mass across the water, and as dusk settled, I turned my lights on. The sky was becoming a dark blue. I followed the road for several more miles, encountering no one. The air was bitterly cold, and I could smell the salt from the water. The trees were thickening, and the factories were fading behind me until I could only catch glimpses of them. They were becoming black with shadows, looming all around me, obstructing my view. The narrow dirt road was so heavily blanketed with deep potholes that it was very slow-moving as I made my way along.

At long last, I rounded a final bend in the road and was suddenly in full view of Puget Sound once more. Ahead of me, a field emerged. There were at least a dozen vehicles parked, and although none had their lights on, I could still see well enough that they were all various makes and models of Law Enforcement. There were several transport vans for the SPD Morgue, and I could see an ambulance.

I parked alongside one of the standard white and blue squad cars and got out. I tried to find the Chief among the handful of Officers milling around. I hadn't seen this much congestion outside of a Police Station in a long while. Catching the eye of a Front-Line Officer, I motioned for him. Hustling over, he nodded his head in the direction of the men along the pathway and tossed me a mask.

I made my way along the trail, following random Men in Blue along a mildly trampled pathway through the brush. It would soon be dark. Whatever was up ahead, the night would soon make this walkway more than troublesome. About a quarter of a mile ahead, the brush began to clear out.

There were men standing on the edge of the thicket, almost as sentries along the wall of thorns. One of them tipped his hat to me, casually, although it was very clear he had looked at the badge on my belt.

The thicket of brush suddenly cleared, and I was standing among dozens of men. A beach was directly to my right, and the sound of seagulls was constant. In the distance, I saw the Chief speaking to another man near the water as he stood on a ridge. After walking a few paces further, I realized it was Officer Stanton, hunched over his electronic clipboard and madly taking notes. I couldn't think of a time I'd ever seen a Research Assistant out in the field, let alone at a Crime Scene. I wondered what it meant and why he was here.

As I waited for him to finish speaking, I scanned the surrounding area. Off to my left, random SPD Officers were sporadically moving around the acreage further away from the beachfront. They weren't close enough for me to take stock of what they were doing, but I could see a dozen or so uniforms walking slowly around before occasionally pausing to bend over and then stand upright again.

I glanced back at the Chief. He was still issuing commands to Stanton, and I didn't want to interrupt. I took a few tentative steps in the direction of the Officers out in the field, squinting my eyes to try and see exactly what they were doing in the fading light.

A sudden thought occurred to me, and as I considered it, I found myself moving slowly through the brush more quickly toward them.

I could hear the sound of the waves as they gently lapped against the shore, and the faint hum of people talking in the distance. But as I took each step toward them, watching the way they all seemed to be doing the same motions, a strange sense of foreboding overcame me. One by one, they each took a few steps, then bent over before almost immediately standing once again and then moving on. It had appeared as though they were picking things up off the ground.

But I was wrong.

I looked down at the ground and finally paused to look where I had been walking. Near my feet, nestled among the overgrown weeds and fallen branches, were red flags.

Markers.

Grave markers.

These Officers were placing red flags as grave markers.

I began walking further into the field, watching the ground with each step. Every four or five feet I passed another red flag.

It was incomprehensible.

I made a full circle, slowly taking it all in. I was standing in the middle of a field now covered with red flags, surrounding me as far as the eye could see. It was a graveyard filled with unmarked graves; endless gravesites filled with discarded Physical Remains.

I barely heard the Chief approach me from behind, so quiet were his footsteps.

He stood alongside me in silence. We watched the men move quietly, awkwardly tagging each unmarked grave. At least fifty red flags. At least fifty Human Beings. People that had once lived among us; people that we had Loved and Cherished. Our Fellow Citizens. Our neighbors. Our friends and family. *Who were they? How many had been reported as Missing Persons in the Greater Seattle Area? How many had Detective Jarrett concealed the cases of? How many were children?*

Decaying Bodies, now nothing more than pieces of meat and bones, left to rot and decompose in shallow graves while worms and other insects feasted on them.

Human Beings, discarded without care, thrown away and buried in a hole like garbage in a landfill, lost to us until now.

I thought back to one of my interviews with Willow Amos, her words echoing in my head.

"There have been times when I have used the facilities and Mr. Kyl's rental trucks for my own purposes after hours and without his consent or knowledge."

"Will you stay?" the Chief asked.

We stood there together, he and I, both in horrified sorrow, silently watching as Evil exposed itself yet again.

Several dozen SPD Officers began processing the scene around us, setting up lights, tables, and overhead tents. With diligence, and steadfast professionalism, my Fellow Officers prepared for a long night, and an even longer investigation—the development of a scene which I had watched many times but was never any easier to process. It was impossible to understand how we could live in a world where we required certain members of our society to Protect both the Living and the Dead from other members of their own kind.

As long as I had done this job—and as long as I intended to do it into the future—it did not seem as though I would ever be able to understand why or how we could wantonly choose to Harm another member of our own community.

The Intentional Infliction of Harm Against Another…
Is a Crime Against Humanity and a Crime Against Ourselves.

There would be no rest for now. Hundreds of Law Enforcement, Medical Examiners, Forensic Specialists, Detectives and Criminal Investigators, and Victim Advocacy Agents would not be resting for a long while. There would be no respite from the obligations of this profession as long as there were questions to be answered, Predators to be captured, black market Criminal rings to eradicate, and Innocent Victims and their Grieving Loved Ones to deliver some measure of Peace and Justice to.

In the distance, I saw the familiar form of Grace walking toward us, her head slowly moving around, taking in the magnitude of the scene as she processed it for the first time.

My heart heavy, I watched her approach with sadness.

I nodded my head in greeting, and found myself more than a little choked up, biting back both seething rage as well as overwhelming sorrow.

She searched my face for answers—some type of confirmation that I was invested; compelling me to *do something about this,* knowing that the only thing that would ever stop such Evil was for Good Men to rise against it and destroy it entirely.

Something deep within me knew that everything we had, everything we were, was changing yet again. We had been too apathetic; we had given too much leeway.

This was what happened when the Rule of Law was not respected; when Law Enforcement was not allowed to do what they were trained and paid to do. This was the price our Citizens paid; it was the same price they had always paid for weakness, compassion, political correctness, and apathy. This was what happened when cancer was allowed to spread without careful monitoring and thorough eradication measures implemented once it was detected.

This was what America looked like when the Value of Human Life was diminished, disrespected, and devalued; it became little more than a dumping ground for the bodies of American Citizens.

Assessment, Planning, Departure

Officer Stanton approached me from my left and handed me his electronic clipboard with the Consent Forms I was required to sign indicating that I was accepting the case. I signed each of the marked tabs, not bothering to read the myriad of documents I knew almost by heart. When it came to the page asking if I was bringing my own team, I looked at both Stanton and Grace, already knowing where they stood, and found it reassuring that the Chief had almost physically seemed to breathe a sigh of relief once he knew that we were all committed to the task at hand.

The next page discussed rates and expenditures, and when I got to the signature line, I looked around the field once more before stating, "I'd like each of you to gather your top five—only the best. The ones with the time and dedication to commit. Transfer all their current caseloads to your other staff; we want them exclusively working on these cases."

They nodded their heads once again, and the Chief asked if I was sure five-man teams with a Lead would be sufficient.

I considered the sizes of the teams based on the caseload, each team would comprise of a Research Assistant and a Victim Advocate doing the legwork and reporting to Stanton and Grace, who would then report to me. With each team handling approximately ten Victims, it would be an exceptionally high workload for at least the next three to six months. It was a mountain of work looming ahead of us, but too many chefs in the kitchen wouldn't make our work product any better. We needed our cases to be investigated in small groupings, but with an open line of communication between each team throughout the process.

They looked around the field, weighing out the workload, the amount of research Stanton's Officers would be responsible for, while Grace measured out the time spent with each of the Grieving families, Death Notifications, follow-ups, check-ins, establishing and building relationships, connecting the Bereaved to counseling and additional resources, the random emotional breakdowns by heartbroken Loved Ones, and overseeing every aspect as they ensured the Victim Compensation Funding, Gemstone Memorialization, and then, eventually, hopefully, Charges, Trials, Convictions, and Sentencing. It was an awesome undertaking ahead of each of them. Overseeing five subordinates each was going to be difficult enough; being the voice dedicated to finding Justice for more than fifty voiceless Victims would become all-consuming as time progressed.

My two colleagues calculated their investment and it almost seemed as if they were already contemplating potential applicants for such important placements. And then each of them nodded their heads, consenting to the staffing, and Officer Stanton prepared the additional forms for everyone's signatures. The Chief supplied his stamp of approval but specified that he wanted the paperwork to allow up to ten staff members beneath each of them in case they decided to expand, and then specified unrestricted hours, travel, and expenses. It was a bountiful contribution, and one that reflected his dedication to ensuring we had everything we could ever need.

Directly following that, the Chief recruited Stanton to make provisions for my own staffing and mentioned that Stanton would be taking his final sets of exams in the upcoming weeks and would then obtain the title of Investigator. He wouldn't be required to shift jobs immediately unless he wanted to, but it would only be to our advantage to have two Investigators on the case since it allowed for substantially greater benefits and doors opening. It was a shrewd way to capitalize off the funding resources as well, allowing for the additional employees to be worked into the budget regardless of whether or not they were enlisted; it ultimately provided us with a buffer should any unexpected problems arise.

It also enabled us to hire virtually any type of government employee, pay them for their time, and because my Investigations were outside of the SPD Chief's jurisdiction, he was neither expected nor required to know how the funding was ever disbursed, and could never be held responsible for anything I funded. The only thing he was expected to do was document where he applied his funding, and because it was essentially just turned over into my investigation, all he needed to do was sign the paychecks.

There was one thing he did following his expenditures, however, and that was to establish and sanctify a separate fund and file for 'up to two separate Independent Consultants'. By establishing a separate acquisition for these two 'Consultants', he provided the means to fund payments for additional resources I might need as part of my investigation.

Independent Consultants were considered Privileged Civilians and were therefore entitled to capitalize off the same anonymity and Security Standards that all Law Enforcement were entitled to have. There would be no documentation or approval for their assistance; they could not be Arrested, Exposed, or forced to reveal their identities. There was no background check and no formal authorization for their assistance, and upon the closing of each case they were left to fade back into oblivion.

One distinction, however, was that such positions had created an Exception clause which allowed—in extremely special circumstances—for such Consultants, after having done an exceptional service to their government and Citizenry, to restore their own Rights and privileges for a job well done. It was all entirely dependent on the exact circumstances and must be the direct result of equal services rendered as to result in such a meritorious reward.

It was a slim shot, but essentially, the Chief had paved the way for Willow Amos to return, and for the two Independent Consultants to have been provided for through funding and acquisitions.

Enlisting the help of Willow Amos might prove instrumental in solving these cases.

Officer Stanton supplied us with the appropriate forms, and with all the solemnity the situation called for, we gave our signature—our word and our bond—to the case at hand. It was a commitment worth making, and even though I had worked on a fair number of high-profile cases, as well as cases that had high Victim counts, I didn't believe anyone in my lifetime had ever been placed in charge of a case of this magnitude before.

I also knew it was another case that would be kept in the dark and concealed from the public eye, at least for now.

"If you don't mind, let's see if we can get Lee down at the SPD Morgue to oversee all of our Victims; I don't want them spread out around the county under different Medical Examiners." I said to the Chief.

He nodded again, and handed the clipboard back to Stanton, advising him to make a note of it.

Stanton scribbled away and then handed me the clipboard again for a final page to sign. I applied my signature to the form and hurriedly opened a new tab so I could scratch out a quick message to him before I left.

"Tag the GOV!!"

Get surveillance on our illustrious Governor. It was time.

I had convinced myself that nothing he had done was so extreme that it had required my immediate attention. I had been willing to overlook far too much; unethical, criminal behavior, abuse of power, and far too many unanswered questions had remained regarding the Governor, and yet I had closed out my case without a backward glance.

I hadn't forgotten about him; I had weighed the issues, considered all my priorities and obligations, measured the risks involved, and then decided—consciously or not—to put my issues with the Governor and his two henchmen on a back shelf for the time being. It hadn't necessarily been my intent to leave it unresolved; I had simply run out of the space and time to justify attempting to investigate him while I was still under his watchful eye, and he was the one with all the power.

Stanton would get things underway, and while I didn't believe that the Chief would oppose our moving forward with an investigation of the Governor, I also knew that sometimes it was better to ask for forgiveness than permission. The Chief was in a difficult position; he was accountable to The People, but also to the government. If the Governor intended to remove the Chief from his position for refusing to play ball, it was imperative that the Chief remain free from even a hint of impropriety. Anything considered professionally unethical would undoubtedly be used against him by the Governor as a catalyst to eject him. For these reasons alone, the Governor was untrustworthy and a dangerous liability for the Chief. For now, it would be better to proceed without the Chief's knowledge.

I handed the clipboard back to Stanton, telling him, "Keep me apprised of what they discover, Stanton, and keep Grace in the loop as well, if you don't mind."

He glanced down, saw my note, and reached out and shook my hand.

"Will do, Sir," he replied.

"Do you still have our offices available?" I asked the Chief.

"Of course; they'll be there when you get back. And Stanton's got your housing situated, right?"

Stanton nodded, confirming it was secured once more and I could return anytime.

"Let me know if you need anything," the Chief said.

I told him I'd touch base, and then told Stanton I'd send confirmation as soon as I had accomplished my mission and was en route back home. He would be flying solo with our new case until I returned, but it was my hope that I would be back before the Medical Examiners were done with their end and we started our Notifications. I knew, though, after having worked with him from the onset of our last case, that Stanton was more than qualified and capable of taking the lead on this.

What he could not do, however, was go where I was about to go. I was the only one that could do what needed to be done.

I turned and started back toward the makeshift parking lot, taking long strides toward the edge of the field and back out onto the pathway. The light was almost gone, but it made no difference; I knew where I needed to go.

FORTY-EIGHT – COLLATERAL DAMAGE

A Fragile Edge

I navigated the pathway slowly, hearing the crunch of overgrown plant life beneath my feet with every step. We had barely crossed over into the official Fall season, but already the moon was out before the dinner meal, and there was a chill in the air that seemed like ominous forecasting of the winter yet to come. The sky was a deep blue as it carried out its final transition, and as I walked, it faded into black for the long night ahead.

I looked down toward the timestamp on my armband, calculating time zones and the tentative travel plans I had formulated in my mind. I would need to establish my contacts tonight to secure everything that I would need by early tomorrow morning. A twelve-hour window, at best, and I would need to get a lot done before that. For tonight, I would return to the SPD Barracks, order a hot meal from the cafeteria to be sent up, unpack, and then pack again—with a decidedly different destination in mind.

Somewhere in there I would establish a line of communication with Stanton and shoot off a brief outline of things I anticipated I would need his help with.

After that, make a call to my folks so they knew I wouldn't be coming over for Sunday dinner after all, and then let them know I wasn't going to be available for at least a week or two, so they wouldn't worry when I didn't answer or check-in.

So, a phone call to the folks, by then my food should be there, and then I would try and get some sleep. I would need to be out at first light, need to be down at the military base located halfway between Seattle and Olympia, and would hopefully be in the air within four hours if all went well.

Slowing my pace, I paused to take stock of the stars that were now filling the sky. It was a beautiful night, and for once it wasn't raining—not a downpour, not a steady drizzle, not even a sprinkle. Given that we were now in October, the rain was upon us almost daily. Tonight, however, the temperature had fallen so low that even the ground below my feet had been solid instead of the usual soggy marshland that was commonplace throughout Western Washington. Looking out beyond the beachfront, the moon was low over Puget Sound in the distance, and the water sparkled under its glow.

There was rustling behind me; someone else on the path now trying to return to their vehicle through the dark and guided only by the moon.

"So that's it?" the voice asked. "You're leaving? Not even a goodbye?"

Grace.

As she took the few remaining steps between us, the moon seemed to capture her in the light perfectly. Her long auburn hair had been pulled back into some type of low bun, her curls escaping around her forehead, cheeks, and neckline. Her skin was so pale she appeared ethereal; almost ghostly.

Looking down at her in the moonlight, it was easy to momentarily forget the urgency and plans I had been sorting through.

We had much to discuss, but standing at the edge of a graveyard as I readied myself to leave the country was hardly the most practical of times. Still, her face searched mine for some type of explanation, and I found myself unable to provide it. Seeing the way she looked at me only made the idea of leaving her more unbearable and reminded me of all the reasons I wanted to stay.

Before I Go ~ A Testament of Love

Were the timing any different; were I able to be as honest and forthright as my own reasonable countenance would have chosen, I would have told her of the many thoughts I had coursing through my head already. But it wasn't the right time or the right place, and I wasn't in the right position to say anything personal to her.

I knew that Daegan Kyl had survived and would still be out there somewhere just as surely as I knew that had he not gone with Willow Amos that she would have been killed sooner rather than later without his protection. They were both going to be vital to my investigation, and now it was necessary for me to find and extract them from the hellish environment they had been dumped in.

I had to leave. I had to go there and try to find them, and I had to do it personally. It wasn't a task I could delegate or pass off for other men to do. I had been the one that had allowed Daegan Kyl to go there, despite knowing what dangers existed. I was the one who had broken all the rules to make it happen and to help him.

It was only reasonable to expect me to be the one who went to find him and extract him from such a place, especially given the reasons for it. They were both my responsibility; it was enough of a burden to bear knowing that I could not do this mission alone, and that I would still be required to solicit the help of others—that I would ask Soldiers to place their own lives in danger for a mission that could have been avoided had I just followed protocol to begin with. I had no right to ask this of them, but I would—and I knew that because they were Soldiers and the men that they were, that they would risk their own lives willingly to save one of their own just as they would any American Citizen.

I didn't expect Grace to understand the reasons behind my work, or to understand why I felt it necessary to go myself. But she did need to accept it and accept the realities of what I was doing.

The odds were stacked against my return. I was going to a very dangerous place.

I wanted to kiss her as I had before; to tangle myself in her hair, to feel her hunger match my own, to share just that one exquisite moment with her once again before I set off. I wanted to hold her close to me, to look into her eyes and whisper reassurances sufficient enough to tide her over until I could return.

I wanted to tell her I would be thinking of her while I was away, and that I thought about her—that I thought about her far too much—and had been looking forward to spending time with her. I could not wait to be alone with her, finally, away from work where we could just be ourselves.

I wanted her to know that even though I was going to be gone for a few days right now that I was going to be here in Seattle for several more months; that the concerns we had skirted around and hinted about regarding the distance between us was now a moot point, since I would be here, staying, at least for a while. To just get her to at least see that a solution had been presented; I would not end up taking up a new case elsewhere, too far away to ever see her or spend time with her—something that would have been the sure death knell for any budding relationship.

At least this way, upon my return, we would be near one another, could continue to cultivate that which had been started, and with any luck, could even manage time away from work with just the two of us. There wouldn't be much available time, of course; as participants in an active investigation, we knew that our time was not our own and there was virtually zero chance to maintain normal professional hours. It wasn't an ideal way to begin a courtship, but it would be better than nothing, and I was glad for the blessing of time we had been granted.

I wanted to put my hand to her cheek, to push the troubled look out of her eyes with the most subtle of touches, to pull her close to me much in the same manner I had witnessed my father comfort my mother, reassuring her with just a look—the conveyance of a shared moment of intimacy where one's thoughts were expressed without words, without confusion, and yet perfectly known by the other person because of years of practice.

I wished, in that flash of an instant, for us to be elsewhere; far into that shared future where we were familiar enough to know that all was well, when we were securely in love and at peace with one another—rather than here, with everything new and uncertain, where words failed and communication faltered—where there were no right answers and I had no earned grace periods on reserve, and where she owed me nothing, least of all a chance.

I wanted to tell her that I was almost certain that I believed she was the one I wanted to spend the rest of my days with; that I wanted to sleep by her side and know she was there waiting for me whenever I returned. I wanted to have a way to express to her that for the first time in my life, I recognized that *it mattered to me* that someone would be here—that *she* would be here—when I returned, and that it was all completely, absolutely terrifying to me to see how strongly I felt about her because I knew what it meant, and it was uncharted territory.

I desperately yearned, the longer we stood there, to surrender to her need for answers and to embrace that look I could see inside of her that I had been trying so desperately to resist. She made me want to abandon all sense of time and obligation, to take her with me, to find somewhere secluded—a place where we were the only two—to delay my departure and seize hold of the moment before us, abandoning everything else for as long as she would allow it.

I wanted to express my desire for her in the language in which I was most familiar and competent; where words were not required to make her feel the things I ached to say to her now that I had been given the chance. I wanted to take her to a place where she would be left with no doubts regarding how much I wanted her, hungered for her, and intended to please her every opportunity I received. She needed to know, by my hands, my body, my mouth, and my words, that I intended to keep her so well loved and satiated from this moment onward that she would never doubt my desire for her again no matter where I had to go or for how long.

I wanted her to remember how greedy I had been—for her time, her thoughts, her attention, her touch. I wanted her to know this entirely—for her to see that I had already been so drawn in and captivated by her that she only needed to understand that today would be the same as ten- thousand days from now, and all I needed before I left was to know she felt the same—and that she was willing to take each of those days with me as they arrived.

I wanted to whisper to her of my secret prayer; that I longed to have someone to share my life with just as I had always watched my parents and their eternal devotion to one another, and that I sincerely prayed that one day I would find someone—the right woman—and she would want me enough to wait for me just as Penelope had waited for Odysseus. God Help Me, but I wanted to be the man worthy of such a woman, and I wanted her to love me as he had been loved. It was selfish, but I needed her to *want* to be *Mine,* and *Only Mine.* I needed her to want *me* to belong to her equally as much.

I was probably a fool, but I wanted to be the object of someone's affection, desires, and passion enough that they were incapable of getting thoughts of me out of their head. I wanted someone to want me as much as I wanted them, and I was willing to wait for the right love story rather than just taking whatever came my way. The world required enough compromise and sacrifice; finding the person whom we were meant to share our lives with was the one time in every person's life that they should not ever succumb to the demands of others, to go against their own instincts and red flags, or to make sacrifices or compromises just to either avoid being alone or to be with someone they told themselves was the right person but they knew was not.

Out of every plan for my life I had ever made, and out of every life decision I was thus far responsible for, the selection for my life partner had remained as the single-most important decision and had always been the subject that I had vowed to myself I would follow the promptings of my heart and the Holy Spirit; that there were many things that were negotiable, but this was the absolute most important evolution and personal growth that I could experience as a Human Being—that of transforming from myself as an individual into the man that would become a Husband, Provider, and Father.

It would be the decision that elevated me from being a single male, beholden to no one other than myself, into being the Head of Household and the Head of Family. It might have seemed old-fashioned for some men and families, and completely alien to those from other places or generations before, but after the Great Reformation there had been such a resurgence in the necessity for Home and Hearth that Family had become the central focal point for many individuals, and I was no different than the generations before me in choosing to prioritize this. Along with the unparalleled necessity for the Citizens of the West to ardently strive to increase their population numbers—heavily promoted through Family Growth Incentives sponsored by national government campaigns—there was a significant up-growth in Christianity and the return to churches as our nations struggled to remember who they were.

We were important, we Men of the West.

We were Necessary.

I wanted to be *very necessary* to the right woman; I wanted to be chosen by her as both partner to her for the rest of her life, but also as the man whom she had selected to become a partner for the parenting that we would one day share in as we raised our family together. It wasn't just a matter of my own selfish desires; it was imperative that we choose the right person because we needed to be capable of raising our children together, as one unit, in the same household. Our own happiness depended on it. Our children's happiness depended on it. The children we produced and set forth into the world depended on our own time and investment. And on a larger scale—a much grander scale than I could ever hope to take personal responsibility for but would still be one grain of sand among many—the future of our Citizenry and Humanity depended upon it.

I wanted to find the love of my life; the One.

More importantly, in my heart of hearts, I believed I already had, and I believed it to be *her*.

Would that I could, all those things would have escaped my lips as easily and as smoothly as I had often heard other men speak. But such was not the case, such was not my way, and as she stared up at me with concern and fear in her eyes, all I could do was stare back at her wishing I could either cross the verbal or physical lines that separated us, knowing that I could not, and due to how things needed to be, would not.

Whether out of Guilt or my own Selfishness, I agreed almost instantaneously when she invited me to follow her home, to come over to her house for a drink and a visit before I started out.

And so, despite the full awareness of what it could mean, and what it could lead to once I was there, I got on my bike and began the drive back toward Seattle, following her home.

A Love Story for the Ages

I thought about her the whole drive over to her house as I followed her. I'd never been there before; I had never even contemplated what sort of dwelling she might reside in. I imagined it would be an extension of herself; well taken care of, modest, small.

I was heading into dangerous territory, and I knew it. I was leaving tomorrow with no return date. It was foolish for me to go to her home tonight, to be anywhere alone with her. It wasn't the same thing as being alone during work hours, or even traveling alone together to and from various locations. It wasn't about sharing lunches or dinners together, and it wasn't even about how she had taken care of me in the barracks a while ago. Each of those situations had been merited, and they had been done with well-defined boundaries.

This…was off course. Unpredictable.

We would be safe if we kept to the script, stayed within our job descriptions, remained committed to the job, and nothing but the job.

If we continued to do that, we were both protected; neither of us would ever get hurt, we would never have our hearts broken or our egos crushed, and we could continue with that tiny little romance that was never really given a chance to develop and probably wasn't supposed to. It kept everything innocent and tender; nothing more than sweet smiles, stolen glances, hopeful fantasies, and longing for one another.

I knew I was the problem behind all of it. I knew that I had crossed the line, messed up the rules, and probably sent out more mixed messages than she knew how to process. I was a simple man and believed that games were best left for children. I had never been one to over-complicate my feelings.

If I said something, I meant it, and unless something changed, I probably still felt the same way. It was probably a comfort for those who appreciate stability and predictability, but a constant source of irritation for those who were more passionate or insecure and required a great deal of attention or affirmation.

I knew how I felt about Grace.

My parents had been married for over sixty years, and so had my grandparents on both sides. Many of my relatives had large families and lengthy marriages; they were vows made with intent, and having large families had been part of that covenant.

My immediate family had carried on with these traditions, and while I was still at an age when many of my peers were single, most were heading down the pathway toward marriage and family. My brothers and my baby sister had all found their own little slice of heaven and were busy growing and raising families of their own. I saw my parents—and countless other parents and grandparents—who had always been together, who loved one another and had built wonderful lives for themselves and their children.

I had always wanted to have that; I had always believed that one day I would. I also believed that it would all arrive as it was supposed to, that it would work out as it should.

I believed in epic love stories because I had always seen them around me. Still, most women found my pragmatic nature to be frustrating and even cold at times; they wanted to be romanced, and I seldom measured up in that regard.

But lately I had found myself wondering about those previous relationships. Maybe love wasn't as difficult or uncomfortable as I'd imagined it was if it was between the right people.

I had watched my father spin my mother around our kitchen my entire life, watching her laugh with joy as they danced without music. But just as much as I knew that to be a symbol of my father's love for my mother, so too was the way she had met him at the door every day as he set off for work, tucked his scarf into his coat, pulled up his lapel so he wouldn't catch a chill, and then kissed his mouth as she told him to come home to her, knowing that his job was not inherently dangerous, but still dangerous enough for her to express concerns routinely. Both were a testament of their love, both seemed terribly romantic to me, yet neither were as overt as what it seemed many women expected to be put out on display in order to win their hand.

At any rate, I had not ever considered myself the type that was inclined to create a love story that anyone would ever put down pen to paper—and God knew I had never been one to make that 'Grand Gesture'—but perhaps there was hope for me yet. Perhaps all I had needed was the correct muse; perhaps it had been that I was missing the right woman. It seemed reasonable to presume that this was often the case in all those epic love stories; otherwise, they would only be unrequited crushes, and the only thing that happened with those is that one person gets crushed while the other does the crushing.

All things considered, maybe it was better to find someone who appreciated the small gestures as if they were grand just because they came from someone who wasn't inclined to do any gestures at all. Surely all that truly mattered was that one's heart was given to someone worthy, and with sincere intentions.

All in all, ultimately what it came down to was me being entirely out of my depth.

All the Reasons I Could Not Stay

I drove from the southern end of Seattle back toward the north, following Grace the entire way and trying desperately to come to terms with the conflicted feelings I was wrestling with internally before I arrived at her house and would be forced to decide.

A picture of her was fused inside of my brain now in a way that was often done by those who were around one another frequently—along with those who were deeply in love. I often pictured her standing inside of my little kitchen area at the barracks as she had that first night when we had been alone together outside of work. It was an image permanently imprinted in my mind—her hair in a high ponytail, dressed in that soft pink fabric, cooking steaks, and blushing sweetly at me as I rounded the hallway and saw her standing there.

I thought of the way she had sat next to me on the chair as I ate, her leg pulled up with her arms wrapped around it, chatting with me about various aspects of the case.

It was a flash into a shared future in which we could build a life with mutual work interests as a cornerstone between us. She was someone who understood the weight of such a career, who would know what it meant to feel brought down by it on occasion. I longed for someone who would love me for all that I did for my Fellow Countrymen rather than resent me for all that I could not do because of my professional obligations. Perhaps she was even someone who could inspire a desire to try and split my priorities a bit better down the road so I could build a family with her without having to choose one or the other.

Maybe it wasn't her, but it was certainly someone *like* her.

I had images of her stuck in my head, and it was a stark contrast to the usual dark ones as they related to our work. My memories of her that night were mine and mine alone; they weren't associated with anyone else, no Victims, no tragedies, no case specifics.

I wanted to make more of those memories.

I wanted to be able to spend time with her away from all this, to be able to get to know her outside of work, to talk of things that were only important to the two of us. I wanted to know her on a personal level, to know what it felt like to have her sitting by my side as we did routine things together—all the things that normal people did who shared their lives with one another. I wanted to be near her, watching a movie while she wore those soft pink pajamas that seemed as though they were made to be touched and held close. I wanted to know what it felt like to fall asleep next to her as she wore them, to pull her close to me as I lay behind her on some cold winter night, and then to know what it was like to wake up next to her and feel her arm sprawled out over my chest or her leg star-fished out over my own.

I wanted all of that, and I knew I could no longer deny how I was feeling about it because it had been a prominent thought in my head since before we dropped Daegan Kyl off at the Transport station.

But the man who wanted to build that life was a very different man than the one currently making his way over to her house at this moment, and selfish fantasies were no longer something that I could afford to lose myself in. As much as I wanted to be able to daydream about such things, and I was not too embarrassed to admit that I had on occasion, I knew that the time for wishing I could casually embark on that type of romance with her was not possible at this point. I couldn't say for certain if we would ever be granted another opportunity or not, but I knew now was not the time.

Nothing good would ever come from my entering her house and setting things in motion in the manner in which I knew she was going to allow me to if I tried. Nothing should be initiated under such circumstances, because she should not be settling for the type of man that would be so cavalier with her emotions or her body, even if that man were me.

I wanted to be many things to her: friend, companion, lover, confidante, colleague, and I could imagine even being husband and father to her children at some point. I could see the potential, and I knew the direction I wanted us to move forward in. But that was all based on the type of man I wanted to be for her, the type of man who was worthy of being those things to her. There were far more ways to end up being *less than* that man, and that was what I wished to avoid.

Above all, I did not want to be the man that this woman invited into her home, her heart, and then her bed, only to leave the next day with nothing more than sweet promises lingering in the air instead of the hard facts and truth of the way things were.

I did not ever want to be among those who were marked; another name affixed to that never-ending roster of self-serving men who had been notorious for having once stood exactly where I was now with a woman, and then let them down bitterly through their selfish actions.

I did not ever want to be regarded as the kind of man that would bed a woman before heading off to war only to end up dead on a battlefield while some innocent, lovelorn young girl was left with a baby in her belly and a broken heart.

In such cases, it was not the men who were left to bear the burden of their actions, because dead men held no such sense of responsibility. Instead, it was the women and the children that were Left Behind who were forced to live with the consequences. If I were to be such a man like those in the past, my name might have been Soiled, but the Dead don't dwell on damage to their reputations, however scandalous. The women left with their Unborn children did, however, and I failed to see how any man, having professed his love for a woman, would leave her to a lifetime in which she could be socially ostracized, demonized and even Victimized all for having simply loved a man wrongly through the critical eyes of a judgmental audience.

But I couldn't change society or social views, and while I knew it was not the same as in generations from long ago when women and their illegitimate 'bastard' children would have been left to endure decades of ridicule and public shaming, I knew it was still not what I would want her to experience as a reminder of my time here. Aside from that, the additional strain of raising a child alone would prove burdensome, and I wanted to alleviate her woes, not compound them.

I would have left her to face the consequences alone. Our shared moments together were but a flicker in her life; a mere hundred days known to one another out of a lifetime comprised of thousands.

She would lead a full, productive, amazing life without me just as she had before she had ever met me, but my actions tonight would dictate whether or not I would selfishly intervene and influence all of the rest of the days of her future. I wasn't sure that anyone ever had the right to do that, but certainly not any self-respecting man who knew what it meant to live a life with honor. I would not be the one who left her after making her life more difficult rather than better.

But it was more than just that; I could not be the one who left her to Grieve for me either. It was not a title, nor a position, that I could ask her to bear. If I left her, as so many other women were left when their men went off to war, it would be a cruel fate to leave her with. The world was too full of Grieving Widows, having been placed into a position where they would spend months, even years, and in some cases the rest of their entire lives, all spent Mourning a man that had once been the center of their world.

Men might die as Heroes and be the ones who sacrificed everything all for the sake of war, but the women and children who were Left Behind were the ones who carried the weight of their absence for the rest of their lives. When it came to the consequences of war, the concentration was always on the brave men left lying dead on battlefields; no one ever considered the Loved Ones all left to Grieve. That was the Ripple Effect of each man's life; the impact he made on every relationship was his legacy. A man could be summarized, and understood, by his legacy.

That was the full Measure of a Man.

And God Help Me, as much as I wanted to claim her as my own for the rest of my days, I knew that it was unfair and selfish of me to do so at this point.

There was a very real possibility that I would not return from Alaska. And if I didn't, I could not be the ghost in her past that she must Grieve for on her own, having been in love with a man who had never been a part of her life. I would be someone who had never been welcomed into her future, or the world she shared with her family.

Part of the Ripple we created included the positive relationships we built with those whom we chose to share our lives with. If she and I were to ever get married, we would be combining both of our own families into the equation. How her parents regarded me would matter a great deal. All of that would have been missed and foregone if I stayed now and disappeared tomorrow. She would have been left to Grieve for someone who no one would have ever known was a person she knew well enough to Mourn, let alone love.

Worse than that, someday she would have met the man whom she would give herself to completely; she would meet him, love him, marry him, have his children, and be all that she was never given the opportunity to be with me. But I would have stolen his place first.

I would have taken something from him that he would have never been able to compete against, because I would have remained a part of her life and heart, cemented in her memories for all time; nothing more than a snapshot of a man whom she may barely recall but whom she remembered made her feel a certain way, and thus continued to hold tightly to in her heart. I would have been a fragment in a lifetime of experiences, love, and happiness, but because I would have become immortalized through my Death, she would have always kept a part of me in her heart—a part that by all rights I had not yet earned the right to claim.

It seemed terribly unfair and selfish of me to want to be that person to her, to want to be remembered or loved by a woman such as she, and for a moment as I thought about it, I was left with a sense of shame and guilt over my selfishness. But having recognized it, I knew it was my ego speaking, wanting to be of such importance to her that I would not be forgotten even if only having shared a brief chapter in time.

None of this was set in stone, either. In order to become immortalized in her memories I would need to die after leaving here, and I had no intention of doing such a thing as of yet. In fact, if all went well, I would go about my business, return completely unharmed within very short order, and everyone else would be equally safe from Harm. And then I would figure out a way to take that first step toward sharing my meager little life with Grace O'Connor, and hopefully be invited to partake in hers.

That was the plan, anyhow. That was as far as I had gotten, and given it had already shifted from where it was yesterday, we were both just going to have to take it day by day and hope it all worked out in the end.

For now, however, I knew that I needed to tread with caution, to appreciate everything that was at stake, and to acknowledge the subtleties of the situation which made it even more imperative that I handle her heart—and body—with more consideration than my own impulsive, foolish, selfish, and yes, even my cave-man desires, would normally bother with.

God Help Me, but I would rather have her hate me for what I didn't do than what I did, even if she never understood why.

Such were the things I had told myself, all the reasons I had given for why I must be the man worthy of being here in the first place; to be above such selfish acts. To show restraint, and maturity; to be worthy of the love of a woman enough to put what was right and must be done above my own selfish desires.

I went through my reasons with the same methodical rationale that I had made most major decisions in my life, and with the same critical thinking and emphasis on logic over emotion that I had been raised to believe all Good Men should learn in order to set a straight course for their lives.

I acknowledged my desires—both physical and emotional—and tried to take into account that she was not going to be without her own emotional investment and feelings, and that everything I did and said would be left between us after I had gone no matter how I chose to behave while I was here.

I felt as though I were Daniel walking into the lion's den; I knew where the dangers lie, but I was unable to stop myself from being surrounded by them.

I knew that there was a better than average chance of my causing more Harm than Good, in never being able to articulate myself well enough to make sense to her and probably avoid her feelings getting hurt in some capacity or other, and I even considered that I was being entirely presumptuous as to her feelings in general.

What did it say about me that I automatically assumed I was going to be invited in, or that I was even reading the signs the right way? What did it say about her if I believed she was as potentially…welcoming…as I believed she would be? At best I was a little rusty and off my game; at worst I never had any to begin with.

I recalled a woman who had once told me I treated my love life as though it were a Crime Scene, and every action needed to be weighed, measured, cross-referenced, and studied for motive and intent.

I watched as Grace slowed her Cruiser down and came to a stop, putting her left turn signal on and then making the turn. I glanced at the sign, signaled, and then turned left, following her.

A quarter of a mile down the road, she pulled her vehicle into her garage, and I pulled my bike up behind her and parked it on the road at the end of her driveway. The houses were spread out over spacious front lawns and far enough out of the downtown area to allow for the privilege of a surplus of square footage and ample back yards. Her home, although it was already dark outside, seemed lovely and exactly as I would have imagined it had I ever given it a thought.

I locked my motorcycle securely—a matter of habit, not necessity—and then followed Grace over toward her front door, electing to keep my helmet in place until we had entered through the front. I didn't have anything on my bike or clothing to indicate that I was Law Enforcement, and her profession didn't require any type of government housing provisions unless she wanted to live within one of the gated communities, so it seemed we were as anonymous as two regular Citizens could be, which I rather liked the idea of.

I stood behind her as she scanned her entry keypad so we could enter, and looked down at her as she walked through the door ahead of me. I watched her as she slipped her high heels off on a mat alongside the hallway, seeing her for the first time in her own surroundings.

It pleased me.

I pulled my helmet off, then my balaclava, and then my gloves and jacket. Finally, nodding down, I asked her if she'd like me to remove my boots, and then lost those as well, leaving one pair of black leather, steel-toed boots next to her own collection of pretty little shoes all neatly lined up in a row.

I followed her into her living room, seeing the way her sweater draped off the back of her shoulders from behind, the way the green of the fabric contrasted with her red hair as she tried to tame her curls by pulling them into some type of loose bun with a clip, and then the curves of her neck, getting lost in her beautiful, creamy skin sprinkled with freckles.

I desperately tried to remember all the reasons I knew I could not stay, but drew a blank. The only thing I could easily recall was seeing the name on the community she lived in, *Tompkins Square Park.*

FORTY-NINE - TO LOVE SOMEBODY

To Love Somebody

I found myself in her living room, against all better judgment, and after having chastised myself entirely the whole ride over to tread with caution, to think about what I was on the edge of starting without any means of controlling the outcome of.

But she had invited me in. *Just a drink before you set out,* she had said. *A proper chance for her to catch up on what she had missed while we were at the field. I could explain where I was going and what my plans were.*

It had been so innocently stated, but she knew as she said it—and I knew as I heard it—that she could no more prevent herself from extending the offer and inviting me than I was capable of resisting my compulsion to accept.

And so, we had taken the time to speak of such things; the home we now stood in, purchased years ago to be near family, the parents still all living nearby in her childhood home, an oil painting of three little girls—all with the same red curls—which she confirmed with a nod of her head to be herself and her two sisters. All the casual conversational pieces which were selected as drinks were made and the guest looked around, discreetly trying to learn about the person whose home they just entered for the first time. The kind of innocent assessment usually done as the guest was trying to get a better sense of who their host was before they ended up making the sort of poor choices that usually resulted in awkward exit strategies and fumbling excuses the next morning.

Her house seemed to reflect who she was, through and through. Several walls lined with dark wood bookshelves overflowed with hardbound books—an extensive collection for these modern times when physical books were rare. The warm, beige walls were half-covered in dark mahogany wainscoting that matched the bookshelves and old hardwood floors.

There were overstuffed pieces of furniture, and a table off in the distance with thick, rustic legs. Everything was comfortable, warm, and inviting, just as she was.

Not that I was there enough to notice, but my own apartment after a decade still had boxes in the spare room that had arrived straight from the Academy, and the only things that matched had been purchased and delivered by my mother or sister. It was a shell of a home for a nomad; this was a home that soothed the restless spirit and kept them from wandering, illustrating once again the boundless beauty created by women and all that they did to build homes, families, and memories.

She was exactly as I had expected: friends, family, a homeowner, a good life, and a future tied to a city that I would probably never need to visit again once I had completed the case we were now embarking on. *Further proof that I should not be here, and she should not want me here.*

It was the very war I had been waging within myself the whole way over. I did not want to be the man who ever stepped into a role I could not fulfill, to make promises that I could not keep, to be presented to another as someone I was not capable of being, or to give hope when there was none to be found.

I had been standing near her fireplace; a gas fireplace that began warming the room and filling the space with its soft light as soon as we arrived. I had no doubt that it would heat up the space; I feared the power of its irresistible incandescence.

Fire was the primary weapon of love, and it always worked in the woman's favor, the flickering of flames, the subtle glow of candles against the darkness. More Good Men had been made vulnerable and rendered powerless by the flattering light cast upon a woman kissed by the glow of a fire than had ever been lost in battle.

When she arrived from the kitchen with two glasses of wine, I only proved history to be true again, offering no counterargument because there wasn't one. Grace, already beautiful and in no need of embellishment, was not merely kissed by the firelight, but instead bathed in it, as if the light itself was made to dance upon the bare skin along her neck and shoulders.

She then handed me wine, and as I smiled down at her, trying desperately to maintain my cool reserve, I knew the stage was set and every ounce of willpower and self-restraint I held would be all for naught with only the slightest change in circumstance. *One glass of wine, one change in physical proximity, or too much sand having been given an opportunity to fall through the hourglass, and I would be done for.*

This was the first time we had been granted everything necessary to create such a moment; we had seclusion, intimacy, no pressures, or stresses other than my impending departure, and nothing to hold us back, *technically*. It was a dangerous gamble even walking through her front doorway; I may as well have been a starved vampire and she my foolish prey, naively believing that an animal could still control his primal desires once offered such tempting fare. God Help Me, but even Odysseus had succumbed to temptation when it was offered.

Every fiber of my Being wanted to be here in this room with her. The slightest invitation—let alone provocation—from her now that I knew it was what she was working toward, and had provided the opportunity for, was going to be nothing short of torture, and a miracle, if I managed to maintain my reserve. I was already fighting against myself to reach out to her, just as I had resisted numerous times already since the day I had kissed her. To ask a man to restrain himself when such beauty was being freely offered was no less than to ask the ocean, full of force and might, to resist crashing upon the rocks in the midst of raging storms.

She came and stood close to me with a book in her hand, opening it with a smile and telling me how she had searched for a long time before finding that particular edition. The page had been signed 'Property of The Watchers On The Wall'. And as she leaned into me, inviting me to read the inscription of one of her prized books, as she pointed out the engravings and other characteristics, her voice was soft, well-acquainted with the words she recited.

I watched her, trying to listen to her words, but mostly just noticing that she was standing so closely I could smell the same familiar, but unidentified, fragrance that over the months I had come to recognize as her scent, and hers alone. Standing in her socks next to me, her body melted against my side. She snuggled up comfortably against me, closer than ever before as she closed the physical gaps between us—the spaces that had always been necessary out of professional duty.

The heat from her skin was barely detectable through our layers, but the subtle pressure from her body brushing against mine was not lost on me. With only the light from the fireplace illuminating our space, I found it impossible to look beyond her.

I watched her as she looked down at the open pages. She had pulled her hair off to the side, allowing the entirety of her neck and shoulder to be exposed only inches away, silently bidding me to cover her pale skin with soft kisses. Consciously exploited or not, the graceful slope of a woman's neck was a hypnotic source of power over men, and served as a subtle means of seduction. I had been held captive by hers on more than one occasion already, and the glow of the fire dancing upon her bare flesh left my mouth dry.

It was then that I realized I was already hers.

And now here we were, right where we both wanted to be.

In this instant, with time moving slower than was ever permitted, as we tried to capture this gift of being present in the moment and leaving everything else outside for the world to contend with on its own while we were gone, I wondered how often throughout history that other men had wished for the clock to stop entirely just for the touch of a woman. How many men had yearned for more time on the eve of a battle, had used their Final Hours to experience the tender touch of a feminine hand, known to them or not. I wondered how many had used their time to profess their love, to make amends, or to make arrangements for the protection and care of their Loved Ones should they fail to return.

I wondered how many men had squandered their time and spent their Final Hours full of memories and regret, and how many would have given up all the wasted days of their lives just to revisit the ones that mattered.

I wondered how many men had sacrificed most of their final night's rest, even knowing how it could affect them the next day, just to ensure they captured as much time with the woman they loved and other Loved Ones before leaving them, future uncertain but outcome bleak, knowing that miracles were not often wasted on battlefields or times of Violence and Bloodshed.

I wondered how many had ridden off to face Violence that was not of their own making, for men who were not of their own blood or obligation, and yet were willing to endure what was surely likely to become their own demise as they stared down the last of their time on this earth. How many men had parted from a woman such as this, a woman whom they loved and who loved them in return, just to go sacrifice their lives and surrender their Final Breath in someone else's battle or for someone else's cause. I wondered if they ever felt it was worth it, or if, in their Final Moments, they would have done anything to trade it all just to be back in the warm, loving arms of the woman that they had once given their heart to, and knew they were going to leave Grief-stricken at the end of it all.

Fate had set the terms for everything we were doing at this moment. I was being given the opportunity I had often wanted but had thus far never been granted the right circumstances to initiate, somehow always believing that such a time would have arrived at some point. But I was realizing that I had fallen into the same trap that most of us were inclined to: that of believing that we always had more time than we were ever given or guaranteed.

Her presence calmed my mind, though she probably did not understand all that had been swirling around in it for the last few hours. There had been considerable disquiet within me since seeing the field from which we had arrived, and it had left me with much anxiety over what was yet to come. Being here, standing near her, gave me a momentary reprieve from the darkness I felt growing within.

Instead, I chose to focus on how she had moved so closely next to me; it was unavoidably intimate. She was reminding me that she was not only a woman—warm, intoxicating, sensual—but that she was here, close enough to touch. She was reminding me that she should be well-loved, often, and never forgotten or left on her own.

By inviting me into her home on this night of all nights she was sharing herself with me, not only the obvious parts, but also her more vulnerable fears and concerns, the fear of my leaving and all that might entail. *She was trying to capture time as well.*

Until now, I had been here every day since the first we had met. The only traveling I had done had been for work-related reasons, and much of it had been done with her by my side. Since my arrival, I had become a fixture within her daily life; long enough to become habit. She had known every day that I would be there should she need me or wish to speak with me. It was entirely possible that there had been a moment in her recent past when she had realized this and found it to her liking; it was possible that she knew that my absence would be noted, and she wanted me to know she did not want that time to begin.

She was telling me that it had been more than three months since we had met, three long months in which we had been around one another day in and day out, working all day long, sharing meals, sharing long drives, talking comfortably with one another about countless subjects as we traveled. The case that we had worked on together as professionals had drawn to a close; she had maintained respect for the professional Code of Conduct, even though it did not directly apply to us as we were from different agencies, but she had waited anyhow. She was telling me that we had invested enough time for her to know how she felt; that she was confident in her actions, and they weren't reckless, nor were they made in haste. She was telling me that she knew exactly what she was doing, and she wanted me to fully understand it as well so I could not attempt to set up chivalrous, yet arbitrary, boundaries or excuses. She might have even known me better than I realized, and was intent on ensuring I did not sabotage anything unnecessarily.

Her eyes had told me long ago that she had feelings for me and that she was unsure of how I had felt in return; she had looked often at me, and I knew there had been times when she was trying to gauge my emotions. I had probably left her confused and uncertain on more than one occasion.

But then, by kissing her outside of the gyrocopter at the Transport Station, I should have bridged the gap between uncertainty and confirmation; there should not have been any questions remaining as to whether or not I wanted her—at least not on the physical level.

But it had been some time since that day at the Transport Station, and I hadn't done anything direct or physical since then. And as with most women, she had allowed me to take the lead in the beginning. She had waited for me to take the initiative, but it seemed the mixed signals with no follow-through had needed a more aggressive response.

Any hesitation over her behavior or boldness seemed to have been lost with the urgency she now felt because I was leaving. I understood why she had invited me here; as we had stood at the edge of the field earlier, I could sense that she, too, had felt it was an inadequate place to say our goodbyes before I left. It was a wildly inappropriate place for personal matters, it had not been private in the least, and the cold weather had made for a hastened departure no matter how well-meaning.

For all those reasons, I understood why she had taken the next logical steps toward ensuring we could spend more time together, and at least muddle our way through a proper goodbye, especially since there really wasn't any way to know when I would be returning. And it had to be acknowledged that there was a possibility that I may well not return at all; it was dishonest and idealistic to try and pretend otherwise. There would be a certain degree of risk involved in my endeavors. I understood why we were here, and why she had invited me; I understood what it was that she wanted from me.

She was here, urging me to step forward and allow ourselves the opportunity to steal some time, to give ourselves the gift of one another.

The quiet, mild-mannered woman that had been patiently playing by the timeless rules which had somehow determined that femininity meant waiting for the man to make his intentions known, for women to sit idly by waiting to get selected on the terms set forth by the man, that woman was no longer abiding by convention; she had obliged, and yet been found wanting as a result. The lack of time that now stood between us was enough of a proponent for action, and if action required opportunity, then she had determined that all obstacles be removed so the course was clear.

There were no doubts that she was fully in control now, and she intended to put an end to the endless circling of one another that led nowhere. We had been in perpetual motion without action for too long. Such bold behavior seemed uncharacteristic for the woman I had come to know, but I had rarely been given time to see her beyond a professional capacity. Actions such as this—this was a different beast altogether, being fed by different desires and needs.

This woman was telling me that she was mine, and the only obstacles that now existed were the ones I created—which essentially declared them for what they were, excuses. She was granting me permission to proceed without any fear of rejection; I was being told that the first move was still being placed on my shoulders, that I was still the lead, but that she did not want me to question or doubt whether or not my advances would be shot down—they would not. She had opened the door; all I had to do was be certain about what I wanted, be sincere in my intentions, and be courageous enough to take the first step which would set everything in motion. She had eliminated the guesswork that was historically known to bury people in self-doubt and angst; only a fool or someone with false intentions would stand on the threshold at this point and still refuse to enter.

I found my own wall of reservations evaporating as the fire played tricks with my eyes. I listened to the sweet, seductive song of the Siren as she read from the pages of her book, and I watched the way her throat gently moved with every word. I saw the way the firelight framed her face before falling to shadows behind the curve of her shoulder. I watched the way her delicate hands held the book as her fingers outlined the beautiful artwork around the text. Her eyes were downcast as she looked at the page, and I looked downward, allowing myself to look upon her face freely, making note of the placement of every single freckle along the ridge of her nose and the side of her face, loving how they splashed across her body as if God Himself had given her a full flick of his red paintbrush just to perfect His work and make her Uniquely Divine in every aspect.

I was caught staring at her when she glanced up at me, and, noticing that I wasn't paying attention, she took the book she had been holding and set it down next to the untouched glasses of wine on the coffee table behind us. Then, with only the faintest of movements, she touched my hand with her own, placing her small, slight fingers near mine, intertwining them gently. I allowed my fingers to close in around hers, welcoming her touch, sensing that she still intended to lead the way at her own pace. She explored the contours of my hand, softly moving her fingers along my own as we stood there, she and I, staring into the fire as our fingers connected with one another slowly, skin to skin for the first time since I had held her hand on our way back to Seattle from the Transport Station.

There had been no mystery when I had taken her hand then; no allure, no sensuality to it. I had merely taken her hand once we were up in the air, kissed the back of it, and then kept hold of it as we traveled; just being grateful to live in the moment and adoring how she had smiled sweetly as she blushed again. It had not been overly romantic, nor had it been intended to evolve into something more physical at the time; I had merely wanted to continue touching her after our shared kiss, and so I had.

I thought of nothing else except the sensuality of our fingers entwined, the contrast between my own rough hands—course, calloused—gently cradling her softness, feeling the delicate curve of her fingers, the feel of her wrist and slender forearm beneath my touch. We stood there, silent, surrounded by darkness other than the faint glow from the fireplace, and the only sound was that of our breathing; each slight intake of breath becoming all the more sensual as my hand began to travel slowly up her bare arm with only the lightest of touches.

I traced my fingers back down to her own, locked them into place and moved my arm slightly, pulling her toward me slowly, turning her so we were face to face, and allowing me to take her other hand into my own as well. She moved toward me, submissively, quietly. I could hear her breathing increasing, a whispered moan of anticipation and desire. I saw her smoldering eyes, and felt the subtle shift in her body as she drew me in.

I could not resist putting my hands along her hips, finally granting myself permission to at least know what it was like to hold her, to have my arms around her, to explore how she melted against me.

I felt myself relax instantaneously; the tension evaporating as the invisible boundary between us was allowed to dissipate at long last. And then suddenly I was pulling her closer, firmly against me, feeling the curve of the small of her back beneath my hands, the shape of her hips, and then wrapping my arms around her as her body softened against my own. I felt her place her hands upon my chest, feeling my quickened heart beating beneath the palm of her hand, made faster with every exploratory move her hands made over my body in return.

She was mesmerizing; she offered another glimpse into who she was, where her mind was, what she wanted from me, what she needed from me. She was sweetly tantalizing, deliciously honest, unabashedly direct. There was nothing coy about her actions or her behavior; she knew herself well, knew what she wanted, and knew how to easily arouse me into such a state of frenzied desperation that all I desired to do was satisfy her.

I was spellbound, and she knew it. I wanted her—to pick her up, to carry her to her bedroom, to devour her entirely and make her mine—and she knew it. She knew that I was helpless to resist her, and I knew it too.

Without any further ceremony she took me by the hand and began leading me toward her bedroom where we would at long last have no distractions beyond ourselves, finally embracing only the moment before us and the gift we were giving of ourselves to one another.

She moved quietly ahead of me, her arm extended and holding my hand within her own, the bare skin of her shoulder and the curves of her body building temptation with each step before me, bidding me to follow her toward what was undoubtedly the closest to Heaven on Earth I would ever dream of being allowed to enter.

I looked at her delicate hand covering my own, saw each slight finger interwoven with mine as they blended together, making one. I looked at her ring finger; the ring finger that called out to me to do the honorable thing, to make her my bride, to give her my heart and then my name before taking a single step further.

And then, God Help Me, without a single sip of wine, without even a solitary kiss exchanged between us, and with only the slightest passage of time, I found it impossible to stop myself from following her.

The Want of Her ~ Submission

I followed her past the furniture, back toward the entry of her living room where the hallway divided; to turn right went back out the front, to turn left meant a darkened hallway, to a room at the end only lit by a faint glow of red.

She left nothing to chance, and as soon as we had cleared the furniture she turned toward me, walking herself slowly backward, bidding me to catch up to her.

Closing the distance between us I pulled her into my arms once again, kissing her fiercely. I knew I could not stay. I knew I should not even tempt the fates by prolonging my departure. But for just one sweet, blissful moment I wanted to know what it was like to be hers, to be in her arms, to be the guy at the end of the story that got the girl he wanted, and everything worked out in the end.

I wanted to pretend, just for one minute, that this was how things could be. To experience what it felt like for normal, average people in my country who could kiss their lovers and spouses, hold their hand, and then go to their bedroom, nothing more than an end to another day, where two people who loved one another lived out their days and nights together. Out of all our gloriously humble emotions, was there anything more profoundly honest than simply acknowledging our desire to be loved, and love in return? To abate the loneliness? To be treasured? She wanted me, and I was weak.

I would have followed her anywhere, but at this moment in time, I would have sacrificed a year of my life just to know what treasures awaited the one whom she had chosen to lead toward the private world only she could create. I would have traded hours of my life for every minute I was able to stay in her company before our time was forced to come to an end. I would have given anything to be the person that she looked at with desire, to see her eyes linger on me for just that long, slow moment, to see that smoldering look revealing the promise of what was yet to come.

If we were honest with ourselves, it was all any of us wanted. But to know that she wanted *me*, to touch me, to kiss me, and that I was not only going to be given this privilege but that I was the source of her desire…it was almost more than I could bear. My longing for her was unlike any other physical encounter I'd ever before experienced. There were not enough wild horses to stop me from seeing what was on the other side of that door.

Men willingly went to war and risked their lives for reasons that might not ever have any value, so quick were they to throw away their one chance to live a long, contented life. What I wouldn't have traded or sacrificed to be the man who could go away and slay the dragons if it meant I could come back here, if I knew she would be looking out her window and awaiting my return, incomplete, inconsolable without me.

I would never be the man who dove headfirst into danger, who risked the life of another or my own, knowing what each man's life was worth. I was not reckless, nor impulsive. But at that moment, as I followed her down the hallway toward her most intimate, private places, I would have stood alongside King Leonidas at the Battle of

Thermopylae before ever surrendering my place in her world or allowing anything else to come between us.

I needed her.

I needed to be near her.

To touch her.

I needed to *belong* to her.

I wanted to feel her body beneath my hands, to explore all the parts of her that as yet were unknown and still unfamiliar, to know her entirely at long last. I wanted to listen to her breathing change, to feel her desire overwhelm her, and to be the cause of it. I wanted to be the man privileged enough to be the one she gave herself to, and to feel her surrender herself to me fully. I wanted to be her lover, not just someone that knew her, that worked alongside her or could be her friend; I wanted to be the man deserving of having such a woman by his side and on his arm. I desired her immeasurably and longed to find the gratification through her that I knew would be unlike any other; to finally understand why it was said that love made all the difference. But what I longed for more so than my own desires was to be the one that gave her pleasure, to be the one who fulfilled her needs; to be the one chosen to be worthy of such a place alongside her. She was a gift; and such a gift was meant to be cherished and appreciated.

I knew that only my fears had kept me away from her until now. I had always held a fear of the Unknown, the fear of becoming entirely enthralled, in being hopelessly enraptured by another person to the point that I could not imagine living my life without them being a part of it. It was a fear of seeking my own happiness, in learning what it meant to touch and embrace a world beyond that of my own making and deriving an equal degree of Pleasure and Joy.

Such happiness had never before been within my grasp and I had never ventured out far enough to try and find it; it had always been something observed, never experienced. There was a fear of being unworthy of such joy, of learning what it meant to be bursting with happiness, of living the life which was that of a contented man. Such a world was a dream to someone like me, something that needed to be held close when it happened, hidden under a bush lest anyone notice it, only whispered about, treasured but concealed—because treasures became the targets of others, quests for their destruction, and ammunition to be used against me—against all Peacekeepers. To love someone meant to acknowledge I was vulnerable to attack; it meant supplying all those who would Cause Harm to me with both the reason as well as the means to do so. To declare my love for someone meant weakness; it meant both she and I could end up hurt.

I had been terrified of not being able to ever pull away from her again once I had both tempted and tasted, supplied, and fed, devoured, and succumbed; of entering a world where someone else's life became more important than my own, where their needs, well-being, safety, and happiness became the defining markers of my own success. I was afraid to love another so exclusively that I risked my world being destroyed through their Loss or Absence; I lived and worked in a world where Pain and Loss surrounded me. To cross that line—to become one of those who were living lives with such risk—especially as those among us who knew the odds, who knew all the statistics and facts—was to be more courageous than I had ever been before, and it was a fear that had consumed me. Fear of having one's heart broken through a break-up was child's play to a man such as myself; I knew of the true Evils that lurked beyond the door, the Violence, the Dangers so terrifying that it was impossible to relax without one hand resting on the trigger and a tight hand clutching my Beloved closely lest I become the Bereaved.

I lived in fear of moving forward because I feared the day when she would no longer be there. I imagined being the husband of Mariam, the father of Katarina. It did not matter what I was capable of handling through my training and work if I could not Protect those whom I loved the most, and it seemed clear that the more people I loved, the greater the threat there was of losing one of them—and loving a woman was the greatest threat of all. I became paralyzed and panicked when I imagined ever surrendering myself over into that world—in ever loving her so much that I could end up a broken man at the end—and I *would* become a broken man; I was sure of it. Because I could not love in half measures, and she was not a woman deserving of anything less than a man who was willing to make her the center of his universe. The fear of Losing Someone had been deeply ingrained within me ever since we had been taught the statistics and risks for Peacekeepers, and then magnified by the relentless barrage of Grief-stricken families I had worked with over my twenty-year career in Law Enforcement.

But until now, until I had held this woman in my arms, it had always been an abstract fear; I had never before desired a woman so absolutely and unequivocally that I could not resist offering myself up to her in the mere hope that she would want me back, that she would find my heart worthy of being joined to her own. Until this woman, my fears had been those of an unknown variety; undefined because the woman at risk of being lost to me was nothing more than a vague idea based on concepts of love that I had never before known to a genuine depth or degree. But now they were real, and she was no longer an idea—she was now standing before me, touching me, offering her body, as well as her heart, into my care.

And yet here I was, and it had somehow all become clear. *None of my fears mattered.* None of it was scary anymore, and none of it had any relevance comparable to what gift I was being offered and allowed to accept.

Most of my time had been spent being near her. Only sleep had separated us, and even then, she had been the last image I had seen as I drifted off to sleep on more than one occasion.

I had listened to her speak to dozens upon dozens of people in countless situations, watched her provide information, support, a shoulder to cry on, and even moments of raw intimacy as she hugged and held Grief-stricken families. We shared stories from our pasts and personal lives as well as provided our professional experiences and expertise to one another without any issues of ego or pride. Our time together had been both casual as well as official; I had witnessed her at our most difficult times with Bereaved Families and found her to be of exceptional strength and reserve—and I had also seen her in soft, pink flannel pajamas with her hair pulled back into a ponytail. She had not intentionally set out to make me drop my self-protective wall, but time spent in her company had left me without much defense otherwise. It had been gradual, built on professional companionship and respect, and done so unassumingly that I had not ever suspected it had truly been possible or capable of happening even as it did.

Now, my only fear was of never knowing, and of never being entrusted with all that she was willing to share with me and me alone. And when she looked at me like she did, her eyes looking up at me with such vulnerability and trust, her heart on her sleeve, it was her faith in me that gave me strength. She made me believe that everything would be all right in the end because we would be with one another and no longer alone.

But it was the way that she placed her hands upon me, the gentleness as well as the fervor, and then how she looked at me with such tenderness, that stole my heart. Every kiss she provided and returned, every advance she initiated, every look she exchanged with me told me she had already chosen me, that she already knew that we would one day stand right here, and that she had been waiting.

Oh, what it meant to be chosen by someone!

All that I was, all that I ever wanted to be, was hers for the taking. I felt her place her hand on the side of my face, her fingers on my neck as she drew me toward her again. Her eyes met mine in the darkened room, and I moved toward her to sweep her into my arms. For just one sweet moment in time, there was nothing else in the world except the two of us, and as the world faded, everything was perfect.

A Love Divine

I entered her bedroom, assessing its space and trying to avoid the most obvious place to release her from my arms. The king size bed in the center of the room was designed to be the focal point, and I longed to see what she looked like upon it.

But instead, I moved with her toward the space in front of the fireplace situated off toward the far end of the room. The large windows and French doors allowed the moonlight to stream in and covered the floor with a soft white glow. I could feel the carpeting below our feet where I landed after walking across the hardwood floors, and realized she had an area rug in the space between her bed and the fireplace.

But the area rug was not all that was there. A handful of pillows and blankets were spread out below our feet, creating a space where we could lie down comfortably. The chill of the night and the darkness of the unlit room was offset by the glow of the fireplace.

We were exactly as she had wanted us to be.

She was Danger. She would always be Danger. I could see it written all over her face. It was in her eyes. She was the one put on this earth to test me; she was my Weakness. She was the source that would draw upon my greatest strengths as a man in every capacity. For her, I would do anything.

I did not want to cross any lines—lines that I had never before needed to set, had never attempted to set, and had never before realized were so difficult to maintain honorably.

I laid her gently down on the blanketed floor, loving the way her eyes held my gaze.

I watched her blush prettily as she was so prone to do, and then pulled her close to me and kissed her once again, slowly, softly.

I wanted this moment to last forever. Everything within me questioned how I could leave her, how I could leave a love this divine.

It was a glimpse into a world that I wanted more of; a moment captured in time that I knew I would carry with me long after I left, and one that revealed to me just how desperately I longed to know this feeling often and well. I knew, looking at her, where it was that I wanted to spend my days and nights from this day forward.

For now, however, I knew I could only stay a while if we behaved; that time was working against me, and there was much that needed to be done. But before I left, before I went out into the Great Unknown, before I intentionally placed myself into Harm's Way and Risked my Life, all I longed to do was lie here next to this magnificent creature, to feel her body close to mine, and enjoy every God-given moment I could. I only wanted to stare into her eyes, to memorize everything about her and this night, and talk of whatever topics we wandered into.

The walls and boundaries had been breached; we had crossed the physical lines that separated most people and kept them from ever forging unions. She knew of my desire for her, and I knew of hers for me.

It was not the same as fully claiming one another. Our actions remained incomplete, and it could not be denied. We were stifling the natural order of things.

But I wanted more than just her flesh; I wanted her mind and her heart. I wanted to know what it was like to have her entirely, and for her to have me. There were so many elements involved in becoming one person out of two; so many things to discover throughout that process. I did not want it rushed or hurried; savoring one another was an investment worth making.

As much as I desired her and wanted to claim her body, to taste and partake in everything she had to offer and that was hers to give of herself, as much as I wanted to mark her as my own, it seemed unfair—cheating—to deny ourselves the opportunity to build upon the foundation that would become the groundwork of our perfect union.

This was the time that would cement us together as Man and Wife for the rest of our days. These were the moments we would refer to when we knew that we were building a legacy for our future that would transcend all things—that our children would emerge from, that the rest of our earthly days would grow out of, and that our eternal love would be founded upon. When someday I was asked how I knew she was The One, this would be the memory that would come to mind.

I did not want this moment, just this small sliver of time between two insignificant Human Beings but a moment that meant everything to *me*, to end.

This was the calm before the storm, and I longed to cherish it for as much time as I had to spare before the darkness descended once again.

Surrender

We lay on her floor for what seemed like an eternity, talking, laughing, and getting to know one another at long last. Time slipped away, and though I knew it had only been a few hours, the little nagging voice within my head told me I needed to get back to the barracks so I could pack and get some rest before morning.

I leaned over and kissed her softly and whispered to her that I had to leave. I found myself both awed by my good fortune as well as slightly saddened by the timing of things as I watched the disappointment register on her face.

She still wanted me here, even after hours of intimacy, after finally being able to know the man beyond the uniform. The realization struck me profoundly, leaving me with that moment of humble clarity when one realized that love was not only staring back at them, but was an inevitability.

I stood, then bent over and extended my arms to help pull her to her feet. She stood across from me, our hands intertwined, and then stretched on tiptoe to kiss me once more. I put my hands on the sides of her face, kissed her thoroughly, and then hugged her closely, intentionally preventing the kiss from becoming too amorous again. All that could wait for another time; hopefully I would be back in a few days…assuming all went well as I prayed it would.

I began to walk toward the door of her bedroom, this time leading her by her hand, pleased to see how reluctant she was to follow me. She walked as if dragging her feet like a child, petulant and pouting. I turned and looked at her, amused enough it made me laugh out loud, pleased beyond imagination to see how resistant she was.

I pulled her close again, treasuring the way her body felt against mine. She wrapped her arms around me, something I felt I would never get tired of.

I kissed her again, allowing myself to savor the moment and the feel of her lips against my own. She was such a delectable temptation it was almost impossible to let her go, to say goodbye. She was hard to walk away from, especially knowing why I was doing it and where I was going.

But I broke away from her, smoothing her hair around her ears, looking deeply into her eyes, allowing my thumb to gently stroke her cheek. I wanted to remember her in this moment, the way she stood there looking up at me. She was a tender woman with a tender heart. It wasn't all that she was, but ultimately, her sweetness and loving nature were part of her very Being. It was as difficult to separate that facet of her character as it was to part ways with her more passionate side.

She gave me a mischievous look, took my hand into her own, and then took several steps backward. I shook my head, smiling, seeing where she was headed, and knew I could not resist such temptation if prompted again. But she was exciting to me; she was dangerous in a way that I'd never before experienced, and her hold over me was strong.

She spun me round, walking me backward several steps until I felt her bed against the back of my legs.

I could have resisted. I could have stopped her.

But I didn't. Being near her felt like Home to me.

Instead, I allowed her to push me down onto her bed, watched as she climbed atop me, and lay transfixed as she took control entirely.

She was…captivating.

I surrendered, feeling the weight of her body as she straddled me, every sense on fire as she did as she pleased with me.

I placed my hands on her hips, allowing them to wander under the edges of her loose sweater, feeling the soft skin of her bare back beneath my rough hands. Suddenly, she stopped kissing me, uprighted herself fully as she sat over me, and before I could even consider what she was doing, she peeled her sweater over her head, revealing her bareness.

Shock and desire surged through me as I stared at her; her face was flushed, her beautiful body on full display.

I looked at every precious inch of her flesh, loving every line, every blue vein I could see through her pale skin against the firelight, and every freckle that covered her body. I wanted to trace my fingers over them, connecting the dots, seeing how many there were, kissing each and every one of them, loving how they belonged to her and only her.

I pulled her back down toward me, kissing her again and again, trying to keep myself from touching her. My desire for her had built up too much to resist though; I flipped our positions, pinning her beneath me, allowing her to feel the full weight of my body atop hers.

I was dancing with fire, and I knew it. I knew what I could handle and what was far too much to bear, and she had crossed that line and I had leapt over it following her. I wanted her, here, now, completely. I wanted to place my mouth all over her body, I wanted to peel off the rest of her clothing and then lose my own, never surrendering to matters of reason or logic again until we had both been fully satisfied.

It was too much. It was torture.

"I can't!" I growled, frustrated.

"I just can't," I repeated, entirely resigned. "Not with you."

I stopped, pushing myself off her, rolling over at first, breathing heavily as I lay there on my back. It wasn't enough. I sat up, my legs over the edge of the bed, distancing myself from her momentarily so I could get my bearings.

She was silent next to me, unmoving. I turned to look at her, reaching out my hand to touch her leg. Without hesitation, her body pulled away from me. She reacted as if burned, her legs retreating instinctually as if from attack.

I looked at her; the expression on her face surprising me as much as her reaction, and then allowed my hand to drop back to my side.

She sat up, grabbing her sweater and placing it in front of her, hiding her nakedness from me. She looked confused, angry, disgusted, hurt. I saw it all flash across her face in an instant and knew I had committed an egregious sin against her that she had no way of understanding, and so was left with her own perception.

I looked at her briefly, saw her avoiding my gaze, and so I surrendered, looking down at the floor. I was so aroused my entire body was shaking; I needed to steady my breathing, control my rapid pulse, get a grip on the thoughts and images of her that were flooding my brain.

I stood, moving myself to the overstuffed chair positioned diagonally from the bed, and sat. I rubbed my mouth and jawline, my elbows on my knees, willing myself to calm down and my passion to subside. I closed my eyes, ran my hands through my hair, took a deep breath.

I looked at her again. Her face looked pained. She was bright red as if blushing, and I tried to extend a hand again to ask her to approach, to come sit with me, to allow me a moment to explain.

She reacted as if I had tried to strike her. Her body actually withdrew further, and I watched as she slid across the bed so she could exit from the other side, pausing only to pull her sweater over her head while her back was turned toward me.

Did she not understand what was happening?

Did she not understand why I pulled away?

The room was silent. Far too silent.

It was the sound of the death of something.

She stood in front of the fireplace for a moment with her arms folded across her chest and her back toward me. I didn't speak. I willed my body to relax so I could approach her, but I knew that something had shifted within that moment that not only killed the mood and whatever intimacy we had established, it had also created barriers that I didn't quite understand.

Much like I was, she was probably asking herself, *"What just happened?"*

I wished I had an easy answer.

FIFTY – WINTER WINDS

Winter Winds

It didn't take a degree in psychology to read her Body Language and know that I was seeing her being self-protective. She had folded her arms in front of herself, and crossed her legs, choosing to sit in a chair on the other side of the room. Her behavior, how she pulled the sleeves of her oversized sweater down over her thumbs, even going so far as to hide her wrists and hands, was self-protective, although she probably didn't even realize she was doing it.

It was still difficult for me to gauge exactly how much my actions had impacted her thus far, but there was no denying I had hurt her deeply in some way.

I didn't have any answers.

I could only do what I believed was the right thing to do—even if it hurt her—even if it killed me—and even if it sent out a Ripple Effect that could change both of our destinies forever.

There were many men who would take that small moment in her life, delight in her body while not even bothering to remember her name, and exploit it for all it was worth without any regard for the consequences. My head and my heart battled fiercely, each vying for control over my actions, each struggling to sort out how to proceed.

I was not a saint. There had been plenty in the past who had not wanted more from me than the physical, and I was happy to oblige.

It had never been my intent to fall short of the mark for any woman, and although they weren't my usual style, I wasn't entirely opposed to one-night stands. I'd spent enough of my youth living away at college and at the Academy to know that sometimes that's all that was desired or required, and fully appreciated that many women were more than happy to make those decisions as freely as men did. I wasn't opposed to any of it, technically; we were animals, after all, and women were equally free to choose whatever path worked best for them.

The only ambivalence or rejection of one-night stands I'd ever really had was in reference to my own sister, and that was where it shifted into something personal. As a brother, the idea of men casually bedding down my sister was not merely uncomfortable, it drew my ire like no other subject could. I felt immensely protective over her—mostly because the idea of men using my sister at their convenience had always left me with a bit of disdain for both men as well as one-night stands.

They were *all* someone's Sister.

Someone's wife. Mother. Daughter.

I just couldn't be that person with her.

I didn't want to be.

I wanted more.

But where we were right now…that was on me. We were here because of *my* actions. I had caused this, and it all rested solely on my shoulders. I was the one that couldn't resist her. I was the one who had allowed it to escalate.

I had to be the man who built our foundation on stone, not sand; we were going to build a fortified home. Emotionally and physically transient men never even considered their role in offering such things; they had no intention of ever being around.

I just couldn't do it. I couldn't make it so obnoxiously *common*.

I'd never even taken her out *on a date*; I'd never even *held her hand* as we walked somewhere. I'd never taken her anywhere for a meal, or an event.

While I fully believed that we could fall in love with one another just through time spent together, even in a work environment, each of us deserved better. I wanted to be able to build a future with her, and lives were built on memories, not encounters.

I was apparently not a very effective communicator.

But then, neither was she.

There were two of us here, neither of us talking, and she didn't want to hear anything else from me; she'd had her fill.

None of this mattered, of course. It was a salve, a Band-Aid on an open wound.

But I was the other person sitting in that darkened, quiet room, and I knew I had just broken something that was priceless. I'd broken something that had been offered to me freely; something that I probably hadn't deserved to begin with.

I was a fool.

But I stood by my actions. I had no guarantee of a safe return.

If all she was going to be left with was memories of me, then let them be good.

A Graceless Exit

In all my days I had never been escorted from a woman's bedroom by such hostile forces that it felt like I had been caught sneaking in uninvited.

Her bedroom was an inhospitable environment which would remain unconquerable and unchallenged until a better man than myself arrived. I had no doubt the room would then reveal its opalescent qualities once again at that point. It would revert back into the same loving environment just as it had been when I first arrived. The fireplace had warmed the room with the vibrant orange glow and as we had touched one another, our skin had appeared flushed and delectable, the flickering of the flames making her pale body as perfect as a Grecian statue.

Her bedroom had transformed though, and had become a cold, sterile, white prison. It had become a hypothermic tundra, a frozen emptiness.

I deserved to be cast out into the darkness after losing her warm embrace.

The warmth from the fireplace didn't matter anymore because the air had become breathtakingly sharp; a blast of bitter winds had swept through the instant I had freed myself from my desire for her. The intimacy we had shared had shattered in the silence.

That hypnotic power she held over me was her greatest strength and served as testament to the depth of my passions for her. But it was also my greatest weakness, and it was not difficult to imagine a day when it was either used against me or the pair of us, whether in anger, or by some unknown third party who knew just how powerful her hold over me was and used it to their advantage.

She had become more important to me than myself; I had used *every ounce* of my willpower to pull away from her for *her* sake, not my own. Would that I could, I would be there still, and the world could sort itself out.

I had *almost* managed it; to leave there without it becoming what it ultimately did. I had almost extracted myself from everything.

But I hungered for her as I never had before, and I hadn't wanted to leave.

Her bedroom had been the only true sanctuary I had ever felt in my lifetime, and it was because she was there, and the rest of the world was absent.

If only I had been able to resist reaching out for her one final time...
But I hadn't.

She had been ravenous, just as I had, and when I kissed her before I left her bedroom, it had been with a hunger that we had thus far managed to avoid. There had been a newfound desperation, because we knew it truly was our last chance, and neither one of us wanted to miss it. She wanted me there just as much as I had wanted to be there, and I could feel her desire for me just as intensely as I knew she could feel mine. When everything else was stripped away, and all that remained were the naked Souls of two people overwhelmed by their primal desire for one another, there was nothing bashful, polite, or rational standing between them anymore; it was pure animal behavior and base, carnal desire and need.

None of the rules mattered, and none of the reasons I had thought about only hours before could even be recalled; I couldn't even remember why I was supposed to resist her—and it made no sense in my head at that moment that there could have been any sort of sufficient reason for *anyone* to stop doing what we were doing.

And then when I could bear no more, when I finally pinned her below me, it was all I could do to proceed slowly. The lush down comforter she had sunk into as I had burrowed myself into her, lying on top of her for the very first time and staring down into her eyes, feeling the heat from her body beneath my own, seeing the way she had clutched the fabric beneath her hand as I had kissed and explored her body—it was all I was going to have to hold on to.

That memory would have to suffice.

Everything was different now.

She stood nearby, having watched me leave her most intimate space and return to the foyer. It was an area where any random guest or stranger might be welcomed and permitted—communal space, impersonal and unfavored.

She was patiently waiting for me to ready myself so I could leave. She was silent, unforgiving, and cold, but she was still there.

She chaperoned me like I was a kid with sticky fingers in a candy store—that was how she waited for the final chapter to be complete before this tragedy came to an end; a stoic sentry guarding the temple. It was all entirely unnecessary; I was a shamed dog having gotten my nose whacked. Her displeasure was punishment enough, my adoration for her resulting in my own self-recrimination more than she was even capable of comprehending. Combined with my own self-contempt and the questions and concerns I now had trapped in my head, I had more than enough to go on for the self-flagellation tour which was about to ensue.

I had spent the required time lacing up my boots properly before I left; a task I would have gladly forfeited to avoid the painfully long awkward silence forced between us, but riding my bike made it necessary, and I had felt small, ashamed, and helpless the entire time. Whatever her goal had been—if it had merely been just to keep that wall between us, at least she could know she had done that part perfectly.

As soon as I finished lacing up my boots I stood, grabbing my jacket, and putting it on. I then picked up my balaclava and shoved it into a pocket, put my gloves in the other, and then finally, picked up my helmet; the last thing which held me here and the first thing that would create a new wall between us as soon as I put it back on. I did all of this with a heavy heart and downcast eyes; the room was silent, but I could see her bare feet off in the corner of my eye and could still feel her watching me.

There had to be a way to talk to her. There had to be a way to salvage this.

Seeing that I had gathered my stuff, she moved past me to the front door.

I followed her, and then held out my hand to her. It was a stupid gesture. I just didn't know what else to do.

She looked at it, unsure of what I was doing, and then looked back into my eyes. I watched as it became clear, and she reached a new understanding. She smiled, briefly;

scornful, full of contempt. Disgust. A micro-expression revealing her true feelings before she closed herself off to me, perhaps forever.

And then, as her expression shifted from the one I had always known—soft, welcoming, concerned—to distant and controlled, an invisible wall materialized between us. I watched, knowing that I was the cause of it, as her delicate, gentle face transformed into an unreadable blank canvas, a porcelain doll with lovely, expressionless eyes.

She deigned to extend her hand and allowed me to hold it within my own for a fraction of a minute, and then she pulled her hand away, letting it drop to her side without any hesitation.

Her hands were an extension of her nature; they were nurturing, tender.

Her hands had cleared away the blood from the back of my head. They had prepared food and nourished me.

She had used her hand to gently run her fingers through my hair as I fell asleep. She had held my other hand in her lap.

Her hand had sat in my own as it rested on my thigh during our return trip from the Transport Station. I had picked it up and kissed her fingers as we glided through the air, separate from the world.

Her hand led the way toward her bedroom. It had made me realize that I should be placing a ring on it and asking her to be my bride.

The same hands had ravaged my body, hungrily, only an hour before.

I wanted to be holding her hand when we were sitting in rocking chairs out on our back deck in the twilight of our lives; I wanted to be able to hold it whenever I saw it sitting there waiting for me...

Now, her message was clear; her Body Language said far more than any words would have been necessary to get her point across. This person did not need to speak; her countenance said it all.

I had been found unworthy of being the source of any feelings, especially the hurt ones, it said. *Of course, we could remain courteous; we were professionals.*

It was the unspoken response of a woman who had chosen self-preservation—and self-respect. She did not want someone who seemingly did not want her back no matter how convoluted his signals had been.

Her eyes pierced straight through me, a thousand-yard stare. It was a dismissal: the audition was over.

She was brutally cold, but I did understand that it had to be this way. It wasn't personal; at least not in the context that she believed it to be.

I understood that I had wounded her pride fiercely.

I knew she didn't understand me or my poorly phrased words in the least. For now, this was how it would have to remain because I was not going to be in a position to do anything about it once I left.

I reached the door. She seemed even smaller in stature now that I had my boots on, and although she only stood at arm's length from me, it seemed clear it was always going to be exactly too far for me to touch.

This fragile creature was an entirely new version of the woman I had come to know.

Distant.

Not mine.

I wanted to reach out to her; I wanted to comfort and reassure her.

But she was unavailable. Had I tried, I would have found her body rigid, unreceptive, and it would have been a pointless exercise in futility. I could not be the one to both cause the pain and then apply the band-aid.

And had I done it, I could not have still held my ground. I was either committed to my stand or I needed to retract everything immediately and grovel at her feet; those were the only two choices before me now.

I sighed heavily, turned the door handle, and wondered as I left her standing there if I would ever be invited back into her world again. Would I ever be welcomed into her home, her heart, or even her friendship? Or was this one of those moments in a person's life by which they were defined and haunted by one choice or another? It was a decision to act, knowing that my choices would always leave an impression on both my own future as well as that of another, and my actions would have consequences.

I had an image of myself as if in some alternate moment in time; it was as though I were sitting on my bike at a set of crossroads, debating which way I should proceed. To turn left or right, to drive forward and into the arms of a woman who had desired me from the start, who had offered herself to me heart and soul and was waiting for me at the other end of the road. A fate uncertain, but a *chance*, nonetheless, to find the one who could have fulfilled my every desire, to love me unconditionally and with unwavering permanence if I were only brave enough to take that initial step.

To turn right was to return home; back to the familiar, the comfortable, and the predictable. It was the certainty of knowing what was safe, what was convenient; the immediate and obvious answer for a man set in his ways and unlikely to take unnecessary chances or risks, especially when the expectation might have been better left to dreams rather than reality. I questioned if it was something that I would look back on from time to time, remembering myself there at the crossroads, always regretting that I never turned left when I had the time and opportunity. It left me wondering if my decision would leave its mark well beyond my own, resulting in a cascading effect of consequences that would serve as a reminder to someone else for the rest of their days; if they, too, would not spend the rest of their life wondering what might have happened had I only turned left.

I moved out onto her porch, and having crossed the threshold back out into the real world, turned back toward her, praying that she would at least meet my gaze or allow me to speak. But she was already gone. She had slipped beyond my view before I could even try once more; she had removed my chance. I didn't even see her face; the door was already closing behind me with nothing of her left except a glimpse of her fingertips across the door frame as she pushed the door closed.

Even still, I stood there, waiting until I heard the locking mechanism fall into place securely, and then finally, started the long walk toward my bike.

I followed the sidewalk from her front porch over to her driveway and then walked along its edge until I reached my bike parked at the end of it.

I was tired.

I walked like I was walking the plank; a man who, after having lived and worked solely on a ship for many years, had forgotten how to swim and was afraid of what lay beyond. But having overstayed my welcome, I was now being escorted off the end of the plank with the tip of a blade at my backside, and not only did no one care if there were sharks or if I would drown, I knew that no one would even look to see what had become of me once I'd gone over the edge.

It wasn't an unreasonable comparison; I had the distinct impression that for as much as she made me feel protective and as though I wanted to keep her safe, I was almost certain that she was the final link to Humanity I was ever going to receive. If I couldn't figure out how to have an authentic relationship with a woman as good as her, as ideally matched—as equally yoked—then what chance have I?

The imagery of my descent into the dark—walking the plank into the Great Unknown—suddenly gripped me with the comparison to that long march from Death Row to my Execution, and it left me with a deep sense of foreboding. I was not one usually prone to feeling self-pity; my work had supplied me with far too many examples of misfortune for me to ever believe that I had suffered or known hardship to the same extent that much of my Fellow Man had.

I believed in living my life with as much grace and gratitude as possible, in doing all that I could to leave after my time here having been used well, and having done more Good than Harm. It was a simple mantra, but it eliminated any chance of self-pity or wasted time; I had stared into the Sorrowed faces of the Bereaved too many times to ever have a day go by in which I was not only grateful to be Alive and Healthy, but to have lived my entire life surrounded by my own Loved Ones—all of whom had mercifully been spared Tragedy and Violence as well.

But at that moment, I felt my jaw-clench as a seething rage overwhelmed me—a level of rage that very few events or people had ever managed to evoke. Yet as I walked back toward my motorcycle, I was overtaken by a feeling of powerlessness due to these mounting new developments which were seizing control over everything so quickly it was making me feel cornered.

More importantly, these new developments were then spiraling out of control and impacting other facets of my work and personal life. I was watching as everything unraveled. I was a chess player and a strategist, but I was not usually required to make my own personal life decisions at the drop of a dime and without careful measure. It was not how I lived my life.

I rounded the front of my bike, a sleek, powerful machine that may as well have served as a Homeric galley as my eyes were drawn back toward the pretty little house with the pretty little wraparound porch; a Craftsman-style replica, as picturesque as any Norman Rockwell painting, complete with a hanging swing at the end of the porch and the soft glow of a porch light casting a warm welcome to all.

Someone's Ithaca.
Someone's Penelope.
But not mine.

Taking a deep breath, I climbed on my bike, and fired it up. I put on my gloves, balaclava, and helmet, taking one last look at her front door before closing my visor.

I raced toward the light at the end of her road, slowing down, turning right onto Holland Road, and then back to the barracks.

I had taken something that had been precious—an offering of another Human Being, the heart of a woman—and I had decimated it. I had caused irrevocable damage to her Soul, just as many of us did to those whom we professed to love. This was something that would mark my Soul just as much as hers; one way or another, we were joined now.

As I made my way along the quiet streets now wet with rainfall, I could not help but question if the sickening feeling in the pit of my stomach was what it meant to be in love.

Without a doubt, I was better equipped to enter a combat zone.
I shouldn't have said anything.
I should have explained myself better.
I shouldn't have left. Not like that.
I should have embraced our time while we had it.
I should have just told her I loved her.
I should have made her mine.
I really fucked it up this time.

FIFTY-ONE – BROKEN CROWN

Broken Crown

    I may not be able to do anything about any of it for the time being—especially since I had to leave and go to Alaska. It was an intermission that I had not planned on, and it would have unexpected outcomes that I could not anticipate or predict at this point.
    I may not be able to invest the time into digging out whatever Evils rested behind the Governors closed doors just yet. And God knew there were still two ICE agents who were going to learn the hard way that they had chosen to stand on the wrong side of the law and the Oaths they had sworn before this was all said and done. I could not live with the man that I was if I walked away from all that I knew and left this unaddressed and unfinished.
    Somehow, someway, I would get Justice for Katarina and her parents. I would find the man who had escaped justice by fleeing our nation and figure out a way to bring him back to America to face the Sentence and Punishment he deserved. I would investigate the Governor and his two henchmen and discover the truth behind their actions. I would discover the root of why the Governor had worked so hard to conceal the Crimes Against Humanity that were Committed against Katarina.
    I would discover the role that Daegan Kyl played in everything and confirm either his own Guilt or Innocence. I would find them, Daegan Kyl and Willow Amos, and I would get to the truth behind the Graveyards and The Angels of Mercy. I would find out whether or not either of them knew about the Second Graveyard—if either of them had been more deeply involved with that hellish, Evil cult of degenerates or not. And God Help Them if they were because I would bring the full weight of both the Rule of Law, as well as the American People, around their throats tighter than any noose they could envision if they had been.
    And if it came to be discovered that I myself had been played by them, that I had Aided and Abetted in providing the means for a Convicted Offender and her Corrupt Sociopathic Thug of an 'uncle' to escape my nation due to my own actions, I would resign from my position just as soon as I handed in my Final Reports and bore witness to the Final Execution being carried out. If I had been so easily manipulated and lied to that I had compromised my own Oath and respect for the Rule of Law that I had not only allowed Daegan Kyl to escape without prosecution, but that I had enabled him, I had no right to even wear my badge or consider myself either an Oath-Keeper or a

Peacekeeper. God Help Me, but I would root it all out before I was done and then let the chips fall where they may.

And if I went down with it, if a career of twenty-two years and a lifetime of being what I had thought was a Good Man, was the price I had to pay for my role in things, then it was the price that I was going to have to pay.

All That Remained

I checked my timestamp to see how much was left of the evening to prepare for my departure tomorrow. There was much to do. I also had some paperwork and planning I wanted to go over with Stanton, including updating my Living Will and After-Life Will and making sure everything was in order should I fail to return.

I had thought about everything I would need packed from this end before heading out, and then made a list of what I would pick up once I was at the base tomorrow.

My own gear that I had on hand was inadequate for going out into the field. Even though much of it was the same issue as our Soldiers, I didn't have anything beyond a few basic uniforms and items here with me in Seattle. What I had back home was probably more than adequate—I did appreciate firearms and tactical equipment, and had a noteworthy investment of gadgets and gear along with my small, private arsenal. But nothing was immediately available or prepped for such a trip, and I certainly wasn't going to lose even more time trying to work yet another task into the itinerary.

So I would be issued the same military tactical gear, weapons, and combat uniforms at the base as the rest of the team that would be escorting me. Wearing any of my current gear—all of which was clearly designated for Law Enforcement—would have been classified as a Suicide Mission; it was better to just blend in with all the rest. They would also double-check that my RFID-Chip was functioning properly in case they needed to Identify, Evacuate, or Transport my Physical Remains.

Which reminded me that I still needed to call my folks before I left; they hated it when it was open-ended and they couldn't check up on me, and Alaska did not have any provisions for worried mothers.

I knew I would have a good team of experienced men with me—men that had similar training as Daegan Kyl and would know how to think like him. Men that would know how and where to begin looking for him if we were unable to locate him through his RFID-Chip.

It stood to reason that it *should* still be active and *should* make this only a three or four-day extraction. If Stanton was able to access his military records at the appropriate level, he should be able to track him, and we'd know in real time where we needed to be. As convenient as it would have been just to access his records directly so we could move things along, to access anyone's RFID-Chip without having met one of the qualifiers—Abduction, Missing Person, Deceased Remains, Active Duty, Charged and Convicted Offenders—it would have been a serious breach of power. So… Stanton and I would just circumvent the details and do what we could to correct the situation that we created; we had bigger issues than whether or not Daegan Kyl felt violated by our trying to track his movements right now.

If we couldn't track him, we would be completely blind on the ground, with nothing more to go on than an approximation of where to begin searching based on a calculation of the time he had been there so far and an overall radius of the area in which he could have traveled.

We would be trying to track a man traveling on foot, and if Willow Amos was still Alive then we would be setting the pace based on what she, an untrained Civilian with no backcountry experience, knowledge, or stamina could manage through rough terrain in cold-weather conditions.

If he had taken my advice, he would have immediately begun by making a wide berth of the Drop-Zone and then making the descent south, hopefully escaping both early snows as well as hordes of Wildmen. It was likely that he had done this, but there was no guarantee, and we couldn't account for things that might have intervened even if he had tried to stay the course.

Regardless of his route, he was skilled enough that he may have traveled in any direction with an equal chance of survival. If that were the case, then heading further north would have put them in the greatest danger from the elements, but it would have all but eliminated any problems with the scavenging, roving renegades who often traveled in packs by the hundreds.

The area in which he could have traveled within thus far didn't seem too vast, but we were also going to be dropped into a heavily populated zone—as had Daegan Kyl and Willow Amos.

We could face difficult circumstances from the moment we entered Alaskan air space, and landing itself could be impossible, even with additional measures in place providing us with more protection and flexibility than the Convict Transports.

We would likely try and use another location as our Drop-Zone. Even an open expanse of field would work if we could find one en route. Our Transport would likely be piloted with a live pilot, as it would grant us more maneuverability and landing options. But no matter where we were able to land, there was still going to be the potential for hostile opposition from the moment the Transport was heard overhead. How difficult our Drop would end up being, whether or not the pilot could fully set-down, whether or not we would be required to use the same designated Drop-Zone if there was inclement weather—all of that remained to be seen. Snow could drastically impede our Drop, our progress, and our Extraction.

And then there was the final element of unpredictability which would by no means make this task any easier: Daegan Kyl himself. The same military training that had given him a fighting chance and was hopefully serving him well now was going to be to our detriment. He didn't know we were coming for him, and he was unlikely to be welcoming. He was trying to survive in an environment where not only was the weather trying to kill him, he was also surrounded by potential enemy combatants in a gorilla-warfare setting. He would be expecting every interaction to result in Violence and control over assets. It was likely that he had already been forced to engage in some form of combat with everyone he had encountered thus far. He would not be easy to locate.

We had millions of miles of untrammeled national forest lands, and the only thing we had to go on was the time and location for his original Drop. He was now somewhere within millions of acres of untamed wilderness at the onset of winter, and while we could safely reduce his potential whereabouts to a few thousand acres, it was still going to take considerable time and groundwork to find him. Essentially, we were going to be trying to track a man that knew how to evade enemies whilst surrounded by millions of them, in what was potentially the most psychologically and emotionally damaging warfare environment known to man. We then had to find him, hopefully still alive, and then try to approach him without any of us getting killed in the process.

I intended to bring both of them home, alive. Hopefully without any of us getting hurt, including the Soldiers who were going to secure our safety.

Ideally, I could get it done without taking the lives of any of the Wildmen either. It would be best if we could avoid them altogether; the last thing we needed were negative altercations with them. But a handful of Soldiers—wearing full combat gear and carrying a small arsenal—would be a very desirable conquest, and we would be hunted and attacked mercilessly until we were so exhausted or outnumbered that each of us eventually fell. It was not a place where we could possibly win if our presence was known.

But I needed to bring them back, so these were necessary risks.

There was a poison growing in America, it was reminiscent of the very poison from the 21st century that had almost destroyed our country, the unity of our people, and had almost led to a Second Civil War. If something was slowly seeping through my country spreading its toxins and contaminating everything, endangering my Fellow Citizens, and preying upon them in their moment of weakness, it needed to be explored, recognized, identified, and stopped.

There was nothing I wouldn't do for my Fellow Man, and if this poison was corrupting our nation, spreading lies that served only to diminish the true Value of Human Life, then I needed to do whatever necessary to put an end to it. I could only pray that the Goodness that I had detected within Daegan Kyl was genuine, and that he, too, felt inherently compelled to help me put an end to it. It was my earnest prayer that he would be able to persuade Willow Amos to render aid. She may have knowledge that had thus far not been discovered—in fact, I was counting on this. I had always believed she had known far more than she had alluded to or provided information about.

It was my most sincere hope and prayer that Daegan Kyl could influence her into rising and becoming a better version of herself. As difficult as it was for me to imagine—or accept—it was entirely possible that the best hope for this case, in bringing Justice to the lives of more than fifty Victims and their Bereaved, in discovering the root source of their Burials and Deaths, and in learning the full extent of the infiltration and growth of these Angels of Mercy, rested in the hands of the last person I would have ever wished.

There would only be one way to know, and only one way to get the answers I needed; I only prayed it wasn't already too late.

The Measure of a Man Worthy

Regret and second-guessing myself were not things I was accustomed to experiencing, but I found myself continuously overwhelmed by my thoughts of her as the evening progressed. I replayed everything a thousand times in the hours after we parted ways. I thought about her the whole ride home, as I packed my bag, and as I wrote a note for my parents and sent it out electronically after having arrived back home too late to call them.

But it was at its worst when I tried to catch a few precious hours of sleep before dawn. She invaded my thoughts as prominently as if she were in the room beside me. I could hear her breath alongside my own, I could see her as clearly as if she were directly next to me. I felt her hand touch my cheek, felt her skin against my own, and felt the warmth of her hands against my flesh.

I saw her smile as she turned toward me in her living room, leaving no possibility for hesitation on my behalf as she pulled me toward her. I saw her as she laid the book down on the table, taking her hand and placing it inside of my own, initiating our contact from the very first moment, confidently.

I saw the look on her face when I stole that confidence from her; the way she had pulled back away from me as if I had jolted her with electricity or burned her flesh.

The desire in her face when I kissed her in her living room near the hallway haunted me; my mind replayed the moment when I had the choice between turning right and leaving or turning left and going down that darkened hallway into her bedroom. I felt the heat from her body as she pulled me near her, as she wrapped her arms around me, as she reached her hands around my neck so she could kiss me. I saw the passion in her eyes; a drunken wantonness that intoxicated and overwhelmed me entirely, and made me crazed with my desire for her.

I recalled how my body had shaken with the want of her as we stood in that hallway, how it was all I could do to pick her up and carry her into the back room rather than just falling to the floor right then as I had ached to. My hands had been tasked with lifting her up, of feeling her body in my arms and completely under my domain. I had wanted to pull her bulky sweater over her head, to free her of that cumbersome, oversized, layered pile of material right then and there, but I had refrained. I had wanted to pull off my overshirt and my t-shirt because I had been overheating, too hot for too long with too many layers, and I could have pulled both shirts off in one swift movement, but I had resisted.

I had, instead, carried her down the hallway and into her bedroom, and against all sense of reason, I had stayed. Even after I saw the fireplace lit, after I saw the blankets and pillows on the floor, after I saw the moon spilling into the room, I had stayed. Even after I saw the inviting bed, I had maintained control. Her bed had called to me to throw her onto it the instant I pushed open her door as she clung to me, breathing heavily in my ear. But even then, I still set her down away from it, tried to distance myself, tried to do the right thing. All to show self-restraint—the agonizing torture I had put myself in just by trying to push my luck, all so I could continue to be near her.

She haunted me; images of her, her sounds, the way she had moved and touched me, all on an incessant, relentless loop in my brain. I heard every intake of breath, every moan, every gasp that escaped her mouth.

She had been completely governed by her desires and her shameless hunger for me, by what she wanted me to do to her, had *begged* me to do to her with the whispered words of a lover. She was on fire, her eyes were filled with a lust and a desire that I had never before found within a woman, and she had offered herself to me. That passion that had consumed her had been entirely for me, because of me. She was a gift; throwing herself toward me as she devoured me with the ferocity of a wild animal in heat.

I was only torturing myself by rehashing it, I knew.

But then I would close my eyes and see her lying across from me, so innocent and pure she looked as though she were confessing her sins in Communion. She had looked at me as if I were not only being offered her body, but also the contents of her Soul. She had been breathtaking in her simplicity; her desire for me was so pure, so forthright.

I knew, in my mind, how things could have gone and what I could have done. I knew that she had been mine for the taking; that she had offered herself to me fully and had I only pushed a little more, had I only taken what I had wanted to take, I could have spent the entire night satisfying my most carnal desires. She had made her feelings known well enough that if I were a less than Honorable man, I could have used it to my advantage and used her to fulfill my own selfish desires probably much sooner than this night had provided for. If I had been anyone other than myself, if I had been as most other men were, I would have used her for my own pleasure regardless of my intentions to leave, and without any regard for how she may or may not have fit into any future plans.

I also knew, mostly without shame, that had she been *any other woman*, had I only had less attachment to her, that I would have stayed, and I *would have* used her just as anyone else would have, because she had willingly offered it, thereby absolving me from any guilt or shame.

I knew that the reason why we were here was not because of what I had done though; we were here because of what was both undone and unsaid, and that was *all* because of who she was and how I felt about her.

I replayed it in my head, all that I could have done differently had I only been a slightly more average man—a man without the uniform and the history that I had.

I could have handled things very, very differently, but I hadn't.

Instead, I gambled, and lost. I had decimated her opinion of me, of the kind of man I was. I had obliterated any sensible chance to explain things to her long before she had shown me the door, and maybe that was what my actions had deserved after my abysmal attempts to communicate effectively with her.

I had gambled, not only with my own self-control, but with my ability to articulate myself, even knowing that I was out of my league and bearing a lengthy history of examples of brief, failed relationships.

And I had *crushed* her as a result.

I could see what I did, and I could see how it went to her very core.

I had made her feel *ashamed*. Whether it was because she felt I had shamed her for her behavior and inability to control herself—her forwardness—or because she thought I did not desire her, I couldn't tell. But she had recoiled from me because I had made her feel ashamed.

Rejected.

Unwanted.

Undesired.

The idea of her feeling as if I found her undesirable was soul-crushing to me. Every time the thought of it entered my mind I wanted to jump up, put on my jacket, and race back to her house, pounding on the door until she let me in so I could explain. I didn't care what time it was; I didn't care what I had to do in just a few brief hours.

It pierced my heart to its core to think she believed that I had not felt as powerful of an attraction or passion for her as she had me, that I hadn't ached with the same urgent and unquenchable longing and need to be fed as she had; that I hadn't wanted to stay with her, unite our bodies, and become as one with her.

I struggled with the idea that she had taken off her sweater and revealed her bareness to me, had shown me her beautifully perfect body that was hers and hers alone, and she thought I had not wanted to touch her. In truth, I had been pushed almost out of my mind with desire. I had fled from her bedroom from having wanted her too much; I had feared my own ability to maintain self-control.

It had been clear that she didn't understand my actions.

It only proved to show that we really were still just two strangers, no matter how deep our attraction or relationship had thus far been able to evolve. For her to not know men well enough to understand just how self-serving, selfish, and ravenous they really were only served as a testament to her own naivety. *No man* would have been able to resist her once she had done that; most men wouldn't have even tried.

I myself had been tested beyond measure; she had taken me to the brink of my own Honor—further than I had ever been challenged by such matters before. I had never expected to wage an internal war between doing what I thought was the right thing and the desperate desires of my own flesh; I had never before needed to tame my needs, feeling as though I were in as dangerous of a situation as any I'd ever before known but with much higher stakes.

I wished I could have explained things to her so she understood; I wished I could have found the words before we had reached that point.

I should never have turned back around and kissed her again.

I should have just kept walking.

I had brought all of this about due to my own actions. I had pushed too far, reached too high, wanted too much. I had been greedy, and arrogant. I had believed myself stronger than I was—able to withstand the fires I was playing with simply because I had never been burned before and thought I could control the flames.

I had learned the hard way that just because I had not ever met my match did not mean that she had not been waiting for me, and that when Satan wanted to tempt someone, he sometimes did it with honey rather than venom.

My entire life I had been told that the true Measure of a Man was to be found in how he dealt with his anger, in how he handled his impulsive nature, and in how well he controlled his temper and propensity for Violence. But Violence was easy; learning to control oneself in matters of Bloodshed—especially when Death was on the line and Human Life was at stake—that had never been a struggle for me. Controlling one's actions was just part of being a Good Man, and for *truly* Good men, the men of our nation and world who were inherently Good and *chose* to be Good, being Kind, Compassionate, and Loving was as instinctual as it was to be Faithful, or to hold a deep and binding belief in God. Such were the men who needed no laws to govern them. They were the Lawmakers and Soldiers, the Peacekeepers, and Warriors. They were the guardians of society, the Sheepdogs who kept the wolves at bay. They were the Cowboys who rose up against the Evil men of the world just because it needed to be done, regardless of whether or not the fight was their responsibility or obligation. Such men did not struggle with self-restraint in matters of Violence, or the Infliction of Harm or Pain on others; it was not who they were.

Instead, they were tested in other ways. The true Measure of a Man was decidedly different than what I had always believed it to be, and when I looked at the man in the mirror, I was not sure how well I had measured up after all. Perhaps life was only meant to be a series of tests; just one long, never-ending string of events that was interrupted from time to time with situations designed to test our mettle and help us prove our worth.

It wasn't our Violence that defined us; men had been Violent from our very origin, when two brothers from the same womb could not even choose their love of one another over Murder. No, the true test of we men had to be determined in matters much closer to our nature; the standard as ordained by God, the person we were supposed to be in His image. Our Violent nature, our Weakness, our Evil, those were expected; we had never controlled our base nature and never would.

But to see how a man responds when faced with temptation, to watch as he crumbles when confronted with loneliness, with his own greed—whether for love, sex, or for money—to see how he battles with his own carnal desires, *that* was how to take stock of a man. Asking a man to stare himself in the mirror and take full measure of his own self-worth by his sexual conduct and self-control, by how well he had treated the women in his past, by how much Respect and Deference he had paid them, by how much he had Used and Discarded them over the years, by how many he had reduced to tears or abandoned with indifference—*that* was the true Measure of a Man.

And by that standard, any woman could determine how to find a man worthy of her and the place by her side.

If he was incapable of addressing his own carnal desires, handling himself appropriately or with the necessary self-control, if he applied pressure for sexual gratification without ever considering the woman even as she tried to graciously decline; simply failing to take the time to even learn the subtleties of the language of Love and Intimacy, or never caring enough to learn, that was how the true weakness of a man, and his internal fortitude were revealed. It did not take Violence to make men strong; it took the test of love, of passion, of kindness and empathy to draw out his internal character and put it on display.

Choosing to respect her autonomy, to believe that she was there to be Beloved rather than to fulfill the base desires of men, to know that men were made to be her Protector, her Defender, and her Champion; *that* was the lesson to be learned. She was meant to be cherished, not used. She was the chosen companion for man; God intended for her to be by his side.

But it was not her *duty* or *obligation* to fulfill the desires of men. She was the *gift* bequeathed to each of us; to be our calm before the storm before we went to battle, and the beacon and the light to guide us home when we were done. She was the *reason* why we tried, and it had been that way since the beginning of time. She had been the reason why they stood at the hot gates of Thermopylae, the reason why Odysseus struggled for twenty years to return home, and why a thousand ships were launched in her name.

She was the solution to the violence, to the hate and rage.

She was the reason why we tried so hard—why we refused to Surrender. She was the Provider of our greatest Gift and Strength: the mother of the children that bound us to her and helped us evolve into the best versions of ourselves.

She was the necessary link between the men we *could be* and the animals that we *were*. We were at the top of the food chain, more capable of advancement and superiority than any other creature on God's earth. But it was only through our actions as men, only by how we chose to regard and treat women, in how well we raised our children, and in how we treated those around us who were Physically Inferior or who needed our help, that we could ever truly discover just how gloriously in His Likeness we could become if we only tried.

Stepping away from her instead of taking her into my arms was the most difficult thing I had ever done in my entire life. I had fought myself from the moment she removed her sweater, and I had believed it to be a lost battle more than once.

Leaving her bedroom, and then her home—that had been a different sort of test, and I had failed that on all accounts as well.

I could have stayed. I could have taken her once and for all, claimed her as my own, made her feel all the passion and heat that we had both felt until that moment and of which we had been driven by throughout the entire evening. I could have left her aching, wanting, breathless, and then spent, content, lying in my arms, satiated and well-loved.

She would have known then, finally understood, exactly how I felt about her and all that I had never been able to say. She would have felt my unyielding desire for her, and she would have known by every touch and moment I shared that I belonged to her; that she had captured my mind and my heart already, but now owned my body as well. There would have been no room left for insecurity or questioning of her value or place in my world after that. I would have laid it all there before her, the Commitment of a man whose Word and Honor mattered above all else.

There had only been two things that I had ever pledged myself to, that I had knelt down and made an Oath worthy of my life; only God and my Sanctity of Life Oath in which I had pledged to always work on behalf of my Fellow Man, to Protect and Defend, and to always fight for the Right to Life. Until her, I had never found or imagined another Cause or Purpose worth pledging myself to, a Sworn Oath made on the altar of God Almighty. But I knew, finally, that such Oaths were meant to extend to the one whom we have offered our heart to as well, a promise to God and our Beloved to do all that can be done for them, and that the Oath we made to them before God transcended all earthly or man-made laws, and was an eternal vow that would serve us in this life and the hereafter, Divinely connecting us and all of the children from our union forever, just as God desired of us.

Even as I had always striven to do all that I could for my Fellow Man and to honor God, I knew that I had never been awake before now, that I had never understood my role on this subject. I had never realized I was intended to find the woman with whom I was meant to create and sanctify this union, and that it was part of the reason for my very Mortal Existence.

All of this was new to me, but I understood it with the same clarity that I knew my duties as a man and a Peacekeeper, and at some point, I knew I would lay all this at her feet and kneel before God with my intentions for her. I understood the depth of my commitment entirely, and I knew it as God intended for it to be known by all His Children.

I could have shown her all of these things, pledged them to her without words and meant them more sincerely than any wedding vow or Oath, because vows and Oaths did not always hold their worth when delivered by those lacking in character or substance, and vows meant nothing if spoken by unbelievers who lacked faith.

I did not doubt that she and I could have managed had we followed the path she had sanctioned; our hearts and minds were sincere, and our intentions were well-meaning. We would have prevailed, in the long run; I believed this. We could have traveled that path and when we parted, we would have both been satisfied, content, blissful. Full of hope. We would have walked with joy in our step, our head in the clouds; that secret smile worn by all who had been well-loved the night before and who knew they were entering into something glorious that made their hearts sing.

We would have parted knowing we had just begun our own love story, and our hearts would have felt as though they were going to burst as we remembered precious moments shared. We would have floated through our days counting the hours until we could see one another again, and willingly sacrificed getting a good night's sleep and being well-rested in exchange for the times where we could shut the rest of the world out so we could lose ourselves in one another's arms.

And even if I had left her in the early morning hours, even if I had stayed, sacrificed all rest, hurried through the myriad of tasks still needing to be done, even if I had stayed there, forfeited the phone calls and preparation I needed to do before I departed, I would have done so without regret. I would have delayed my departure, postponed my travel arrangements for another day even though I knew it could have negative consequences greater than myself.

I could have—and would have—sacrificed it all just to be with her, and I knew when I looked at her that I wanted to be lost in her eyes far more than I wanted to be taking a perilous journey into the Great Unknown and moving toward Harm and Chaos. Even as I realized I was going there to potentially save another Human Being's life, the life of someone who needed me far more than she did, I could have prioritized my time with her. Even then, I still would have delayed leaving, selfish or not.

And eventually, when I finally did leave, when reality demanded we return and re-engage once again, we would have affirmed our love for one another wholly; I could have left her as I needed to, and she would have known that I would return as soon as it was possible. She would have been confident in my devotion. She would have been left with no doubt of my love for her, of the life and future I wanted us to have together. I could have conveyed that even if I was never able to find quite the right words, even if I was never able to fully articulate exactly how I felt. She would have known because I would have been able to show her; every tender touch, lingering look, passionate kiss, and the millions of other little things that Good Men did to show their Loved Ones that they loved them every day could have been done by me just as they had been done since the dawn of time.

I thought of her, the woman that I had found lovely from our first encounter onward, but who had become more beautiful with every passing day since. The woman that I had grown to respect and trust—admire even—for her professionalism and dedication to her work; a woman that had known her own worth, the value of her contribution, and had worked by my side tirelessly these last three months. She was the woman I had quietly studied and learned the nature of, her demeanor, her personality, her quirks, and her qualities. She was the one who took care of the Hurt and Wounded, granting them permission to Grieve by offering to take the load, to carry their burden and tend to the practicalities of their circumstances for them in their stead. And just as she had cared for them, she had been the one who had arrived at my home and fed me, who had taken care of me, held my hand, nursed me, and stayed by my side. I had found her to be alluring, charming, an enchantress, a nurturer, an educator, a caregiver, and a leader. She was everything I could have ever dreamed of.

She was the woman that one married, not the one used out of convenience and then dismissed. She was the one that deserved to be courted, romanced, and seduced; not the one that needed to provide easy conquests just to capture the attention of a man.

And I knew that she did not quantify this to be something of such low regard. I knew she was not giving of herself in such a manner that was unworthy of either of us; she never intended for this to be *an event,* but rather *a beginning.*

I knew that we would have been establishing our foundation, and it was a pathway toward happiness. It was the first physical step toward setting aside the individual self and choosing to become part of a whole; the merging of two into one. The pathway was one that brought out the best of Humanity; it was an offering to God as we made our pledges toward selflessness, vulnerability, intimacy, sacrifice, honesty, and trust. We would have found ourselves standing before an altar, in front of all of those whom we loved, the merging of our lives and families, promising ourselves and all those who loved us that we would take care of one another, love one another, and cherish one another. A promise. A commitment to each other and a vow sworn unto God Almighty, none of which was ever meant to be broken, forgotten, or disregarded, but in the world of man, all too often was.

She needed to know that I was not the man that would break such promises, and I could not begin a life with her based on my own selfish desires any more than I could have left her for them. She needed to believe that when I was able to be by her side, I would be, no matter where my work and travels took me, that she would always be my highest priority when it was necessary.

She needed to know that I couldn't stay because I knew I could not provide the rest to her afterward, that I could not guarantee my return, and thus she was not mine to claim, even if she was offering and willing to accept the terms. She should not *have to* accept terms or compromise in matters of the heart; that was the whole point. She deserved to have a love story worthy of the ages, we all did, and only I could hold myself to the standard I believed the situation merited.

I did not want to speak in terms of what she 'could have' before I left our nation and traveled into one of the most dangerous lands left on earth. I did not want to part ways handing her nothing but praise for her beauty, declarations of my desire for her, and gallant, sweeping gestures promoting a future that I could no more promise and guarantee than I could wave my arm grandly toward the heavens and declare the moon would shine fully every night until my return—all just for her. It was false flattery at best. It was an embarrassing, desperate manipulation of words done by both young and old men alike and had been done with such recurring predictability that she ought to have been as embarrassed about falling for it as I would have been for attempting to do it. Aside from our ages and stations in life, I could only pray that she was not wishing for me to be a man prone to such brash, over-the-top romantic gestures. I feared she would have been very disappointed in me if that was what she required; it simply was not who I was or could ever comfortably become.

But of my heart, if she would have me, it was hers.
If she desired me, I was hers.
If she intended to treasure me, I would always be there.
That was what I could promise her because *that* was who I was.
I was loyal to a fault. Devoted beyond reproach.
Eternally faithful and invested.

Like so many other Good Men out there, I was as constant as the North Star for the woman that owned my heart, and for a woman who understood the value in such steadfast commitment, I was as much of a prize as she was.

I was not without my faults—all of which she would discover soon enough, and most of which she had already been subjected to. But I was also not without my positive qualities and charms, either. For the right woman I believed I was absolutely worthy of being her Chosen one. Among my strengths, perhaps, was my willingness and preference to being entirely, thoroughly, wholly devoted to one woman. All I wanted was to find the right one who would love and accept me as I was and allow me the privilege of doing the same. Nothing more, nothing less.

As for my heart, like so many others out there, it had been handled roughly a time or two. I had never professed to being a knight in shining armor; I was merely a Peacekeeper, more than a little damaged and set in my ways, and always beholden to the Greater Good rather than my own needs. I had paid my dues already, even if my rite of passage had not been paid in the tears of a broken heart, even if I did not have a past riddled with other women and an extensive history of long-term relationships. Love came in many forms, and I had loved and loved well. And with that love I had learned the most important lessons of all, the lessons that had taken the boy and turned him into a man worthy of holding a woman's heart for Safekeeping.

I was a Peacekeeper. I had dedicated my entire adult life to the pursuit of Justice, to helping my Fellow Man as they came to terms with the Losses of their Loved Ones through the worst Tragedies conceivable in a world that was supposed to be under the Protection of our Heavenly Father. I had fought for them, cried *for* them and *with* them, raged for them, and Grieved for them. I had always tried to do right by them and to secure Justice on their behalf; I had fought for those who were unable to fight for themselves, relentlessly.

If anyone knew the capacity of what it meant to Love Another, to see the results of what it meant to give one's heart to another, it was the Peacekeeper. They bore the scars of Humanity every day—every time they put on their uniform and took to the streets, they knew the power of both Love as well as Hate. They knew the cost that love could exact each and every day; they knew the risks of what it meant to Lose someone Beloved. They knew the fears that came with knowing how costly love could be, and how easily it could all be lost—that all of it could be Stolen from them in the blink of an eye. They knew the uncertainty, the fear, the bravery, and the courage it took to love another person in a world that could just as easily Take their Loved One away from them as they were Taken from those whom they served within their communities. They knew what it meant to have no guarantees, that it could all be Taken Away in an accident, a trauma, a crisis of mental health or terrorism, or through one of the senseless, devastating, unforgivable Acts of Violence that plagued our nation even when they shouldn't.

I knew the Pain and Fear that came with Loving Another. I knew the risks, knew the odds, knew the panic that coursed through my body. My fears were well-grounded; I had witnessed enough tragedy to know that nothing was ever going to be written in stone, and I could never become involved with anyone without putting their life in danger because of my profession and those who hated everything that we stood for.

I knew that there was a risk in loving me, risk in being the wife or child of a Peacekeeper, and that the risks had never gone away entirely because Evil itself could never be fully rooted out and destroyed. I knew that for her to love me she would have to shoulder the weight of my possible Death every time I left her arms and became a Public Servant. She would be joining the ranks of a club where no wife or child was ever entirely free from the fear of the Loss of their Loved One, but to be with me meant accepting that if I was willing to take an Oath to Protect the Sanctity of Human Life, and was willing to risk Losing my Life in the Line of Duty for my Fellow Countrymen, then she must be too. She needed to understand that it was part of the package that she must accept if she were going to claim me as her own.

I knew the fears of what it meant to try and reach out to someone even without their being a Peacekeeper, to try and forge a bond and build a relationship despite the anxiety and misgivings I held so closely within. I heard the call for love with just as much power and force as my own needs were demanding to be accounted for. I felt myself drawn in with a gravitational pull even as I knew how terrifying the journey was going to be. I heard myself acknowledge that my need for Love, Companionship, and Desire longed to be counted and validated. I knew the risks, and still, despite them, despite knowing how afraid it made me to take that step—for her, *I was all in.*

I knew I didn't have as much to offer as many men. I knew I was set in my ways, I was unyielding in some regards, and that my career placed me as a high-risk bet. I was never going to be as available and accessible as others could be, that as long as I worked in such a field, I would be required to make sacrifices of my time and body just as anyone connected to me would, *especially* my wife. I knew I would miss important milestones, anniversaries, and events; that I would leave a woman on her own more nights than not, and if she were not strong enough, if she did not have enough independence to lead a personally fulfilling life on her own, that the loneliness and fear would eventually prevail in the end, and we would never survive.

I knew that the statistical odds for Peacekeepers were not much better than those of our Soldiers, and that a productive career was not always conducive to a successful marriage. I knew that she would face her own demons and tests if she were to align herself with me. There would be times when I might never know for certain whether or not I was still important enough for her to choose me, or if she herself would end up questioning things. There might one day come a realization that after all of her time being on her own, she was better off alone, or she may decide she needs to be with a man who could meet her needs more often and was home by six every night.

I knew I prized my Honor and the man in the mirror more highly than most. But it was the Honor and the Heart that made the man, and those were the two strengths that could carry any relationship through the storms which undoubtedly lay ahead. My Honor, as with my Heart, had both been tested and proven solid; they had proven their worth. They had been put through the fire and found uncompromising when pushed upon by outside forces. My Honor was something that could not be Taken from me, while my Heart was mine—and mine alone—to Give freely to another. And while I knew it hadn't ever really been tested in the manner in which I was willing to give it to her, I knew that if it was freely given in the same manner that I had used it to love my family and my Heavenly Father, then it would be up for the task.

I belonged to her; and that would not change unless some tremendous force of nature intervened and altered everything.

Until that happened, my Heart was hers, if she wanted it, and for as long as she wanted to keep it. And just as I would have to, she was going to have to put her faith in someone she had no reason to trust as well as something she could neither see nor know with any degree of certainty to be a safe bet. That was the essence of faith; that was the test. It was what made it such a beautiful leap for each of us to make; it required us to let go of our weaknesses and the historic truths we thought we knew, all in an effort to grab hold of something new, even if it seemed terrifying as we did so.

She would have to make the decision to give me another chance or not, to decide if my excuses were worth hearing or not, and it would all need to be done based on her own desires and fears. She was going to have to decide if trusting in me was worth allowing me the opportunity to get close enough to her to possibly hurt her again. Only she could decide if the advantages outweighed the risks; if potentially being able to fall in love with me was worth starting over once I was home again—assuming I came home at all.

No matter what I did to repair or explain things, no matter what grand gesture I could supply, ultimately it came down to her ability to allow me back into her life and her heart; she would have to choose to let go of the hurt I had caused and forgive me. In order to have her own epic love story, she would have to place her trust in another person again—someone who had the capacity to hurt her, even to destroy her. Someone that had already let her down, and that would undoubtedly let her down again before it was all said and done.

It would either be worth the risk, or it wouldn't.

I would either be worth it or not.

All I could do was wait and pray.

There was only one thing that stood between the two of us and knowing how our future unfolded.

Alaska.

MILITARY OATH OF ENLISTMENT

I, (name), do solemnly swear (or affirm) that I will support and defend the Constitution of the United States against all enemies, foreign and domestic; that I will bear true faith and allegiance to the same; and that I will obey the orders of the President of the United States and the orders of the officers appointed over me, according to regulations and the Uniform Code of Military Justice. So help me God.

LAW ENFORCEMENT CODE OF ETHICS

AS A LAW ENFORCEMENT OFFICER, my fundamental duty is to serve Mankind; to Safeguard Lives and property; to Protect the Innocent against Deception, the Weak against Oppression or Intimidation, and the Peaceful against Violence or Disorder; and to respect the Constitutional Rights of all Men to Liberty, Equality, and Justice.

I WILL keep my private Life unsullied as an example to all; maintain Courageous Calm in the face of Danger, Scorn or Ridicule; develop Self-Restraint; and be constantly mindful of the Welfare of Others. Honest in Thought and Deed in both my personal and official Life, I will be exemplary in Obeying the Laws of the Land and the regulations of my department. Whatever I see or hear of a confidential nature or that is confided to me in my official capacity will be kept ever secret unless revelation is necessary in the performance of my Duty.

I WILL never act officiously or permit personal feelings, prejudices, animosities or friendships to influence my decisions. With no compromise for Crime and with Relentless Prosecution of Criminals, I will Enforce the Law courteously and appropriately without Fear or Favor, Malice or Ill Will, never employing Unnecessary Force or Violence and never accepting gratuities.

I RECOGNIZE the Badge of my Office as a Symbol of Public Faith, and I accept it as a Public Trust to be held so long as I am True to the Ethics of the Police Service. I will constantly strive to achieve these objectives and ideals, dedicating myself before God to my Chosen profession Law Enforcement.

THE AMERICAN'S CREED

I believe in the United States of America, as a government of the people, by the people, for the people; whose just powers are derived from the consent of the governed; a democracy in a republic; a sovereign Nation of many sovereign States; a perfect union, one and inseparable; established upon those principles of freedom, equality, justice, and humanity for which American patriots sacrificed their lives and fortunes.

I therefore believe it is my duty to my country to love it, to support its Constitution, to obey its laws, to respect its flag, and to defend it against all enemies.

— William Tyler Page

Written, 1917
A Resolution passed by the U.S. House of Representatives on April 3, 1918.

The Watchman On The Wall

The word of the Lord came to me:
"Son of man, speak to your people and say to them,

If I bring the sword upon a land,
and the people of the land take a man from among them,
and make him their watchman,
and if he sees the sword coming upon the land
and blows the trumpet and warns the people,
then if anyone who hears the sound of the trumpet does not take warning,
and the sword comes and takes him away,
his blood shall be upon his own head.

He heard the sound of the trumpet and did not take warning;
his blood shall be upon himself.

But if he had taken warning, he would have saved his life.

But if the watchman sees the sword coming and does not blow the trumpet,
so that the people are not warned,
and the sword comes and takes any one of them,
that person is taken away in his iniquity,
but his blood I will require at the watchman's hand.

Ezekiel 33: 1-6

Printed in Great Britain
by Amazon